The
MX Book
of
New

Sherlock
Holmes
Stories

Part VIII – Eliminate the
Impossible:
1892-1905

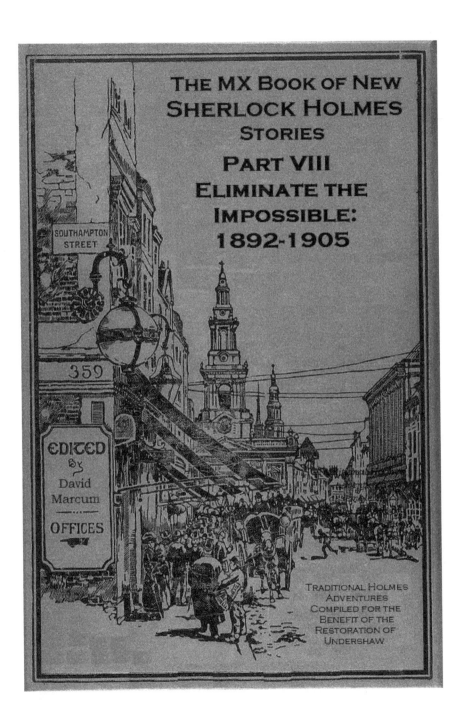

THE MX BOOK OF NEW SHERLOCK HOLMES STORIES

PART VIII
ELIMINATE THE IMPOSSIBLE:
1892-1905

SOUTHAMPTON STREET

359

EDITED
By
David
Marcum

OFFICES

TRADITIONAL HOLMES
ADVENTURES
COMPILED FOR THE
BENEFIT OF THE
RESTORATION OF
UNDERSHAW

ISBN Hardback 978-1-78705-205-5
ISBN Paperback 978-1-78705-206-2
AUK ePub ISBN 978-1-78705-207-9
AUK PDF ISBN 978-1-78705-208-6

Published in the UK by
MX Publishing
335 Princess Park Manor, Royal Drive,
London, N11 3GX
www.mxpublishing.co.uk

Illustrations by Sidney Paget
Cover design by Brian Belanger
www.belangerbooks.com and *www.redbubble.com/people/zhahadun*

CONTENTS

Introductions

Adventures

(Continued on the next page . . . .)

(Continued on the next page . . . .)

The following can be found in the companion volume
The MX Book of New Sherlock Holmes Stories
Part VIII – Eliminate the Impossible: 1892-1905

These additional Sherlock Holmes adventures
can be found in the previous volumes of
The MX Book of New Sherlock Holmes Stories

(Continued on the next page . . . .)

PART III: 1896-1929

PART IV – 2016 Annual

(Continued on the next page . . . .)

PART V – Christmas Adventures

(Continued on the next page . . . .)

PART VI – 2017 Annual

(Continued on the next page . . . .)

COPYRIGHT INFORMATION

The following contributions appear
in the companion volume
The MX Book of New Sherlock Holmes Stories
Part VII – Eliminate the Impossible: 1880-1891

Editor's Introduction:
"Eliminate the Impossible"
by David Marcum

"*N*o *ghosts need apply.*"

So says Mr. Sherlock Holmes to Dr. Watson near the beginning of "The Sussex Vampire", one of several tales in The Canon that initially seem to involve the supernatural, the unexplained, or the impossible. In this one, Holmes has just been invited to consult on a matter related to vampires, leading him to state, "*It's pure lunacy.*"

We expect nothing less from Holmes. He approaches the world in which he lives with the assumption that all is rational and explainable. In *The Hound of the Baskervilles*, he states that "*I have hitherto confined my investigations to this world.*" And it is the rules of *this world*, with its defined physical laws, understood causes-and-effects, and observable entropy and quantifiable phenomena that allow him to inexorably build his cases, piece by piece by piece. If Holmes were to consider the possibility of interference or involvement from some supernatural element in the solutions of his investigations, then every truth that he might establish would count for naught as some unquantifiable *X*-factor could be used to explain away every damning point. "*I know that it's my knife that killed him,*" the criminal might state, "*but it must have been the ghost that held it!*" And who then, in a world where the impossible could *not* be eliminated, would be able to say for sure that it hadn't?

In both the pitifully few sixty stories of the original Canon, as well as the many adventures that have been brought to us over the years from Watson's Tin Dispatch Box by so many other later Literary Agents, Holmes refuses to acknowledge the influence of the paranormal. However, he is often presented with situations that *seem* at first to have unexplainable origins and impossibilities that apparently cannot be eliminated without acknowledging some sort of improbable elucidation beyond human ken.

Holmes's scientific and skeptical approach was quite appropriate for those years in which he was in practice. It was a time when old beliefs were grinding against the new modern era, and men of science like Holmes were leading the way into the future. Holmes stated that "*[t]his agency stands flat-footed upon the ground,*" a policy that he held to time and again, approaching his investigations

1

from a footing in fact, not fancy. This stance served him well. It has been noted elsewhere that Sherlock Holmes was in the forefront of developing modern forensic methods for criminal investigation. For example, in 2002, the United Kingdom's Royal Society of Chemistry posthumously bestowed the "Extraordinary Honorary Fellowship" upon Holmes as "the first detective to exploit chemical science as a means of detection". And there's a very good reason that Scotland Yard's national computer system, developed for major crime enquiries by all British police forces, called is called *HOLMES* (*Home Office Large Major Enquiry System*), and that the Yard's training program is called *Elementary*.

Yet, even as Victorian and Edwardian societies were modernizing in terms of a respect for and advancement of science, much was still mired in the past. New knowledge widened the gulf between the haves and have-nots, and there was so much that was still culturally rooted in the old ways – including an idea that it wasn't a good thing to abandon ancient beliefs too quickly, and a sneaking suspicion in the back of many people's minds that there was some truth in the notions of ghosts and monsters and beasts and curses of all descriptions.

Perhaps this is what led to the easy acceptance of spiritualism during and beyond the years of Holmes's active practice. The Victorians had a fascination with death, as reflected in the rise during this time of extremely ornate cemeteries, along with the many curious customs related to dead bodies, including making strange photos while posing with the dead. Interest in archaeology increased as artifacts were brought to England from around the world, with many of them – such as the Egyptian mummies that can still be viewed today at the British Museum – only fueling the fires of interest in the unusual ways that the dead are treated. And certainly people wanted to know more about life *after* death – either for the promise of an easier afterlife as a reward for the trials upon *this* earth, or simply for the comforting knowledge that loved ones, and one's self as well, would continue on in some way following the transition from this physical plane to the spiritual.

The uncertainty of those years when Holmes was in practice, with upheavals in the social order and the seemingly endless parade of newly invented machines and technology, contributed to an unsettled sense that this new science wasn't able to explain everything after all.

2

As this innate and curious void, held by the masses who wanted to hear more about this other unexplained world, cried to be filled, it is no surprise that literature did its part to provide answers of sorts for people from all walks of life. Ruth Robbins, a Professor of English Literature at Leeds Metropolitan University stated in *The Guardian* ("Ghost Stories: Why The Victorians Were So Spookily Good At Them", December 23, 2013) that the much-easier availability of the printed word, coinciding with the Industrial Revolution of the second half of the nineteenth century, profoundly changed the way that supernatural stories were presented. Prior to this time, ghost stories, for example, had been primarily shared orally. With access to relatively cheap books and periodicals, people could now read these spooky tales on their own – and there was no shortage of them.

Ghost and monster stories played right into the existing gothic tradition, that form of literature known for its sense of foreboding, along with the feeling of a deepening mystery with every turn of the screw, and the hair standing up on the back of one's neck. Among the practitioners and purveyors of this type of narrative was one of my favorites, Charles Dickens, rightfully credited with so many things, and also one of the early scribes of ghostly yarns. He's famous for *A Christmas Carol* (1843), but there was also its prototype, "The Story of the Goblins Who Stole a Sexton", buried in Dickens' first novel *The Pickwick Papers* (1837), and also "The Signal-Man" (1866).

Dickens was preceded in the telling of these thrilling tales by many other pioneers in the field, including Edgar Allan Poe and Mary Wollstonecraft Shelley, and followed by others, such as M.R. James, Robert Louis Stevenson, Henry James, Bram Stoker, Gaston Leroux, and Sir Arthur Conan Doyle.

The latter, Dr. Watson's Literary Agent, contrived a number of supernatural stories throughout his career, including the Egyptian-themed "Lot 249" and "The Ring of Thoth" – or so I'm told, as I've never actually read anything written by Conan Doyle besides the historical middle sections of *A Study in Scarlet* and *The Valley of Fear*, and the introduction to *The Casebook of Sherlock Holmes*. A man of science himself, Conan Doyle's odd pivot to an interest in spiritualism began in the mid-1880's, progressing steadily throughout his life from being merely curious to a fervent missionary as he became one of its indefatigable and vigorous defenders. Even as that occurred, one can only imagine his acquaintance, Sherlock Holmes, shaking his head in either pity or disgust.

3

In the original Canon, there are a number of occasions when Holmes is approached to investigate something that has some apparent connection to the supernatural. *The Hound of the Baskervilles* stems from an ancient family curse. "The Adventure of Wisteria Lodge" has connections to voodoo. As mentioned, "The Sussex Vampire" seems to involve a blood-sucker attacking a child. "The Creeping Man" concerns the possible transformation of a man to a beast through suspicious and unproven science, and "The Devil's Foot" is a chilling case where something can drive men mad – or kill them. Even "The Copper Beeches" and "The Speckled Band", while not specifically supernatural, cannot avoid a sense of creeping horror. Then there are the untold cases – a giant rat, a remarkable worm unknown to science, and the cutter *Alicia* vanishing into the mist. And that doesn't even begin to account for all the subsequent narratives provided by later Literary Agents wherein Holmes seems to face the impossible.

The examples are far too numerous to list completely here, but the list wouldn't be complete without mentioning stories in various collections like *The Irregular Casebook of Sherlock Holmes* by Ron Weighell (2000), *Ghosts in Baker Street* (2006), the Lovecraftian-themed *Shadows Over Baker Street* (2003), and the ongoing *Gaslight* series (see below.) Holmes battled the supposedly supernatural in countless old radio shows, including "The Limping Ghost" (September 1945), "The Stuttering Ghost" (October 1946), "The Bleeding Chandelier" (June 1948), "The Uddington Witch" (October 1948), and "The Tollington Ghost" (April 2007). And of course, one mustn't forget the six truly amazing episodes of John Taylor's *The Uncovered Casebook of Sherlock Holmes* (1993), published in the same year as a very fine companion book. Then there's George Mann's audio drama "The Reification of Hans Gerber" (2011), later novelized as part of *Sherlock Holmes: The Will of the Dead* (2013).

An especially good radio episode with supernatural overtones was "The Haunted Bagpipes" by Edith Meiser, (February 1947), later presented in comic form as illustrated by Frank Giacoia, and then again adapted for print by Carla Coupe in *Sherlock Holmes Mystery Magazine* (Vol. 2, No. 1, 2011)

In addition to numerous radio broadcasts, there were similar "impossible" television episodes from the old 1950's television show *Sherlock Holmes* with Ronald Howard, such as "The Belligerent Ghost", "The Haunted Gainsborough", and "The Laughing Mummy". The show was rebooted in 1980 with Geoffrey Whitehead as Holmes, and had an episode called "The Other Ghost". Films with

4

Holmes facing something with other-worldly overtones have included *The Scarlet Claw* (1944), *The Case of the Whitechapel Vampire* (2002), and *Sherlock Holmes* (2009).

From the massive list of similarly themed fan-fictions, one might choose "The Mottled Eyes" or "The Vampire's Kiss". There are countless novels, such as the six short works by Kel Richards, or Val Andrews' *The Longacre Vampire* (2000), or *Draco, Draconis* (1996) by Spencer Brett and David Dorian. One shouldn't ignore the narratives brought to us by Sam Siciliano, narrated by Holmes's annoying cousin Dr. Henry Vernier, all featuring supposedly supernatural encounters. Then there is Randall Collins' *The Case of the Philosopher's Ring* (1978) and the different sequels to *The Hound*, including Rick Boyer's most amazing *The Giant Rat of Sumatra* (1976), Teresa Collard's *The Baskerville Inheritance* (2012), and Kelvin Jones' *The Baskerville Papers* (2016).

Holmes has battled Count Dracula in too many encounters to list, but in almost every one of them, he finds himself ridiculously facing a real undead Transylvanian vampire who can change to a bat. Often, Holmes is simply inserted into the Van Helsing role within the plot of the original *Dracula* story. I've always ignored each of these, as the *real* Holmes would never encounter an imaginary creature such as this. The one exception so far has been a book that I recently read, Mark Latham's *A Betrayal in Blood* (2017) – finally, a Holmes-Dracula encounter that I can enjoy and highly recommend.

A list of this sort is really too long to compile, and this shouldn't be taken as anywhere close to the last word. There are numerous supposedly impossible circumstances or supernatural encounters of one sort or another contained in many Holmes collections, tucked in with the more "normal" cases, and these are but a few of them:

- The Case of the Vampire's Mark", *Murder in Baker Street* – Bill Crider
- "The Night in the Elizabethan Concert Hall in the Very Heart of London" *and* "The Night In The Burial Vault Under The Sanitarium At Soames Meadow", *Traveling With Sherlock Holmes and Dr. Watson* – Herman Anthony Litzinger
- "The Adventure of Jackthorn Circle", *Sherlock Holmes: Mysteries of the Victorian Era* – Rock DiLisio
- "Sherlock Holmes, Dragon Slayer", *Resurrected Holmes* – Darrell Schweitzer

- "The Adventure of the Phantom Coachman", *The MX Book of New Sherlock Holmes Stories – Part IV: 2016 Annual –* Arthur Hall
- "The Adventure of the Talking Ghost", *Alias Simon Hawkes* – Philip J. Carraher
- "Lord Garnett's Skulls", *The MX Book of New Sherlock Holmes Stories – Part II: 1890-1895* – J.R. Campbell
- "The Ghost of Gordon Square", *The Chemical Adventures of Sherlock Holmes* – Thomas G. Waddell and Thomas R. Rybolt
- "The Case of Hodgson's Ghost", *The Oriental Casebook of Sherlock Holmes* – Ted Riccardi
- "A Ballad of the White Plague", *The Confidential Casebook of Sherlock Holmes* – P.C. Hodgel
- "The Adventure of the Dark Tower", *The MX Book of New Sherlock Holmes Stories – Part III: 1896-1929* – Peter K. Andersson
- "The Adventure of the Field Theorems", *Sherlock Holmes In Orbit* – Vonda N. McIntyre
- "The Haunting of Sutton House", *The Papers of Sherlock Holmes Vol. I* – David Marcum
- "The Chamber of Sorrow Mystery", *The Outstanding Mysteries of Sherlock Holmes* – Gerard Kelly
- "The Shadows on the Lawn", *The New Adventures of Sherlock Holmes* – Barry Jones
- "The Deptford Horror", *The Exploits of Sherlock Holmes* – Adrian Conan Doyle and John Dickson Carr

When I had the idea for the theme of this anthology, I wasn't sure how it would go. I'm a strict traditionalist. I want to read more and more Canonical-type stories about Holmes and Watson – and nothing about "Sherlock and John"! – and that's what I write and also encourage in others as well. Many has been the time when I've started reading a new Holmes story, only to realize that, no matter how authentic the first part is, the end has veered off into one-hundred-percent no-coming-back supernatural territory – Holmes is battling a real monster, or facing a full-fledged vampire or wolfman, or perhaps a brain-eating fungus from another planet. There is a misguided belief that, just because someone wishes it to be so, Holmes is interchangeable with Abraham Van Helsing – and he most definitely is not.

6

As someone who has collected, read, and chronologicized literally thousands of Holmes adventures over the last forty-two-plus years, I'm dismayed when this happens. As I make notes for each story to be listed in the massive overall chronology that I've constructed, I generally indicate when a book has "incorrect" statements or segments, and that includes notes identifying those parts of a story that were really and truly written by Watson, as compared with paragraphs or pages or chapters that were clearly composed and added by some later editor who has taken Watson's notes and either changed parts, or stuck in completely fictional middles and endings to fulfill their own agenda. Sometimes the story goes so far off into the weeds that even pulled-out pieces of it can't be judged as authentic, and the whole thing is lost.

In terms of the theme of these books – *Eliminate the Impossible* – I owe thanks to Sherlockian Jeff Cambell. In the past he's found some tales from Watson's Tin Dispatch Box, and also (with Charles Prepolec) edited several anthologies, including two of my favorites, *Curious Incidents* Volumes I and II, featuring totally traditionally adventures, and *Gaslight Grimoire* (2008), *Gaslight Grotesque* (2009), and *Gaslight Arcanum* (2011), each with a more decided supernatural bend. Jeff and I were emailing about things Holmesian back in June 2016, and it was then that I had the idea for this collection's theme. We discussed it in a few emails, and I realized that I was enthusiastic about an anthology of apparently supernatural investigations, *but with rational solutions* – just like "The Sussex Vampire" and *The Hound of the Baskervilles.*

I sent out invitations, and the response was overwhelming. Just like the first volumes of the MX anthologies, which grew from one to two, and then from two to three, this two-volume set started with the idea of being a single book before greatly expanding, as more people wanted to join the party. (Sadly, Jeff Campbell was going to write a story, but his own editing duties for the upcoming *Gaslight Gothic* took his attention elsewhere.)

As I had explained to the participants, this book would consist of what seemed to be supernatural tales, but with real-world rational endings. However, I left the door open just a crack – if there was some sort of hint at the end that more had occurred than could be easily explained, possibly even something a bit supernatural, I was okay with that too – this time. After all, I think it's arrogant for us to think we have figured it all out, and that something doesn't exist simply because we can't see it . . . yet. To paraphrase Hamlet: *There*

7

are more things in heaven and earth, Watson, Than are dreamt of in your philosophy.

I did hear a bit of sarcastic push-back. One person referred to this as a "Scooby Doo book", but I firmly declare that there is a plethora of different kinds of stories in this volume, and none that have the sense that the culprit would have gotten away with it if not for that meddlesome consulting detective.

These two volumes contain stories where Holmes faces ghosts and mythological creatures, possessions and prophecies, impossible circumstances and curses. Some begin with the impossible element defined from the beginning, while others progress for quite a while as "normal" cases before the twist is revealed. As with all Holmes adventures, this collection represents one of the great enjoyments of reading about The Great Detective – the reader never knows where each tale will lead. The narratives might be serious or humorous, workmanlike or heart-breaking.

The reader might encounter a ghost story or a police procedural or a caper, set in London or in the country, or early or late in Holmes's career, and either a comedy or a tragedy. And while each of the adventures in these volumes is categorized by Holmes *eliminating* the impossible to obtain, however improbable, the truth, the various impossibilities contained within these covers are presented in an incredibly varied and exciting manner. I'm certain that you will enjoy all of them.

As always, I want to thank with all my heart my patient and wonderful wife of nearly thirty years (as of this writing,) Rebecca, and our son, Dan. I love you both, and you are everything to me!

I can't ever express enough gratitude for all of the contributors who have donated their time and royalties to this ongoing project. I'm so glad to have gotten to know all of you through this process. It's an undeniable fact that Sherlock Holmes authors are the *best* people!

The royalties for this project go to support the Stepping Stones School for special needs children, located at Undershaw, one of Sir Arthur Conan Doyle's former homes. These books are making a real difference to the school, and the participation of both contributors and purchasers is most appreciated.

Next is that wonderful crew of people who listen to my complaints and manic enthusiasms, read my Sherlockian thoughts and dogma, and offer support, encouragement, and friendship, sometimes on a nearly daily basis, and sometimes more irregularly as daily business gets in the way of replies. Many many thanks to (in alphabetical order): Derrick Belanger, Bob Byrne, Steve Emecz, Roger Johnson, Mark Mower, Denis Smith, Tom Turley, Dan Victor, and Marcia Wilson.

I want to thank the people who wrote forewords to the books:

- Lee Child –Many people might not realize that in another life, you worked at Granada Television from the mid-1970's to the mid-1990's, during the glory days when Jeremy Brett's Holmes was being produced. Thanks for your perspective on The Great Detective.
- Michael Cox – Thank you so mjuch for giving your thoughts about pastiche and the making of the Granada Holmes series. And I especially thank you for making sure that those programs adhered to the TRUE Canon and the TRUE Holmes!
- Rand Lee – I can't thank you enough for writing a foreword and giving some information about your father, one of my favorite writers of all time, Manfred Lee, half of *Ellery Queen*. As I've explained elsewhere, Ellery's adventures are some of the best stories anywhere, period. Go read them, people!
- Roger Johnson – Several years ago, when I first found one of Watson's old notebooks and prepared it for publication, I sent a copy to Roger, because it really mattered to me that he review it. He was very receptive, and we began to email. Since then, I'm glad to have become friends with both him and his wonderful wife, Jean Upton. Roger always takes time to answer my questions and to participate in various projects, and he and Jean were very gracious to host me for several days during part of my second Holmes Pilgrimage to England in 2015. In so many ways, Roger, I can't thank you enough.
- Melissa Farnham – Thanks for the work that you do, and personally for taking time last year, when I was able to attend the Grand Opening event at Undershaw, to take my picture while I was sitting in Conan Doyle's study. I'll never forget it!

Thanks also to Jeff Campbell for sparking the initial idea of this collection, Rich Ryan, (who put me in touch with Lee Child, leading

9

to Mr. Child's foreword for these books,) and James Lovegrove, who answered a question about storm directions at Holmes's retirement villa.

And last but certainly *not* least, **Sir Arthur Conan Doyle**: Author, doctor, adventurer, and the Founder of the Sherlockian Feast. Present in spirit, and honored by all of us here.

As always, this collection has been a labor of love by both the participants and myself. As I've explained before, once again everyone did their sincerest best to produce an anthology that truly represents why Holmes and Watson have been so popular for so long. These are just more tiny threads woven into the ongoing Great Holmes Tapestry, continuing to grow and grow, for there can *never* be enough stories about the man whom Watson described as *"the best and wisest . . . whom I have ever known."*

David Marcum
August 7th, 2017
The 165th Birthday of Dr. John H. Watson

Questions, comments, or story submissions
may be addressed to David Marcum at
thepapersofsherlockholmes@gmail.com

Foreword
by Lee Child

Not long ago, series editor David Marcum e-mailed me to remind me that the deadline for this foreword was coming up fast. At that moment I was reading an in-depth true-crime story in a prestigious weekly magazine. The case involved a man found dead in his car. There was evidence of a pre-existing heart condition, and of recent sexual excitement, and of a low dose of a certain dangerously stimulative drug in his system. The drug in question was obtainable only through a particular type of doctor's office. There was a twenty-minute window during which the alleged perpetrator's movements were not accounted for. The prosecutor developed a narrative whereby the alleged perpetrator must have had both prior knowledge of the victim's heart condition and foreknowledge of his upcoming sexual excitement, thereby allowing him to use a small – and therefore hopefully undetectable by taste – dose of the drug to lethal effect. The perpetrator was alleged to have taken a fast, circuitous twenty-minute there-and-back route to the crime scene, where he was alleged to have delivered the mild-but-fatal dose in a go-cup of Dunkin' Donuts coffee. No other explanation would fit the facts. The journalist called it a "Holmesian solution". My eyes were on the word "Holmesian" when David's e-mail pinged in on my phone.

Coincidence? To some extent, but not as much as you think. Sherlock Holmes is by far the most deeply embedded fictional character in our adult culture. Beyond by far. His penetration as a metaphor, worldwide, into every area of discourse is unparalleled. In fact my own character, Jack Reacher, a brainy detective but famous as a wanderer who eschews possessions, was once described as "*Sherlock Homeless*". By a journalist in Spain. People make Holmes puns even in foreign languages.

How did this happen? Let's agree Conan Doyle was a fine, original writer, but he wasn't unparalleled or by far the best in history. When reading The Canon we are entirely satisfied, but we know Holmes isn't world famous more than a century later because of the quality of the prose alone. The plots of the stories have a better claim to immortality, being necessarily complicated and ingenious, and often unhinged enough, in a Victorian way, to sear themselves in our memories. But are plots enough that around the world probably a thousand journalists a day use a Holmes metaphor in their work?

The conventional analysis is no, it's the character that counts. It's Sherlock Holmes himself. But I think that's incomplete. Sherlock Holmes is two things: What he is, and what he does. His character and his process supply two different needs. One is primary, and the other is secondary. As a person, he's fascinating, compelling, and deserves every bit of his enduring appeal, but what he does is much more important.

First, he explains the incomprehensible. That has been a universal human desire dating back to the earliest reaches of our prehistory, ever since we first glanced at the stars with enough new intellectual capacity to wonder what they were. We retain powerful ghost traces of that desire today, and we carry equally powerful primeval memories of the satisfaction – the joy, even – we feel when our questions are answered. Holmes first excites our desire, and then brings the joy. Because we understand the conventions of narrative fiction, we know all along we will get the explanation, so the twin emotions are blended. We wonder why, say, red-headed men are being lured to a certain place, and we thrill with the delicious feeling of knowing, just knowing, we're going to find out soon, and it's going to be good. Whether by fantastically smart design, or fantastically good fortune, Conan Doyle has Holmes stroking and massaging a DNA remnant ten million years in the making.

And second, Holmes gives us the deep human pleasure of seeing something done superbly well. It's why we love the great magicians, and the great athletes, and acrobats and gymnasts and jugglers. Sherlock Holmes gives us the mental equivalent. Our separate indrawn breaths in our individual reading places add up to stadium-sized gasps. Like his physical counterparts, Holmes's ratiocination can be dazzling, and is never less than solidly satisfying. It's something done well, which is always a pleasure.

As will be reading the stories in this book. They are all solid, non-gimmicky, respectful, disciplined celebrations of The Canon. They're about taking one step further into the world we imagine so vividly. They are about thinking your way into the front room in Baker Street, and staying there a spell, and looking around, and asking, "What if this happened?" The result: These stories, and the pleasure of seeing something done well.

Lee Child
New York, July 2017

Foreword
by Rand B. Lee

My father, Manfred B. Lee, would have loved *Eliminate the Impossible.* Co-author with our cousin Frederic Dannay of the *Ellery Queen* mysteries, Dad was a Sherlock Holmes fan from boyhood. Born Emanuel Benjamin Lepofsky in 1905 to a poor blue collar Jewish family in Brownsville, a suburb of Brooklyn, New York, young Manny's early world was not that different from Holmes and Watson's. Gaslight illuminated the neighborhood where he grew up. "Iceboxes" kept food from spoiling, cooled not by electricity and chemicals but by chunks of ice delivered by the iceman. Automobiles, airplanes, and motion pictures were still thrilling novelties, and communication was accomplished by letter writing, telephone, or telegraph. There were no ATM's – if you wished to get cash from your banking account, you needed to visit the bank, in person, before closing Monday through Friday.

My father's early years were marked not only by the humiliations of poverty and anti-semitism, but also by the horrors of World War I, the global influenza epidemic, and the Great Depression. I have always felt that the logic-driven rationalism of the Sherlock Holmes mysteries, in which Holmes's observational skills and scientific acumen brings balance and closure to even the most gruesome puzzles, satisfied Dad's craving for justice and the triumph of reason over chaos. In the character of Ellery Queen, the gentleman detective, Holmes's powers of reasoned observation were reincarnated, softened a bit by Dr. Watson's capacity for empathy.

Rand B. Lee
May 2017

Where Pastiche Begins . . . .
by Michael Cox

In the early 1980's, when I set out to make the best possible Sherlock Holmes series for television, I gave no thought to the question of pastiche. In my innocence, I thought that our films would be based fairly and squarely on Conan Doyle's original stories and that was that. To begin with that belief held true. The first of *The Adventures*, no matter which collection of stories they came from, were entirely faithful to the originals with very few additional flourishes.

Then we reached the adventure of "The Greek Interpreter", and I have to admit that an element of pastiche began to creep in. It happened because the grammar of film demands a different structure from the grammar of prose fiction. Conan Doyle brought the story to a curious conclusion. Once the interpreter has been rescued, he presents us with a series of unanswered questions about the fate of the villains. On the screen this would have left us feeling unsatisfied and deprived of a climax. So we supplied our own answers. I believe that they were in the style of the original and I hope they were satisfying as well as exciting. Above all, they obeyed the film maker's imperative: *Don't tell me, show me!*

As time went by, we took more liberties with the stories, although we were always determined to keep the original plots intact. Our most substantial addition was the one we made to "The Final Problem". This is a curious detective story because there is no problem to solve and no mystery for Holmes to tackle. There is simply the battle of wills between The Master and Moriarty which leads to the shocking finale at the Reichenbach Falls. So we added a crime: The theft of the Mona Lisa and Holmes's success in recovering it through his pioneering study of fingerprints.

Over the years that the series ran, we changed Watsons and the production team also changed. I moved into the background, and after more than thirty episodes disappeared altogether. When these changes were introduced, the scripts remained faithful to Doyle, but towards the end there were some extraordinary lurches into pastiche. Chambers Dictionary rather unkindly defines this as "a jumble", and "The Eligible Bachelor" (or "The Unintelligible Bachelor" as one critic described it,) is a good example. Unhappily, "The Last

Vampyre" is another. Both these episodes suffered from the schedulers' demand for two-hour films, rather than the shorter format with which we began. Holmes has usually been happier in short stories.

Unfortunately, the writers were not aware of the very sensible rules which David Marcum has laid down for the contributors to this anthology. Neither (dare I say?) were the creators of the BBC series *Sherlock*. But you are in good company here. You can sit back and enjoy the additions to the Holmes Canon between the covers of this book. They all show a proper respect for that great storyteller, Arthur Conan Doyle, and add to our enjoyment of the world he created.

Michael Cox
Producer, *The Adventures of Sherlock Holmes*
Granada Television 1981-1985
March 2017

"Rubbish, Watson, Rubbish!"
by Roger Johnson

Sherlock Holmes made his opinion absolutely clear. He dismisses the legend of the Baskerville family as of interest only to "*a collector of fairy tales*", and when Dr. James Mortimer confesses uncertainty as to whether the phantom hound of the legend has returned to Dartmoor, Holmes says, "*I see that you have quite gone over to the supernaturalists.*"

On another occasion, when the topic of vampirism in rural Sussex is raised, he exclaims, "*Rubbish, Watson, rubbish! What have we to do with walking corpses who can only be held in their grave by stakes driven through their hearts? It's pure lunacy.*"

But more familiar perhaps is his statement a minute or so later: "*This agency stands flat-footed upon the ground, and there it must remain. The world is big enough for us. No ghosts need apply.*"

Arthur Conan Doyle had been interested since childhood in the supernatural, mainly as a concept in fiction. It was not only for the "tales of ratiocination" that he revered Edgar Allan Poe, and ACD himself wrote some excellent ghost stories, including "The Leather Funnel", "Lot No. 249", "The Ring of Thoth", and "The Captain of the *Pole Star*". In the early 1880's, perhaps inspired by a lecture he attended at the Portsmouth Literary and Philosophical Society, he began to take a serious interest in the theory that the dead have merely passed from one sphere of life to another, and that they can communicate with the living. It was not until some three decades later that he became a leading advocate for spiritualism, but the belief was there, growing, all along.

It's important, incidentally, to realise that Conan Doyle thought of spiritualism in terms of scientific research and discovery. He was by no means the only trained scientist to believe that communication with the dead was possible, and was not "supernatural" in the usual meaning of the word, but rather the revelation of a higher level of nature.

Yet he never inserted his spiritualist beliefs into the Sherlock Holmes stories. Some think that he might have done so if he had been fonder of the detective, but there's very little evidence in the stories of any deep religious faith or adherence to a philosophy such

16

as Buddhism. To Sherlock Holmes, they would have been as disruptive as – well, as grit in a sensitive instrument or a crack in one of his own high-power lenses. [1]

More to the point as far as this book is concerned, Conan Doyle never had Holmes confront actual ghosts, vampires, werewolves, or anything of that sort. *The Hound of the Baskervilles* and "The Sussex Vampire" are firmly in the tradition that we might call "the impossible explained". Over a century before, the novels of Ann Radcliffe – notably *The Mysteries of Udolpho* – had made the device very popular, but Conan Doyle added the important element of logical reasoning to prove that the supposed supernatural was nothing of the sort. And in doing so, he harked back much farther in time, to the story of Daniel and the idol in the Old Testament Apocrypha. [2]

"No ghosts need apply . . . ." And yet, for many years pasticheurs have refused to take Sherlock Holmes at his word. The results (are you surprised?) have been variable. The trend began, or at least became fashionable, with Loren D Estleman's novel *Sherlock Holmes vs Dracula, or The Adventure of the Sanguinary Count*, and the aristocratic Romanian immigrant has been by far the most popular choice of supernatural opponent. Fred Saberhagen, in a series that begins with *The Holmes-Dracula File*, actually posits a blood relationship between the detective and the vampire.

Holmes, with or without Watson, has faced the cosmic horrors of H.P. Lovecraft's "Cthulhu Mythos". He has opposed evil Faeries, and been recruited to assist the famous psychic sleuths John Silence and Thomas Carnacki. There are anthologies with titles like *Gaslight Grimoire, Shadows Over Baker Street, The Improbable Adventures of Sherlock Holmes*, and *Ghosts in Baker Street*.

Some of these books and some of the short stories are of high quality: Well conceived, well executed, and immensely entertaining. Ron Weighell's *The Irregular Casebook of Sherlock Holmes*, though rare, is well worth looking out for. His knowledge of the occult is matched by his knowledge of Sherlock Holmes. The great bulk of Holmes pastiche, however, makes one nostalgic for the days when it was a good deal harder to get a book accepted for publication.

Fortunately we have the ideal antidote in David Marcum, Steve Emecz, and all the contributors to the present volumes. They know that when Sherlock Holmes investigates an apparently supernatural phenomenon, he should (a) find that the occurrence is actually down

17

to natural causes — and (b) that the natural causes were made possible by human agency.

What more could one reasonably wish for?

Roger Johnson, BSI, ASH
Editor: *The Sherlock Holmes Journal*
June 2017

NOTES

1 – A character for whom the author had more regard, Professor George Edward Challenger, was introduced to spiritualism, and indeed converted, in *The Land of Mist*. Conan Doyle used Challenger to make what he believed to be an important statement, but artistically the story is all wrong. Challenger was always the outsider, the man who *challenged* scientific orthodoxy, the heretic who was proved right. That's an essential element of *The Lost World*, "The Poison Belt", and the other Challenger adventures . . . but not *The Land of Mist*. Given Conan Doyle's absolute belief, Challenger should have been the one attempting to convince the others – Malone, Summerlee, Roxton, and the rest – of the truth of spiritualism. Instead, he is the belligerent embodiment of scientific conformity, more like Summerlee of old than his own self.

2 – He was evidently familiar with this particular tale, which is considered canonical by the Roman Catholic Church, as Holmes adopts the Prophet Daniel's device at a crucial point in "The Golden Pince-Nez".

A Word From the
Head Teacher of Stepping Stones
by Melissa Farnham

W e now draw towards the end of our first year in Undershaw, and the young people under our watch truly feel like they are part of history.

> *A man should keep his little brain attic stocked with all the furniture that he is likely to use, and the rest he can put away in the lumber-room of his library, where he can get it if he wants it.*

– Sherlock Holmes
"The Five Orange Pips"

In the fast paced world we live in, these words are both of truth and demand. Enhancing young people's metacognition skills to ensure a well-stocked attic is paramount as we prepare them for the world they will one day step into.

Melissa Farhnam
Head Teacher, *Stepping Stones,* Undershaw
July 2017

Undershaw
Circa 1900

Undershaw
September 9, 2016
Grand Opening of the Stepping Stones School
Photograph courtesy of Roger Johnson

Sherlock Holmes (1854-1957) was born in Yorkshire, England, on 6 January, 1854. In the mid-1870's, he moved to 24 Montague Street, London, where he established himself as the world's first Consulting Detective. After meeting Dr. John H. Watson in early 1881, he and Watson moved to rooms at 221b Baker Street, where his reputation as the world's greatest detective grew for several decades. He was presumed to have died battling noted criminal Professor James Moriarty on 4 May, 1891, but he returned to London on 5 April, 1894, resuming his consulting practice in Baker Street. Retiring to the Sussex coast near Beachy Head in October 1903, he continued to be involved in various private and government investigations while giving the impression of being a reclusive apiarist. He was very involved in the events encompassing World War I, and to a lesser degree those of World War II. He passed away peacefully upon the cliffs above his Sussex home on his 103rd birthday, 6 January, 1957.

Dr. John Hamish Watson (1852-1929) was born in Stranraer, Scotland on 7 August, 1852. In 1878, he took his Doctor of Medicine Degree from the University of London, and later joined the army as a surgeon. Wounded at the Battle of Maiwand in Afghanistan (27 July, 1880), he returned to London late that same year. On New Year's Day, 1881, he was introduced to Sherlock Holmes in the chemical laboratory at Barts. Agreeing to share rooms with Holmes in Baker Street, Watson became invaluable to Holmes's consulting detective practice. Watson was married and widowed three times, and from the late 1880's onward, in addition to his participation in Holmes's investigations and his medical practice, he chronicled Holmes's adventures, with the assistance of his literary agent, Sir Arthur Conan Doyle, in a series of popular narratives, most of which were first published in *The Strand* magazine. Watson's later years were spent preparing a vast number of his notes of Holmes's cases for future publication. Following a final important investigation with Holmes, Watson contracted pneumonia and passed away on 24 July, 1929.

Photos of Sherlock Holmes and Dr. John H. Watson courtesy of Roger Johnson

The MX Book
of
New Sherlock Holmes Stories
PART VIII –
Eliminate the Impossible:
1892-1905

Sherlock Holmes
in the
Lavender Field
by Christopher James

Retired now, he spends his days beekeeping
and playing Bach's sonatas on his violin.
At night, he feeds his case notes to the fire
allowing old enemies to slip from his mind.
But today, he is standing in a field of lavender
showing me the sky: how the cirrus uncinus
is a blur of angels returning to heaven; why
the altocumulus floccus is the pipe smoke
of a thousand problems. At the edge of the field
is a man in a black topper, a statue of Napoleon
in one hand, a pistol in the other. *Look*, my friend
says: a single bee buzzes inside a gold snuff box.
Holmes lifts the lid and lets it spiral into the air,
woozy with freedom, as the bullet sings by.

The Adventure of the Lama's Dream
by Deanna Baran

My friend Holmes had long ago determined to trade his rooms overlooking the streets of London for lodgings upon the chalk cliffs and thyme-scented downs of the Sussex coast. Sometimes he spoke of botany, and sometimes of philosophy, and sometimes of apiculture. Privately, I suspected it would remain but a fanciful dream. I doubted that the kittiwakes and gannets would provide him with the mental stimulation he required. As he once said, he was a brain, and the rest of him mere appendix, and such a one is never meant for a retirement consisting of little more than golf club and tackle box.

Likewise, for one who had led a life of excitement, influencing events upon the international stage, it was almost an insult to imagine him spending his declining years in an arm-chair before the fire in the presence of a conscientious nurse-maid. No, I was certain this old hound would run to the view-halloa till the very end, and where else was a better setting for his activity than London, the very centre of our Empire? No matter how much energy he had expended during the course of his career, and how deserving of retirement he may be, I knew it would be selfish – nay, criminal! – for him to bury himself in obscurity and rob Britain of his unique and irreplaceable talents.

"It's not the edge of the world," said Holmes kindly, breaking in upon my reflection. "Only the edge of our great island."

"Eavesdropping upon my thoughts!" I exclaimed. "Come now, I thought you were of the opinion that such displays were pretentious in the extreme."

"Even a child could have followed your thoughts as they cycled through your brain," he explained, unruffled. "Since your eye fell upon the correspondence from my agent upon my desk, your lip has not uncurled from its disdainful sneer. You glanced at my scrapbooks upon the shelf, calling to mind my long and illustrious career. You shake your head pityingly to yourself. Perhaps you think it a loss to society, or perhaps you doubt my ability to make such a drastic transition at this stage of life."

"I was imagining you with no greater ambition in the world than to correct the flaw in your swing! I believe you would go mad within the month from the banality of retired life in the countryside."

"On the contrary, I suspect you, your wife, and your patients would be grateful for the peace and quiet, without the worry of my appearing like a jack-in-the-box and hauling you off to Cardiff one moment and Inverness the next."

"We all got accustomed to it a long time ago," I said, rather more gruffly than I had intended. "But, see here, London is so full and alive. I think you would miss all of the people, the places, and the amenities that one finds in a metropolis."

"It hasn't been easy to trade St. James's Hall for the Queen's Hall," countered Holmes. "London isn't the same these days as even a decade ago. Ah, there is no constant like change! Although I suspect such an observation even pre-dates the concept of the city."

"The museums, the concerts, the colorful characters," I said. "For example, I heard some positive things from some of my lady-patients regarding a very popular and successful series, 'Cosmology of the Orient'. The lectures are given by a man who spent twenty years in Lucknow, and he speaks of his experiences with the *gurus* and *faquirs*. Now, there's a man who you would be unlikely to encounter upon the pleasure pier at Hastings."

"Do you think that scholarly lecturers do not take seaside outings?" asked Holmes. "And besides, may I remind you, you are not the only one in this room who has docked at Bombay."

"I had forgotten that," I admitted. "You speak so rarely of the happenstances of that interlude, it is easy to overlook that you yourself spent no little time in the East. I don't suppose you might regale me with a tale that would rival that of the paid lecturer?"

"So much time has passed, I don't see the harm in it," said Holmes thoughtfully. "Of course, you realize that Tibet itself was, and still is, barred to Europeans, and those caught trespassing and all who would aid them in their intrusion can only have expectations of torture, mutilation, and frequently, death. Yet it was the very doorstep to British interests in India, and much of the last century was a chess game on a grand scale between the Tzar and Her Majesty to determine whose influence would reign over the vast expanse of Central Asia. Also pray remember that the Emperor of China was not sitting idle during all this time, and so one can imagine that Tibet was quite the cauldron of international interests, especially during the period in question. You know all this, having been a pawn in Afghanistan yourself.

"However, just because the official position is 'no foreigners allowed', in practice, the rule is truly 'no foreigners allowed, except for those we in power care to make an exception'. So, as I found it personally prudent to lie low in anonymity, the Foreign Office found a way to make use of me during this period when I found it useful to not be myself. Even with my talent for masquerade, there was no way I could disguise my European heritage in such an environment: The mere gray of my eyes would have been sufficient to betray me, let alone my height, for I was as Gulliver among the Lilliputians. Besides, the Tibetan language is so full of idiom, I could have spent a decade in study and still tripped over my phrases. So, if I had to be obviously European, I could at least pass for Norwegian for those who must needs be aware of my presence, as Norway had no political baggage that would make my presence awkward for my hosts, or lead to unpleasant speculation amongst those who had no business speculating.

"The country itself is in the hands of the lamas themselves, as far as is permitted under the administration of the *Qing ambasa*, and they guard their temporal power with feudalistic fervor. There are dozens of lamasseries throughout, some clinging to sheer cliffs, others more prosaically erected upon the vast plateau. In all places, the air was thin and cold, and I doubt I ever felt truly warm during all my time in that country. In addition to my unofficial official duties, Sigerson took a little time to compose a few articles for various ethnological journals on the subjects of Tibetan art, religion, cuisine, and music. It lent colour and credence to the disguise. I don't suppose you ever went back and read any of them?"

"You had never mentioned their existence," I said. "You know that I read the medical journals myself."

"They're very fond of their tea," reminisced Holmes. "But it's easier to drink if one imagines it to be soup. Jewels, as depicted in art, look remarkably like turnips. Their music is best appreciated at a certain distance – approach too close, and it's positively barbarous. A barnyard or a nursery would be more melodic. I suppose that was the way it was for much of the country: Perceived at a distance, it was the stuff of fairy tales beyond the dreams of Haroun Al-Raschid. But when investigated up close, it could be rather grimy and even tawdry. For example, the massive Potala Palace of Lhassa would overwhelm the residence of any of the crowned heads of Europe – and yet few of the rooms are ever used, let alone cleaned, and the whole of it is pervaded by this unique scent, a mingling of the sweetness of incense and putridity, an odor that is so uniquely

31

Tibetan that I have never smelt it duplicated anywhere else in the world. You would have had a fine time describing it, Watson – the dim glow of the butter-lamps, Milton's star-powdered sky, corridors of mystery, dreams of empire, the glint of gold, the rustle of brocade. And yet, contrasted with the realities of those who begged in the shadow of its palaces – the cripple with his severed tendons, his neighbor with his nose sliced off, their companion with his eyes gouged out. It was no mythical fairy-kingdom then!"

"I suppose every land has its unfortunate souls," I mused. "Goodness knows there is more than one neighbourhood I would not care to venture into after dark without a sturdy policeman at my side."

"You are aware that regardless of where I travel, small problems seem to be drawn to my attention as iron to a magnet. In addition to my unofficial official business performed on behalf of the Foreign Office, I found the solution to a handful of matters which had inconvenienced and perplexed my hosts. This feat I credit entirely to my powers of observation and deduction, as, as I remarked, I had little grasp of the language itself, and many of the little signs I would normally expect to find upon the person of a British subject did not translate into this culture."

"But on the other hand, I'm sure you picked up a wealth of observations regarding caste and rank," I suggested. "'This is how a trader sneezes; observe the distinctive way in which a labourer walks; please take note of the warrior's unique method of expectoration!'"

Holmes fixed me with a stern eye for having made light of his beloved science of observation. "You know as well as I do that caste has no place north of the Himalayas, whereas, yes, individuals in different classes do have their own mannerisms and conventions. A costermonger cannot masquerade with any success as an archbishop; a pilot is not indistinguishable from a parliamentarian at twenty paces."

"Pray continue," I said humbly, fearing that he would not resume the broken thread of his narration.

"Thus it was that one of the other lamas requested the honor of my presence at his lamassery. His status was such that my keepers found it fitting to indulge this whim. I found myself conveyed to an isolated mountain fastness. Each of these lamas in this country, you see, is the custodian of a particular school of thought, or line of teaching, and is trained up from youth by the students of his predecessor. In this particular place, the throne was shared by two

32

individuals who were considered the reincarnation of their tutelary deity: The young man, a lad of seventeen at the time, held the position of the 'Heart' reincarnation, whereas his co-principal was a man of surely no less than sixty, who claimed to be the living 'Speech' of their god. Together, as the two halves of their living god, they formed the head of their establishment, teaching dogma, performing divinations, and conducting sacred rites."

"Living god?" I asked blankly.

"Most of the lamasseries have at least one," said Holmes carelessly. "Many of the lamas themselves are astonishingly cavalier about it, but it is their bread and butter, and they generally enjoy giving the populace every possible chance to accumulate merit by exercising the virtue of charity. The result is a certain amount of cynicism regarding the whole thing. This attitude crosses over into the common people as well. There was a most interesting song I was able to transcribe, although ultimately it was rejected, for although it was of great ethnographic interest, it wasn't fit for print. Granted, they do have genuine respect for some of the lamas, especially for some of the very elderly ones. And I know Kipling's lama exists here and there in quiet obscurity, striving to follow the great Example beneath the leaves of the Pipul. But most of the men I encountered in this portion of my wanderings were very much – men.

"Of course, there were other leaders as well who kept the lamassery running. There was a Superior-General, of sorts, who acted as the spiritual and temporal chief. A second man was head of the internal police, who made sure those within observed regulations and all was in order. There was the Chapel-Master, in charge of rites and accoutrements, and the Treasurer, keeper of the great historic and artistic treasures, the accounts ledger, and the strong-box. This quartet shared in the power of the Heart Lama and the Speech Lama, although the latter two were most certainly the figureheads of their particular sect. Of course, they all had grand titles in their own language – you really ought to refer to *An Overview of Management and Governance in a Tibetan Lamassery*, which I don't think actually saw print until the autumn of 1893 – but I forget the terms now. As I said, their class had a reputation for rapacity, and more often than not, it was well-deserved. That's why I was rather taken aback when the Heart Lama invited me into his presence for a private meeting and confided in me, through the services of my trusted translator, whose unspoken secondary duty it was to monitor my doings and report upon them to my hosts.

33

"'I am no superstitious peasant,' he began – that was the part that I found rather droll – 'but I find my heart greatly troubled by a persistent dream which has been plaguing my rest. I fear I am being warned for my life.'

"'Pray describe your dream,' I said, and he explained how, night after night, he watched as faceless men plotted his death in secret, and then proceeded to enact their foul plan. He did not recognize specific identities, but it was obvious that the party consisted of several leaders of the lamassery, for who else had the hubris to destroy their living god? He observed the sequence of events as though it were a stage play. Night after night, he watched them offer himself a cup for refreshment, and he watched himself quaff it in all innocence. In almost no time, their victim's eyesight grew dark and he writhed upon the floor, tearing his garments in excruciating pain. Night after night, he attempted to warn himself before the deadly draught was consumed, but in vain: He was silent and invisible to all. Knowing things, as one does in dreams, he was aware that this dream version of himself would not live an hour and, as the dreadful knowledge settled upon his consciousness, he would awaken. As a consequence, his diet had become even more ascetic than usual, and he consumed nothing which might possibly conceal poison.

"'That is very wise,' I applauded his caution. 'Food and drink are often more difficult to poison than the literature would lead one to believe, for it can cause discoloration or unusual visual characteristics: An unwonted change in texture or odor, an unsavoury flavor, or any number of small, subtle signals to suggest that all is not right, before the fatal dose may be consumed. But it is best to eat plain, simple food and drink, and prevent a potential poisoner from perceiving opportunity.'

"'But surely I cannot live with this sword hanging over my head!' exclaimed the Heart Lama. 'I am certain I am in danger, but I do not know whom to accuse and in whom to confide.'

"I felt pity for the poor man, for he was young, and he, acclaimed as a living god, carried out his existence in relative isolation, possessing no refuge for this crisis. He had no friends, no confidante, and a frankly dubious faith. I promised to do what I could, but as you are aware, it is harder to prevent a crime than it is to bring home guilt regarding one that has already been committed. I suspected that his foes, should they prove to exist, would merely bide their time until his vigilance relaxed, for no man can remain in a perpetual state of nervous tension. It is contrary to human nature.

"As his enemy was unknown and his fears were based upon shadowy dreams, I resolved to make the acquaintance of the top men of influence, to better familiarize myself with the personal relationships that within the community. I sat with the Speech Lama and listened to him opine about the *Qing ambasa*, whom he hated with a vengeance. I shared tea with the Superior-General, who had resided within those walls for a good threescore years, and, through my gracious translator, questioned him about Tibet of the past, and his lamassery specifically. You'll find Sigerson submitted that interview to the journals as well: *Sixty Years A Tibetan Monk*. The Treasurer was more than happy to show me the artistic treasures hidden deep within inner chambers. All the smoke and grease and dirt of the ages couldn't hide the sheen of burnished gold. Countless niches were inhabited by the imagery of deities wrathful and benign, set in precious stones. Haroun Al-Raschid would have approved! I followed the Chapel-Master as he laid out the accoutrements for divers ceremonies: Bells, horns, and drums one day, masks another, always the censers and the chalices and the curl of incense. No hand but his was permitted to gather the sacred objects in preparation for ritual, and no hand but his was allowed to put them back into their storeroom. And I spoke with the head of the internal police. He was rather a brutish man, in charge of a gang of rough monks, whose primary responsibility was keeping order during times of festival. One comes across men of his type often enough: Not particularly ambitious to expand beyond his sphere, but jealous of the temporal power he does wield."

"Despite the romanticism of the setting, they all sound like a remarkably ordinary assortment of men that one might find as part of the staff in any institution," I remarked.

"Men are men, and there is nothing new under the sun! One learns to recognize the type, and the measure follows," said Holmes placidly.

"About this time, ill omens began to circulate. The sort of whisperings that were never quite traceable to the original source, but all were familiar with the portents of death and disease and ill-fortune. Was it a coincidence, or was someone attempting to set the stage so that when foul play occurs, all would accept it as prophecy fulfilled, rather than black villainy? Having nothing solid with which to work, I could not make progress, and I knew I would be recalled to Lhasa sooner than later. The matter of the Heart Lama's dreams would have to be filed away amongst those vague little half-cases which occasionally cross my path, yet never develop into a definite problem."

"I can see why you never told me of this particular adventure," I said. "It seems to have all the correct elements for a good story – a forbidden kingdom, an isolated monastery, men who are worshipped as gods, prophetic dreams, and intrigue afoot! To have been forced to leave before the adventure was fully developed must have dissatisfied you."

"Ah, but it did develop," said Holmes. "For it was about the time I had come to this realization that the Heart Lama's enemy made his move. As in fencing, one cannot make an attack without leaving some small opening and thus exposing himself to counterattack. I was sitting in the Great Hall, listening to the chanting of the monks accompanied by sundry instruments, and wondering if that trumpet I saw was indeed made from a human femur with copper end-pieces, when their ritual was interrupted by a cry of anguish. The Heart and Speech Lamas had been sitting side-by-side upon the bench of their shared throne, each ringing his own bell and intoning the phrases in their language at whatever intervals were dictated by the nature of their ceremony. Now, however, the Heart Lama sat, writhing in pain, clutching his right hand, and the rest of the monks, the ceremony having been broken, looked on in astonishment and confusion.

"Needless to say, I leaped into action. His right hand was badly blistered, and worsening before my eyes. I knew that it was the sort of thing that would cause death before the sun set, if I did not procure the antidote."

"Antidote, Holmes? Surely this isn't some case of crime by a 'hitherto unknown Oriental poison', my dear fellow! That's rather difficult to believe, that there is some poison out there which gravitates towards the victim's right hand, and proceeds to blister him to death."

"Come now, Watson," said Holmes. "As a doctor, surely you recall that different poisons work in different ways. Many poisons work by ingestion. Some are be poisoned through the air itself, as with poisonous fumes. And some poisons work by touch. Surely you recall the Death of Hercules and the Blood of Nessa from your schoolboy days?"

"Ah!" I said. "So the poison was applied to an object the assassin knew he would touch, with the confidence that it would never be traced to him."

"Indeed!" said Holmes. "In that part of the world, there's a small amount of literature on the subject, although it can be difficult to separate the science and the chemistry from the astrology and the magic. Sigerson had no interest in submitting *this* information to the journals: The British criminal has his arsenic and his Prussic acid. He does not need additional suggestions from the East. Sometimes a contact poison might be applied to the handle of a fan, or a handkerchief used to wipe sweat from the brow. It might be applied to a shirt, or to trousers, or to any other garment that comes in contact with the skin. Occasionally, it is even applied to the pillow upon which one sleeps. Once the poison itself dries, none would be any the wiser until it did its dreadful deed. If this particular poison goes untreated for six hours, it usually results in fatality. Death is swifter when it comes in contact with particularly vulnerable parts of the anatomy."

"Did he die?" I asked.

"Not that day, nor the next," replied Holmes with tranquility. "I was able to recognize it for the classic concoction of crowfoot mixed with the milk of *calotropis procera*. It's thoroughly mixed with a piece of wood from the caltrop plant, after which the evildoer uses it to anoint the chosen article to bear his poison to its victim. The antidote is a charming little folk-remedy that includes a hare's stomach, a wood-pigeon's brain, and camel's milk. Camel's milk being difficult to come by in that region, I substituted some yak-milk, and the salve turned out admirably. A follow-up remedy included juice squeezed from sebesten leaf, which is a member of the borage family and readily available. I was pleased to find that pumpkins are grown by Tibetans, and was able to put my hands on some pumpkin seed oil as well, which further encouraged the poison from gnawing into his body. It was no easy task, and required many treatments, but the important point was that his life was preserved, and this unseen enemy finally had a face."

"How could you possibly have brought it home to anyone in particular?" I asked.

"It was fairly obvious, friend Watson," said Holmes. "What object was the Heart Lama handling with his right hand at the time of his distress? His bell, of course. Obviously, no one could have meddled with it after the sacred articles had been set out for the ceremony, with the entire monastic population trickling into the hall and milling about beforehand. From a distance, in the gloom, I could not differentiate between the Heart Lama's bell and the Speech Lama's. They were certainly identical in tone. Did each man had his own dedicated bell, or was a matter of chance? But it was of no consequence, because if it had been meddled with prior to being locked away after the previous day's use, the Chapel-Master, too, would have blistered his hands in handling it, either in the putting-away or the bringing-out. The fact that the Chapel-Master was unscathed showed that he was well aware of its tainted nature, and had exercised caution in the process of taking it from the storeroom to setting it in its place before the throne in the Great Hall. I was less certain that the head of the Internal Police was not one of the co-conspirators, so I made sure to make my accusation very publicly. The Internal Police took to their task with gusto, for beatings are common in Tibet, and frequently accompany investigations and judicial proceedings alike."

"Evidence under torture? Was it admissible?"

"They beat suspects, they beat witnesses – it is all the same in their system in their interest in discovering truth," said Holmes. "You really must consult those ethnographic journals. It's remarkable reading."

"And what was his motivation?"

"It was readily obtained that, in the opinion of the Chapel-Master and his co-conspirators, the Speech Lama and the Superior-General, that my friend the Heart Lama was a little too intrigued by the *Qing*. They determined that a friend of the *Qing* had no place in the leadership of their society, especially in one of such an influential position and so close to the age of his majority. It was necessary for the lamassery to begin their search for their next Heart Lama's incarnation. That would give them another opportunity to raise up a more tractable youth to the ideals of their institution, and even should his successor likewise prove to be too close to the officials from the East, it would at least buy them another couple of decades' time."

"I see. They were just men after all," I said thoughtfully. "It was a pity, though, that the poison was administered through his bell, and not in his drink, as in his dream-warning. That would have been a most colorful touch, should it have turned out to be a truly prophetic warning from beyond."

"Ah, that dream of his," said Holmes. "In the process of gathering confessions – the Internal Police were very dedicated to their work! – it also came out that this was not the first time that untimely death had been visited upon the incarnation of their living god by their hand. The Speech Lama and the Superior-General, who was not quite so high-ranking at the time, disposed of the Heart

Lama's direct predecessor in a similar way, when they determined that he did not play his part appropriately. But on that occasion, they had concealed some pulverized *opoponax* in his drink. The symptoms of this sort of poisoning are a sharp sweetness in the mouth, which changes and develops into a great foulness, followed by a sudden onset of blindness, an overwhelming anxiety, and a difficulty in breathing. Those so afflicted will tear their clothes and beat their heads against the wall in their suffering, which does not last long, as it has been known to be fatal within two hours and certainly within four if the remedy, which is a complicated one, is not readily at hand. But as the current Heart Lama had been so ascetic in his diet, they had had no opportunity to introduce *opoponax* this time around, and so they had resorted to a more oblique attack."

"Holmes, you mean to say that in his dream, he witnessed his own murder in his past life, and it served as a warning to avoid the same fate in this one?"

"Not *his* past life," corrected Holmes. "According to their teaching, it's more of a mental continuum than a matter of self, no matter how highly individuated it may be. But there are more things in heaven and earth, Horatio . . . !"

The Ghost of Dorset House
by Tim Symonds

At eight o'clock on an April evening in 1894 a ghost came upon an intruder in a great London mansion and began to chase him through pitch-black staterooms and corridors. While this unusual event took place, a hansom cab was returning me to my surgery in Kensington from a visit to a patient in the fashionable district of Knightsbridge. I stared sleepily out at the deserted gas-lit streets. To judge by our twists and turns, the cabbie was treating me to a tour of the townhouses of the nation's aristocracy – the Salisburys, the Derbys, the Devonshires. Devonshire House in particular was the site of the most exclusive social affairs, the centre of London's political life, though one from which I had been excluded since the death at the Reichenbach Falls three years earlier of my great friend and comrade-in-arms, Mr. Sherlock Holmes, England's greatest Consulting Detective.

I took out my pocket-watch. Ten past eight. By the most direct route I would expect to reach my quarters by half-past, but with an overturned Park Drag blocking the way ahead, the driver diverted from Park Lane and started along Deanery Street. To the left stood a gate-keeper's lodge made of brick and heart pine. From it, a drive led to a vast house shaped like a parallelogram, the grounds circled by a massive stone wall. Any thought I might have entertained of a pick-me-up nap over the last stretch of the journey was ended by sudden frantic shouting. A man, his face strained with fear, came rushing from the lodge, shouting "Police, police!" in a high, panicky voice.

I threw down the window and called out, "My dear fellow, what on earth's the matter?"

He gasped, "Something's going on in the Great House, sir. There was a light inside when no-one's meant to be there. The light went out and crashings and screams began, screams so terrible, sir, it's hard to reconcile them with the order of Nature."

"And you are?" I enquired.

"Sykes, sir." He pointed at the building behind him. "The lodge keeper."

"So, Sykes, you rushed up to the house at once?" I enquired in an ironic tone.

"No, sir, I did not," came the lodge keeper's petrified reply. "Not for a minute. The Master makes light of it, in fact he pooh-poohs it, but the staff say the house has become haunted. Not terrible screams like just now, but someone – more like *something* – straight from Hades, Lord preserve us, rushing through the corridors and rooms at night for weeks, its torso guttering like a lantern."

"Your Master being the Duke of Weymouth?" I asked, remembering the title of the ancient family which owned Dorset House, for that is where we were.

"Not the Duke, sir, no," the lodge keeper replied, his chest still heaving with fear. "The house is let to the American Ambassador to the Court of St. James. Mr. Hammersmith's his name. He occupies the house, but he's away. I haven't seen hide nor hair of him for three days. The house has been quite empty."

"What of the other staff?" I enquired.

"All away," came the reply. "The Master sent them away too. All except me."

I stepped from the hansom, unhooking one of the carriage lamps.

"Lead on, my good fellow," I ordered the trembling lodge keeper. "The cabbie can fetch a constable. As to whether a doctor may be required, considering the ghastly screams and bangings you say you heard, I am myself a member of that profession. As such," I added, a trifle sententiously, "I'm not given to a belief in the Occult."

"*You* may not, sir," Sykes asserted, "but even famous men believe in things like ectoplasm and rappings and ghosts returning from the Other World. A demon from Hell, sir, is what we reckon it is. The cook's already got her things together and gone back to Devon."

It was not unexpected to find the doors at the impressive main entrance firmly locked. A hard push indicated it was also bolted. We circled the outer walls until my companion exclaimed "There!" A window had been jemmied open. We entered and shortly came to a wide hallway running the length of the ground floor. A line of antique statues lay as though scythed down, terracotta heads and arms and legs scattered several feet from their torso. Just beyond, the shattered glass of an oil lamp glittered among glossy black shards of a Bucchero pot. A heavy inundation of blood commenced some five yards beyond the figurines, but not on the marble floor. Instead, it was a foot or so to the side of a wide doorway at a height of about five feet. Judging by the explosion of blood, the impact of the man's face on the wall had badly damaged the nasal mucosa.

41

My companion issued a low whistle.

"Someone must've banged him hard against that wall, sir," Sykes marvelled. "Who'd ever 'ave thought any man would have that much blood in 'im!"

A trail of bloody shoe marks commenced immediately beyond the door, crossing to the foot of a grand staircase. I had seen this particular configuration in Afghanistan, at the Battle of Maiwand. A bullet from a long arm Jezail rifle sent me reeling off the field in the arms of my orderly, my shoulder haemorrhaging blood, soaking my boots until they began to slip and slide on the surface of the rocks.

"Now that's interesting, sir," the lodge keeper exclaimed. "Despite doing all that smashing of statues back there, he's still trying to keep as quiet as possible. Look how he's tiptoeing along."

I replied tersely, "I doubt if the smashing was on purpose. And certainly he wasn't tip-toeing."

"Then why are there just toe-prints in the blood, sir?"

"Look at the length of his stride, man. The wretched fellow was running, running desperately, running for his life. He cannonaded willy nilly into those statues. His lamp smashed against the pot, but still he carried on at speed, even though – to judge by that wall – he must have been running in the pitch dark."

"So where do you reckon he is now?" my companion whispered.

"We'll follow the trail and find out," I replied.

Minutes later, Sykes's question was answered. A man lay motionless on the floor. In life he had been between fifty and sixty years of age. The face was split wide at several points across the forehead. The nose was badly broken. Around an outflung arm lay a scattering of jewellery.

"A thief all right," my companion muttered, his voice muted at the sight of death. "That pair of emerald cuff-links, them's Mr. Hammersmith's."

"You can turn on the lights now, Sykes," I ordered.

A switch clicked three or four times.

"They're not working," the lodge keeper called out.

I asked, "Would your Master have ordered the electricity to be turned off while he's away?"

"Never has before," came the reply. "Quite the contr'y. When the place is empty, he likes me to come up at night and check all's well. Not that I've done so lately," he added.

"Can you show me where the electricity enters the house?"

"I can, sir. We'll have to go back through that window. It's a bit to the left of it."

"One more thing before we go," I said. "The rings and the cufflinks . . . pick them up and hand to me."

I stood over the dead man and let the handful of jewellery dribble out of my grasp. The spread was contained to within the original foot or two of the outstretched hand.

We encountered Inspector MacDonald when I was clambering through the window to the outside, though it was his revolver I saw first. For several seconds he and I stared at each other. Noting the epaulettes, I broke the silence with, "There's something you should see back there, Inspector."

The policeman's lamp came closer to my face.

"Good heavens!" he exclaimed. "Why, it's Dr. Watson!" The inspector waved the revolver with a slightly embarrassed air and put it into a hidden holster.

"I'm gratified you recognise me, Inspector," I replied. "My cab was passing on my way home when Sykes here came running out of the lodge."

I pointed towards the now-invisible holster. "I didn't know our police were armed."

"Special duty, Doctor," came the friendly but non-committal reply. "There's a lot of very important people in this district, not least the prominent member of the *Corps Diplomatique* who lives in this house. Now tell me, what have you found in there? Cadavers galore?"

"Not galore, Inspector," I replied. "But certainly one cadaver."

"A very dead cadaver," added the lodge keeper emphatically. "Blood everywhere."

"Before I take you to the body," I told MacDonald, "we must discover why the electricity isn't working in the house. Our friend here is about to show me the outside connection."

The lodge keeper led us forward and pointed at a waterproof box down low. "There, sirs. That's what they call the disconnect box. It's where the 'lectricity comes in from the big new station at Deptford East. The Duke of Weymouth always likes to be first with anything new."

"Hold back a moment, There's a good fellow, Sykes," the business-like inspector interrupted sharply. "Before anyone steps too close, someone get some light right over the box."

The lamps flooded two or three square yards or so of damp earth.

"See there, Dr. Watson," MacDonald said. "The wire's cut. Someone's been standing by the disconnect box with sacking over his shoes, and recently too. There are just flat impressions of the soles. I expect the corpse you found had sacking around his shoes?"

"No, Inspector," I replied. "As you'll soon discover for yourself," I added grimly.

MacDonald stepped forward a pace. "You see!" he exclaimed, standing back with a tiny section of wire in his hand. "As I suspected. The cunning blighter. He didn't just yank the cable out of the socket. He cut an inch out of it to stop it being repaired too quickly."

I took the short piece of wire from him, turning it end to end.

"Why," I asked, "would a burglar need to cut the electricity off when it was clear the entire house was empty? A thief could find everything he wanted with just the lamp he'd have with him."

"That's a fair question, Doctor," MacDonald admitted. "Perhaps as a precaution?"

"Possibly," I agreed, "but at a considerable risk. At the very least it would indicate a burglary had taken place. A hunt would commence the minute anyone returned to the house."

"So why do you suppose it's been cut?" MacDonald continued. He pointed at the piece of wire in my hand. "Cut it certainly was."

"That's the question I believe our dear departed friend Sherlock Holmes would ask," I admitted, a momentary sadness overtaking me.

Inspector MacDonald threw me a sympathetic look.

"Bad deal about Mr. Holmes," he said.

I nodded. For readers in parts of the world so remote that even such earth-shattering news never reached them, I should explain that hardly three years earlier, my great friend Sherlock Holmes and I had been in the remote Alpine village of Meiringen when Holmes had finally encountered that greatest schemer of all time, the organiser of every deviltry, Professor James Moriarty, for a once-and-for-all showdown. As was revealed in "The Final Problem", I was tricked into abandoning Holmes for a supposed medical emergency back at the hotel. Moriarty and Holmes grappled at a cliff edge before plunging into the boiling waters of the Reichenbach Falls, held for eternity in each other's iron grip. So died a friend and comrade-in-arms that I shall ever regard as the best and the wisest man I have ever known.

As though Holmes himself had prompted it, an idea flashed into my mind. I gesticulated urgently at the lodge keeper. "The burglar's tools, man. Where are they? He must have had a bag with him."

"By the broken pot, sir," Sykes responded. "There's a carpet-bag there. But why . . . ?"

"Quick," I said, "go and fetch it." I pointed at the severed wire. "It may well contain the answer to this."

Minutes later, the bag lay open at our feet. One by one, I took out a supply of burglar's tools – a small crowbar, a jemmy, a chisel, and a screwdriver, none showing any signs of wear – and last of all, the object of my search, a pair of wire-cutters, lying at the very bottom. With the inspector and lodge keeper watching keenly, I snipped off a further quarter-inch from the piece of electric cable and held it up to a lamp.

"I think, Inspector," I said rather dramatically, "you'll see There's a difference between the two cuts. These pliers are sharp. They sliced through the cable. On the other hand, whoever cut the wire in the first place used a blunt pair of pliers. The wires were pretty well squeezed apart, not cut. Those well-worn pliers were the ones which cut off the electricity."

"Which means . . . ." said Inspector MacDonald.

"It was done by someone who wanted the intruder inside the mansion with no electricity."

"But why?" MacDonald queried. The Aberdonian accent was growing stronger, as though he was about to break into Doric.

"Answer that, my dear Inspector," I replied, "and we are a long way towards solving this mystery."

It was time to take Inspector MacDonald to the shattered figurines and on to the corpse. On our way, I pointed out the trail of scarlet shoe-prints.

"Inspector, look at each step. There's just the toe of the shoe marked out in blood, the intruder's own blood. He started to flee for his life, and he continued even after his lantern was dashed to the ground, leaving him in complete darkness. It must have been panic of the highest order which caused him to continue at such speed, even though he was crashing into walls and cannonading off staircases. At all costs, he had to get away from something utterly terrible."

I held my lantern close to the marble floor. "As you'll note, there's a second person present. He's the one with cladding over his shoes. He must have cut the electricity."

"Then, Dr. Watson," queried the inspector, "if the second man was pursuing him, why didn't they grapple with each other? There's no sign of a struggle."

"Because," I replied, "the pursuer had no intention of seizing him. Inspector, you have been an avid reader of my stories in *The Strand*?"

"Every one of them, Doctor, without fail, I can assure you," came the reply.

"Then let me test your powers of recall. In which of Holmes's cases did I write: '*There was one thing in the case which had made the deepest impression both upon the servants and the police. This was the contortion of the Colonel's face. It had set, according to their account, into the most dreadful expression of fear and horror which a human countenance is capable of assuming.*'"

At this the inspector broke in with "'*More than one person fainted at the mere sight of him, so terrible was the effect.*' Why, Doctor, that's easy! 'The Adventure of the Crooked Man'."

I bent down and turned the corpses head towards him. "Take a look at this man's face," I ordered. "As you will see, it could hardly be more contorted from terror." I turned to the silent lodge keeper. "Sykes, would you say we're five or six rooms from the shattered lamp?"

"Six, yes, sir. From just this side of the state rooms. Them's down that end of the house, Inspector, near the room the Master uses for his private study."

"Whoever chased this wretched creature could easily have grabbed hold of him a long way before they reached here," I continued. "There's one more thing of note, Inspector. Whoever or whatever was chasing him wasn't holding a lamp, or at least it wasn't lit. Otherwise, his quarry – only a yard or two in front of him – would hardly have crashed into walls or tripped up stairways. The two of them hurtled along in the pitch black, the one just behind the other . . . ." I pointed down at the corpse. ". . . but only the one was cannonading into walls and door-jambs."

"The phantom, sir!" the lodge keeper cried. "*Now* do you believe . . . ?"

"Sykes," I interrupted sharply. "I hope my cabbie has been good enough to wait for me. Would you be kind enough to return to the street? Tell him I expect to be there in a few minutes. Don't provide him with any lurid details, only that we have found a body. Do you understand?"

When Sykes left, MacDonald asked, "If the pursuer could have grappled with him at any time, how do you explain the distance they ran?"

"Capturing the intruder wasn't top of his priorities. What else would explain it? He wanted him to reach such a pitch of terror this man's heart or brain would explode, as I believe the autopsy will show. Which the pursuer achieved wonderfully well."

"Just like the case of Sir Charles and the Hound of the Baskervilles?" the inspector asked, a rather disbelieving twinkle in his eye. "Everyone at the Yard has heard of the Hound."

"Exactly like the Hound," I replied. "Such intense fear as I believe our cadaver here suffered in his last moments alive can cause a disorganised heart movement, a quiver. Not the regular beat required to sustain life. Driving someone to their death this way is as much murder as firing a bullet through the vital organs."

I turned to face MacDonald head on. "Now, Inspector, I expect you've already come to the same conclusion as I? That something took place here quite unique in the annals of crime."

He shook his head. "I'm baffled. Unique in the annals of crime, you say? I can't hold with Sykes's theory of a ghost, though the idea of being chased all that way in the utter dark has got me a bit spooked, I must admit."

I replied, trying hard not to appear triumphal, "Let me remind you of one of my friend Sherlock Holmes's favourite axioms: *"How often have I said to you that when you have eliminated the impossible, whatever remains, however improbable, must be the truth?"*

The bushy eyebrows were raised. "And what might that truth be?"

"At least you and I appear to agree on one fundamental," I parried.

"Which is?"

"This is not the work of some Risen Dead, as Sykes is inclined to believe."

"I think I can accept that, Doctor," came the smiling reply. "And then?"

"The living being who perpetrated this dastardly deed knew exactly which way the dead man would have to flee – towards this door, along that corridor. His knowledge of the house must have been extensive. Inch-for-inch, in fact."

"I'll go along with that, yes. Next?"

47

"The pursuer took care to have a handful of Hammersmith's jewellery at the ready."

"Why in heaven's name would he do that?" MacDonald exclaimed.

"To salt the corpse. Look at the close spread of the jewellery. When a man crashes to the marble floor the pieces should be flung from his grasp far and wide. Instead, we found them more or less as you see them now, contained to within a foot or two of his hand."

"Very good. And?"

"Last but very far from least, the murderer has a characteristic which neither the dead man, nor you nor I nor Sykes, have in common with him, a condition normally considered a disability, but one without which his fiendish plan may have ended in complete failure."

The eyebrows rose even higher.

"A *disability*?"

"A vital one," I affirmed.

"There's no evidence he was lame."

"Not lame," I replied.

"Then?"

"Blind."

There was a moment's astonished silence before Inspector MacDonald emitted the loudest guffaw I had ever heard.

His hand reached out and gripped my arm, his shoulders heaving. "My dear Doctor," he gasped finally, "I assume this fellow Sykes told you?"

"Told me what?" I asked, taken aback by this unexpected reaction.

"Or did I tell you back there on the terrace? Though I don't recall doing so, but perhaps I did!"

"Inspector, you or Sykes may have told me *what*?" I persisted.

"Why, the only blind person around here is the American Ambassador himself!" and once more MacDonald went off into a paroxysm of laughter. "I hope," he spluttered, "you aren't suggesting it was the Ambassador himself who chased the housebreaker from here to Kingdom Come!"

We returned in silence to the back terrace.

"If he's the only blind man in the household," I recommenced, "then, yes, I point the finger at the Ambassador, Inspector. He would know how to find his way unfailingly through every door and up and down every staircase in the pitch dark, avoiding any obstacles – even

Etruscan statues – on the way. Sykes told me a demonic figure has been glimpsed running through the corridors and rooms in the dark of night for the past several weeks, '*its torso guttering like a lantern*'. The staff were frightened enough to plan to quit *en masse*. I suggest it was the Ambassador practicing for the events of this evening."

"My dear Doctor Watson," MacDonald replied, wiping tears of laughter from his eyes, "even if you are right, it's entirely conjecture. '*Its torso guttering like a lantern*', you say. What of proof? If I take in the Ambassador of a friendly State for questioning on what we have here, I'll become the laughing stock of the Force. My chances of rising through the ranks will be rather less than zero. I'd find myself running an alehouse in the Out Skerries. No, I'm afraid that at best I'm going to have to report death by misadventure, certainly not *malum in se*. What's more, I think we'll find the denizens of every grand house around Mayfair saying 'Well done and good riddance' at the demise of anyone caught stealing their valuables or family heirlooms, even at the hands of a ghost."

Courteously MacDonald saw me back to my carriage.

I was within a quarter-mile of my residence when the driver rapped on the roof.

"I was just thinking, sir," he called down. "You asked me back there if I'd seen anyone hurrying out of the grounds while you were up in the big house."

"And you replied 'no-one, except Sykes', delivering my message to you."

"I did indeed say no-one, sir. But you didn't ask me if anyone *come* to the lodge, did you, sir?"

"I did not," I agreed. "And did they?"

"They did. A growler comes speeding around the corner from the direction of South Audley Street. The cabbie jumps down and takes a box pushed out from the cab itself. He drops it at the lodge door, clambers straight up on the Clarence, and off they shoot. Gone in a second. If I'd got a better sight of him, I'd report him for whipping the horses like he did. I went over and took a gander at the box when Mr. Sykes fetched it in. It was marked Diplomatic Bag. There was a seal attached to it."

"Cabbie!" I shouted out. "Return us immediately to Dorset House. Quick, man! Get us back there within fifteen minutes and There's an extra guinea in it for you."

Warily the lodge keeper opened the door. It was clear he was still distraught. I had to repeat my question before he pulled himself together.

"A box, sir?"

"A diplomatic bag," I said. "Sealed. It arrived when we were up at the house."

"Ah, that one, sir," came the reply. "It's over there, among the other Diplomatic bags. They arrive any time of the day or night. Look at 'em – cardboard boxes, briefcases, crates. All sealed."

"Open the new arrival!" I cried.

"Sir!" the lodge keeper protested. "Only the Ambassador hisself is allowed to break the seals!"

"Open it at once, man, if we are to solve this bizarre crime," I said sharply. "Otherwise, I shall hold you responsible for letting the trail go cold."

The lodge keeper broke the seal. I bent down and lifted out a piece of blood-stained sacking.

"Well, I'm damned," a now-familiar voice spoke suddenly behind me. It was Inspector MacDonald.

I held out the sacking. "This what he wrapped around his shoes, Inspector. It not only prevented us from comparing his shoes to the imprints outside, but it meant he was utterly silent as he chased his victim around the house. And," I continued, reaching down to retrieve a pair of wire-cutters, "I think we know what these were used for."

I lifted out the final item, a black garment tailored to fit a man of about six feet in height from head to toe. Daubed on it in luminous paint, flickering like a thousand glow-worms, were the bones and skull of a human skeleton.

"Inspector, we live in an age when a white sheet and some dark shadows are quite enough to frighten even the most cosmopolitan victim to death. This outfit was as effective as if he'd taken a new Army & Navy Colt and blown the intruder's brains out."

MacDonald's brows knitted. "Well," he said cautiously. "I think we may have enough. The Met will be appreciative, Dr. Watson, I'm sure about that. You, Sykes, take some wax and reseal the box and its contents. Say nothing to anyone about it. Do I make myself clear? I'll want to know if the Ambassador himself seems especially keen to collect it."

The cabbie drove me home. Jubilant as I was, a sad thought recurred time and again over the journey. If only Holmes had been

50

alive to hear a blow by blow account of how I helped MacDonald solve the murder. Alas, my old friend's bones were entangled for ever with those of Moriarty, the "Napoleon of Crime", in some *danse macabre* at the foot of those distant Falls.

In view of the inspector's words when we parted, the reader may imagine my dismay and irritation when, two days later, tucked deep in the inner pages of *The Daily Telegraph,* I read:

> *Burglary in Mayfair – A string of burglaries may now come to an end with the discovery of the corpse of a house-thief within the premises of a grand house in Mayfair. "Swag" in the form of valuable jewellery was found at his side. He was pronounced dead by a passing doctor. The deceased's clothing gave no clues as to his identity. No relative has come forward to claim the body.* Scotland Yard Inspector Alec MacDonald told The Telegraph, *"Any premature death is an unfortunate occurrence but we are confident the recent spate of burglaries near Dorset House will now cease.*

A week later, the departure of the American Ambassador was widely reported, "*a popular figure among the* Corps Diplomatique, *whose blindness proved no impediment to the successful commission of his duties.*"
Ambassador Hammersmith, it was explained, had decided to return to the United States of America after being "deeply disturbed" by the recent discovery of the body of a burglar in the house he occupied on Deanery Street, London.
I flung the newspaper to one side. "*He was pronounced dead by a passing doctor*" hardly described the role I had played. I cancelled my day's patients and go for an extended walk to overcome my disappointment. Even a common-or-garden burglar deserved justice.
Back at my quarters later that afternoon, an encounter took place of such magnitude that all thoughts of the case were blotted from my mind. My old comrade-in-arms Sherlock Holmes returned from the dead.

Twelve years later, I was to discover what truly lay behind the death of the intruder. The case had been curious enough, though in retrospect I was myself inclined to laugh (albeit grimly) at some of its grotesque and fantastical features.

51

I was on my way for a constitutional in Regents Park when threatening clouds diverted me to the Junior United Services Club, where I could spend a convivial hour in the dry with commissioned officers past and present, above all those of the 19th Punjabi and the 28th Indian Cavalry. Instead, the first person to catch my eye was MacDonald. He was seated alone, chin on hands, his great sandy eyebrows bunched into a yellow tangle. At his side lay two or three folders. I was beckoned over with a friendly wave.

"Thank goodness for a familiar face!" he exclaimed. "I confess I feel like a sore thumb sticking out among all these senior officers."

His would-be host had as yet failed to materialise.

I pointed at the insignia of rank on his shoulders, a crown above a Bath Star, known as "pips", over crossed tipstaves within a wreath. It was very similar to the insignia worn by a full general in the British Army.

"I read of your promotion to Commissioner of Police of the Metropolis, MacDonald. Congratulations."

"In no small part due to you, Doctor," he replied in his still-strong Aberdonian accent. "I became a man marked out for promotion the moment you solved the Dorset House murder for me."

My forehead furrowed. "But you reported it as a mere burglary. It didn't even rate a snippet in the *Police Gazette*."

"Paradoxically, that's because it turned out to be the most important case Special Branch had worked on for years! Every editor in Britain was ordered in no uncertain terms not to print a word."

I beckoned to a steward. "What's your tipple, Commissioner?"

"Whisky would be nice."

An unexpected silence fell upon our conversation. My companion gnawed a thumb, staring at me thoughtfully. At one point he surreptitiously ran a hand over a side-pocket.

The glasses arrived. MacDonald leaned forward.

"I'm not in a position to tell you precisely why, Dr. Watson, but it's extraordinarily fortuitous to meet you like this. First, remind me, have you signed the 1889 Official Secrets Act?"

"I have," I replied.

"Then you'll especially recall Section One (c), '*where a person after having been entrusted in confidence by some officer under Her Majesty the Queen with any document, sketch, plan, model, or information*' . . . continue please!"

"'. . . *wilfully and in breach of such confidence communicates the same when, in the interest of the State, it ought not to be communicated*'. I do indeed," I replied, smiling at the officialdom.

"Does this mean you're about to tell me more about the Ghost of Dorset House?"

"I am, yes. A great deal of water has flowed under the bridge. You'll find what I am about to reveal to you a very pretty matter indeed. You know Ambassador Hammersmith is dead? Trampled by a bison he kept as a pet."

And so over a generous tot of fine Glen Garrioch, Commissioner MacDonald went on to fill in with remarkable detail matters of which I had known nothing.

"The Ambassador," he began, "was a born and bred American, but a direct descendant of Junkers, members of the higher *edelfrei* nobility. At some point, his paternal line adopted the name Hammerschmidt. On arrival at Ellis Island, the father's name was anglicised by an immigration official and became Hammersmith. The son's loyalties, second to his native land, America, grew attached to the young and intemperate Kaiser Wilhelm. The American developed a great deal of sympathy for the German Emperor's hatred of the British Empire."

"Are you saying the Ambassador was a threat to England's safety?" I asked.

MacDonald nodded. "More than you would ever guess," he replied gravely, "but we'll return to that in a moment. It seems Hammersmith had come to believe he was being watched by the British Government. Over the three months leading up to the events of that night, he had reported several break-ins. Petty thefts – silverware, some cash, that sort of thing. The claims explain why I was on the spot so quickly. I was on permanent watch in the neighbourhood. Despite my vigil, no-one was apprehended. In retrospect, we can see the thefts were entirely imaginary, but cleverly designed to influence the authorities. He was setting up the scene for the murder. The police coming to investigate the mysterious death of an intruder would readily assume the corpse was a cat-burglar who'd tried his luck at Dorset House once too often and met his come-uppance.

"At most, the coroner would register it as an unexplained death and leave it at that. Hardly a week goes by in any of our big cities where someone isn't found dead in the course of carrying out some crime or other – falling off a roof, tumbling down a steep flight of stairs. The Ambassador must have thought he could get away with murder without the slightest suspicion falling on him, and I have to say, Doctor, had you not been passing by at that moment, that would have been the most likely outcome. None of us would ever have concluded a blind man could be the murderer. As it was, that was your remarkable deduction. The discovery of the skeleton suit confirmed it, though I was not ready to say so in front of Sykes. The moment your carriage sped on its way, I called in a dozen colleagues from Special Branch. We reconnected the electricity and went through the house with a tooth-comb."

As he spoke he reached into a pocket and withdrew a small wooden box about an inch by one-and-a-half inches.

"We found this under a stairwell." He passed it across.

"A miniature camera?" I asked, turning it over and over.

"A bespoke camera developed for Special Branch by the camera-makers J. H. Dallmeyer. I brought it with me today in relation to another appointment, but I think that you should have it, Doctor. It has a completely silent shutter and a special lens for close up copy work. The dead man was probably using it at the very moment the 'phantom' rushed in on him, but being blind, the Ambassador wouldn't have known."

I stared from the camera to the Commissioner in bemusement. I began, "Why would a burglar have a . . . ?" when once again, as though Holmes were hovering at my side, the answer came to me. "You mean the victim wasn't a simple sneak-thief after all?"

My companion slapped a hand on his thigh in pleasure. "Special Branch!" he cried. "The nation's security was entrusted to him. Special Branch had their suspicions about the Ambassador's repeated use of diplomatic channels to contact Berlin. Unknown to me, they put a man on to watching Dorset House, observing who came and went. The fellow knew his job. Not once did I catch sight of him. Then Hammersmith was seen driving out in his automobile, followed by a Clarence containing several pieces of expensive luggage. The servants departed soon afterwards, each carrying enough possessions to keep themselves in clothes for several days. The house was left completely dark. An opportunity to enter the mansion had presented itself. That's when they took the decision to break in. Who could have known it was a cunning trap!"

MacDonald pulled out a rolled-up photograph. "Take a look at this," he urged, handing it across. "He only had time to take two snaps but they provided the proof we needed. Hammersmith was providing Germany with copies of top-secret documents of international importance. The one in the photograph shows the likely deployment of the Royal Navy's Ironclads in a first encounter with the Kaiser's High Seas Fleet if he proved stupid enough to challenge Britain's vast naval power."

I passed the photograph back. "You mentioned a second snap?" MacDonald looked around cautiously and showed me a second photograph. "This one's of a document *from* Berlin. It's the most egregious of all."

"The Parliamentary and Financial Secretary to the Admiralty!" I gasped. "My Heavens, MacDonald, surely that would have provided a *casus belli*?"

"If the assassination attempt had succeeded, no doubt it would," the Commissioner agreed. He pointed at the photograph.

"Thanks to this, we were able to thwart the plot. If our poor blighter had lived, he'd have been awarded a gong in Her Majesty's Birthday Honours, that's for sure." What was more, the Commissioner continued, a warrant to search Dorset House revealed more stolen and copied documents under the floor-boards, "and this little curiosity." He passed across a file titled *The History of Hammersmith District*. It contained a yellowing newspaper clipping dated late November 1803, some ninety years earlier than the events of that night. Somebody was roaming the nocturnal streets and lanes in a white sheet.

> *One night a heavily pregnant woman was crossing near the churchyard about ten o'clock . . . when she beheld something . . . rise from the tomb-stones. The figure was very tall, and very white! She attempted to run, but the ghost soon overtook her, and pressing her in his arms, she fainted. Found hours later by neighbours, she was put to bed in a state of shock and died there.*

Commissioner MacDonald said, "You were right, Doctor. His intention was to frighten our man to death. And that must be where he got the idea."

"My heavens, MacDonald," I cried. "Adding all this up, it must have been dynamite! But the newspapers said the Ambassador took voluntary retirement? He wanted to spend more time on his buffalo ranch in Utah."

"Not exactly voluntary, Doctor. The Prime Minister passed the evidence to the American President. Within twenty-four hours, Hammersmith had packed up his goods and chattels and was gone. He 'retired' from the Diplomatic Corps soon afterwards."

I recalled the photograph in *The Times*, a smiling Ambassador boarding the *Majestic* for the Atlantic crossing.

"There was no way we could charge the fellow in a British Court, but that didn't stop Her Majesty's Government declaring him *persona non grata*," MacDonald continued. "My report was received with relief in the highest quarters of the land. Special Branch was glad to see the back of him. It put an end to a very troublesome thorn in England's side." Leaning closer, he whispered, "It wasn't long before I found myself up for a significant promotion." He gestured at the pips on his shoulders. "You can see I haven't looked back since. I've a very great deal to thank you for."

As he uttered these words, over his shoulder I saw the steward directing an apologetic looking man towards MacDonald's leather armchair. I recognised the visitor at once, the holder of a very high public office.

I thrust the camera into a pocket and stood up. As I did so, I whispered, "I shall go now, Commissioner. This has been a most exceptional half-an-hour. I have just deduced you must be here to brief our recent Foreign Secretary, now Prime Minister, on Hammersmith's shenanigans, or you would not have had such an archive with you, let alone the camera."

The Commissioner's face turned ashen. "Good Lord, Doctor Watson, how on earth did you . . . ?"

I replied, "Elementary, my dear MacDonald! To judge by his expression, an approaching Prime Minister is about to apologise to you for being so tardy, but I am entirely indebted to whichever matter of State it was that kept him."

I patted my pocket. "And who knows what Sherlock Holmes and I might get up to with this treasure of a camera."

The Peculiar Persecution of John Vincent Harden
by Sandor Jay Sonnen

It was on a spring evening in 1895 that Sherlock Holmes first received a plea from Mr. John Vincent Harden of South Carolina, in the United States of America. One of the boys from the Cardison Hotel had followed Mrs. Hudson up the stairs. Abiding by instructions given him by Mr. Harden, it was only to my friend that he would give up the sealed envelope in his possession.

"The Cardison is a private hotel on Exeter Street," Holmes said to me. "It is by the Lyceum Theatre." He took the opener from his desk, made a clean tear of the envelope, scanned the paper inside, then glanced at the clock and shook his head. He pondered a moment, then turned back to his secretary and spent a moment using his own stationary, afterward sealing a sheet of it inside a gummed envelope before handing it to the lad.

"You come to me from John Harden, the tobacco industrialist. He is staying at the Cardison?"

"He is, sir."

"Take him that straight away."

"Yes, sir," said the boy, before turning and nearly running out the door.

"I'm sorry, Mr. Holmes," said Mrs. Hudson. "The boy was insistent. He would not leave, would give the note he had only to you, and he followed me about until I let him come up with me." Our landlady seemed annoyed at herself for the freedom she appeared to have given the youth.

The hour had become late. Holmes handed me the note.

Mr. Holmes, (it read)

I know you from reputation and can only pray I have the address correct. Should this reach you by means of the young man to whom I have entrusted this letter, write me a return note that you will be able to come to my suite at the Cardison Hotel tonight at half-past nine.

My nerves have been taken to their breaking point.

57

"How holds your constitution this evening, Watson?"

"It bares up," I answered.

"Will your plans for this night allow you to accompany me?"

"I shall join you to see this man."

"It is a rather interesting time to call. He is alone here in London. He must be, otherwise he would have sought other means to deal with this."

We alighted from our hansom, and the Cardison's doorman directed us to the manager. We were given a page boy who took us to the mid-floor suites, leading us to a double door of oak that demonstrated we were at one of the more special rooms within the hotel. A parlor maid in the service uniform of the hotel's staff answered the door, and before us was an ornate entryway. She told us we were expected and ushered us into the small area of tile. In the living room beyond stood a man in his late fifties, dressed in his American suit and black western boots, stitched with embroidery and artistry. It was black threading on black leather, and only careful examination would show to an observer that this detail identified an understated expense. Looking above the boots showed he wore wool trousers, and on the man was a coat of the same material, a handsome dark gray with light pin-striping. He wore a waistcoat and dark tie, and on the sofa nearby was a short black top hat.

"Good evening, Mr. Sherlock Holmes," the man said to the both of us. "I am John Vincent Harden of Charleston, South Carolina. I know of your reputation for solving problems for people that can sometimes involve an investigation. I thank you for coming immediately, as I have a deep problem, and from it I have become very troubled."

"Your note provided no explanation as to whatever you need, but I am at your service. Here is my colleague, Dr. John Watson."

The man sighed. "Please be seated and I will share with you my problem, and then you may say if you can give to me your assistance in what has become a strange series of events. In truth, if I were in my native land, I would have available to me those who could help in an instant. But I must stay in London on business, and for that reason I need turn to someone capable of working in the elements of . . . the fantastic."

That word alone was enough to move my friend into the room and seat himself across from our host. We turned down any libation, but he insisted that we enjoy with him one of the many cigars that were in several boxes on the large table before us.

"Well," said Holmes, "you are indeed known for your cigars. My friend was reading about your coming to our city to expand the sales of your product. Dr. Watson and I do discuss tobacco, but I also take an interest in it for professional reasons. I admit to reading the story in *The Daily Telegraph* over a week ago, where your arrival was heralded as an important step in spreading commercial contacts with the Kingdom and with Europe."

"This is one of my own mark, Mr. Holmes. Dr. Watson," the man explained. "The bands of gold and blue at its surround is of my design. My father's family crest is used to make a statement by which those who appreciate tobacco can tell they are having an experience of quality.

"In America, we have a number of tobacconists who manufacture many varieties of product. Some impress the purchaser purely due to cost. This is not one of those. This is for an evening of pure enjoyment. The gold on the band added to the blue – the blue being used for our standard – is our way of denoting our finest tobacco made by our most careful attention to detail. The plant is grown of perfect seed, unblended and taken from a soil now in its fifth generation of planting and cultivation.

"I can go on about this process in relation to this particular cigar, but it is enough for now that you know it is our finest commercial offering, not including the specialty cigars we offer under commission. The Havana-grown Larga Vista is very popular and has come to define my company. The mark has made my company in every way. Fame, a good write up by the experts, and naturally sales. It was a lengthy, seven-year struggle, but now I know the sweetness of success. Last year, I sold near eighty-million of these, and we mean to break better records this year. They are twenty-five cents more than those in which a machine is used for manufacturing, but our customers will pay that."

"I do know something about cigars and their construction," said Holmes, "and tobacco in general, so the description of your special tobacco's growth as plants and the making of them into the kind of cigars which your customers most appreciate is not lost on me. And I am an enthusiast as well."

"Then you may enjoy this experience. It is, in fact, why I sailed to Southampton and made my way to London. I arrived two weeks ago with two-thousand of the Larga Vistas in hand, and at your customs in Southampton is my cargo of several thousands of boxes of twenty-four, which will be used to begin sales. I've entertained potential distributors here in London, meeting with their principles and putting together their offers. These parties, spaced one every few nights, were each nothing short of great successes, and it is fair to say I will make for myself several millions in your pounds sterling, as well as francs and marks and lire, and other values in foreign currency, over the next few years, based on exclusive distribution agreements, each of seven years for the European markets.

"And now you know my business," finished Mr. Harden in his southern American accent, where the word *my* was pronounced in a softer manner, and with a touch of sentiment, as though he was letting Holmes and me in on one of his most personal interests.

"Then if you do not mind the interruption, Mr. Harden, our coming to see you this evening does not have to do with the cigars you brought by ship?"

"In truth, I cannot say. It doesn't make any sense that what has happened would be because of my business. No, sir. This appears to be personal. I have no other way to place my ideas into words without letting you in on the notion that in some manner, I'm being persecuted." Harden, who had up to this time been steadfast in his presentation as a man of fortitude, now showed dread.

"Then tell us," said Holmes.

Harden looked at my friend and at me. He made a frown of a kind and straightened his coat for a moment, then looked up.

"The very night after these first-stage meetings were concluded, I went to bed late, and a brandy and two of my cigars meant that when I did drop off, I would have a deep sleep. Then, in that very foyer to these rooms – " the man pointed to the space beside the front door to the apartment " – there was a noise which took me from my bed, though it was a long time until I was fully awakened.

"I made my way out into this room, and in the darkened atmosphere – for there was not a candle lit at this three o'clock hour – " again the man pointed " – I saw before me a table alien to the room, with no similarity to any of these furnishings. It was rounded and covered with a red cloth, which I thought might have been velvet or something similar."

"How could you, Mr. Harden, determine in the darkness the material from which it was made?" my friend asked the man.

"Mr. Holmes, I could *see* the cloth, because on top of the table was a stack of skulls, painted green and orange and red. Several of them, one atop the other, created a small triangular shape – a pyramid shape of skulls – and in each of them was a small flame

60

thrown by a shortened, deeply melted candle. This made the entire area glow in an eerie manner, for the candles themselves were of similar colors. The moonlight, seeping through the open shades of those windows, also lit up the pile of skulls and gave it this Hallowe'en-like illumination."

"The windows themselves?" asked Holmes.

"The windows had been opened, and have stayed open since the day I moved in. Naturally, the cigar smoke warrants that. But we are two floors above the street, and you will see there is no nearby balcony or piping on the wall outside the windows. There is no way to climb up and enter into these rooms."

"This is certainly, even at first blush, in the realm of the fantastic," said Holmes, looking toward the entry of the room. "As you say, you are persecuted, meaning that this must have been the first of a series of events. But let us not stray from the first of them just yet. What did you do then? I presume your room's private hotel staff had retired to their own quarters, and no one remained in service in any of the rooms within your let?"

"Quite so, Mr. Holmes. At that moment, I was all alone. For a while, I was aghast at what I had beheld, but after a lengthy minute, I gathered my wits and lit two of the lamps and saw the display for what it was. Just as I had described it, but now with less menace, while taking on more of a forensic study. I left my rooms and, taking the main stairs, found the night man on duty at the front desk. A bit groggy but in a serviceable manner, he followed me up the stairs. Upon entering the room, we found that the whole of the setup was gone. All of it. Skulls, cover, table – all gone!"

"What do you estimate this pile of skulls to have been in size?"

"Ha! I can do better than estimate! Before I ran downstairs to bring up help, I took hold of it and know it was very substantial. I shook it and it barely yielded. Its weight was formidable. It could not have been taken by someone easily, and yet it was gone when I returned. No one followed me down. No one but myself was on the main stairs when I came down."

"I'll examine the hall, though likely to little avail due to the many days between the event and this evening. What said the day staff?"

"I needn't tell you that I had no real sleep afterwards, from four until the dawn. Certainly I called for coffee when the kitchen opened, and was by then fully dressed. I called the manager to my room at half-past eight. There was, as you know, no evidence of this thing, and the man wondered over my certainty of the event. The house

61

detective visited me at ten, and together we looked all over the room and the hall, and naturally the service stairs too. There was not a trace to be found of any skulls or cloth or candle-use or table. The kitchen had no staff at the ground level, but certainly the night girl and boy were there, laundering piles of clothing and bedding, polishing shoes, and cleaning suits. I wasn't above going to these areas with the detective to see what anyone dragging such a piece down the stairs would have encountered, and who they would have had to pass in order to make it to the door to the service entrance, or the alley way beyond, where they would have had to pass the carts bringing food and materials to the hotel, and everything else that you may imagine is necessary."

"The detective's final opinion?"

"Naught. What was there for him to say? He did wonder at who I knew in the city, and whether any of my friends or acquaintances would have a rag on by playing me the fool. I told him that was out of the question."

"So you have no such people, and those you do know would only want you to experience the most excellent evenings, one after the other."

"Exactly."

"But you are here, sir, and have not been harmed. So whomever did this, along with whatever else you haven't yet discussed with me, apparently doesn't have a sinister intent, in as much as bodily harm is concerned."

"Of course not. It is a *persecution*, not an *assault*. Whomever is behind this wants me of sound body in order to experience the results of their scheme."

"Then their next mental attack took what form?" Holmes asked.

"A few days later – no. A few *nights* later, I wasn't yet asleep. Once more it was late, in that the maid had retired to wherever she stays in this place, or back to her home, and I was by myself enjoying a scotch and cigar. That telephone there at the desk buzzed. I answered it, and the girl downstairs told me there was a call for me from the Trafalgar Exchange, which I found later meant that it came from a post office at the square there, with a fulltime telephone for use at all times, day and night.

"I didn't understand this at the time, but I know now how your system here in England operates. I've met the people who oversee the telephone there at night, and they were of no use in remembering anything. But that is all by the way. The girl put through the call from the post office, and over the wire came a blood curdling voice, not of man nor woman, but rather a creature."

Harden looked to Holmes and saw his look of strange interest. But he, not knowing my friend's excitement over such details, misunderstood and acted as if he had been rebuffed by the man he had turned to for help.

"You believe me to be unnecessarily bizarre, Mr. Holmes."

"Not at all, not at all. I am intrigued and quite interested."

"The voice spoke the same phrases three times, as if to be an incantation of some kind – though I had no understanding of it, and did not in the least recognize it whatsoever."

"Do you remember the exact words of this incantation?" asked Holmes.

"I remember much of the passage, and it's now into my memory. 'Thou has transgressed. Thou has taken the fruits of the labours of the fields. The witch of the fields will slay thee. Azaka Meyday. Azaka Meyday. Azaka Meyday. He is the witch of the fields and he will have his way.' More of the same. After the first of the versions of these groups of phrases, I demanded to know who it was, but the voice merely repeated the incantation again, and in this overly evil and sly manner, with an intentional scare built into the sounding of the sentences."

"'The witch of the fields', you say? 'Azaka Meyday', being given as a name of a kind? And you have taken the fruits of their labours? Well, does that mean anything to you? Whomever staged this telephone call, and presuming it is in relation to the diorama left in your entry, has specifically designated you as their unmistakable target. It makes no sense for it to be done that way, unless you understand its meaning immediately. Otherwise, why toy with you in such a way? There must be a reason for it all."

"As you say, Mr. Holmes. But it makes no sense to me. I've had no association with anyone of this name during my professional lifetime. Naturally I made enemies when I was in my twenties, but my enemies were men whose names I didn't know, and they did not know mine."

"You refer to your participation in the Southern War in your country."

"Yes, Mr. Holmes. We had no witches or Azakas from those times. And I was not political. After the war's end, I returned to my father's farm, where he had just lost the family of four slaves who worked our fields. We weren't that well off to begin with, and there's no reason why my father or I – my father has passed on –

63

should be singled out, because we were average cotton farmers. We didn't have a plantation, but merely a crop. There were many families better off than we were, and the family who lived with us as our slaves left our farm halfway through the war and disappeared, severing any connection with us whatsoever. My father was nearly fifty at that time, and though there were men who fought at that age, he did not.

"During the war, President Lincoln announced that any slaves in states that were the enemy to the United States, which included our slaves, were free and could make their way to the North. Naturally, South Carolina did not acknowledge this freedom, but a year later we did not have the power to police the slaves who left their masters, and it was as good as if we had accepted this edict of freedom. So the family left, and if we owe them something, there are a lot more who were in my position who owe a lot more. If the Joe Buck family came to me, I would give them jobs if that's what they wanted, but it's never happened. They wouldn't need to go about this torment."

"So you do not believe this is the work of that family or a descendant?"

"Of course not, Mr. Holmes. I deal in a world of plain reality, and not in one of scaring one another to achieve an end."

"But the torment will not cease."

"No sir, it persists. Last night, the phone call occurred once more. 'Thou has transgressed. Thou has taken the fruits of the labours of the fields. The witch of the fields will slay thee. Isadore. Isadore. Isadore. He is the witch of the fields and he will have his way.' The name was changed, but only that."

Holmes sat riveted by what the man had told him.

"I take your problem very seriously, Mr. Harden, as well as an in interest in preventing your persecution. I'm also professionally curious over the method chosen by your adversary. It's quite singular in my study of criminal behavior. As we agree, what can be the purpose of making a torment that includes references by which the victim is unaware of their meaning?"

"What can you do for me then, Mr. Holmes?"

"I'll need to study this. What a man has designed, another can unravel. These words must mean something, and we live in a tangible world defined by space and reason. I don't promise miracles, but I do promise to you my industry. If you'll put your trust in me for two or three days, I will come to you again when I have a fresh development."

Our host rose. "I can ask for nothing better, Mr. Holmes. I'll await that time. And I'll send to you news of any new thing done against me by this person or persons."

"Person," said Holmes, himself rising.

"Only one?"

"Yes. At this instance, I know enough of that to be certain."

During the following morning, Holmes returned to the hotel to look about the many areas that had been unavailable to him the previous night.

"This hotel detective is unimaginative at the least. He didn't see the connection between the movement of two mattresses from a storage room to the alley outside and the disappearance of the skull display that was set out to frighten his guest. He thought it was the work of tramps attempting to steal them. I examined them. They had splashes of red and green wax, and were set out to lessen the fall of the display. As Harden said, table, cloth, skulls, all gone in an instant – all dropped from his window to the alley. Three o'clock, and no one would be there, and no one on the ground floor would have heard the disturbance of the fall."

"And the ability of a trespasser to lay in wait on the upper floor itself?"

"That, too, was very possible, Watson. For the service door is left ajar for the breaks of those people Harden met before they went off night duties – the men and women dealing with the overnight laundry and cleaning the guests clothing. Their work room is only two doors from the door, and that door is often partly open. A man could go from the alley to the door, and so to the back stair. It is a risk, but not a bad gamble in the great scheme of life."

"What will be your next ploy?" I asked him.

"This afternoon, I began research using the resources of the British Museum and Reading Room. I'll need the weekend to look deeper into this matter. What I know so far is that something about the persecution of John Harden is based in spiritualism, a religious practice that is strange and irreverent." He took his favorite long stemmed pipe from the mantel, for use when his mind was especially vexed, and he didn't move from his chair for the rest of the evening.

On Saturday, Holmes was put out of his way by a visit from a Miss Violet Smith, previously unheard-of, who had come to consult my friend without an appointment on a matter which at first appeared commonplace, but would eventually become quite horrible. Miss Smith was a most beautiful woman who had been offered higher-than-market pay to teach music during the weekdays at an estate in Surrey, very near the border of Hampshire. It was because of her beauty and kindness of spirit – and a certain insistency that her plea be heard – that Holmes set aside time to listen to her statement. It had, however, come at this crucial moment in his research related to those matters of the occult that appeared to form the basis of Harden's unique form of persecution.

Holmes, unable to leave to go to Farnham, where the young woman had been employed, sent me in his stead on the following Monday. I proved on the occasion to be of no real value to him in the matter, though I did indirectly allow him to work on Harden's problem. During my day in the country, Holmes had an interview with a person whose history was elemental to his learning about the artistic display by which Mr. Harden had been tormented.

He was also able to revisit the British Museum's Reading Room, a place which had on more than one occasion given him a valuable understanding into the history and purpose of a given artifact. Finally, he spent some time attending the mass given at the Roman Catholic Church of Saints Alban and Stephen, just outside of Hatfield.

Despite his researches, he determined the next day to travel to Farnham himself in hopes of producing some substantive facts related to Miss Smith's problem. He returned late that very day, after having been in a fight at one of the town's country pubs with a man named Woodley. That invigorated him and had a positive effect on the Harden case as well. He found himself in the unusual circumstance that he had worked throughout his profession to prevent, with one investigation already begun now overlapping a second. During the week, Miss Smith's letters to Baker Street became more ominous, and Holmes found his thoughts divided between the needs of his now very definite clients, both in danger.

The day after Holmes's fight at the inn found the arrival of a package, sent to him from the Cardison Hotel, with the strangest imaginable contents. I rose and walked into the sitting room to find my friend at the dining table, excited and filled with vigor and resolution.

"Look there," he said to me. "Friend Harden sent it to me by means of one of these boys who serves the Cardison. I didn't have the heart to awaken you to look at it when it arrived, and enjoyed some of this morning by myself. It has allowed me to settle my thoughts."

Inside of the plain box was a sack that reminded me of beggar's homely purse, made of a poor material and wound by a knotted cord. I opened this and found inside nothing but dirt. Also in the box was a small set of pipes, made of wood and having the look of being used over time, pitted and worn.

With these items was a note from Harden:

Mr. Holmes, (it read)

At near three o'clock this morning, there was the sound of a rattle against my door. I don't know for how long it was made, but when I opened the door, there was only this, left just outside of it in the hallway.

This has now made me deeply angry, as much as it has left me upset over some impending doom.

What does this all mean?

J.V. Harden

Strangely, this omen did not disturb my friend, but rather quite the reverse. That morning saw a new man in Holmes, and he apparently had asked our landlady for more of our dinner from the previous evening. I would have none of that, and when she came around, I asked instead for fresh coffee before I broke fast with a more traditional morning meal. However, Holmes's interest in eating meant he'd had a mental breakthrough in some form or another.

"You made a reasoning of importance."

"Most assuredly, Watson. A new understanding, and I'll play the cards for all they are worth. It's all wrong, you know. All wrong, and we're looking at things from the inside out. Now, with a fresh taking-in of all that is about us, we can live in the harsh world of reality. It's less romantic, but should you ever put pen-and-paper to this affair, you will clean that all up."

"Your jesting at least means that your disposition has improved."

"I'm going to reward myself upon the conclusion of friend Harden's problem, and Miss Violet Smith's endangerment, if we take seriously her letters over what's overhanging her joyful spirit at Chiltern Grange. Sunday afternoon, I'll attend a discussion led by a young man whose family are all refugees, having adopted England as their home. The young man, Mark Hambourg, is from a family that is making the case for adding Franz Liszt's 'Sonata in B minor' to the repertoire. I would very much enjoy what he has to say about that work, which is now nearly fifty years old, and whether there is a revisionist view of it. If I bring both the Smith and Harden matters to a successful conclusion, I'll have certainly earned my listening to what the young man has to say, and whether its pedigree should be improved. Revisionist! Ha!

"In an hour's time, if you'll finish your breakfast and join me in what should be an easy hunt for a cab, as the hour will be close to ten o'clock, we shall investigate our own revisionist view of what has been placed before our eyes. We may then determine who it is that has been working to persecute our client. By that, I mean Mr. Harden, not Miss Smith.

"At the same time, I don't wish to stray too far from home, as I'm expecting another letter from Miss Smith, sent from Chiltern Grange, to ask whether she should attempt to last there until the weekend, or perhaps stating that she is interested in an immediate departure before her usual Saturday morning return to her mother, never to return to Mr. Carruthers' employ."

We were in a hansom, rattling through London on what had become an April of continuous foggy days and nights. The past few days had put into clear understanding exactly why my friend didn't like it when one case interfered with another. It had become difficult to keep both persecutions separate from one another, if indeed Miss Smith's being followed was a form of persecution in the same way that Harden's torment was, as in the latter case there could be no doubt. He had been faced with the collections of skulls as a direct, enemy action. Miss Smith's being followed by a man with a great beard didn't necessarily carry with it the same danger – there could be a design of purpose that might not be persecution.

"I see with new eyes, Watson. I had incorrectly viewed these warnings, these fetishes – as both my research and a priest I met at that church I visited used that expression specifically – as the genuine articles of threat and fright, for that is indeed their underlying purpose. But they are not genuine. That has been my faulty premise. If we revise our understanding of the tableau, we then ask ourselves how it is possible for one to know the appearance of the fetishes but not the substantive meaning behind each of them.

"We are left with the conclusion that their maker is not then a practitioner of *Vodou*, but merely an observer of the use of the articles. This means that he lacked the language. How does a man

68

lack the language but know the surface details of the forms? Because he never conversed about them. Yet he must have seen them. And to see them, he had to penetrate into the heart of the living areas to where he knew that Harden had also been. Not an easy task to do, and to find *Vodou* when even the new government that now directly represents the population of Haiti has declared it to be occult and unlawful."

"You speak in riddles," I said to him.

"I do not mean to be mysterious for its own sake. John Vincent Harden's persecution is based in the iconography of Haitian *Vodou*, a religious practice removed from Africa by the captured slaves forced to live in the Caribbean Islands, and in this forced removal, these things that are the symbols of its practice have been conflated with those of the Catholic faith."

"And so you spoke with someone associated with the Catholic faith to help you in this matter?"

"I did. And it was not so simple finding someone with any of this knowledge. It is simply too esoteric, and therefore not on the mental fingertips of the average reverend father of that faith. One has to have experienced it in some way."

"You were not able to do that, I should think," said I.

"No. That is so. My knowledge comes from the only two writings made by those who have visited into the heart of one of the areas where these beliefs have been practiced. One is from the seventeenth century and by a priest. The other is by a French historian, and my knowledge of that language, which serves me well, was stretched to its limits due to the unusual subject matter."

"Why has this unknown tormentor of Harden chosen the symbols of the *Vodou* religion as his means of persecution?"

"Therein lay my problem, which is now no longer a problem. That is, it is not the problem it had been previously to me as I began my research. As I began to form my views on the matter, I was thinking of an islander who was versed in *Vodou*, and was calling upon one of its various charms and spells related to vengeance in order to bring a harm upon our client, while at the same time having him to reflect upon something related to his past where he would have been involved in a group where *Vodou* practice was part of its culture. And so that must be. But it is only today, reflecting on this new fetish Harden sent this morning, that I am brought to a new and correct understanding of the true nature of a concept that was discussed by the French author – that of *syncretism*."

"That word is new to me," I said.

69

"Syncretism is a rarely used expression for what has become the method of how these originally African symbols and holy persons from one belief system are combined with another to disguise the actual purpose of the practicing previous symbols and holy persons. Some cultures do this outright and without guile. Merging one pantheon with another can bring about a new version of dogma from which parishioners may worship. And yet, the term 'new' does not make sense in the accepted understanding. It is a newer version of a previously ordered canon. A new version of the canon blending old ideas.

"The expression was just as new to me as it was to you. Typical use of the term is where one culture conquers another culture, especially one pagan group forcing control over another, and the invaded culture accepts the new gods but also uses the imagery of their previous gods while the honoring of the new ones. But there is a darker side to it, one based in using the newer gods or divine persons to surreptitiously honor the previous ones. That is what became of the *Vodou* pantheon once its practice was outlawed. It became an outlawed faith by the French in Louisiana and by the islanders themselves in Haiti. But the practitioners would not give it up, and took the visages and descriptions of the holy persons identified with the Catholic faith and merged them with the older Haitian gods, demigods, witches, and the like, as a means of continuing their appreciation of *Vodou*."

"Fascinating. An otherwise elegant solution to such a merge of culture."

"True. But you can see the built-in problem. Should an uninitiated observer take in the overt practice but not know of its details, he walks away with an incorrect understanding of what he thinks that he sees. Such a thing has happened in this case. Any man who in fact understood *Vodou* would never combine its practice with Catholicism, as he would have no need to either disguise his practices or combine them with the majority view. He would simply go about his *Vodou* ways, casting his charms and leaving his fetishes as they in fact appear in the older more accurate forms."

"How will you find this man, then?"

"The field is already considerably condensed, as I've made inroads into what I believe is the pool of people most well-placed to have chosen this elaborate form of bother to Harden. The man we seek would have been actively involved with the islanders, but not too actively involved in the depth of their studies. He would be a

70

priest who saw from the outside the members of that faith practicing their religion, but he didn't realize the syncretism."

Upon our arrival, we walked into Harden's sitting room, whereupon Holmes removed his hat. I noticed Harden's reaction to seeing the plaster on the corner of his forehead where I had treated Holmes's injury the day before, following his visit to the public house in Surrey, where he had met Mr. Woodley in combat.

"Mr. Holmes, your mouth is broken at your lower lip," said Harden.

My friend chose not to discuss the matter. "That is for another time," said Holmes. "But I would report to you that I have a nearly connected case. However, there is one crucial piece missing."

Holmes walked to one of the room's sofas. "Come join us," he said, "and answer a few questions, and we'll explore more deeply into what has to be at the heart of this matter." This was an unusual turn, in that Holmes appeared to have become host in his client's own rooms.

Still, Mr. Harden complied, and a moment later he was opposite Holmes on the other sofa, while I took a chair that was offset to their positions, allowing them to have their conversation without my interference in the scene.

"Well then, sir," said Harden, "that bodes well, and yet does not leave me settled."

"Just so. I myself have the same worry over the matter. I have before me appearance but not substance. It's a strangeness itself within a greater mystery. But on the good side of the ledger, it does proffer the notion that you yourself may be able to help me regarding some points pertaining to something that I presume is a part of your past."

Holmes leaned forward and took one of Harden's precious Larga Vista cigars from the box on the table between them. It was only a brief moment to get it going, and before its first puff, he began his inquiry.

"Your soil is in its fifth generation, or so you stated. Yet your company was incorporated under the laws of South Carolina, only some seven years ago. Your first attempt at a field of tobacco wasn't on the island of Cuba."

"No, it was not," replied a weary Harden.

"It was in the French area of Hispaniola."

"You were told? By whom?"

"I was not told. I understand this is the case. Your adversary has made it understood to me. I believe he wishes for you to understand it as well."

John Vincent Harden looked coldly at my friend, who was now reclining and apparently becoming quite expansive in the enjoyment of his host's cigar. Holmes calmed his movements, but blew a ring of smoke in the air above the both of them before lowering his eyes to the man across from him. Harden gave back very little in admission.

"Come now, Mr. Harden. You know something of what you have experienced these past several days. Would you not rather be straightforward than coy? You don't wish to begin? Then I shall forge my way through the morass and see if I can find the treasure.

"Seven years ago, you were looking for good soil and hard workers at the cheapest price. It is nothing to be ashamed of, as you were starting a venture and in need of the shortest route to immediate profits, and this meant land that was the most kind to your object of tobacco growth. But you sought a parcel where those in authority had little or no mechanism for protecting the workers under their sway. You settled on Haiti for this purpose, and I presume that you undertook a series of tests to determine whether the land and the people would be in harmony to achieve the pilot version of these Larga Vistas of yours.

"Soil doesn't possess the power to torment a man, and we must therefore accept that someone has been at odds with you for some time now. For over a year, I should think, though he would have had seven to ruminate upon his design.

"What happened to your Haitian workers, Mr. Harden?"

"Nothing I could have foreseen, Mr. Holmes."

"But the result was still a bitter end for some. Or all."

"I was not certain."

"That makes little sense. You would have used your power to send out for any report of intrigue."

"All right. Fine. I was back in the Carolinas, expecting shipment, by the time the mischief was made known to me. A man that I had employed as overseer of the crop was unethical. He didn't keep the promises that he made to the natives in the Haitian portion of that island."

"I am sorry, Mr. Harden, but to advance your case, I must ask you what it means that this man was 'unethical'." Holmes had ceased his freely moving about upon the sofa, and now looked directly into Harden's eyes.

"There were others in my employ who worked under this man. They made vague comments about the natives not being fully compensated for their labor. There were some disputes."

"Certainly you had the power to look into the matter yourself? This was still at the beginning of establishing your company. Weren't those fields intended to be cultivated for the following year's crop? How is it that you intended to build up a long-term use of the land without a personal knowledge of its use, and presumably of the population with whom you would hope to have a long term relationship?"

Harden had become more uncomfortable with each passing question. Accusing his client was not typical of Holmes, but the man, I presumed, had to be in a position to have at least some of the answers that he needed to get to the heart of the matter in which he had become engaged.

"I think that, even though you have done a very satisfactory job up to this time, Mr. Holmes, perhaps it might be in our mutual interests if I remunerate you for what you've done to this point and then we go our separate ways. It appears that your investigation is trying to paint me as my own adversary – as if I'm the madman out to bring this attack upon myself – if indeed that's what it is."

After a moment's quiet pause, Holmes shook his head, stating, "You, sir, are able to recompense to me what you will over the matter thus far. It will have no effect on my own actions from this point forward.

"That is a strange business arrangement, sir!" cried Harden with some bitterness, looking across at my friend with indignation and a certain anger.

"This is a strange case, and I will fix my solution upon the unusual aspects of what has become apparent to me. I've researched some of the more illustrative factors of what has been put before you by our unknown friend, and have gained some understanding of the tableau that is the central theme of your terror. This understanding points solely in the direction of Haiti. You, or those in your employ, or specifically this now-mentioned servant of yours working in your name, robbed those people of their payments, or created a series of supposedly justifiable expenses upon them, the same way that the Americans have done in their settlement of the western interior, creating a group of company towns and stores wherein workers find, at the end of the project, that in fact they owe more than they have made.

73

"There are other examples of how an overseer so placed can affect the same bitter outcome. Regardless of the technique, the result is always the same. I use the word 'robbed' because it fits, even though men positioned like yourself may choose a different expression. But the truth is, I wish to meet this man who is tormenting you, and your payment to me is now secondary to such a meeting."

"So that is now your game, Mr. Holmes."

Holmes stood. "You began this game, sir, and made its first salvo. I cannot promise that I will finish it for you, and I don't know that I owe anyone such a duty. But, as I've stated, I will meet with this person and find out from him what it is that he wishes for a conclusion to his actions."

Together, Holmes and I left the room, leaving Harden displeased and furious.

We took the midday train from Charing Cross to Hatfield Station, and after nearly an hour in a hired carriage, our driver delivered us to the church that Holmes had recently visited, named for Saint Alban and Saint Stephen.

"You return, Mr. Holmes!" said the man who greeted us. "And today of all days. We're having our own celebration in honor the consecration for Westminster Cathedral in London. The foundation stone will be laid in a few months. I wish that I could go, but that cannot be so. May I know your name, sir?" This man in holy garb was buoyant and registered great pleasure at seeing my friend again in his presence.

"Dr. John Watson, Father."

"I am Father Lawrence. Please, if you should write this adventure of your friend's, do not succumb to any *Romeo and Juliet* references."

"Be assured that I'll restrain myself," I told him.

Holmes allowed himself a smile. "I need to bother you once again, and this time I seek not a concept, but a man."

"Of course. How may I help?"

"He is a priest who would have spent some time in America. A man of some artistic abilities. A man who would have assisted a more experienced priest when they were on a mission of some kind in Haiti. This would have occurred some seven years ago. Since that time, he would have become involved in church matters here in England, and most probably in London, but this last point is not a strict requirement."

74

The man was stunned. "Mr. Holmes, you describe Father Frances Daystrom to his last detail. He is most certainly all of the things that you have said. He is in the heart of London, and has been for over a year. He came here from Charleston, in America, where he has been working on stained glass for the cathedral there. He is here for a similar artistic purpose. It's interesting that you mention that quality above other parts to his history, for he is attached to the Westminster Diocese, and works under those who are responsible for the building of that new cathedral. Naturally, he will be at work on the art there for some years to come."

"How do you know of his work in Haiti, Father Lawrence?"

"Ah, this is no secret, and you should have well asked about his assisting one of our church's most honored missionaries in the West Indies. For he was called upon to aid this well-regarded priest, Father Roland Nelson. Father Nelson had a younger assistant, but the man became very ill and could no longer serve. A new assistant was chosen by the diocese, and this was Father Daystrom. However, he was only there for a few months. It is strange you mention a period of seven years as one of your descriptions, as Father Nelson died just that many years ago, or near to that number. Just after his work in Haiti."

"Thank you, father," said Holmes. "You've done me a world of help."

Returning to London, we took a cab until the streets became so bottled up that it became necessary for us to alight and walk some blocks to Holmes's destination, a vast open space in Westminster where a ceremony was in progress. We were held up for twenty minutes, as it was either wait or go back from where we had come, and I was able to witness some sort of ceremony in the distance, with men in holy orders of the Catholic Church presiding over the event. There was eventually a polite but vigorous applause without cheer, and this signaled an end. We understood this to mean we could now advance into the building that was the headquarters for the Diocese of Westminster and its Clergy House.

"We are having a celebration this afternoon, Mr. Holmes," said a young priest, a clerk in the hierarchy of the church's personnel. He walked into the guest area where we waited for the attention of anyone who would see us without an appointment. "But certainly," he continued, "we do have a man matching your description. He's here as you said he would be. He is from America, but his arrival was very surprising, even for our diocese."

75

"That is less a surprise to me," said Holmes to the young man. "This place, this house I mean – it's attached to some type of rectory, is it not?"

"Certainly."

"And that building is one of several which together form this campus."

"Of course, Mr. Holmes."

"And this man came to you with a letter, but without an overall scheme."

"Just as you describe."

"Then who is his current superior?"

"Ah. I see. Well, he was placed naturally under the supervision of Reverend Father Michaels, an auxiliary bishop to His Most Reverend, The Archbishop Vaughan. Building the cornerstone has been Father Vaughan's life work. By that, I mean that it is to see the Cathedral rise in London. The man you seek certainly came at just the right moment to contribute to Father Vaughan's vision. I myself have seen his sketches, and they are of the finest quality."

"All of these gentlemen I see filing through your doors below – these would be the Archbishop, his auxiliary bishop, and Father Daystrom?"

"Yes, Mr. Holmes. The ceremonies have concluded, and there will be some wine poured for the clergy. I fear that you will be at some wait until Father Daystrom is available to you. This party they are about to enjoy may go on for some time. The Archbishop will be presenting Father Daystrom's drawings to the clergy this afternoon. They are certain to appreciate his contribution."

"I do appreciate the nature of their celebration. Yet my time is also limited, and I shall be altering Father Daystrom's agenda to some degree."

Holmes stood and walked to the throng of holy men making their way through the grand entrance of the building, just below us where the stairs joined the large room. He stood looking down at them all, a singular being by himself at the top of the stairs they were all about to ascend.

"Father Daystrom," he called. "My name is Sherlock Holmes. I was curious as to whether you would consider sharing with me some conversation, perhaps in one of your more secluded cloisters."

The men as a group stopped midway up the stairs. Each of them looked from Holmes to the man that he had addressed, located toward the end of the procession. After some assorted voices and low murmurs, the man spoke.

76

"Welcome to the Clergy House, Mr. Holmes. I shall be at liberty another time. Now I am in service to His Most Reverend Father." He leaned his head toward a bespectacled man of dark hair in an arch bishop's mitre.

"Oh, I am sorry to have incommoded you on such a day. Perhaps, then, you will not mind if I ask the priest who has been serving me here to direct us to such a place where my friend and I might be alone and enjoy the rest of the afternoon. I shall be passing the time enjoying a Larga Vista cigar."

The reaction given by the man, whom I now understood to be Father Daystrom, was one that had obviously been intended by Holmes, as he was immediately flustered. He recovered quickly, and appeared to be on the verge of responding, but his speech was interrupted by the central figure to whom all of the men had given their deference. Complete silence fell as he addressed my friend.

"Mr. Holmes. I am Father Herbert Vaughan, in service to the church, in so much as this diocese is concerned. As you have decided to speak to one of our flock – well, to one whom we have taken into our fold recently, and whose interest we love and will protect – do you not believe you would have some courtesy in more carefully approaching our brother, instead of toying with him before us and before his colleagues?

"I do not know of this 'Larga Vista' of which you speak, but this *'long view'*, as it would translate, is not lost on me, nor upon any of us. I dare say it has some double meaning. Please allow our train to enter above and into our own celebration room near to where you stand, and then wait but a few moments time. Any service that the good father or my office can give to you will then be made available. Is that, Mr. Holmes, not more charitable than throwing at Father Daystrom some hidden allusion?"

Sherlock Holmes bowed to the archbishop, demonstrating not only his appreciation for the man's magnanimity, but also that he, Holmes, was acknowledging that his bravado had created some form of trespass, and that he wished to make amends for what he had done. He moved back to where we had originally stood before the men had arrived, once more joining me by the seats placed at the top of the landing for those who would beg an audience with one of the senior members of the clergy.

The group of holy men walked up the stairs, past us, and continued into a room, followed by the young priest who had been our host. But as he passed Holmes, Father Daystrom peripherally eyed my friend with a look of enraged scorn.

A quarter-of-an-hour later, the young priest opened the door for the very man, who left their private celebration and walked to where we sat. Holmes and I rose to meet him.

"I believe our discussion would best be served in a place of the sort that you suggested. Please follow me.

Father Daystrom was dressed in the simple black that was typical of his order, with only his white clerical collar denoting his association with the Catholic priesthood. I had seen him earlier with a festive sash about him, but that had been removed, and his style had become taciturn and businesslike. He was probably in his mid-thirties, with rosy cheeks over a dark complexion, brown hair that was short and neatly combed, and generally with lines more associated with travel and the sun, rather than wear from life's worries.

Together, we left the hall dedicated to the clergyman's administration of the diocese and followed him to an archway in the shade, looking out at the interior of the vast property in the heart of London. The buildings, from an interior point of view, obscured anything of the city beyond.

"So, Mr. Holmes," said the man after we sat. "You found me, or you found me out, and then found me. I should say that if Harden hadn't consulted with an expert, he would have become none the wiser, and I would still be making my sketch-work for the cathedral's stained glass, and you would be working on something altogether different. Were my set pieces so easy to connect with me? Why isn't Harden with us? Are you indeed going to jibe at me with one of his tobacco leafs rolled into the Cuban version of what was originally a Haitian product? I suppose you've figured out that part by now."

"What I have figured out is that you have chosen a very clever way to persecute John Vincent Harden, basing it upon something he would understand, yet not fully understand. But the swerve to it is that you didn't realize yourself that you haven't the depth of knowledge upon which to draw an accurate version of what is to be the basis of his torment. So you accidentally threw in front of him an iconography that was the symbolic equivalent of gibberish.

"Neither of you penetrated deeply enough to learn what *Vodou* actually was – unlike Father Nelson, who had spent so many years in the western region of Hispaniola that he did become acquainted with the details of the religion."

The man did not hide his utter surprise at what Holmes had learned about him, almost as if by magic. "I admit that knowing of you – or at least knowing of your reputation as I do – pales as a very poor counterfeit to hearing you speak. You indeed possess powers that are not of this world, Mr. Sherlock Holmes. So says His Holiness, to this day, as reported by him to his closest intimates. It was Archbishop Manning of this same diocese, the predecessor of the man whom you just met and who spoke with you on those stairs, who urged His Holiness to seek you out directly, Mr. Holmes – for you to travel to Rome as you did, and discover for him a solution related to the cameos that were taken from one of the palaces."

Holmes tilted his head toward the man for a fleeting acceptance of the praise being awarded to him. Then, he said, "Did you wish for this interview to include Mr. Harden? You are correct that I chose not to include him at this time, but that is easily remedied."

"I wish nothing more than the man know the harm his overseer inflicted upon the people of that island. They worked the fields for months under the suggestion of Father Nelson, and the man's heart was crushed after all of the trappings of Harden's men left. Harden was an absentee landlord, devoid of any real interest in what became of his first attempt at cultivation. How," Daystrom continued, "did you come to the conclusion I was involved?"

"Cultivation," said Holmes. "Your use of both 'Azaka Medeh' and 'Saint Isidore the Farmer', to use the correct names, as a blended being meant that my search had to conform to a very specific standard of a man with a very specific history. Even the small fetish you left, a bag of earth and pipes, are the accouterments of this being, and your knowledge of them showed you to be such a man.

"Your correct use of skulls, but your failure to understand they would never be colored as they were done so by you, showed you to be such a man. You had to be a holy man, and you had to be junior to another father who knew far better than you knew about the people and their practices. It was one of several things that caused you to have less of a pedigree along this line than that of Father Nelson. Your late arrival in Haiti, and only in service to your superior in ways that would not require you to know the people and their history but be more of a helper than a pioneer, made sense to me of who you had to be.

"You had to know something about *Vodou*, but not enough to know *why* one who cared about the religion as a believer would never for his own sake revere Isidore *as* Isidore. You had to be a man who could travel as needed, and your profession allows for that, if one has a talent that is sought. Indeed, you fit that factor perfectly. Your artistic skills must be greatly appreciated."

79

"I truly enjoy the staining of glass. To be honest with you, I do not take a pride in my art or in its creation. Unlike my recent misdeeds, I hold to it only in the most Christian understanding of giving, without conceit."

"I will take you at your word, Father Daystrom, as I have only heard of your labors on the stained glass for the cathedral in South Carolina's Charleston. I reasoned that you were instrumental in working with Franz Mayer and Company to make the glass for that structure."

"And I will return there, now that Archbishop Vaughn has approved my designs for the Westminster Cathedral. Many can go five lifetimes and not be able to see even one cathedral be erected. I am twice blessed to have been able to work for the making of two, both within the same decade."

"You shall not return until you settle matters with friend Harden. He does perhaps deserve your treatment of him in the manner you have chosen, but then again he may deserve a more honest approach. I will not render judgment. But it is time for you to deal with him, man to man. You should let him know about the harm he caused, especially to Father Nelson and how he was crushed."

Father Daystrom turned in his chair. "I am torn between the ideal of Christian charity and an admitted anger for what became of one of the most decent men I had ever worked with. I wasn't his apprentice for very long, but it was enough for him to teach me to bring others to The Christ, without telling them that their culture was bankrupt or evil, as too many of my brethren persist in doing. I wonder. I wonder if Mr. John Harden has truly reflected on his crimes."

"You and I both know that is for another to decide. He can, however, be placed in position to perform the reparation of giving to those islanders the value of their labor that was initially cheated, and by doing so, fulfilling earthly justice."

"Then I shall visit him in his rooms. Though I do not know what I will say to those to whom I give service here at the Clergy House."

"Fortunately for me, those kinds of questions do not fall into my work."

"Yes. They are the difficult ones, certainly. I cannot yet give to you thanks, Mr. Holmes. It is because I have not yet fully appreciated where this will all lead, and I will not be thankful unless my spirit takes me to such a place."

"Fairly spoken," said Holmes. "But aside from your thoughts about my involvement, I am certain that you will find your way to

80

grant Mr. Harden some forgiveness, should he fall in with your plan to compensate the islanders."

"A path to forgiveness is always made for those who ask at the time of their good acts. In this instance, Harden's soul is in his own hands."

The Case of the
Biblical Colours
by Ben Cardall

ACT I

We all have those moments in time in which we remember exactly where we were and what we were doing – the very first instant that I saw my dear Mary smile, or the first time that I heard my friend admit he could be beaten, and by a woman no less. For artists, it might have been the passing of Van Gogh, or when a sporting enthusiast is able to witness the first county cricket match. My point is simply that for me, this case represented a marker in what my dear friend Sherlock Holmes referred to as a "locked room" mystery.

It was a particularly humid summer's eve in July, 1896. All was quiet outside, except for the distant chatter of the hooves and wheels in the street as the carriages were pulled by. Holmes and I were enjoying a discussion of matters for the logician. I say *enjoying*, as I was fast becoming a man out of my depth, and Holmes's eyes were getting wider due to his passion for the topic at hand.

"Oh, Watson, it is a simple matter when you have learnt to think as I have. Many is the time I have relayed to you that the little things are often the most important. I present you with these gambits of mine to challenge your faculties."

I must confess that I did appreciate his challenges, as on more than several occasions I could follow the deductions made. However, in my current mood, I could feel my frustrations growing, as opposed to my critical vision.

I tried to hide the fact that I was playing for time. "Run it by me once more to see if I have all of the details correct in my head, as I am not allowed a pencil to make notes."

"You do not need notes, Watson!" Holmes's excited state increased, his frustrations no doubt matching my own. "Once you can see your way to the one deciding fact, a thing so apparently inconsequential that it would be glazed over by the untrained eye, then the whole riddle becomes a matter of simplicity.

"Once more then, Doctor. A couple, who for the purposes of this riddle have been targeted to be murdered, unbeknownst to them

82

of course, have arranged to meet for drinks at night at a local hotel. The lady arrives late, and a little out of breath due to her rush. They enjoy their drinks, each having the exact same ones I might add – iced raspberry lemonade and wine – and a few moments afterwards, the husband falls down dead. I put it to you that with this evidence alone, I could tell you how the husband died and why the wife did not, as well as the tools for the murder as well."

"Definitely murder then, as you have already mentioned as much," I mused aloud.

With an almost playfully magnanimous sense, Holmes replied, "Yes. However, I do want you to go a little deeper. The actions of the people are key, and I will tell you that it was a hot day, if it helps you get there a little faster."

"Though I appreciate the assistance, it does appear to be maddeningly unhelpful."

"Imagination, my good friend! Use your imagination! Go through the actions of both as if doing it yourself – " Holmes began and then stopped mid-sentence, as if stifled by some unshakeable thought. "And if you could call to Mrs. Hudson to please to let the constable in, this new case appears to be a matter of most importance. Oh, and Watson – make the young man a cold beverage."

I was completely befuddled – not at my friend's brilliant mind, though that same feeling would come moments later – but in this moment at the apparent random chain of events that my friend had imagined in his head and then verbalised. Were it not for the somewhat profound knocking upon our front door and ringing of the bell, I fear that I might have been stuck in that instant for a considerable time. I was literally shaken to my feet.

My friend looked at me with an all-knowing smile, and I felt that I was supposed to know more about it than I did. So as requested, I went down to Mrs. Hudson's kitchen, filled a glass of water, added a piece of ice, and made my way back up the stairs. Upon my return, who should be standing there but a young man, a constable to boot, having entered in my absence, and gasping for breath. I merely gestured toward him with the water, which he literally ripped from my hand and drank with such speed that it looked as if it were giving him life. Then, with thanks, he handed me the glass.

Holmes, still grinning with delight, encouraged the young man to sit and tell us what he had to say. I must have been simply staring unblinking at my friend's apparent premonition of the not-so-distant future and the constable's arrival, for he said, "Watson, that can wait until later. The constable has a matter of some urgency and he needs our help."

"I was sent strictly for you, Mr. Holmes, by the inspector," said the man, now slowly bringing himself back to normalcy in my chair.

"And being new to his career," Holmes continued in my direction, "he does not appear to know that when I am called, Dr. Watson will never be far behind. I can assure you, my good man," he then said to the constable, "that Lestrade is very well informed on this matter. So what has happened at the church that has you all so stuck?"

The constable looked at me as though my friend were speaking some sort of foreign language, and I were the only one who could translate it. "Both of your feet are virtually bathed in sacramental wine," I said. "Were you not so tired from your run, I would imagine that you would have smelt it."

"Blow me," the constable stated. "Every fibre of me wants to ask how on earth you gentlemen caught that. However, first and foremost, I must carry out my duties. Mr. Holmes, I am required to accompany you to the scene of the most curious crime that I have seen. I am to tell you that the room is locked, and that nothing has been touched that we can see."

"I fail to see why you would need my assistance for that. Call a locksmith."

"Well, that's the thing, you see, sir. We can see four dead men from the window, and the door has been locked from the inside, and the locksmith there says that it's nothing to do with the lock. The door just won't open. No one is prepared to smash a window on account of it being a church, sir. So the inspector asked that I recite these details to you exactly. Between you and me, sir, I think he's trying to ask for help without specifically asking for help."

"Well, that is an intriguing matter, and you are absolutely correct that Lestrade would never admit to needing my assistance in front of so many ears – something I will spend more time upon in the future. For now, gentlemen, downstairs! We have a trip to make."

Holmes then seemed to appear in his coat and hat as if a conjuror had stepped into our rooms. Not a moment later, we were in a cab heading for the church.

ACT II

Little did I know that our destination was one of the better-known churches of London – so vast, and at the same time so stunning, that one could believe that someone might hide in the shadows for an age. We pulled up outside, and my curiosity must've been visibly bursting, as my friend smiled and said, "The constable is still pressing on your mind, Watson, and I fear you haven't paid a moment's notice to the little challenge I laid before you."

"You're quite right, Holmes, though I believe from your reaction that the two must be connected in some way." Holmes let out a cry at my feeble attempt to curry favour for a clue.

"Watson, you have hit upon the trail. However, the connection between the riddle and this investigation is only a matter of happenstance, as if penned to illustrate the purpose of my challenge. The point of the riddle and the policeman isn't that they are linked through themes or a particular item – it's that one salient and often over-looked piece of information, because of its commonplace sensibility within the setting, can be potentially the most lucrative when it comes to solving a puzzle. The riddle simply highlights a particular way of thinking that is beneficial for deduction.

"The man and woman meet for drinks. She arrives late, out of breath on a hot day. They have the identical beverage, served over ice. However, the thirsty woman drinks hers immediately, while the man sips his more slowly. Soon, he dies. Now, think – do you see anything in connection to the way the constable drank the water that you provided and the woman in the story?"

I thought, and then I began to dimly understand. "When the constable handed me the empty glass, the ice that I'd placed in it was still nearly whole."

Holmes smiled. "Exactly. He drank quickly due to his thirst, so the ice hadn't had a chance to melt – the same as for the thirsty woman in the story. While her companion, the man drinking at his leisure, allowed the ice to melt, its substance diffusing into the beverage. Both drinks had *poisoned ice*, but only the man's had time to become effective.

"Now, as regards the prediction of the constable's arrival – you know my methods. My senses are always working, and I had simply heard a faint but expedient sound of police-issue shoes approaching quickly in the street outside through our marginally open window, giving me the man's job and age, and thus allowing me to infer his position and rank. Someone running down Baker Street at that time must have had a pressing matter, and running at all when he could have caught a cab shows his inexperience, and also that he would need to quench his thirst."

I had that same feeling of wanting to kick myself for not having seen something that was right under my nose the whole time, and Holmes flashed me his all-knowing grin which, in times like this, I could admittedly do without. As we turned to the very obvious scene of the crime, judging by the amount of policemen gathered around the window and closed door, Lestrade greeted us. "Right, then, Mr. Holmes. We have a door sealed from the inside that no locksmith knows how to open, four dead men, and a room that has yet to be touched since whatever has happened, happened. No one associated with the church," he added, "saw a thing."

"And this?" Holmes pointed at a scattering of broken wine bottles near the doorway.

Lestrade grimaced. "An accident. After we had arrived, one of the constables turned from the window in shock and straight into a delivery man."

Holmes glanced at me. "Thus the smell of sacramental wine upon our young constable friend." He then turned to peer at the door, followed by a lengthy view through the window. Finally, he said, "Two things, Lestrade. You're going to need a few more men or a pickaxe of some description. And can someone please fetch me a Bible?"

"A Bible, Holmes?" I enquired. "Surely you, of all people, do not need to seek comfort in such a book."

"On the contrary, my dear Watson. It is merely a source of fact-checking at this stage, and I use the word 'fact' in the loosest sense. This scene is already representative of a battle that has been going on throughout the ages." As grandiose and potentially interesting as that sounded, Lestrade beat me to my question.

"I know that you're dying for someone to ask, Mr. Holmes, but before you continue making such outlandish statements, could you please explain yourself?"

"The pocket squares, Lestrade, the pocket squares!" He gestured toward the window. "Surely you observed that each of the four men within that room have matching squares, folded in the exact same manner, alike in every way except for their markedly different colours. They are obviously arranged to attract attention. Red, white, black, and green. Did neither you, nor anyone else, ever pay attention in Sunday School?

"Given that we are in a church," he continued, "it is interesting to note that the poor souls we see before us are quite infamous in London circles for renouncing the church, or at least the way of thinking that it glorifies. I would know their faces anywhere: Charles Livingston, Daniel Manning, Lincoln McConnell – who moved here from North America not six months ago to pursue his work in the sciences with this group – and Martin Noland, the latter being the most religious of the group, as he comes from a family of priests, and in that same vein, the most infamous of the dead men, due to his outspoken nature."

"I realise that I am very stupid and you are very clever, Mr. Holmes, but would you please make your point?" Lestrade rebuked. "What in God's name do pocket squares and a pickaxe have to do with anything?" This was another of those important moments that I shall remember for quite some time – Lestrade rarely admits to being the lesser man in any situation, and yet here he belittled himself and praised my friend in the same breath, even if sarcastically. Though Holmes would later remind him of this instant time and again in order to quieten him when needed, it was understood between the three of us that Lestrade was merely snapping in a moment of frustration, caused by one too many problems occurring all at once.

"The pickaxe is a simple matter: You will need it to open the door, as it has been sealed shut with a concrete mixture from the inside – you can see it there, escaping from under the bottom of the doorway. Now, before I go any further, you must allow me to enter the room first to observe and to collect valuable data, lest your men trample something of importance, like the – "

"Holmes, please stay on track," I interrupted, noticing the pallor of the inspector's face change to a deep red.

"Yes, of course," Holmes continued. "The scent of fresh concrete is still in the air, coupled with the fact, as I mentioned, that some has slipped underneath the doorway as it has set. This shows two things: Whomever the killer is, he or she is not in that trade, as such a sloppy thing would never have happened if a craftsman were involved, and the other is that the killer could still potentially be sealed inside with the bodies."

"*Pickaxe now!*" Lestrade cried. I pressed for an answer that perplexed me much more. "Why the Bible?" I asked softly. Holmes must have been in a particularly good mood, for he was able to recite his thoughts and deductions without a growing sense of annoyance at being forced to slow down.

"I *did* pay attention in Sunday School, Watson. Over the years, my proclivities as a logician have led me into a battle with circular belief systems of faith, time and again, and as such, I've read the Bible cover-to-cover on more than one occasion. '*Know thy enemy,*' Watson, '*know thy enemy*'.

"Proverbs?" I asked.

"Sun Tzu," he replied. "The attic that I've created in my head can often be a little vague if I haven't visited a specific part of it in a while, particularly that place that holds the Good Book. Still, I strongly recall that the Apocalyptic Horsemen were represented by *colours* – red, white, black, and green – colours that match each of the prominently displayed pocket squares in the jackets of these unfortunate gentlemen. Have you found one?" he asked suddenly, as if I had been about the search for a Bible all along.

It was a simple matter to locate one, given that we were in a church. I was only gone a few minutes before returning with the book in question. Holmes flipped quickly to the back and nodded, as if his suspicions had been confirmed. I looked to see that the door was very nearly prised open. Lestrade, of course – feeling hugely important with his commands of "Faster!" – grew louder and more impatient. At last, the door was undone, and all went silent, bar one. Holmes used his handkerchief to push open the door as wide as it would go and then took in a huge breath. He hung his head moments later in what seemed like disappointment. However, we did not have long to wait in order to find out why, as my friend – ever the dramatist – didn't intend to miss a valuable opportunity here. This, was another singular reason that this case stands out for me – the little things indeed.

"There is no cause for alarm, gentlemen, for all who are inside are quite deceased. You have my word.

I must confess that, as familiar as I was with death, the macabre nature of the setting was most affecting. For an instant, I felt the tension catch in my throat.

"I implore you," said Holmes, "give me at least five minutes within the room, no more, to gather evidence so that I may put this to rest at once."

Lestrade gestured him inside with some urgency. In matters of this nature, however, Holmes, never to be rushed, was always careful and cautious, as well as taking time to drink in every last detail in that singular way of which only he seemed capable. There were occasions when he reminded me of a bloodhound, not least of all because he was prone to smelling victims and crawling around on the floor, examining it through his glass lens. Yet, I looked twice when I saw him, with my own two eyes, taste some powdery residue that he spotted near one of the dead men, whom I soon learned was Daniel Manning.

Then, in a flash, it was over. He jolted to his feet and motioned for the inspector to begin his side of the investigation. "That's quite enough to get me started, Inspector. I would recommend that you take the water jug from the table, as well as the glasses, as there are no injection marks or any other signs of the poison being ingested in some other way. Make no mistake: This is murder, and it was unsuspected. Watson, come! We have a cult to find. They are dabblers in the dark arts, so be prepared to see some curious wonders."

With that, Holmes left the room to hail a cab. This, then, was the performer of whom I had grown so fond!

ACT III

We returned to Baker Street, and no sooner had we entered the rooms than Holmes lit a pipe – a sure sign that something had puzzled him greatly. I was hesitant to ask, as one of a few things usually happens: Either I have missed something important, or Holmes will let his excitement get the better of him and talk far too quickly for a clear understanding. Or if I'm very unlucky, both.

"Holmes, I must confess: With what we have, I'm quite perplexed by it all. Sealed shut from the inside, and all murdered, with no apparent culprit inside. He – or indeed she – must have been an apparition of sorts." I thought that I would try to beat him to the punch on at least one of the points.

"Watson, the matter is this: We must eliminate the impossible. Ghosts are not real, despite what people will believe, and until I see one, I shall steadfastly hold my belief. There are four dead men in a room, only one of whom would be needed to seal it from within. If it was a joint suicide on all counts, it would then be a contrived spectacle, intentionally used to make a statement about their cause. Instead, it's murder. All of the men were in reasonably comfortable positions, which one would not expect of anyone who has been poisoned, as they clearly were. Therefore, someone moved their bodies to more relaxed positions afterwards. The real question that I have for myself at this point is how this connects to the apocalyptic nature of the Bible, and – if there was a fifth person with them –

where did he or she go afterwards, if indeed he or she went anywhere at all?"

"How could this other person leave if they were sealed shut from the inside?" I asked

"Now, Watson, you are asking the important questions!" He puffed quietly on his pipe before rising. "I must go out. I believe that, with a bit of research into the backgrounds of the four dead men, I'll be able to find a trail leading to those who have an interest in this affair."

And with that, Holmes donned one of his many indiscriminate jackets and was out the door. I was unsure as to whether it was because he knew that I might ask more questions, or that he was simply giving a fine performance. He did not return that night. Occasions such as these always left me on edge, as I was never sure if my friend was going on some type of reconnaissance mission or using his ability to blend in so that he could slip into a less-than-reputable part of London, as he was prone to do when a matter of this sort vexed his mind. Also playing on my mind as well, aside from the concern for Holmes's well-being, was the question of how could the murderer – he, or even she – have still been in the room? Nothing slipped by my friend when he was given full capacity to let loose his skills.

It was a beautiful morning when I awoke to discover, sitting in a chair at the foot of my bed, none other than Sherlock Holmes himself. He had a look on his face that allayed my previous concerns, only to ignite another. This was no ordinary problem for him; this had shaken him. One could always tell when something had truly disturbed him. I had seen it during the times involving *The Woman*. He didn't blink, he barely moved, and most importantly, he didn't smoke. I didn't quite know how to ask what was wrong, or what he had seen that troubled him so, though I was grateful that I didn't have to wait long to find out.

"Watson, you know me to be a man of logic and well-founded skills, based upon reasoning and evidence. Much of the time, I observe evidence that admittedly others cannot – or choose not – to see, but it is evidence nonetheless. However, I must confess that I have no satisfactory explanation for what I saw last night. Well, I have no satisfactory explanation *yet*, except for the fact that I should not have seen what I saw, for quite simply it cannot exist. Still, I saw it – I saw *him* – plain as day, and with my own two eyes!"

"Holmes, what the devil is going on? Whom did you see, and why are you sitting in my room?"

"I saw what I was told was Daniel Manning's ghost. I saw him, not moving, but almost as an apparition. I heard a voice, but have no way of knowing if it was his or not, as I have never heard the man speak. However, others around me seemed quite excited by the fact that they could hear the voice of someone that they knew and recognized."

I gestured before I spoke, and clearly my dear friend knew what I was going to say, again for he answered it before I uttered a syllable.

"No, Watson, they were not twins. I feel you misunderstand what I am saying. This wasn't simply a person in an excellent disguise – this wasn't even a *person*. What I saw managed to keep its form *as others passed through it*. I could find neither an explanation, nor a mirror, nor some sort of projection machine. But one thing is certain. I need to go back and carry out further inspection. Until that time, however, I remain, I confess, at a loss as to how I saw those things."

He stood and began to pace. "A quick investigation narrowed my interest to Daniel Manning, who has been associated for some time with a prospering religious movement, located in a house in the East End. Suitably disguising myself, I made my way inside, during a meeting that was taking place there last night.

"The place can only be described as a 'cult-house'. It was during the ceremony that I saw young Mr. Manning, knowing for certain all the while that he was dead. I watched as people passed through him. The only thing I can tell you for sure is that the attendees were passing through the . . . the *apparition* on purpose, as if to overstate the fact of its appearance. They seem to value this as the great proof of their belief, as well as it being an aid in convincing the undecided masses with whom I stood. Watson, these people – these *believers* – have the potential to be very dangerous indeed, as there were more than several prominent scientists there. If they are to be indoctrinated, then believe me when I say – and no dramatisation would be needed – the next generation will be at risk."

Now, I may not be in league with my friend, but I am smart enough to know that science and religion and all the other things of a mystical nature have been at war for centuries, and at any time when one side is doing particularly better than the other, then usually a great many people are in danger. Holmes and I would need to control this quickly.

Holmes remained most perturbed for the rest of the day, until he decided that we should return that night to the "cult-house", as he continued to call it. Thus, we found ourselves that evening approaching a nondescript building in the East End. To many, it would simply be a darkened corner of an even more ghastly and gothic-looking alleyway in the heart of London. Blink and one would have missed it while walking by, as it seemed to blend into the other looming buildings surrounding it. Yet, it was the type of place that might affect anyone's mood, simply by sight alone. As we arrived there, at what I understood to be the next meeting, Holmes's sights were set on something much more tangible and "of this world", as he put it – *data*. My friend was in desperate need for a solution to this problem, as it was an itch that he simply could not scratch.

I was of a mind that we were going to be quietly and surreptitiously entering the house, but Holmes simply wandered in, without a care being paid to keep the fact that we were on a secret hunt. "Holmes!" I whispered as loudly as I could without discomfort, "Shouldn't we be a little more careful?" This as my friend rummaged in his whirlwind way through the drawers and cupboards of the entrance room.

"Nonsense, Watson. I spent last evening amongst the peers of this den. That is more than enough time for me to know its workings. Now, at any moment there is going to be a very large gentleman coming through this door. It is of the upmost importance that you not give him any reason to be alarmed."

"Whatever do you mean, a large gentleman?" I said.

"He is the protection for the place. There are some very familiar faces that walk the halls here, which is why this group has the potential to be such a threat. Now, my friend, did you have the foresight to bring your revolver?"

I nodded. It was all that I could do not to be propelled into action, and yet the sight of this "large gentleman" when he arrived was enough to allay any urge that I had. He was at least seven feet tall, and not only did he have to duck down to get through the doorway, but he had to step sideways through it as well. He reminded me of the carriages that only large horses could pull. In that moment, it was very clear why, with his magnitude, he represented a one man force: Having others to help him would be merely laughable.

I turned to find Holmes, hoping for some guidance regarding what to say, as I was quite out of my depth. He wasn't there. So much for the non-stealthy approach. I hadn't heard anything when he

92

vanished. Looking into the jet black eyes of this mountainous man must have only taken a few seconds, but it felt like a lifetime. I couldn't let my mind run away with me, musing on all the feats of strength of which he must be capable, and thinking how feeble my bones would be under his dinner-plate-sized hands. No doubt he would quickly determine that I was there for reasons with which he would be less than happy.

After those few lifelong seconds, a frail greying northern man stepped in, introducing himself to the guard with what must have been some form of a secret handshake, as it was quite unnatural to see. The man then nodded toward me and stated, "This is my friend's first outing into the ways of this world. I am keen to open his eyes to the possibilities."

Two things made sense in that instant: I must have looked like a clueless child to these men, and the man from the north was in fact Sherlock Holmes. This was clearly the disguise he had used when he was here last.

Leaning in, Holmes whispered, "I found nothing in the entrance but whispers of my youth and books on science and conjuring." His expression then went vacant as we were shown into a gaggle of people, sharing quiet words as if in a doctor's surgery. I knew better than to ask what was happening. Holmes needed to work, and I was more than a little intrigued with what I was about to see. I turned to ask him about it, and much to my surprise, he was gone again. I was shocked to see a great many respected scientists in the crowd, as well as politicians and even members of the Yard, though I only counted two of those. It would be a few weeks later when I would be able to question them about their involvement with this cause and hear their embarrassed explanations.

An aging man entered the pulpit at the centre of the stage in front of us. Were I in a different location, it might have looked as if we were about to watch a show.

"My friends, it pleases me to see so many familiar faces, and a few new ones as well. We are here to celebrate in the knowledge that the followers of our cause can experience an existence without end. A few days ago, our brother Daniel was taken by the Horsemen as a punishment for his non-belief. I spoke with them and pleaded for his return so that he might continue to do the work for us and our way of life." He smiled. "And they informed me that he would return. *And he has.*"

I expected him to dance around the topic at hand a bit more, but no. Here was a man that stated unequivocally that there is life after

93

death, and also that he had been in direct contact with the Four Horsemen of the Apocalypse. I didn't know whether or not I was more concerned about the forthright nature of his speech, or the fact that so many people around me seemed to believe in what he was saying. It was a feeling of uncertainty that I had experienced too many times in my life, but not so strongly since that fateful day at Reichenbach in 1894. This, and for many other reasons, is why this case stands out in my memory. I say again, I saw and heard a man that night who stated outright that he spoke with the Four Horsemen of the Apocalypse.

"Your continued support and allegiance to this cause," continued the aging man, "has pleased so many of our constituents and spiritual friends. The time will come when you can show your dedication. But until that time comes, let me show you why your aid is so valued. Let's talk to Daniel.

"I understand that for belief, proof is needed, and I offer it to you simply. My boy," he called, "come back to this plane and share with us the wisdom of your existence. Come back and show us why we value our time in *this* household. Come back and let us rejoice in the knowledge that what we do here, in his room, protects us and binds us for all time."

At that moment, in a flash of light, I also saw what Holmes had seen the night before – *Daniel Manning*! He was there – or at least some part of him – floating in the middle of the room, and looking exactly like the dead man that had been in the sealed room, right down to the clothing and the prominent pocket square. Although his spirit, if such that it was, appeared only in shades of blacks, whites, and greys, the fold of cloth suggested red, as had the one that was on the body on the previous day. The phantom's mouth was slightly ajar but not moving, and yet we heard his voice, albeit muffled and difficult to understand. The leader informed us that this was due to the trans-dimensional distance.

"Under my guidance, I will now ask our new friends, including the colonels and army doctors among you, to come up and meet Daniel."

I froze. He came down into crowd time and again, and one at a time we were encouraged to go up onto the stage and talk to the apparition, and then to pass through him. Many around me stated that the apparatiion sounded exactly like Daniel Manning, whom they had known during his lifetime. On stage, people asked ridiculous questions, obviously in some attempt to prove that what they were seeing was not real, and each one left the stage dumbfounded at the answers, and even more so after walking *through* him. Then came my turn. I had no questions. I merely observed, and could see nothing but lights and a body, floating there before me. I walked through the apparition, and it was as cold as the fear I had felt years before when I believed that my friend had died. On my way back to the crowd, Holmes was standing there, this time looking slightly pleased. This was a huge comfort to me, as I had just had my world turned upside down.

ACT IV

We returned to the rooms at Baker Street to find Lestrade waiting for us. He had that same look of impatience that I recognised as "being beaten to punch" by Holmes again, and I was brought back to this world, as I knew that this was when I would actually get to see a performance – a performance of one of the sharpest minds of our generation.

"Well, what is it, Mr. Holmes? Some of us have to work and can't simply spend our days wearing makeup and going about the town."

"Are we simply solving the murders, Lestrade, or also the reasons why?" Holmes asked.

Lestrade grew flustered with impatience as he attempted to chastise my friend about the two being intrinsically linked. Before he could begin, however, Holmes told him of our experience at the old house where the cult was ensconced.

"The murders and the reason are in essence connected," Holmes continued, "but there is much blame to go around, and we will eventually need to track down and question a great number of people. First things first: The powder that you found on the ground by young Mr. Manning's body was Magnesium, was it not? It certainly tasted like it."

Lestrade turned to me as if to confirm that he had heard what he had heard. I merely gestured in such a way as to indicate that I was not shocked to hear that Holmes would taste Magnesium, and also that I had no idea how he knew that he could taste it without coming to any harm.

"Four dead men, one with Magnesium beside him. Do you find it suggestive that such a powder was found with the bodies? Oh well, more about that in a moment. First I will explain and let you in on a secret of such severity that you may be reminded of a conjuror

95

revealing his secrets. When I saw the ghost of Daniel Manning, or what looked like the ghost of him – I can't even say that now without feeling some form of anger at myself for being taken in by it! – I *knew* that is must be some sort of illusion.

"On my way through the halls of that place, that cult-house, I found a few things that were the turning points in this case – specifically a camera, and a few books on magic and conjuring. My friends, have you ever heard of Pepper's Ghost?"

Our glum expressions were enough to show Holmes that we had no idea what he was talking about, for we couldn't even formulate a question.

"Go with me on a journey, if you will, a journey of imagination. Two men form an organization, religious in nature, but decidedly dishonest. Now imagine three other men who make it their business to question religions, and are on the cusp of disproving and dismantling this growing cult."

"Charles Livingston, Lincoln McConnell, and Martin Noland!" I asserted.

"Very good, Watson! And the two men who started the cult would be Daniel Manning and his father."

"Is that the man who spoke to the crowd?" I asked.

"I believe not. From my research of the organization, Manning's father tends to keep to the shadows. That is how he was able to maneuverer so well when faced with the efforts of the other three to dismantle and disprove their cult, which would essentially destroy their source of money and with it, the power that it provides for the Mannings.

"But then – something happens. The three men working to expose the cult unexpectedly have the opportunity to take on someone whom they believe is an informant, but is in fact a double agent. It's a case of the old 'I have served evil but now I want to do good, so I'll tell you about the evil in order for you to *think* that I am good, while I am still actually evil' routine."

Lestrade looked at me and raised his eyebrows. I smiled, and Holmes continued. "Daniel Manning, still working secretly with his father while acting as if he has turned against the cult, manages to convince the other three that a meeting to discuss proceedings will be best. They do so, at the church where the bodies were found, for who would expect that they would assemble there? The very nature of the setting adds to the Mannings' plan. It was likely presented as safe neutral ground. There, Daniel Manning poisons the other three with

96

something in the drinks – you did find poison in the water jug, did you not Lestrade?

"We did."

"Excellent. Manning poisoned the other three, Livingston, McConnell, and Noland. It was then that the elder Manning joined him, helped him to arrange the bodies, and proceeded to take photographs of Daniel for use later."

"Photographs?" I asked.

"Of course. This is proven by the presence of the Magnesium, an important component of flash powder. Although the photographs of Manning, later used in the illusion of his ghost, could certainly have been made elsewhere, creating them at the scene had certain value in creating the effect. Then, with the other three dead and the photographs complete, the elder Manning departs, leaving Daniel to seal himself inside the room with the dead men. I have some theories about how the materials used to seal the room were hidden as well, but I'll address that later. The advantage to all of this, as explained to Daniel Manning by his father, would be that the cult, having perceived an outside threat, has managed to destroy all three enemies to their cause, leaving one faithful servant alive."

"But Holmes," I said. "Manning's son died."

"Yes. Despite what Daniel Manning was told of the plan, the elder of these two evil cult leaders had other ideas. Daniel, under the illusion that he was serving his father, the elder leader, by creating a 'miracle', sealed himself in with the three other men, using concrete around the door. Then he sat down. He and his father had already placed the four Apocalyptic pocket squares to add extra portents of doom and then arranged the bodies in a semblance of comfort, to seem as if they had died peacefully in their chairs.

"After Daniel sealed up the room with concrete to add to the locked-room illusion, he seated himself as well, taking something given to him by his elder master, having been told that it would leave him unconscious, to be found later within the room as a supposed fourth but lucky victim. The death of the other three would serve to reinforce the beliefs of the cult – and encourage donations! Unbeknownst to Daniel Manning, however, the material that he added to his own drink, supposedly something quite a bit different and more harmless than what was given to the others, had also been poisoned by the elder cult leader, his own father, leaving a beautiful symmetry for the Four Horsemen illusion.

"In the meantime," Holmes continued, "the leader of this cult had prepared well, knowing what he needed for the next part of his

97

plan. As I mentioned, he had previously taken several pictures of Daniel Manning that would serve to represent to a full-length image of the man, as he appeared just before his true death. That brings me to Pepper.

"We were taken in by a conjuror's illusion. It works quite simply, based upon the reflection of light through a clean plane of glass. There was a book in the cupboard of the entrance hall pertaining to that very trick. With the power of belief, all that one needs to make it happen is to tantalise with an idea, a suggestion, and then have a piece of evidence or proof to back it up, and the circle of thinking has been established.

"Magical performances and mesmerism give the audience something that they cannot refute. Now I ask you: If you saw something of that nature, in a setting that was outside of a theatre, would you immediately assume a trick, or would you consider the possibility, even a slight one, of something else?"

In that one crystallising moment, everything that my friend had been telling me from the beginning of this case rushed back to me, including the meaning of the riddle with the poisoned ice cube and the thirsty constable that came calling. It occurred to me that it must always be this way for Holmes – seeing the one fact, the one salient detail, that could break apart an entire puzzle. In this case, my friend had observed a camera and a reference to a magic trick, and that had set his mind ablaze, allowing him to make connections that might not otherwise have been made, purely because, as he sometimes put it, his emotional qualities had become inextricably intertwined with his eyes.

"Did you notice that many people seemed to accept that the voice we heard was that of the dead man? I believe that it was being produced off-stage by Daniel Manning's father. Who better to produce a similar voice than a member of the same family? I'm certain that it was coming out of those long metal horns shoved into the corner of the room.

"We are a product of our surroundings, and those that surround us. Words, dialect, and cadence from Daniel's father would have sounded very familiar to those around us, those that knew him, and it's thanks to this 'trans-dimensional distance', as the man on the stage put it, the voice that we heard could be so easily mistaken for Daniel's, when in fact it was his actual father's voice.

"*He*, then, is the architect of this whole case, the whole cult, and indeed the whole problem. *He* is the man whose reach has the potential to rival another criminal mastermind that we have faced in our time. We find the father, and we find the poison, and put this whole problem to bed, as he is the real murderer who also took his own son's life to keep his cause going in the eyes of all those he relied upon to move silently in the shadows."

Act V

Lestrade needed a few drinks and nearly fifteen minutes to go over the details of what he had just heard, until we were all upon the same page. We then headed back to the church to find the materials used to seal the departed souls into the room. Holmes led the charge, as usual when he was chasing a lead. To him, finding these materials would prove his reasoning. We entered the room and went straight to the bookcase in the corner.

"It occurs to me, Watson, that books can be used for a great many things, both good and bad, and in some cases in which I've been consulted, they can literally be used as weapons. In this case, I believe we will find our materials hidden amongst these pages."

I was of the opinion that if books contained the tools needed to seal one's self in a room, then they would be a little more obvious, negating the entire purpose of the search. Holmes had told me that he knew that the materials had to be hidden somewhere, as there were no compartments that could not be seen, no drawers or cupboards, and most importantly, there was no cellar and no other openings to the room. I had thought that Daniel Manning might have used his hands to smooth the mix into the seams of the room, which meant that he would only need to hide the concrete mix itself. Holmes was all too quick to point out the many reasons why this was impossible, including the fact that there was no trace of concrete on the dead man's hands.

At that stage, the search didn't need to be delicate, as we knew exactly what we were after, and all the other evidence that could possibly be collected from the room had already been taken. Therefore, the books were merely pulled from the shelves, I was clearly looking in the wrong place, as I was hugely disappointed when I saw nothing remaining on the shelves after all of the books had plunged to the ground. Holmes, on the other hand, began to flip through the pages of what looked like every single book that he could get his hands on.

He then stopped and began to smile a huge, all-knowing, moderately conceited, and partially relieved smile. "Watson, when I said the books held the key, I meant it literally." He turned one of

99

them around to show that it had been hollowed out and – as he had foretold, like some sort of spiritual man himself – within was a dirtied trowel. We also found the remainder of the concrete mix that Daniel Manning had used, hidden in the plant pots and mixed in with the soil. Holmes pointed out that lilies were never that particular colour, and their smell was unnatural as well. To this day, I still remain happily uncertain of just how many senses Holmes has, or how finely tuned they are.

"Now on to the next game, gentlemen – finding the father!" Lestrade summoned a pair of constables and we found a growler to transport us to the cult-house. Soon we were standing outside. "Of my two trips exploring the literal catacombs in the bowels of this building, I discovered only one locked door, and I was robbed of the time I needed to gain entry. In that we have quite literally eliminated the impossible, because I have searched the other rooms and found no other data, then the one that remains must be the truth – or in this case, our missing link."

Holmes led us inside. There was no sign of the gigantic man – in fact, the house seemed to be deserted completely. Holmes moved with confidence to a back hallway and straight to the door in question. It was akin to a front door in the middle of a hallway, for it had the most grandiose of door knockers. It looked as though someone had taken great pains to demonstrate just how much money they had, and this was an extension of their wealth and taste. It was enough to make one wonder about the treasures that one would find on the other side. The simple act of knocking before entering told us that, whatever was in this room, even the cult itself wanted it kept secret from the other members. It was for this reason that I believe Holmes had such excitement in his eyes – a puzzle within a puzzle. It isn't very often that these come along for my friend. He let his mood get the better of him, I fear, for he knocked on the door quite loudly, and a voice that we recognised beckoned us inside.

The door itself was quite a heavy struggle to push open, and once we had, it took several moments to drink in the details of the room. Sheets of paper covered in scrawled scriptures were strewn about the floor, and what seemed to be a few hundred pins were stuck in a map of the whole country. A small vintage library stood in one corner, and weaponry and gothic ornaments were on every shelf. In another corner, hunched forward in his chair, was a man that not only sounded, but looked, very familiar as well.

Holmes stepped forward "Mr. Manning, Senior. After being thrown out of Oxford all those years ago for your conduct and addiction to substances, your bitter feud with that world has sent you down the wrong path. Though you are a skilled builder, I must confess that what you have built here is not something of which you should be proud."

"Who are you?" uttered Mr. Manning in a startled breath.

"Had you spent any time in the real world, you would know precisely who I am. I am here simply to ask why you conspired in the murder of three respected men, what exactly you plan on doing with the gun that is currently resting under your left hand, and why did you murder your only son?"

Manning Senior continued to stare vacantly at Holmes, clearly in shock. My friend, taking this as his cue to continue, did so. "I can see that you are a man who has been blinded by the dreams of power and have regretted your actions, but that does not tell me why. I need to know! And while *La Palina* is a fine brand, you may not smoke in my presence until you have explained to me your part in this. Now, talk to me and unburden yourself."

Lestrade had remained uncharacteristically quiet throughout this whole ordeal. He was either still unsettled, or was simply a bit behind. However, he looked like he was about to speak when Mr. Manning cried, "Get out of my head! What are you?"

"You see, that's the thing with belief, isn't it?" asked Holmes. "You operate with what you've been given, and when that isn't the whole story, when that isn't all of the facts, you are forced into making up your own mind, based upon the evidence at hand. That is what I deal in. I am not anything but an observant man, and I assure you that the signs are in this room for all to see. But it is only I, Sherlock Holmes, that chooses to see them."

"I have heard the name before," said the old man, "and yet I never get to see or hear much of the outside world these days. This whole saga is gathering speed, and is quite tough to hold on to. It only started as a way to show that arrogant community that I can make them believe in whatever I want them to – that they don't hold all the answers. If they'd only listened to me when I was there, then we wouldn't be here right now.

"The answer is a simple one, Mr. Holmes." My friend nodded. "I needed a way to make my story real. I needed a way to give these people *evidence*, a way to show them that what had gone on for all the years before had all been for something. I'll confess that we have committed some severe atrocities in the past – "

"Attacks on royalty throughout Europe, thefts of both art and jewels, and arson." Holmes interrupted.

"It seems you know more about the goings on of my organisation than someone of this world should. Then you'll understand that I needed to give the people something to convince them, and sacrificing my son was the easiest way to do it. I wanted to regain control, as my leadership was being contested, you see. I could do all of that, and more, with a few well-timed drinks and a magic trick."

"Your own son – !" I began, but Holmes raised a hand.

"The drinks," he said. "You lured some of your enemies to the church, and worked out a plan with your son to murder them, while you told him that his would be a miraculous recovery. But he had to die as well, with coloured pocket squares added to the mix to suggest an association with the Four Horsemen. And then, you were cold enough to make use of his death through a photographic image and distorted voices."

Manning nodded. "A simple magic trick is all that it took to gain blind allegiance from some of the finest minds in this land! You will probably understand the rest." Mr. Manning let out small silent movements that resembled laughter, but he had deep set sadness in his eyes, I agreed wholeheartedly with Holmes in assigning regret to him, for he looked, underneath it all, to be in a great deal of pain. It is this reason why I believe that he confessed so readily to Holmes, and by extension to myself and Lestrade, as he wanted this to end, and to possibly find some peace.

"Come on, up you get. You're under arrest," Lestrade said proudly. Mr. Manning cradled the gun in his hands a little before standing, which set us all on edge for just a moment. Then, he sighed and gave it up, and he was escorted out.

In the weeks that followed, we would learn just how deeply this organisation had actually been set within the country. Life-sized photos of numerous other dead men and women showed up in many places, which gave some indication of just how wide-spread the planned colonisation of England was under the rule of this evil group. This truly had been the cusp of something quite catastrophic. If they hadn't experienced such an internal battle, resulting in Manning's need to murder his own son in order to remove his enemies while giving himself some added credence, then I might be writing about a different case altogether. We would later learn of Mr. Manning's suicide in his cell, as evidently his impending judgment was something for which he could not wait.

102

So, as I remarked at the beginning of this affair, the reasons why I shall always remember this case are many, and they are why it will always stand out in my mind. I felt that I understood my dear friend's methods just that little bit more, but I also gained more of an understanding as to how he used them, and what continuous work that it must be. In a city that had its best and brightest swept under the rug of circular belief, it was my friend that stood against the tide to show them all just what "having an intellect worth using", as he put it, was for.

My most favourite reason for recalling this case, however, and one that makes me smile even to this very day, was that my friend, Sherlock Holmes, with his razor-sharp observational and deductive skills and unparalleled logical prowess, was stopped dead in his tracks, if for just a little while, because he believed that he had seen a ghost!

The Inexplicable Death of
Matthew Arnatt
by Andrew Lane

As I recall, it was during the autumn of the year 1896 that I was offered an unexpected view through a window into the childhood of my friend and colleague Sherlock Holmes. The landscape of that childhood was something that he had kept hidden from me, and from everyone he knew, for most of his life, and so the sudden realization that he had actually once *been* a child, with a family and a best friend, was something that took me aback.

Holmes and I first met when he was almost twenty-seven years of age and I was nearly two years older, but although I had often conversed with him about my own formative years – including my upbringing in Australia, my return to England, my time with the 66th (Berkshire) Regiment of Foot in Afghanistan, my service in the Second Anglo-Afghan War, and my wounding at the Battle of Maiwand – all I knew of his was that he had a brother, and even that took him seven years to reveal to me. He knew everything about me; I knew virtually nothing about him. That was the way he preferred it, and I accepted it.

1896 was a quiet year for us. The criminal underclass appeared to be slumbering, and, while I had my medical duties as a place to retreat, Holmes had a stark choice between updating his files and resorting to the needle. Fortunately he took the former course – as far as I can tell. The only cases of substance that we had were the one I have previously alluded to in print as "The Veiled Lodger" and another, which I have not yet committed to paper, involving a gentleman by the name of Simeon Wilkins. He had disappeared without a trace twenty-five years before and then reappeared in April of that year, claiming that he had been abducted by pixies for what had seemed to him to be a few days but, which had turned out, when he emerged from their lair beneath an ancient oak tree, to be two-and-a-half decades. Holmes quickly determined that the Simeon Wilkins who had disappeared had actually moved to America under a different identity and subsequently died, whereas the one that had emerged from the roots of the oak tree was actually his illegitimate son and murderer. The whole charade was an attempt not to gain access to Simeon Wilkins's fortune, for there was none, but instead to raise publicity for a planned tour of theatres during which the son, impersonating the father, would speak of his time spent with the diminutive woodland folk who had supposedly taken him – for a hefty appearance fee, of course. I recall with some shame that I said to my friend, "It was an obvious explanation, was it not?", following which he observed, with his characteristic dry wit, "All things are obvious when viewed through the lens of hindsight. The trick is to see them clearly at the time."

Having said that the year was quiet, it was, as I recall, a heavily overcast September morning when Billy, our page, ran in to our rooms at Baker Street.

"Telegram, Mr. 'Olmes!" he trumpeted with admirable volume but questionable originality, for the provenance of the envelope he passed to my friend was clear for all to see.

Holmes ripped the envelope open, scanned the contents, threw it down on the breakfast table and retreated to his bedroom without a word.

I could not help myself: I retrieved the telegram from the marmalade dish and perused it.

Matty dead, come quickly, it said. Four stark words.

I stared at the slip of paper, attempting to make some sense of it. Assuming that it was not written in code – and that was a bold assumption, considering the recipient – then it was at the same time a notification that someone known to Holmes had died and a request for help. Looking deeper, given the telegram ran to only four words, there seemed to be some understanding there that Holmes would not only drop everything in order to comply with the request – there was no explanation, no background – but also that he would know exactly where to go.

I knocked on my friend's bedroom door. I heard no response but, after a decent time spent waiting for one, I entered anyway.

Holmes was sitting cross-legged on his bed, staring at the wall.

"An acquaintance?" I ventured. "Please accept my condolences if that is the case."

"An old friend," he said. His tone was calm, but I could sense turmoil beneath the placid surface. "Perhaps my oldest. Matthew Arnatt – Matty for short. We met when I was fourteen. I have no idea how old *he* was, because he had no birth certificate and, when I knew him, no family. We met in Farnham, where I had been sent to stay with relatives on the basis that my mother was ill and my father had been sent to India with his regiment." He paused for a moment long enough that I thought he had finished speaking, but then he went on.

105

"He was a rover, a survivor, and something of a rogue and a thief, but we quickly became inseparable. We travelled widely."

"And yet," I ventured when it seemed as if he would vouchsafe no more information, "you did not stay in touch?"

"He found writing tedious and difficult, while I abhor casual letters. When I settled in at Cambridge to study he decided to keep on travelling. We drifted apart, and only met by accident on three occasions after that, but we had both changed enough that there was little to talk about."

"What did he do?" I asked.

"He imported silk from India and cotton from Egypt and had them made into fine dresses for high-class women here in England. He told me on the last occasion we met that he had married a girl in Dorset, and that they were living on a barge on the River Frome. "He shrugged. "He could have afforded a large house with the money he had made from silk, but he preferred the barge. He was, at heart, always a traveler."

"And now he is dead. How – " I stopped, conscious of how stupid my next words were: " – how do you feel?"

"People die," he said, still staring at the wall. "My mother and father are dead, as are their mothers and fathers, and one day Mycroft and I will join them. I am afraid to say that you, too, will die. It is the one thing in life we cannot avoid – the inevitable full stop at the end of the sentence. The only choice we have is how well that sentence is written, and in that regard I think Matty acquitted himself very well." He snorted. "Certainly, for someone that never learned to write properly."

"And the telegram?"

"From his wife, I presume. As I recall, her name is Ellie."

Abruptly he launched himself from the bed and started ransacking his chest of drawers, throwing items of clothing into a leather valise.

"I – " I started, and then hesitated.

"You wish to come too," he said without turning, "but you are unsure how to broach the subject, as you suspect I may wish to travel alone. In point of fact, I would value your companionship."

By custom, I always have a travel bag prepared, as I cannot count the number of times in the past my friend has suddenly leapt up out of his chair and exclaimed, "Quick – to Cardiff!" or wherever. Holmes himself does not pack in the normal sense – he just throws clothes and grooming essentials willy-nilly into a case on the basis that he can purchase whatever else he needs when we get to where

106

we are going. Often, rather than drag everything that he has purchased back to Baker Street again, he will just abandon his new possessions in his hotel room, or even at the station. He claims it is the most logical way to travel, I counter that it is wasteful.

The train to Dorchester leaves from Waterloo, and takes many hours. I settled down with Daniel Defoe's *A Tour Thro' the Whole Island of Great Britain* – at the time my favourite book for dipping into – while Holmes sat voraciously examining the many and various national and foreign newspapers and periodicals he had scooped up from a vendor at the station. I slept for a while, and when I woke up, bleary-eyed, at a country station named Ringwood, I found him staring moodily out of the window. Suspecting that he was remembering other times, I diplomatically closed my eyes and went back to sleep.

Dorchester is a historic market town whose antecedents date back to prehistoric times. According to the well-informed Daniel Defoe: "*The town is populous, tho' not large, the streets broad, but the buildings old, and low; however, there is good company and a good deal of it; and a man that coveted a retreat in this world might as agreeably spend his time, and as well in Dorchester, as in any town I know in England.*" Looking back now, I could not disagree with him. We arrived at the station and took rooms at the Station Hotel which, like Defoe's description of the town itself, seemed "*populous, tho' not large*".

"Shall we visit your friend's widow?" I asked Holmes. "Ellie – was that her name?"

He shook his head. "I would prefer to consider the evidence first. In this case, the nearest evidence is the body of Matthew Arnatt."

The local doctor also acted as the coroner – Dorchester being Dorset's county town. We found him in his office, and explained our business. A short, stout man with a bald head but a luxuriant white handlebar moustache, he was initially reluctant to let us see the body, until Holmes mentioned that he had known Matthew Arnatt. At that point, the coroner suddenly grinned. "Oh – Sherlock Holmes! Of course you may see the body. Mr. Arnatt often spoke of you, and your childhood antics. I hadn't made the connection."

Childhood antics, indeed. I filed that away in my mind for later consideration.

"You knew Matthew, then?" Holmes asked.

"Not well, no, not well at all, but we sometimes drank together. He was a garrulous man, with a whole fund of stories that few of us

107

believed but many of us enjoyed." He leaned forward conspiratorially. "Is it true, Mister Holmes, that he once fired a poisonous toad from a catapult into a man's mouth?"

The corner of Holmes's mouth twitched. "It is indeed true. I was there. Matty was fortunate enough to get away with some blistering of the skin. The man whose mouth got in the way of the poisonous toad was not so lucky."

Again, I filed that away for later discussion. There had to be a story behind that, and I wanted to hear it.

The coroner took us next door, to the cold room where the body was kept. He gestured to me to pull the sheet from the body – a professional courtesy from one medical man to another. I did so, aware that Holmes was watching the process with gimlet eyes from one side.

Matthew Arnatt was a man in early middle-age, small but burly, with skin that suggested he had spent much time in the open air. I noted broken veins on his nose, which I ascribed to a fondness for drink, but it was the obvious wound in his right temple that immediately attracted my attention. I noticed pitting of the skin as well as burns, soot, and tears, and a marked peeling of the epidermis and dermis.

Before saying anything, however, I made a quick but comprehensive examination of the rest of his body. Holmes would have been cutting in his criticism had I not considered *all* of the evidence. I saw no evidence of any other wounds, nor was there any sign of blistering within the mouth that might have been caused by poisonous substances.

"Without conducting a full autopsy," I said eventually, stepping back, "I have to say that the obvious cause of death appears to be the *actual* cause of death. This man was. I believe, shot at close range." I turned to the coroner. "Suicide, or murder?"

He shook his head. "Neither is the case. No, neither."

Holmes pushed himself away from the wall. He had been attentive all the way through my examination – attentive and apparently emotionless, although I had no idea what was happening behind those steel grey eyes of his. "Accident, then?" he said. "Knowing Matthew as I did, I find that hard to credit. He was a meticulous man."

The coroner nodded. "Indeed," he said. "To my knowledge, the local constable is still checking the course of events. He has yet to come to a firm conclusion."

"There were other people present?" Holmes asked.

108

"Indeed there were. Three others in the carriage where the shooting took place."

"Including his wife?"

"No." The coroner shook his head sadly. "Poor Ellie. No, she was not present when he died."

"The death occurred in a carriage – stationary, or moving?"

"Stationary."

"But there *was* a gun?"

"There was a gun, which the constable now has in his possession." The coroner glanced from Holmes to me and back again. "The problem, as I understand it, is this: All four people present had examined the gun just before the unfortunate event and agreed that it was unloaded. The constable examined the gun immediately *after* the event, and could not find any evidence that it had been fired. The weapon was not hot, as it should have been, or even warm, and there was no characteristic smell wafting from the barrel of the hot gases that would have propelled the bullet, had there been one."

"But there *was* a bullet?"

"Indeed. I retrieved it from the victim's skull with a pair of forceps." He gestured to a nearby table. "It's in the kidney tray, over there."

Holmes nodded to me to take a look. Holmes's knowledge was, of course, immense, but there were certain areas where he was willing to step back and let other experts take their place. On medical matters, and when it came to guns, he always deferred to me. Sometimes on horses too, although he would point out wryly that my knowledge of the equine world might have been extensive but it did not enable me to predict winners on the racetrack any better than a rank ignoramus.

As I crossed the room, Holmes said, "And this weapon – where had it come from?"

"It is owned by Mister Gorringe – a local livestock auctioneer. He had it with him, to show everyone. Part of an extensive collection of firearms he possessed. Quite the collector, apparently."

I pulled a cloth from the kidney tray and looked at the bullet. There had been no attempt at cleaning: A small puddle of congealed blood surrounded it, and I also noticed traces of brain-matter. In deference to the fact that it was evidence in a fatal shooting, I did not touch it, but I did move the tray to roll it around so that I could examine it from various angles.

"Point four rimfire?" I asked.

109

The coroner nodded. "Point four one, in actuality. I measured it. A one-hundredth of an inch difference is very difficult to spot – you have a good eye, to have got as far as point four."

"And the gun recovered from Mister Gorringe?" Holmes snapped. "What type was it?"

"A Colt New Line revolver, I saw it myself."

"Also point four one caliber," I observed. "The caliber of the bullet is consistent with the weapon."

Holmes moved to the white-tiled table and leant over the body. If I hadn't known that he had been well acquainted with the dead man, I would not have been able to guess from his demeanor. "Where did the death occur?"

"The carriage had just come to a stop outside the Station Hotel."

Holmes glanced at me. "Convenient for us," he observed. Turning to the coroner, he said, louder, "There were four people in the carriage. Was anybody outside?"

"Many. The hotel was full that night. It is popular with commercial travelers and with locals."

"And you were there." Holmes turned and stared intently at the coroner. "You saw events as they transpired." These were not questions, but statements.

The coroner nodded. "I was drinking in the snug that night, yes. How did you know?"

"You said you saw the weapon, and you identified it as a Colt New Line revolver. It would have been confiscated as evidence immediately by the constable, and taken to the police station. I can conceive of no reason for you to have seen it, unless you were there at the time."

The coroner sighed. "You want me to tell you how a man – an acquaintance of mine, if not a friend – could have been shot, just ten feet away from me, by a gun that patently had not been fired for years and had dust in the barrel. I wish I could tell you. The only explanation I have is the same one you will get from anyone present – the Blaelock Revolver, as it is known around here, is a cursed weapon. Other men who have held it, over the years, have been shot by it, and yet the weapon has always been shown to have been unloaded at the time, and displaying no evidence that it had been fired." He shook his head. "This room is a place of science, Mister Holmes. If I am going to talk to you of cursed weapons then I would rather do it in a tavern, with a pint of good practical beer in front of me. Can we meet later, when I have finished work?"

"Indeed," my friend said. "And I would suggest that the Station Hotel is the obvious place to have that meeting."

"I was afraid you might say that," the coroner said sadly. "I have not wanted to go back, for obvious reasons."

"But it is the scene of the crime," Holmes added, "and therefore our investigations should progress there."

As he and I left, he said, "I shall go and pass my commiserations to Matthew Arnatt's widow. She still lives in the barge on the River Frome that Matty first arrived here in. I would be grateful, Watson, if you could talk with the local constable. Introduce yourself, explain our presence here, and take a look if you can at that weapon."

"You don't want me to come with you to console the Widow Arnatt?" My feeling was that, of the two of us, I was far better placed by character to console a grieving person, but my friend disagreed.

"We share something, she and I," he said, "although we have never met. This is something I should do alone."

I wondered if the reason for my friend's reticence was that he did not want me hearing stories about his childhood. Perhaps I was being uncharitable.

I walked the short distance to the local police station. The constable was in, and I quickly explained our business there. I then had to stand outside while he locked the door, crossed to the post office and sent a telegram to Inspector Lestrade at Scotland Yard, who I had mentioned in my introduction. He made me a cup of tea while we waited, and we made small talk for a while. He seemed a good sort: Of farming stock, with a thatch of ginger hair, and he had a fund of interesting stories about petty crime in the vicinity. Fortunately, Lestrade was at his desk, because a reply came within the hour.

"'*Trust them both*'," the constable read. He looked over at me. "Succinct, this Inspector Lestrade."

"Can you tell me the details that led up to Matthew Arnatt's death?" I asked.

"I can tell you what I saw when I arrived, and what I was told." He closed his eyes and leaned back in his chair. "This was last night. Matthew Arnatt had been at home, but he was picked up by the carriage of Jacob Gorringe so that the two men could travel to the Station Hotel. Mister Gorringe has a business auctioning horses, cattle, sheep, and pigs in the area. His family have lived here for generations. On the way, they stopped three times – once to pick up one Frederick Darley, a farmer, and once again to collect Paul Furnell, who rents out agricultural machinery to local farmers at decent rates. The four men had a long-standing monthly arrangement to meet for an evening's convivial drinking."

"You said they stopped three times," I pointed out, "but you have only mentioned two."

"The third stop was back at Mr. Gorringe's place. Discussion in the carriage had turned to Dorset's reputation for the supernatural, and from there to a weapon that Mister Gorringe had recently obtained from America to go in his collection, a Colt New Line revolver which Mister Darley had expressed interest in buying, so they returned to get it. The weapon was made twenty years ago, and in the intervening time it had passed through several hands. It had also – " he opened his eyes and stared at me, " – please be aware, Doctor Watson, that I am only passing on what I was told, and I am not making any judgement on how true it might be. Anyway, the weapon had also gained a reputation for causing the deaths of anyone with blood on their hands who picked it up and fired it at their own heads. It was said that the Blaelock Revolver would seek revenge for any death it came across."

"Any loaded gun would be likely to cause the death of someone who picked it up, pointed it at their own heads and pulled the trigger," I pointed out, although I knew already where he was headed.

"That's the thing," the constable said, placing his hands flat on the table and leaning forward. "Every single death allegedly attributed to this gun, from first to last, happened even though the gun was unloaded at the time!"

I waited a moment to see whether he was going to add anything, but he just stared challengingly at me, hands on the table.

"That would seem . . . unlikely," I said carefully. "Who was the first victim?"

"Apparently it was a craftsman at the Colt factory named Wilhelm Blaelock. He picked the finished weapon up and held it against his forehead, joking with his workmates. "If there's any justice in this world," he said, laughing, "then I should die right here, because my hands fashion these little engines of destruction." So saying he pulled the trigger, and immediately died from a bullet to the brain. His workmates checked the gun, which was fresh off the production line and therefore should have been unloaded. It was. There was no cartridge in any of the barrels, and no sign that the gun had been fired." He took his hands off the table and shrugged. "Or so

112

the story goes. Since then apparently eight people have died under similar circumstances – bravely, or foolishly, depending on your point of view, challenging the curse that apparently follows the weapon around. Eight, including Matthew Arnatt."

"The story seems implausible, on the face of it," I said carefully.

"Perhaps it is, perhaps it is, but look at the evidence. The carriage stopped at Mr. Gorringe's house, where he retrieved the Blaelock Revolver. The men examined it while the carriage took them to the Station Hotel. Mister Gorringe, Mister Darley, and Mr. Furnell have all since attested to me under oath that there were no cartridges in the gun's chambers. There was some banter over the Blaelock Curse, which was generally agreed to be ludicrous. They all agreed to test the gun. Mister Gorringe placed the gun to his head and pulled the trigger. Nothing happened. 'There,' he said. 'I have never killed a man, nor ever intend to. The proof is there.' He passed the gun to Mister Furnell, who said, 'I am a Christian man and I have never taken a life.' He pulled the trigger, and again nothing happened. The carriage was just arriving at the Station Hotel then, and Mister Arnatt snatched the gun from Mister Furnell with a cry of, 'I have done things in my life of which many might disapprove, although I did them all in good faith and to save a friend. If this gun is cursed, then so be it, but on my life I do not believe it is.' He put the gun to his forehead and pulled the trigger." The constable blinked, and looked away. "It fired, killing him instantly."

I tried to consider what Sherlock Holmes might have asked under those circumstances.

"How quickly did you arrive on the scene?" I asked.

"Immediately." He blushed, and examined his fingernails. "I happened to be in the Station Hotel on other business. I heard the gunshot and rushed outside."

"The carriage?"

"Both doors were closed, on the basis that the horses had been spooked by the gunshot and were rearing up, and it was dangerous to get out. Someone assisted the driver with the horses, and as soon as they were calm we got Mister Furnell, Mister Darley, and Mister Gorringe out. They were in shock, of course. Mister Arnatt was still in the carriage, dead, with the Blaelock Revolver clutched in his hand."

"You examined the gun, of course?" I asked.

"Immediately. No cartridge was in any chamber, and the barrel showed signs of dust. Had I been the gun's owner I would have given it a thorough clean and servicing before I tried to fire it, lest it explode in my hand."

"And the carriage – any open windows, gaps in the cushions, holes in the roof? Anything that might have allowed someone outside to fire in?"

He shook his head. "That was, if you'll forgive me, one of the first things I thought to do, having secured the revolver. The carriage was sealed. A man could have submerged it in water and survived in there until someone pulled him out."

I sighed. I have to admit, a part of me wanted to glean some clue, find some obscure piece of evidence that would enable me to say to my friend: "I believe I have solved the case!", but I could not think of anything.

"One of the other men shot him!" I suddenly said, the thought hitting me unexpectedly.

The constable shook his head sadly. "There were three men in that carriage, and none of them saw another one take out a gun and fire it."

"You searched them?"

"There was no need. One murder and one victim leaves two witnesses. I repeat: Nobody saw anyone pull out a gun, and let me remind you, Doctor Watson, that a gun is not a small thing. Had any of them been armed, I would have noticed it, on their belts or weighing down their jackets. And, as I said, I searched the carriage. No weapons had been left behind, save the Blaelock Revolver itself."

"Might I examine the weapon?" I asked.

He looked at me skeptically. "Have you ever held a gun before, Doctor Watson? Would you know what you were looking for?"

"I trained on a Tranter .44 revolver and a .577 Snider–Enfield breech-loading rifle during my time at Sandhurst," I said quietly but firmly.

He had the grace to look embarrassed. "Sorry, Doctor – didn't take you for a military man at first. Of course you can look at the gun."

He crossed to a locked cabinet, and from it retrieved a cardboard box. Inside lay a silver-coloured revolver with a curved wooden grip. I picked it out and examined it carefully. It was chambered for seven rounds. I pulled back the hammer and checked it, then I pushed out the cylinder and did the same. All seven chambers were empty. Finally, with the cylinder out – I am a very cautious man when it comes to firearms – I squinted down the barrel.

"Not only has this weapon not been fired recently," I said; "I would be surprised if it had *ever* been fired. It looks as pristine as the day it was made, and as dusty as a display weapon gets."

"When, according to the stories, its first act was to shoot the workman who finished it." The constable held up a hand. "I know – it is just a story."

I put the gun back in the cardboard box and handed it to him. "Thank you," I said. "You appear to have been very conscientious in your work. I am, I confess, baffled."

"As baffled as I am," the constable admitted ruefully.

I returned to the Station Hotel then, and waited in the lounge with a glass of whisky until my friend returned. During that time, I turned the matter over and over in my mind, looking for some crack, some weakness, some way of breaking through to the solution inside, but nothing occurred to me except the possibility that all of the men were in it together, and had conspired to hide the evidence and cover up for each other. But if that were the case, then surely there must have been easier ways of killing Matthew Arnatt? Why the charade concerning the Blaelock Curse – a charade that would have fooled only the man who was to die?

When Sherlock Holmes arrived at the hotel, he was noticeably more taciturn than usual. I presumed that the meeting with Ellie Arnatt had resulted in tears and emotions – neither of which he was particular enamored with or indeed prone to himself. I fetched him a glass of sherry, and told him everything I could remember about what I had heard from the constable.

"Instructive," he said, tilting his head back and staring at the ceiling.

"I have a question," I said, "but I do not think you will appreciate it."

"Then it concerns Matthew Arnett."

"It does."

"You want to know if he had blood on his hands – whether he had ever killed anyone."

I nodded. "I do."

"The question is irrelevant to the matter at hand, but yes – he saved my life on several occasions by taking the life of the person who threatened me. And him, I should point out."

I carefully phrased my next sentence. "If he was the only one in that carriage who had committed murder, then perhaps it is true – the gun only fires when in the hands of a person who has taken another life."

115

"Balderdash!" Holmes exclaimed. "And what does this gun do – fire phantom bullets propelled by phantom gunpowder? It is too ridiculous for words." He picked up his glass of sherry and drank it in one go. "I trust implicitly your examination of the Colt New Line, of course, but I need to look at that carriage."

"It is back at the police station," I said. I checked my pocket watch. "Nearly five o'clock. If we are fortunate, then the constable will still be there."

The station was only a few minutes' walk away, and Holmes crossed the intervening ground in a rapid stride that was only a little bit short of a run. I introduced him to the constable, who then took us to a yard out back where a carriage was stored. It was a four-wheeled double brougham, red in colour, battered and muddy with the wear of the road. My friend threw open the door and stood looking for a while, taking in all the details, before climbing in and closing the door again. As the constable and I watched, the carriage rocked on its metal springs, bouncing as Holmes threw himself around inside.

"Takes these things seriously," the constable observed.

"He does indeed."

"He won't find anything."

"Ah," I observed, "but that's the point – it's *him* not finding anything, not somebody else telling him that *they* didn't find anything."

The constable nodded. "He'll be wanting to see the Blaelock Revolver, then?"

I sighed. "I rather think he will."

Holmes eventually climbed out of the brougham. Before I could say anything, he was climbing up into the driver's seat. From there he crawled across the roof, checking every inch, and then slid down to the luggage area on the rear. After that he dropped to his hands and knees and rolled beneath it, looking intently at the underside. Finally he climbed to his feet and approached us, brushing himself down. His expression was alert. "Nothing," he said. "Not a chink of light or a breath of fresh air could get into that vehicle if the windows were up and the curtains drawn, and those windows have not been opened since last summer."

"With the greatest respect to the constable here, are you sure it's the same carriage that Matthew Arnatt died in?"

He nodded. His expression, which had been relatively cheerful, took on a saturnine cast. "Yes," he said shortly. "The evidence is unquestionable."

"And by evidence you mean – ?"

116

"Blood and tissue." He walked away abruptly.

The constable took us inside, to his office, where he handed Holmes the cardboard box. Holmes checked it over, then threw it casually back inside. "You are correct, Watson – that weapon is hardly capable of firing."

"Then we are at a loss."

He shook his head. "Never that. We still have the witnesses to speak to." He glanced over at the constable. "Have they been allowed to leave?"

"No, sir. I asked them to stay on at the hotel, while my inquiries were under way."

"Then let us return there."

We found the three men – Jacob Gorringe, Frederick Darley, and Paul Furnell – sitting together morosely. We knew it was them because the local coroner was at another table, and nodded towards them when we entered. I thanked him.

Holmes grabbed a chair and placed it at the table. "You will not mind if I join you," he said, sitting. I took a chair from another table and slipped in beside him.

"You'll be the detective fellow," a portly man with mutton-chop whiskers said. "Holmes, is it?"

"Holmes it is. And you are – ?"

"Jacob Gorringe." He turned to a tall, thin man with a receding hairline wearing tweeds beside him. "This is Furnell, and that – " indicating a smaller man with protuberant ears " – is Darley. Has that half-hearted excuse for a constable told you whether we can go home or not, and when I can get my pistol back?"

"Not until this matter is sorted," Holmes replied, "and I should mark that the constable seems to me to be a careful, meticulous man. You should be grateful you have him. I know many worse."

Furnell snorted. "If he's that clever," he said, his voice thin and whiny, "then he should have sorted this thing out quicker. It's obvious what happened. The gun is cursed, like they say, and it only kills people who themselves have killed people."

"I must say," Gorringe said, "I didn't think Arnatt had it in him. Dark horse, that one."

"Don't speak ill of the dead," Darley muttered. His voice sounded deeper than his diminutive size would have indicated. He glanced at Gorringe. "And I still want that pistol of yours, when you get it back. I'll pay a fair price."

"A little macabre, isn't it?" I asked calmly, "wanting to buy a weapon that's just killed a friend of yours."

117

"Better to buy something that has a history to it," Darley observed, affronted. "I miss Matthew, I do, but not buying the gun that killed him won't bring him back. And besides, it's like a memorial to him."

"And besides," Gorringe interjected, "Darley here has a weakness for collection objects that have some link to the supernatural. Knives used in satanic rituals, stones from haunted houses, dresses that have been said to come to life and move around without anyone in them – he's a sucker for that kind of thing. Can't say I believe in it myself, but I'll take advantage of any man that does." He turned to Darley. "The price has gone up, of course, now that the Blaelock Curse has been independently verified."

"You are an auctioneer, Mister Gorringe," Holmes said. Turning, he went on: "You, Mister Furnell, are a farmer and you, Mister Darley, rent out agricultural machinery. Do I have this right?"

"Right on the nose," Gorringe said, rubbing his arm absently. He seemed to be the natural spokesman for the group.

The door to the snug – which was already nearly full – opened, and the constable came in. He nodded to me, then squeezed in at the table with the coroner, although he seemed more interested in what was going on at our table.

"I'd like to go over the events of that carriage ride," Holmes said, indicating to the landlord that he should pull pints of beer for everyone in the snug. "Can you tell me exactly what happened, moment by moment?"

"Again?" Furnell whined. "We've been over it and over it, and we just don't know what happened."

"Don't worry about working out what happened – that's my task. Just give me the facts. First, tell me where you were all sitting, then start when you, Mister Gorringe, got into your carriage alone."

The men glanced at each other, and then Jacob Gorringe led with the tale, with Darley and Furnell interjecting. Their story was in all particulars the same as I had heard from the constable and, in more abbreviated fashion, from the coroner. Those two gentlemen were both listening in from their table, and a few times I glanced across at them to check their reactions. They nodded at me, confirming that what was being told now was as it had been told to them.

Halfway through the story, the landlord arrived at the table with a tray of beers. Holmes took it from him, set it on the table, and handed a tankard to Gorringe. The auctioneer reached out for it with his right hand, then hesitated, withdrew his hand and extended his

118

left one to take it. "Twinge of rheumatism," he said. Holmes nodded sympathetically, although I'd never known him to be sympathetic in his life, and passed Darley and Furnell their tankards. I had to reach across and get mine myself. Such is the way of things.

"The carriage drew to a halt and the driver called down that we'd arrived here, at the Hotel," Gorringe said, "and that's when Matthew put the gun to his head. He looked us all in the eye, and he said, 'I have done things in my life of which many might disapprove, although I did them all in good faith and to save a friend. If this gun is cursed, then so be it, but on my life I do not believe it is.'"

"You recall those exact words?" Holmes asked raising his hand in interruption.

The three men nodded.

"They're burned into our memories," Furnell rumbled. "Always will be, 'til we die."

"Then he raised the gun to his forehead, smiled, and pulled the trigger." Gorringe's rather large face seemed suddenly gaunt. "And he died."

"Let me go back, just a fraction," Holmes said. "Picture the scene – all of you in the carriage, Matthew Arnatt holding a gun to his head. He has not pulled the trigger yet. What were each of you doing?"

"I was looking at Matthew," Furnell said. He looked around. "Wasn't I?"

"You were," Darley confirmed, "and I was reaching into my pocket for a handkerchief."

Gorringe nodded. He put his elbow on the table and leaned forward, chin on his hand, then winced and moved back to his original position. The rheumatism again, I presumed. "I was watching Matthew too," he said. "He'd made such a show of it all."

"No," Darley interrupted, "you were reaching out for the gun. I remember."

"That's right!" Gorringe exclaimed. "I'd forgotten. Yes, because we'd stopped I wanted to take the revolver back. He was going to pull the trigger, nothing was going to happen, and I was going to take it from him and laugh." He paused, somberly. "But that's not what happened."

Holmes leaned forward. "And you had all examined the gun in the minutes before it fired, and found no ammunition?"

Gorringe nodded. "That gun could not fire. I would stake my life on it." He winced as he realized what he had said.

119

"No sound of smashing glass?" Holmes asked. "No derangement in the upholstery of the carriage? No splinters of wood?"

"None," Darley answered for them all.

Holmes took a swig of his beer and sat back. "When I knew Matthew Arnatt," he said, "he was a believer in ghosts and supernatural powers, but by the time we went our separate ways, he had realized they were nothing but flummery and fakery and foolishness. He put that gun to his temple knowing that there was no way it could have fired." He paused. "And indeed, it didn't."

Silence fell across the snug as everybody hung on his words.

"I have already ascertained from the coroner that Matthew often talked of his past," Holmes went on, holding his glass up and looking at it critically. "For that reason, I assume that it was generally known that people had died when he had been present and that he had been responsible, although never in a way that could have – or indeed *should* have – led to police action. And that means, in a group where the other three people had *not* been responsible for a death, that he was the odd one out. And that difference was exploited."

"Now wait a minute," Darley interrupted, his high voice pitched even higher. "There's a lot of things happen in this world that nobody can explain."

"This," Holmes said, setting the pint glass down, "is not one of them."

"The carriage was sealed," Furnell objected. "It's been examined and examined again. When those doors were closed nothing could get in or out."

"Exactly." Holmes looked at each of them in turn. "Which means that whatever weapon fired the fatal shot was in the possession of one of you."

Silence fell, for a few moments.

"None of them had a weapon, Mister Holmes," the constable called from his table. "I already told you that. I checked them."

"You were looking for a normal size revolver." Holmes paused for a few moments, then turned to me. "Watson, are you aware of a weapon called a derringer?"

I nodded. "It's a small gun, made for ladies' handbags. Ladies in America," I hastened to add. "I'm sure no woman in England would use such a thing."

"Then your experience of English ladies is not as extensive as mine," he said with a thin smile, "at least in the area of firearms." He glanced around the snug. "I could hold a derringer in my hand," he

120

went on, "fingers curled, and you would never know it was there. A derringer typically has a single barrel, barely longer than one's little finger. The range is highly limited, but at short range the effect can be deadly. Mister Henry Deringer – with one '*r*', strangely – invented the weapon and specialized in so-called 'pocket pistols', but other manufacturers make them. Remington, in particular, sell a .41 calibre derringer-style weapon."

"The same calibre as the Colt New Line," I said, stunned.

"Indeed."

I had to protest. "But surely, even with such a small weapon, somebody would have noticed it being held?"

"Held, yes, but what if it were strapped to a man's forearm, under his shirt sleeve and his jacket sleeve? What if it were fired when the man extended his arm? It would look to any who observed as if, perhaps, the man was scratching himself, but in reality he was pulling the trigger through the cloth."

By now everyone but Holmes was staring at Jacob Gorringe. The constable was halfway out of his chair.

"How's that arm of yours, Mister Gorringe?" Holmes asked calmly. "I noticed you scratching it earlier, and of course you changed hands when you reached for your beer. I am sure that, if we look, we will find a burn on the skin of your forearm, on the inside, where the gun was strapped." He smiled thinly. "Fortunate we have two medical men in this small room. I presume you have not sought treatment for it yet?"

The next few minutes were a cacophony of events, as Gorringe overturned the table with a roar and attempted to bolt for the door, but was bought down by the concerted efforts of the constable, Holmes, and me. The constable and I tackled him, rugby style, while Holmes threw his tankard, catching Gorringe on the back of the head. Furnell and Darley accompanied the constable out of the snug, assisting him in carrying the struggling and cursing auctioneer.

By the time things calmed down, Holmes had procured more pints of beer for the two of us. I set the table back up, and we sat down. The coroner, who had watched the whole thing in bafflement, joined us.

"How did you know?" he asked wonderingly.

"The deduction was simple," Holmes said, "once I removed the supernatural possibilities. The Colt New Line revolver couldn't have fired, therefore it didn't. No other weapon could have fired into the carriage from outside, therefore none did. The only remaining possibility was that one of the men inside had a concealed weapon

121

small enough not to attract attention. I was unsure which one it was until I noticed Mister Gorringe favouring his left arm. I tried an experiment with the beer, which confirmed that his arm was injured. Given that the best place for the weapon was strapped to his right arm, which we have heard was extended towards Matthew Arnatt when Matthew died, it was likely that Gorringe had sustained a burn – quite a serious one, I should think." He glanced at me. "Remind me to tell the constable that the Remington derringer is, in all likelihood, hidden somewhere here in the Station Hotel."

"And the motive?" I asked, astounded. "What possessed him to do such a thing?"

"Oh, motive is for the courts to determine, and there I can only enter into the realms of speculation. Matty, when I knew him, had a finely-honed sense of natural justice, and I hope that I may have helped him out with some lessons in logic. Mister Gorringe, the auctioneer, had already indicated in his own words that he would happily take financial advantage of people. I do not think it a stretch to say that Mister Gorringe was probably fiddling his auctioneering business, passing cheap animals off for expensive ones, and that Matty suspected. Matty, being the person I knew, would have confronted Gorringe with his suspicions, most likely during the part of the carriage ride when he and Gorringe were alone. Gorringe decided to take action, and came up with a spurious yet convincing reason to return to his house to retrieve the Blaelock Revolver, whose history could be used to his advantage, along with another weapon from his collection. And so it played out."

"And that history?" The coroner was frowning. "Was that true, or was it fictional?"

"True, in the sense that people believed it," Holmes said, "but fictional in so far as the events did not occur. At least, I do not believe they occurred. I was not there, so I have no direct knowledge."

We sat in silence for a while, each of us thinking his own, inviolable thoughts.

"Will you stay for the funeral, Mister Holmes?" the coroner asked eventually.

Holmes shrugged. "A funeral is for the living, not the dead. The dead do not care anymore. Attending will not help me to come to terms with something I have already accepted. Watson and I shall return to London."

I reached out and put a hand on his arm.

"We shall stay for the funeral," I said quietly, but firmly. "It is a mark of respect for someone who has passed over, and it would comfort his grieving widow. And besides," I added, when Holmes opened his mouth to object, "if the situation had been reversed, Matty would have been at *your* funeral."

"If only to take advantage of the free food," he said with a mordant smile. He glanced at me and nodded. "I have said it before, Watson – I may have intelligence, but you have wisdom, and that is a much rarer thing."

The Adventure of the
Highgate Spectre
by Michael Mallory

Those who are familiar with my good friend and associate Mr. Sherlock Holmes through my transcriptions of the adventures that the two of us have shared over the years will no doubt think of him as a man with few personal weaknesses. This impression is likely due to my presenting him in my writings as a man who can overcome virtually any obstacle, from without or within, through sheer force of personality and intellect alone. There is, however, a side to my friend that I have not shared with my readership, and that is his humanly vulnerable side. For all his vast accomplishments, Holmes can still be "cut to the quick" by circumstance, and retreat into a dark, defensive corner.

That was the state into which he had fallen this past October, the result of his highly-publicized failure to solve the case of the Egyptian mummy theft from the British Museum, and a dearth of cases since, combined with the threat of a libel suit from a spiritualist, whom Holmes had characterized as a charlatan in a letter to *The Daily Mail*. In an effort to raise him out of his emotional depression, I scanned the daily newspapers, looking for accounts of any crime, or even strange happenstances, which might serve to engage his intellect.

"Look at this, Holmes," I said one afternoon, studying a page of *The Times*. "It appears a solicitor has been murdered in Bloomsbury."

Holmes remained as silent as death.

"Is that not of interest to you?" I prodded.

"Not in the least," he whispered hoarsely.

"But a man has been murdered."

"I am quite confident the police will be able to handle the situation."

I threw the newspaper down on the floor. "Look here, Holmes," I cried, "I have taken as much of this as I intend to. I am not going to sit here and watch you drown in a maelstrom of self-pity!"

"What is it you intend to do, then?" he asked.

"Well, I . . . ."

The truth was, I was at a loss as to what to do. The situation, and Holmes's mood, remained morose for another two days, by which time I was considering forcibly committing him to Barts for examination. The respite finally arrived when, on a particularly gloomy, foggy evening, Mrs. Hudson announced that we had a visitor. Holmes initially refused to see the caller, but I put my foot down. "Please show the person in, Mrs. Hudson."

The man who walked into our rooms looked to be around fifty years of age, and was slightly under medium height, quite lean, and wore a heavy tweed suit. He bowed upon seeing me. "I should like to see Mr. Sherlock Holmes," he said in a thin, reedy voice.

"This is Mr. Holmes," I replied, gesturing toward my friend. "Please, sit down, Mr . . . ?"

"Turley. Arthur Turley. And I prefer to stand, if I may."

"As you wish," I said, taking a seat myself.

Holmes looked up at the man and said, "I am very sorry to learn that the man you have served faithfully has died."

"Thank you . . . but . . . how on earth did you know that?"

"It is my business to know."

"I have heard, Mr. Holmes, that you were a man of remarkable abilities, and now I see the veracity of that judgment," Turley said, bowing. "I do indeed serve the Helmsdale family of Blackwelton House as butler, and my master, Lord Helmsdale, has indeed passed away, which is the impetus for my being here."

After a long moment of apparent indecision, Holmes finally said, "Go on."

"You are most kind," the man said, bowing again. "From the papers, Mr. Holmes, I have learned that you do not believe in ghosts."

"Please do not tell me you are in the employ of a spiritualist."

"No, no. But as I said, my master died one week ago, and was buried at Highgate Cemetery. Since then . . . well, I don't know how to say this, exactly . . . but it appears he has been seen walking outside the crypt."

Holmes covered his eyes with his hand. "I have heard enough. Watson, kindly show Mr. Turley out."

"No, wait, sir. You misunderstand me," Turley said quickly. "Like you, I do not believe in ghosts, shades, or spirits of any kind, save for distilled ones. But her Ladyship, the widow of my late master, has become convinced otherwise."

"By some mountebank offering his services as a medium, no doubt."

"No, sir, by her own eyes. She herself has seen the figure of Lord Helmsdale at the cemetery."

Holmes slowly sat up to full attention. "Hysteria, fuelled by grief, perhaps?"

"Forgive me, sir, but her Ladyship is not given to hysterics. Grief, of course, but not hysteria. The fact that his Lordship was a relatively young man of forty-seven makes his death even more tragic."

"Has anyone else witnessed this alleged apparition?"

"A gravedigger employed by the cemetery reported seeing a figure, but had no way of recognizing him. It was her Ladyship who made the identification."

"How did your master die?"

"Malaria, sir."

"Good heavens!" I cried. "In England?"

"Lord Helmsdale spent his youthful years travelling the globe. He had a particular affinity for Australia, spending an entire year there. That is where his Lordship contracted the disease. Upon returning to England, he thought himself cured, but was plagued with periodic recurrences of illness. The last one proved to be too much for him."

"I see," Holmes said. "How long have you been in the service of the Helmsdales?"

"My entire life. My father served the family before me."

"So you knew your master when he was a young, adventurous man?"

"Oh, indeed, sir."

"Mr. Turley, my remarkable abilities, as you have called them, are failing to inform me what exactly it is you wish me to do for you."

"It is for her Ladyship, really," the man answered. "I am hoping you will be able to convince her that there must be some other – far more worldly – explanation for the apparition she has seen. It is, I fear, weighing heavily upon her mind."

"Has anyone attempted to convince your mistress so?" I asked. "You, perhaps, Mr. Turley?"

"Oh, sir, it is not my place to contradict her Ladyship. As for Mister Jeremy, well, his mind is often on other matters."

"Who is Mister Jeremy?" Holmes asked.

"He is the son of Lord and Lady Helmsdale, and a rather spirited lad."

"And heir to the estate, I presume?"

126

"Yes, sir."

"Where is Blackwelton House located?"

"Near Hampstead Heath."

"That is good, since I am not much in the mood for a long rail journey to some godforsaken moor. Very well, upon your return, kindly inform Lady Helmsdale that she will be receiving visitors tomorrow morning. Now, Watson, you may show Mr. Turley out."

I did so, and returned to the room elated to witness Holmes filling his pipe and demonstrating the kind of energy I had not seen from him in weeks. "Well, Watson, an interesting fellow, wouldn't you say?"

"A bit obsequious, I should think. But really, Holmes, how did you immediately discern that the man was a servant whose master has recently died?"

"You said it yourself, Watson," he replied, lighting his pipe and drawing in a great puff of smoke. "He was more than a bit obsequious. He bowed to us, and not simply in the manner of a courteous gentleman, but in a practised, even ingrained way, the way a servant would bow to a master. Then, of course, there was the matter of his clothing."

"His clothing? I noticed nothing about his clothing. His suit was certainly not a butler's uniform."

"Precisely. Those were his personal clothes, which is why they were in such excellent condition, even though they were rather old and out-of-fashion. A man who normally wears a uniform and only dons civilian clothing on the odd day or evening off, perhaps once a week or less, possesses a suit that will last much longer than the norm. I daresay he will be wearing that same suit ten years from now. So, having established the fact that he normally works in a uniform, what sort of uniform might it be? Given the man's age, I ruled out the possibility he was a soldier, and one glance at his shoes argued against his being a policeman. Unlike his suit, Turley's shoes were new and of a very high quality, the sort of shoe one might expect to see accompanying a butler's uniform."

"You never cease to astound me," I said. "But how did you deduce that his employer had recently died?"

"Oh, really, Watson, that fact practically advertised itself! Hanging out of the man's right jacket pocket was the torn end of a strip of black crepe. There was also a slight indentation in the material of his coat on the upper arm of the left sleeve, signifying that he was in mourning and wearing a black arm band. I can only surmise that the band came apart as a result of being transferred from

127

his butler's jacket to his thicker, rougher tweed one. So who would he be mourning? The fact that the fellow wore no wedding band argues that it was not a wife or child, so in view of his position, the obvious deduction is that it was for his employer. Now if you will excuse me, Watson, I fear I must retire early. Swimming against a maelstrom of self-pity, as you so colourfully put it, can be wearying."

By the next morning the fog had lifted, but had been replaced by a light rain, which cast a pall over much of city. No one building, however, looked quite so foreboding in the grey dampness as the imposing edifice of Blackwelton House. It was located, as Turley had said, not far from the Heath, but appeared to sit alone within the countryside, as though shunned by other houses. As our hired growler proceeded up the carriage drive, I could make out Turley, now clad in the uniform of his profession – and with a new black arm band – standing in front of the house, an umbrella at the ready. As we pulled up, he dashed down and shielded us from the rain as best he could on our walk to the front door.

"I have been awaiting you, Mr. Holmes," he said, opening the door for us. "Lady Helmsdale is in the day room. I shall take you there."

The interior of Blackwelton House proved to be a study in contrasts. It was a combination of the traditional and the modern, with both gas lamps and a telephone sharing a room, while stately oil paintings of past family members hung alongside framed photographs. Had the weather been more pleasant, the day room would have been light and airy instead of bleak and shadowed. Attired in mourning wear, Lady Helmsdale sat sombrely in a chair, her handsome face etched with sorrow. "Madam," Turley said, bowing, "may I present Mr. Sherlock Holmes, and Dr. John H. Watson."

She rose and extended a hand, which Holmes took. "I understand why you gentlemen are here," she said, "and I pray you have not made the journey on this miserable day in vain, because I also know what I saw."

"I am here, Madam, to inquire into exactly what you observed at your late husband's crypt," Holmes said gently.

"I saw him, my Edward," she replied. "I assure you, sir, I know . . . knew every line and shadow of his face. We were married three-and-twenty years. It was he."

"Was anyone with you at the time, anyone who also saw the apparition?"

128

"No. I was driven to the cemetery by our coachman, but he did not accompany me to the crypt. I have been told that an employee of Highgate has seen him as well, but know not the circumstances. Mr. Holmes, I do not wish to be rude, but I find simply talking about this most disturbing."

"My apologies, Madam," Holmes said. "If you would indulge me in two other matters, we will trouble you no more today."

"What is it you wish?" she asked, wearily.

"Why do you think your husband has returned from the grave?"

The poor woman appeared to deflate. She held her hand over her breast as though to staunch the bleeding out of her life, and lowered herself onto a chaise. "I am terrified that he has come to take me with him," she whispered. "I am very tired. Please go now, all of you."

"I have one request left, Lady Helmsdale," Holmes said.

She waved a hand by way of permission to proceed.

"Do you have a picture of your late husband?"

"Of course I do. Why do you ask?"

"I should wish to borrow one."

"What for?"

"So I may recognize his Lordship if I pay my own respects at his grave, and he decides to return and accept them in person."

Lady Helmsdale regarded Holmes with an expression of indignation. "Now you are mocking me," she said.

"I assure you, Madam, I am not. I have no doubt you saw a vision of your husband."

"Turley, find a picture for him," she sighed. "Now please leave me, gentlemen."

Once we were outside of the day room, the servant said, "Mr. Holmes, I feel I must apologize to you on behalf of her Ladyship. I'm afraid she is not quite herself at the moment."

"Apology unnecessary," Holmes said. "As I told your mistress, I never doubted for a moment her veracity. When I said I believed she saw a vision of her husband, I spoke the truth as well. But a vision is not the same as a restless spirit."

The butler disappeared into another room and a few seconds later, a young man came down the stairs. He appeared of university age, and carried himself with authority. "You there, who are you?" he demanded. "What are you doing in my home?"

"Your home?" I questioned.

"Indeed, Watson, for this, unless I am mistaken, is Jeremy Helmsdale, her Ladyship's son."

The young man approached us in a forceful manner. "I believe I asked who you were."

"I am Sherlock Holmes, and I have come at the behest of your butler in order to speak with your mother."

"My mother is in a weakened condition and is not to be disturbed, is that clear?"

"I have no further business with her."

At that moment Turley returned and bowed to his young master. "Forgive me, Mister Jeremy, I did not realize you were here."

"Obviously not," Jeremy Helmsdale snapped. "What have you got there?"

"A photograph. Your mother offered Mr. Holmes a photograph of his Lordship."

"Let me see that," the young man said, grabbing the photograph out of the butler's hands. Upon glancing at it, he appeared to blanch. "This is their wedding picture! She offered this?"

"Your good mother offered the loan of a photograph, and this one was the smallest and easiest to remove from the frame," Turley said, (though I thought I detected in the expression of the servant a certain note of defiance.) From what I could see of the photograph, it showed a much younger version of the woman he had just encountered, with a sturdily-built, dark-haired man.

"I refuse to let this out of the house."

"But sir, the photograph is her property."

"We shall see," Jeremy Helmsdale said. "Where is she?"

"The day room, sir," Turley said.

The young man marched into the room, and within seconds we heard the sound of a rather heated conversation.

"Oh, dear," the butler muttered. "I fear I have made a muddle of things."

"Perhaps we should leave now," I offered. "If the young man is the lord of the house now, we would do best to obey his wishes."

"While Mister Jeremy inherited the title upon his father's death," Turley said, "he cannot yet fully claim ownership of the estate, since his Lordship's will has yet to be found."

"He died intestate?" I asked.

"No will has yet been found, sir," the butler reiterated.

I could discern from the expression on Holmes's face that his mind was turning like the wheels of a locomotive at top speed, but what particular ground it was covering, I knew not. Moments later, young Helmsdale returned, quite red in the face.

"Very well, take the damnable photograph," he said, thrusting it into Holmes's hands. "But I caution you, all of you, not to cause my mother any further distress." He then stormed past us and went back up the staircase.

"I trust you will handle that photograph with care, sir," Turley said, as he walked us to the door. "It was taken but a few years after his Lordship's return from Australia."

"Indeed?" Holmes replied, examining the photo before tucking it inside his coat. "I shall guard it with my life."

Turley then summoned the family coachman to transport us back into the city. Once ensconced inside in the carriage, Holmes withdrew the photograph again.

"That was quite a family row over the lending of a photograph," I said.

"Not *a* photograph, Watson. *This* photograph. You saw young Helmsdale's reaction upon seeing it. There is something about it that is particularly meaningful, but I do not as yet know what." He continued to study it as the carriage clopped down the road, and then looked up and muttered, "Yes, quite possibly."

"What is it, Holmes?"

"A hunch, Watson, merely a hunch."

"Can you not tell me?"

"I have always found hunches to be like paintings – best revealed only when completed." Then he leaned out the window of the coach and asked the driver to take us to Highgate Cemetery rather than return to Baker Street.

The cemetery was not far from Blackwelton House. Upon our arrival, Holmes requested that the driver remain at the gate until our return. We set out to explore the necropolis on foot. Fortunately, the earlier rainfall had settled into nothing more than a sombre, wet mist, which cast a singularly foreboding shroud over the place. If it were indeed possible for a person to return from the grave as an apparition, Highgate Cemetery at this moment would seem the likeliest place.

"What are we looking for?" I asked Holmes, as we trudged down well-maintained pathways cut through a labyrinth of graves, headstones, crosses, sleeping angels, and Madonnas frozen in stone.

"A sign of life," Holmes replied.

"I fear you have chosen the wrong haystack in which to look," I muttered.

After we had passed a small crescent of classically-styled tombs, Holmes suddenly pointed and cried, "There!" At first I saw nothing, but then noticed the movement of a man working the earth of the graveyard. "That is our sign of life, Watson. Even on a day like this, life and work must go on for a gravedigger." Walking over to where the man was working on a plot of earth that appeared only half-emptied, Holmes stood and looked at the fellow for a few moments, then asked, "Might I have a word with you, my good man?"

The gravedigger stopped shovelling and looked up. His face was lined and weathered, but he was neither bowed nor impaired from the hard physical labour. "What'cha need, guv?" he asked.

"Are you the only digger employed here?"

"Naw, but I seem to be the only one they send out in this kind o' weather. Nice sunny day, when it's a pleasure to be out o' doors, that's when the young'uns turn up."

"A shilling for your trouble," Holmes said, reaching into his pocket.

"Yes sir!" the man said, all but leaping out of the hole. Since he barely came up to Holmes's shoulder, I could not help but wonder how he emerged once the grave was finished. "What can Toby Plummer do for you?"

"Were you by any chance the digger who spotted a strange figure in the proximity of Lord Helmsdale's crypt?"

"Helmsdale . . . oh, crikey! That was me, all right. I was workin' on a plot and saw this bloke out o' the corner o' me eye. Tho't 'e was just a mourner, maybe got lost or somethin' . . . it happens here all the time, guv . . . so I called out to him, but then he seemed to just vanish."

"Did you see him clearly?"

"Oh, aye, but it weren't no one I know."

Holmes reached inside his coat and pulled out the photograph. "Could this have been the man?"

Toby the gravedigger studied the picture. "Blimey, that's him all right! Clothes is a bit different, but that's 'is face, I'd swear to it!"

"You are positive?"

"Nobody's ever accused Toby Plummer o' sayin' a falsehood for the sake of a shilling. That's him, all right."

"When you saw this man, did he appear to be doing anything in particular?"

"Don't foller you."

"Was he merely standing, or walking, or looking confused?"

132

"No, none o' that, but . . . well, this is barmy, it is, but I got the idear that 'e was lookin' to find a way to get into the crypt. But that can't be right."

"Could you take us to Lord Helmsdale's crypt?"

"Well, I could, but I really got to get this 'ole dug before nightfall. New owner's takin' it tomorrow."

"Would another shilling cover your services as a guide?" Holmes asked.

"Lor' love ya, guv," Plummer said, accepting the second coin. "Let's see, Helmsdale . . . this way." For the next five minutes we walked down what seemed like every pathway in Highgate Cemetery, past ever more tombs and graves. Then he stopped. "That's it right there, guv," he said, pointing at a red-stone, hexagonal construct. "That's the Helmsdale crypt."

"Thank you, Mr. Plummer," Holmes said. "You can go back to your work now. We will be able to find our way out."

"We will?" I asked, uncertainly. As far as I was concerned, we were in the maze of the Minotaur.

I followed Holmes as he inspected the perimeter of the crypt, which seemed solid enough to withstand a siege. As far as I could tell, anyone who wanted inside of this small edifice would have to wait to earn entry. "Yes, it would be easy to disappear from view here," he said, finally.

"It would?"

"It is far more effective to turn the corner and hide when there are six corners, as opposed to four."

"With whom, or *what*, are we dealing, Holmes?"

"I am not yet certain, but we are finished here. Let us return to the comfort of Baker Street."

"Are you positive you can find your way out?" I asked.

"You are not required to follow me, if you have doubts."

Of course I followed Holmes, who naturally led me to the entrance of Highgate Cemetery far more expeditiously than I might have imagined. The Helmsdales' coach was awaiting us, though the driver's countenance betrayed a certain annoyance at having to remain stationery in the foul weather. Once we had settled inside the coach, Holmes said, "Tell me, Watson, what do you make of Arthur Turley?"

"Well, I could not help but notice that he and young Helmsdale did seem to be at odds. Yet he seemed completely devoted to Lady Helmsdale."

"Yes, interesting, that."

"Holmes, you don't think that Turley somehow killed Lord Helmsdale!"

"I do not, Watson, for the simple reason that, had he murdered his master, I would be the last person he would wish to involve in the case. But I do believe that the obsequious servant knows more about what is occurring here than he is revealing."

"Do you think he has information regarding the missing will?" I inquired.

"I don't know. But there is someone who might." Holmes once more thrust his head through the coach window and called to the driver. I heard him ask, "Did you have occasion to take your late master to visit his solicitor?" This was followed by the coachman's voice, but I could not make out the words. "Take us there, if you would," Holmes said, pulling back inside the coach. "According to the coachman, Helmsdale's retained the services of a lawyer named Granger, who has offices in Gordon Square. Perhaps he will be able to shed light on whether or not a will was drawn up."

"Granger, you say?" I muttered, struggling to remember where I had recently either heard or read that name. After several blocks it came to me. "Great Scott, Holmes! Do you remember when I read to you that newspaper account of a solicitor being murdered in Bloomsbury? His name was Westcott Granger, as I recall."

Even though seated, Holmes rose to a position of attention. "Gordon Square is within the boundaries of Bloomsbury," he said, then again thrust his head through the widow and cried, "Make haste, driver!"

We said nothing more until the carriage arrived in front of the solicitor's office, whose door was adorned with a black wreath. Holmes dismissed the coachman, stating that we would find our own way back to Baker Street. As the carriage clopped down the street, we rang the bell for the establishment. After a minute or two, a young man with a ruddy complexion and a crop of unfettered red hair opened the door. "You gentlemen are not clients, are you?" he asked meekly.

"We are not," Holmes said, "though there is a matter regarding one of your clients, Lord Helmsdale, in which we are involved."

The young man sighed. "Come in."

The interior of the office was so bestrewn with papers and files (all lying haphazardly on every available surface) that it appeared as though a small bomb might have gone off recently. "Since Mr. Granger's unfortunate death, clients have been arriving daily,

134

desiring to know the status of their particular cases, and I simply cannot keep up," the fellow said.

"You were Mr. Granger's legal clerk?" Holmes asked.

"Yes sir, Thomas Pryce, and you are . . . ?"

"Sherlock Holmes."

The young man's eyes widened. "Are you going to solve the murder?"

"That was not initially my intention, though please feel free to tell me what you know of the matter."

"Only that I went home like usual one night, and when I came back the next morning, I was surprised to find the door unlocked. Mr. Granger was sitting in his chair, with a bullet hole, here." He pointed a finger at his chest.

"Did Lord Helmsdale ever come here to the office?"

"I recall seeing him a time or two, but I never had any personal dealings with him, of course. Mostly, though, Mr. Granger went to his house if they had business."

"Did your employer keep an appointment book?" Holmes asked.

"I kept it for him, sir."

"May I see it?"

Thomas Pryce went to a smaller desk in the cluttered office, presumably his, and came back with a record book. He handed it to Holmes, who turned to the last page that contained any entries. "Granger's last appointment was with a Guy Steersdene . . . yes, of course."

"Oh, I remember him," Pryce said. "He spoke with a strange accent."

"Do you happen to recall if Jeremy Helmsdale, the son of his Lordship, had been in to see your employer?"

"Oh, that one, yes sir. Something of an argument resulted. The door was closed so I couldn't hear it all, but it had something to do with Lord Helmsdale's will."

"Young Helmsdale was probably angry that it could not be found," I said.

"I can't say as to that, sir. All I know is the fellow stormed out in a fury, muttering something about requiring a Burke and Hare."

"Burke and Hare?"

"Yes sir. I assumed it was Bow rhyming slang, you know, where 'Burke and Hare' stands for 'chair.' I figured he had gotten some bad news and needed to sit down, like maybe he'd been disinherited."

"Think very carefully," Holmes instructed the redheaded youth. "Did Helmsdale say *he* required a *Burke and Hare*? Or that *it* would require a *Burke and Hare*?"

"Since you put it that way, I think the latter."

"When did you last see your employer alive?"

"When he was talking to Mr. Steersdene," the clerk replied. "Mr. Granger told me I could leave early that night, so I did. He said he'd lock up. I got the idea he had something sensitive to discuss with the gentleman."

"If this Steersdene chap was the last to see the man alive, wouldn't that mean he must be the murderer?" I asked.

"A reasonable conclusion, but unproven," Holmes said, handing the book back to the law clerk, and after thanking him, we started to take our leave. However, the young man called us back.

"I think one of you dropped this," he said, holding out the wedding photograph of Lord and Lady Helmsdale.

"It must have fallen from my coat," Holmes said, taking it. "Thank you, Mr. Pryce."

"That's a picture of the one you were asking after, isn't it?"

Holmes turned to him and smiled. "Yes, it is."

Holmes hailed a cab to return us to Baker Street. On the way he remarked, "The picture of this case is becoming clearer and clearer, Watson. It is, in fact, nearly revealed."

"For once, Holmes, I see exactly where your deductions have led," I said confidently.

"Do you, indeed?"

"Of course. Lord Helmsdale must not really be dead."

"What brought you to that observation?"

"Does not the fact that two people, independently, have identified the man in that picture as Lord Helmsdale, including one who has seen him in person, the legal clerk, predicate such a conclusion?"

"I did not hear Pryce identify the man as Lord Helmsdale," Holmes countered.

"But he did. He said this was the man you were asking about."

"I was also asking about the last person whose name was listed in Granger's appointment register, which was a man named Steersdene."

I looked at the photograph again. "How possibly could this be a man named Steersdene, unless Steersdene and Lord Helmsdale are one and the same? But that cannot be!"

"Watson, Watson, you see, yet you do not comprehend," Holmes said, and then fell silent.

I was more confused than ever in regards to this bizarre case as we arrived in front of 221b Baker Street – a situation in no way aided by the fact that Holmes lacked any sign of exiting the cab. "You go on, Watson," he said. "There is something I must attend to. If you would, build a roaring fire in anticipation of my return, as I feel I shall need it. That's a good fellow." Then after requesting the driver take him to the nearest post office, the hansom sped away.

Once back in our rooms, it took quite some time to get the fire going, but I trusted Holmes would be satisfied with the result upon his return. I found it inviting, at any rate. With little else to do, I took to my writing desk and made notes of the case so far, hoping that setting them down in ink might result in a pattern that led, somehow, to clarity. In that, I was quite mistaken.

Holmes remained out until a little after four in the afternoon, at which time he burst through the door, shed his coat, and laid it over a chair by the fire. "Thank you, Watson," he said, doffing his tall hat and then warming his hands. "The heavens have not let up their punishment of we mere mortals."

"You sound positively philosophical, Holmes," I commented.

"I can afford to be, having solved the case of the Highgate spectre."

"Is it this Steersdene fellow, then? If so, who is he?"

"It is not yet my place to say, though all will be known shortly. This evening, in fact."

"This evening?"

"Yes, we are to return to Blackwelton House, where I believe this matter will be concluded, but not without an element of danger. Is your service revolver at the ready?"

"My revolver? Of course." I went to the drawer in which I keep it and withdrew it. "You believe things are going to come to violence?"

"We are playing a deadly game, Watson. I dare not assume otherwise." He rubbed his hands in the warmth of the fire. "But now that I am becoming warm, I find myself also becoming quite hungry. Would you consult Mrs. Hudson as to the availability of some supper?"

"Build a fire, forage for food . . . you know, Holmes, you might want to think about hiring a valet," I grumbled, but I did as he requested.

Mrs. Hudson was good enough to provide a two servings of cold ham with mustard, some bread and cheese, and a pot of tea, which I carried upstairs myself. After supping, Holmes checked his watch and then pronounced, "It is time to put this conundrum to rest." Once he had replaced his watch in his waistcoat, he reached into his coat and from an inner pocket withdrew the wedding photograph. "We mustn't forget this. Take up your revolver, Watson," he said, as he went once again for his more-or-less dried coat and hat.

Holmes said maddeningly little during the ride to Blackwelton House, except to encourage the driver on to ever greater speed. In no time we were out of the cab and up to the door of the house, which was answered by Turley. "Good evening, sir. Good evening, Doctor," he said.

"Is her Ladyship in?" Holmes asked.

"Yes sir, as is Mister Jeremy."

Holmes rushed past the butler and went instinctively to the day room. Upon seeing him enter, young Helmsdale demanded, "What do you want?"

"To return this, of course." Holmes took out the photograph and laid it on a table. "I have no further use of it."

The young man approached Holmes, fists clenched, as though he were about to strike a blow, though Holmes did not flinch. "Just as we have no further use of you. Good day, sir."

Ignoring him, Holmes turned to Lady Helmsdale and said, "Madam, I have some information regarding your ghost that you may find disturbing."

"I will not allow this tommyrot to continue a second longer!" Jeremy Helmsdale cried. "My mother has been through enough!"

"She must know the truth, unpleasant though it may be."

"That is it! I intend to telephone the local constabulary and have a man sent here to remove you!" He brushed Holmes aside as he marched out of the room and into the foyer, where the telephone sat on a small table, yanked the receiver off of the cradle, and pumped it until someone picked up at the other end. "Metropolitan Police, and quickly," he said, then waited. "Yes, this is Jeremy Helmsdale . . . make that *Lord* Helmsdale . . . of Blackwelton House, and I require assistance in removing a trespasser from the premises. What? What do you mean you were about to telephone me? Why? What? No, no, never mind." He replaced the receiver. By now, Holmes, Lady Helmsdale, and I were all in the foyer. "The sergeant said another

138

sighting of the ghost in Highgate has been reported," the young man told us."

"Then there is no time to lose!" Holmes cried. "Turley, call your coachman immediately! Watson, the game is afoot!"

"What do you think you're doing?" Jeremy demanded.

"I am engaging transport to Highgate Cemetery, where we must go to put an end to this matter."

"I am coming with you!" The young man ran upstairs and returned moments later brandishing a pistol.

"What are you planning to do with that?" Lady Helmsdale demanded.

"To put an end to this matter myself."

"I will join you as well," her Ladyship said.

"That is not necessary, Madam," Holmes told her.

"I said I am coming, if for no other reason than to prove you wrong. Turley, fetch my wrap."

The four of us – Holmes, Lady Helmsdale, Jeremy, and myself – piled inside the carriage, when it arrived in front, while Turley, equipped with a lantern to use as a weapon against the increasing darkness, took a seat next to the driver. We proceeded in all haste to Highgate Cemetery, and upon arriving at the entrance, we poured out of the coach, as Turley leapt down from the driver's seat, clutching a welcome light.

"Lady Helmsdale, I believe it would be better for you to remain here with the coach," Holmes said with some urgency. It was to no avail, however, as her Ladyship pulled up the bottom of her dress and she hastened behind her son, who was running toward the family crypt. Holmes, the butler, and I followed through the winding paths of the cemetery (and how I wished I had thought to bring an electric torch of my own!), but the Helmsdales arrived there moments before.

"There!" Jeremy Helmsdale cried. "There he is! Bring the lantern!" Turley rushed to him holding the light aloft, and in its beam, all of us could recognize the very image of the man in the photograph. In his hands: An iron jemmy! Lady Helmsdale gasped, but her son, appearing not surprised at all, shouted, "Damn you to hell!" and withdrew his pistol, firing shot after shot into the startled figure. After the sixth round, all sounds ceased . . . even those made by our breathing . . . as the black-clad figure of Lord Helmsdale remained upright, untouched by the bullets!

"You see?" Lady Helmsdale cried. "It is Edward's ghost! He cannot be killed!"

139

"Tommyrot!" young Helmsdale cried, throwing the pistol aside. "The gun worked fine mere days ago!"

"Your revolver, Watson, quickly!" Holmes shouted, and I withdrew it from my coat, but upon seeing the weapon in my hand, Jeremy charged me, wrenching the revolver from my grip and knocking me to the ground. I had only barely risen again to my feet, ready for combat, when I heard six more rounds fired, none of which appeared to have any effect whatsoever on the figure, who still stood before us!

"I . . . cannot . . . what are you, dammit?" Jeremy shouted, dropping my revolver. At that moment Lady Helmsdale fell into a swoon and Holmes rushed to her, catching her, and gently lowering her to the ground.

By this point, our macabre party was joined by three members of the local police force, whose torches provided more illumination. "What were those shots?" one asked.

"A form of confession," Holmes said, pointing a finger at young Helmsdale. "That man is a murderer."

"Look, the man is still there and alive!" Jeremy cried. "I have murdered no one!"

"No one except a solicitor named Westcott Granger, some days back, when your pistol still worked fine."

Rather than deny the accusation, Helmsdale attempted to flee, but was quickly captured by the police. "Unhand me!" he shouted. "Do you not know who I am?"

"You. sir!" Holmes shouted to the mysterious man who had somehow survived a dozen bullets. "Do not even think about attempting to flee. You cannot escape. We know who you are."

"I'm not running," the man said in a guttural voice that betrayed a strange, thick accent.

"Mr. Holmes . . . please tell me who this is, and what all this means," Lady Helmsdale asked breathlessly.

"Your ghost, Madam, is Guy Steersdene from Australia. Your son's half-brother."

"My . . . son's . . . half . . . ." With that, the poor woman fell into a faint on the wet ground.

The police detained Jeremy Helmsdale on suspicion of murder, and also the mysterious Steersdene for questioning; in particular, what use he had planned for the jemmy in his hand. Holmes was characteristically remiss in explaining anything further to me until we had seen Lady Helmsdale home. She was, understandably, quite distraught, and I was able to recommend a calming solution for her.

140

Had I brought my medical bag, I could have administered it on the spot. As we were about to leave Blackwelton House, Holmes turned to Turley and said, "As for you, I know not whether to commend you or reprimand you."

"I, sir?" the butler asked, guilelessly.

"Do not think me a fool, my good man. I know you have directed the investigation of this case as completely as Richard D'Oyly Carte stages an opera. Once you had involved me, you volunteered information about a missing will, assuming, I imagine, that I would consider the possibility of a battle for the estate. You repeatedly mentioned Australia, knowing that would be implanted in my mind as a clew. You even selected that wedding photograph, among all others from which to choose, knowing there was a significance to it. You have known everything from the moment you stepped into my rooms in Baker Street. Why, therefore, did you involve me?"

"I did not know *everything*, sir," Turley replied. "Lord Helmsdale did inform me of the truth regarding Mister Guy, and that he had instructed his solicitor to track the lad down and summon him to England. His Lordship wanted to see him before he died. Her Ladyship had no idea. As for Mister Jeremy, I certainly had my suspicions regarding the death of the solicitor, based on statements he made about the man prior to the murder, but I had no proof of anything."

"Why in heaven's name did you not go to the police, even if you had only suspicions of murder?" I demanded.

The man appeared shocked by the suggestion. "Sir, it is simply not my place to accuse any member of the family of anything."

"Not your place?"

"A butler must remain loyal, sir. But I would be lying if I did not confess that my suspicions weighed heavily upon me, which is why, Mr. Holmes, I decided to seek you out, knowing that you would be able to prove what I merely suspected."

"Then, Turley, I commend you," Holmes said, offering his hand, which, after a moment of confused hesitation, the butler took. "Do you suppose we could prevail upon your coachman once more, in order to return us to Baker Street?"

Holmes remained silent as we were being driven back home, at least until I provoked him by saying, "Don't tell me, then. I was only by your side every step of this case."

"Tell you what, Watson?"

"Well, what significance does that blasted photograph hold?"

141

"It's significance is it's age, Watson," Holmes replied. "The late Lord Helmsdale would have been a man of twenty-three or twenty-four at the time, roughly the same age as Guy Steersdene, who is, of course, the natural son of Helmsdale, having been born in Australia during his Lordship's period of adventure. Even for a father and son, the resemblance between the two is remarkable, but only at the same age. Had I been given a more contemporary photograph, I doubt the gravedigger would have been able to identify the man, and the solicitor's clerk would have named him immediately as Lord Helmsdale."

"So you realized there was an illegitimate heir simply through the photograph?"

Holmes smiled. "That, and his name, of course."

"His name?"

"Really, Watson. *Helmsdale*. Another word for *helm* is *steer*, is it not? And pluralizing *helm* – *helms* – provides us with *steers*."

"While another term for *dale* is *dene*," I acknowledged. "Now it seems so obvious."

"Brilliance is the art of pointing out the obvious to the obtuse, Watson. Not that you fall into that category."

"Thank you. So is Guy Steersdene, or Guy Helmsdale, the real heir to the estate?"

"That is precisely what Jeremy never wanted to test in the courts. Since Guy Helmsdale was born before his Lordship married and fathered a son legitimately, he could hold a claim as heir to the estate. Jeremy learned of Guy's existence, most likely from his father, and he vowed to prevent him from making such a claim. His plan was to hide the will until he could murder his half-brother, at which time the will would miraculously be found, but Guy Helmsdale would not."

"He must have found an effective hiding place, if even the lawyer did not know where it was," I said.

"It was chillingly effective, but it was not the case that Granger was unaware of its location. Remember the legal clerk, Pryce, speaking of an argument taking place in the solicitor's office, over the will? I believe that Jeremy forcibly removed it from Granger's custody, and then impetuously made the '*Burke and Hare*' comment as he left. The solicitor must have deduced where the young man would sequester the will, and I believe passed that information on to Guy Steersdene the evening of his murder. Jeremy must have followed Guy to the solicitor's office, watched, and waited for his elder half-brother to leave. By then, Pryce had also left the premises.

142

Knowing Granger was alone in the office, Jeremy confronted him and forced him to reveal that he had informed Guy as to the will's whereabouts, and then killed him, so he could inform no one else."

"For heaven's sake, Holmes, where was it hidden?"

"Where it remains to this moment, inside the crypt of Lord Helmsdale. Jeremy buried it with his father."

"Good lord!"

"Jeremy's statement that it would require a '*Burke and Hare*' to find the will makes perfect sense, given that Burke and Hare were grave robbers."

"Wait a moment." I blurted, "When we encountered Steersdene tonight, he was holding a jemmy . . . was he attempting to break into the crypt?"

"Yes, and fortunately, we were able to prevent him. Steersdene hoped to retrieve the will to prove his claim, and his previous sightings as a 'ghost' were simply to try and figure out how to get into the crypt. It appears he is as incompetent at stealth as his half-brother is at holding his tongue under stress. Now, Watson, I trust all your questions have been answered."

"Not by a long chalk," I responded. "There's the matter of Steersdene's ability to survive twelve bullets fired at close range."

"That is simplicity itself. Once I had connected the clues and deduced that Jeremy was out to murder Steersdene, I thought it best to have the bullets in his pistol replaced with empty cartridges. Blanks, I believe the military calls them. Earlier this evening, when I left you at Baker Street to build a fire, I proceeded to the post office to telephone Turley and ask him to do exactly that, since he would know the proper calibre of Jeremy's pistol. Then, imagining what he might try to do when his pistol proved faulty, I decided to offer him a second harmless weapon . . . yours, to be precise. While I was out, I also obtained blank cartridges for your service revolver, and replaced the bullets while you were down procuring our repast from Mrs. Hudson. It seemed the best way to keep Steersdene alive."

"Good heavens. What will happen to Steersdene now?"

"I doubt he will be charged with anything, and once the shock has abated, I feel certain Lady Helmsdale will see fit to recognize him as an heir to her husband, particularly since her own son will likely be hanged."

I shook my head. "Well, if nothing else, Holmes, I trust the successful resolution of this matter has restored your faith and confidence in yourself. I wish to see no more black moods or depressions."

"What it has restored, Watson, is my appetite. Mrs. Hudson's cold ham did little to assuage it. What do you say we ask the coachman to drop us off at Simpson's in the Strand for dinner?"

The Case of the
Corpse Flowers
by Wendy C. Fries

In my long association with Sherlock Holmes, I was privy to the particulars of many unusual cases and to the even more unusual ways that my companion went about solving them.

Perhaps one of the strangest occurred many years after I moved into 221b Baker Street when, in the aid of a botanist friend, Holmes appeared to deduce the sun.

Though I had watched Holmes solve a great many intriguing puzzles, some with the most obscure of clues and the most remarkable of solutions, I was still sometimes awed by Holmes's powers of observation, and in this lingering admiration I was not alone. After my companion had solved in a single hour a problem that had been plaguing Scotland Yard for weeks, even Inspector Lestrade was moved to mention it.

"I really don't see how you knew that about budgerigars, Mr. Holmes. Sometimes your knowledge does boggle the mind."

As the case in which the budgerigar had starred was just concluded, Holmes and I were enjoying a rare quiet moment and good tea at the inspector's desk.

We could afford this time for once, as Holmes's plans that afternoon were no more urgent than collating a series of newspaper editorials on the state of London's wretched sewers, though it's safe to say his interest was in no way the same to that of Sir Joseph Bazalgette, who'd created the over-burdened network below our streets and who spent many years working on their improvement. No, instead Holmes used these yellowing articles as something of a treatise on access points to this vast underground web, taking careful note of the availability of key routes during high tide. In short, Sherlock Holmes was making do with the mildly-interesting busy work he sometimes used to fill case-fallow periods.

My afternoon was likewise indolent, with nothing more pressing than jotting notes on the case just concluded, and with that in mind I agreed with Lestrade. "Holmes, you talk about the brain as an attic which should contain only vital lumber. Then you go on to know the rare colours of captive budgerigar?"

My friend shrugged while accepting a refill of his tea. "I do my best to clear my mind of useless *minutiae*, such as the name of a stage siren's royal beau or the state of Constable Gleeson's roses, but alas, some things resist purging, Watson. When you've lodged with a parakeet-raising landlady during your college years, one who taught hers to say 'Won't you play the Vivaldi again, Mr. Holmes?', the fact that only the violets are to be found in captivity is one such resistant fact."

We continued chatting in this casual vein until we were interrupted by two seemingly unconnected events, the second almost immediately following the first.

"Mr. Holmes?" Young Constable Gleeson, who did indeed go on about his roses, politely knocked on the inspector's open door. "A message for your sir, sent on from Baker Street."

"Thank you, Gleeson," Holmes said, taking the telegram and quickly reading.

"Intriguing. This is from a friend at the Royal Botanic Gardens at Kew. I once worked with Madame Levin on a little case before your time, Watson – a small matter about stolen seeds, not over-important on the face of it. Madame Levin was attempting to grow plants from a rare tropical seed, plants which could go on to have important medical properties. And profits.

"In the end, the thief was Madame Levin's assistant, and his motives and financial gain were both expected and mundane. The whole thing was a trifle I'd forgotten until now. Less mundane was Madame Levin's collection of plants and her knowledge of them. After the conclusion of the case, we developed quite a rapport, and she has since helped me on one or two small matters. Now it appears I may once again be able to help her."

Holmes handed me the note and while he collected our coats I read the message aloud.

> *Rare corpses blooming worldwide. Appreciate your thoughts. Today noon. Green glass.*

As I finished, Gleeson came running into the inspector's office.

"There's been a fire at the paper warehouse, Inspector. Cupboard's suddenly gone up in flames. Nearly took two clerks and the whole factory with it before they managed to break the door down and put the fire out."

146

Why this might be of interest to Scotland Yard was soon explained, though young Gleeson seemed a bit awkward in relaying the rest. "The clerks, the ones that almost got it, they say it's unnatural what happened 'cause that room, the one where the fire started, it's always locked they say, always. They reckon you'd need someone who can do what that mentalist Mister Lemezma can do – you know, the one at the Alhambra Theatre who talks to spirits and starts fires with his mind and the like?"

Holmes nearly hooted, but put on a mock serious face quite quickly. "Well, it's a good thing this is on your side of the street, Lestrade, I'm afraid spirits are not at all Watson's or my purview."

"Yes, yes, well thank you again for your help with that small matter previously, Mr. Holmes. Always a pleasure." The inspector pushed past us, and I spotted a bit of a self-important smirk as he added, "And of course good luck with your little gardening case. Come along, Gleeson, we'll soon get to the bottom of this."

With that, the inspector dashed off, and we were soon following out the door, though at a more leisurely pace.

"Now, Holmes, you're not interested in Lestrade's ghostly locked room mystery?"

My friend shrugged. "We both know it's not a spirit who starts a fire. It's a man with a match, or something similarly mundane. Besides, it's no matter to us as we've already got a case. If you're not pressed for time with other things, I think you might find this excursion out to Richmond intriguing, Watson."

"I'm in no great hurry, and am happy to enjoy our rare November sun. Lead on."

Lead Holmes did, and we soon found ourselves boarding a District Line train heading to the Royal Gardens, where my friend provided a bit of background about the case.

"Madame Levin has been a botanist at Kew for ten years now, specialising in growing scarce plants with the idea of making them less so. She had a bit of notoriety a half-dozen years back when she shared several of her successes with the Orman Garden in Egypt and the Arnold Arboretum in America. It seems some thought Kew should keep its successes, and any potential profits from them, strictly to itself."

Every medical man knows that science is full of small developments with the potential of lucrative outcomes. "Much like foxglove leading to the digitalins that help cardiac patients, for example?"

147

"Apparently so. Madame Levin won out in the end through sheer doggedness and unexpectedly deep pockets, using both her free time and her family fortune to visit botanic gardens worldwide, sharing not only her techniques, but cuttings and seeds, too."

Instead of answering my very natural question of what these things had to do with corpses and blooms, Holmes claimed the need to think, and so we spent the rest of the trip in easy silence.

By the time we reached the gardens not much before noon, the day had dimmed with scudding clouds, though the gloom seemed to have had little effect on the park's visitors. Hundreds of men, women, and children wandered along its dozens of winding paths and through its spectacular glass houses.

As we followed one of the paths ourselves, I could see palm fronds pressing against the graceful curves of high-arched roofs of some of those houses, and I glimpsed the reaching arms of tall cactus through the foggy glass of others. Having not been to Kew for many years, I enjoyed the twists and turns of the lengthy paths we took to our destination, which turned out to be a green-tinted glass house, tucked unobtrusively behind the rock gardens.

Holmes reached for its door, which bore a hand-lettered sign: *Closed for the Remainder of the Week.* "Welcome to Madame Levin's domain, Watson. Green Glass has been her duchy since she arrived, and her subjects are an extraordinary lot." With a smile, he opened the door and gestured me through.

The instant we entered the shimmering glass house, I knew the why of Holmes's sly smile as well as the reason for the sign on the door. The odor inside that high-roofed room was absolutely foul.

"It smells like rotting meat in here!" I exclaimed, barely resisting the impulse to cover my mouth and nose.

"A faultless deduction old man," laughed Holmes, turning toward the woman hurrying toward us.

"So good to see you again, Mr. Holmes!" she called, her French accent faint but still melodic. "I did so hope you'd come – that is, if you weren't too busy chasing criminals across London."

Holmes took the woman's hand briefly, then gestured to me. "You've been reading my friend's stories, I see. Madame Levin, may I present Dr. John Watson, medical man and author. Watson, this is Madame Françoise Levin, botanist *extraordinaire.*"

A woman in her fifties, faintly tanned, with a streak of gray in her dark hair and a dirt-smudged canvas apron around her waist, Madame Levin made a dismissive but pleased sound. Then, with the languid speech of someone who lived long in the tropics, she said, "I

148

never expected that solution to the newspaper story with the mutton merchant, Dr. Watson. I do hope to see your version in print someday."

After assuring the lady that it was my companion's unexpected knowledge of deer breeding that brought the case to its successful conclusion, Holmes moved on to the matter at hand, saying simply, "Do tell us about your corpses, Madame Levin."

With a gesture, the botanist invited us to the far back of her domain, where we came to a stop before two very strange, very large flowers . . . and the overwhelming source of the putrid odor.

"Here in Green Glass House, we specialise in growing rare plants *from* seed and *to* seed, Dr. Watson, but none are more rare than these two beauties, our *titan arums.*" Gesturing to the eight-foot tall plants and the single massive bloom taking root in each of the pots before us, Madame Levin said, "With the intense carrion odor of their blooms, I suspect you've already guessed why they're called *corpse flowers*, Doctor?"

"The scent is astonishing! Like rotting meat, decaying cheese, and unwashed clothes all in one. Something rather like a college hall of residence!"

Madame Levin laughed loudly. "The scent is meant to attract pollinators like flies and beetles, and while it is quite extraordinary, what makes corpse flowers truly astonishing is the fact that they bloom only once or twice in a generation, and then for just a single day, sometimes two."

She gazed fondly at her immense charges. "They appear dormant for so long that you really have no true sense of their beauty until they bloom. A simple bulbous green plant hurls itself skyward overnight and then unfurls one of these stunning maroon spathes, what you might call a petal, but which is actually a gargantuan leaf. To me it looks for all the world like the frilly skirt of a pretty lady. For a plant that may weigh well over two-hundred pounds, with a central spadix taller than a man, the whole effect is surprisingly delicate, don't you think?"

As if catching herself, the botanist laughed again and said, "Listen to me. You've not come to admire, you've come because of these." Withdrawing a handful of telegrams from the pocket of her apron, Madame Levin held them out to Holmes. "These blooms and these telegrams are the reason I contacted you," she said. "We've received an unexpected flurry of messages from gardens in Tokyo and New York, Johannesburg and Cairo, all of them saying the same

149

surprising thing. In the last day or two, it seems everyone's *titan arums* have begun growing and then blooming."

I must have looked confused, for Madame Levin gestured to her plants again. "I promise you, Dr. Watson, the growth of a corpse flower is startlingly obvious. A plant can sprout as much as eight inches in a day – that is quite natural. What is decidedly *unnatural* is for them to do so all at the same time. Therein is the real mystery."

Instead of looking at the telegrams, Holmes began making a circuit around the titanic plants. "These other plants, Madame Levin, the ones in Cairo and so on – they aren't from your own stock are they? Plants you might have given to the other arboretums?"

"Not a one, Mr. Holmes, but even if they were, differing climates and care guarantee that the plants wouldn't all bloom at the same time." The botanist gestured to the telegrams. "Which might explain why some of my colleagues attribute supernatural forces to the simultaneous emerging of the blooms."

Holmes paused in his pacing. "I assume you don't take such ideas seriously?"

"Oh, *titan arums* have always offered a bit of titillation to those who like to believe in strange and occult forces. Quite aside from their extraordinary ability to grow so quickly and their graveyard scent, you just can't call something a 'corpse flower' without inflaming imaginations.

"Now, I know the supernatural isn't your area, Mr. Holmes, which is why I was so hoping you'd be able to make something sensible of this little mystery."

As if he hadn't already had his fill, my companion peered closely at the mysteries in question, going so far as to take a hearty sniff of the wretched things. Then, with a brisk nod, he promised to consider the problem and return in a day or two. With that, we returned to Baker Street and a fire already lighted by our landlady.

Over a warming dinner, we talked about the budgerigar case and other trifles, then afterward took to our chairs by the fire. I began writing up notes and Holmes settled in with one of his big books of clippings, occasionally jotting things on a scrap of paper. Long hours passed in such companionable silence, and it was about the time I was trying to decide between an early bed or finishing a rather poor first draft that I realised the stack of books beside Holmes chair had grown.

"Do you really think you'll find something about Madame Levin's dreadful flowers in your clippings?"

"Dreadful? Come now Watson, I'd have expected a doctor to be more open-minded!" With a stretch and a yawn, Holmes clapped his book closed. "In answer to your pointed question, I have a vague reply. You see, I know that there's something that I *already know* which will help with Madame Levin's little plant puzzle, but it's eluded me. I thought it might be in one of these, but despite a good many hours looking, I haven't found what I'm looking for."

I couldn't imagine what Holmes could hope to find in one of his books about gigantic plants that rarely bloomed and which smelled like rotting flesh when they did. His tomes tended more toward notable crimes, but he had more than once discovered a useful clue in his yellowing papers. "Well, good luck to you. I suppose it isn't quite the crime of the century or a locked room mystery, but it's good to see the case is providing you with *some* diversion."

Holmes tossed his book onto the wobbling stack beside his chair. "Speaking of locked rooms, I wonder how the inspector got on with his paper factory fire. I may pop round tomorrow to – Oh!"

As if surprised by my friend's sudden exclamation, the pile of poorly balanced books finally slid across the floor. "Watson, you've gone and done it again!"

Failing to explain in what way I'd been illuminating, Holmes bolted from his chair with an eye on the mantel clock. "If I hurry, I may just catch him."

"Where are you going?"

"To the Diogenes, to ask Mycroft about the summer I was five," he replied, slamming the door behind him.

Holmes returned as I was putting aside my pipe and the novel I was doggedly trying to finish.

"I didn't expect to find you still up, old man."

"I was curious to hear what you'd found out from your brother."

Holmes dropped hat and coat onto the nearest chair and himself in the one across from me. "Well, don't let me keep you, my boy. We can do nothing about what I learned until morning."

"And then?"

"And then we shall go to the telegraph office."

"Are we sending a telegram?"

"No, no, no. We're going to ask the clerks if their equipment has proved shocking lately. Good night, Watson."

Though we had a case on, which usually meant early rising and bustle, breakfast the next morning was a leisurely affair. Holmes was ruminating over his second cup of coffee when he said, "Watson, I am of the opinion that nothing's better for the digestion than purpose. As such, and as soon as we're done here, I think *our* purpose is to visit the Westminster telegraph office, and then almost certainly the one in Leicester Square."

When we arrived in Westminster a half-hour later, we found the telegraph office chaotically busy. This led to a long wait for what turned out to be a short visit.

"You've received forty messages in fifteen minutes," said Holmes by way of greeting the harried boy behind the counter, "and sent only two."

The lad pulled out a blank sheet, presuming Holmes wanted to be the one to send message three. "The machines have been completely barmy here, and just about everywhere all yesterday and this mornin' sir, workin' and not, messages bein' delayed and then comin' in in fits and starts. Regular ghost in the machine sort of thing. Do you got a message needs sending?"

After deliberation, Holmes wrote several short missives and gave these to the boy, explaining their contents to me as we hailed a cab. "I've sent telegrams asking acquaintances at observatories in America, Australia, and Scotland whether they've seen any mysterious lights in the night sky. I expect I already know their answers because you were wrong, Watson."

As our cab rattled on toward Leicester Square, I exclaimed, *"I was wrong?"*

With a lift of his pointed chin, my friend looked out the window and murmured, "Yes. You see, I do have *some* knowledge of, and interest in, astronomy."

Quite soon *we* had a great deal of interest in the state of the Leicester telegraph office, which was even more busy than the one in Westminster, though for reasons entirely different.

" – And some of the wires took to sparking, Mr. Holmes, like fireworks. We had to disconnect the batteries for safety's sake, but here's the thing about that: Some of the machines kept right on working anyway, even with no power. We've settled things now, but it was spooky, real eerie-like for a while, I don't mind saying."

Holmes gave the jittery clerk's arm a commiserating pat. "I think you'll find the worst of it over now, Mr. Brian. I predict today you'll find your equipment far less uncanny."

After this we were again on foot, this time to Scotland Yard, not so far away. There Holmes seemed entirely unsurprised when the front desk constable handed him two telegrams. "Boy just delivered these for you, Mr. Holmes."

My companion read his messages, crowing in delight. "Exactly as I thought, Watson! An aurora was spotted over Melbourne, old Adams says. '*Bright as blood*', he enthuses. The other telegram is as I expected, too."

"And what did you expect?"

"Proof that botany is a bizarre business, and that spirits did *not* set fire to the paper warehouse, of course. Now let's go tell that to the inspector."

Lestrade was busy with other things when we finally found him, and he waved off Holmes's question about the blaze the day before. "Oh, that. There was nothing to it. I'm sure it was just a clerk having a secret smoke where he ought not. Certainly it was negligence and nothing more."

"Didn't Gleeson say that they had to break down the door and that the room was locked from the inside?"

Lestrade waved again, annoyed. "Yes, that's what both clerks insisted. They also said no one but the manager had the key, and that *he* was off all week in Durdle Door or some similarly silly-named town. I'm sure they're either forgetting that someone else has a key, or they're covering up for the real culprit."

Holmes agreed that of course this must be the answer, then he asked a simple question. "Lestrade, did that locked room by any chance contain telegraph paper?"

Lestrade narrowed his eyes. "Well, the factory makes all types, actually. Specialises in paper for broadsheets mostly, but yes, that's what was in that particular cupboard. Apparently such paper is filled with chemicals that make it a bit tricky, which is why they keep it off by itself. Why? What is it you know?"

Holmes glanced at his watch. "Only that we must be keeping you from important things. Let the Good Doctor and me know if we can help in any future endeavors. Good day, Inspector."

The sun was high in a cold, clear sky when we reached the District Line, again on our way to the Royal Botanical Gardens. Instead of pressing my friend for details, recognising the serene and self-satisfied expression he often had when a little problem had resolved itself, I took the opportunity to rest mind and body with the train's rhythm. In this way the journey passed quickly, and it wasn't long before we were again meandering park paths toward Madame Levin's Green Glass House.

"I took the liberty of telegraphing this morning Watson, letting Madame Levin know we've found an answer to her question."

"And that answer is?"

As he did the day before, Holmes took the handle of the greenhouse door and ushered me ahead of him. "It's inside."

Madame Levin's office was tidy, warm, and offered a welcome respite from the stink of her over-large charges, though we had noticed their blooms already fading as we passed through the greenhouse.

" – And the answer to your conundrum is as simple as the sun, Madame Levin," Holmes said, accepting a cup of tea.

"Have you ever heard of the Carrington Event? It was quite news-worthy a few dozen years ago. Though I was only a small child, I do remember the papers breathlessly reporting a massive solar storm and its wide-ranging effects here on earth.

"A friend in Australia tells me that sun spot activity is extraordinarily high right now, though it isn't quite at the levels reported by Mr. Carrington that day in late summer of 1859. During that particular solar event, aurora were seen across America, and were in fact were so bright that morning birds warbled their songs at one a.m., and labourers reported to work, thinking it was daybreak.

"Other effects less benign included surges of current so great that delicate telegraph wires melted, and telegraph papers, some of which are coated with special chemicals, spontaneously caught fire without aid of match or spark. More relevant to us, several botanical gardens at the time reported that some of their autumn-dormant plants were suddenly blooming.

"So you see Madame Levin, your rare ladies in their frilly skirts were doing what plants always do – blooming in response to the sun."

It would be another week before Holmes and I had much to occupy us, so at Baker Street, we again took up the occupations of idle gentlemen. Holmes started several mycology experiments with a variety of mushrooms given to him in thanks by a colleague of Madame Levin's and, once he had this series of improbable proceedings underway, my friend returned to his detailed notes on London's web of sewers.

After recording a few particulars about the case of the corpse flowers, I began writing *The Problem of the Violet Parakeet*, an occupation the engrossed me until dinner, over which I teased my friend. "Holmes, you do realise that today you deduced the sun?"

After a moments reflection Holmes shrugged. "I suppose from a storyteller's point of view it might appear that that's what I did."

"This storyteller has a question. That trip you took to see your brother? What on earth did Mycroft have to do with all of this?"

Holmes pushed away his plate and patted his pockets for his pipe. "What does Mycroft have to do with anything except everything? It sometimes seems my brother's fingers are in every pie."

"Surely even Mycroft can't make sun flares?"

Holmes unearthed his pipe – not on his person but under a pile of papers stacked on the dining table. "To be honest, when I was a child I wouldn't have put it past him, self-important and serious as he was. In actual fact, I'm not sure I'd put it past him now.

"At the time though, it was my brother's blustering self-importance which helped to lodge the memory of the Carrington Event in my mind. Though I'm sure I was busy with the important studies of every five-year-old, I do remember that summer day when Mycroft was so bad tempered, so annoyed, that even my flighty attentions were drawn. I tagged after him as he paced through the house, muttering and complaining and saying dour things like 'Technology Sherlock! Technology! Beware the vagaries of technology!'

"He didn't explain much more than that, so it was only later I learned that my twelve-year-old sibling was closely following political contretemps in both Sri Lanka and Bombay. The wide-spread telegraph outages, and therefore the delay of news, had caused his foul temper that day and it got no better the next, when the papers were filled with breathless news of minor fires and melted wires instead of the international intrigue he craved.

"Even that wouldn't have kept this *minutiae* in mind all these years later, if it wasn't for a little boy's ability to hold a very big grudge. You see, the real reason I remember the Carrington Event is because the day it happened, Mycroft had promised to take me to see the new clock tower that had gone into operation over the Houses of Parliament, just that May."

I poured my friend and myself more coffee. "Holmes, did you deduce the sun and solve the puzzle of the corpse flowers because you didn't get to visit Big Ben when you were a five-year-old child?"

Holmes tapped the stem of his unlighted pipe on the rim of his cup. "Apparently so."

The Problem of the
Five Razors
by Aaron Smith

Sherlock Holmes's method of digging to the truth of any particular mystery has always been rooted in several rules of operation. First, and perhaps foremost, among these is that he first must eliminate the impossible. This is not difficult for Holmes, for he is a man of reason, of science, of logic, and believes that the world is governed by physical laws which do not change willy-nilly from moment to moment, day to day, or case to case.

Belief in the impossible or improvable has never been a feature of his personality. There is not an ounce of faith in Holmes, for he always requires evidence.

However, this is not to say that faith and belief in the seemingly impossible have not played a part in the cases upon which Holmes and I have worked, but it is always the other individuals involved who suffer these delusions.

This was perhaps never more clearly demonstrated than during one autumn when a series of savage attacks put fear into the hearts of Londoners and money in the pockets of the newspaper men who related the gruesome details to the public.

Holmes and I were aware of the case for a short time before we became personally involved, for how could we not notice the papers that screamed for our attention with such article titles as "Mayhem at Midnight" and "Blood Stains the City Streets"?

It was on the day following what was assumed to be the third incident, and Holmes and I had just been brought our morning coffee by Mrs. Hudson. I glanced at the early paper and said to Holmes, who was watching the smoke of his pipe swirl up toward the ceiling, "It has happened again, it seems."

"What's that, Watson?" Holmes asked, shooting me a look of irritation as if I had snapped his reverie in two.

"Those vicious assaults, Holmes?"

"The faces being slashed," Holmes recited from accounts of the previous events, "as the victims passed some dark alley or doorway in the late hours and were surprised by a black-clad man wielding a razor."

"Indeed." I had been chilled by the horror of such attacks since first reading of them. "And Scotland Yard seems no closer to identifying the fiend."

"Because," Holmes said, "there is not a clear mind among them, they tend to trip over one another in their chase for glory, and not one of them, with the exception of Gregson on his good days and Lestrade when he accidentally plucks the proper string, knows how to look at what is right in front of his eyes."

"And now, Holmes," I said, for years of working alongside the detective had taught me something about judging his moods, "you are itching to involve yourself in this bloody business."

"'This bloody business', as you call it, must end," Holmes said as he stood. "Do you not concur?"

"Of course," I said, as I, too, left my chair. "Three innocent people mutilated by a madman is three too many. To the Yard, then?"

"No, I believe it would be better to converse privately with one of our frequent allies on the police force. We might avoid interference from Scotland Yard supervision in that way. Come along."

Thirty minutes later, I followed Holmes into a small pub. It was barely past breakfast time and the place was nearly empty, but I spotted a familiar figure at a table in a dim corner.

"Inspector Gregson!" I said in surprise. "You knew he would be here, Holmes?"

"Of course I did. Do not be alarmed by the inspector's habit of imbibing so early in the day. One drink will hardly intoxicate a man beyond the ability to do his duty, and perhaps it even helps keep his nerves in check. As you know, Gregson has had some difficult cases this past year, and I believe he is now involved in the investigation of the slashings."

Sherlock Holmes considered Tobias Gregson the best of Scotland Yard's detectives, an opinion which could be interpreted as either a compliment to Gregson or an insult to the Yard.

"Shall I buy you gents a pint?" Gregson asked as we joined him at his table.

"This is not a social visit," Holmes said. "I assume you are to some extent involved in the most prominent mystery of the day."

"If you mean the lunatic with the razor, indeed I am," the inspector confirmed.

"Little progress has been made, at least according to what the press reports," Holmes stated.

"You'll get another on that count."

"Will you accept a bit of assistance," Holmes asked, "or shall Watson and I travel the difficult road of discovering for ourselves what facts you could easily volunteer?"

"Not a word to my superiors, then?"

"You have my word," Holmes said, "and Watson's as well."

I nodded.

"Tell me what you know of the case so far," Gregson said.

"Only what the papers say. Three victims, two men and a woman, seemingly unconnected by blood, business, or social circle. Each attacked in a dark place late in the night by an assailant using a man's shaving razor as his weapon. Each cut across the face several times. That is all."

"As little as it is, everything you have just said is correct, Holmes, except for one fact."

"What is that?"

"There have not been three victims, but four."

"A fourth!" Holmes said with the excitement he often demonstrated when a vital piece of information had made its way to him. "A victim of whom the newsmen were not aware?"

"Yes," Gregson continued. "It was the first, actually. Several days before the other attacks began to occur, and, thus, before we could see a pattern, a first body was found. Unlike the others, who survived the attacks, this one was dead when discovered."

"So our razor-wielder is a murderer."

"Yes, but we have yet to determine if he killed intentionally."

"Do explain, Inspector."

"When dawn broke one morning, the body of a young woman was discovered on the street in front of a tall building which houses many flats. The face had been badly damaged, and many of the bones had been broken. Due to the nature of the injuries, it was first believed that she had tried to cross the street in the darkness and had been struck by a carriage. It was only after what we now know to be the second and third slashings, that the injuries were reexamined and it was found that some of the damage to the face had been done by a keen blade."

"The razor."

"Yes. The poor girl – a Miss Riker – had been slashed across the face while standing atop the roof of the building in which she lived. Her parents, when questioned, revealed that she often sat upon the roof, reading. A book was found there, with the place where she had stopped reading, marked by a handkerchief left between the pages, presumably when she realized she was not alone. She was attacked there, and then fell from the roof. The further damage, leading to her death, was inflicted by impact with the hard ground."

"It seems to me, Inspector," Holmes said, "that this young woman being attacked upon her rooftop is a much more purposeful crime than the incidents of those who were perhaps randomly chosen when the opportunity arose in the darkness of street-level shadows."

"We thought so, too, Holmes, but nothing in her life could be found that would seem to be a reason any man would wish to do her harm. She was only nineteen years of age, had no suitors, no enemies her parents were aware of, and rarely left her home."

"I see," said Holmes. "Tell me of the other victims."

"A shopkeeper of thirty with no record of criminal behavior; a recently discharged sailor of Her Majesty's Navy, aged forty-one years; and another young woman, also of nineteen years, who lives with her rather wealthy father. No notable connections between them."

"And all attacked in the same manner?"

"By their own reports, yes."

"I should like to meet them and to examine the remains of the first victim."

"The first has already been cremated, I'm afraid, and my superiors will not approve of you speaking with the others."

"They need not know."

"You wish me to sneak about behind their backs? If they discover my subterfuge . . . ."

"Do what you must, Inspector, before more innocent blood is spilled."

We received a message from Gregson late that day. In a plain envelope delivered by messenger was a note containing three names and addresses, along with the statement, *"Please refrain from revealing from whom you acquired this."*

Holmes and I wasted no time leaving our Baker Street rooms and hurrying to the closest address on the list. We arrived at a cheap flat in a rundown building. Our knock was answered by a short, round man with muscular arms featuring an assortment of tattoos. Still-healing cuts ran across his tanned and weathered face, three slashes in all, one down the left cheek, one across the chin, and the other horizontal on the right cheek.

159

"Mr. Ralph Bartlow," my friend said, "I am Sherlock Holmes, and I would very much appreciate a few moments of your time."

"You coppers?"

"No," Holmes said. "I am investigating the series of crimes to which you were a victim, but I hold no official status with the police, nor does my associate, Dr. Watson."

"Then why investigate?"

"Because someone must. May we come in?"

"Aye."

We followed Bartlow inside and sat upon wooden chairs, with mine tipping precariously, as one of its legs was shorter than the other three.

"Tell us, if you will," Holmes said, "what occurred on the night you received those injuries to your face."

"I was a damn fool," Bartlow said. "Walkin' home on the dark streets, I was. Even with a few pints in me, I should have had my ears open and my eyes peeled. You know how many fights I won in the navy? More than I can count! So I shouldn't a' let some scoundrel get close enough to carve up my face, but I did. Came at me from the dark, dressed in black to match the shadows, right up to his mask."

"What sort of mask?" Holmes asked.

"Nothin' fancy," Bartlow answered. "Just a wool piece that covered the whole face, 'cept the eyes, like you'd wear in a snowstorm."

"I see," Holmes said with a nod. "And then?"

"Well, he comes up behind me, see? And puts a hand on my shoulder, so I turn around to see who's there, thinkin' maybe I'm about to have my pocket picked. And the blade comes up!"

"And," Holmes interrupted, "the razor was wielded in the assailant's right hand and came down along your left cheek, then skidded across your chin as you moved back a step, and then cut straight across your right cheek as you began an attempt to turn your face away from further harm."

"Yessir," Bartlow said, his face taking on the look Holmes often evoked when he stated facts the interviewee had not yet revealed. "But how did you . . . ."

"Your face, much like a book, tells a story, Mr. Bartlow, and the tale does not end with the strokes of the blade, for it also tells me that the man who cut you was nearly a foot taller than you, and quite slender, and, of course, right-handed."

"Aye, he was tall and thin, like you, Mr. Holmes. The same size as you."

"And what happened after he damaged your face? Did he attempt to finish the job and kill you?"

"No, and he didn't try to rob me either. He ran away. I didn't understand, and I still don't. Why cut a man if you don't aim to kill him or take his money?"

"I promise you I will share the answer to that question with you as soon as I have determined it for myself."

And with that, Sherlock Holmes stood and marched out of the shabby little flat. I shook the hand of the retired sailor and said, "Be sure to keep those wounds clean until they have fully healed, Mr. Bartlow, for infection is still possible."

The next morning, Holmes and I visited the bookshop run by Jeremy Gladdon, the next victim on Gregson's list. It was a small store with a somewhat disorganized manner, but a paradise, I assumed, to bibliophiles. Shelves were piled high with volumes, and a glass case behind the counter boasted what I supposed were, as the American, Poe, said in one of his works, "*Quaint and curious volumes of forgotten lore*".

Gladdon was a soft-spoken, polite young man who had heard of Holmes and warmly welcomed us.

"I'm honored to meet you both," Gladdon said, "though I had hoped, upon hearing the bell, that you were customers, for business has been slow since I reopened the shop after my days in hospital. These confounded wounds," he rubbed his face, where the marks of violence had healed a bit further than those etched on the cheeks and chin of the retired sailor of the night before, "are frightening away half my customers and making the other half nervous, for a scarred man, is, I suppose, not as easy to talk to as a smooth-faced fellow."

"Describe to me, Mr. Gladdon," Holmes said, interrupting the shopkeeper's lament, "the person who injured you."

"He moved fast," Gladdon said, "swung that razor right at me and I never saw it coming. He must have been young to move so quick! And strong, with thick arms. Couldn't see his face, though."

"Yes, yes," Holmes said, "I am aware that he wore a mask. How tall was he?"

"Not a short man, but not as tall as I am," said Gladdon, who was approximately the same height as Holmes.

"Thank you for your time, Mr. Gladdon. That will be all." Holmes barked as he turned and marched out the door.

"I'l join you presently," I called at Holmes's back. I felt sorry for Gladdon. The young man had answered our questions politely and done his best to assist us. I felt obligated to help him in some small way. I thanked him and purchased several of his books before leaving the shop to find Holmes standing outside, smoking and tapping his cane in an impatient rhythm.

We hired a carriage to deliver us to the third address. As we rode, Holmes asked, "Do you see, Watson, what happens when we compare the account we have just heard from Gladdon to what Bartlow told us last night?"

"There were," I said, "differences in the two stories. Bartlow, last night, reported the attacker as being as tall as you, while Gladdon, who is your height, said he was a bit shorter. And Gladdon described the slasher as a muscular man, while Bartlow said he was quite thin. However, Holmes, it was dark during both attacks, and they happened quickly, and unexpectedly. That could very easily explain the disparities between accounts. Also, a man who looks tall and thin to the short, stout Bartlow might very well seem shorter and thicker to the tall, slim Gladdon. Are you seeing something I am not, Holmes?"

"Perhaps, Watson, perhaps, though I am not yet certain."

Our carriage had entered a wealthy neighborhood and came to a stop in front of a lovely yellow house with blue curtains in its large front windows.

We were admitted by the maid and led into the office of a man of about fifty with a white beard.

"You are Holmes and Watson, I take it?"

We nodded.

"Inspector Gregson informed me you would be coming. I am Reginald Christopher."

"The father, I assume, of Miss Juliet Christopher?" Holmes asked.

"Indeed, and I thank you for involving yourselves in this dreadful business. Gregson is a good man, but Scotland Yard moves slowly and I desire justice for my daughter."

"If we have any say in this matter," Holmes said, "you will have your justice. May we see your daughter?"

"You may speak with her," Christopher said, "although your actually seeing her may be another question entirely. You realize that it has only been two days since her assault. Were we poorer people, she would still be in hospital, but I thought it better to bring her

162

home to rest in privacy. A nurse and physician come around thrice daily to see to her. Clara will take you upstairs."

The maid left us at the door of a room on the second floor. Holmes and I entered.

There was a large bed at the end of the room, but it was cloaked in shadow, as the curtains were closed and the room's lone lamp had been placed in such a way that it cast its light at the door, and thus straight into our line of sight, making it impossible for us to see more of the bed's occupant than a slim outline of a body reclined against a stack of pillows. Other than the grim strangeness of the small figure hidden in darkness, the rest of the room looked like the bed chamber of any young lady of an affluent family. There was an expensive chair, several framed photographs, a pleasant painting of a pond reflecting sunlight, and a dresser upon which sat the usual trinkets of young womanhood: A hair brush, a music box, and a scattering of jewelry which Holmes pushed around with his long fingers as if the items were chess pieces before turning to the young lady.

"Miss Christopher?" Holmes asked.

"You are the detectives?" a soft voice responded from the shadows.

"I am Sherlock Holmes, and this is my associate, Dr. Watson. Will you speak with us?"

"I spoke with the policemen, and they have not caught the monster who has ruined my life!"

"We are most certainly *not* the police."

"Will you find him?"

"I will do everything in my power to do that."

"And will you kill him?"

"That will be the decision of the court. It is not our place to say – "

"It should be *my* place to say! He killed me! Now I want you to kill *him*!"

"Miss Christopher, calm yourself."

"Mr. Holmes, go to Hell!"

I knew the situation would only worsen. What I saw before me was a distraught young woman, having just been through a traumatic experience, and probably still feeling physical pain and emotional confusion. In such a state as that, to be confronted with Sherlock Holmes on the trail of answers to a mystery and when he is at his most driven, can only lead to disaster. Holmes's genius has often made it difficult for him to put aside his bloodhound nature and reassure those in need of his help. I had to intervene.

163

"Miss Christopher," I said. "May I call you Juliet? Although you are, I am sure, in great pain and uncertain of what the future may hold for you, we are trying to help. But anger, justified as it may be, will not answer certain vital questions which must be addressed if we are to learn who did this to you. I beg you to forgive Holmes's somewhat gruff nature and bring this talk back to what it should be, a quiet conversation between friends. Will you do that for me?"

"I will try."

"Good. Holmes, ask your questions calmly."

Holmes gave an indignant snort, but spoke clearly and gently. "How did you come to be alone on the street so late in the evening, Juliet?"

"I had gone to the theatre with my friend, Margaret. We were supposed to take a cab home, but I felt so happy after the play that I decided to walk. Margaret lives in the opposite direction, so we parted ways."

"And you were soon surprised by the man who attacked you?"

"Yes. I had turned left down an empty street and thought I was alone, until he jumped from the shadows and had that . . . that sharp thing in his hand and . . . ."

"You need not relate precisely what he did. But, I must ask, do you recall what he looked like?"

"He was dressed all in black and his face was covered by a mask, so that only his eyes were visible to me. And they were terrible eyes, wild and deep, and he glared at me as if he were a demon as he swung the razor! My God, it was like a nightmare! Those eyes! I saw straight into them, for he was of the same height as me!"

"And how tall are you, Juliet?"

"I am five feet, two inches tall."

"And do you recall the shoes you wore that night? Did they add much to your height?"

"Perhaps an inch."

"I see," said Holmes, and I could hear the rising fascination in his voice, for I understood what had just occurred and how the game had changed. "I have one more request of you, Juliet, and it may be an uncomfortable one. Will you show us your face?"

The poor girl let out a little shriek, then said, "Must I?"

"It is of grave importance, I am afraid," Holmes told her.

"Both of you?"

"Do you wish only one of us to see?"

164

"Yes. Your friend, for he speaks with a gentler voice, while you frighten me. I . . . I am sorry. It is good, I think, that you frighten me, for perhaps you will also frighten the monster when you find him. I mean no offense."

"And I take no offense. Dr. Watson, will you please be so good as to . . . ."

"Of course, Holmes," I said as I walked closer to the bed.

"I will wait outside," Holmes said, and he gripped my shoulder to stop me for an instant and whispered, "I trust you know what to look for," before continuing on his way and closing the door behind him.

I turned the lamp around so that it's light shone on the bed, and I witnessed the terrible harm that had been done to the face of the unfortunate young woman.

Once I exited the bedroom, Holmes and I walked downstairs, said goodbye to Mr. Christopher, and returned to our carriage. As the horses began their trot back toward Baker Street, Holmes looked at me expectantly. Concern crossed his face, rare as that was, and he said, "Watson, your hands tremble."

"It was terrible, Holmes!" I said.

"You have seen many injuries, Watson, for it is your profession. Yet, this instance bothers you?"

"That poor girl! The damage done to her face was most dreadful, worse even than the mayhem done to Bartlow or Gladdon."

"Was it worse?" Holmes asked. "Or did it seem worse because from your point of view the ruin of a young female face is a harsher tragedy than the scars given to a man?"

"Perhaps you are correct, Holmes, but it is still a terrible thing, and she now fears that she will never find a husband. I assured her that love is blind, but I have little faith in that sentiment."

"Our chore is not to plan Miss Christopher's future," said Holmes, "but to avenge the wrong done to her. Now that you have expressed your horror, will you please tell me of your findings in a clear, concise way."

"There are at least two of them, Holmes. Even if we assume that Bartlow and Gladdon were attacked by the same razor-wielding man, although perhaps you are correct that they were not, there is most certainly another, for not only are Miss Christopher's injuries consistent with slashes made by one who stands at about her height, a very short man indeed, but those cuts were made in the opposite

165

direction from the marks on the two male victims' faces, which indicates, if I am not mistaken, that this criminal was left-handed."

"It does, Watson. It certainly does. So we have two, perhaps three, and maybe – for we have very little information on the woman who fell to her death after being attacked – as many as four."

"What is our next avenue of investigation, Holmes?"

It often happened that our most efficient means of communication with our allies, especially when trying to keep certain aspects of an investigation secret, was the gang of street urchins we occasionally employed. Holmes had named them the Baker Street Irregulars, and they now took to the task of ferrying messages back and forth between Holmes and Gregson.

By this method, Holmes informed Gregson of the fact that there had actually been multiple attackers, and then asked the inspector for the locations of the slashings.

Once we had received the requested information, we began our journey to each of the specified places. The sites of the attacks on Bartlow and Gladdon yielded no new information, for it had rained in the days since those incidents, and things like footprints and bloodstains do not resist water well.

Our final stop of the day was the narrow side street where Miss Juliet Christopher had been savagely cut by a very short man.

Even in daylight, it was clearly not the sort of place a young woman should have ventured. Little more than an alley between buildings, it was dirty, shadowy, foreboding.

Holmes glanced around the narrow space, then got down on his knees and crawled, peering at the ground so closely that his long nose nearly poked at the grime and muck of the street. Finally, he stood and muttered, "Nothing!"

He marched back to the main avenue and continued on his way. I hurried to catch up. Holmes was silent the rest of the way back to Baker Street.

"What?" Holmes shouted as he pounded his fist on the table in our flat. "What causes such a series of events as this to occur?"

"I do not know," I admitted.

"Of course you don't, Watson. And neither do I. If this were the work of one man, I would assume it was some dark obsession that compelled him to roam the night, carving deep ruts in the faces of random citizens of London. But we now know it to be the work of at least three different men, all wielding the same sort of weapon, all wearing the same attire. So the question remains: Why? And the lack of connections between the victims makes the puzzle even more bewildering. If this was to prove some political point, they would do something to draw more attention to their acts, such as leaving messages written on the walls, or sending letters to the newspapers. And if it was some elaborate scheme of revenge, there would be some common thread or mutual history among the victims. Why would three men take razors to a former sailor, a bookshop proprietor, a wealthy young woman, and a poor young woman, none of whom knew each other? "

"The answer will come to you, Holmes. It always does."

Holmes did not reply. He had closed his eyes, and I knew that meant he was searching every piece of information he had so far acquired about the case – every image, word, or fact.

Many minutes passed. I had no way of knowing how long Holmes would be lost in thought and memory, so I intended to have Mrs. Hudson bring supper, but before I could walk to the door to call for her, Holmes exclaimed, "Of course! It was there! It was everywhere! And I saw it, but I did not *see!*"

"What did you *not* see?" I asked.

"Watson, I have just revisited, in the eyes of my mind, the places where we interviewed each of the three victims. Something was there with us in each of those places, with each of those people. But it is only now, having searched my memory, that I realize this. In the morning, we will see if I am correct!"

"Can you not tell me now?"

"In the morning, Watson. In the morning."

Immediately following breakfast, Holmes and I returned to the Christopher residence. Holmes quickly explained to Reginald Christopher that he had further questions for Juliet, and we were led upstairs.

The curtains had been pulled back this morning, and Juliet was fully visible to us as she lay in bed. The wounds to her face had been covered with fresh bandages, but her eyes shone with better spirits than she had shown the previous afternoon.

"Good morning," I said.

"Dr. Watson, Mr. Holmes," she said with a nod. "Have you found him?"

"I'm afraid not," I told her, "although you may help us to do so by answering more of Mr. Holmes's questions."

"Please ask."

Holmes turned and walked to Juliet's dresser, stared down at the assortment of items, and picked one up, held it so that she and I could both see.

It was a small pendant on a silver chain. I stepped closer to Holmes and saw that it was a beautifully made representation of the sun, but a sun with a face that showed an expression something like a man about to burst into laughter, though the laughter could have been interpreted as malignant rather than jovial. And, across the face, were three lines that radiated outward to form three of the rays of the sun. It was an odd image, somehow disturbing in that the three lines reminded me of the cuts made to the faces of the three slashing victims we had seen, though the placement was different, just as it had been different on each of the mutilated faces.

"How did you come to possess this necklace, Juliet?" Holmes asked.

"I purchased it with some money my aunt gave me for my last birthday."

"When was your birthday?"

"Nine days ago."

"Why did you select this piece?"

"For no particular reason other than that I liked it. I found it amusing and quite unusual."

"Where did you buy it?"

"From a street peddler, a ragged old woman. I realize it was probably stolen, for she had fine wares on her small table, but I liked it too much to care."

"Would you know her if you saw her again?"

"No, I don't think so. Those street people all look the same to me."

"Were you wearing it on the night you were attacked?"

"Yes . . . yes, I was. I thought it went nicely with the dress I wore to the theatre."

"Thank you, Juliet," Holmes said. "That will be all."

Ralph Bartlow looked disheveled and half asleep when he opened the door to his flat.

"What do you want, Mr. . . . . I forget your name."

"Holmes is the name," Holmes reminded the sailor, barging into the flat. "And I want a good look at your left forearm."

I followed Holmes in and immediately looked at the retired sailor's arm, which was a field of tattoos. I saw it then, and I was amazed. Among the palm trees, anchors, native girls in rude poses,

168

and names of ships on which Bartlow had, presumably, been part of the crew, was an image nearly identical to that featured on the pendant worn by Juliet Christopher: the sun with the face near to laughter, and marked by three strange lines that extended out into rays of light.

"Do sit down, Mr. Bartlow," Holmes said, and the startled seaman tumbled into a chair and stared up at the detective. Holmes pointed at the sun-faced illustration on Bartlow's flesh. "When did you acquire that tattoo?"

"Long time ago. Don't recall exactly when."

"Where?"

"Some port along the way. You see how many tattoos I have. You expect me to remember them all?"

"Who applied it to your skin?"

"That, I remember. Strange woman, she was. Wild-haired and wild-eyed. Said it was a charm and would protect me from drowning. What sailor worth his weight in the salt of the sea wouldn't want a thing like that drawn on his arm?"

"What sailor, indeed, Mr. Bartlow?" Holmes said. "If you recall anything else about the subject, do contact me. Watson, give this man the information he will need."

I always kept a few of Holmes's cards in my coat pocket, and I now passed one to Bartlow, who gave it a glance and dropped it onto the small table beside where he sat.

As we left Bartlow's flat, Holmes asked, "Do you see now, Watson? Do you see what I failed to see before?"

"I do, Holmes," I answered, "and I am fascinated. To Jeremy Gladdon's bookshop next, then?"

"Yes, Watson, yes." Holmes increased his walking speed. The thrill of the hunt was upon him now, and no man could stand in his way.

I saw it as soon as we entered the shop, before Gladdon had a chance to properly greet us. There, on the shelf behind the counter, sat a small volume with a dark red cover, upon which had been etched in a golden color the sun-faced symbol we had seen on Juliet's pendant and Bartlow's tattoo.

At Holmes's command, Jeremy Gladdon took the book down and handed it to him.

"How did you come to possess this book?" Holmes demanded.

"People often come here to sell me their old books," Gladdon explained. "Much of the time, they bring me rubbish and I must decline, for my shelves are already well-stocked, but this was such a curious volume that I purchased it."

"From whom?"

"So many people come in and out of the shop. Let me think. A woman. Yes, a woman sold me the book!"

"Watson," Holmes said, passing the tome to me, "look through this, will you, while I continue this conversation?"

"Gladly," I said, and began to page through the volume as Holmes questioned Gladdon.

"Describe this woman," Holmes said.

"She was old, perhaps seventy, well-dressed, but did not appear wealthy."

"Do you recall anything she said as the transaction was made?"

"Only that she said, 'Finally, someone demonstrates taste in literature. Many other merchants have refused to purchase that book.' She was polite and our business concluded, I believe, to both our satisfaction. She received a reasonably good price for the book, and I now possess an interesting item for my shop."

"Have you read it?"

"Only a bit of it. It is a religious text of some sort, though not of any set of beliefs common to London. An esoteric volume, you might call it."

"May I borrow it for a time, Mr. Gladdon?"

"If it will be of help to your case, Mr. Holmes, I see no reason why you should not take it with you. Although I do not understand its relevance."

"All will become clear in time," Holmes said. "Come, Watson."

I continued to read the small book as we were driven back to Baker Street. As we disembarked from our carriage, Holmes called to a passing boy.

"Arthur! Arthur, come here and earn a few pennies!"

The child, an Irregular of perhaps nine years old, hurried over, his eyes wide with joy at the promise of money.

"Yes, Mr. Holmes?"

"Do you know Gregson, the Scotland Yard man?"

"Yes, sir. Wiggins had me deliver a message to him for you just yesterday."

"Excellent," Holmes said. "Go and find him, and ask him to come and see me presently."

"Yes, Mr. Holmes," Arthur said as he turned and ran off, eager to earn his pay.

Holmes sat in silence for most of the next hour while I read the book Gladdon had loaned us. It was not very long and was, as Gladdon had said, a strange religious text, centering on a creation myth, crediting the origin of the universe and the human race to the work of a deity called Grillik. There was, as one might expect, a note explaining that the original version of the book had been written in a language no longer known to mankind, though the translator was not credited.

According to the story, Grillik inhabits no physical body most of the time, but can take a human host and speak through the borrowed body. Grillik, the tale continued, has not walked among humanity for many ages, but will return, in his human host, when his followers find the right vessel for him to dwell within and act through. This person will be distinguished by the three lines upon his or her face, because Grillik, in his spirit form, also bears three lines from which the light of his power emanates.

However, the reader is warned, the marks cannot be intentionally etched into one's face for the purpose of attracting this god. The Scars of Worthiness, as they are called in the book, must occur by chance, for no man can claim to know who the rightful vessel will be. One must first claim the Sigil of Grillik without understanding its significance, and then, only after this sign is in their possession, may the Scars manifest, and only one will wear the lines in their correct configuration.

"And there, Watson, we have it all explained for us!" cried Sherlock Holmes when I had related the general message of the tome to him. "Religion rears its ugly head again and causes men to harm one another. It is clear what has happened here! This woman, whoever she is, arranged for random people to possess this sigil, in the form of a piece of jewelry for Juliet Christopher, who could have chosen any trinket but was drawn to that one, or on the cover of that book for Jeremy Gladdon, who was one of several shop owners offered the volume, and in whatever form the first victim possessed the symbol, which is a matter I am certain Gregson will clarify for us upon his arrival here.

"Then, once these people had chosen the sigil, this woman's minions, fellow followers of this cult of Grillik, watched them and waited until an opportunity arose to attack them and haphazardly slash their faces in the hope that the wounds would fall in the proper configuration. Of course, they seem to not have had much success in this bizarre endeavor, as the first victim died, and the marks upon the faces of Gladdon, Christopher, and Bartlow do not match what we

171

see on the cover of the Grillik Bible! And what this means, Watson, is that the mayhem will continue!"

"Horrible," I said. "But one thing strikes me as odd."

"Ralph Bartlow," Holmes said.

"Yes. His Sigil of Grillik has been there upon his flesh for years, he told us. Do you think he lied?"

"No, he spoke the truth. The color of a tattoo changes with time, and Bartlow's sun-face is no recent addition to the gallery that is his arm."

"Then how did the London-based followers of Grillik find him, if not through their game of baiting their victims with pendants or books?"

"That is the key, Watson! That is how we will find these believers in an obscure cult. One of them must have come into contact with Bartlow and seen his tattoo, and decided that he must be tested for the role of Grillik's host."

Our discussion was halted by Mrs. Hudson, coming in to announce an arrival.

"Inspector Gregson to see you, gentlemen."

Gregson entered and sat.

"Inspector," Holmes said, "do you recognize the symbol on the front of the book Watson is holding?"

"Good lord!" Gregson said. "The girl who fell from the rooftop had that very same image in her possession, stitched on the handkerchief she had used as a bookmark!"

"Ha!" Holmes let out a noise of triumph. He proceeded to tell Gregson all that we knew so far.

"Intriguing," said Gregson when Holmes had completed his tale.

"Watson," Holmes said, "what does the book say will occur after Grillik has entered his human host?"

"The dreadful rubbish one would expect, of course," I answered. "The reborn deity will lead the faithful to war against the unbelievers, and blood will be spilled."

"Of course," Holmes said with a sad sigh. "What is religion without brutality?"

"Shall we go and question the sailor again?" Gregson asked.

"At once," Holmes said, and in a flurry of motion grabbed his coat and hat and hurried for the door.

Bartlow was not pleased to see us. He had been drinking, as shown by his slurred speech and strong smell. But he immediately recalled the answer to Holmes's question.

"Yes, something of the sort did happen. Was a day or two before I got cut. I was down at the docks where I've still got friends from the old days, and this man was painting a pretty picture of the harbor. I stopped to watch, and he turned to me and glanced down at my arm. He had this look like he'd seen a ghost or some such thing. And then he blinked a few times, and I could have sworn I saw a tear trickle down his cheek. Then he turned and went right back to his picture. I walked away, but I turned and looked back at him a minute later and some other fellow had stopped to talk to him, and I saw them both look in my direction. All the rest of that day, I had a feeling I was being watched or followed, but, to tell you the truth, I forgot all about it until you asked me just now."

"What did this painter look like?" Holmes asked.

"A little barrel of a man, short and thick."

"And his associate?"

"Taller, thinner."

"Of my size?"

"Thereabouts."

"Could he have been the man who attacked you?"

"I suppose he could've been. The bloody son of a cow!"

"Mr. Bartlow, we will return in an hour's time. Sober yourself and be ready for a trip to the waterfront."

Holmes marched out and Gregson and I followed.

We stood far back from the water's edge and watched as Bartlow pointed out the painter, who seemed to be in the habit of practicing his art at the docks quite often. He was, just as the retired sailor had said, a sturdily built man of small stature. Perhaps, I thought, the same man who had mutilated the face of Juliet Christopher.

We observed for a short time and saw the painter's confederate, a taller, slimmer man who brought a drink to the artist and stood there talking, smoking, and watching his friend run a brush across the canvas.

The taller of the two soon left and wandered a short distance down the docks. Holmes proceeded to walk toward the artist. Gone were the detective's coat and hat, and his sleeves were rolled up. As he walked away from Bartlow, Gregson, and I, we could still see the small black mark upon his arm, the Sigil of Grillik, a false tattoo Holmes had copied from Bartlow's mark.

What I saw transpire next was Holmes stopping at the painter's side and stretching out his hand to point at some detail of the work-in-progress, thus putting the tattoo in the artist's line of sight. The painter turned toward Holmes, his head changing position so quickly and his body shaking with such a tremor of surprise that he dropped his brush. Holmes spoke, the artist replied, and the conversation went back and forth for several minutes. Finally, Holmes turned and walked away as the artist, watching Holmes depart, stood mopping perspiration from his brow.

We had agreed to meet Holmes a short distance away, far enough that we should not be seen to be awaiting him.

Holmes arrived at the rendezvous point and I was, just as I had been when he had unveiled his work an hour earlier, mightily impressed by the false scars he had applied to his face, the lines precisely matching the Scars of Worthiness.

"Mr. Bartlow, I thank you for your assistance," Holmes said. "You may return to your flat and your drink."

"You'll arrest him and hang him, won't you?"

"Not until we have found them all," Gregson said. "Off with you now, Bartlow."

The sailor shuffled away.

"He believed it, didn't he?" Gregson asked.

"Like a stupid sheep," Holmes said. "Those who want so badly for a thing to be real will often trust the flimsiest of evidence for the silliest of myths. I altered my voice slightly to sound as though I were unused to speaking with a human throat, and I scolded him for the method by which he and his fellow cultists have tested those who chose the sigil. He now truly thinks I am Grillik taken a man's form, and he is most eager to have me show myself to the rest of his gang of fools."

"Where and when?"

"At the home of one Mrs. Mildred Hardcastle."

"The widow," I asked, "of Jonathan Hardcastle, the famous explorer?"

"The same," Holmes answered. "It makes sense that a man who spent much of his life traveling the various regions of the world would have come into contact with a little-known religion like that of the worshippers of Grillik. Perhaps it was he who wrote the cult's bible. In any case, his wife was somehow indoctrinated into the idea and now leads this band of criminals in carrying out their supposedly

174

holy mission. Tonight, at eight o'clock, this will end, and Ralph Bartlow, Jeremy Gladdon, Juliet Christopher, and the even more unfortunate young woman who did not survive will have justice, or perhaps vengeance, depending upon the course of the encounter."

Holmes's last words to me before we left Baker Street that evening were, "Watson, I trust I do not have to remind you to bring your revolver."

I patted my pocket where the weapon rested.

The Hardcastle house was a large manor not far from the Christopher residence. Inspector Gregson, accompanied by three constables he had specifically chosen for the job, waited outside, hidden behind a tall row of bushes, while Holmes, still in his Grillik guise, and I walked up to the door and knocked.

The artist opened the door and cast a suspicious look my way.

"This one assists me in adapting to the ways of human flesh," said Holmes in the strange voice he had developed for the occasion. "He has earned my trust."

The artist led us in, and we walked down a long hall and through a set of wide doors. Inside, we were met by a grey-haired woman and three other men, the tall one from the docks and two others, one tall and thin, though not as tall as the one we had seen previously, and the other slender but of only average height. All were dressed in robes of dark colors. They kneeled as we entered.

Mildred Hardcastle was the first to speak.

"Lord Grillik, we welcome you, and ask that you guide us in the way of truth and power."

"Power, I cannot provide," Holmes said, "but I know something of truth. Truth lies in the laws of nature, of science, of reason, and of evidence. Faith comes not from the words written in a book of fanciful symbolism and poetic declarations, but in what can be detected and measured and verified by the senses and the repeated results of experimentation. You have been misled by your eagerness to have something to believe in, no matter how intangible and absurd those beliefs may be. And four innocent people have paid the price for your gullibility, one with her life, three with their faces. This will stop now."

"You are not Grillik!" the artist cried out.

Holmes glanced over at me, smiled. "You see, Watson, how one of them comes to his senses?"

"Holmes, look out!" I cried.

175

The five of them moved all at once, each producing a razor from the folds of their robes or, in the artist's case, from a pocket.

I drew my revolver and shouted, "Gregson!" hoping the inspector was still within earshot.

Mildred Hardcastle, unsteady on old legs, stumbled and fell to the floor, where she lay whimpering.

I raised my weapon and fired, the bullet striking one of the tall cultists in the shoulder.

The other tall one reached Holmes and took a swing with his razor, but Holmes dodged the swipe, grabbed the man's wrist, and twisted until the blade fell to the floor, at which time Holmes landed a solid punch to his assailant's jaw.

The door burst open behind us and Gregson and his men stormed in, the inspector wielding a pistol and warning, "Be still, all of you!"

The robed ones halted. The razors fell to the floor. The constables made use of their handcuffs on all but the pitiful, fallen Mrs. Hardcastle, to whom I tended. She had broken her hip in the fray and had already descended halfway into an abyss of shock. It was my sworn obligation to help her to the best of my abilities, but I predicted she would not live long enough to face a judge and jury.

The four male followers of Grillik were sentenced to spend many years in prison. Mildred Hardcastle died in hospital. After her funeral, which few attended due to the shame now attached to her name, Juliet Christopher, whose soul was now, I feared, forever tainted by bitterness and sorrow, spit on her grave.

The little book with the Sigil of Grillik on its cover was permanently given to Sherlock Holmes, for Jeremy Gladdon did not want it in his shop. It now sits in one box or another among the many souvenirs of the many strange cases in which Holmes has been involved over the years.

The Adventure of the
Moonlit Shadow
by Arthur Hall

As my long association with my friend Mr. Sherlock Holmes progressed, we shared many adventures of an unusual nature. Most were brought to a satisfactory conclusion, but there remained some with aspects that were beyond explanation. It is one of these that I propose to relate here.

The first light of a late November day was settling on the city as I let myself into our lodgings in Baker Street. Tiredness lay heavily upon me, but I considered the loss of a night's sleep a small price to pay – I had remained at the side of my patient until his fever had at last begun to subside. I reached the top of the stairs having made little noise – I did not wish to disturb Holmes, who was a late riser – and opened the door carefully. I quickly saw that such precautions were unnecessary, for he sat fully dressed at the breakfast table and apparently in good spirits.

"Watson, my dear fellow!" he cried. "Do come and join me. I see that you are in need of sleep, but a good serving of Mrs. Hudson's bacon and eggs will fortify you first."

I took off my hat and coat and sat opposite him. "You are up unusually early, Holmes."

"Much to the contrary," he said after he had called out to our landlady. "I have not been to bed."

"You caught Nicholls on one of his night raids, then?"

"Indeed we did. I had deduced his intentions correctly. He was captured in the act of breaking into the jeweller's premises, and Gregson now has him behind bars."

"And so," I observed as Mrs. Hudson laid my breakfast before me, "we have both had our successes."

He nodded his head but said no more, and watched in silence as I ate. While we awaited our coffee, he began to open a pile of letters, to which he had paid no attention until now.

"The late post from yesterday," he explained. "I had left before it arrived."

"One envelope has a coat-of-arms," I pointed out.

Holmes raised his eyebrows and used his breakfast knife as a letter-opener. His hawk-like expression changed as he read the document.

"What do you make of this, Watson?"

I took it from him and read the few words, which were written in an ornate script.

I have proof at last, and it is indisputable. But there is little time. I beg you to come at your first convenience. Bring Lestrade if you can.

Trentlemere

"From someone of your previous acquaintance, obviously," I deduced. "Also, he knows Lestrade."

"Indeed. Lord Trentlemere has cause to remember us both."

"I cannot recall such a case."

"That is hardly surprising. You and I saw little of each other for a while, following your marriage. The Edmund Saunders affair took place during that time."

I nodded. "That name is familiar to me."

"The newspapers made much of it, but the fact remains – Saunders is a murderer who escaped the rope." Holmes frown deepened. "But perhaps not for much longer."

"This letter then, refers to new evidence that has been discovered?"

"Apparently, but that remains to be seen. Lord Trentlemere's obsession with proving Saunders' guilt has been unceasing over the years."

"Will you tell me about the case, Holmes?" I asked, unable to contain my curiosity.

He leaned back in his chair with a look in his eyes that I have rarely seen – remembering an unsuccessful case.

"Lord Trentlemere is among the kindest and most courteous men that it has ever been my good fortune to meet," he began. "Yet his reaction was hostile at the outset when his daughter, Leone, was courted by Edmund Saunders. At first, his Lordship told me, it was no more than instinct. He felt that something about the young man was not genuine. Secretly, he employed agents to explore Saunders' background. Their findings were that his claims of family connections and wealth were false, as were those of leading an honest life."

178

"The man was a criminal?"

"He was, and he demonstrated it in the extreme when, having been convinced by her father's evidence, Leone faced him with it and told him that their courtship was at an end. Her strangled body was found in a country lane shortly after."

"That is appalling. Was Saunders arrested?"

"Yes," Holmes said thoughtfully. "Lestrade went to Norfolk to investigate and make the arrest, only to find that there was no substantial evidence. Saunders had friends who swore that he was in their company at the time the murder was said to have taken place. Scotland Yard could discover no proof, and that was when Lord Trentlemere called me in. Much to my everlasting regret, I could offer no assistance. Saunders is one of the most careful and vicious villains I have come across. Both his Lordship and I were convinced of tje man's guilt. Indeed, he all but admitted it with his insults and taunts, but nothing that would stand up in a courtroom ever came to light. Since then, Saunders has been suspected of several robberies and another murder, but still he has escaped the net."

I shook my head. "Intelligence and evil are a combination forged in hell."

"As you say, Watson. For a time, Lord Trentlemere was a broken man, but the flame of revenge burned within him. He swore that Saunders would hang, and devoted himself to bringing this about. Paid agents, and his Lordship himself, buried themselves in an intense examination of Saunders' life, with the object of discovering any incriminating aspect. Until now this has met with no success, though Lord Trentlemere occasionally receives anonymous and taunting letters, as do I, to ensure that we do not forget Saunders' triumphs over the law."

"This is monstrous, Holmes!"

"I am sure his Lordship would agree with you. However, it seems that he has accomplished his purpose, and wishes me to verify it. I can only hope that, as the letter says, there is no mistake."

"So you will go to Norfolk. Doubtlessly, Lestrade will accompany you?"

Holmes shook his head. "Lestrade is away on a case in Brighton."

"Then, if you will have me, I will take his place."

"Watson, you are exhausted. You must rest."

"I will wash my face in cold water," I said as I stood up, "and put on a clean collar. After that, I am at your disposal."

As I made my way to my room, Holmes was already reaching for his Bradshaw.

It had begun to rain heavily as we left Baker Street. Now, as our train steamed from Liverpool Street Station into open countryside, the sky grew ever darker.

"Why do you suppose Lord Trentlemere's letter was written with such urgency, Holmes?" I asked. "After all, he has patiently studied Saunders' activities for several years."

He turned away from the window. "The phrase, *'there is little time'*, struck me at once. Probably he is ill, for his health was never good."

"One wonders then why he did not summon you by means of a telegram, which would have reached you more quickly."

"Lord Trentlemere has his peculiarities, like most men. He never sends telegrams because he believes there is a lack of privacy there. The telegraphist, you see, is aware of the contents even before the message is sent. Also, Lord Trentlemere's estate is some distance from the nearest Post Office."

I nodded my acknowledgement, and there was silence between us for a while. Sometime after mid-day, we made our way to the dining coach where an excellent steak-and-kidney pie was served, and on our return to our reserved smoker, the incessant beat of the wheels against the tracks quickly lulled me into sleep.

"How long have I slept, Holmes?" I asked as I awoke.

He stared through the window still, as if he had not moved since returning from our luncheon, at the driving rain and the near-darkness.

"Four hours and ten minutes. I trust you feel refreshed."

"Yes, but I must apologise. I have been poor company."

"You were in need of rest, and I have done much thinking during the time. The conductor called out a few minutes ago – in ten minutes we will arrive in Norwich."

As we approached the station, I caught a glimpse of the Foundry Bridge, which spans the River Wensum. The train slowed and came to a halt, and we stepped out to be confronted by the long red brick and stucco station building. People moved about in droves, shaking soaked umbrellas and huddled in rain-capes as they found shelter beneath the ironwork and glass concourse.

Holmes stopped to study a timetable affixed to the waiting room wall.

"This way, Watson," he said after a moment. "We must catch the local train to Queen's Mount."

180

We purchased further tickets and were soon settled in a much smaller train that rattled away down a branch line in response to a quick whistle-blast. The darkness was total now, and the rain more fierce than ever.

"What station are we bound for, Holmes?" I asked my friend.

He produced his tobacco pouch and his old briar, which he began to fill. "Little Tensdale is the nearest to Lord Trentlemere's estate, if my memory serves me well. It is no more than five miles distant."

Indeed, Holmes had only just finished his pipe and I a cigarette before we alighted at a small country station. A single gas lamp shone above the door of the station master's office where two men, one in uniform, stood deep in conversation.

As we approached, the train belched out a cloud of steam before setting off backwards in the direction of its arrival.

"Good evening," Holmes began. "Would you be kind enough to tell me where we can hire a trap?"

The station master straightened his uniform jacket, and they both turned to face us. "Not here, at this time of night, sir. Where was it you were wanting to go?"

"We are heading for Lord Trentlemere's estate, but if there is no transportation available perhaps you could direct us to a hotel?"

The station master rubbed his unshaven jaw. "The Fox and Feather should be able to put you up for the night. It is, I would say, no more than half-a-mile from here. What d'you say, Tom?"

The other man knocked out his pipe and smiled. "I think we can do these gentlemen better. I have to pass the estate on my way home to Little Tensdale, and I can let them off by the side entrance. That is, if they don't mind getting wet in an open cart?"

Holmes assured him that we did not, whereupon he produced and put on a seaman's oilskin and led us to on overhanging clump of trees opposite the station. The horse tethered beneath stamped his hooves as if impatient to be away, and Holmes and I scrambled into the cart. Tom climbed aboard, glanced back once and, seemingly satisfied that we were adequately seated, shook the reins. The horse acknowledged the signal at once, and we set off at a brisk pace. Holmes and I wrapped our coats tightly around us, and pulled our hats further down onto our heads.

In a short while, we found ourselves on a dark and uneven country track, with the sinister shapes of bare trees on either side. In the distance, a rumble of thunder warned of worse weather to come. I was able to make out the beginnings of a tall fence to our left, which

181

continued until Tom drew the cart to a halt. "There it is, sirs. You see the gap in the fence? If you go through there, there's a field to cross and then a bridge over the stream. After that, you climb the hill and you're in front of Trentlemere Hall. The only other way, from here, is to the far right along the edge of the forest. There's a stile, but it's a treacherous path."

We jumped down from the cart. Tom touched his cap and thanked Holmes for the coins that were pushed into his hand. He wished us well and continued on his way. No more than a few moments passed before he was lost in the darkness, with the sound of the horse's hooves growing steadily fainter. After passing through the fence, we could see, faintly, that a narrow path had been worn across the sodden field. Gusts of wind blew the long grass against our legs like whips, but we both wore stout walking boots and were able to make our way forward.

"Stay close to me, Watson," Holmes said, "in this darkness we could lose our way, or each other."

Certainly there was not the faintest light to be seen, and any attempt to use a dark lantern would have been immediately foiled by the wind. Tom had indicated that a straight course would take us to the bridge, and we endeavoured not to waver and trudged on for perhaps half-an-hour. Finally, we reached a great oak, and we could see a darker line among the blackness which we took to be the first trees of the forest.

"There!" my friend exclaimed, and at the same moment I heard the roaring of the swollen stream.

I followed Holmes to where the land began to rise, just ahead. It was then that something fantastical, something which I have never been able to explain satisfactorily, even to myself, occurred!

Another clap of thunder was followed by a streak of lightening which lit up everything around us. Holmes had stridden a little ahead of me, and between us a man appeared with his arms held up in warning. I had but a momentary glimpse of him, and he was gone.

"Holmes!" I cried. "Stop at once!"

My friend obeyed, and in the darkness I fancied he smiled. "How did you know, Watson?"

"Know what, pray?"

"Look before you."

I leaned to glance ahead. Another step would have taken us into the dark chasm left by the shattered bridge. The waters had risen to the extent that part of the structure had been carried away, while the remainder hung precariously from the opposite bank. The stream had become a raging torrent.

"How did you know?" Holmes repeated.

"A man came out of the darkness and warned us. You must have seen him."

"I saw no one. Yet the warning was a timely one. Where is he now?"

I looked all around us. "In this weather, and without light, I cannot tell."

"The nearest hiding-place is the oak we passed, and that is too far away. Could you have imagined our benefactor?"

"I think not. He was so near, I could have touched him."

Holmes touched my shoulder, indicating that I should squat down. I did so and he did the same, forming a shelter between us for the vesta that he produced from his coat. In its flare, I saw my friend's puzzled expression, and I became similarly mystified as I realised his intention. He moved the flame over and around the patch of mud where the man had stood. There was no impression, no footprints – the surface was completely unmarked. He shook the vesta out, and I sensed that he looked at me critically.

"Doubtlessly it was the lightning, old fellow. It is easy to see what is not there, when the eyes are confused by such a brilliant flash."

"But Holmes, I could have sworn!"

"A hallucination, nothing more. I am told they can be very convincing."

"I suppose it must have been," I said, feeling rather foolish.

He stood so close, that I felt his body turn to our right. "Now we must proceed along the edge of the forest. You will recall that Tom mentioned that it is an alternative route."

As we moved towards the trees, the cloud cleared, allowing a shaft of moonlight to pierce the darkness and aid our progress. The ground was uneven in places, and we sometimes stumbled as the downpour, a little lessened now, beat against us.

"I see it," said Holmes, after we had travelled about half-a-mile. "The stile is beyond that bent pine."

This proved to be the case, and we entered the forest at that point. At once we found ourselves in a place of silence, a quiet that was broken only by the rain dripping from the branches. Moonlight shone onto the forest floor in patches where the branches above grew less thickly, lending a spectral glow to every clearing.

183

"Tread carefully," my friend advised, "there are thick roots underfoot."

And so we continued, endeavouring to maintain a straight course to emerge within sight of Trentlemere Hall. We trod through saturated leaves and gnarled twigs for a while, before approaching a fork in the path.

Holmes stood still, his thin figure barely visible, deciding which direction we should pursue. Then to my absolute amazement, I saw the vision of the man that I had imagined earlier appear again before us. He stood in a pool of moonlight, pointing along the right fork and meeting my astonished gaze with a stern stare. He vanished in an instant and this time I said nothing, for fear that Holmes would begin to doubt my sanity. I had thought that he had seen nothing, but as always, he had seen more than I.

"It was a moonlit shadow, Watson, nothing more. The patch of light amid this dense darkness causes our eyes to play us false. Come, old fellow, let us take the right fork, for that seems to me the most likely way out of here. Take care!"

I was greatly relieved that I was spared an argument with Holmes, for the apparition had saved us before and for some reason I felt it would not have failed to do so again. A few minutes later, an overhead thunderclap preceded a sudden lightning strike which immediately brought down a heavy branch. In the poor light I could see that it was large enough to have crushed us, and that it had fallen upon the left fork where we had stood a few minutes before.

"We seem to have had our share of luck this evening," was his only comment.

Nor was that the end of the strangeness of that night. Careful to return to the same course, we avoided several thick groups of trees that proved impassable. This took us some time, but on emerging, I saw that the trees ahead were thinning, and that the night sky was visible a short distance beyond.

Once more, the apparition stood in our path, holding up a hand and pointing to the flooded earth with the other. Holmes made no sign that he had seen anything out of the ordinary, but he too, studied the forest floor.

"We have seen this before, Watson," he said. "Remember the lair of Stapleton, on Dartmoor?"

With that he lifted a thick, dead branch from among the fallen leaves and hurled it before us. It was then that I realised that what I had taken for a clearing ahead was a concealed patch of mud or

184

swamp, for the branch lay on the moss-covered surface for but a moment and then was sucked down out of our sight.

"Good heavens, Holmes!" I exclaimed. "If we had tried to cross that, we would have vanished without trace."

"Most likely, but the sheen on the surface looked unnatural, even in this sparse moonlight. It was then that I remembered our previous experience."

We retraced our steps, testing to ensure that the ground was firm until we found a place where a change of direction was possible. It was a wide detour, for the black and dangerous patch was spread over a greater area than we at first thought. Moonlight faded and returned several times, and the denseness of the trees and the blackness proved formidable, but at last we left the forest behind and emerged into an open field.

Before us was the stream, but narrower here and running with much less fury. The bridge was built higher than that we encountered earlier, resting on piled wooden trestles that had probably saved it from destruction. The rain had dwindled considerably, as we made our way up the gradual incline leading to the unfamiliar shape of Trentlemere Hall.

As we approached, I noticed that several downstairs rooms were lit, and one above. We found ourselves at the rear of the house and followed the terrace to the front, where a wide drive led away into the darkness to meet with the road.

We stood saturated before a wide iron-studded door, and Holmes knocked loudly. Footsteps echoed inside, getting louder, and the door creaked open.

A black-clad butler faced us, his expression solemn. "Good evening, gentlemen."

"I am Sherlock Holmes, and this is my associate, Doctor Watson. We received a summons, in London, from Lord Trentlemere."

The butler bowed his head. "I am aware of that sir. Come in, please."

We were shown into a pleasant drawing-room, with drawn curtains and a roaring fire, for which we were most thankful. The butler left us, taking our soaked hats and coats and assuring us that Lord Trentlemere would be with us shortly.

As we warmed ourselves, Holmes pointed above the hearth at the heavily-framed portrait above.

"That is Lord Trentlemere," he remarked, "as I remember him. The likeness is excellent."

A moment later we were joined by a young man of no more than twenty-five. Who announced himself as Lord Trentlemere. I saw surprise cross Holmes's face.

"You were expecting my father, of course," the young man said. "I regret to inform you of his death, early this morning. He is free of pain now, and reunited with my mother."

We expressed our condolences. For a while we talked, sitting in comfortable armchairs and drinking brandy, about Holmes's previous association with the Trentlemere estate.

"My father left instructions regarding the documents concerning the murderer of my sister," the young man said during a lapse in the conversation. "He was most explicit, and satisfied at last that his years of study had not been in vain." "Do you know the nature of his evidence?" Holmes enquired.

"No, but I can tell you that it has been examined by more than one group of solicitors, and that we have received assurances that it is valid and legally binding. My father said that you, Mr. Holmes, would know how it should best be used."

"Indeed. The documents will be in the hands of Scotland Yard upon our return to London tomorrow."

The young man smiled for the first time. "Excellent. I can see that my father's trust was not misplaced. And now, gentlemen, there is a meal and a room prepared for you. I expect you will wish to retire, after an arduous journey."

We rose and followed the new Lord Trentlemere out of the room. At the doorway, I looked back at the portrait above the hearth, at the face of the man with the eye patch and drooping moustache. The face of the apparition that had warned us thrice this night of calamities that lay ahead.

My friend glanced at me as if he had read my mind, and I wondered as to what his cold and logical brain had made of the strange events that had occurred during our journey.

I would learn nothing if I enquired, for in Holmes's view of life, everything has a normal explanation.

Until now, that had been my view also.

The Ghost of
Otis Maunder
by David Friend

Since several of the most stimulating cases investigated by my friend Mr. Sherlock Holmes first became a matter of public record, my own name has become better known than any provincial medical practitioner may reasonably deserve. Although, with some justification, it is Holmes who has remained the keen focus of attention, I have had occasion myself to be greeted enthusiastically by followers of his exploits. These instances, of course, do not present themselves when such good people see my face but when they recognize my name. Although not troublesome in itself, this does become a bother when they are also patients and insist on asking questions of my famous friend, instead of allowing me to minister to them.

The instance of which I shall record occurred one cold November day in 1896. Sherlock Holmes was back in the country after a five-week, cross-continental case involving his former nemesis Brigadier Horrigan and the Nostradamus legacy and I had not yet welcomed him home. I was instead serving as a *locum*, undertaking my duties as I had for several weeks. The fog was swirling languidly without and pressed against the windows as though it wanted to come in and join me. I wanted dearly to return to the hearth and read *An Outcast of the Islands*, but considering the number of patients waiting in the hallway, it seemed I would be occupied for some time.

"I had not the devilish notion just where she was stepping out each night."

"Raise your arm, please, Mr. Bickerstaff," I asked politely. The old man was too distracted by his own words to detect my weariness.

He lifted his left arm mechanically, but did not cease his chatter. "Just why, I asked myself, was the blessed Effie visiting the house next door?"

"Er . . . your other arm, Mr. Bickerstaff. The arm you are so concerned about."

My patient managed to obey the instruction, but continued nonetheless. "And as I read on – with still no answer of my own and worrying for poor Mr. Grant Munro – your clever friend Mr. Holmes

187

had sorted it as well as always." He shook his head with awe, his white curls shaking with the motion.

"Perhaps you can bend your elbow for me," I requested.

"It was Effie's first husband in the house, you see." He began to lift up the wrong arm again, but I stopped him. "She had been married once before to an African-American lawyer named John Hebron."

"Mr. Bickerstaff, I urge you to concentrate." There was pleading in my voice now.

"They had a daughter together named Lucy, you see. It's believed he had died of Yellow Fever."

I returned behind the desk and sat down heavily with a sigh. "Mr. Bickerstaff, you are aware I was with Holmes at the time? And I understood the situation comprehensively enough to write it all down?" I looked at him squarely. "Which is the only way *you* know about it."

Mr. Bickerstaff stared at me for a long moment. I truly believed he was now grasping the point. "It was the daughter's face Mr. Munro had seen in the window!"

Even war does not prepare a man for such things.

"Am I right in saying, Mr. Bickerstaff," I said, trying to remain unflustered, "that you have no real ailment to speak of? That the only reason you have visited today is to discuss the remembrances of my friend, Mr. Holmes?"

My patient suddenly looked quite awkward and I decided I had heard enough.

I marched out of the room and found over two dozen men and women waiting without. I had never seen the place so occupied. I turned to face them all with a grim and, I thought, forthright countenance.

"Can everyone here who does *not* wish to consult me for genuine medical purposes but instead to discuss Sherlock Holmes please leave?"

For a moment, nobody moved, and I felt a flicker of relief. Perhaps I had misjudged the situation and this was to be a regular day at the practice after all. Then, in one fluid movement, my supposed patients suddenly arose from their seats and began heading for the doors. There were so many, and so close, that their bodies ploughed determinedly into mine and I felt myself being pushed back and rendered off-balance.

The doors shut behind them and I was left in an empty waiting room. I sighed deeply, trying to rid myself of the annoyances of the day. Then the consulting room door opened and I realised one of them still remained.

"You see, Effie had hidden the girl because she though thought – "

"Mr. Bickerstaff!" I yelled.

Without giving him another moment to respond, or to explain anymore of the retched case, I took the little man by the shoulder and frog-marched him to the door. Slamming it closed after him was the most satisfying thing I had done all day.

I was heading back to collect my coat when I bumped into Mrs. Agnew. She was a short, elderly woman with a permanently knotted brow.

"Mrs. Agnew," I said lamentably, "it's been an absolute fifteen puzzle here this morning. If I screw my eyes shut and think hard, I can almost remember when this was a normal practice and the patients wanted nothing more than medical advice. Now, all they do is press me for news about Holmes. Has he had any baffling cases recently? Can I speak about them? When will there be another account?"

I would never describe Mrs. Agnew as a sympathetic person, even if she did spend her days around the sick and infirm, and she was typically indifferent now. "Can these people not simply visit Mr. Holmes himself?"

"I thought so, too," I agreed. "He told our landlady to keep them away. One man kept pestering him to find his missing cat and began knocking on the door at all hours of the day and night."

The old lady could not have looked more cross if she had been harassed herself. "What did Mr. Holmes do?"

I smiled with dark humour. "Holmes poked his head out of the window and catapulted the fellow with a stone."

Mrs. Agnew seemed to think this was a sensible idea, so I elected to leave before she suggested I try it myself. With no other patient waiting to consult me, a free afternoon clearly beckoned. I felt weary, as though I had already worked a whole day. Despite my friend indirectly causing such interruptions to my professional duties, I decided to return to him at Baker Street.

With a slow and leisurely gait, I set off in that direction. I began passing Georgian houses and hansom cabs patiently waiting for customers. The mentioning of a previous case by Mr. Bickerstaff brought to my mind many others. I wondered about my friend's former clients: Mr. Jabez Wilson, the red-headed pawnbroker, and the strange circumstances involving the *Encyclopædia Britannica*;

Miss Mary Sutherland and her suitor, and Mr. Victor Hatherley and his thumb. I realised, poignantly, that neither Holmes nor I had ever encountered such clients again. He helped them at the time and they, satisfied, returned to their lives, melting back into the millions that made up our metropolis. How they lived or what they then did was as much of a mystery as the ones they had presented to Holmes in the first place.

Such nostalgia, however, would be entirely alien to my friend. Rarely had he made known his memories. The ones he had conveyed were inevitably bound up in another adventure. Clients to him, I fancied, were merely vessels bringing to him a perplexing problem. In his own small way, he cared for them, in that he was happy to end their distress, and certainly endeavoured to save their lives, but foremost of all was the case itself. It was a way in which he could marshal his motor signals. The moment the case was solved, the client was of no further use to him, and he looked with impatience to the next.

As I perambulated down Baker Street, I believed only companionable silences and the occasional quiet conversation where to follow. However, when I reached the door, it jutted open suddenly and I found my friend standing framed on the threshold. He was wearing his top hat and frock coat and clutching his cane. He did not even cast me a glance as he stepped purposefully forward.

"Quickly, Watson!" he cried.

He gestured urgently to a dog-cart across the street and it lumbered over to us. Holmes jumped smoothly aboard.

"What is all this?" I asked, bewildered, as I dropped down beside him.

Still, Holmes didn't look at me. He was studying his pocket-watch with beetled brows. "I have had a cable from Inspector Bradstreet," he said. He looked about him, searching for shorter routes to whatever destination he was so keen to reach. "Nothing interests me less than the news of an arrested murderer, Watson. By definition, all mystery has withered to nought. However, this matter is unprecedented. I dare say you remember Miss Violet Hunter and how her position as a governess in Winchester brought her some considerable concern."

"Yes!" I exclaimed. My mind swivelled back ten years. "Her employer, Mr. Runcastle, forced her to resemble his daughter, Alice, as he had locked – "

"Watson, I share full knowledge of the case in question. I did, after all, solve it myself."

190

I realised, with a wince, that I had repeated Mr. Bickerstaff's mistake from earlier that afternoon. "But what of it?" I said, desperate to understand. "What is going on?"

Holmes's face tightened, his head hung low. "I am afraid," said Holmes, "that Miss Hunter has been arrested for murder."

"What in the –?"

"Horace!" he barked at the cabbie, who swerved to a hasty halt outside the police station.

Holmes leapt out. He headed for the entrance, his strides long and loping. With a firm push, the doors swept open and he entered the foyer. I finally reached him and can bear witness to the fierce look in his cold-grey eyes.

A wiry young man was moving swiftly past in a curious half-run, his arms hung still and his feet like those of a duck paddling through water.

"Constable Cook!"

The man stopped and turned. "Mr. Holmes!"

My friend stepped closer and I noticed he was keeping a tight grip on his cane. "I must see Inspector Bradstreet at once," he said seriously. "It is a matter of great importance."

The constable led us through to a small, cramped room on the west side of the building. Inspector Bradstreet was hunkered over a desk, his not inconsiderable weight pressed hard against the wood as though it were trying to push it away. I had not seen him since the business of Sir Thaddeus Fowler and the Onandaga treasure, though I knew he had solicited Holmes's help on several subsequent occasions, not least with the business of the Hangleton Witch. He lifted his large, bearded head and looked at us in surprise.

"Inspector," said Holmes, as Cook took his place beside the door. "I would appreciate it if you could furnish us with the facts." He didn't take a seat, nor did he take off his hat.

Inspector Bradstreet's brows were raised so high they were almost obscured by his hairline. I observed in him a faint air of triumph, as though he were pleased to have solved a case without the help of London's famous consulting detective. But Holmes had not come here to give his congratulations, however much Bradstreet would have liked him to.

"Mr. Holmes, I am sure you can understand that this case is now closed."

There was a rickety chair opposite and, without a glance, Holmes seated himself on its edge. "It is about to be open again," he said quietly. "Why have you arrested Miss Violet Hunter?"

191

His stare was absolute and seemed to displease the Yard man.

"The same reason we arrest anyone," was the terse reply. "Because she's guilty."

Holmes leant back. "You belong in the music hall!" he said bitterly.

"Holmes!" I admonished.

Constable Cook, I noticed, had taken out his notebook and had begun scribbling furiously.

"Don't write any of this, Cook!" said Bradstreet impatiently. He turned back to Holmes with an awkward look. "The constable here is recording some of my cases," he explained. "Much as Dr. Watson has with yours." He sounded guilty and looked suddenly embarrassed. I wondered if Holmes would feature at all in the chronicles of the cases they had shared.

My friend looked as though he was about to emit a derisive laugh and I spoke quickly to stop him. "We would like to see Miss Hunter," I said, my voice firm.

The inspector looked irritated. "You will be wasting everyone's time," he warned. "As I said, the case is closed. But, by all means, cause yourselves embarrassment. It would make an amusing addition to my memoirs."

Constable Cook led us on another journey across the police station, during which I caught glimpses of other associates from cases past, all crooked over desks, including Inspector Patterson, Inspector Gregory, and Constable Pollock. We finished up in the cells, and Cook revealed to us Miss Violet Hunter.

She had been sitting on a bench and had risen at the tinkle of keys. Her appearance was much the same as it had been years earlier, when Holmes had rescued her from the sadistic Mr. Jephro Rucastle. Her face was pale and lightly freckled, her hair still curled and auburn, while the only difference I could see was the look of frozen horror in her eyes which I suspected she had held for some time.

"Mr. Holmes!"

She stepped widely towards us, relief spread across her face.

Holmes moved to the bench and sat down as though he himself was now a prisoner. "Miss Hunter," he said earnestly, "if we are to help you, you must tell us all."

Miss Hunter was still registering the surprise of our arrival. She lifted a hand and rubbed her temple, clearly trying to focus. "It is such a shock to see you," she said quietly. She quickly marshalled and slowly began pacing the cell. Within moments, she was telling her tale.

"My life has recently become one of change," she said. "I became betrothed last summer to a young man named Mr. Marcus Housley, an Alderman in Penshurst. I have become a schoolteacher since I last saw you and have also been a headmistress. A few weeks ago, I received a letter. The headmaster of an independent school, a Mr. Otis Maunder, was retiring and had recommended me as his successor. Well, I could scarcely believe it." She shook her head, still apparently bemused. "Not only was it strange to receive such a letter without warning, but I had never met this gentleman. However, I knew better than to disregard such an offer and accepted it gladly. I went there and started work. The name of my predecessor, however, kept returning to me, and queerly, I began to feel as though I had heard it before.

"I spent the first Friday unpacking my belongings in my office. In one of the drawers of this desk, I found lots of old photographs, mainly of the school through the years. There was only one portrait, a framed photograph covered in dust. In it was a man I supposed was Mr. Maunder. It must have been from long ago, as he looked to be in his late thirties, with thinning dark hair combed briskly to the left and a cool, absent stare, as though he wasn't aware he was standing for his likeness at all. I thought again of his name, and it seemed to tug at something at the back of my mind.

"Then I remembered. My late father, Pheaphilus, had mentioned him quite frequently at one time. They and two others had set up the Sevenoaks Secretarial College for Gentlewomen. If I remembered rightly, it came to light that Mr. Maunder had embezzled funds. However, instead of informing the police, my father and his friends were lenient and agreed that Mr. Maunder should simply leave the firm. I remember Father being disappointed, but apart from that, it is all I recall about the affair.

"I finished sorting and my new secretary, Mrs. Burton, appeared. She is quite a gentle lady, with a grey bun and an open, pleasant face. I wanted to ask about Mr. Maunder. It still troubled me why he would recommend me for such a position. Perhaps, I considered, he was grateful to my father for not telling the police of what he had done.

"Mrs. Burton told me how he had departed from the school quite quickly, leaving only a hasty recommendation for his successor, and had died soon after from heart failure. I asked what she knew, if anything, of the secretarial college and, at the very mention of it, the old lady's face turned sour. She said she didn't know the particulars, just that he had been forced to leave, and had

193

always been bitter and furious because of it. Whenever the girls at the school expressed an interest in proceeding to that college, Mr. Maunder virtually forbade it. He said the people there had done him a great disservice and he would never forgive them. He would, apparently, tremble with the rage it brought him."

"That night, I continued with work far into the evening. It had turned quite cold and I tested the fire. Then, as I often did while a governess elsewhere, I took a walk around the grounds. The moon was out, and though dimmed by clouds, I could clearly make out the lake. I moved towards it, breathing in that brand of evening air which is so fresh and chilled that you can taste it. All I could hear was silence. With the school behind me, I could only see woods and country ahead. I looked towards the lake, a couple of yards distant, and saw how it stretched far and deep into darkness. And that was when I noticed something.

"A curious shape seemed to have formed and was slinking slowly across the water. It was a good way out from the edge, not at all near the shallow part, and at first I had to strain my eyes. It was a man, I could tell, but his footfalls were firm upon the water. How in the world was he doing it? My heart began to race. As he moved closer, I recognized his face. It was the young Mr. Maunder, just as he had been in the photograph. My throat was suddenly dry, and I couldn't even muster the energy to scream.

"'Avenge me!' wailed this impossible spectre. 'Avenge me!'

"Breathless, I span around and dashed back in the direction of the school. I was breathing heavily, even hoarsely, as I stamped across the grounds, and my feet were hurting like never before. I found my way inside and didn't stop until I had reached my office and shut the door. For a reason I didn't even register, I turned the key in the lock and stood as far away from it as possible. There, in the darkness of the office – a room which didn't look at all familiar anymore – I cowered. Shivering with fright, I turned away, my eyes falling to the desk and the photograph of Mr. Maunder. Quite witless, I took it from its frame, tore it in two and threw it into the fire.

"I needn't add that I barely slept that night. Even on the morrow, the memory of whatever it was I had seen haunted me still. I felt compelled to tell someone, and so I told Mrs. Burton. The old lady humoured me, of course, telling me it was the excitement and nerves of starting in a new position. But I knew what I had seen. I think myself practical, Mr. Holmes, and it was in such manner that I set about researching Mr. Otis Maunder. I searched in various books

194

and documents and asked others too. I learned how he had become headmaster in the late '60s after leaving the college he had set up with my father and two men named Edwin Luckett and Nathaniel Farley. Both men lived in the nearby village of Riverhead. I heard again that Mr. Maunder had never forgiven any of them, and that while they had become rich and successful, he had become progressively miserable until he recently resigned.

"In looking for papers which could help me in my quest, I happened upon a letter. I am not of a mind to pry into other people's correspondences, Mr. Holmes, but I read the first line almost accidentally and I confess its bluntness gripped me. I remember it vividly:

I sense there are spirits here in this house. Nobody may believe me, but it is what I know to be true. In the dark of night, when the world is otherwise silent, I can hear noises. I wander and hope to find them. Alas, I have not yet, but I shall one day and I dread it. I even consider leaving here and escaping once and for all. But something makes me stay. A sort of indescribable hold.

"Naturally, I was staggered. The handwriting was rough, as though the person writing it was scared."

"Was there an address?" asked Holmes. He had remained sitting, his head tilted back against the bars, his eyes closed.

"No. It appeared to be unfinished."

"Proceed."

"Well, it frightened me even more. I felt like he had led me to this letter, to prove to me that what I had seen was real. I was desperate to speak to those who had known him. It so occurred to me that I should find his former associates – presumably, the people his ghost wanted me to avenge. I took a trap to Riverhead and saw Mr. Luckett and Mr. Farley wandering the village. I wondered what I could say. Part of me wanted to tell them what I had seen, but I was worried they would consider me mad. I was still undecided when a policeman passed.

"'You want to speak to those men?' he asked curiously.

"'I mustn't,' I said. 'What I have to say would only scare them.'

"And so I returned to the school. I decided that I must now forget what I had seen. I was still trying to do this, some days later, when the police arrived. They began questioning me immediately. In

195

Riverhead, they said, two middle-aged men had been stabbed to death in their houses. Their corpses had been covered in violets."

I jerked back a step in surprise. "Violets?" I repeated. I looked at Holmes, but he did not seem the remotest surprised.

"They had been picked from the surrounding gardens," Miss Hunter explained. "As no violets could now be found in any garden at that end of the village, they believed I was responsible – that a clue had been deliberately left as a twisted joke. The killer was a violet hunter, and I am a Violet Hunter. The police discovered that I had been asking about both men, had traced them to Riverend, and had watched them. One of their own constables was a witness! They also spoke to Mrs. Burton, who told them how convinced I was that I had seen the ghost of Otis Maunder. They believe me insane, Mr. Holmes, and want me to hang!"

As she finished, Miss Hunter and I turned to Holmes expectantly. He remained still. If he had been anyone else, I would have assumed he had fallen asleep. But then, his eyes blazed open and he sprang to his feet. He moved to the door of the cell, about to leave, then whirled suddenly around like a sequined cobra.

"Miss Hunter," he said quietly. "I cannot promise you anything."

It occurred to me, as we left the cells and the eerie silence of those within them, just how little we knew about Miss Violet Hunter and whether, as a medical man, I could vouch for her mental stability. Perhaps, I considered, her experience at the Copper Beeches had affected her more than we had realised.

I met Holmes in the corridor, his long loping legs having conveyed him there faster, and gave voice to my concerns.

He pondered a moment. "It is true that some cases may take their toll on those with a weaker constitution than others," he accepted. "Your old friend Mr. Percy Phelps, for example, was a man in deep distress."

"Yes," I said, nodding at the memory. "He doesn't work for the government anymore, apparently. The pressure didn't sit well with him."

Holmes sniffed. "As I recall, it wasn't his personal qualities which afforded him the position in the first place."

"Do you suppose that the matter at the Copper Beeches could have affected Miss Hunter's mental health? Years later?"

Holmes paused again, his brow furrowed. Then his eyes seemed to spark and, turning on his heel, he headed off down the corridor.

I tried my best to catch up. "Where are we going?"

196

"The Yard's forensic alienest."

Ten minutes later and two floors above, Holmes and I entered a dimly-lit room. It was lined with bookshelves with small, curtained windows, and a narrow desk in the corner. A short man was seated behind it. Dr. Marcellus Chappell had a wide, domed forehead and a bushy Van Dyke beard, rather like Carl Zeller. The hair on the back of his head was brushed up untidily, as though he wanted to remind people that he had at least some of it left.

"My name is Sherlock Holmes and this is my friend and col – "

"Ah," said Dr. Chappell in surprise and let out a hand for my friend to shake. "It is good to meet you, Mr. Holmes." He stared at my friend and hadn't, it seemed, even seen me.

I coughed lightly. "And I'm Dr. Wat – "

"I have enjoyed reading your observations, Mr. Holmes," the alienist interrupted.

Holmes smiled thinly and I could tell he was greatly pleased.

"I shall be writing another soon," I promised.

Dr. Chappell turned to me for the first time with a frozen expression. "Excuse me, but I was referring to Mr. Holmes's monograph on enigmatic writing." He looked at Holmes. "Who is this?" he asked bluntly.

Holmes made no effort to disguise his amusement. "This is my friend, Dr. Watson," he said. "He has written up some of my exploits for an undiscerning public."

Dr. Chappell nodded cautiously. "I am unfamiliar with such work," he said.

Holmes looked even more delighted. I expected him to substitute my friendship for that of this other doctor at any moment.

"What can you tell us about Miss Violet Hunter?" I asked the alienist testily.

Dr. Chappell's eyes widened at the remembrance of our curious client.

"I concluded that Miss Hunter is mad," he said candidly. "She has convinced herself that she had seen Mr. Maunder's ghost. She may even believe that it was possessing her. As I see it, Miss Hunter was suffering from guilt."

"Guilt?" I echoed. "Why must she feel guilty?"

Dr. Chappell continued as though I had not said a word. "We have spoken extensively about her experiences," he said, looking at Holmes. "I understand her father and Mr. Maunder, among others, had founded a college together, but Mr. Maunder had been forced to resign. It would seem he was willing to forgive her father and, as a

197

symbol of this, he recommended Miss Hunter to succeed him as head-teacher. She felt she could return this favour by punishing those who had wronged him."

"But that would be . . . ." Any word I considered seemed somehow inadequate. "Don't you think?" I added, omitting the word entirely.

Dr. Chappell, nevertheless, seemed to understand. "Miss Hunter is clearly unwell," he reminded us. "This was hardly the action of a sound mind."

I could see the doctor's reasoning, but somehow did not want to accept it. I seized upon the question of the violets.

Dr. Chappell tilted his head ponderously as though he was only now considering the matter. "I would suggest Miss Hunter's subconscious mind had selected the violets and left them on the bodies as a clue to her identity," he said. "It is not an unusual occurrence for the culprit to desire capture and therefore punishment for his crimes, particularly if there is a large degree of guilt involved, which there may be in this case, as Miss Hunter perhaps feels she has benefited from her predecessor's death."

"And the ghost?" I asked.

"A vivid dream," said Dr. Chappell dismissively. "They can often be confused with reality. If I recall, Miss Hunter believes she encountered the ghost at night time, which would make perfect sense."

"It would indeed," Holmes agreed. I had almost forgotten he was there. "Thank you for your time, Dr. Chappell."

"Not at all. I look forward to more of your monographs, Mr. Holmes."

Holmes's mouth curved into a smile.

We moved towards to the door, but then I paused. "Perhaps," I added hopefully, "you may like to read one of my accounts of Mr. Holmes's cases."

Dr. Chappell's eyes dimmed at the words. "I only read academic journals," he said blankly and returned to his work.

A short hour later, Holmes and I were taking a train from Charing Cross to Sevenoaks. Holmes was silent for much of the journey and stared blankly at the floor, as though there were not any sumptuously golden fields lying flat beyond the window. After a while, I too was seized by thoughts of that mysterious phantom striding across the lake. On reflection, that month, so suspiciously near to All Hallow's Eve, was a decidedly unnerving one, and would also see us contemplating the wrath of a Peruvian vampire.

The rest of the afternoon was spent visiting the school over which Miss Hunter had presided, and speaking with those who had known her. Mrs. Burton, her secretary, attested that Miss Hunter had confided in her about the alleged ghost. The old lady seemed quite shocked at the subsequent events, but was certain that her headmistress was unwell.

Holmes also managed to discover that another teacher, Mr. Lucian Devitt, was the only person who found Miss Hunter's presence at the school disagreeable. This was due to the fact that he had expected to inherit Mr. Maunder's position himself. We met him briefly in one of the many labyrinthine corridors, and he certainly seemed unconcerned about the circumstances in which his headmistress had now found herself. He was an astonishingly long-limbed man with jagged sideburns and flamboyant curls, though his stare alone made him worthy of note. It was cold and intense, his damnably blue eyes seemingly fixed so hard that nothing would pry them away. Thankfully, he became distracted when he recognized one of the boys – the school's most infamous practical joker, apparently – and began telling him off.

It became clear that we were to spend more than just a day in Sevenoaks, and Holmes suggested I find us accommodation for the night. I went to the village and settled upon The Ploughman's Inn. It was a quiet and comfortable place, and Holmes was to join me there that evening for a steak and ale pie. I waited for him at the bar and mulled over the ghost who walked on water.

In our time together, there had been moments when I'd had cause to question the rational outlook of my friend, not least during the Erasmus Brew case of 1889. Both as a doctor and a soldier, I had borne witness to occurrences which could not be explained by anyone but the churchman. I pictured what Miss Hunter had seen that night upon the water and I tried to adopt my friend's certainty.

A little after six o'clock, Holmes joined me. I noticed a gleam in his eyes which could only tell of success.

"I have had a most invigorating session at the school library," he said.

"Good to hear," I said between mouthfuls.

"Miss Hunter's father, Pheaphilus Hunter, was indeed in business with Otis Maunder, Nathaniel Farley, and Edwin Luckett," he said. "They were rather entrepreneurial men, having noticed the growing demand for female clerks and the need to equip them with the skills of shorthand and typing. Luckett had a friend, G. E. Clark, who had founded a secretarial college in Southgate Road, and

199

wanted to do the same here. So it was that the four men founded the Sevenoaks Secretarial College for Gentlewomen. They hoped it would emulate the success of Skerry's College, which provides young men with civil service training and has colleges all around the country. However, it soon became apparent that Maunder was embezzling funds and, just as Miss Hunter said, the other three men did not inform the police. This, by the way, is Maunder."

He had taken out a photograph and I examined it with interest. Mr. Otis Maunder had been stout and of medium height, with only a few forgotten hairs left on his head, and a downturned mouth which made him appear somewhat brusque.

Holmes was about to speak again when he noticed something through the window of the pub. "Ah!" he said. "Come, Watson." He leapt from his chair and threaded quickly through the inn's other customers. "This," he told me in a low voice as we made our way outside, "will be Ambrose, an odd-job man from Sturridge. I had the landlord summon him here to clean the windows quite urgently."

"Why would windows need to be cleaned urgently?" I asked.

"Because we won't be here for long, Watson, and this man is the son of Otis Maunder."

We turned a corner and approached a figure pressing a rag against one of the windows. He looked nothing like his father. Whereas the older Maunder had been paunchy, Ambrose was tall and lithe, his face thin with sucked-in cheeks, and a pencil moustache sat astride his mouth.

"Good evening," said my friend merrily. "We would like to speak with you about a young lady named Miss Violet Hunter."

The young man turned and eyed Holmes suspiciously. "I'm not talking about her," he said quietly. He seemed to grip the cloth harder and turned back to the glass. "I'm busy."

"If you insist," said Holmes, "Watson here will wash those windows for you."

I looked at my friend in surprise. "I will?"

"Most certainly," said Holmes, as though he himself was offering to help.

Ambrose paused reluctantly, but nodded to a bucket on the ground. I picked it up and stared into it with distaste. It was half filled with dirty water, with pieces of old moss and floating dead beetles. I shook my head resignedly, squeezed the cloth out and applied it firmly to the window.

"How do you feel about your father's – ah – *ghost* being seen?" Holmes asked the young man.

200

"It's not true," he said stonily. "It's a fairy tale. Margaret Oliphant nonsense."

"Have you considered asking Miss Hunter about it? I don't think you have visited her yet, have you?"

The young man's lips pulled back into a bitter grimace. "And I won't either," he said. "My father has been dead five months and now this mad woman is trying to start rumours. I won't have his memory upset like that."

Holmes nodded, as though none of this was unexpected. "Your father once embezzled funds from a company he ran with his friends."

I paused in my endeavours, shoulders sagging with disappointment. Holmes was capable of tenderness and tact, but exhibited it with astonishing inconsistency.

"I won't have his memory upset by you, either," Ambrose said harshly.

"We already know it to be true," Holmes pointed out. "I grieve to tell you that speaking ill of the dead is a necessity in my profession."

Ambrose seemed to consider for a moment. "He needed the money." He said it quickly, as though he had been bursting to support his father for a long time and was now finally able to. "But he always thought the other three should have given him a second chance. And I did too."

Holmes nodded, unsurprised. "One other matter, Mr. Maunder, to which I hope you will submit your attention." He fished a piece of paper from the inside pocket of his coat and presented it to the young man, who looked at it indifferently. "Is this your father's handwriting?" he asked.

Ambrose shifted, unsure. "It's been a long time," he said, "but I think so."

"Thank you," said Holmes. I glanced back at him and noticed his smile was less fleeting than usual. He was clearly pleased about something.

We returned indoors and found our table again.

"I didn't like to mention his mother's alcoholism," he volunteered before I could even ask. I looked at him incredulously. "The letter I showed him," he explained. "It is the one Miss Hunter found. It seemed to describe how his father thought there were spirits roaming the house at night, how he could hear them, how they frightened him, and how he was considering moving away just to be rid of them. Rather, of course, the letter wasn't about ghosts at all."

201

"What is it you mean?"

"His wife was addicted to drink," he said. "She swore to her husband that she was addicted no more, yet she hid these bottles of spirits in the house. He became suspicious and was determined to find them. She would drink them at night, coming downstairs and taking them from their secret hiding places, where they would tinkle and unknowingly disturb him upstairs. In his despair, Maunder even considered leaving her. The letter was written to his son, wherein he explained the situation, and the handwriting was shaky, as Maunder was upset. "

I was about to congratulate Holmes when I noticed his face twisting into a perplexed frown. "There's something else," I detected.

He nodded. "I cannot say here," he said, his eyes flitting fretfully about the snug.

We took the stairs to the first landing, each of our rooms in opposite directions. Holmes stood over the banister, his hands gripping it tightly as he spoke. "Otis Maunder," he said, "never forgave his former associates. He was resentful of his lost opportunity. The other three went on to become wealthy and Maunder did not. He was furious. Ambrose admits that he is too. No doubt the old man poisoned his mind. I believe that, before he died, Otis Maunder thought of a plan in which he could exact his revenge.

"Pheaphilus Hunter, of course, had since died, and so it was necessary to punish his daughter instead. He discovered that Miss Hunter was now a teacher and headmistress and was, as it happened, searching for a new position. Maunder retired and recommended Miss Hunter as his successor. He fully intended to carry out the rest of his plan, but died of heart failure before he was able to. I fancy that Ambrose knew of what his father was up to and decided to continue himself."

I stared at my friend keenly. "What was the plan?"

Holmes let go of the banisters and threw his hands up in the air as though admitting defeat. "It is a hypothesis which cannot work," he said. "I believed that it was Ambrose who Miss Hunter had seen that night. Just how he managed to walk on water, I do not yet know. But I was sure it had to be him." He smiled grimly. "But Ambrose looks nothing like his father. Even if he had stuffed a cushion up his shirt, he would still not have looked convincing. From the moment we learned this ghost was supposed to be Otis Maunder as a young man, I wondered why. Surely a ghost would look like a man at whatever age he died, not as he was in his prime? Alas, Ambrose

202

could not, I fancy, look like the photograph of his father which Miss Hunter had seen. His father carried too much weight. In other words, we still do not know what happened."

The following morning, we took a dogcart to the school, but Holmes elected not to trouble any of its staff again. Neither of us spoke for some time. I followed my friend through the grounds and noticed with concern how sombre he seemed. He moved briskly, the ground dipping slightly into a curve, and reached the lake.

"How, Watson? How?" he murmured as I joined him.

I was about to reply when he suddenly charged into the water, splashing like a mad seal until he finally halted, over two yards away. The water came up to his knees.

"There would have to be a platform of some sort," he speculated.

Again, I was about to answer him, when he jumped up and, in another splash, disappeared beneath the surface. There he remained for what felt like minutes, until I began feeling rather worried. I stared hard into the water but could not see through the murkiness. Something, I felt, was wrong. I stepped forward and was about to totter into the stillness myself when there was a sudden burst a mere foot away.

I smiled with relief as I watched Holmes, curled into a ball near the very edge of the lake, unfurl into a stand. Every inch of him appeared soaked. He clambered out, dripping onto the ground.

"Find anything?" I asked.

Holmes shook his head and water sprayed off his hair. "Nothing. Just blackness, mud, and moss."

He looked about him, his face tight with concentration. He was searching for something. I looked about me but could see nothing unusual. His eyes then widened and one side of his mouth twisted shyly into a smile. "Halloa!" he cried and sprang forwards into a run. He stopped some yards away, then bent down, picked something up, and held it aloft like a schoolboy who had just won a prize.

"A dead fish," I said upon seeing what it was. Holmes examined it minutely. "How do you suppose it got so far from the lake?" I asked. "I know they can leap out of a stream, but they couldn't get this far."

Holmes remained mute and I knew I would get no answers – at least, not yet.

"Come, Watson," he said finally. "We shall discover nothing more here."

He turned and, with surprising dignity, walked off, still dripping water wherever he went.

We returned to the Ploughman's Inn and he took the opportunity to change into dry clothes. I thought it likely that we would be staying for a few days and asked the landlord if the rooms were to remain available. It was typical of my friend, however, to suggest something completely contrary to my expectations. When he returned, I noticed a keen look of determination on his face.

"We must return to London," he announced.

And so it was that we met with Miss Hunter again. This time, we shared her cell with Inspector Bradstreet, who took prime position on the bench, and Constable Cook, who seemed again to be making a series of copious notes.

"How do you spell *aquiline*?" he asked me.

"I don't," I lied.

Holmes brushed a piece of fluff from his sleeve with a weak-fisted wave. He was set to begin. "It occurred to me, Miss Hunter," he said, "that we only ever had your confirmation that the man in the picture was indeed Otis Maunder."

Miss Violet Hunter looked shocked. "Mr. Holmes! Are you accusing me of lying?"

Holmes's expression almost mirrors hers. "Not in the least," he said. "I simply mean that you would not know what a young Otis Maunder looked like. The photographs in the drawer did not include any other. I am suggesting it was not the late Mr. Maunder in that picture at all."

Miss Hunter, Inspector Bradstreet, and Constable Cook all shared the same frown.

"Who could it have been?" she asked.

"His son, Ambrose," said Holmes. "I was always convinced it was he, though I could not reason just how he had managed it. But then it became clear. Instead of using a photograph of his father, of whom he looked nothing alike, he used a photograph of himself. He put it in an old frame, covered it with dust and planted it in the drawer. He wanted you to believe it was his father, and you did not question the implication for a moment."

Holmes gestured to me, clearly unwilling to continue his explanation himself.

"Ambrose," I said, remembering what Holmes had told me on the way back to the capital, "had his father's key to the school and every night he would steal into the office and check to see if the photograph had been moved. When he found it was missing, he knew it was time to put the rest of his plan into action. As an odd-job man, he does a little work in the grounds every now and then. He had seen you walking around the lake and learned that it was your custom to do so every night. Holmes and I have visited the lake. Now, if we remember, the end you saw is rather narrow at only two yards across, and the ground beside it is only an inch or two higher. There is also quite a curvature in the ground's formation, meaning that it can retain water when it rains and make a puddle."

"I believe," Holmes went on, "that soon before you ventured out for your walk, Miss Hunter, Ambrose came to the lake and filled a bucket with its water. He then poured it thickly across the ground and kept doing so until he had created a very large puddle, as Watson just indicated. It stretched out wide until it reached the edges of the lake itself. From a distance, the join between lake and puddle could not be discerned. To all purposes, the lake had been extended a little. Ambrose then positioned himself in the middle and waited.

"Soon after, you arrived, Miss Hunter. In the dim moonlight, with the barest hint showing from behind the clouds, you did not have the surest notion of where, precisely, you were standing. Neither did you realise that the lake was apparently nearer than usual. All you knew was that a figure was out on the lake and moving towards you. His feet, in fact, were touching the ground underfoot but, from all outward appearances, he was walking on water. To your startled eyes, Otis Maunder had returned as a ghost!

"Over the following few days, you learned of his life and death, and that his former associates Edwin Luckett and Nathaniel Farley lived in nearby Riverend. You even visited the place and saw them from afar, which not even Ambrose could have anticipated. He worked in many gardens, and had been in Riverend for a couple of weeks already. He collected together a bunch of violets. He then visited both of the men's houses and killed them, leaving the flowers on their corpses. He hoped the police would understand the message – and they did. The killer was apparently announcing himself as a violet hunter, and you are indeed a Violet Hunter."

Inspector Bradstreet's face had paled. He looked from Holmes to our client and back again. Constable Cook, meanwhile, struggled to keep speed with Holmes.

"They believed you were quite literally mad, leaving a cryptic clue as you avenged Otis Maunder. And with the questions and the spying and this talk of a ghost, it is no wonder they had you see an alienist."

Miss Hunter looked awed. "But we can understand your conviction," I added, at pains to sooth her. "I'm sure even Mr. Holmes himself would have been deceived."

"I wouldn't quite say that, Watson," said Holmes harshly.

"But Mr. Holmes," said Miss Hunter, "how do you know this?"

Holmes lifted a hand like a magician producing a pigeon. "You ripped the photograph in two and threw it into the fire. Considering your temper at the time, you were too distracted to tell if it had properly burned. I checked, and I was fortunate, for one piece had fallen behind the lumber." He took it from his pocket and revealed it to us. It was the upper half of the photograph and was clearly Ambrose, not his father.

Inspector Bradstreet looked sceptical. "What about the lake?"

"Upon inspection of the ground nearest to the lake, I found a small, dead fish. Ambrose had clearly scooped it in his bucket before pouring the water onto the ground. He was too rushed to notice it. I had visited Ambrose and had also seen pieces of moss in the bucket which I believe had also come from the lake. I tried to have Watson retrieve it, but he started washing windows instead."

Miss Hunter remained worried. "But how will the police stop believing it is me?"

"Rest assured," said Holmes, "I would wager that even the Inspector here will secure a confession from Ambrose Maunder. Leaving you, Miss Hunter, free to marry Mr. Marcus Housley and continue your career as a headmistress."

Miss Hunter's frown cleared as he said this. "Mr. Holmes," she said, "I cannot adequately thank you!"

Holmes opened the cell door and she sauntered happily out of it.

Cook followed us, frowning at his notes. "I don't think I've copied this down properly," he told me. "What's the fish got to do with anything?"

Inspector Bradstreet remained sitting on the bench, frowning at the wall and thinking over all he had heard. Holmes quietly closed the door of the cell, locking the oblivious inspector inside. My friend looked at me with a mischievous smile and a finger raised in silence and I said nothing as we moved away.

"*Now* the case is closed, Inspector!" called Holmes, and I could hear the man's guttural cry of indignation as we left.

The Adventure of the
Pharaoh's Tablet
by Robert Perret

Left to his own devices, my friend Sherlock Holmes would hardly set foot outside of Baker Street, preferring that the cases which provide his livelihood be brought before him, rather than requiring him to venture out. His sustenance would come from Mrs. Hudson, his chemical supplies brokered by telegram, his tobacco and newspapers delivered by standing arrangement. Indeed, I daresay it was providential for Holmes that Stamford found himself in a position to arrange our meeting. My stories brought Holmes a certain fame, and with that fame came cases too *outré* to be solved second-hand, and clients too demanding to allow Holmes to remain seated in his club chair by the hearth of 221b Baker Street. Then again, on a dull day such as this, in the dreadful month of September, I could at least serve as the great detective's personal secretary, for as of late his post would accumulate unopened in the nooks and crannies of the flat. Holmes had come to feel that cases of sufficient import and intrigue should be pleaded in person, or at the very least by telegram.

So it was that I sat at the table with letter opener in hand, gutting envelopes like fish. Most of the queries were trite and banal as Holmes feared, but those few that seemed to me to hold some interest I would read aloud. Holmes's response was often no response at all, although a few elicited a weary sigh, and others were plucked from my hand and fed to the fire. Such was the case for the card currently pinched tightly between my fingers. Holmes was grasping the other end and we were in a tug-of-war.

"We've nothing else on," I said.

"You've struck upon a combination of the two least interesting topics in the world. First, ancient history, that dreary subject wherein there is nothing left to happen and every aspect has been exhausted. Second, mumbo-jumbo, or parlor tricks for the simple-minded, who, by the way, never appreciate it when I pierce the veil of their intellect with the blade of rational inquiry."

"Professor Morgan's salons are quite exclusive, Holmes. To be honest, I'm surprised that you were even invited. Thus far, they have been the purview of royalty and captains of industry and government."

"Dull company, indeed."

"If you suppose the professor a charlatan, then take this as a challenge to expose him."

"I am being invited to play *his* game by *his* rules. My attendance would be an implied endorsement, and should the illusion prove insoluble to me in the moment, a validation of the professor's absurd claims."

"Ah, you fear the man is your mental superior."

"I can count my peers on one hand, and Professor Morgan is most certainly *not* among them."

"I shall send the RSVP, then."

"If, at the same time, you make a reservation for a late supper at Simpson's, then I suppose the evening will not be a total waste."

After I had dispatched the message, I spent the rest of the afternoon infused with a great sense of satisfaction. I had managed to pry Holmes loose from his chemical bench for at least one night. I also looked forward to seeing the professor's metamorphic tablet myself. No doubt Holmes was right and it was a simple parlor trick, but the thing had a certain notoriety and cachet this season in London, and it would be a coup to be among the select few to have seen the thing. The thought of capping it all with some roast beef and Yorkshire pudding didn't go amiss. I warmed my stomach with some brandy in anticipation and pondered what question I might ask the all-knowing tablet. Before I knew it, I was roused from my daydreams by the chiming of the clock. I quickly shaved and slipped into my evening suit, which hung ever pressed and ready but rarely used in my bureau.

Holmes had made no concessions to the refinement of the event or the illustrious company which we were about to join, remaining in the same clothes he had worn earlier in the day. Thankfully, when he exchanged his housecoat for a jacket and combed his hair, the effect was not wholly unsuitable. As a bit of a celebrity known for his Bohemian habits, Holmes was allowed a certain degree of latitude, much like a painter or a musician. Mrs. Hudson straightened my tie and simply *tsked* at Holmes as we stepped out into the fine London evening. At this time of day, cabs were easily hailed and soon we were clopping towards Hightown Manor, London home of Lord and Lady Grantlee. When we arrived, I saw the place had been strung with paper lanterns, giving an Oriental impression to the proceedings. We were received at the door by a fatigued butler. These seasonal homes were easy postings for much of the year, but the staff were forced to severely muster when the Grantlees came to town.

"You are the first to arrive, Mr. Holmes and companion," he intoned. "Please, repair to the sitting room and I shall pour a drink for you."

"Nothing for me," Holmes said. "My faculties shall remain sharp."

"Very good, sir."

"As one of naturally dull faculties, I may safely take you up on your offer," I said.

The man bowed slightly and we were left alone in the sitting room. The walls were papered in pink with a trefoil motif, and the furniture was rosewood polished to a high sheen. Everything that might reasonably be gilded was, and a few other things besides. On one wall was a hunting scene, the autumn trees painted in warm colors. On the opposite side a painting of a ruddy cheeked woman gazed benevolently down, pearls trickling down from her ears, around her neck, and down onto her bodice. Her puffed sleeves alluded to an older era, but something in her countenance belied a modern understanding of the world, and I suspected this depiction was of the current Lady Grantlee.

The warmth of my sherry had just begun to spread across my cheeks when the next guests arrived. He was a man of receding hairline and sagging countenance, and his suit was of fine material, but a conservative grey and well worn. She, on the other hand, wore a dress of a violent purple hue cut in what I understand to be the latest fashion, and yet the material and construction was cheap, even to my eye. Holmes had no doubt observed all of this and more by the mere reflection of the window, before turning around and offering his hand to the man in a supercilious fashion.

"Deputy Mayor Umberton. I don't believe we have had the pleasure," Holmes said.

Umberton sputtered as he shook Holmes's hand, unaccustomed to being recognized. "And you, sir?"

"Mr. Sherlock Holmes, consulting detective."

"And you must be Dr. Watson," the man nodded to me. "Obviously I know who *you* are, but how do you know me?"

"It surely isn't because he has done anything of interest to a detective," the woman said, sidling up to Holmes.

"My wife, Mrs. Umberton," Umberton sighed.

"My friends call me Dolly."

209

"Indeed, Mrs. Umberton? As you say, the Deputy Mayor's career has been beyond reproach. An unimaginative drone plugging away for the good of the hive."

"Why see here . . . ."

"Your suit is bespoke, Saville Row. Harrington and Son, if I am not mistaken. The habiliment of the powerful, and yet I daresay you own but . . . three . . . suits, and they are pressed into constant service. By contrast, most men who own such a suit easily own a dozen more and wear them only a few times a season, tossing them well before they develop shiny elbows and frayed cuffs. You have the poor eyesight of a man who squints at documents all day, but not the calluses of a man who writes, nor the sleeves of a man who types. A solicitor perhaps – but then, a solicitor would have never ceded control of this conversation so easily. A scholar would never forsake his spectacles, nor have spent a tenth as much at the tailor. A politician then, but not one who shakes many hands, not a senior functionary. Cross referencing the known facts in my mental index, I arrive at you, Deputy Mayor."

"Astounding!"

"Deduce me, next!" Mrs. Umberton cooed.

"I hardly think it will be the attention you desire, dear lady."

"My friends will be positively envious that the famous Sherlock Holmes applied his deductive reasoning on me."

"Unlike your husband's suit, your raiment is a cheap imitation, perhaps passing muster at a distance, but up close surely any person who cares about such things must see right through the deception. So, you do not spend much time in direct proximity with the elite to whom you aspire, but if seen in passing, through a carriage window perhaps, you wish to appear current and en vogue. A woman's wedding ring is telling in many ways, amongst them that it is the best piece the groom could afford at the time of the happy nuptial. Yours, a modest but precious band, is in line with your husband's place in the world, as is your necklace, your earrings, your brooch, your hairpin, all just as we would expect them to be for a man of a middling government career's means. And yet this perfume . . . ." Mrs. Umberton flushed now, "ambergris and civet, rare floral extracts from the sub-continent, that cost a pretty pound."

"You are mistaken, Mr. Holmes," she said, now shying away.

Holmes pursued, "I assure you I am not. I have quite the olfactory sense, and I am developing a treatise on the topic. Perfume, being always artificially introduced to an environment, is an invaluable detection tool. It can linger for hours after its wearer has departed, and a custom scent like this is as singular as a fingerprint."

"I assure you, Mr. Holmes, this is but a common scent from a bottle presented to me by my loving husband."

"Perhaps," said Holmes, smiling to himself.

"Let the lady be," came a booming voice from the doorway. "Perfumes and cosmetics are no fit subject for a man to know of in any event. Let the ladies have their feminine mysteries. We've worlds to conquer."

This new speaker was an aged man in elaborate military dress. I, of course, immediately recognized the eccentric plumage of a veteran of the Crimean War. His white whiskers were carved into an elaborate design upon his face. His skin remained a dark chestnut against his white hair, as if the sun he had absorbed almost four decades prior continued to roast him. His watery eyes were nearly lost in a web of wrinkles. At his elbow hung a striking young woman, her skin an exotic bronze, her amber eyes upturned ever so slightly. A high-necked dress of emerald and gold held close about her. I felt my bile stir as my first thought was that the man, this ancient Colonel, had somehow absconded with a child bride after developing a taste for the exotic during his time in the collapsing Ottoman Empire.

"My granddaughter, Elizabeth," he said directly to me, as if reading my mind, soldier to soldier. "She goes in for all of this spiritual rot, as did her mother. Too much savage blood still in her."

"And you, Colonel?" I said icily, putting a stop to any further insulting comments.

"John Mathers, 1st Brigade of the Light Division, marched on Sevastopol. I've seen what happens when magic meets lead, and I'll tell you which one wins out every time."

"Excellent. Our little party is now complete," said a man now entering. It was easy to recognize the professor, who, as the man of the moment, had been depicted in every newspaper and upon dozens of posters and flyers. Immediately behind him was the living incarnation of the painting upon the wall. As depicted, Lady Grantlee had a mischievous twinkle in her eye as she came in and graciously welcomed everyone.

"Let us get down to business, shall we?" the professor said. "I have invited tonight some of the greatest skeptics in London, for it is a trifle to amaze the uncritical, but an achievement to convince those such as yourselves. I am confident that when you have witnessed the metamorphic tablet of Ra-Atet, you shall be my greatest disciples."

"Ha!" scoffed the Colonel. "Have at it then, I mean to be at the cribbage table at the Officer's Club before the hour has elapsed."

"Grandfather!" chided the beautiful Elizabeth.

"Think nothing of it, my child," said the professor, "I understand that men such as yourselves do not stand on ceremony, and have no need for pomp and circumstance. Therefore, I shall ask Lady Grantlee to retrieve the tablet in the most expeditious manner."

The Lady nodded to the professor and produced a key from her bosom. With measured steps, she paced the room and unlocked a great cabinet. Inside was a velvet wrapped parcel, a large glass bowl, and a variety of phials and beakers, each labeled with hieroglyphics.

As the Lady began to transfer the things from the cabinet to the table, Holmes spoke. "May I inquire as to why Lord Grantlee is not present?"

"I hesitate to say," Lady Grantlee responded. "But I suppose we are among trusted company, and so I may reveal a little. My husband and I have become convinced of the authenticity of the fortunes predicted by the tablet. The transcendent Pharaoh Ra-Atet has given my husband business advice upon which he currently acts. I'm afraid it has taken him abroad, but when he returns our family's wealth will be secure for generations."

"And now you host these salons for others?" Holmes asked.

"The Pharaoh asked it of us, and it is so little in return for the boon he has bequeathed."

"And you, Professor. Why does the Pharaoh not favor you with a fortune?"

"As an academic, I do not seek material wealth, but this rediscovery will etch my name in the annals of history. Please, Mr. Holmes, everyone, come see for yourselves."

We pressed around the table, peering at the blank slate before us. I was hard pressed to decide if rock could look ancient, but I supposed at the very least it did not appear to be freshly chiseled. Holmes reached for it, but the professor stayed him.

"I'm sorry, Mr. Holmes. Without knowing how the spell works, I hesitate to do anything to break it. Only I may touch the tablet."

"I see. Perhaps I could handle it through the velvet, as Lady Grantlee did."

"Perhaps, after my demonstration."

"Ooh, ancient mummy magic. I can feel it radiating through my whole body!" Mrs. Umberton said.

I looked to Elizabeth, who said nothing but was transfixed by the stone. Her grandfather was chomping his cigar in impatience.

The Deputy Mayor was tugging at his collar and remained a step back from the table's edge.

"One of you may ask a question of the tablet."

"Oh, let me do it!" Mrs. Umberton declared.

"My granddaughter is the youngest, and should have first crack at your little game. It would do her good to see it for the fraud it is."

"To be honest," said the professor. "There is one of you I was hoping to impress most of all. I would like to give this honor to Mr. Holmes."

"I should like to decline."

"Really, Mr. Holmes? Surely no one is better placed to put the tablet to the test."

"I share the Colonel's opinion that this is a charade, and you have now tipped your hand that tonight's demonstration was planned specifically to fool me. I say let the Deputy Mayor ask a question. He wants nothing to do with this business, and thus is the closest thing we have to a neutral observer."

"What a waste!" said Mrs. Umberton. "To throw away a mystical consultation on the most boring man in the room. You'd do as well to have the chair ask a question."

The Deputy Mayor's jaw clenched and he stepped forward. "Very well, Great Ra-Atet, I have a question for you. Will I ever again know a moment of happiness?"

It was the professor's turn now to take measured steps around the room to the cabinet, from which he placed the bowl and retrieved one of the beakers. "The healing waters of the Nile. Ra-Atet draws his strength from this precious fluid, the mother's milk of the world."

"How did you select among the many bottles?" Holmes asked.

"The particular bottle is trivial. Each is but a sip from that life-giving confluence, packed out discretely. The Egyptians guard the water most jealously."

"Even so, why keep the water in separate jars?"

"Why do you isolate the specimens in your scientific studies, Mr. Holmes? To prevent cross contamination for one. To minimize the chance of losing everything to a careless breakage for another. Further, the water has a spiritual integrity, and to jumble it all up would be to lose all of that."

Holmes curled his lip with contempt but said nothing. The professor now uttered a Coptic prayer while gently pouring the contents of the beaker into the bowl. When it was full, he reverently lifted the tablet and laid it down in the water. After a few moments, the water became hazy and then opaque. Holmes leaned over the bowl, intently gazing down. The liquid bubbled and fizzed, releasing an eerie, dense vapor that crawled over the edge of the bowl and across the table. When finally the fluid was again at rest, the professor reached down, probing for a moment before pulling forth the tablet, now inscribed in an unsettling, willowy script. At first I thought it to be more hieroglyphics, or some ancient cuneiform, but at last I saw it to be English, merely inscribed with strange spacing and overlapping letters.

"What does it say?" Mrs. Umberton cried.

"*The House of Umberton knows relief already, before truth, and an end to ruination.*'"

There were gasps heard round the room.

"That didn't really answer the question, did it?" Holmes said.

"It says Umberton, clear as day!" said the Deputy Mayor.

"The great Pharaoh Ra-Atet knows our name!" Mrs. Umberton cheered.

"I'll inspect that tablet for myself, if you don't mind!" said the Colonel.

"I'm afraid the tablet is in a delicate state after transmogrification."

"I'll just bet it is," the Colonel said.

"Grandfather!" Elizabeth tugged at the man's sleeve with her delicate fingers.

"You had said I might examine it?" Holmes said.

"If you come back in the morning, something can be arranged," the professor replied. "In the meantime, I shall provide you with a rubbing. And you as well, Mayor Umberton, of course."

Lady Grantlee produced sheafs of paper and a thick charcoal, with which the professor transferred the image on the stone.

"You must send word of the accuracy of Ra-Atet's prediction," the professor said. "Promise us!"

"Perhaps we could tell you in person, at your next salon?" Mrs. Umberton said. "I expect there will be more famous people there?"

"Delighted to have you, my dear lady. Now, the spirit of the Pharaoh is exhausted. Let us all retire for the evening and wait to hear the Deputy Mayor's happy report!"

Holmes and Elizabeth took this last opportunity to peer down into the dark water, a reflection of Holmes's suspicion and the girl's wonder peering back up at them. The professor had encircled Holmes with a convivial arm to lead him away, and Lady Grantlee was pressing the rubbing into my hands. Of a sudden we were back on the street. The Umbertons were already climbing into their carriage.

"It was simply divine," said Mrs. Umberton, "and did you hear, we can come back again! I must send a letter to absolutely everyone."

The Deputy Mayor himself looked ill as he sunk back in his seat.

The Colonel stepped in front of us. "Mr. Holmes, as a modern man of reason, you know as well as I do that what we just witnessed was poppycock. And the way we were hustled out of there afterwards, that seals it. You can prove the man is a fraud, can't you?"

"Not yet, but a fraud he must be, and so the evidence must be as well. I mean to take the professor up on his offer and inspect the thing tomorrow."

"I'll stand you three gold sovereigns and an evening at the Lion and Sabre if you can prove it."

"The satisfaction of proving the truth of the matter shall be enough."

"Mr. Holmes shall graciously accept the prize as well," I hastened to add. Our income was fickle but our expenses were not. Mrs. Hudson would have my head if I let that much trickle through our fingers.

"Make sure you are truly seeking the truth," Elizabeth said. "The answer you seek may not be the answer you want."

"Perhaps we could consult with you further on this matter, Miss?" I interjected.

"Get in the carriage, Elizabeth," the Colonel said. "You don't need to be wasting Mr. Holmes's time, and no one needs to be wasting any of yours." He eyed me as he pulled himself up into his seat and they clattered away into the night.

The next morning, we received word of the success of the tablet's prediction, but not from Deputy Mayor Umberton, but rather from our old acquaintance, Inspector Athelney Jones.

"A proper hash you've made of this, Mr. Holmes," Jones said as he removed his hat.

"I beg your pardon?"

"The Deputy Mayor's home robbed, right out from under your nose."

"I have never had the misfortune of attending Mr. Umberton in his abode."

"Maybe not, but you knew it was going to happen."

"How could I?"

"You heard the Sphinx's riddle. The Deputy Mayor told us so himself. '*The House of Umberton knows relief already, before truth, and an end to ruination.*' While I think you take all too much credit for the luck and happenstance which places criminals in your lap, even I will admit you have a knack for little puzzles. Even Mr. Umberton himself easily cracked the code once he came home to a burgled house. If he can do it, Mr. Sherlock Holmes would have known the answer to the riddle right off the top."

"Yes, well, the Sphinx is a Pharaoh and the riddle is a fortune and it is a trivial matter to see the solution to any puzzle that has already been pieced together. You yourself excel in the field, Inspector."

"Ta, Mr. Holmes, but that still doesn't explain why you allowed the burglary."

"I allowed nothing."

"That's not the way it looks, Mr. Holmes."

"I've an appointment with Professor Morgan to view the tablet this morning. Why don't you come along? It may clear a few things up."

The three of us climbed into Jones's carriage and were soon back at the Grantlee Manor. Lady Grantlee herself soon attended us in the familiar parlor.

"I had expected to speak with the professor," Holmes said.

"He has been summoned by half of London to provide assurances after last night."

"Last night?"

"Well, Mr. Holmes, I struggle to put it delicately, but the events of last night showed that the deductions of a famous detective do not hold a candle to the predictions of the Pharaoh Ra-Atet."

"Is that what was shown?"

"Did the Pharaoh not predict exactly what was to occur? Even with that prediction in hand, did you not fail to prevent the robbery?"

"I believe I have the professor's permission to examine the tablet?"

"I suppose he did say yesterday evening that he would allow it." Lady Grantlee carefully stepped around the room in a now familiar pattern. She extracted the tablet from the locked cabinet and carefully laid it upon the table.

Holmes set upon it with his magnifying glass. Gently he lifted a corner of the tablet from beneath the velvet and let it drop to the table again.

216

"Please be careful, Mr. Holmes. This is already an unprecedented liberty you are being allowed."

"What of the Nile water? Might I inspect that?"

Lady Grantlee moved to block Holmes. "Even I do not handle the water, Mr. Holmes. Further, that was not part of the agreement you had with the professor."

"Alas, I suppose you are right. One last thing before we leave, Lady Grantlee. My partner Dr. Watson has misplaced his pocket watch, and I suspect he may have left it here by accident. The clasp is loose, you see, and comes easily undone."

I wasn't sure what Holmes was up to but I casually moved my hand to my vest pocket to obscure my watch. I was much surprised when my thumb met the vacant lining of my vest. There was a twinkle in Holmes's eye as he patted his own pocket.

"I am not aware of any pocket watch being discovered."

"I'm afraid I really must insist. It is a plain watch of little monetary value, but it has passed from his father to his brother and now ultimately to Watson himself. I know it to be of great sentimental value. I imagine a reward would not be out of order, should one of your staff have discovered it."

"Ah, yes, indeed," I said to Holmes. "There will certainly be a just reward when my watch is returned."

"Fine, but then I really must ask you to conclude our visit. The professor will no doubt gladly receive you at a more convenient time." She moved to the doorway and called back into the house, "Charlotte, Petunia, come here!"

While her back was turned Holmes seized a beaker from the cabinet and, uncorking it, poured the contents over the tablet which then hissed and fumed.

"Mr. Holmes!" Lady Grantlee gasped. "This is outrageous! You will leave at once and you are not welcome to return!"

"Wait!" said the inspector. "The tablet is forming words."

They were so shallow as to be barely perceptible, and contained entirely within the liquid splash, but plainly enough the tablet read: *Easy lies and sneaky hands reveal the desperation of Sherlock Holmes.*

"Dash it, Holmes, if you have dragged me into a mummy's curse, I'll have you breaking rocks for the rest of your days!" Jones said.

"Go now! You are not welcome in this house!" Lady Grantlee said.

"Take the tablet into evidence, Inspector, and the so-called water as well."

"I'm going nowhere near that thing! Besides, the only act of which it is evidence is your boorish behavior."

"Tell Professor Morgan that he can expect the three of us for his weekly salon, and that the inspector will be bringing his handcuffs," Holmes said.

"Don't you worry, I'll be telling the professor all about this, and writing to my husband as well."

I saw Holmes's face fall for just a moment. "Until then, Lady Grantlee. I do apologize, I sometimes forget myself in the pursuit."

"I can't believe what I just saw, Mr. Holmes! The metamorphic tablet of Ra-Atet is real, and it is out to get you!" said the inspector.

"I can't believe what I saw either," Holmes said. "Just make sure that you are back here this Saturday evening. I'm going to give you the arrest of the decade. You'll have your cuffs on the wrists of the spirit of Ra-Atet, or you'll have them on the wrists of Sherlock Holmes."

Holmes would see no other callers that week, spending the days out of the flat. I was able to gather that he had commandeered the chemical lab at St. Barts, eventually leaving with a laden satchel. For a shilling, I was able to prise from the Irregulars that Holmes had sent them running all over London with a shopping list of strange ingredients to be obtained from the most unusual vendors. Following him myself, I watched him disappear into the King's College secret archives. He was out all night that time. On another night, I saw Holmes hunched over his chemical bench, tendrils of smoke cascading down.

"You've almost cracked it, Holmes!" I said. In reply he lobbed a pestle in my general direction without even looking up.

At long last Saturday evening had arrived. Holmes sat perfectly still in his chair, his long, slow breaths evident from the gentle billowing of his pipe. I had often seen Holmes like this, perfectly composed, perfectly at ease. It was only while waiting to spring the final trap on his prey that he achieved this state of transcendental composure. I ate my roast and his as well, knowing that he would take no food until the case was through. Inspector Jones knocked shortly after dinner and we were off. When we arrived at Grantlee Manor, the Umbertons were present, as was Colonel Mathers and Elizabeth. The room was packed, in fact.

"It seems word has circulated that the Pharaoh Ra-Atet and the great detective Sherlock Holmes mean to have it out," the professor smirked.

"I told absolutely everybody," said Mrs. Umberton.

The Colonel leaned into Holmes conspiratorially, "You've got him, old boy, I can see it in your bearing. Good hunting!"

"I have to express some surprise," said the professor. "Ra-Atet already revealed you for the cad you are."

"I agree that a cad has been revealed by this tablet."

"Why trade barbs with me when we can hear directly from the Pharaoh?"

"Capitol suggestion."

The professor nodded at Lady Grantlee, who began her customary procession around the room. The crowd parted easily before her. She extracted the key and turned it in the lock, the mechanism easily audible in the silent tension. The bowl was produced, and the wrapped stone. Lady Grantlee gently folded back the covering, as if she were unswaddling an infant. The silent crowd now began to murmur. She laid it down to rest in the bowl.

"You've had a week to try to outsmart Ra-Atet," said the professor. "What question do you put forward?"

"The only possible question," Holmes said, slipping into a dramatic register. "Oh, most venerable Pharaoh Ra-Atet, I bow before your secret knowledge and testify to its ultimate truth, I beg of you to reveal that which I cannot, and demonstrate the mastery of genuine wisdom here before these assembled witnesses."

The crowd, myself and Jones among them, murmured in surprise.

"Have your bracelets at the ready," Holmes whispered.

An empty smile played across the professor's face, but only for a moment. With a miniscule shrug, he proceeded to the vials of Nile water and plucked one forth, holding it up to the crowd as he began his Coptic incantation. He paused just as the liquid was about to leave the container and cocked his head at Holmes one last time. My friend, for his part, had folded his hands together and stooped contritely. I widened my stance and shifted back and forth on the balls of my feet. Holmes would genuinely assume that pose for no man – he was a viper lulling his prey before the strike.

The water trickled from the glass and began to sizzle upon the surface of the tablet. A malicious grin now split the professor's face. He dumped the rest of the container out into the bowl, and it smoked and bubbled and churned. It was Holmes's turn to smile now.

219

"Pluck it out, reveal the truth to us all professor."

Morgan's face had dropped, beads of sweat now bespeckled his brow. "Wait!"

"Wait? Wait for what? The Pharaoh has endured the eons to convey this message to us. Surely the least we could do is bring it into to light."

"Show us, Professor!" Mrs. Umberton cried. The crowd pressed together expectantly.

Morgan hesitantly dipped his hands into the bowl, as if he were afraid to touch the water. The tablet was revealed, for but a moment when the professor shouted with rage and attempted to smash it upon the ground. Holmes seemed to have anticipated such a result, for the snatched the tablet from the air the very moment it left the man's hands.

"Colonel Mathers, would you do the honor?" Holmes presented the tablet with a flourish.

"With the greatest of pleasure," the Colonel said, before mumbling to himself as he attempted to decipher the strange writing. "My word!"

Elizabeth gasped, and then looked upon Lady Grantlee with that natural sympathy that is the special domain of women.

"What is it?" Lady Grantlee demanded.

"Clear out, you lot of benighted poppets," bellowed the Colonel. Some responded at once to his commanding voice, others needed to be prodded by myself and Inspector Jones. Holmes stood fast, barring the exit of Professor Morgan.

"You had best sit down, my Lady," Elizabeth said, taking Lady Grantlee by the arm and leading her to a chair.

"I don't understand," Lady Grantlee said.

"Handcuffs, Inspector Jones, and don't let the professor out of your grasp," Holmes instructed.

With great sadness the Colonel turned the tablet over to Lady Grantlee. I looked over her shoulder to see the following inscription: *Morgan a fraud, Lord Grantlee murdered in Hampstead, SH.*"

"How can this be? I receive a letter from Lord Grantlee today."

"In fact, you received a telegram."

"Yes."

"Telling you that Lord Grantlee had set sail for Panama to settle a contract personally."

"Yes, but how . . . ."

"Of course, the ship-to-shore telegraphs gave the perfect excuse for short communiques, all in type. The story would allay suspicion for weeks, maybe months. At any time this fictional Lord Grantlee could be disposed of far overseas."

"Fictional?" asked Jones.

"I'm afraid the genuine Lord Grantlee lies under the lakes of West Hyde. An Inspector Caldecott made short work of that nefarious accomplice after I traced back along the lines the telegram Lady Grantlee received. That last, corruptible operator was easily convinced to reveal the sender, for he stood to lose his job or his life."

"But why would you do this?" Lady Grantlee shouted at the professor. "We have shown you nothing but kindness and charity."

The professor simply snarled and strained at his restraints.

"I am afraid that to a vicious mind, kindness is seen as weakness. And Professor Morgan has become quite vicious thanks to his association with the last living remnants of an ancient society of assassins."

"Absurd!" cried Lady Grantlee.

"His published work reveals his long affiliation with the desert encampment of Abu Shad, and also that he was following the classic arc of going native. His phraseology borrowed more and more from ancient Oriental scrolls, until he suddenly ceased publishing. That incantation he uttered over the tablet is actually from a Demotic *stelae* and invokes a spell of deceit and camouflage. It is essentially a cutthroat's prayer for protection."

"How could he, and you, command the tablet?" asked the inspector.

"A-ha! That is indeed ingenious, although the credit is due to some ancient alchemist and not the professor." Holmes lifted the tablet above the bowl and began pouring the contents of other bottles upon it. "By delving into Haliburton's *Collectanea Ægyptiaca*, I easily determined that the glyphs on the labels were gibberish. That, of course, identified Morgan as a fraud." There was more smoking and hissing and soon he presented to us a tablet completely crisscross with diagonal lines, a tessellation of hundreds of diamonds looking much a serpent's scales."

"What is this?" Jones bellowed. "You have completely destroyed the evidence."

"To the contrary, I have revealed the mechanism of the professor's charade." Holmes produced two small jars from his pocket, packed with what appeared to be mud. You simply press one compound into the cracks like mortar, leaving open the spaces that form the letters you desire. You then fill those cracks with another compound. The two compounds both dry to look just like the stone of the tablet, but each is soluble in a different solution. By utilizing the right dissolver, the professor was able to revel only the letters he wanted. For my demonstration, I utilized only the base compound meant not to be dissolved and one dissolvable compound, but I believe the professor had developed a system for laying different messages on top of each other, so that depending on the question he could reveal a particular answer."

"That is why the writing looked so strange," I said.

"Indeed, it is remarkable he was able to craft decipherable messages at all."

A haughty sneer twisted Morgan's face,

"And that is why he was so sensitive about the bottles," said Lady Grantlee.

"Yes. The tablet could be prepared in advance, but the bottles and the revelation were performed live with no room for mistake. He needed to be exactly sure of which bottle revealed which message."

"I've never seen anything like it!" Jones said.

"I don't think many have in a millennia or more. This kind of ancient spy craft is largely impractical, except for magic tricks."

"And schemes against the gullible." Lady Grantlee began sobbing. Elizabeth held her shoulders.

"It was a scheme hatched over millennia and forgotten again for as long," Holmes said. "I flatter myself to be a competent chemist and performer, and yet even with my encyclopedic knowledge of criminality, I was stymied for a time."

"But how did the professor predict the future, as he did on several occasions?" Jones asked.

"His predictions amount to confessions, for he committed every predicted action himself, or had them committed anyway."

"The burglary of our house?" demanded Mrs. Umberton.

"Amongst many other deplorable acts."

"Again, I ask to what end?"

"Professor, do you care to lecture today?" Holmes asked. The man just barked.

"I expect, Lady Grantlee, that shortly you would have received telegrams inviting you to join your husband in Panama, and instructing you in the mechanics of transferring the goods and wealth of the Grantlee estate there. Once completed, you would prove as disposable as your husband, and the professor could carry on his researches in comfort as a wealthy expatriate of the Crown. Money

222

would answer any questions asked there, and your disappearance from England would be well-explained.

"By the time your family or friends raised a definitive alarm, Professor Morgan would be far beyond your, or even my, reach. As with so many of his ilk, his hubris was his downfall. To tweak my nose was sheer folly."

"Perhaps he meant to hang the whole affair on you, Mr. Holmes?" Jones offered.

"Or discredit me at the least. As promised, Inspector, one would-be Pharaoh, bound and ready to be buried."

The trial kept the professor and Lady Grantlee in the papers through the winter. She weathered it admirably well, he much less so. The fame he so courted ensured his ultimate rendezvous with the hangman, and I for one can't say I'm sorry for it. Colonel Mathers made good on his promise to toast us and gild our palms. To this day he sends us news of strange little mysteries he believes need debunking.

I cannot pry from him a single word about young Elizabeth. We saw the Umberton's but rarely, and it seemed from their reticent manner that they never quite shook the suspicion that Holmes could have prevented their burglary. Holmes himself seemed quite pleased with the outcome, and while predictably Athelney Jones received the credit, Holmes consoled himself with the collection of strange books he had liberated from the library. He would have a new assortment of tricks soon, I imagined. As for me, I was happy enough to sit by the window and supply a few more stories for the old dispatch box. I put this tale aside for a day when it will do the unfortunate Lady Grantlee no more harm.

The Haunting of
Hamilton Gardens
by Nick Cardillo

"Good God," I said as I returned my cup of coffee to the saucer, nearly losing a large quantity of my drink. I stared at the morning newspaper in my hand and tried to make sense of the headline. No matter how fast the cogs in my brain worked, however, I remained just as surprised as when I had first come across it.

I see that I have once more fallen into the pattern of telling these tales wrong end foremost. To begin, it was a cool, autumn morning in 1897. I had been away from Baker Street – and London for that matter – having spent two weeks in the country in the company of an old friend from the Fifth Northumberland Fusiliers. It had been a gratifying trip, though at the end of the time, which was spent in much reminiscing and relaxing out-of-doors, I found myself exhausted. I had fallen asleep on the train back to the city and, arriving at Baker Street late, had ascended the steps to my room in silence. I could see light emanating from the door to the sitting room and knew that Holmes was still up, no doubt lost in thought, wreathed in a fog of thick pipe smoke. However, being far too tired to announce my presence, I went up to my room and virtually collapsed upon the bed.

I managed to rouse myself early the following morning and, after I had set about putting away my things, I shaved and dressed and made my way downstairs for breakfast. Sherlock Holmes had already risen and dressed and was languidly flipping through the morning edition of *The Times* when I entered the sitting room. My friend greeted me warmly and said that there was much to discuss, though, he told me, he would wait until after I had broken my fast to begin his oration. I sat down at the breakfast table, poured a cup of coffee, unfolded the copy of *The Star*, and promptly let out the exclamation of surprise.

"You have seen the paper then?" Holmes asked.

"Yes," I stammered. "Holmes, what does it mean?"

I returned my gaze to the sheet of newsprint and the large headline which had grabbed my attention. It ran:

Sherlock Holmes Wages War on Prominent Spiritualist

"If you read the article, I daresay that you shall learn very quickly what it means," Holmes said, not without a touch of stinging sarcasm in his voice. "What's more, the reporter for *The Star* might be able to relay facts to you more concisely than I ever could."

I regarded the newspaper in my hand with some contention. I was not a frequent reader of *The Star*, for I found it to be overly lurid and in poor taste. I could still recall the autumn of 1888, during the horrible Jack the Ripper murders, that it was *The Star* which carried the most sensational details of the case, sparing little thought for the public at large, or for the kith and kin of the murderer's victims. I shall not stress mention of that foul business, for our involvement in that matter is one which I am afraid I can never make public.

In hindsight, I should have found its presence on the breakfast table curious in the extreme, but I supposed Holmes had gotten a copy for his own amusement. I looked at the writer's name.

"'*Mr. William Parker*'," I read aloud.

"A rather amiable young man in his own way," Holmes said. "Oh, come now, Watson. Do not regard that piece of pulp with such derision. Allow me ten minutes more and you shall hear the business through to the end. I cabled Mr. Parker this morning after I rose and requested that he come 'round to Baker Street to relay the whole situation to you."

"You asked him to come around just for my benefit?" I asked, rather touched.

"And for mine, too," Holmes added. "It can never hurt to hear the details of a case again. I very nearly have the thing solved. But my solution lacks evidence. And evidence is the one thing I need if I am to win over Sir Jeffrey Curbishly."

"I take it then that this Sir Jeffrey is the prominent spiritualist?"

"Precisely," Holmes said. "Sir Jeffrey – and a great deal of London – has also reached a conclusion to this whole, nasty business, although his culprit is rather difficult to go and clap irons upon, I'm afraid."

"Oh? Why's that?"

"Because, my dear Watson," Holmes said, "Sir Jeffrey points the finger of suspicion firmly at the Devil himself."

I confess that a faint chill ran up my spine at these words. A moment later, the bell chimed below. Holmes extracted his watch from his waistcoat. "Excellent," he said noting the time, "Parker's five minutes earlier than expected."

My friend rushed out of the room and left me in stupefied silence until he returned a moment later with a young man following behind. He could not have been more than six-and-twenty, and his young face bespoke of some *naïveté*; it was obvious that the young man was not as world-weary as Holmes or I. He was well-dressed, and carried a bowler hat in his long, dexterous-looking fingers.

"Mr. William Parker," Holmes began by way of introduction, "allow me to introduce you to my friend and colleague, Dr. John Watson."

"A pleasure to meet you, Doctor," Parker said. "I have read all your accounts of Mr. Holmes's work."

"Thank you," said I.

Holmes gestured for our guest to sit. "You will forgive the Good Doctor for a few moments while he breaks his fast. It would be remiss of me should I not allow him to enjoy a hearty meal on the day after his return from the country. All the same, I should like you to go over the details of this case – for both the Doctor's benefit and my own."

Parker settled back in his chair. From his inner breast pocket, he withdrew a small, black notebook which he opened. "Well, I suppose I ought to begin with a few particulars about myself. I am a reporter for *The Star* and I have been in my present situation for nearly four years. In that time, I have reported on dozens of stories of all varieties. Some of us at *The Star* have a bit of a specialty; I am afraid that I have yet to find mine. While I may be young (and not as experienced as some of the other writers on the paper), I like to think my skills set me apart from the others. I am something of a favorite of Mr. Parke, the editor, as well.

"This current matter was brought to my attention two weeks prior by an associate of mine who lives in the region of St John's Wood. It was he who brought me to the attention of Mrs. Emily Cardew and her daughter, Lillian, who currently reside at No. 41 Hamilton Gardens.

"Some description of the neighborhood might be in order for you to accurately perceive what section of the city with which we are dealing. As one can imagine, the area is quite nice – surely one of the more upper-class regions of London. The homes which make up Hamilton Gardens are part of Alma Square, and they are small, two-story affairs which stand in rows, one beside the next. I feel as if this is an important fact as skeptics – such as Mr. Holmes – could make the claim that the family is trying to move into a more salubrious section of the city. Still, as they already reside in one of the more

226

fashionable districts of London, that claim *does* seem to be easily refuted.

"Onto the principal people in the case." Parker turned over a page in his notebook as I settled into my chair and reached for my own. "The woman is Mrs. Emily Cardew, formerly Miss Emily Melville. She is thirty-six years of age and has lived at 41 Hamilton Gardens with her daughter for three years. Her daughter, Lillian, is eleven. Mrs. Cardew was of good social standing – her father having held a minor position in Her Majesty's Government Twelve years ago, she was left a good deal of money by her father, who had a minor position in Her Majesty's Government. That same year, she wed a young officer – Lieutenant Cardew – who, the following year, was killed in the Mahdist War, just before the birth of his child."

"The name is familiar to me," I said as I took it down. "Having served in the Afghan campaign, I have tried to stay abreast of my fellow military officers."

"The Lieutenant was a decorated officer, Doctor. Anyways, Mrs. Cardew lived off of her late father's money, as well as that of her late husband, and she was also supported financially by the lieutenant's family, to whom she had grown quite close. They helped her raise her child and school her. Through it all, Mrs. Cardew never seemed intent on marrying again, though she had gained something of a reputation in society. And, for what it is worth, I found Mrs. Cardew to be a very handsome woman on the occasions when I spoke with her.

"Now, as I mentioned, Mrs. Cardew and her daughter moved into 41 Hamilton Gardens three years ago, and by all accounts their time there was happy and quiet. Neighbors – including my associate – said that they kept much to themselves, but they were always very friendly in passing. On occasion, some of the other school children in the neighborhood would go to play at the Cardews', or Lillian was invited to play at another's house. Their quiet routine was not altered until two weeks ago.

"Mrs. Cardew stated that in the early hours of the morning of 3 October, she thought that she heard the sound of someone moving about in the house. At first, she believed it was nothing. But she heard it again a few moments later – this time even more loudly than before – she sat up and lit a lamp. The sound grew nearer, and a moment later she saw its source: Her daughter, Lillian, was walking in her sleep. Lillian entered her mother's room and stood in the doorway, appearing almost to sway to and fro, before she turned and went back the way she had come."

227

"Did Lillian routinely suffer from somnambulism?" I asked.

"According to her mother, never," Parker replied. "And, I am afraid that that fact makes what follows all the more distressing. Mrs. Cardew said that the following day, Lillian had no memory whatsoever of the incident, despite her mother's many efforts to question her daughter about it. Lillian was fine for the remainder of the day and even went to play with one of the little girls who lives in the neighborhood."

"Did that little girl's mother have anything to say about Lillian Cardew?" Holmes asked.

"When questioned about it, she said that there appeared to be nothing wrong with Lillian whatsoever. Nevertheless, once more, in the early hours of the following morning, Lillian Cardew rose from her bed and began to walk in her sleep. Yet this time Mrs. Cardew insists that she could hear her daughter muttering something under her breath. Later, when she questioned her daughter, Mrs. Cardew discovered that Lillian had no memory of having woken in the night, but there were dark circles under her eyes which she attributed to the lack of sleep following two consecutive nights of sleepwalking.

"So, in order to get to the root of the problem, Mrs. Cardew endeavored to sit outside her daughter's room. In the event that her daughter was roused from her sleep once more, she would be on hand to tuck her in. Mrs. Cardew says that once again in the early hours of the morning, she was roused from sleep (having drifted off herself) and found that her daughter had sat upright in bed and was murmuring once more under her breath. Mrs. Cardew lighted a lamp and drew closer to Lillian's bed and discovered, quite to her horror, that Lillian's eyes appeared to have rolled back in her head. The whites of her eyes shone brightly in the guttering flame of the lamp."

"And what was young Lillian Cardew muttering about?" Holmes asked.

William Parker adjusted his tie nervously. "She was speaking some sort of nonsense about the house being her own, and that she and her mother would have to leave immediately. She repeated that phrase over and over again: '*This house is mine. This house is mine.*'"

I looked to Holmes. His face was cold and unreadable. He had closed his eyes – absorbing this information once more – but whether he found the story credible or not, I could not say. I have always been a rational man, but this new development suddenly put Holmes's cryptic statement about the Devil in a whole new light. I confess that for an instant, I knew not what to think and I reached for my cigarette case to momentarily steady my nerves.

Without opening his eyes, Holmes said: "I trust, Mr. Parker, that you shall not object to Dr. Watson lighting a cigarette? I confess that I am rather craving my first pipe of the morning."

"By all means, gentlemen."

Holmes reached for his pipe and began to fill it with tobacco from the Persian slipper on the mantelpiece. "Speaking objectively," said he, "I can understand where the rumors of *demonic possession* are originating. You know as well as I that the facts in this case are very much in their infancy. Please continue, Mr. Parker."

Holmes struck a match and lighted his pipe as Parker continued. "Well," he said, "Mrs. Cardew decided that the next course of action would be to speak with a doctor. A medical man was brought to the house – one Dr. Douglas Flaugherty – and he conducted an examination of Lillian Cardew. I have interviewed the doctor on two occasions, and both times he told me outright that there was nothing at all the matter wrong with the girl."

Holmes suddenly stood from his chair and moved to his desk where he rifled through a pile of papers. He extracted from the stack a folded-up copy of *The Star* and read aloud: "Your own words, Mr. Parker: '*Dr. Flaugherty says that Lillian Cardew's pulse and breathing were normal. There appeared to be no sign of any illness, and even an inspection of the girl's eyes – which often yields up unseen evidence from the brain – could conclude nothing.*'"

"Precisely, Mr. Holmes," Parker said, "but Lillian's condition didn't get any better. In fact, it only got worse. Following the doctor's examination, Mrs. Cardew believed that, perhaps, her daughter was suffering from a mental disorder. Over the course of a few days, she corresponded with a physician on Wimpole Street who is a follower of the psychoanalytic theory currently being pioneered by Dr. Freud. Mrs. Cardew was prepared to take Lillian in for a consultation, when, once more in the dead of night, Lillian had another outburst. This was one was far more violent in nature, and she appeared to be gyrating madly on her bed. She thrashed about in her sheets and uttered oaths of the most deplorable nature. Gnashing her teeth and snarling, she continued to repeat: '*This house is mine.*'"

"And," said Holmes, "there was a witness."

"Yes," Parker replied. "Mrs. Ellen Mortimer. She is a friend of Mrs. Cardew's and was, in fact, the mother of the girl who Lillian went to play with only days before. Mrs. Mortimer had already said that she could see nothing wrong with Lillian Cardew but, having seen how frightened her mother was getting over the whole business, Mrs. Mortimer insisted on spending the evening with the Cardews."

"And this Mrs. Mortimer witnessed the violent outbursts of which you spoke?" I asked.

By way of an answer, Holmes quoted from the same article:

> *"I watched in horror," said Mrs. Mortimer, "as little Lillian Cardew convulsed wildly on her bed. It was as though she was a puppet being conducted by some great, invisible hand pulling at strings from above. All the while – as she convulsed, twisted, and knotted herself up on her bed – she said things, truly horrible things, in a voice which I swear could not have come from the girl I have known so well. I knew in that moment that this was no longer an earthly matter. This little girl had become possessed by some malignant, evil power whose might I dare not attempt to contemplate."*

"All rather lurid stuff. The morning after this display, Mrs. Mortimer implored Mrs. Cardew to seek out the services of a priest."

I sat for a moment in stunned silence. "A priest?" I said at length. "To perform an exorcism?"

"Quite right, Dr. Watson," Parker replied. "As the matter stands, no such action has occurred, leaving this story without an ending. It is for that reason that so many newspapers have been scrambling to fill in the details of the story thus far."

"And in doing so," said Sherlock Holmes as he returned to his seat, "your newspaper – as well as the other papers which have covered this incident – have created something of a sensation in London. There are few in all circles of society who have not spoken of the curious haunting of Hamilton Gardens."

"It is remarkable," I said at length. "It is simply too fantastic to contemplate."

"Tell me, Parker," Holmes said, "in your interview with Mrs. Mortimer, how did she strike you?"

"She was a quiet, reserved woman," Parker said. He opened his notebook and consulted his notes. "She is forty years of age – four years Mrs. Cardew's senior – and has been married to her husband for fifteen years. They have two children: The first is the same age as Lillian Cardew, and the other two years younger. I found her to be a very amiable woman."

"Did it strike you as an out-of-character act for Mrs. Mortimer to suggest seeking the aid of a priest to perform an exorcism?"

"No. In my interview with her, Mrs. Mortimer described herself as 'religious and God-fearing'. It is, I suppose, somewhat natural than for her to seek a theological explanation for this turn of events."

Holmes once more withdrew his watch from his waistcoat pocket. "My, how the times does fly, Mr. Parker. I shan't keep you longer. And yet, there are one or two things which I think would be invaluable to me. First and foremost, are there any photographs of Mrs. Cardew and her daughter?"

"For the sake of her daughter, Mrs. Cardew refused our photographer to take pictures."

"That is unfortunate. I would find them most illuminating," Holmes said. "Secondly, what church does Mrs. Ellen Mortimer regularly attend?"

After Parker had supplied the name and address of the church, he excused himself from our room. Holmes closed the door behind him and, as soon as we heard the front door close downstairs, he let out a loud burst of laughter.

"Forgive me, Watson," he said as he crossed back to his chair. He eased back and crossed one long leg over the other. "My laughter is ill-advised, for we do tread in dark territory I'm afraid."

"You aren't seriously suggesting that the poor girl has become possessed by some demon, are you?"

"I should hope that you know me well enough, Watson, that I refute that explanation wholeheartedly. No, despite what the majority of London's populace may believe – and what the ignorant Sir Jeffrey Curbishly insists on proliferating – this is a simple matter of deception."

"By Mrs. Cardew?"

"Yes," Holmes replied languidly. "And she has involved her daughter in the scheme as well. I am certain of it."

"But what motive should they have for doing such a thing?"

"That is one of the few pieces of the puzzle which I have been unable to put into place. Until I can do so, I am afraid that my rational explanation shall be ignored."

"When were you first consulted on the matter?" I asked.

"Only days ago," Holmes answered. "I confess that I had not been following the case, being preoccupied with far more important matters. When Parker turned up on my doorstep asking for my opinion, I could not help but become involved in the business. Apparently after finding a cogent explanation for the Baskerville business, I have gained something of a reputation in certain circles as a debunker of ghosts."

Holmes spoke in a tone which did not mask his evident derision. Filling his pipe once more, I was about to do the same when we were arrested by the sound of the bell ringing below. A moment later, Mrs. Hudson entered with the card of our visitor. Passing it to Holmes, he glanced at it before smirking mischievously and handing it off to me.

The name of our guest: Sir Jeffrey Curbishly.

The man who entered our sitting room moments later was tall and broad-shouldered, carrying in his gloved hand a silk top hat and wrapped in an expensive-looking greatcoat, done over with a fur collar. He appeared to be in his mid-forties, for his temples had begun to grey, giving him an air of authority which complimented his learned-looking countenance. As he stepped into the room, I watched his dark eyes meet Holmes's. My friend arched an eyebrow ever so slightly and then wordlessly gestured toward the settee. Curbishly silently crossed the room and took a seat, his eye still trained on Holmes's with peculiar intensity.

"Ah, Sir Jeffrey," Holmes said, feigning a cordial tone as he struck a match and relighted his pipe, "I do not think that you have had the pleasure of meeting my friend and colleague, Dr. John Watson."

"I have not," Curbishly replied. "It is a pleasure, Doctor. I have read your accounts of Mr. Holmes's work with keen interest."

"Now then," said Holmes as he settled back in his chair, crossing one leg over the other in a deceptively languid manner, "what brings you to my home?"

"You know very well what brings me here." From his inner breast pocket, Curbishly withdrew a folded-up copy of *The Star*, the same one which still sat on our breakfast table. "This article."

"You must not blame me for the rather cavalier use of the phrase *wages war*. I usually hold the journalistic profession in some esteem. But I do believe that the amiable Mr. Parker did overstep his boundaries at his typewriter."

"This is not a simple matter of semantics," Curbishly retorted. "This is a blatant attempt to tarnish my image."

"I never did desire to do anything of the kind," Holmes replied. "In fact, Sir Jeffrey, I do hold your *scientific* work in high regard. I could not think of a more suited figure to be knighted for such contributions to the field as yourself. Still, since you have begun spouting this spiritualist claptrap, I cannot help but consider you a particularly nasty impediment to solving this case. That is – as you should know – my sole desire in the matter."

It was Curbishly's turn to smirk now. "Ah, you cannot admit when you are wrong. You cannot help but fight back when you've been bested. You should know as well as I that this business is firmly rooted in the supernatural."

"I do not see what leads you to such an assessment," Holmes retorted. "All of the evidence which has been made public to me suggests a rational explanation."

"Then perhaps you would care to explain the Ouija Board . . . and the other reported supernatural phenomenon which are connected to 41 Hamilton Gardens?"

"Pardon me," I said, "but what do you mean when you refer to the Ouija Board?"

Curbishly smirked again. "Have you been holding evidence from the Good Doctor in order to further your case?"

Holmes rolled his eyes.

"Allow me to elucidate, Doctor. Perhaps you may not have known, but I was one of the first people who was involved in this business after it took the public's attention. I have, for some time, been something of a public figure after I began a serious study of spiritualism. What started out as a passing interest in the subject – certainly you cannot deny asking yourself what happens after death – soon became a passion of mine. In my studies, I came to learn more about the spirit world. But I have also come to learn about a host of other entities which exist outside our own world. It is one of these entities that is responsible for the haunting of Hamilton Gardens.

"Imagine if you will, Dr. Watson, a soap bubble floating in the air. It – for the purpose of this explanation – represents the world in which we live. It is composed of all the settled orders of nature and laws of science which I have held dear in my line of work and which you, no doubt, also studied greatly before becoming a doctor. I ask you, Doctor: How likely is one to find a single, isolated soap bubble floating in the air? It seldom occurs. There are other soap bubbles which float and bounce around alongside of it. And these other bubbles represent their own worlds. They do not operate in the same manner as our world does. Some of these worlds are merely worlds of ideas and concepts, filled with intangible notions. Others are far more perceptible. They are the worlds inhabited by those who have shuffled off this mortal coil.

"The other difference between the real world and the analogy which I have just presented to you is that it is impossible for two soap bubbles to interact with one another. Should the two collide, they would burst. Picture instead, if you will, Dr. Watson, the bubble which represents our world attaching itself to one of these other bubbles. A clear link between the two has been forged."

I cast a glance in Holmes's direction and found my friend with his eyes closed, pulling on his pipe. His brow was knitted with a look of derision. Holmes – ever the skeptic, ever the rationalist, who believed only in what could be calculated, observed, and studied – could not help but find Curbishly's talk impossible to digest. I tried not to mirror my friend's contempt towards the spiritualist. I thought that there could be something to be gained from his words which might stimulate something in Holmes and lead him to a conclusion.

"There are many methods in bridging the gap between our world and another," Curbishly continued. "Perhaps the most common sort is the séance. I perceive that you are familiar with the practice, Doctor?"

"I am," I replied. In our time together, Holmes and I had been called in to investigate spiritualists who would con the public out of their money with cheap trick shows and conjuring tricks at such séances.

"The method which figures directly in the case of Lillian Cardew is the aforementioned Ouija Board – a device which is used to contact spirits from another world. The person using the board is guided by the hand of a spirit and may communicate with them in this manner. I have seen a number of successful demonstrations of the Ouija Board in my time. Still, these devices do present a hazard for the user, and I believe that young Lillian Cardew fell victim to a spirit after using a Ouija Board.

"As I mentioned already, Doctor, I was one of the first people to be involved in the Hamilton Gardens case. I met with Mrs. Cardew and observed her daughter from afar. When I visited the household, I could see young Lillian Cardew laying in her bed in a terribly weakened state, still groaning and muttering under her breath in a voice which I am certain was not her own. With her mother's consent, I was able to search through a few of the girl's possessions and came across a Ouija Board. It was a crude, make-shift type, but spirits are not particular. Mrs. Cardew insisted that she had never seen it before. Nonetheless, I was certain now that the board had to be connected to Lillian's strange behavior, and I endeavored to find out when she had used it. I spoke to a number of the children who reside in the neighborhood. One of them told me of how she and Lillian had been playing with the board one day.

"Armed with this knowledge, I began to investigate the house itself, No. 41 Hamilton Gardens. Before Mrs. Cardew moved into the residence three years ago, it was occupied by the Wheelwrights – Horace and Patricia. According to my research – which I can easily verify should you desire it – Patricia Wheelwright died eight years ago. Her husband died two years later. You may ask what connection this has with the rest of the case. I shall tell you: According to the child with whom Lillian Cardew played with the Ouija Board, the spirit who they managed to contact was named *Horace*."

"And you believe that the ghost of Horace Wheelwright is responsible for the strange goings-on now?"

"Not quite, Dr. Watson." Curbishly leaned forward in his seat. "You see – to return to my soap bubble analogy – just as one bubble can connect to another, imagine a number of soap bubbles connected like the links of a chain. In this way, an entity from one world could travel through various worlds and into our own. This is undoubtedly frightening for, as I have been quite vocal pointing out, I believe that the Devil – or one of his agents – his responsible for possessing and corrupting Lillian Cardew."

Sherlock Holmes snorted loudly.

"Just as the spirit of Horace Wheelwright made it into our world," Curbishly continued unabashed, "I believe that a demon used the poor man's spirit as a means of free transport. Unwittingly, Lillian Cardew was corrupted by the demon as she used the Ouija Board to communicate with the spirit world."

"What evidence do you have to support this claim?" I asked.

"There can be no other explanation," Curbishly replied with steadfast resolve. "I have read the witness's testimony, and I can assure you that there is no possible way for a young girl to contort herself and writhe as she did under her own power. It is simply a physical impossibility."

Sir Jeffrey Curbishly sat back on the settee with a smug expression etched on his face. "Well," he said at length, "what do you have to say to that, Mr. Holmes?"

For what masqueraded as an eternity, Sherlock Holmes sat calmly pulling on his pipe. At length, he laid it aside, sat back in his chair, and pressed the tips of his fingers together in his usual gesture of contemplation. "I do not believe a word of what you have to say," he quietly said. "You have put forth no evidence to support your claim, and in my line of work, cold, hard evidence is an imperative component to solving any problem. Therefore, Sir Jeffrey, I shall not resolve to do anything about the newspaper headline to which you

235

took such offense. If all-out war is what you desire, then I shall only be too happy to oblige."

"What are you saying, Holmes?"

"I am saying that I can present a logical explanation to the Hamilton Gardens case in twenty-four hours' time. And, what is more, I needn't even leave my rooms here at Baker Street to do it. I am in possession of nearly all the facts and, what I do not know off-handedly, I can ascertain with the help of Dr. Watson and my other agents. By the time that the last edition of *The Star* goes to press tomorrow evening, you shall find my explanation therein."

Another palpable silence descended over the sitting room, Sir Jeffrey Curbishly staring into space. I could see in his eyes a look of befuddlement, and I could read the man well that he was the sort who always believed that he was in in total control of any situation, but for once in his life he seemed to know not where to turn. Curbishly drew in a deep breath and stood from his seat.

"Very well, Mr. Holmes," he said as he placed his hat back on his head, "if you wish to act in this manner, then I shall not do anything to prevent you from making a fool of yourself. I fully expect you to be a man of your word."

"My word is my bond, Sir Jeffrey."

The ghost of a smirk flashed across Holmes's face and, wordlessly, Curbishly turned sharply on his heel and exited the room. As soon as he had pulled the door shut behind him, Sherlock Holmes laughed. "I hazard a guess that Sir Jeffrey felt rather the part of the fool," Holmes said. "Surely he came in here with the intent of winning me over to his point-of-view, and if he succeeded not with me then certainly with you, my dear fellow. Have you ever heard someone deliver such drivel with such authority? Oh, Sir Jeffrey Curbishly would make a handsome sum for himself if he made his living in the prosperous con artist trade."

"But do you think that what you have done is wise, Holmes?" I asked. "I have never been one to question your powers, but certainly you have made your situation needlessly complex by imposing on yourself confinement to this place?"

"Hmm? Oh, I beg pardon, Watson. My mind was elsewhere. You need not worry about me." Holmes rubbed his hands together delightfully. "I shall relish this game between Curbishly and me. And a game it shall be. If I know Sir Jeffrey as I think I do, than he will doubtlessly take this rivalry with deadly seriousness, and I would not be in the least bit surprised to find a man posted on the opposite side of the street to ensure the fact that I do not break my word and leave these premises."

"Then what do you intend to do, if you are indeed going to be a veritable prisoner here for the next day?" I asked.

"I shall first send a telegram to the amiable Mr. Parker and tell him of this new development. This is the sort of stuff the press simply takes to like a fly to honey. And then, I shall see if Mrs. Hudson is willing to scare us up some luncheon. This case has already consumed our morning and now part of early afternoon. We shall no more speak of it."

Holmes was true to his word and refused to speak of the matter whilst we dined. In the meantime, he pressed me for information about my two weeks in the country, and I was only too willing to share my reminiscences of the past fortnight.

Just after we had had our dishes cleared away, Billy, the pageboy, scampered up the seventeen steps to our rooms carrying the latest edition of *The Star*. Holmes zealously paged through it and let out an exclamation as he clapped eyes on the desired article.

"Ah, Parker has done his job up to snuff once more," Holmes said.

Sherlock Holmes Challenges Spiritualist
to Game of Wits

According to the great detective, Mr. Sherlock Holmes himself, he is close to providing an explanation for the mysterious events which have transpired at No. 41 Hamilton Gardens which have so enraptured the public. Holmes says that he refutes the assertions of noted spiritualist, Sir Jeffrey Curbishly, who has provided a supernatural explanation for the case. In order to prove Curbishly wrong, Holmes has endeavored to solve the case in twenty-four hours without leaving his rooms in Baker Street. This reporter shall carry the story as news develops and will print Holmes's explanation of the case when it is provided to him.

"That article will certainly incite Curbishly's temper," I said.

"Just what I hoped to do," Holmes remarked with a wry grin. "While Sir Jeffrey may have taken matters to an extreme when he accused me of wishing to tarnish his image, I confess that there is

237

some latent bullying behind my actions. I do it not entirely for myself though, old friend. If Curbishly continues to proliferate his fantastic theories, then dozens of hapless and unsuspecting people will continue to believe in his words and fall right into the hands of the charlatans and tricksters we have spent time exposing. There is more at stake in this case than is readily apparent."

Holmes moved to his chair and took a seat, stretching his long frame out and once more pressing the tips of his fingers together.

"Well," I said at length, "you do not have much time. If this really is a game of wits between you and Curbishly, what is your first move?"

"I feel as though a visit to the scene is imperative," Holmes replied. "I confess that I have yet to venture forth to Hamilton Gardens, and seeing as it is impossible for me to do so now, I must ask for your help, my dear fellow."

"I shall only be too happy to help in any way that I can," I answered.

"Excellent!" Holmes cried. "Then away you must to No. 41 Hamilton Gardens. The place has become a center of attention in this city, so there is some police activity there. I would not be surprised should you meet a constable or even good old Stanley Hopkins in the midst of your sojourn. But make your way to the house tonight and report back to me everything you see and hear. As Parker told us, the scene is a most unusual one for events of this kind to transpire. I shall ask you to perform one small but utterly vital task for me: I shall need you to procure for me a photograph of the two women concerned in this business. That should be the last link in the chain for me to build my case."

Silence fell over the room as Holmes then seemed to forget all about the events of the morning yet again and busied himself with his chemical apparatus. I, feeling as though I should wait for my friend's directive before going on my mission, settled in with a book and my pipe and wiled away much of the afternoon in a contemplative silence.

Mrs. Hudson brought us our dinner and we ate, Holmes most heartily, which was most gratifying for me, as I knew of his bad habits in foregoing sustenance when he was occupied with work. After our supper was cleared away, Holmes inspected his watch and drummed his fingers anxiously on the table. He lit a cigarette and cast a dark glance into the street below.

"The hour approaches when you should make your way to the scene," he murmured with a foreboding undertone in his voice.

I drew up to the window where Holmes stood and parted the curtain to cast a glance into the thoroughfare below. Just as Holmes had predicted earlier, there was a man standing on the opposite side of the street. He was dressed in a handsome but simple suit of clothes and appeared to be in the process of lighting a pipe. Holmes let out a bemused exclamation.

"Judging from the none-too-small pile of matches by his foot, I should say that our friend has been standing in that spot for at least two hours. Sir Jeffrey is certainly the competitive sort. I shouldn't wish you to be accosted by the fellow – though I clearly laid down the rules that my agents are free to come and go as they please – so I would recommend leaving by the back."

Only moments later, I had bundled myself up in my greatcoat and bowler, had descended the staircase, and left out the back door. I made my way along the road until I came to the main thoroughfare and hailed a hansom. Once ensconced in the cab, I sat back and let the events of the day play out in my mind. It was cool in the cab – the autumn air had turned biting and cold quickly. The chill which passed over me only made my mission all the more tense. *What was I to find?* I asked myself. Though I was by no means won over by a supernatural theory, what horrors might await me at this house which was so shrouded in mystery and horror? These thoughts occupied me until my hansom drew up outside the very dwelling and I alighted, feeling, for an instant, unsteady as my boot touched the cobblestone pavement.

The road was narrow, lined on both sides by buildings of a small but comfortable-looking nature. A set of neat steps ascended towards the doors of each building and, should there not have been a constable posted outside the door to No. 41, I might have figured that it was just as innocuous a residence as any other building on the boulevard. I slowly approached the uniformed officer and I could see his face – a youthful countenance with a large nose and bushy mustache – register a look of familiarity with my own person. All the same, it was evident that the man could not place my name.

"Sorry, sir," he said, "no one's allowed in."

"But I have come under the express orders of – "

Before I could finish, the door to No. 41 opened behind the constable and the youthful Inspector Stanley Hopkins faced me in the doorway. "Dr. Watson! I must confess that I am not very surprised to find you here!"

"Good evening, Inspector," I replied. "I take it then that you have been reading the latest edition of *The Star*."

Hopkins patted in his inner breast pocket. "I just got through with it. You know how I respect Mr. Holmes, but I must admit that I rather think his ego has gone to his head this time around. Step aside, Constable McWilliams. This man may come through."

Stanley Hopkins opened the door wider and I stepped over the threshold and into the house. I found myself standing in a small foyer which opened up into a modest sitting room, furnished with a few chairs and a settee. A low fire burned in the grate on the opposite side of the room and, as I followed the inspector into the house, I saw the figure of a woman, perched on the edge of the settee. She appeared to be gazing deeply into the undulating flames.

Hopkins cleared his throat and the woman turned about quickly. She was a tall, handsome woman. Her beauty was not diminished by the redness around her eyes and the tears which still festooned them. Clothed entirely in black, I would have perceived her to be in mourning. Knowing her situation, however, I figured that she was not far afield from grieving.

"Mrs. Cardew," Hopkins said gently, "I would like to introduce you to Dr. John Watson. He is a personal friend of mine, as well as the friend and biographer of Mr. Sherlock Holmes, the detective."

"How do you do, madam?" I asked. I took her hand in mine. Her grip was weak and, considering her dainty appendage, the lady seemed suddenly very fragile to me.

"It is a pleasure to meet you," she replied softly. "I had read that Mr. Holmes has taken an interest in Lillian's case."

"He most certainly has," I replied. "I am here acting on Holmes's behalf."

"I am desperate to get this matter settled, Dr. Watson," Mrs. Cardew replied. She returned to her seat and gestured to one of the chairs. I sat as she withdrew a handkerchief from the folds of her black dress and dabbed at her eyes. "Can I be of assistance to you or Mr. Holmes in anyway?"

I was not sure how to advance from here. Holmes's instructions were vague in the extreme. I found myself now with little idea how to proceed. The overwhelming sense of dread which had seemed to settle over the household did nothing to ease my nerves. I suddenly remembered how keen Holmes had been to see photographs of the mother and daughter, and the mission which he had given me.

"Perhaps you can be of assistance to us, Mrs. Cardew," I replied. "Do you have any photographs of you with your daughter?"

"Oh, of course," she said. She rose and moved further into the sitting room. I joined her at a small bureau. It was covered with an

240

assortment of papers and, atop it, two framed pictures, each of the mother and daughter. I could see new tears welling up in Mrs. Cardew's eyes.

"These photographs are my only solace now," she said as she pressed her handkerchief to her eye again. "Only this afternoon, that reporter, Mr. Parker, came around and asked if he might borrow one of them. I refused and told him that they were the only memories of the little girl I so love."

I knew that Holmes would be pleased to hear that Parker had made the attempt. But, seeing as I was playing the part of the understanding supporter, I was obligated to exclaim, "The nerve of the fellow!"

Mrs. Cardew returned the frame to the bureau top and turned on me suddenly. "Oh, Dr. Watson! Will my little girl ever be better? I don't care what has caused her to act this way. I simply want her to be the same, smiling child whom I raised for eleven years."

"I am confident that she will recover," I replied. I gently took hold of her hand once more and patted it. "Some of England's finest minds have taken an interest in this case. I am certain that your little girl will be returned to you."

I nimbly reached out my other arm and, with an amount of stealth which I think would have impressed even the most seasoned of thieves, I slipped one the pictures into the folds of my coat.

"Thank you, Dr. Watson," she said. "Is there anything else which I may do to assist you?"

"I think not," I replied.

I turned to Stanley Hopkins. "There have been no developments, I take it?"

"I'm afraid not, Doctor. Dr. Flaughtery called 'round earlier this evening to tend on Lillian. He's still upstairs now. He has come up with nothing, I'm afraid."

Though I knew that it was hardly my place to interfere, I took pity on the poor woman. As a doctor, I had to help her in some capacity and, perhaps without knowing entirely what I was saying, I had asked if I could also take a look at Lillian Cardew. The faintest ghost of a smile crossed across the edges of Mrs. Cardew's mouth.

"You said yourself that some of England's finest minds have taken an interest in my daughter's case," she said. "As a despondent mother, I would not be doing all that is in my power to see her get better if I denied one more of England's finest minds to examine my girl."

I politely waved away Mrs. Cardew's compliment. I cast a nod to Hopkins, who slightly nodded his head in approval. Then, gesturing for Mrs. Cardew to lead the way, I followed her to the narrow staircase. As I mounted the steps behind her, I suddenly felt an overwhelming sense of dread overtake me. With each step, I was nearing the spot of the strange goings-on which had captivated and horrified the nation. What was I to find on the other side of the door leading to Lillian Cardew's room? As we reached the top step, I felt a numbness surround my legs. I took hold of the wooden banister to support myself.

Mrs. Cardew tapped on the door. From within, I heard a voice call out and we stepped inside. The man I took to be Dr. Flaughtery was standing over the girl's bed. He held a dainty wrist between his fingers and stood watching the hands of a watch tick away before him. He put it back into his waistcoat pocket and gently returned Lillian Cardew's arm to her side on the bed. She was wrapped in her sheets, which covered all of her petite frame in a tight shroud.

"Doctor," Mrs. Cardew said addressing Flaughtery, "I would like to introduce you to Dr. John Watson. He asked if he could examine Lillian."

"By all means, Doctor," Flaughtery replied, stepping away from the bed.

I approached the bedside and what happened next still haunts me to this day. In a swift movement which caught everyone in the room off-guard, Lillian Cardew jumped up from her lying position and stood upon the bed. It was Lillian Cardew, but one could be forgiven for thinking otherwise, as she looked nothing like the pleasant, little girl who had stood dutifully by her mother's side in the photograph I had seen only moments ago. She was wrapped in her nightdress and her hair stuck out wildly in all directions. Beneath the dark locks which covered her face, I could still see her eyes which had gone over white. She gnashed her teeth together like some wild animal and, before I could move, she had jumped from her bed and leapt at me.

I confess that fear had rooted me to the spot when the girl grabbed hold of my arm while she had launched herself into the air. Pandemonium broke out as both Flaughtery and Mrs. Cardew rushed to my side. Both were effecting to pry the little girl from my sleeve. Lillian let out a guttural snarl, not unlike the hiss of an angry crocodile – a sound which I am unlikely to forget from my days passing through India.

242

The two managed to wrench Lillian from my arm, but once they had done so, she spun around and lashed out at Flaugherty. I saw her fingers connect with his cheek and he tumbled backwards, the traces of the scratch marks crimson on his face. He fell backwards as Stanley Hopkins rushed up the stairs and stood in the threshold of the room, his gaze locked on the strange tableau within. Composing himself quite quickly, Hopkins rushed into the room and took hold of Lillian. Together, we endeavored to force the girl back onto the bed and, as we held her down, Flaughtery regained his composure, stood, and rummaged through his Gladstone bag. He produced a syringe and, rushing forward to Lillian, thrust the needle into her arm and pushed the piston down. She went limp only seconds later, leaving the three of us to stand around in shock and exhaustion.

"The sedative I gave her should keep her out for a few hours," Flaughtery said breathlessly.

"What came over her?" Mrs. Cardew asked.

"I have no idea," Dr. Flaughtery responded. He dabbed at his bleeding cheek with his own handkerchief and endeavored to catch his breath. "She was like a wild animal. I've never seen a person do anything like it this side of an asylum door."

The doctor's words did nothing for Mrs. Cardew. She made her way out of the room and silently descended the staircase back into the sitting room. Hopkins and I followed shortly behind and, when we found our way into the sitting room, Mrs. Cardew had sank once more onto the settee and was convulsing with an onslaught of fresh tears. The whole scene left me in a state of utter stupefaction and I took my leave. There was nothing that I was looking forward to more than a drink and the warm fire of Baker Street.

As I rode homeward, ensconced once more in a hansom cab, I knew that my dreams would be haunted by the face of Lillian Cardew. I was inclined to agree with Dr. Flaughtery as I sat back against the plush interior of the hansom. I had never seen any person act the way the little girl did that night. Though I was loath to admit it, I – only for an instant – entertained the notion that some supernatural hand may have played a role in this bad business. Was this evidence, I wondered as the cab drew up outside of 221b Baker Street, that the Devil can play a hand in the affairs of men?

"It certainly sounds as if you had an eventful evening," Sherlock Holmes said, rather more cheerily than I would have liked, at the conclusion of my tale. He was wrapped in his preferred dressing

243

gown and stretched out before the fire, filling his pipe with tobacco from the Persian slipper while I sat opposite and nursed a brandy.

Lighting a match and applying it to the bowl of his pipe, Holmes tossed the stub into the fire and sat, pulling on his pipe for what seemed like an eternity. "You will," he said at length, "be glad to hear that my evening here has proved to be quite fruitful as well."

"Oh? Why was that?"

"The photograph," Holmes replied. "It was, as I thought, quite illuminating."

Standing, Holmes moved to the table, where he picked up the picture with which I had absconded and pressed it into my hand. I stared into the content faces of Mrs. Cardew and Lillian. Nothing about them seemed to suggest the misery and hardship which both now endured. Had Holmes been in one of his more philosophical moods, I might have made a comment about the Hand of Fate, but I resisted. I handed the photograph back to my friend.

"The picture is of use then?"

"It is invaluable," Holmes said with a grin. "It truly is the missing piece."

"You've solved it then?"

Holmes held his index finger aloft. "Not yet," he said. "This development has raised a question or two of its own which I endeavored to answer this evening. I've sent a few telegrams and – with luck – I shall receive an answer to all of them on the morrow."

I downed the last of my brandy. "Well, go on Holmes, let me hear it through!"

"Ah, I am afraid that you shall have to wait, my dear Watson. As I mentioned, the case hinges upon a number of pieces of conjecture, and it would be remiss of me should I tell you my solution without facts to support it. Besides, you ought to know me well enough that I cannot resist a touch of the dramatic. The denouement of this affair will take place here, in this very room, tomorrow evening."

Holmes returned his attention to the photo. He seemed to consider it intently for some time before I heard him murmur, nearly inaudibly under his breath, "She does look quite young, doesn't she?"

I stared up at Holmes from my seat, my attention arrested by his cryptic comment. "Lillian Cardew?" I asked.

"Yes," Holmes replied. "She is quite young."

"The girl is only eleven years old," I countered, not a little peeved at my friend's usual, enigmatic manner.

244

"Is she?" came his unexpected reply.

So saying, Holmes laid his pipe aside and moved away from his chair. "It has been a rather taxing day for the both of us," he said. "I would suggest a good night's rest. I shall see you in the morning, Watson."

Crossing to his room, Holmes stepped inside and closed the door behind him. I huffed. Sometimes, I told myself, Sherlock Holmes could be the most infuriating of men. Despite what we had both been through that day, he still refused to share his results. Still, I knew Holmes's methods well enough by now not to be too upset. I poured myself another brandy and stared into the flames in the fireplace for some time. Nodding off, I roused myself and made my way to my bed.

It was a fitful sleep which came to me that evening. Visions of Lillian Cardew still burned in my memory like an ember. I recall that I woke more than once during the seemingly endless night. I could still hear the hisses which the little girl made. I could see her eyes which had gone over white. Finally, knowing that sleep would never truly come, I rose early, washed, dressed, and made my way down to our sitting room. I sat about with a book for some time before Mrs. Hudson brought a pot of hot coffee, which did go some way to restoring my spirits after the sleepless evening.

Per his habit, Holmes slept late and, when he did sweep into the sitting room, he seemed cheery and in good sorts. We breakfasted and, at the conclusion of our meal, he moved to his usual chair and spread the first edition of the paper across his knee.

"This is a most curious development," he said.

Passing the page to me, I read the bold headline:

Famed Haunted House Burns in Mysterious Fire

"Good lord," I murmured.

"Would you be so kind as to read the article, Watson?"

No. 41 Hamilton Gardens of St. John's Wood, [I began] *which has, of late, gained some reputation as a haunted house following a series of disturbances that have garnered much public attention, caught fire in the early hours of the morning. The only occupants of the house, Mrs. Emily Cardew and her eleven-year-old daughter, Lillian, are, as yet, unaccounted for. Inspector Stanley Hopkins of Scotland Yard – who was already posted at the house following the series of disturbances – refused to comment whether or not the family is believed to have perished in the flames.*

"'The matter of the supposed haunting of No. 41 Hamilton Gardens has incited some public interest in the past few weeks. Noted spiritualist Sir Jeffery Curbishly has been involved in the matter, as has the famed detective, Mr. Sherlock Holmes.

"I would not be surprised in the slightest of Sir Jeffrey uses this development to his advantage," Holmes said once I had finished reading. "To Sir Jeffrey, there are no earthly occurrences. That fire was not an accident, nor was it caused by some human hand. Surely, it was the Devil who burned the house down, bathing his demonic disciples in hellfire!"

"Do you think they perished in the fire, Holmes?"

"Unlikely in the extreme," Holmes retorted. "And now, I must wait until I receive the answers to my telegrams. I am, unfortunately, working against the unstoppable forces of bureaucratic red tape. An answer could be hours away."

Holmes wordlessly moved to his chemical apparatus and continued to work in silence.

Busying himself with his test tubes and beakers, he sat quietly as I finished perusing the paper. Only a quarter-of-an-hour had elapsed before there came a ring from the door below. Holmes sat up, a grin crossing his face. Standing, he opened the door and met Mrs. Hudson in the threshold, relieving her of our visitor's card which she carried upon a small, silver tray. Holmes studied it and wordlessly gestured for our landlady to show the guest in.

Holmes turned to me and smiled like a cat who had just eaten a canary. "An answer to one of my telegrams has come sooner than anticipated, Watson."

A moment later, Holmes greeted a tall, distinguished-looking woman, dressed in mourning, at the top of the stairs and showed her into the sitting room, where he briefly introduced me and then took his place before the fire.

"You might be interested to know, Watson, that our distinguished guest is Mrs. Henrietta Cardew, mother of the late Lieutenant Cardew. I contacted her last evening, and she has done me a tremendous service by replying as promptly as she did."

Though I perceived that the woman who drew into our sitting room would have normally held herself with a regal bearing, she moved into the room slowly and under great duress. She had stripped off her gloves and held them tightly in her hands, wringing them anxiously. I knew at once that the poor woman was consumed with thoughts for her daughter-in-law and beloved grandchild.

"I extend my thoughts and best wishes to you, Mrs. Cardew," I said, as Holmes gently led the woman to the settee. "I know how trying this morning's news must be for you."

"It is only because I know that you are so intimately associated with all of this terrible business, Mr. Holmes, that I came as quickly as I did. Therefore, if I can be of any service to you, it would take a great weight off of my mind. Emily had been so consumed by the tragic events which have surrounded her and Lillian for the past few weeks. I truly fear for her. She had shut herself away completely and refused to see me."

"Her actions surprised you no doubt?"

"They most certainly did," Mrs. Cardew replied. "But, I suppose, I can understand her."

"I understand it that you have been providing Emily with something of an allowance ever since the untimely death of your son."

"I have, Mr. Holmes," Mrs. Cardew said, seeming to take umbrage with Holmes's questioning tone. "Emily was quite beside herself after my son's death. Then she returned to England with the baby. I felt morally objected to assist her in any way I could."

"And you have continued to look out for Lillian's interests to this day?"

"Why, of course I have. The dear, sweet girl deserves only the best in my mind."

Holmes drew himself up before the fire. "And how long did you intend to carry on financially supporting Emily and Lillian?"

"Mr. Holmes," the woman said impetuously, "I fail to see the point – "

Holmes quieted the woman with a look.

"I had intended to support Lillian until she was of legal age, of course."

Sherlock Holmes crossed to the table and plucked the framed picture from the tabletop. "Mrs. Cardew, the question I am about to pose to you will seem unusual, but would you be so kind as to identify the woman in this photograph?"

Holmes handed the photograph to the woman and she stared at it intently. "It's Emily," she said. "But who is – ?"

"Who is the young girl with her?" Holmes asked.

"Yes," she replied, her tone wavering, filled with confusion.

Holmes took the photo from Mrs. Cardew's hand and returned it to the table. "Thank you very much, Mrs. Cardew. You have indeed been of invaluable assistance to my case."

With a few words of reassurance, Holmes managed to cajole the woman to follow him out of the room and, once he had bundled her away in a cab, he returned to the sitting room where I still sat, my face a mask of bewilderment.

"What is the meaning of all this, Holmes?"

"All in good time," Holmes retorted.

It was only moments after our last guest had departed that the bell chimed below once again. Holmes saved Mrs. Hudson the trouble of having to mount the seventeen steps to our sitting room by greeting the guest in the foyer. I moved to the door and heard my friend exclaim pleasantly as he opened the door and guided our client through. I was greeted by the sight of Holmes showing an austere-looking woman into our sitting room where he gestured for her to sit.

"Miss Primm," he said, "you have, as I understand it, been in charge of the St. Isidore Home for Children for the past twenty years."

The woman peered over the top of the delicate pince-nez which she wore on her pallid face. "You understand quite well, Mr. Holmes."

"Excellent," Holmes replied. "I realize the question which I posed to you in my telegram is one you may be hesitant to answer, but it is imperative to solve a baffling mystery, and it will bring to book two dangerous scoundrels: Did a woman going by the name of either Cardew or Melville adopt a child from your foundling home around twelve years ago?"

Miss Primm shifted uncomfortably in her chair. She drew in a very deep breath as she stared, fixated at one point upon the carpet before she said, "You should consider yourself quite lucky, Mr. Holmes, that when I received your telegram early this morning, I consulted my register at once. I can tell you most definitely that a woman answering to the name of Melville adopted a girl from our home."

"This girl," Holmes pressed, "what was she like?"

"Oh, she was a lovely baby," Miss Primm said, her grim countenance lightening as she reminisced. "She was a beautiful girl, though rather sickly, I'm afraid. But Miss Melville seemed like such a caring young woman that we had no qualms whatsoever in sending the girl off with her."

"Thank you," Holmes said. His face was a mask as he showed Miss Primm to the door. Then, silently he returned to his chemical apparatus.

Knowing that this would occupy him for the remainder of the morning, I decided that there was nothing for me to do but decamp to my club. I set out and, as I hailed a hansom, I cast a glance across the street. I could see Curbishly's man standing on the opposite side of the road, his eye still fixed upon the window of our sitting room, where Holmes was visible at his task. I chuckled in spite of myself as I rode off.

I spent my morning and afternoon in solitude. I perused the papers at length and sampled a fine port. I also played billiards with my customary partner, Thurston. His attempts to spark conversation regarding the Hamilton Gardens business were not as fruitful as he would have wished, I am sure, for I was unable to supply him with any true answers.

It was nearing five and I was making my way out of the club when I happened to catch sight of the latest edition of *The Star*. Its front page leading article declared – just as Holmes had surmised – that Sir Jeffrey Curbishly had put forth a supernatural explanation for the house fire. Hailing another hansom, I rode back to Baker Street, keenly aware that my long wait to hear Holmes's solution was almost at an end.

I didn't suspect that our sitting room would be as full as it was when I arrived. Holmes stood before the fireplace while Stanley Hopkins had taken my friend's customary chair. Mr. Parker was seated in my own seat, and Sir Jeffrey Curbishly sat uncomfortably on the sofa.

"Glad that you have joined us, Watson," Holmes said airily. "I am just about to present my explanation for the Hamilton Gardens business."

I took a seat at the breakfast table and, once Parker had extracted his notebook from his inner pocket, Holmes drew himself up and began.

"From the beginning," said Holmes, "I never accepted that there was anything remotely supernatural about the Hamilton Gardens business. Though the case did appear to have some fanciful aspects, I resolutely believed that this was the work of some person. The only person – or persons – who could have been responsible was Mrs.

Cardew and her daughter. I did not know how or why they would do this. That is, until I happened to make a chance remark about 'the prosperous con artist trade'. This, in itself, was what truly started the cogs working in my mind. Mrs. Emily Cardew and her daughter were not what they appeared.

"But, I asked myself, why should they wish to create an elaborate ruse about demonic possession? As Mr. Parker told me, Mrs. Cardew was quite well-off financially. Her late father had a position in Her Majesty's Government, and she was supported by the family of her late husband. Their house was situated in one of the better regions of the city, meaning that the family was not trying to move from their quarters. Despite all of this, I knew something for certain: The appeal of money can persist, even when one is well off. Simply put, gentlemen, we have been witness to one of the most elaborate and deceptive schemes which I have ever witnessed.

"Once I began to question the character of Mrs. Cardew and her daughter, I sent a telegram to my brother, Mycroft. He occupies a position in Her Majesty's Government, and I wondered if any such person as Mr. Melville, Mrs. Cardew's father, actually existed. He responded to me only hours ago and told me that there was no record of anyone by the name of Melville having a daughter named Emily who had occupied any governmental position. This lie was only the first in a series. I sent another telegram to the public records office and requested a birth certificate for Lillian Cardew. They too had no record.

"Prior to her marriage to Lieutenant Cardew, what do we know about Emily Cardew? It appears as though those specifics were fraudulent in the extreme. Mrs. Cardew is no longer the long suffering woman who Mr. Parker portrayed her as, but rather a woman whose past is a mystery. Having borne no child, one wonders just who Lillian Cardew is. It was for that simple reason that I wanted to see a photograph of the young woman and her daughter. Perhaps you gentlemen are unaware, but one of the simplest methods to determine someone's age is to simply look at his or her face. Between the ages of twenty-five and thirty-five, the first few visible lines of age are evident around the eyes and on the forehead. While I knew that it would be a challenge to determine this from a photograph alone, I figured that it would be the best method of age identification for me without leaving this room."

Holmes crossed to the breakfast table and once more picked up the photograph. He plucked his convex lens from his inner pocket and held the glass directly over the picture. "Though it is rather

250

difficult to perceive," he said, "the faintest lines around the eyes and forehead are visible to my lens on the face of Lillian Cardew. Lillian Cardew was not Emily's child, gentlemen. Rather, she is her *sister*."

There was an audible intake of breath from everyone in the room.

"The ruse was one of the simplest variety. Did I not comment last evening, Watson, that the person who was said to be Lillian Cardew truly *did* look like a little girl of eleven? No one would have questioned her for an instant.

"After I had determined that Lillian Cardew was also not who she appeared to be, I spent my evening poring over some of my indexes and clippings. I came across reference to a pair of sisters – performers – who were quite popular in small, traveling venues throughout England. The younger sister was particularly popular. She appeared to be a young girl despite being then in her early twenties. She was also an accomplished contortionist. You will doubtlessly recall the words of Mrs. Ellen Mortimer: '*Little Lillian Cardew convulsed wildly on her bed. It was as though she was a puppet being conducted by some great, invisible hand pulling at strings from above*'. An eleven-year-old girl could not have acted in such a way, but a limber woman certainly could.

"As I followed this line of investigation, I found that these sisters had left the sideshow and had married. It was something of a disappointment to ardent appreciators of vaudeville, though the sisters returned to the stage only a year later. What had become of the marriage no one knows. Anyhow, their spouses were surely only the first in their schemes: Find a financially stable young man, marry him, collect his money, and leave him shortly thereafter. This time around they played too bold a game.

"This morning I questioned Lieutenant Cardew's mother, Mrs. Henrietta Cardew. She told me that she planned on continuing to support both Emily and Lillian until Lillian grew to legal age. Therefore, Emily has the perfect avenue by which to elicit money from her late husband's family for many years. I believe that Emily grew to be financially dependent upon the Cardew's, and would have continued to live in a manner to which she had become rather accustomed had the real Lillian Cardew not suddenly died."

"What on earth do you mean, Mr. Holmes?" Parker cried.

"Consider, gentlemen: There must have been a real Lillian Cardew. Mr. Parker told me that Emily was close to the Cardew family, a fact which was substantiated by Mrs. Cardew herself. She *knew* the child. But I also spoke to the head of the Saint Isidore

Foundling Home this morning who informed me that about twelve years ago, a young woman calling herself Melville adopted a young girl. This could, one supposes, be coincidence, but I do not give credence to such theories. The links in the chain of events were beginning to be forged.

"What Emily did not anticipate was that the child was a sickly one. Doubtless, the girl eventually succumbed to some illness, but Emily was not prepared to lose the cash-flow which her mother-in-law continued to pay to her and her daughter. Emily persisted the falsehood that her daughter was alive and well, moving into Hamilton Gardens and having her sister impersonate her daughter and make friends with the neighborhood children. But as time went on, her inlaws wanted to see their granddaughter, and they needed to increase the distance between them and the Cardew family, so they concocted the elaborate scheme of demonic possession. It was all rather more *Grand Guignol* than they anticipated, I believe, and quickly grew beyond their control, but it did suffice. That is – until the popular press became involved."

"But how could we have fallen for their story?" Parker asked.

"That was the simplest part of it all," Holmes replied. "Though I applaud your work as a journalist, Mr. Parker, I am afraid that even you did not question all aspects of your story. As all journalists do, you followed the tantalizing tale to its source and never quite looked back. I would also not be surprised if you were taken in by Mrs. Cardew. You told me that you found her to be quite a handsome woman. I know that I am the exception to the rule, as most men do not allow their brains to govern their hearts. What's more, I shouldn't be surprised if Mrs. Mortimer, the witness to Lillian Cardew's possessed antics, was not chosen at random. You told me that Mrs. Mortimer called herself a 'God-fearing' woman who regularly attended church. It was not an out-of-character act to suggest that a priest be brought in to perform an exorcism.

"And lastly, there was Sir Jeffrey Curbishly. Sir Jeffrey's theories regarding demons from beyond our world excited the public and gave you much fodder to report upon, Parker. In cases like this, the power of the press can be quite a force."

"But about the fire?" Stanley Hopkins asked.

"The fire was doubtless set deliberately," Holmes replied. "As I do not routinely number modesty among the virtues, I feel quite at liberty saying that as soon as Mr. Parker's article went to print saying that I would deliver a solution to the mystery in twenty-four hours' time, Emily and Lillian Cardew knew they had to act quickly. I would not be surprised, Inspector, should you make a formal examination of Mrs. Cardew's bank account, that you would find it empty. Obviously, they took off with their accumulated money and burned the house down, only to further the claims that this business was not of an earthly origin."

"Incredible," I heard Parker murmur as he furiously took notes, "absolutely incredible!"

"I would imagine that they will find England an inhospitable place," Holmes continued as he lit a cigarette. "They are, after all, quite well known. I would be very much surprised if they have not taken the boat train for the Continent."

Slipping his watch from his waistcoat pocket, Holmes continued, "They have quite a head start, Inspector, but I am quite confident in your abilities, should you wish to give chase."

"I think I shall do just that," Stanley Hopkins said as he jumped from his seat. He shook Holmes by the hand, and a moment later he was out the door and bounding down the steps.

"And I think I had best be getting this story to my editor," said Parker, making his way out of the room.

Sir Jeffrey Curbishly stood, his eyes filled with contempt, saying more than he could ever hope to verbalize. He made his exit in virtual silence. Once he had gone, Holmes closed the door behind him.

"Not a bad way to while away two days' time, eh, Watson?"

"That was quite clever of you. Well done."

Sherlock Holmes slipped into his customary seat once more. "It really was a simple business, once I managed to look beyond the sensational dressing. I believe this was the perfect showcase to support one of my little sayings: As a rule, the more bizarre a thing is, the less mysterious it proves to be."

"I'm inclined to think that you're quite right," I replied.

Holmes tossed his cigarette into the fire. He stared into the flame for what seemed like an age. "The pair were quite the devious duo. But, on to other matters. You will have no doubt observed me hard at work for the past two days at my chemicals. I have recently become engaged in another matter which is proving to be far more difficult. Allow me ten minutes to give you the pertinent details, my friend, and then, provided that Sir Jeffrey was kind enough to call off his watchdog across the way, I would find your assistance at the scene most invaluable."

The Adventure of the Risen Corpse
by Paul D. Gilbert

There had been little doubt in the minds of anyone who had actually lived through and survived it that the late October of 1897 had been the coldest and most severe in living memory.

Throughout the entire fortnight which had led up to the night of Halloween, the temperature had struggled to barely rise above freezing, and it had left everyone in dread of the sinking of the sun, for it was then that the thermometer truly plunged.

On the night of the thirty-first of that unholy month, Sherlock Holmes and I were besieged within our sitting room by the necessity of staying warm, and also by the scarcity of worthwhile clients.

Admittedly, our visitor's chair had been in almost constant use throughout that time, but Holmes and I had both agreed that neither the affair of the Avaricious Philatelist, nor that of the Outraged Wife, were worthy of his talents, nor of inclusion in my ever-expanding chronicles. Inevitably, the constant redundancy to which Holmes's remarkable faculties had been subjected led to an increasing frustration within him, and his finely tuned nervous system was being stretched to its very limits.

Holmes had spent much of the day scouring the agony columns within all of the important newspapers, and then angrily condemning each one onto our life-preserving fire. My protests at his flagrant abuse of potentially worthwhile reading matter fell upon deaf ears, and he then turned his attention to the deserted street outside.

Each evening's severe frost had been accompanied by an impenetrable dark grey fog that seemed to absorb the decreasing temperature. Consequently, only the hardiest of individuals would dare to venture outside on such a God-forsaken night – or perhaps those set upon a mission of the most dire and vital consequence.

"As you know, Watson, I do not hold any truck with the superstitions and rituals that seem to accompany the eve of All Hallow's Day. However, if there were to be a night when the spirits might arise from their graves and when the Devil's minions could be drawn to dance merrily upon the realms of mortal men, then this surely would be the one."

"Really, Holmes, I must confess that I am most surprised to hear you, of all people, give voice to such sentiments. During the affair of the Sussex Vampire, I recall you using the phrase, 'no ghosts need apply', when you dismissed the notion of a real vampire completely out of hand. Surely a mere meteorological phenomenon such as this could not be enough to stimulate the imagination of the world's most renowned logistician?" I jovially declared.

Holmes waved me towards him with a broad sweep of his arm. "Watson, tell me, have you ever seen a fog so dense and capable of such obscurities? The few souls brave enough to venture out-of-doors on this portentous night appear to step through the portals of a toxic wall of vapour, never to re-emerge. The wild imaginings of ancient folk could have done far worse than to describe such an apparition as the rising and disappearance of a spirit, would you not say?"

"They lived in a dark and unenlightened time, Holmes, when superstitions and heresies formed an integral part of their culture. Indeed, even today, when the moon rises over the eve of All Hallow's, a tradition still exists whereby men tell tales of a spirit world beyond their own. However, nowadays this is born more of a desire to thrill and amuse, rather than the fact that they harbour a true belief in such things."

"Well said, Watson. Spoken as a true man of science, I must say." Holmes gave me a hearty slap across my back and then moved over to the port decanter.

I did not follow him immediately, however, for I felt strangely compelled by the phenomenon that had so stirred my friend's imagination. My mind had never been as closed as Holmes's when it came to matters of the paranormal. My own personal experience at the conclusion of the "Reluctant Spirit" affair was largely instrumental in causing me to accept, at least, the possibility of such singularities. On the other hand, my friend was always inclined to believe in a more logical and scientific explanation for any of the more bizarre cases that had been presented to us down the years, our encounter with the Baskerville's hound being a prime example.

Baker Street was as empty as I had ever seen it, but as I gazed down upon the few hearty souls that still trod upon its paving, I noticed how each one of them seemed to be constantly drifting in and out of a living, ethereal realm of ether. As urgent as their missions may have been, the lack of visibility induced a reluctant caution that slowed their passage to a stuttering crawl.

Then I saw her!

255

My attention had been drawn towards this apparition more by virtue of her conspicuous behaviour than her appearance. The horrendous conditions rendered it impossible to distinguish any of her features, other than her slim build, above-average height, and long flowing hair. However, it was hard not to have been intrigued by the fact that she was the only person on the street without a coat. Furthermore, she was dressed from head to foot in a flowing, diaphanous white material that belied the treacherous temperatures.

However, even if I had been indifferent to this implausible detail, I would have been a poor associate of Sherlock Holmes indeed had I not been drawn to the fact that this lady was moving at a speed that was nothing less than reckless in such dire visibility. Her frantic haste was made the more obvious by the cautious and shuffling progress of her fellow passers by, who eyed her with brief, horrified glances of disbelief.

Nevertheless, her most striking and distinguishing feature was her voluminous head of the most vibrant strawberry blonde hair that I had ever seen. This billowed out dramatically behind her as she made her perilous passage along Baker Street.

I was on the point of calling Holmes over, that he might share this most singular anomaly, when I realised that there was something most familiar about this rash young woman. I baulked at the thought of passing on my observation to Holmes, because had I done so, he would surely have dismissed me as an illogical buffoon.

Nevertheless, something in my manner had surely alerted him to my dilemma and he joined me at the window with a lithe, single bound. He took no obvious pleasure in my perplexity. On the contrary, he seemed as concerned as I had been and gazed down upon the scene below with the eyes of a hawk. He pressed his right forefinger against his lips as he tried to fathom the unfathomable.

Alexandra Gordon had been tried and convicted of a most heinous crime over six months previously, and her punishment for having drowned her own young daughter had been the harshest sentence of all. Despite an almost irrational belief in some quarters in her innocence, and a heartfelt protest that had echoed around the place of execution, Mrs. Gordon had been condemned to the gallows.

Although Holmes and I had not been actively involved in the case at any stage, Inspector Lestrade of Scotland Yard had been so horrified by the details of the crime that he had immediately rushed round to Baker Street to give voice to his obvious revulsion.

The details of the matter could not have been any clearer or palpable. The close neighbours of the Gordons all bore witness to the fact that Alexandra and her husband had been constantly at one another's throats for as long as anyone could remember. However, during the weeks that culminated in the tragedy, matters had taken a more dramatic and violent turn for the worse. The screaming and hollering were now accompanied by the sound of crashing doors and broken furniture, while the wailing of their long-suffering baby daughter was more than anyone could bear to hear.

Time and again the police had been summoned, but upon each occasion, Ralph Gordon had managed to convince them that nothing out of the ordinary had been taking place, and that theirs had been no worse than any other form of domestic strife. On the night in question, however, their protests of innocence could not have been further from the truth.

The rows and sounds of violence that night had reached an unprecedented crescendo and finally, amidst a barrage of awful insults and threats of violence from her drunken husband, Alexandra Gordon had been seen running from their little house in Bermondsey with her young daughter, Annie, bundled up within her arms.

She had sprinted away from the drunken lout, whose level of intoxication had rendered him incapable of giving a worthwhile pursuit, and then she had made directly for the river. Once there, and in full view of a throng of dumbstruck onlookers who had been drawn towards her by her manic screams and irrational movements, she raised her child above her head and hurled her daughter into the swirling tides below.

The events that then followed had been graphically described by the press, and Mrs. Gordon's crime immediately created outrage amongst the general public. Her escape was cut off by the angry mob and she was held in check by several among them until the police arrived to take her into custody. Under the circumstances, her arrest was probably the best fate that she might have expected, as the crowd were surely in the mood to have lynched her there and then. She had offered neither protest nor resistance while being led away by a group of constables, nor did she look back even once to discover the fate of her baby girl.

Our old friend Lestrade had been put in charge of the investigation, and he immediately instigated a thorough search of the rushing waters, using as many officers as Scotland Yard could spare. Their numbers were swelled by dozens of concerned members of the public, but all of their efforts were heartbreakingly unsuccessful and futile.

The search was resumed the following morning, at low tide when it was thought that the seeping mud banks might yield their ghastly treasure, but to everyone's surprise and consternation, no sign of the tragic child was ever found.

Despite the absence of a corpse, the trial did not go well for Alexandra Gordon. The Crown Prosecutors were able to produce dozens of witnesses on their behalf, all of whom were eager to offer their own version of the events by the river. Each one corroborated the testimony of the other, and before long there was very little doubt in the minds of all those present that Alexandra had deliberately drowned her daughter.

Rather bizarrely, Mrs. Gordon offered not a single word in her own defence, and she just sat there throughout the entire proceedings, staring blankly in front of her, showing neither emotion nor remorse. Some amongst those who were seated close to her would even report afterwards that she betrayed a strange and enigmatic smile during the whole trial, and she displayed not a sign of concern for her own inevitable fate.

Consequently it was left to her publicly appointed lawyer to point out that she had been reacting to the most mitigating of circumstances. After all, her husband had often been prone to the most violent and threatening behaviour imaginable and he had frequently been heard to even threaten the life of their daughter. Surely, he had reasoned, such domestic turmoil would have gone some way to creating the mental instability that Mrs. Gordon had displayed on the day in question?

Certainly, anyone who had seen her that evening would have been left in no doubt that her behaviour had been irrational, and therefore she had been deemed capable of any sort of violent action. Nevertheless, the only testimony that she offered was her assertion that she only did it to save her daughter from further abuse at the hands of her husband.

Naturally enough, the judge and his jury were unanimous in condemning her, and at the appointed date and time, Alexandra Gordon was summarily executed by the noose. Her execution received as much press coverage as had her trial, and therefore everyone soon became familiar with the appearance of the notorious child killer. She had died with her beautiful strawberry blonde hair in a bun and wearing a flowing, white, diaphanous gown. Strangely, it had only been at the very end, when there was clearly no chance of redemption, that she finally broke her silence and pleaded for mercy

258

in a manner that reached a hysterical crescendo. Of course, by then it was to no avail.

Once Holmes was by my side, I pointed tentatively through the window towards the mysterious woman in white.

"Holmes," I whispered, "I have just seen the ghostly form of Alexandra Gordon"

"Really, Watson, I know that it is the night of Halloween, and that our recent conversation may well have stirred your unusually fertile imagination, but that is surely no reason to abandon the use of all reason. You know as well as I that the tragic Mrs. Gordon was hanged in full public view, these six months past."

"I am fully aware of that, Holmes, but there is also no escaping from the evidence of my own eyes."

At that precise instant, the spectral woman emerged once more from the murky miasma that had engulfed her but a moment before. That she seemed agitated was obvious even from such a distance and through such awful visibility. However, the cause of her agitation was not as yet obvious to us. Even Sherlock Holmes, despite his unshakable faith in the ideology of pure logic, could not deny the existence of an image that threatened to shake his beliefs to their very foundations.

Suddenly and uncharacteristically, Holmes slapped me on my back with a force and with a light-heartedness that belied the sombre situation that now confronted us.

"So, are you up for a spot of ghost hunting, friend Watson?" he asked.

"Well, of course I am," I declared.

"Then come along, Doctor. The journey begins!"

Holmes dashed off to his room and a moment later he re-emerged, as well prepared for the elements outside as I had ever seen him. Not only was he wearing his heaviest coat and muffler, but his hat was tied down with an extra scarf and his favourite brown blanket was draped dramatically around his shoulders.

However, by the time that I had returned from my room with my own hat and coat, I was disturbed to note that my friend, despite his great encumbrance, had already fled down the stairs and had disappeared into the all-enveloping mire outside.

I am not ashamed to admit that I found the surreal surroundings to be not a little disconcerting. Baker Street, with which I was obviously well familiar, now assumed the form of a mysterious and resounding wasteland. Every step that I took was with great care and trepidation, and echoed as if it had belonged to someone else.

259

I crossed the street, a cautious step at a time, towards the spot where I had last seen the vision of Mrs. Gordon, and my arrival on the opposite curb seemed to be nothing less than miraculous, once I realised how much of the obscured traffic that I had fortuitously managed to avoid.

Mrs. Gordon had been travelling in a northerly direction, so I began my search by doing likewise. Despite my caution, I found that collisions with my fellow travellers were almost unavoidable under such hazardous circumstances. I wasn't the only one, however, and before too long I seemed to be surrounded by an eerie cacophony of apologetic and disembodied voices.

There had been no sign of Holmes at this point, and so I continued my search alone. However, once I had gone about a hundred yards or so, I reasoned that my quarry must surely have managed to do an about-turn without my having observed her do so. While I considered my next option, I paused for a few moments with a cigarette and I leant my back against a wall for reassurance.

I became conscious of my rapid heart beat and my deep and heavy breathing. All the while, I chastised myself for having allowed my imagination to overrule my sense of the rational at such a time. Had Holmes not been next to me when I had first gazed down from our window, I was certain that by now I would surely have been doubting my own judgement. Surely such a vision in white should not have been so easy to conceal? Where had she managed to hide and, perhaps more pertinently, where was Holmes?

I peeled myself away from the wall and began to retrace my steps. As each passer-by emerged briefly from the gloom, I found my pace and heart rate quickening. I was almost frantic by this point, and once again my shoulders were colliding with those of the other lost and confused souls.

My next accident, however, had not been greeted in such a civilised and harmonious manner. A vise-like set of bony fingers had grabbed hold of my right arm and an East End accent shouted aggressively at me. "'Ere, steady on guv, where do yer think you're going then, in such a 'urry?"

I apologised profusely while trying to extract my arm from the ruffian's hold. Then the tone of the voice suddenly modulated and I was now being addressed in a more familiar fashion.

"Watson, I have found her!" With incredible relief, I recognised Holmes's voice at once, despite the hoarse whisper that he felt compelled to employ.

"Thank goodness for that," I responded. "I was beginning to wonder whether she existed at all"

"Oh yes, Watson, Alexandra Gordon is real enough, and she has taken refuge in the very same empty house we once employed in ensnaring Colonel Sebastian Moran, of such ill repute."

The coincidence was not lost on me, although I could not, for the life of me, comprehend how she had managed to escape her prescribed fate on the gallows.

"Refuge? From what?" I asked, my mind a befuddled mess.

"Not from what, Watson. The question should be: *From whom*? I assure you that the solution to our little mystery is grounded in the material and not the ethereal world," Holmes inevitably confirmed.

At that moment, he pressed his forefinger against his lips, imploring me to total silence. He pushed me back into the darkest recesses of the shadows, making sure that we were both obscured from the object of his concern.

As it transpired, this took the form of a large, drunken ruffian in the most tawdry of attire. He stood at no less than six feet in height, and his bulky physique was covered by a huge, battered greatcoat that had clearly seen better days. A misshapen, black top hat was tilted to one side of his enormous head, and he brandished a gnarled, heavy stick with an evil intent. His uncertain and swaying movements indicated that he was certainly under the influence of a great deal of alcohol.

I cursed my lack of foresight, as I realised that my trusty army revolver was still lying uselessly within its drawer in my room. Then, to my great surprise and consternation, Holmes suddenly stepped out from his place of hiding and brought his loaded cane handle crashing down upon the ruffian's wrist! The lout was clearly more surprised than even I had been, and his cry was one more of astonishment than of great pain.

His club clattered to the ground and I lost no time in claiming it before the fellow could make a move towards it. His initial reaction was to take a swing at Holmes with his wayward right fist, but once he realised that there were two of us, and in spite of his heavily intoxicated condition, he knew that his game was up.

"Who the devil are you, then?" the man bellowed.

Holmes's only response was to prod him sharply in the middle of his back with his cane, indicating that he should mount the steps and enter the empty house without any further delay. As we opened the door, the shrill wail of a baby suddenly echoed down from the floor above and chilled the blood of all who heard it.

"This gentleman is Mister Sherlock Holmes," I declared proudly, and at once the drunken lout's attitude changed most markedly. The very mention of my friend's name produced an immediate sobering effect, and he acquiesced to Holmes's demands without the need of any further persuasion.

"After you, Mr. Gordon," Holmes suggested, and once again Holmes's words took the man off of his guard.

"Mr. Gordon?" I muttered in a tone of whispered surprise.

"Yes, Watson. I fancy that you and I are about to witness a most unusual form of a family reunion." Holmes raised his right eyebrow, and he displayed a most enigmatic and mischievous smile as we followed Gordon up the stairs and towards the sound of the crying baby.

As we crept slowly up the narrow, creaking staircase, another voice, belonging to a mature and frightened woman, echoed down to us, and we knew that the creak of the bowing wood had once again alerted the occupant of the upper floor, as it had when Holmes and I waited for the arrival of Colonel Moran several years before.

Passing through the doorway of a small room leading off from the first floor landing, we saw at once the source of the sad sound of the crying baby. For there, huddled in the far corner of that dark and bitterly cold room, was the terrified form of Alexandra Gordon with her sobbing child wrapped in an inadequate blanket, clinging feverishly to her mother for protection and for warmth.

I froze in horror at the thought of two such tragic spirits sitting there, immediately in front of me! Yet the logical side of my brain told me that this simply could not be so. Admittedly, I had never met Mrs. Gordon, but the description of her in all of the newspapers and Lestrade's subsequent report to us mirrored the vision in front of me down to the finest detail. Even her most singular apparel, although appearing in the confines of the room more substantial than my earlier observation had perceived, confirmed my unlikely hypothesis.

Nevertheless, I took a deep breath and tried to convince myself that the likelihood of someone actually resembling Alexandra Gordon so closely was a more likely scenario than the supernatural one that had instinctively occurred to me. However, the presence of the child was a far harder one for me to accept.

"Watson!" Holmes snapped me out of my bizarre reverie with a sharp call of reprimand, for which I was immediately grateful. "As a man of medicine, you should realise that the eye does not always paint the most complete or accurate of pictures. The three dimensions of which we are aware are only a minute fraction of what

262

lies beyond, and should be dismissed until you can prove their revelations.

"Now, would you go back to our rooms and bring across your notebook and pencil, after asking Mrs. Hudson to personally take urgent word to Inspector Lestrade while you are on your way? Unless I am very much mistaken, he will have a most vested interest in this little gathering."

Before my departure, Holmes also asked me to assist him in securing a set of cuffs which he had with him around the bloated wrists of Mr. Gordon. Although our detainee was subdued enough at this moment, I was glad to help ensure that he remained so during my brief absence. Then I set out upon Holmes's bidding without a moment's hesitation.

Despite having endured many years of my friend's incorrigible behaviour and unreasonable requests, even Mrs. Hudson now baulked at this, his latest liberty. Not for one minute would I have expected her to make her way to Scotland Yard in such conditions, but on such a night, even a call upon the butcher's boy, who had delivered our messages on so many occasions, seemed to be a treacherous enough prospect for her.

Nevertheless, once I had briefly explained to her the motives behind Holmes's request and the events that had led to it being made, our landlady grabbed her hat and coat without a moment's further hesitation and set out upon her perilous mission.

I dashed up the stairs to fetch my writing implements, but when I was halfway back down again, I decided to rectify my omission from before and returned to my room for my revolver. By the time that I had returned to the empty house, I was both breathless and agitated for, despite the restrictions of the handcuffs, Gordon still seemed to be a most threatening prospect.

It was with a sense of great of relief that I discovered my fears to have been totally unfounded. The child was still crying, Mrs. Gordon was shaking uncontrollably, and neither Holmes nor Gordon had moved a jot.

"You have done well, Watson!" Holmes greeted me, once I had confirmed that Inspector Lestrade had been sent for, and he waved me towards a most precarious-looking chair, that I might begin to take my notes.

"I am certain that on a night such as this, it will be some considerable time before the Good Inspector makes his appearance. However, we can use the wait wisely by asking these good people to explain the most singular set of circumstances that have led us all here tonight. Although I fancy that we shall obtain a more lucid interpretation from *Mrs.*, as opposed to the rather inebriated *Mr.*, Gordon!" Holmes declared.

Holmes moved across to the tragic woman and child and, in a tone of tenderness that belied his cold, logical temperament, he encouraged her to explain everything whilst placing the blanket he had worn gently around her shoulders. Mrs. Gordon had cowed in terror at the sight of her husband entering the room, but she seemed to be reassured by the sound of Holmes's voice. Even the baby appeared to be soothed by Holmes's manner, and when Mrs. Gordon began to speak, her daughter fell into a sobbing silence.

"My friend, Doctor Watson, was quite convinced that he had seen not one but *two* ghosts on this most auspicious of nights. However, I trust that you have a more rational explanation for how you came to escape the gallows, and your daughter the murky depths of the River Thames?" Holmes encouraged the wretched woman with his softest and most charming of tones.

It took a few moments for Mrs. Gordon to finally gather herself, but once her weeping had subsided and she had taken several deep breaths, the much maligned woman began to tell her most singular of stories.

"I met this animal when I was a young barmaid at the pub in Bermondsey, which he had virtually turned into his second home. Like a little fool, I soon fell under his spell of charm and easy manner, ignoring the good advice of my friends and family.

"They all warned me that his drinking habits would eventually lead to no good, but I ignored them. After all, he was earning a good living down on the docks and he was constantly lavishing me with flowers, meals out, and the occasional night spent at the local Music Hall – "

Holmes interrupted her with an impatient smile and by raising his right hand in front of her.

"Forgive me, Mrs. Gordon, but when I said that we should have plenty of time till the arrival of Inspector Lestrade, I did not mean to say that we had an eternity. Perhaps you would be good enough to move forward to the more relevant facts?"

She nodded and apologised breathlessly before continuing, but I was not really sure why Holmes thought it imperative that her story should be concluded prior to the arrival of our colleague from Scotland Yard.

"Well, not to make a labour of it, within six months of our having met, this monster and I were wed! He had decent lodgings close to the river and, with my mother's warnings still ringing in my ears, I moved in with him at once. Our lives continued pretty much as they had done before, and I had no reason to regret my decision . . . until that fateful day."

"The day you fell pregnant?" Holmes asked quietly.

Alexandra Gordon nodded profusely and emotionally.

"Ralph changed horribly from the very moment that I broke the news to him. The nights out suddenly stopped, he barely looked at me, let alone have a conversation, and he would come home from the pub roaring drunk every single night.

"If I ever dared to broach the subject of his change in behaviour, he would fly into a violent rage, hurling the furniture about and threatening me with all sorts of unspeakable acts. This was my life, before the birth of sweet Annie. However, after what should have been such a beautiful and memorable moment in my life, it became intolerable.

"Luckily, my mother suggested that I give birth at her home, and she insisted that we extend our stay with her during the days immediately after Annie's birth. In fact, she treated us so well and it was so peaceful there, that I even considered not ever returning to Ralph and his drunken ways.

"But he was having none of it. I was his wife and that was an end to it. He stormed round to my poor mother's home, and I am sure he would have had her door down had I not agreed to return with him there and then. For her sake alone, Annie and I returned to him that very night and he promised to change his ways if we did so.

"I had no choice, Mr. Holmes. My mother lived in a quiet neighbourhood and I had no wish to bring any shame upon her. Besides, her nerves had always been rather fraught, and her condition had certainly not improved since the sudden passing of my dear old father from consumption. Therefore, I feared that her deteriorating health might be irreparably damaged by any further drama. Besides, I thought that having young Annie about the place might have had a calming effect upon him and keep him away from that dreadful public house.

"How wrong I was. He took no more interest in young Annie than he had done in me, and before long he took to the habit of bringing his mates back with him from his drunken exploits. They were as loud and obnoxious as he was, and they were all constantly causing confrontations with our neighbours, despite the cries of my baby girl.

"As you know, Mr. Holmes, violence from a husband to a wife is no crime in the eyes of the law, and the police only offered me the advice of leaving home. I was at my wits end, until my sister, Rose, devised what I thought to be the perfect plan. Oh, I curse the day that I ever agreed to it, Mr. Holmes, and you must not chastise me for having accepted what I considered to be the only course left open to me. I would never have hurt a hair on Rose's head – she was my closest friend and dear sister – and her plan seemed to be fool-proof.

"Despite Rose's confidence in her plan's success, I still hesitated in putting it into practise. However, when Ralph began to threaten my darling baby with the kind of abuse that I had already suffered, I realised that I had no other choice.

"No one could chastise a woman in such a deplorable predicament!" I assured her, while glaring malevolently at her husband who sat quietly, almost obliviously, in the opposite corner of the room. "You have clearly suffered much." I pointed towards several bruises and abrasions, some of them quite clearly recent, which ran up and down her left arm. She pulled her costume ever closer to her shivering form, and I feared she was hiding still more of her malevolent husband's atrocities beneath it.

Holmes grunted in my direction for my having interrupted Mrs. Gordon's narrative, as if he somehow sensed that Lestrade's arrival was going to be imminent. I could not help but wonder if he already knew the conclusion to Mrs. Gordon's story, but he still wanted to hear it in her own words for authentication.

"Although Rose and I are not twins, I would swear that it was only our closest relatives and friends who could ever tell us apart. Her plan took full advantage of this similarity. This brute's threats and rages were intensifying each day, so we wasted no time in putting her scheme into action.

"We bundled up a wooden doll in a set of Annie's baby clothes and then wrapped the whole thing up in one of her blankets. For good measure, we weighted it down with my clothing iron, to ensure that it would never see the light of day again.

"You see, Mr. Holmes, we reasoned that the only way that we could ever have this monster off of our backs for good was to convince him that Annie was dead and that I was a murderous lunatic! As you know, the first part of our scheme worked like a charm. Rose wore my clothes and threw the doll in the river. Then she was arrested in my name, and I fled with Annie to a small but comfortable room, close to my late aunt's home in Faversham, while my husband was out at work. Here I thought that we should remain

266

safe and secure, hidden until the truth could safely be revealed, when I would appear with Annie and explain the scheme to the authorities. Mercifully, I suppose, our ailing mother was so ill by this time that she was oblivious to what was occurring, remaining blissfully ignorant of both mine and Rose's plights, and the further horrors that were about to unfold.

"Oh, what a fool I was, to think that such an evil and devious man could be so easily duped! My poor Rose endured everything, even the rigours of the trial, confident to the very end in the knowledge that, when all had been done and dusted, I would appear at the judge's door with Annie, the supposed victim, safely in my arms, explaining everything. I cannot imagine the agonies that she must have gone through, once she finally realised that I was not going to come and save her. The subsequent stories of her hysteria on the day of her execution, and her futile attempts to convince them that she wasn't me, have broken my heart beyond repair!" At this point Alexandra Gordon finally gave way to tears, as the thought of her beloved sister's torment welled up inside of her.

"I do not know how, but this evil and vindictive man managed to find us at our cottage, and his final act of maliciousness was to keep us captive while the sorry deed was carried out. I still cannot understand how a man who once had loved me could have behaved with such cruelty. Despite my pleading for my sister's life, over and over again, he decided to stay away from work just to keep me prisoner and prevent my poor sister's salvation." The tragic woman paused for a moment while she wiped away her heartfelt tears.

"By then, it was too late. I had given up. I've stayed with him all this time, until this morning when it finally became too much and I tried to escape yet again. My closest friend, Gladys Fowler, discovered that I was still alive and offered to put us up when we both thought that the coast was clear. However, she reluctantly agreed with me, once I had pointed out the dangers in which she would be placing herself if I took her up on her kindness. It was she who suggested this empty house as a last resort. Although I knew that he was in pursuit of us once again, in my desperation I prayed that the fog and his drunken state would prevent him from finding our final place of refuge . . . ."

The sound of a growler, pulling up immediately below us, galvanised Holmes into an urgent and quite alarming course of action. With the key already in his hand, he whipped the hand cuffs from Gordon's wrists in a single movement, while first ensuring that I had my revolver trained upon the man before he did so. "Quickly

Watson, strike me!" Holmes insisted, while indicating my free hand and his right cheek.

"I shall do no such thing!" I responded defiantly.

"For their sakes!" he implored and with a passion such as I had never seen from him, before nor since.

Faced with such a display, I had no choice but to carry out his bidding, and I released a left hook against him with all of my might. My fist found its mark and Holmes fell to the floor with a thud, while his right cheek bone began to swell and bleed profusely.

My action was so well-timed that he had a moment to smile appreciatively up at me just before Lestrade and two of his men burst clumsily into the room.

The inspector stood rooted to the spot, finding it impossible to either speak or move, while he took in the implausible scene that he was now confronted with.

"What kind of devilry is this?" he demanded in a shrill voice of bewilderment. Lestrade's normally taut, emaciated face was now contorted in total confusion as he contemplated his next action. He pointed towards Mrs. Gordon and her child.

"You two are supposed to be dead!" he exclaimed.

Holmes leant himself up on his elbow and smiled benignly at his former antagonist.

"That clearly is not the case, Lestrade."

The inspector's face exploded in a deep red flush of rage and frustration. "But I saw this woman swing from the gallows!" Lestrade exclaimed.

By now Holmes was back to his feet, with the handkerchief that he had held to his cheek totally saturated in his own blood. He took Lestrade gently by his elbow and led him to the corner of the room, from where I heard them whispering in great earnest for several minutes.

Evidently Holmes had explained something of the matter to the inspector, for Lestrade's manner to the mother and child was altogether more sympathetic than it previously had been, when he returned to the centre of the room.

Lestrade ordered his constables to place Gordon under immediate arrest.

"What's this all about?" Gordon protested. "I ain't done nothing wrong! Is it a crime to want to take my wife and child back home with me? It's my marital right. We are all men of the world and know that every now and then, the women need to be reminded of their proper place."

"Sadly, you are correct, Mr. Gordon, and your unspeakable actions are not punishable by law. However," Holmes reminded him with a victorious smile, "I think you will find that assault certainly is."

"Who am I supposed to have assaulted, may I ask?"

"Why, Mr. Sherlock Holmes, of course!" By now, I had realised Holmes's original purpose, and I had no intention of allowing this blackguard to walk away Scot free by not following his lead.

With his cries of protest echoing throughout the empty house and well beyond, Gordon was dragged away by Lestrade and his men towards the wagon that awaited him downstairs.

"I shall be around later on for some words with you, Mr. Holmes," Lestrade sneered as he left the room, but his threat was obviously a benign one.

Over the years, I had often witnessed Holmes manipulate the law to suit his own interpretation of justice, and certainly not always with my approval. However, on this occasion he had my wholehearted endorsement.

"I do not know for how long the police will be able to hold your husband, Mrs. Gordon, but I am certain that it will be time enough for you to make a permanent escape from your tormentor." As he spoke, Holmes slipped his note clip out from his jacket pocket and he thrust several notes of value into the reluctant hand of the bewildered woman.

For my part, I passed her a card containing the address of some of my people in Goole, where I knew that she could remain safe and well, until such time as she was able to make her own way in the world once again. I promised to wire them without a second's delay, to tell them of her coming.

"May a thousand blessings be upon you both!" Mrs. Gordon cried as she slowly made her way back up onto her feet. "Although it was my beloved sister who made the ultimate sacrifice, I shall never forget your kindness. We shall leave for Goole at once."

Holmes ensured that our old friend, Dave "Gunner" King, was able to shepherd them safely to Euston Station in his cab before we finally returned to our rooms opposite.

"Well, Holmes, I must say that for once I completely approve of your flagrant abuse of the law of the land," I proclaimed proudly over a glass of port and a rather fine cigar. "It just goes to show that even your cold and rational exterior can be melted by the sight of a woman and child in the direst need." I teased.

"That creature deserves far more than our justice system is able to administer to him, but I am content to know that we have saved two lives here tonight. However, you should not concern yourself unduly, Watson, for every rule deserves to be broken just the once." Holmes smiled. "By the way, you have a fearsome left hook for a man of medicine!" He laughed while stroking his swollen cheek gingerly.

I drained my glass and extinguished my cigar before turning to the door.

"Good night, old fellow," I called out over my shoulder as I left Holmes standing by the window with a full pipe ready to be lit.

Later, I concluded my bedtime ritual with a final cigarette by the open window, which I closed urgently upon hurling the remains to the street below. Then, as I began to close the drapes, I was taken aback by the sight of a small single light emanating from the first floor window of the empty house opposite. It was a faint orange glow, that seemed to be coming from a candle recently lit, an apparition that defied a logical explanation.

Then – I saw her! A tall, slim woman, gliding back and forth behind the window, dressed only in white . . . .

The Mysterious Mourner
by Cindy Dye

It should come as no surprise that in my role of biographer to my friend Sherlock Holmes, I have often been approached by those too diffident to contact Holmes directly. I first noted the phenomenon after *A Study in Scarlet* appeared, and upon the publication of *The Sign of Four* the floodgates truly opened. Old schoolfellows wrote me, not to reminisce, but in hopes of an introduction to Holmes. My patients were quick to mention their conundrums, some of them coming to me for that sole purpose, and the fellows at my club made a regular habit out of pointing out little puzzles – two-thirds of which I could "solve" myself without any recourse to the art of detection. I even found myself being accosted at my favorite restaurants and my tobacconist by supplicants for my friend's aid.

In fact, before Holmes's confrontation with Professor Moriarty, only twice had I brought a mystery to his attention without being asked to do so. I took to carrying cards which listed Holmes's consultation hours, which discouraged the merely curious and provided an acceptable alternative to the truly desperate. Holmes, as always, took on cases when they interested him or required his specialized skills, regardless of how they came before him. Although it appeared to me that he bent a trifle more when one of my genuine acquaintances appeared in our sitting room. The matters were often minor – mysteries Holmes could dispose of without ever leaving his chair – but he met them with unfailing courtesy. Which perhaps emboldened me, long after his miraculous return to London, when I found occasion to importune him on my own behalf once more.

It was late in the winter of 1898, and I was making the all-too-familiar railway journey to Brookwood Cemetery. Whilst I was still in practice, I had visited my wife Mary's grave quite often, taking my chance to step away from the funerals of patients or colleagues to bring her flowers, or to sit a moment in contemplation of the simple stone which had been all I could afford to give her. But since Holmes's return, those opportunities had dwindled. His services were in great demand, and I, as his biographer and companion, had few occasions to attend some acquaintance's solemnities, and even fewer free days to set aside for solitary excursions.

271

I should explain, to those of my readers unfamiliar with London, that the great city had outgrown its burial grounds at the mid-century. One of the responses to that dilemma was the founding of the London Necropolis Railway, formed to bring funerals to Brookwood, some twenty-odd miles away, where there was still ample room for the deceased to be interred without first removing the bones of those who had gone before them. It is a sensible arrangement for the dead, who can rest undisturbed, but a burden to those who mourn them. The fare is reasonable enough, but the cost in time prevents impulsive visits to the cemetery, even for the wealthy. The funeral train runs but once a day in each direction, departing its own dedicated station near Waterloo late in the morning and returning at mid-afternoon. There are ordinary trains which share the line, of course, and which run at more convenient times of day, but they stop at the village station, which adds another mile of walking to each leg of the journey – no great burden in summer, but treacherous and unpleasant when the paths are mired in mud or ice.

And poor weather or no, this was the anniversary of my wife's death, and a journey I could no longer defer.

The day was damp and cold, the station crowded. There had been an ice storm the morning before which had precluded the operation of the service, and while the company had added carriages to accommodate the accumulation of first- and second-class mourners, by the time I reached the ticket desk only third-class seats remained. I made no objection; the army had inured me to hardships, and travelling with Sherlock Holmes upon his adventures had more than once required perching amidst the milk churns of a morning. Still, I was careful to secure a window seat once aboard the third-class carriage, where I could attempt to distract myself from somber contemplations.

Holmes I had left tucked up in bed with a hot water bottle, a plate of dry toast, and strict orders to take his next dose of the infusion of gentian and ginger I had prepared for him as soon as he felt able to keep it down. He had recently completed an investigation which had required a variety of disguises, none of which had allowed for the fastidious hygiene which might have spared him from the ravages of the complaints which were endemic in the poorer sections of the city. Lestrade had hauled him home two days before, triumphant and miserable, and quite willing to be cosseted by Mrs. Hudson and myself until he had shaken off what his informants by the docks called "the three-day collywobbles". That concession, and his relatively low fever, indicated that he was suffering no more than

272

a minor gastroenteritis, else I would have had the excuse to remain at Baker Street. My friend was never a happy convalescent, and the days when he might choose to ameliorate his condition or stave off a black mood with cocaine were not all that far behind him. But I would have been disconsolate and out of temper, I knew, had I been home, and Holmes knew it too, for he had arranged for Billy to collect the bouquet of hothouse flowers I held in my hand.

As the train left the grey stones of the city and the snow cover brightened in the absence of coal dust, I became aware that I was being observed. This was not an unfamiliar sensation, given my association with the world's foremost observer, but in his absence it was an unwelcome one. I turned my attention from the fog-shrouded view of Richmond Park to study my fellow passengers. The third-class carriage is not designed for privacy: Although the arrangement of the paired benches and aisle mimics the compartments and corridor style of the other carriages, it can easily hold a hundred passengers. Three extended families and a half-a-dozen clusters of tradesmen had scattered themselves across its broad benches, and I could see the tops of hats all the way down to the door leading to the front of the train. Closer to hand, three people had joined me in the set of facing benches near the vestibule, two tradesmen and a woman.

One of those tradesmen, a small, pale, elderly man with a tonsure of grizzled grey and the mien of a wizened apple, was the one watching me. He wore a suit that had been altered and mended and patched so often that there was reason to doubt how much remained of the original cloth. When his gaze met mine he nodded, blinking and grimacing, as his work-scarred fingers fluttered in the direction of the lady who shared my bench seat.

She was stout and straight-backed, and not a scrap of skin showed beneath her veils. An older woman, I assumed, for the black dress she wore was a dozen years out of fashion, and much of its jet ornamentation had been lost to time and wear. My nose told me she was fond of gin, and despite the waft of camphor, I could see that her cloak was moth-eaten along one sleeve, so I thought perhaps that in her widowhood she had fallen on hard times. Her hat had certainly seen better days, although the lace suspended from it was for the most part intact. Her gloves, too, looked newer than the rest where she held them clasped before her, but gloves are easily knit if a ha'pence for wool can be spared from the rent.

I thought my scrutiny discreet, but she rose abruptly and walked away down the train. In a moment, she was through the door, and no sooner was she out of sight than my tatterdemalion observer transferred himself into her place. "You saw her, didn't you?" he asked in an excited whisper.

"I did," I said. "And you've taken her seat. I'm sure she'll want it when she returns."

"Oh, she won't come back no more," he vouchsafed to me. "She don't never come back no more once she knows she's been seen." He nodded again, as if his head were too heavy for his neck.

"Is she that shy then?" I asked, thinking of the lady's all-encompassing attire.

"She's not shy," he said, conspiratorially. "She's dead."

"Dead?" I echoed, falling into my companions secretive tone out of surprise.

"Dead!" he asserted. "She's a ghost. She haunts the train." He laid a finger alongside his nose. "You saw her, but you won't see her no more. You'll see. She'll be gone, completely gone, by the time we gets where we're going."

I was momentarily dumbfounded. "She seemed very solid for a ghost," I ventured.

"Well, she didn't buy no ticket, I promise you," my informant said. "I watched this time. She never did."

"Just turned up on the train, like always," the other tradesmen chimed in wearily. He was a fresh-faced youth, not much more than twenty, and had yet to grow into the black woolens he wore. "Please excuse my Uncle Ruben." He stood up to gather his elderly relation back to his original seat and then took a moment to hand over a trinket that his uncle immediately began examining and adjusting. "I assure you, he is quite harmless."

"And no harm done," I replied. "Do you take this train often?"

"Every Monday, if the weather permits," the boy said. He fumbled in his vest pocket and then leaned across the compartment to offer me a card. His hands, like his uncle's, bore the nicks and scars of a craftsman, if not in the same quantity. "Jonathan Horner, at your service."

"John Watson, at yours," I said, reciprocating with my own card. I looked at his. It was very new, still smelling of the printers' ink, and it revealed that the Horners dealt in fine ornamentations made at a reasonable price, funerary decorations a specialty.

"Funerary decorations?" I asked.

"A new venture," he explained. "Basketry for flowers and insets – cartouches and *memento mori* made of horn, that sort of thing." He extended an arm so that I could see the elaborate horn cufflink at his

274

wrist – a carven hand grasping a sheaf of flowers, black as jet, but with a different quality in the light. "People still do buy buttons and small things, but there's less call for them than there was."

"And you come on the train to sell your work?" I asked, curiously, nodding to the small basket which rested on the seat beside Uncle Ruben.

"Oh no. We sell things in town, usually. But much of what people can afford is wickerwork, so we check to make sure it hasn't been blown over, and mend anything that might need mending," young Horner explained diffidently.

"Ah," I said, realizing that I had seen the company's offerings or something similar, now and again, scattered amongst the headstones. "It's kind of you to set the things you've sold to rights."

Jonathan Horner flushed at my words. "It's a practical sort of kindness," he confessed. "Nothing shows to best advantage if it's face down in the mud. But at least it gives Uncle Ruben the chance to tell my father tall tales." He smiled at his uncle fondly,

"Your father is . . . ?" I enquired.

"Dead these two years gone. It was the cartouche we made for his stone that got people to asking if we could do the same for them." Horner said. For a moment he looked out the window at the telegraph poles appearing and vanishing in the mist. But he composed himself and turned once more to me, nodding to the clutch of hothouse flowers I held. "And you? Who are you visiting?"

"My wife," I said, simply, and took my own turn looking out into the grey. We were well along now, and the train was slowing to make the switch onto the cemetery siding. "Today is the anniversary of when I lost her."

"My condolences," Horner said, and we might have slipped each into awkward reminiscence but that his uncle spoke up.

"Those won't last, you know," the old man said, pointing to my bouquet. "They might not even make it through the night."

"I do know," I said, with all the patience his age and simplicity demanded. "But I didn't want to visit empty handed."

"Leave them for the ghost; take this instead," he said, offering me his handiwork. I took it out of sheer surprise and discovered it to be a rose made of ivorine and gold wire. "That'll last your lady a long time. And the ghost likes flowers. I've seen her take one when no one is looking." He cocked his head and frowned. "No one but me, that is. I was looking. But no one else was. I was going to give her this one. But I expect she'd like yours just as well."

275

"It's a beautiful rose," I said, for it was. The craftsmanship was exquisite. And by the dismay on Jonathan Horner's face it wasn't meant to be handed off to a chance stranger, however polite, on the train, nor yet left behind for a ghost that didn't exist. "But isn't it promised to someone already?"

Uncle Ruben considered the question. "Jacky? Is it? I thought it was for the ghost."

"Is that what . . . ?" Young Horner bit back an exclamation and took a deep breath before answering. "We told Mr. Hendrickson we'd show him a sample of our work. Remember, Uncle? In case he wants to offer them in his shop."

"Then what can we leave *her*?" Uncle Ruben asked, his expression crumpling. "It's best to be kind to the dead, you know."

"Yes," the younger man said. "But not with six shillings worth of gold wire and two days' work."

"I'll leave her one of my flowers," I said, for it seemed best to soothe the old man before our discussion disrupted the fresher grief of the other mourners in our carriage, and I was touched by his determination to be kind. "I'm sure that will be sufficient. Ghosts have difficulty carrying things, you know." I extracted a gardenia from the knot and offered it and the crafted rose to the old man as the train slowed to a stop and began to reverse down the spur line into the cemetery.

"Thank you," Horner said as he rose and took possession of the shell rose. "If you'll excuse us, the first places we must visit are nearest the north station."

Uncle Ruben, who was content to take the gardenia and tuck it into position at the corner where the back of the seat met the wall, nodded to me. "She won't take it while you're here," he said. "But it will be gone all the same when we go home."

The train came to a stop, and as my companions gathered their things to go, my curiosity got the better of me and I rose hastily, to see if I could spot the "ghost" once more. But there was no sign of her, neither in the carriage nor on the platform. I even went to the vestibule and looked out the of the other side of the train as it started to move on to the southern station, but the plantation of cedars there and the steep drop from the train steps made it unlikely that anyone encumbered with skirts would attempt to leave that way. That left the other carriages, which a brief reconnoiter proved clear of ghosts, if not elderly ladies in black with disapproving glares. I turned to go collect my hat and found myself under the equally critical eye of the conductor.

I did consider, briefly, whether I should ask him if he had observed the ghost, but in the face of universal disapproval, I chose discretion and merely nodded as I passed him on my way back to my seat. There my hat was waiting but, I noted with surprise, the gardenia was gone.

During the return to London, I did not immediately return to my seat. A gentleman had slipped on an icy path whilst we were still at Brookwood, and I had been called upon to bind his ankle and assure his wife and children that no serious damage had been done otherwise. They invited me to stay, but it occurred to me that I had a fresh opportunity to walk the train, and I demurred. By the time I reached the third class carriage, my search as fruitless as before, I found that the Horners had been absorbed into the periphery of two of the families. I found a place nearby and listened as the adults discussed the ceremonies with grim satisfaction, and the older children interrogated each other in order to determine whether they should be friends or rivals once back in London. Uncle Ruben was amusing the smallest children with paper birds folded after the Japanese fashion, and a story about Bartholomew Fair, but his nephew looked up from and nodded a greeting.

When we reached Woking, where the train stopped for water, I went to join the other men on the platform for a cigarette. Rather to my surprise, Jonathan Horner followed me. I waited for him to gather his nerve to speak. "Dr. Watson," he began, "do you . . . I mean . . . ." I expected him to ask me whether I was the Dr. Watson who knew Sherlock Holmes. But for once it was my own expertise which was wanted. "Do you make house calls? Uncle Ruben isn't fond of most of the medical profession, but he likes you."

"I'm not really taking on patients at the moment," I said, and Horner's face fell so quickly I relented. "But I can certainly take a look at your uncle. Have you reason to be concerned?"

Horner brightened, but he ducked his head. "I'm afraid we might be asking too much of him. He's closer to eighty than seventy, you see, and this whole business of the ghost has me worried."

"'Well, he's not hallucinating," I said, thoughtfully. "We both saw the lady too. And she certainly isn't upon the train now."

"But there has to be a reasonable explanation for that."

"And I share rooms with a man who might have one," said I. "Can you bring your uncle by for a consultation once we reach the City?"

"My sister will be waiting tea on us," Horner said. "Could we come in the evening?"

"Certainly," I agreed, and I shook hands with him on it, already thinking about what Holmes would think of my visitors.

By the time I walked in the door at Baker Street, the falling temperatures had transformed the fogs of the morning into a fresh snow. Mrs. Hudson pounced on me with the brush the moment I came through the door and kept me on the mat until she was satisfied that I wouldn't trail flakes through the house. "It's time you were home," she said, giving my shoulders a final sweep. "He's been up and down, calling for this and that and complaining of ennui."

"That's excellent news," I said. "A bored patient is halfway to recovery."

"He'll be investigating the mystery of why your tea is burnt in a moment," she replied tartly, shooing me up the stairs. "But do tell him that Alice has gone to the booksellers at Charing Cross to find the titles he asked for."

"I shall," I promised, before heading up to my room to change into my dressing gown.

Holmes wasn't in his bedroom, although a neglected cup of tea on the stand and a drift of newspaper scraps on the coverlet were evidence of his day's occupation. Instead, I found him in the settee, propped up with pillows, more newspapers strewn on the floor beside him, and his commonplace book open on his knees. His face was still flushed, and his eyes were brighter than was his wont, but his smile assured me that he was indeed feeling much more himself. "Ah, there you are, Watson," he said, setting aside his scissors and glue pot. He had dressed in trousers and shirt and dressing gown, though his feet were only in thick socks and slippers.

"Here I am," I said, pulling the stethoscope and thermometer free from the bag I fetched from my desk. "Did you rest at all while I was gone?"

"When I had to." He grimaced. "Which is far more often than I prefer. I am afraid I make a very impatient patient."

"It isn't worth the practice to become a good one," I said, and took a few moments to assure myself of his symptoms. His condition was improving steadily, without question, and I blessed his iron constitution. I chided him for depending on it, all the same, as I set my bag back in order. "We are neither of us as young as we once were."

278

He nodded, but his eyes were on my hands. "You've taken on a patient, I see."

I couldn't help but smile. "I would ask how you know," I said. "But I'm sure it will have something to do with a smudge of dust on my left elbow."

He laughed. "Watson, you know that if you smudge an elbow it will generally be on your right," he said, but couldn't resist going on. "This morning you put away your tools by merely dropping them into your bag. Now you are being much more careful. Are you going out again tonight?"

"No. My patient is coming to me, as soon as he's had his tea," I said, for his words had a wistful note. "But we shan't disturb you if you would rather read or work on your files. I can take him up to my room."

"Nonsense, Watson. I've used our sitting room for consultations often enough. It's your turn tonight. I can retreat to my room and read."

"Mrs. Hudson said you've sent Alice for books."

"Reference works," Holmes said, the corners of his mouth downturned. He waved a languid hand at the newspaper debris. "The papers are devoid of interest, but when I examined our bookshelves in hopes of diversion, I saw that we need a new almanac, a gazetteer of the North American continent, and the latest Bradshaw."

"That will hardly amuse you," I observed. I knew from my own experience how welcome any diversion would be from his ailment. And I wanted, very much, to present him with the mysterious events of my morning. "But I doubt my patient will mind if you were to stay whilst I examine him."

Holmes canted his head at me, his expression stern but his eyes a-twinkle. "You're up to something, Watson."

"Perhaps," I conceded. "How do you feel about ghost stories?"

He raised an eyebrow. "I think they are pernicious twaddle," he said, "even though you do tell them well. Why?"

"Because I have a new one."

My recitation was interrupted – once by the arrival of Mrs. Hudson with my tea – and far more frequently by Holmes, who, once engaged in the tale, kept pestering me for details. The lamps were lit and casting a halo of light into the falling snow by the time I recounted the return to London. I had just begun to recount the return trip when the bell rang below.

"That will be the Horners," I said, finishing off the last bite of cake before hastily bundling away the newspapers and mess. "Will you stay, Holmes?"

"I think I shall, if your visitors make no objection." Holmes moved to ensconce himself in his usual chair by the fire. He no doubt looked well enough to anyone who did not know his usual vigour, but he only nodded, instead of rising, when Mrs. Hudson announced our visitors and ushered them in.

I made introductions, and Jonathan flushed, twisting his hat in his hands as he looked to me.

"I didn't realize you were *that* Dr. Watson, sir. I've read your tales in *The Strand*. It's an honor to meet you." He bowed to Holmes. "And an honor to meet you, as well, Mr. Holmes."

Holmes inclined his head in acknowledgment. "Watson showed me your card. Are you by chance related to Josiah Horner, of that unusual construction in Hosier Lane then? You know the place, Watson, the narrow Elizabethan house with all of the patterned horn buttons pressed into its wattle and daub to form the name."

"Indeed I do," I said. "I passed it quite often on my way to find my luncheon after a morning of lectures when I was a student at Barts, although I had no idea the family had continued. Why, the house appears quite old enough to have survived the Great Fire."

"And so it did, sir, although the first Josiah was long gone by then. According to our family tradition, it was his grandson who stood upon the roof and stamped out each falling ember or spark. We've been in Smithfield at least as long as the animal market there, turning horn and bone, and liverymen in the Company of Horners from its inception. Both the name, and the craft, have been passed down through the years, though the hornwork itself was banished from the City because of the smell before I was born, so now we must work with other materials or lose our home," Jonathan Horner's eyes fell, and he fidgeted with his hat for a moment longer before blurting out, "And I'm very sorry, Mr. Holmes, but I'm afraid that we have no problems worthy of your attention, nor the funds to ask you to solve the ones we do."

Uncle Ruben had wandered over to the mantelpiece, and now he looked up from his examination of the curious inlaid box where Holmes kept his watch, fob, and cufflinks when they were not upon his person. "We have problems?" he asked his nephew, ingenuously.

"Two that I can see," Holmes said. He held up one long finger. "You seem to be meeting a ghost on a regular basis." He held up a second finger, "And that ghost appears to be more avaricious than

280

the usual spectre." He smiled at the elderly man. "I was hoping you could tell me how you came to meet her."

Uncle Ruben brightened and perched on the end of the settee nearest Holmes. "Do you like ghosts, Mr. Holmes? I saw one when I was a boy, and I waited a good long while to see another." Behind him, I signalled to his nephew, who was quite astonished by the direction of the conversation, to keep his peace until things came clear.

"I'm interested in anything unusual," Holmes said, deploying all the charm of which he was capable. "And your ghost seems quite unusual. Dr. Watson tells me that he couldn't tell she was a ghost at all."

"Nor could I at first. But ordinary folk don't disappear, now do they?" Uncle Ruben lay a finger alongside his nose. "That's when I knew."

"She disappeared?" Holmes exclaimed. He snapped his fingers. "Like that?"

"No, no," Uncle Ruben chortled. "She gets up and goes along the passage through the door. But she doesn't come back. And if you go to find her, she's not there. Not a scrap of her."

"And do you see her every time you ride the train?"

"Not always. But often enough. You can come along and try to see her too, next Monday."

"Why Monday?" I asked.

"Well, I ain't never seen her on a Tuesday," said Uncle Ruben. He hitched around to get a better view of his nephew. "Have you seen her on a Tuesday, Jack?"

"I don't know," Horner said, sinking onto the other end of the settee. "I never really look for her. And we don't often go any day but Monday."

Uncle Ruben patted him on the knee. "Jack's always fretting about something when we take the train. Keeps him busy, worrying does, though he'd be better to be working with his hands. And he don't believe in ghosts, none. Never saw one the way I did, so he don't believe. He got believing educated out of him."

"But you've seen the one on the train," Holmes said, directing his gaze to Jonathan Horner.

"Of course I've seen her," Horner said tiredly. "But she's just an old woman."

"Have you seen her face?" Holmes asked. "Or her shoes? Watson was singularly uninformative about either."

I sighed and took my own seat. "I told you, Holmes. Her hems were too long, and her veils too thick."

"And yet I've seldom seen a woman whose veils were so opaque that even her profile was imperceptible." Holmes turned to the Horners. "You were sitting opposite her. Could you see her face?"

Jonathan Horner frowned and bit his lip. "Not that I recall."

"She hasn't no face," Uncle Ruben said cheerfully. "Just eyes, now and again. But she has boots, right enough. Even a ghost needs feet."

"Pointed toes or round?" Holmes asked.

"Square!" Uncle Ruben crowed. "Waste not, want not, even for a ghost!"

Jonathan put his head in his hands. "Uncle . . . ."

"Those are men's boots, Jacky. Might have been her husband's once, if he was a soldier." Uncle Ruben lifted his own foot, to display a boot which had been mended nearly as often as his suit. "They last a good long time, do soldier's boots, if you keep the polish bright."

Holmes laughed and got to his feet, reaching for his pipe upon the mantel, too engrossed in the mystery to pander to his convalescence. "Here's a man after our own hearts, Watson! Tell us, Mr. Horner. What else have you observed about the lady? Does she appear every time you take the train?"

"Nay. I've not seen her more than a dozen times. But she's never once missed my gifts to her." He cast a raised eyebrow at his nephew and crossed his arms with an air of distinct satisfaction.

Jonathan groaned. "Uncle, if you'd only said you were taking the things for her, I wouldn't mind so much. You've made most of them, after all. But does she really need them? Especially the shell roses?"

Before Uncle Ruben could come to his own defense, Holmes intervened. "What's this about?"

Jonathan sighed. "Doctor Watson told you that we make ornaments and things? Well, for the past few months, some of them have been disappearing. I never thought that Uncle Ruben might be behind the pilferage, because he keeps everything he thinks he might have a use for, but now I've discovered that he's leaving gifts for a ghost."

"And have you ever seen her collect these gifts?" Holmes asked Uncle Ruben. "Does she pick them up and put them in her pocket?"

Uncle Ruben frowned, thoughtfully. "No. No, not in her pocket. And I've never seen her pick one up, nor even touch one, not since the first time."

I was not the only one who blinked. Holmes looked, for a moment, like he'd bumped his nose into a wall. "The first time?" He settled back into his chair, his pipe still unlit and his eyebrow flying. "What happened the first time?"

"I thought that I heard her crying." Uncle Ruben turned to his nephew. "It was last spring, when we were seeing what could be done with the Parkesine we had on hand. You remember, Jack? And we couldn't find a glue that would hold, so I was mending the pieces with wire?"

"Parkesine?" Holmes asked, and I was glad of it, for the name was unfamiliar.

"An early type of synthetic ivory," Jonathan explained. "The original manufactory went out of business, but somehow Uncle Ruben acquired all of the leftover stock."

"Waste not, want not," Uncle Ruben agreed. "And your father was the one who knew Parkes, Jacky-boy. In any case, I could see that the lady was unhappy, and you were off talking to the Waterstones about their standpiece, so I began to talk to her, explaining what I was doing. She grew very still, but when I offered the rose, she took it. You came back a moment later, and when I was done talking to you, she was gone." He snapped his fingers. "Disappeared."

Holmes set aside his pipe and steepled his fingers. "Watson said that this morning she got up and walked away."

"Aye, she does that. Goes through the door towards the baggage, but if you follow, you'll not find her. And she might have slipped away that first time, I grant you, but even then, where should she go? There's nothing at the back of the train but the coffin carriage, and that's locked."

"He did try following her once," Jonathan Horner confirmed. "But there still has to be a logical explanation."

"I can think of three," Holmes said. "The most likely is that the lady is not a lady at all, but someone in disguise. A young, energetic man who wears the all-encompassing dress and veils to prevent being discovered. He cannot hide in the coffin carriage at the beginning of the journey, but he can gain access to it – perhaps with a copied key – during the journey, where he removes the feminine garb and conceals it before taking a position where he can jump off of the train as it stops to reverse course down into the cemetery."

283

"But why?" I asked. "The fares for the Necropolis Railway are low, but not that low."

Holmes smiled. "Granted. But think, Watson. The funerary train does not leave from Waterloo station. If you needed to travel to – say, Aldershot, or one of the barracks nearby – and you wished to avoid detection by the military authorities, the game might be worth the candle."

It was all of seven miles from Brookwood to Aldershot proper, I knew, but that was no barrier to a soldier, especially if he could travel cross country. "You're thinking that he might have a reason to overstay his weekend leave."

"A family, perhaps, whom he is reluctant to leave." Holmes made a moue of dissatisfaction. "Which, unfortunately, does not explain the disappearance of your flower this morning."

"There were children in the carriage," Jonathan Horner offered. "One of them might have collected it."

"Or the guard," I said. "He would have walked past whilst I was searching the train."

"The guard would explain the disappearance of Mr. Horner's other offerings," Holmes agreed. He looked to our guests. "Have you never checked with the company for lost items?"

"I've asked the guard," young Horner said, "But if your theory about the lady is correct, then the guard must be helping her. Him. Complicit."

"Or she could be a ghost," Uncle Ruben said, grinning. "Who likes flowers."

Holmes smiled back. "And is perfectly satisfied with them, no matter what they're made of. Perhaps you should construct hers out of paper? Waste not, want not, after all."

Uncle Ruben slapped his knee. "Fair enough!" he cried. "Fair enough! Will that do for you, Jack?"

Young Horner laughed. "I'll even help you make them, if you'll teach me," he said. He stood and offered a hand to Holmes. "Thank you, sir. It's been an honor to meet you. And you too, Doctor," he added turning to me.

I watched out the window as Jonathan Horner took his uncle's arm and escorted him off to the Underground station. With the question of the ghost resolved, I had taken a few minutes to examine the old man and found him remarkably sturdy for his age. But it was my friend who had truly allayed the younger man's fears. "That was a grand compromise, Holmes," I said.

"A problem solved, if not a mystery," he granted. "And don't think I am unaware of why you brought it to my attention."

I turned to find him curled up in his chair, contemplating the fire. He looked tired. "I have long since abandoned any hope of disguising my thoughts from you, Holmes," I said. "And you must admit that Ruben Horner is a worthy addition to your collection of unique acquaintances."

Holmes's lips twitched. "He is that!"

I took my chair and reached for my notebook, so as to record the conversation before the details grew dim. "What made you think of a disguise?" I asked.

"The lady's lack of a face suggests that beneath the heavy veils there must be a black mask, obscuring details – a mustache, perhaps – which would ruin the illusion. And why else the gloves and the long concealing skirt? The deterioration of the jet decorations suggest that the person within the dress is unacquainted with needle and thread, even while the new gloves seem to indicate that the lady is an accomplished knitter. So someone associated with the 'ghost' cannot easily get to the dress for repairs, but can deal with gloves, which might be carried home in a pocket. A wife, presumably. And why hide a marriage? Insufficient rank, yes? You're the military man, Watson."

"'Captains *may* marry, Majors *should* marry, and Colonels *must* marry'," I quoted. "And you're right: For privates and corporals, matrimony is very much frowned upon." I found my own gaze drifting to the flames as I considered our theoretical young soldier and the wife for whom he would risk the stockade to gain a single more night together. "Would you mind terribly if we never confirmed your hypothesis?"

"You know I could be wrong," Holmes said, gently, "The only love involved might be love of the bottle."

"I know," I said. "But I should hate to shatter Uncle Ruben's illusions." Nor my own, come to that.

Holmes studied my face for a moment before nodding. "There's no need," he conceded. "It's hardly as if it is worth smuggling illicit goods from London to the suburbs by such elaborate means. Our soldier may collect paper flowers for his wife, if she exists, for all I care, and no harm done. The Horners are content, and I have been saved from boredom. But now I am tired." He pushed himself to his feet and started for the bedroom, pausing only for a moment to touch my shoulder. "Goodnight, Watson."

"Good night, Holmes."

285

The Adventure of the Hungry Ghost

by Tracy Revels

"**I** will not return to *Journey's End* – I shall send for my belongings, or sacrifice them, but I shall never return to that Godforsaken place. Yet I must know what happened there, and why I was attacked. Even if the truth is that devils and ghosts are real, I must know it. Otherwise, I will certainly go mad."

The words were spoken with dramatic force by a young man who had burst upon us on a warm spring evening just as we were settling down to smoke our after-dinner pipes. His name was Reginald Humphreys, and he had the look of an esthete, with pale skin, rakishly long hair, and a foppish frock-coat trimmed in purple velvet. His right hand was wrapped rather clumsily in bandages, and he had entered our rooms without a cane or hat, breathless and drenched in perspiration, as if he had dashed across half the country for a consultation.

"I was just telling my friend Watson that the criminal classes have been showing a singular lack of imagination this season," Holmes replied, motioning for me to offer our guest some brandy to steady his clearly rattled nerves. "Perhaps we should give the diabolical a try if mortal felons prove so wearisome. Drink your glass, Mr. Humphreys, and tell us your story."

Our guest nodded, bolting down his libation. He pulled a handkerchief from his checkered vest to dry his brow. Though the words came freely, I could tell he could command coherence only with the most determined effort.

"You should know, Mr. Holmes, that I am a hermit by inclination. I am the only child of parents who died when I was an infant, and I was raised in the household of a maiden aunt. I much preferred the company of my books to that of other schoolboys, and the single year I spent at the university, where I was forced to take lodgings with a most uncouth set of rascals, confirmed my ambition to lead a solitary life. Some time ago, I had a modest success with a book of poetry, and I came to believe that if I could retire from London and reside in a dreamy, lonely place, my pen would catch fire. Living on my pitiful royalties and a small allowance from my aunt, I found myself in a slow retreat to ever more secluded and

286

impoverished locales. Finally, thinking that exposure to the wind and waves might summon my muse, I turned to the Cornish coast. Do you know the area?"

Holmes gave the slightest of smiles. "I know it well."

"Then you have perhaps heard of a place called Widow's Bay. I packed my meager belongings and travelled there in hopes of renting a cottage for the season. Much to my dismay, the house agent could show me only rat-infested huts that I would not condemn a convict to be locked in, or elegant villas that would better suit royalty on holiday. I despaired of finding lodgings, and was just about to order the agent to return me to the station when he asked me a fateful question.

"'I say, would you have any objection to living in a haunted house?'

"'Haunted!'

"'So I have been told by the last two fellows who rented it. Both left in the middle of the night, long before their leases expired. One even threw the key through my window, he was in such a hurry to be away.'

"'It sounds like some crumbling old manor. I doubt it would be to my taste.'

"The agent – a stout man and jolly man, Falstaff's twin – shook his head. 'Crumbling? No, sir, not at all! It is a fine house, overlooking the ocean. It was built by Ebenezer Worth, a sea captain from America. He named it *Journey's End*, and he lived there until his death, which I believe was about two years ago. He left no kin except a nephew in America, who has instructed that the house be rented complete with all its furnishings.'

"'It costs a small fortune, then.'

"'Oh no – the price is most agreeable.'

"I confess my curiosity was aroused, and I agreed to consider the place. The agent snapped the buggy reins, and soon our trap was bouncing down a narrow road toward the ocean. We came over a steep hill, and I beheld the dwelling.

"It was a strange house, three stories tall, of a style I had never seen in England. The agent explained that Captain Worth had constructed it to resemble the homes of wealthy men in his native Nantucket. The house was only a few steps from the cliff's precipice, and a hearty gale might, it appeared, drive the entire edifice into the sea. We approached the house through a weed-choked yard. Though the structure appeared sound enough, the condition of the paint and the closely shuttered windows indicated its lack of regular occupants.

There was one ancient elm to shade the dwelling, and, beneath the elm, a strange stone cairn. I asked the agent what the odd pile of rocks signified.

"'That? Most likely the grave of the captain's dog. He had quite a mongrel, all black and hairy, nearly the size of a calf. I used to see it waiting for him when the captain came into the village for supplies. His only companion, that dog. The Captain was a bachelor and had no friends in the neighborhood – rather grim man, as I recall. Right this way, if you will.'

"If I had found the exterior odd and forlorn, the interior of the house was, in contrast, utterly fantastic. It was in a perfect state of preservation. The kitchen was fully stocked with pots and pans, and contained an oven of the most recent design. Each room was decorated with relics that would have been the envy of any museum. There were stuffed birds, mammals, and reptiles, great elephant tusks carved with curious scenes, native weapons of fiendish design, prints of exotic lands, and a library containing books in more languages than a university faculty could translate. The master bedroom was particularly fine, with mahogany furnishings, and a bed with velvet curtains and an ornate brass headboard."

"'How can such a wonderful place be haunted?' I asked, as we retired to the study, where a great portrait of Captain Worth gazed down on us from above the mantel. The agent was already spreading out a contract on the desk.

"'I do not know. The previous tenants left few details, other than to say they would not spend another night beneath this roof. Perhaps they found the atmosphere oppressive.'

"I sniffed the air. While the entire house had the musty odor of disuse, the study was exceptionally rank. I could not pinpoint the source of the unpleasant smell, but it seemed peculiar to the room, as if something had decayed within the walls. I mentioned this to the agent, who quickly struck a line through the rental price, reducing it by half. I am a man of reason, not a spiritualist, but the romance of the mansion appealed to my imagination and the rent to my pocketbook, and so – quite foolishly – I signed the papers.

"My first days were filled with the usual problems a bachelor has in taking up a new residence. I sought a housekeeper, but none of the good women of Widow's Bay would agree to employment at *Journey's End*, even on generous terms, for the house had acquired something of an evil reputation. At last I was able to find a girl, the daughter of the tavern-keeper, who was willing to work for me. Helen is deaf and mute, and her father permitted her to go into

288

service provided she could return home every evening on her little pony. It was an agreeable arrangement, as she confined her efforts to cleaning the house and preparing meals, and I had no desire for the idle chatter another woman might have inflicted upon me. I directed her attention to the study, but soon came to the conclusion that she could not disperse the evil smell, no matter how diligently she scrubbed.

"Despite its odor, the study held my attention, for it was a veritable cabinet of curiosities. The shelves were filled with ornate scrimshaws, dazzling samples of minerals and precious stones, odd miniature creatures preserved in amber, and strange, almost diabolical fossils. Beads, totems, and grotesque masks indicated the late captain's interest in pagan rituals, and, upon forcing open one rusty iron chest, I found a collection of shrunken heads and mummified hands. I came to think of Captain Worth as a natural savant, a man of such remarkable talents and knowledge that surely the world should be mourning his loss.

"The captain's portrait became an especial object of contemplation to me. Nearly life-sized, it showed the man aboard his vessel, one hand resting easily upon the ship's wheel and the other shoved inside his pea coat. The dark, indistinct background of the painting gave the impression that a storm was rising, that the ship might be sailing into danger, yet its commander faced the elements with steely-eyed indifference. From the very first, I felt there was something strange and inhuman about that picture, which portrayed the captain as a man completely lacking in warmth and sympathy.

"But there was something more – something suggested in those murky black and grey oils, as if the artist had longed to depict a presence *behind* the captain, a malignant creature peering around the captain's elbow. More than once I climbed upon a stool and held a lamp close to the canvas, only to find nothing but competent if uninspired brush strokes. It was only when I moved away that I perceived the unformed image. And when I sat at the desk, with my back turned to the picture, I felt as if I were being watched."

I glanced at Holmes, knowing that while I was enthralled by the young writer's tale, my companion lacked patience for such "poetry". Indeed, Holmes's brows had drawn tight, and I suspected he might be preparing to toss this prospective client into the street for wasting his time.

"If the painting disturbs you so," Holmes said, with some asperity, "then throw a sheet over the thing."

Mr. Humphreys shook his head. "I considered it, but thought myself foolish. I could have endured the portrait if that was the only unpleasantness – but when food vanished from my plate, into thin air, I began to be more alarmed."

Holmes reached for his pipe. "A hungry ghost! Ah, now your story becomes truly intriguing. Carry on."

"Helen is at best only a serviceable cook, but upon my fifth night in the residence, she produced a Cornish game hen that promised, based on its aroma, to be superb. I had asked her to bring the meal to the study, and as she placed my dish before me, she signaled that she wished to immediately depart. A storm was coming and the poor girl was anxious to be away from the house. I nodded my consent and went outside with her to make sure she was mounted on her pony and galloping away before the rain and wind began. I returned to the study in haste, my mouth watering, for the smell of a well-cooked bird had overcome the room's unwholesome odor. But, upon opening the door, I beheld an empty plate. My meal had been completely consumed."

"By a rat or by a cat?" Holmes asked.

"By neither. I keep no pets. And even if a rat had somehow made its way onto the desk where the plate rested, it could not have carried off an entire bird without a trace and gobbled up all the vegetables. My glass of wine had been overturned, and nothing was left upon my plate but a hint of sauce. At just that moment the storm began to rage and my nerves became unbearable. By luck I had some laudanum, and I swallowed a draught and did not awaken until late the next morning.

"The following afternoon, I was in the study again, perusing one of the volumes of poetry, hoping to make some headway on my own couplets and telling myself that the missing food had some bizarre but logical explanation. Glancing up from my book, I noted something lying in the unlit fireplace. At first, I thought I was only beholding a shadow, but then a draft of air came down the chimney and the thing in the fireplace stirred. I rose and crept closer, kneeling slowly. It appeared to be a clump of long, dark hair. Trembling, I leaned closer, willing myself to grasp the foul mass, when something abruptly pinched my shoulder. I gave a cry and fell to the rug, only to find a hideous, leathery-faced old man standing over me.

"Who the devil are you?" I cried.

"I beg your pardon," he said, in a rough but civil tone, "your maid would not speak, and I decided I could not wait for her to gather your attention. My name is Ambrose Coffin, and I was first mate to Captain Worth for nigh twenty years. I am here to tell you that if you value your sanity, your life, and your soul, you must leave this house."

"You cannot imagine the effect this rough intruder had on me. He was clearly a poor man, dressed in an ancient mariner's coat, his long gray beard much stained from a foul pipe that he had clenched in the black stubs of his teeth. But my curiosity proved stronger than my fear or my displeasure at his rude entry. I offered him a chair. Mr. Coffin sat for well over an hour, spinning a tale in a crude Yankee dialect. I will give you the essence of his words without their abominable accents.

"Captain Worth, Mr. Coffin claimed, was once a fine man and a bold commander. Fearless and resolute, he was the master of the *Lurker*, a clipper ship he had inherited from his father, who was one of the richest men in Nantucket. For forty years the captain sailed around the world, roaming wherever he might find trade. He possessed a superior mind and a cleverness that seemed almost supernatural; upon landing on any shore, no matter how primitive, he could quickly master the language of the natives. He read books, studied the stars, and knew more medicine than the ship's surgeon. He eschewed liquor, gambling, and profanity, and he was never overfamiliar with his men, who signed up eagerly for each new voyage, because of the captain's reputation. Many an old Yankee sailor now lives in comfort because he was once a crewman on the *Lurker*.

"Captain Worth had, it seemed, only one fault. He was not a religious man, and though he did not forbid his men their devotions, he never joined them. He was a rationalist who had no hope of heaven nor fear of hell. His obsession was with the material world, and he was a great collector of oddities and specimens. It this mania for collecting that brought about his doom and damnation.

"The *Lurker* had dropped anchor at a tiny, unnamed island in the Pacific, where the crew conducted a brisk business for over a week, as their captain bargained for valuable spices and exotic feathers, yielding only worthless glass beads in return. Just as the vessel was preparing to depart, a delegation of native warriors, all arrayed in bones and paint, arrived bearing a large wooden chest. The box was decorated with ghastly images of the island's gods, but the crewmen quickly perceived that the chest also contained air holes and emitted foul odors. The men could not understand their captain's parlay with the natives, but they watched as he directed the warriors to deliver the chest to a dark place deep in the cargo hold. Once the ship had passed from sight of the island, Captain Worth summoned the crew onto the main deck. He told them he had been given a valuable gift by the chieftain, and that he would tend to if himself. No man was to approach the chest, or touch it, or attempt to look inside it. To do so, he warned, would be to court disaster.

"These words – and the odd noises and foul stenches that came from the great box – naturally aroused the seamen's curiosity, but knowing that they would lose their share of a great profit, and perhaps rouse their captain's temper, they stayed away.

"All but one.

"Young Jeremy Banks was the cabin boy, a lad of no more than nine. The child was the pet of the crew, and he could think and talk of nothing but what might be inside the box. The men warned him not to pry, but one night, when the *Lurker* was still a thousand miles from land, the boy snuck down to the hold. With a candle in his hand, he attempted to peek inside the chest. He had no sooner pressed his eye to a hole in the wood than the Captain, who had come to tend to his prize, seized him by the collar.

"All hands were summoned to witness Jeremy's punishment. The crewmen begged for the boy to be forgiven as the lad trembled and wept. He would not say what he had seen, but his eyes budged, and his breath came in convulsive gasps. Even as the sailors spoke up, arguing that Jeremy was guilty of nothing but childish mischief, a madness descended upon the master of the vessel. Heedless of the crew's pleas, Captain Worth pronounced sentence, and before the men could move as a body to stop him, he hurled the hapless boy overboard. Whipping a pistol from his belt, he threatened to shoot the first man who dared go to young Jeremy's aid.

"After that, misfortune trailed the *Lurker* like a snarling beast. A plague swept the crew; a dozen men died and were buried at sea. The ship was damaged in a storm, and much of the cargo was lost. When the *Lurker* made port in Nantucket, Mr. Coffin vowed to have proceedings launched against the captain, but the remaining men would not support him, for they were heartsick and longed only for the comforts of home. Mr. Coffin learned that Jeremy's widowed mother had perished while they were abroad, and Captain Worth informed his most trusted mate that he had tired of the ocean and planned to retire. Mr. Coffin struggled with his conscience, thinking that as much as he loved his master he must avenge the innocent boy, but before he could resolve himself to betray his captain to the authorities, he found that the *Lurker* had been sold and Captain Worth had vanished.

"Years passed. Mr. Coffin also retired from the sea, and converted to an evangelical church. His new piety led him to seek out his captain and see if he had ever repented of his sin. In some manner he learned that Captain Worth had moved to Cornwall, and so he followed him. At last, Mr. Coffin at arrived at *Journey's End*, at midnight, just as a full moon rose overhead. But as he came close to the house, he beheld a hideous sight.

"It was the captain, still a strong and imposing man, though his hair had grown long and his beard had turned gray. He was kneeling by the elm tree, next to a large mound of stones, wailing in grief. Next to him, howling piteously, was a coal-black dog. Something about the scene, so unnatural and unholy, caused Mr. Coffin to take flight. He paused for just a moment at the top of the hill, looking back toward his old master, who was now prostrate across the stones. Mr. Coffin attempted to summon the courage to return. Then a hideous cry filled the air and the man fled beyond the rise."

"One moment," Holmes interjected. "Who made the cry? Was it the captain?"

"I asked him that very question. He said the sound seemed to arise from somewhere *within the house*."

Holmes nodded, as if a private thought had been confirmed, and signaled for his client to continue.

"I thought the story ended, but Mr. Coffin told me that, try as he might, he could not help but feel a moral obligation to his captain. He believed that the man had cursed himself by killing the cabin boy, and he wondered if guilt had driven Captain Worth mad. So, a month later, he returned to try and speak with the old man, but arrived just as the hearse was departing *Journey's End* for the cemetery. He made inquiries and learned a secret. Captain Worth had perished naturally, of heart failure, but it was the circumstances of how his body was found that caused dark gossip in the community. The captain kept no servants, and had it not been for the arrival of a tinker, who had an appointment to sharpen knives, the man might have rotted where he fell. Captain Worth was found clutching a strange item to his breast – a bright red dress, made of satin and silk, complete with an ornate bustle, the size that a small child would wear."

I looked up from my notes with a start. Holmes gave a puff of his pipe.

"Yet the captain was a bachelor, devoid of female relatives?"

"He was."

"What about the dog?" I asked, looking down at my scribbling. "Was it faithful until the end?"

"No, strangely enough, Mr. Coffin learned that the dog had died a week before the master. A local shepherd mistook it for a wolf, and shot it."

Holmes stared up at the ceiling, his fingers placed together. "I sense your tale is not concluded, Mr. Humphreys."

"Indeed, for the worst was yet to come. Mr. Coffin had grown quite incensed as he told his story, and made all manner of dire prophecies as to what misfortunes would befall me if I did not give up my lease immediately and vacate the premises. He seemed certain that the house was somehow cursed by its builder's sin. But then it occurred to me – for I am not a stupid man, I trust – that I had only Mr. Coffin's word for all that had transpired in the life of Captain Worth. For all I knew, the mariner could have been a God-fearing gentleman and this Mr. Coffin some type of swindler or confidence man. Perhaps he wanted the house for himself – perhaps he had learned of some treasure hidden within! Or maybe Captain Worth had buried a fortune beneath the stones, like some pirate of olden days. I decided I would not obey Mr. Coffin's order, and I turned him out rather brusquely. He shrieked a string of oaths hardly befitting a Christian, but he tramped away without further mischief.

"I returned to my chair by the fireplace, wearied beyond measure. As I settled down, I recalled the strange clump of oily hair I had seen in the grate. I looked down, and imagine my horror when I perceived its absence, as if some invisible hand had whisked it away while I was engaged in Mr. Coffin's storytelling, or in the brief instant that I saw him to the door. I immediately sought out Helen, communicating the mystery to her on paper, but she denied she had ever been in the study.

"I passed a long and restless afternoon. I attempted to dig up the cairn, thinking that I might find a treasure buried there, but the stones were so heavy I could not move them. That evening, I sent Helen away early, making do with just a pot of tea and some crackers for my supper. My mind would not stop working. Why did things vanish in the house? Had the old sailor spoken the truth? If so, what was the significance of the tiny dress found in Captain Worth's dead hands? All manner of devilish ideas crept into my brain, especially after I heard a noise, a long, lingering wail just as Mr. Coffin had described. God help me, but the sound came from nowhere – it had no point of origin, no obvious source. It was as if the house itself had moaned! Once again I restored to my laudanum bottle for succor.

"I tossed in my bed all night, a prisoner of the most hideous dreams. At times I seemed to see a vision before me, a dark, grimacing thing with a face caught between a beast and a man. Then, abruptly, there was a sharp pain in my right hand. The drug had me so thick that I could not respond, but the pain came again and again, stinging and hot and tearing. It felt like I was being devoured! At last my conscious brain was triumphant and I roused myself with a cry, flailing my arms. Blood splattered across my face. I looked down to find my right hand was . . . ."

He had been tugging at the bandages around his palm, and now he held out his hand. It was savagely mutilated, almost chewed, as if something with razor-like teeth had been gnawing on his flesh. The wounds had been badly treated, and I insisted on fetching my bag. I quickly bathed the mauled flesh and redressed it, providing Mr. Humphreys with another much-needed glass of brandy as I worked. I looked up to find Holmes standing beside me.

"A house determined to consume its resident is a rather frightful thing indeed. I think, Watson, that we had best take ourselves to Cornwall without delay."

By the next afternoon, we had engaged a suite of rooms at the Golden Mermaid, an antique tavern that passed for a hostelry in Widow's Bay. Mr. Humphreys had given us the key to *Journey's End* and a message to deliver to his little housekeeper. The paper stated quite clearly that her services were no longer required and that he had no intention of ever returning to that hellish abode. Holmes, however, had written a new note, this one saying that her master would be abroad for a week and that we, former tutors of his university days, would look after the place for him. Helen was to prepare supper for us that evening, and Holmes had included a long grocery list as well as a fat purse so that she could fulfill our particular culinary request for Cornish game hen.

Holmes had spoken very little on the train. Mr. Humphreys had gone off to lodge with his maiden aunt, leaving the field free for our investigations. As we neared the coast, Holmes's mood seemed to brighten. He even hummed a selection of music hall tunes as the train approached the station. I found myself unable to contain my curiosity – why this sudden cheer?

"To be frank, my good Watson, I feel we are on holiday again."

"Yet it is a dismal and grotesque case that calls us here."

"I would hardly say that! Grotesque, perhaps, but not dismal. I believe this story may yet have a happy ending."

"You propose to put the ghost to rest?"

"No, I intend to feed it."

Following that baffling intelligence, Holmes refused to say more. We left our suite at the Golden Mermaid for the haunted house, walking the three miles from the village to *Journey's End* at a brisk pace. Reaching the top of the hill, we paused for a moment to take in the scene. The gnarled tree and the strange cairn were clearly visible. The house was badly painted, with warped boards showing in places, yet it was still an imposing structure, rather majestic in its isolation. The girl's pony was grazing contentedly near the door, but it perked up its ears as we approached. Holmes offered the creature the apple he had purchased at the tavern while chatting with the owner about Captain Worth.

"He bought so few groceries," the proprietor had told us. "He must have had the appetite of a bird. I wouldn't be surprised if he starved to death! Doctor says it was his heart that caused him to perish, but what do doctors know?"

"Very little, indeed," Holmes had answered, far too cheekily for my taste.

Helen, who was at work in the kitchen, greeted us with a curtsey and a rash of notes inquiring whether we would like the bedrooms aired. Holmes assured her that our only interest was in the study, where we would take our meal when it was ready. We retired to that room, finding it exactly as Mr. Humphreys had described. A veritable museum of oddities and curios, it was somehow both fascinating and repellant. Holmes paid little attention to the relics, but spent much time inspecting the walls and examining the seams of the woodwork with his lens. He poked his head up the chimney, but withdrew very quickly.

"You note the smell?" he asked.

"I do. I am surprised that our client could ever become accustomed to it."

"What would you say it is?"

"I do not know. It seems a mix of many things, rot and decay but also as if an army of tramps lived just in the next room."

"Precisely, and yet – ah, this will serve nicely!"

Holmes plucked down a heavy fisherman's net that had been draped across a shelf. With a deft toss, he swung it from the large gas lamp just above the desk. I was sent to fetch string, and when Holmes finished his engineering he had created a serviceable trap that would dangle just above the head of an unwary diner. Holmes moved a large oriental screen from one of the bedrooms, placing it opposite the desk and the fireplace.

A short time later, Helen brought out the plates. Holmes had ordered a gargantuan meal that would have fed an entire company of hungry men. The savory aromas soon changed the smell of the room, and after dismissing the girl, we feasted. At Holmes's urging, we talked loudly of inconsequential things. We rattled the silverware, clinked our glasses in merry toasts, and made outlandish comments on the exceptional deliciousness of the meal.

"I am stuffed!" I announced, not needing Holmes's cue to give a loud belch. "I could not eat another bite."

"Nor I. But it is late, and we should be returning to our hotel."

"What about these dishes?" I asked, feeling rather like a bad actor in a music hall melodrama. "Shouldn't we take them to the kitchen and wash them?"

"Fine gentlemen like ourselves do the dishes? Perish the thought, Watson. I'm sure the girl will return in the morning to tidy things up. Here, old fellow, into your coat."

We pretended to remove ourselves from the house, dimming the lights and loudly slamming the door. But at the last moment, we had removed our shoes and drawn back into the hallway. We tiptoed to the silent study, kneeling down behind the screen.

"We should not have a long wait," Holmes warned in a whisper. "Keep your bag and your revolver close."

It was a most uncomfortable watch, with both of us in a crouched and wary position. Once, my knees gave a loud pop, which I was certain earned me a grimace from Holmes, but as the room was inky, I could not see his face. I wondered what manner of beast we were stalking, but I could conjure up none that fit all the particulars.

Holmes's ice cold hand suddenly seized to my wrist. There was a scrambling sound, and patter of small things falling. It came from the direction of the chimney. I peered through the narrow slit we had cut in the screen, but saw nothing. Then, in a heartbeat, there was something oozing from the fireplace. It moved in fits and starts, too shadowy in the darkness for me to see its true form. It panted like a dog, but wiggled and writhed in such an unnatural way that it took all my courage not to bolt from my hiding place. With a grunt the black, trembling thing hurled itself into the chair Holmes had vacated and seized the remaining bird on the platter. There was a nasty sound of flesh being rent, followed by gurgling and gulping, and then suddenly the string connected to the fowl was pulled tight and the net above the desk released.

"Now, Watson! The lights!"

A scream split the air. The shapeless thing was encased in the net, but had kicked over the chair and, with frantic shrieks and struggles, was slithering back toward the chimney. Holmes fell upon it just as I reached a lamp.

"Quickly! A needle! Sedation!"

For an instant I could only stare at what Holmes had pinned. It was a foul, filthy creature – a naked, grime-besmirched, long-haired boy, of not more than five or six years of age. Holmes's attempts to soothe him were met with the fierceness of a tiger, as the child tried desperately to sink his teeth into my friend's arm. I quickly filled a syringe with morphine, and in moments the sad child was limp in our grasp.

"My God," I gasped, "what is he?"

"*Who* is he?" Holmes corrected, gesturing for me to bring the café of water that had been left upon a sideboard. Holmes scrubbed the youth's face with a handkerchief, and while his ministration made but little difference in removing the accumulated filth of the years, it allowed us to see that the child's features were a mix of the European and Pacific Islander, with nut-hued skin, inky black hair, and delicately slanted eyes. "Watson, we are looking at the heir to *Journey's End*, young Master Worth."

"But – who is his mother? And how did he come to be in such a ghastly state?" I demanded, noting his small limbs and protruding ribcage. It was clear to me that the youth was near death from starvation.

"I believe that should we imitate the resurrection men of old, we would find this boy's mother buried in the cairn beneath the elm. Recall what Coffin said about the 'gift' the natives presented to Captain Worth, and his feverish desire – to the point of murder – to keep it a secret. The gift was a native woman, a concubine."

I shook my head fiercely. "Why the need for secrecy? If the captain was an irreligious man, why would he have hesitated to take a native woman as a bride?"

"Recall the dress, Watson, the garment that he clutched in his death throes. It was no larger than a child would wear, yet made for a woman: His 'wife' was a pygmy or a dwarf. Shame, or fear of it, forced him to keep the secret, yet his lust for her was fierce, or he would have freed her on some foreign shore."

298

"But the boy appears normal! Why treat him with such cruelty?"

I could see from the way Holmes held the child, with such gentleness, that he was greatly moved by his plight. My friend had always been an ally to children, valuing the company of his unruly little Irregulars above the society of dukes and barons. "It is mere conjecture at this point, but perhaps Captain Worth blamed the child for the mother's sickness and death. The wail Coffin heard was not the house, or a ghost, but a mistreated toddler. Captain Worth could not expose the child's existence, lest he be questioned about the mother's disappearance, so he brought him up in this house alone – hardly a healthy environment for an unwanted child. When his father died, the boy turned feral. He retreated to the hidden compartments of the house, the only safety he knew."

"And he has lived inside this house, slowly starving, all this time?"

Holmes nodded, and together we wrapped the child in a blanket. "When the house was rented, he could steal food and provisions. When the house was untenanted, no doubt he ate rats or other vermin that he could catch. I noted a number of places where this room could give access to secret chambers, much like a priest-holes of the Civil War era. Captain Worth no doubt constructed the dwelling with such hidden rooms so that he could whisk his native lady into one of them, should any guests abruptly arrive."

I shook my head. "How horrible."

"At times, I believe that the devil learned his tricks from mankind, not the other way around. Come – let us see if we cannot find a better home for this poor little fellow, who was so hungry that he tried to eat his own guest! Considering the circumstances, I will readily forgive his cannibalism."

Unlike so many of my friend's investigations, this one had a happy epilogue. The lad, who was given the name Edward by the good sisters of the Widow's Bay Orphan's Home, quickly rallied upon receiving medical care and nourishment. He spoke not a word of English, but his mind and body quickly began to grow. Within a year he was proving one of the cleverest boys in the home. Mr. Landly, the tavern-keeper, became his guardian, and little Helen was soon his dearest friend. In due time, the boy came into his inheritance, and the sale of the house and its many oddities provided for Master Worth's education at Oxford. Just a few months ago, Holmes drew my attention to a notice of a fashionable wedding of a

young Cornish barrister, who had married a lady said to be deaf and
dumb, and nearly a decade his senior.

In the Realm of the
Wretched King
by Derrick Belanger

I, John H. Watson, take pride in my role as biographer of the great detective, Mr. Sherlock Holmes of 221b Baker Street. I have retold many of his fine adventures, including those involving the laughable Red-Headed League, a certain Noble Bachelor, and a notorious pair of severed ears arriving in a Cardboard Box. I scribe so that the public may regale in my dear friend's feats of the mind, and all can know his seemingly superhuman methods of deduction. Yet the adventure contained on the following pages I write not for the public but for myself. Indeed, the matter itself is hardly a memorable one, save for the use of my dear friend's method of untangling a truly complicated web of a puzzle. And yet, I find my skin crawling and my mind unsettled when I reflect upon the mystery involving the writings of Mr. Adam Smith, an American folklorist and supposed prophet. Truth be told, the mystery has a rational explanation, and Holmes would chuckle at my implication that there was something beyond the fathomable in the episode's conclusion, something beyond his logical deductions.

And yet, I find myself waking to my own nightly feelings of sheer terror, and my mind wandering to the darkest incomprehensible thoughts which have, at times, left me to question my own sanity. It is for those reasons and those reasons alone which I tell this tale. My hope is that by transcribing the events on paper, my mind will return to the rational, and I will fully accept the conclusions of the wisest man I have ever known.

The adventure began on a brisk spring Sunday at the conclusion of the nineteenth century. Holmes and I had lunched at Simpson's and returned to Baker Street via the Underground. Mrs. Hudson was out for the afternoon on a shopping excursion with her friend, Mrs. MacDougall. The sky was overcast, and there was a gentle breeze in the air, just enough to make the street lights sway slightly back and forth. As we were walking home from the Baker Street Station, I tightened the scarf around my neck, for the wind was cool enough for my neck hairs to stand on end and face to redden from the chill. Holmes wore his deerstalker flaps down and seemed to have sufficient warmth for our stroll home.

When at last we made it to 221b, there was a rather unusual horseless carriage parked at the pavement curb.

"Holmes, what do you make of the wheels on that vehicle?" I asked as we reached our dwelling.

"Ah, Watson, you are referring not to the wheels themselves but to the pneumatic tires adorning the vehicle's wheels. Those are the latest addition to Mr. Benz's most expensive carriages. They are made of a thick rubber and filled with compressed air, and designed to give a smoother and more comfortable carriage ride. I'm sure my client will have no problem extolling the virtues of his luxuries."

Client? I almost asked aloud but caught myself, for why would anyone but a client of Holmes be parked in front of 221b Baker street in a fancy vehicle? As I was thinking this to myself, an impeccably dressed driver in a dark suit coat adorned with large gold buttons promptly stepped from the vehicle, went to the passenger side, and opened the door for his employer.

Out stepped a stern and imposing figure. He was tall, standing well above the Holmes's height. His shoulders were broad, his hair, from what I could see of it below his black top hat, was the color of clouds. His face was framed by bushy sideburns, and his skin was thickly lined with age, as if the man had been chiseled out of clay by a modern artist. His grim, bronze-colored eyes and his dour expression added to the gentleman's aura of unpleasantness.

"Mr. Holmes," the man stated firmly. "I have been waiting for a quarter-of-an-hour to see you."

"I do not recall a scheduled appointment," Holmes responded firmly, his silver eyes meeting the gaze of this austere client.

The man sneered and responded unsympathetically, "I do not take kindly to waiting, Mr. Holmes, whether or not I had an appointment. My time is precious, and I do not want to waste another minute of it. Shall you invite me in, or will I tell you the details of my problem out here with the three of us standing upon the pavement?"

"As much as I enjoy the din of the traffic, I believe that we would be more comfortable inside," Holmes responded. He stepped to the door of our flat, unlocked it, and swung it open. "After you, Mr. Monroe."

The client glowered, but nodded his consent and went through the door to the entryway, followed by me, and then Holmes, who closed the door behind us. He then stepped past us to the foot of the stairs.

"I don't recall telling you my name." Monroe brusquely stated.

"That's because you didn't. Now, kindly take the book and papers you are concealing under your overcoat and follow us up the steps to our flat. There, we shall all find comfort."

Mr. Monroe started to let out a low growl. Holmes ascended two steps, then paused and stated, "If you follow, I shall explain all."

Monroe held himself, and no sound escaped his mouth except his steady breathing. He then walked to the stairs and ascended, following Holmes. I did the same, taking up the rear.

"Your identity," Holmes said as we climbed, "was easy enough to ascertain. A wealthy American munitions manufacturer who rides the streets of London in the latest contraption by Mr. Benz, and has publicized engagements with both the Prime Minister and Queen Victoria is very easy to identify.

"As for the book and papers, the size and shape of the volume you hold curled in your hand, tucked below your arm, was easy to detect. While it could possibly be a box holding some weight, the way your fingers are spread and the top of your palm is held outward, it is clear you are cradling the pages of a closed book and not the flat of a package. As for the papers, a light cloak such as yours cannot completely deaden the sound of crisp pages crinkling against the clutch of your hand and the leather cover of the tome. I noted the sound as you stepped past me in the entryway. Now, here we are."

We had reached the top of the stairs, and Holmes opened the door to our sitting room. I took Monroe's cloak, seeing that Holmes was correct that the gentleman had a thick leather book and several loose papers clutched against the left side of his body. Holmes invited Monroe to sit in the sofa. Then he and I busied ourselves to make the room comfortable. Holmes added some scraps of wood and paper to the firebox and then started the flames. I poured three glasses of scotch, and pulled three Cuban cigars. Soon we were seated, our bodies heated by the fire, our bellies warmed by the drink and smoke.

"Now, Mr. Monroe, what brings a busy man such as yourself to my doorstep on this fine day?" Holmes started.

Monroe, who had never ceased scowling at my friend, bluntly replied, "With your reasoning skills, shouldn't you be the one to tell me?"

Holmes's lips curled up into a mischievous smile. "I can tell much about you, Mr. Monroe. I can tell from the bags under your eyes that you have not been sleeping well. From your attire that you care very much about your appearance, so much so that you apply a slight bit of whitening makeup to cover for the wrinkles which come with age. You – "

"That's enough, Mr. Holmes. I did not ask to hear about my appearance."

"Very well," Holmes smirked and leaned back in his chair. The detective was rather smug and pleased with himself for pointing out the vanity of his client. "You asked me to tell you your case. That is beyond my reasoning skills. I know it involves that tome resting on your lap, and the withered parchment pages by your side. Anything beyond that would be guessing. So, please enlighten Dr. Watson and me for I, myself, am rather curious why a notorious munitions manufacturer such as yourself is sitting in our rooms. I'd expect you to be at home proudly overseeing your company's profits from the American War with Spain."

"Watch your tongue, Mr. Holmes," growled Monroe. "Despite the rumors to the contrary, I wish that war had never started in the first place. I take no pride in profiting from the war in the Spanish islands and blame the newspapers for riling up the American public. My nephew is currently serving on the *USS Newark*, and I would give away all of my profits to have the boy home safe."

I nodded somberly at Mr. Monroe's explanation and found a new respect for the man.

"But I did not come here today because of the vicious rumors against me. I came because of this and what it foretells!" Monroe held up the book and papers and shook them in the air.

Holmes motioned with his hand for Monroe to explain.

The client lowered his hand and began telling his story. "To explain my case, I have to start many years ago. My grandfather started our company in the days of the American Revolution. He was an excellent mechanic and engineer, and he made his name with small explosive devices.

"At the end of the Revolution, Grandfather Monroe knew that his income would be significantly reduced. He still had a contract with the young United States government which would sustain him, but he wanted more, and knew that there were riches to be had elsewhere.

"My grandfather traveled to England, and since his name was known for the destruction caused by his weapons, the King was happy to have Grandfather work with his military. Afterwards, Grandfather traveled to France and to Germany before returning home. In this voyage, he made deals with several other munitions manufacturers, and thus laid the groundwork for my family's global empire."

At this point in Mr. Monroe's tale, I glanced over at Holmes. I could not fathom why Monroe was telling us a piece of his family history which was over a hundred years old. Holmes was in his usual meditative stance, his elbows resting on his legs and his fingers steepled before his eyes, offering his full concentration on the matter at hand even if it seemed, from my perspective, to have no connection to events in the nineteenth century.

"Now, gentlemen," Monroe continued, "when my grandfather returned to the States, he was a wealthier man, but he was in no way a more satisfied one. He was obsessed with knowing where the next war would start, where he could earn the most money. He started making connections in the governments of many nations to give him information of potential conflicts, but this was not enough. To truly know the future was his goal, for if he knew the future with certainty, he would be able to maximize his profits, break into other areas of business, and even profit enough to the point of becoming the wealthiest man in the world.

"This became Grandfather's life goal, and it consumed the man. He first began experimenting with tools of fortune. He sought readings of the I-Ching and Tarot, consulted spirits through séances, Ouija Boards, and mediums, and began studying Christian rituals of old which have long been abandoned by keepers of the faith. Over the years, as these attempts at seeing through the veil of time failed, Grandfather started exploring other even more fiendish methods of obtaining that which he wished to see. He began seeking out practitioners of the dark arts, those that worship multiple gods, even demons and devils. He traveled to visit the pyramids of Egypt, took part in savage tribal rituals, and according to my father, he even participated in a human sacrifice led by a coven of witches and warlocks in a secret underground location in the hills of eastern Tennessee.

"Of course, this was all voodoo nonsense and quackery. Grandfather built our family empire through hard work, shrewd negotiations, and excellent business acumen, yet the old fool felt that he had failed in life for not being able to see the future. So strong was his obsession that he could not tell that he had, through his own volition in many ways, he had been able to foresee it, but not through mystical means. He had achieved this through applying logic and strategy in the capitalist market system.

305

"After Grandfather passed, Father took over and kept the business successful. He branched out into even more countries and increased our global sales, all without the aid of voodoo mumbo-jumbo. Then I did the same when the torch was passed to me.

"All of grandfather's occult nonsense has largely been forgotten, all was proven fake." Here Monroe paused, his expression went from gruff to sour, and he looked pained as he softly spoke his next few words. "All were fake, save one particular artifact he collected. And that, gentlemen, is the reason I am here today."

"You refer to the papers and the book you hold on your lap," Holmes stated.

"I refer to the papers. The book is the key to understanding the papers and possibly into seeing a glimpse of what is to face us in the next hundred years. I know, gentlemen, that I sound as loony as my grandfather, but I swear to you that I am not. Tell me, Mr. Holmes, have you ever read of the American folklorist, Adam Smith?"

Holmes leaned back in his chair and held his chin with his right fist, his eyes darting upwards as his inner machinations worked to retrieve such knowledge from the storage of his brain attic. "Adam Smith . . . Adam Smith . . . ah, yes!" Holmes said with a snap of his fingers. "The man who collected stories about the strange and macabre."

Holmes turned to me and said excitedly, "Watson, Smith was a resident of New Hampshire who traveled throughout the colonies, interviewing Indians and recording stories of such oddities as monstrous wild men living in Appalachia, people from the stars mating with members of various Indian tribes, giant birds in the mountains of Virginia attacking villagers and abducting children, prehistoric water beasts living in lakes and streams in Vermont, and other odd phenomena, such as the raining of fish, frogs, and blood from the sky. Don't look so stricken, Watson – the man was far ahead of his time. He would collect the stories, but whenever possible would provide a rational explanation for the mysteries. I found his theory that blood rain was caused by microscopic pollutants in the atmosphere most practical. Perhaps, in this age of advancement, he shall be proven correct on that front."

"Really, Holmes," I sputtered, still trying to grapple with the lunacy of all Monroe had previously said, "I did not think you had an interest in such matters."

"I am interested in only one such matter, my dear Watson, and that is knowing the truth. Adam Smith collected stories of the absurd, analyzed them, and then drew conclusions based on the rational. In my humble opinion, he was far beyond his time," Holmes concluded, then quickly turned his attention back to Monroe. "Now tell me, Mr. Monroe what does an eighteenth century folklorist have to do with your problem?"

"He has everything to do with it, Mr. Holmes. You are correct that Adam Smith was a researcher and a rationalist, but there is a myth about the man, a mystery which still lives to this day.

"Like yourself, Adam Smith was a man obsessed with knowing the truth. Legend has it that before his days as a folklorist, Mr. Smith visited a supposedly haunted Indian burial ground near Goffe's Falls in his home town of Bedford, New Hampshire. This burial ground was notorious for its supposed *thinning*, which means its wall between our world and the spirit world was thinner within its boundaries.

"The burial spot is well known, and I, myself, have visited it on several occasions and have felt absolutely no effects. For Mr. Smith, the result was supposedly much different. When he entered, he at first felt nothing, then he heard strange warped whisperings as if the voices were speaking both forwards and backwards at the same time.

"Most people would have turned and run away at hearing such oddities, but Smith was no ordinary man. He tried to determine if the sounds he was hearing were conversations of others in the vicinity muffled by the sounds of rushing water and echoing off the nearby rock walls.

"Smith felt that no one was within the vicinity besides himself, and was going to check if the sound, through various vibrational effects, was actually traveling from miles away. It would explain the oddities people hear in the area and the myth about the thinning."

"An excellent theory," Holmes stated, impressed. I could tell that the more Holmes heard of Smith, the more he admired the man.

"Yes, but if we are to believe the legend of Adam Smith, then we are to believe this theory was quickly disproven. For as Smith was about to exit the circle and explore if his theory was correct, he was visited by a strange man. Out of the ether before Smith appeared an albino giant. Bald headed with large black pupil-less eyes, a nub, almost flat nose, and a thin expressionless mouth. This man was present but not present, only vaguely materialized in our world. The creature asked Smith what he would like to know. Smith, who did not seem taken aback by the creature, as if it was no less common then seeing a fellow traveler upon the road, responded, 'the truth'.

"The giant nodded its head and then disappeared. Afterwards, Smith left the circle, traveled back to his family homestead, and that evening, wrote a series of letters to various witnesses of unexplained phenomena. The next day, Smith traveled to see a man he had heard of living in the town of Merrimack who claimed that while chipping away at a stone on his property, he had discovered a frog trapped inside of it. *The Merrimack 'Toad in the Hole'* would be the first published article of Adam Smith, appearing in the Merrimack Gazette on August 14th, 1763."

Holmes gave out one of his odd, silent chuckles. "And so, the myth is that the rational Adam Smith received his powers of observation through otherworldly means. Sounds like what some of the officers of the law have said about me, aye Watson?"

I smiled at Holmes, though refrained from laughing outright. There was something unsettling about the story of Smith, and I could tell that there was more that Mr. Monroe had to say on the matter.

"I concur, Mr. Holmes. However, this story came from the lips of Smith himself, and was confirmed by none other than his publisher, Andrew Gardner. From the years of 1763 to 1768, Smith traveled the American colonies, collecting stories of the supposed unreal. Throughout that period, Smith did not often speak of his own strange encounter, but he did say it to a few people within his small inner circle of friends. He also told them of a powerful after-effect of his request to know the truth. While Smith was able to puzzle out the true meanings of Lake Monster sightings (he put forth that they were dislodged pieces of debris which bubbled to the lake's surface), he also learned of a much more gruesome truth, that which would occur hundreds of years in the future.

"Smith died in 1768 while recording a story of a warlock who lived in a cave in the woods of Kentucky. There was an earthquake which caused the roof to collapse, killing both Smith and his interviewee.

"The day after his death, a package arrived in the office of Gardner House Publishing. It was a manuscript entitled *The Complete Work of Adam Smith, Folklorist 1763-1768*." Monroe paused to hold up the book in his lap. He then held up the papers. "It also contained this."

"What is the significance of the papers?" I asked as Monroe handed the parchment papers over to Holmes.

"They are the opening pages to Smith's one fictional story," Monroe explained, and Holmes read the title aloud.

"*In the Realm of the Wretched King*. Not the most jolly of titles."

"But it reads as though it is a whimsical tale of a humorous wedding between the daughter of a wealthy plantation owner and a Northerner named McGill who pretends to be a rich distillery owner but is really a pauper smitten with the lass. The story goes off into all sorts of silly hijinks, some involving the servants of the house, others involving the grumpy father discovering the true status of McGill, but supposedly, in the end, McGill discovers that he has inherited a distillery from a distant uncle and he really is wealthy. The two leads are married, and they live happily ever after, as happens in such poorly conceived drivel ever popular with the ladies of the world."

"Supposedly?" I asked as Holmes was quietly reading over the handwritten manuscript.

"Yes, Dr. Watson, supposedly, for save the eight pages Mr. Holmes holds in his hands, no one has ever read the story. We know that basic plot outline from the letter which Mr. Smith wrote to Mr. Gardner and included in his manuscript.

"Smith explained to Gardner that the full story is contained within the pages of this book, his complete work. Smith hid the story, so to speak, within these pages. One only need to decipher the story from the folklore text and one can read *In the Realm of the Wretched King*."

"Why would Smith go to the trouble of hiding this romance in his folklore collection?" I could not fathom a reason and found these events most absurd.

"Because, Dr. Watson, within this hidden story Smith hid something else. He hid his vision of the future."

"But why go to all that trouble?" I asked.

"Because the future he saw was too terrifying to behold. He saw countries scarred by the ravages of war, mass executions of people through poisonous gas, graves miles in length, ovens used to cook those who disobeyed the Wretched King."

Holmes interrupted Monroe and asked him for his copy of Smith's book. Smith removed an envelope from inside the front cover and then handed the book over to Holmes. The detective then flipped through the book, eyeing the content and comparing Smith's handwritten pages. Holmes showed no reaction to Monroe's wild tale.

"Grandfather acquired those pages at the auction of Gardner Publishing's assets when the company folded. Once he read the pages, he believed he had something that was truly mystical. Father also knew this to be true, and when the work was passed to me, I learned the secret as well. Yet, over these decades, no one has ever been able to crack the code and read the entire story. No one, 'til now."

At this admission, Holmes put down the book and papers and gave Monroe his full attention. "Go on," Holmes said forcefully.

Monroe held up the envelope he had removed from the interior of the book. "A month ago, I received this letter from a man housed in a mental institution here in London. This Ned Walker claimed that he had solved the mystery of Smith's story. To prove it, he sent me copies of the pages you hold in your hands, Mr. Holmes, plus two additional pages. The man is telling the truth."

"But if this Walker has solved the puzzle of Smith's encrypted tale, then why do you need my services?" Holmes enquired.

Monroe slammed his fist down. "Because Walker is hopelessly insane. I have visited him twice, Mr. Holmes, and on both occasions he spent the entire time talking to a China doll and asking me to play games of draughts and chess. Every time I would ask him for the secret of the story, he would chuckle maniacally, mutter to his doll, and then ask me to play a game.

"He knows the secret, Holmes, but getting it out of the man may be even more difficult than solving the puzzle yourself," Monroe concluded.

Holmes sat back in his chair. His face had turned blank, and not being able to read his expression worried Monroe. The businessman blurted out, "You will be well compensated for your actions, Mr. Holmes. I shall pay you five times your normal fee for accepting this case, and ten times if you are successful."

The blank expression on Holmes's face turned to a deep frown. I thought for sure he would reject the offer, even though it was extremely lucrative. Holmes kept that frown for nearly a minute before he let out a long sigh and said, "Very well. I will accept your case."

Mr. Monroe nodded and offered Holmes his hand. They shook and Monroe said, "I need to leave for Germany in three days' time."

"Mr. Monroe," Holmes said matter-of-factly, "If I can decipher the code on my own, you will have your story within twenty-four hours. If I need the assistance of Mr. Walker it will take me no more than forty-eight."

"Thank you, Mr. Holmes. I will let it be known that a message from you takes top priority. Once you've puzzled it out, you contact me immediately."

"Very well, sir."

Holmes asked Monroe to leave the book, papers, and the letter from Mr. Walker. Monroe agreed, said his goodbyes, and soon was off in his jalopy.

When the entrepreneur was gone, I asked Holmes why he took on such an odd case.

"Do not fret. I do not believe that Smith was anything more than a very good folklorist, and it appears, very good with encryption as well."

"So you do not believe Monroe's story that Smith could see the future?"

"My dear Watson, the idea is preposterous," Holmes chastised. "I accepted Mr. Monroe as my client because I wanted the challenge of breaking Smith's code. Looking at the first few pages of the story and comparing it to his complete works has shown me that the code is most advanced. In fact," Holmes added while putting down the papers and standing up, stretching his arms towards the ceiling. "I must away for a while. I am afraid I may not be able to join you for dinner this evening."

"Why, Holmes, is this about the case?"

"It is in part. Good afternoon, Watson," he said and grabbed his hat and cape. Then he left.

I was taken aback by Holmes leaving in such a blunt and off-putting manner. He gave me no reason as to why he had to go in such a hurry, nor did he invite me along.

While I thought this was eccentric for Holmes, the *V.R.* spelled out in bullet holes on the wall reminded me that this, for my good friend, was a relatively minor infraction of decency.

With Holmes away and with no particular plans for the afternoon, I decided to read up on Mr. Monroe myself. I first consulted Holmes's index file. Most of the information I uncovered there included the basics of Mr. Monroe being a munitions manufacturer. However, there were two items of interest. First, Monroe was not as opposed to his study of the occult as he had claimed. One clipping explained that Monroe had participated in a séance held at the American White House to try and contact the spirit of President Abraham Lincoln.

The other clipping concerned the sightings of mysterious airships over the American West. I recalled Holmes mentioning the phenomenon and even Thomas Edison consulting him about the purported aerostats. The massive airships were first reported in California in 1896 and then the sightings traveled further east. Speculation was that the device or devices were created by Edison

311

himself and that he planned to bring an airship over Washington D.C. or New York City in broad daylight as a major source of publicity.

Of course, the airship never materialized and the papers moved on to other stories of interest. The clipping was a letter to the editor expressing the belief that Mr. Monroe could be the man behind the airship flap, and that the devices were actually a new aeronautical weapon to be used by the U.S. Armed forces.

This letter was nothing more than speculation, yet Holmes had included it in his file. Could there be some truth to the accusation?

Next, I moved to the parchment containing the excerpt of Smith's story. Though I do not enjoy being critical of a fellow author, the work was the most maudlin and poorly executed I have ever read. The dialogue was florid, the jokes lurid, and the undertones horrid. One particularly dreadful scene involved the male servant of Miss Alexandria modeling one of the lady's dresses. There was one line in this scene that caught my eye, though. When Miss Alexandria chastises her servant, she says something like, *"Tee-hee, you silly man. Do not let the Wretched King know of your private charades."*

To which the servant replied, *"Ah, my sweet and beautiful lady, if the Wretched King in his infinite wisdom were to sniff out my true stripes, I would be roasting in the glorious oven and you along with me. Gardens would grow from our intermingled ashes."*

Later in the tale, towards the end of the fragment, McGill is visiting a distillery to learn the terms of the trade to fool Alexandria's father. There are some crude attempts at humor involving the rhyming of the words yeast and beast, but again there is an odd line in which McGill notes the strong stench of fermentation. *"My nostrils caught a waft of the fermenting rye, and for a moment I feared the King's death gas was upon me. When I realized it was no more than the normal odors of a distillery, I got down on my knees and prayed to our Wretched Lord, for he and he alone holds my fate in his hands. He would decide whether my nightingale would be mine or if my fate would be to lie in a mass grave with my fellow subjects."*

I found these asides to be distasteful, and made the amateur narrative that much worse. I went out for dinner and returned to find that Mrs. Hudson was back from her trip but that Holmes was still out. What was keeping my friend away for hours?

To pass the time, I turned to Smith's complete folklore collection. This book was the opposite of the depravity found in *The*

Realm of the Wretched King. The scholarship was excellent, the explanations clear and concise. Smith's deductions on some of the unexplained phenomena he was investigating were worthy of Holmes himself. In one instance, he exposed a spiritualist who claimed to bring forth a malicious spirit. Smith was led to an empty room with a wicker chair in the center. Hovering above this woven chair was a cloudy figure with a human face. While most would have been enchanted with the spirit, Smith lit a match, inspected the room, and found the ghost was no more than a trick developed using smoke and mirrors.

When the witching hour approached, I had read half of Smith's book. Holmes still had not returned. I decided to get some sleep, as I had a busy morning ahead of me with a number of scheduled patient visits.

As tired as I was that night, I slept little, tossing and turning in my slumber. I had hideous night visions of the Earth scarred with great slashes. Inside these slashes were thousands of men, soldiers, writhing, screaming, tearing the flesh from their faces and gouging their eyes as an odd syrupy black cloud engulfed them.

Then my mind switched to a school setting where masses of bald-headed children were assembling kites in a school room as vast as a warehouse. The school resembled a factory system, and each time a group of students completed a set of kites, a teacher would collect them, then take them to the furnace and toss them in, as if their work was pointless. As more and more kites were tossed to the flames, the furnace grew in size until it touched the ceiling and wanting to expand more, its mouth opened ever wider. The beast sprouted tentacle limbs which slithered out, knocked the teachers aside, and grabbed the kites for itself. The eldritch beast swelled as it consumed more and more. It sprouted bulbous eyes and insect-like mandibles.

The students worked furiously, yet could not keep up with the creature's demands, and eventually its tentacles came for them. The octoploidal beast snatched the children and tossed them into the flames at an alarming rate. Their shrieking bodies burst into flames, their skin sizzled and crackled. The smell of charred flesh overtook my senses, and I awakened to my own terror, my body shivering, my sheets drenched in a cold sweat.

I clutched at my heart and found it pounding. From outside my room I heard Holmes call out to me, asking me if everything was alright. From the sound of my howls of terror, I was surprised that he did not knock the door down out of concern for his Boswell.

313

"Watson, whatever is the matter?" Holmes asked as I came down from my chamber. He had the folklore book and manuscript spread out on the dining table with his own notes scrawled out on copious sheets of paper.

I noticed that my friend had large bags under his own eyes and that his silver orbs were cracked with bloodshot lines. I told Holmes of my nightmares and then, noting his own haggard state, asked if he suffered the same night terrors.

Holmes poo-pooed my suggestion. "No, of course not, Watson. I returned here rather late last night, slept a few scant hours, and rose early to begin working on deciphering the book." Holmes's lips curled downward into a deep frown. "Unfortunately, I have made little progress. If I continue at this rate, I shall have to reach out to a madman for assistance."

"You mean Mr. Walker?" I asked.

"Indeed," Holmes answered after a loud yawn. "I will spend the morning working on the issue, and if need be, after a brief nap, I shall seek out Mr. Walker this afternoon. Would you care to join me, Watson? I shall be away again this evening."

"Again Holmes?" I blurted. "What the devil are you up to?"

"It is a private matter, Watson."

"I see," I answered and dropped the matter.

Over the years, I have written of my adventures with Holmes, most involving me and a few in which Holmes retold stories of his past. What I have not shared with my readers is that there are more than a handful of adventures each year in which I have no involvement. With the popularity of my highly regarded writings on the exploits of the great detective, a number of clients have insisted that I have nothing to do with their cases. Holmes calls these matters his private cases, and though I would keep their affairs as secret as my friend, I fully understand and sympathize with these clients who request the utmost discretion.

Holmes and I had breakfast and discussed the news of the day, including the progress in the war between America and Spain. The United States had scored a big win by destroying the anchored Spanish fleet in Manila Bay. With this victory, it appeared incredibly difficult that Spain could mount a comeback without issuing forth many more troops. I thought Mr. Monroe would be pleased that his nephew would most likely return home safely in the near future.

I said my goodbye to Holmes and then spent the morning and early afternoon with my patients. Holmes sent me a message asking me to meet him at a private mental hospital hidden away on Upper

Brook Street. I believed that I would have to regrettably inform Holmes that I could not join him, for I had a late afternoon appointment, the last on my calendar for the day. As fortune would have it, that patient cancelled, and I was able to join Holmes as he met with Mr. Walker.

I took a hansom over to the fashionable area. As I traveled into the affluent neighborhood, I thought of how fortunate Mr. Walker was to be housed in luxury. London's public asylums were woefully crowded and underfunded. Many doctors ruled their patients with an iron fist, the inmates suffering under their own wretched kings. Instead of treatment, they received cages, straitjackets, and powerful sedatives. The Empire had made such progress in our march toward enlightenment, yet this was a retreat toward our barbaric ancestors.

Mr. Walker's treatment was much different. I met Holmes in front of what appeared to be a private home. No one from the outside world, even the neighbors, would be able to tell who the residents were in this mansion. There were no bars on the windows. The greenery was well manicured, and I was certain that the elite who shared the neighborhood had no idea of who was housed within the building's walls.

Holmes and I were greeted at the door by two burly gentlemen who could have been officers of the law. Holmes handed the men a letter from Mr. Monroe explaining the purpose of our meeting.

Even with the letter, the men escorted us to a waiting room where a smaller man with well-trimmed greased-back hair and a *petit* handlebar moustache greeted us. "The famous detective Sherlock Holmes and his assistant Dr. Watson," the man said suspiciously, his English strongly accented. "It is good to meet you. I am Mr. Lamont and I help manage the affairs here."

"You wish to have our identities verified," Holmes said, cutting through the pleasantries.

Lamont ran his hand through his slicked black hair and eyed the guards nervously. "*Oui, monsieur.* We have a duty to keep our residents safe from the prying eyes of the outside world, and we are rewarded handsomely for doing so. Currently, Mr. Monroe is being contacted via the telephone to verify your purpose and identities. Please understand that we would not want to admit a Nellie Bly into our home. That would be problematic, no?" he asked in a thick Parisian accent. Holmes agreed and then Lamont asked him about a case from years past.

"Now, one man I know had visited you long ago, Mr. Holmes about a matter involving a rather expensive aluminium crutch . . . ."

315

Mr. Lamont asked Holmes several questions about this case, one which I had never scribed. Holmes answered the questions asked, none of which would violate his client's privacy, and Mr. Lamont seemed satisfied. After a short time, another tall man in dark clothing entered the waiting room and whispered a message to Mr. Lamont. "Your identities and the purpose of your visit have been verified, Mr. Holmes and Dr. Watson. Please wait one moment here. A doctor will arrive shortly to escort you to see Mr. Walker."

"They certainly are thorough," I commented to Holmes as we waited. "I am rather impressed."

Holmes simply nodded at my statement.

"Why, if it isn't good old Johnny-boy Watson!"

Both Holmes and I looked up at this interruption, and I mirthfully replied to the gray-haired doctor who had entered the waiting room, "Lefty Johnson, you old scoundrel!"

I rose and shook hands with Lefty, who was Dr. Johnson. We had been childhood school chums before parting our ways in life.

"Why, I haven't seen you since that convention in Cambridge two years ago," Lefty said. "Are you planning on attending this summer's conference?"

"Of course, my friend." We chatted for a while longer before I heard a slight cough from Holmes and realized I had forgotten my manners.

"Holmes, this is my friend, Dr. Johnson," and I explained our connection to the detective. Lefty was a pugilist who received his name for his strong left hook.

"I was the fighter, Mr. Holmes, I had to be. Your friend here was the lothario. There was no other way to compete with Johnny-boy for the eye of the ladies."

Holmes pleasantly chatted with Lefty for a moment or two about boxing, but I could tell that the detective wanted to move past the pleasantries and meet with Mr. Walker. Lefty would be our escort.

We left the waiting room and were finally allowed to enter the premises. Lefty led us up the marble steps of the ornate spiral staircase. At the top were several large rooms, all locked.

Two well-dressed tall gentlemen stood as sentries on either side of the hallway. A reporter who snuck into the house would assume these two to be servants, not guards, from their attire.

"Please understand, we must keep up our appearances," Lefty explained. "The doors remain locked, but the prisoners are given the utmost care. When visitors arrive, they must be thoroughly vetted, and then a doctor must accompany them to see a patient. The families of our patients pay dearly to receive such care. Ah, here we are now."

We had arrived at the room of Mr. Walker. Lefty unlocked the door and we entered an exquisitely decorated chamber. The room had large bay windows overlooking the grounds, casting significant light into the room, decorated with ferns, flowers, and other exotic plants giving the humid chamber the feel of a room at a botanic garden. In the center of the chamber sat Mr. Walker before a stone table engraved with a patterned board for draughts or chess.

Walker was an odd looking fellow with a flat nose and large bulgy eyes, almost ichthyan in their appearance. He grinned at seeing us and rose from his seat. "More visitors, aye Caliban," he muttered and walked towards us with a shambling gait. The squat fellow was slightly hunched, with very few threads of hair covering the top of his head. When he met us he smiled, and I felt revulsion when I saw that his teeth had been filed down to resemble fangs. He offered his hand to shake, and though repulsed, I took it, finding it to be so sweaty from the humid air in his room as to feel slimy, like the slick scales of a newly caught trout.

Holmes and I introduced ourselves to Walker, and when Holmes said his name, the bulbous eyed freak chuckled to himself and muttered, "Another Holmes today, heh . . . heh . . . . What you make of that, Caliban? So many that want to play in the realm of the Wretched King." I heard a strange mischievous laugh come from the corner of the room in response to Mr. Walker's statement. It sounded like a child, but it was difficult to determine whether the voice was male or female. "We must get the pieces out, yes Caliban, the pieces," Walker added and shambled off to a cabinet in the corner of the room.

""I hope you are prepared to play games for the next few hours," whispered Lefty to Holmes and me.

"That voice?" I asked.

"That's Caliban. Mr. Walker is a talented ventriloquist."

I was going to ask who this Caliban was, but then I saw it.

Mr. Walker returned to the table, clutching a pouch in one hand containing his game pieces and holding in his other a broken, dirty china doll. The thing was in poor shape, with a chunk of the face gone, a hole where the right eye should be. When we sat around the game table, Walker put the thing on his lap, and I could see that the doll's long faded white dress was not only caked in dirt, but that green speckles of mold had begun to form on it.

317

"I believe we shall start with draughts," Holmes said, pulling his seat up to the table on the opposite side of Walker. He removed a notebook and pencil from his pocket and set them on the side.

"Hee hee hee," giggled Caliban. "Yes, continue with draughts. This Holmes is a glorious subject of the Wretched King."

"No ovens for him, aye Caliban?" asked Walker, setting up the game.

"We shall see," squeaked Caliban. "We shall see." Then it giggled maniacally.

The game then commenced. Holmes won the first round and Walker the next two. The game then changed to chess, where Walker lost three and returned to win the next three. The game then returned to draughts. At every move either player made, Holmes made note in his book. It was not long before I had ascertained that there was something to the pattern of the games, a secret code. Neither player was playing to win. Rather, they were speaking to each other through the games.

Lefty and I sat watching the two players for several hours. So mesmerized was I by the game playing that I did not even notice the sun setting, nor Lefty lighting the lanterns of the room. It was not until a knock was heard at the door that my attention was diverted. Lefty answered the door and a guard whispered something in his ear. He nodded and then motioned for me to join the guard in the hallway.

"Yes?" I asked.

"Telephone call for you sir, a Lady Espinoza," the guard explained.

"Espinoza? Called here?" I questioned. "How the devil did she know my whereabouts?"

Neither man answered my questions. Lefty said he had to get back to the room with Walker, and the guard simply escorted me to the telephone. Lady Espinoza was my wealthiest client. She was a great supporter of my writing, and only sought me out as her doctor so that she might mention to her friends that she was the patient of Sherlock Holmes's colleague. She paid me handsomely for my work, but she was also an eccentric and at times, a hypochondriac.

I answered the call and she explained rather hurriedly that she believed her pulse was weakening, and I must hurry over to save her. She would pay five times my usual fee.

I grumbled but consented to her request. Though I would need to cross the city to get to her residence, I was going to receive a considerable recompense for my inconvenience.

After ending the telephone call, I realized I would be hard pressed to hail a hansom in that neighborhood at that hour of the evening. Fortunately, when I explained my dilemma to the guard, he revealed that they had contracted with a cab company, and a driver was available for my use.

I wrote a quick note to Holmes explaining the situation and handed it to the guard. He accepted it, and then his eyes shifted around suddenly making certain no one was around.

"Dr. Watson?" he asked in a low tone.

Yes," I said.

"I just wanted to say how much I enjoy reading your stories. It's an honor to meet you and Sherlock Holmes."

I waved off the compliment, as they were starting to become more and more common, but thanked the man. Then I thought of something that Walker had said earlier, and added to the guard, "The other Holmes who visited this morning?"

"The burly fellow," the guard said, then realized he may have revealed private client information.

"No need to worry," I told the ashen faced man. "I was just going to say how fortunate that you got to meet Sherlock Holmes."

"Oh, yes," he smiled. "I wasn't sure if the man was real."

The night was another long one for me. After the carriage dropped me at the Espinoza estate, I was surprised to find the Madame suffering from a real malady. The elderly woman was bedridden and suffering from a debilitating headache, fatigue, and nausea. After going through several tests, I determined that she was suffering from overuse of a popular brand of freckle ointment which contained a high amount of lead. She argued with me over her diagnosis, and I could see that it was a disagreement that, no matter how strong my evidence, I could not win. Such is the curse of a woman's vanity!

Fortunately, her lady's maid saw the seriousness of her lady's condition and we conspired together to come to a solution. After Lady Espinoza fell asleep, her maid emptied out the bottles of freckle ointment and replaced the contents with a harmless resin.

The driver was courteous and waited for me to finish conducting my visit, and afterward he dropped me off in Baker Street. Weary from the day's labors and knowing that I had a full schedule the next day, I climbed the steps to our rooms and found the sitting room door unusually locked. I used my key and entered a dark chamber. Holmes hadn't yet returned. Whether he was still with Mr.

Walker or working on his other case did not matter to me. I was exhausted and no sooner had I climbed into bed then I fell fast asleep.

Queer visions returned to me that evening. I found myself returned to the Battle of Maiwand, though instead of facing Afghan warriors, slick plumes of black smoke crossed the battlefield. Soldiers were engulfed with the oily tendrils and screamed out in sharp pains. Some tore the flesh from their faces and gouged out their eyes, driven mad from the thick dark clouds. I tried to flee, but all around me was the inky black death. Surrounded and with nowhere to go, I put the end of my rifle in my mouth and pulled the trigger.

I awakened, clutching my chest, breathing rapidly, and covered in sweat. My death had only occurred in my dream. At least I hadn't screamed this time, I thought to myself.

When I came down from my chamber, I was surprised to find that Holmes's door was still closed. Perhaps he was sleeping late, or possibly he never returned home. After I had dressed and breakfasted, he still hadn't risen. I had a full schedule and did not tarry to see my friend, though I was interested to see if he had made any progress on deciphering the narrative of the Wretched King.

My morning was as busy as expected with the usual seasonal maladies. It was on my way home that I stopped and purchased the evening edition of *The Times* from a newsboy at the entryway to an underground station. While I rode the train back to Baker Street, my eye caught an article on the second page which froze my graze. The headline screamed that Monroe, Holmes's client, had died. He had been found in his bedchamber that morning from what appeared to be a burst heart. The rest of the obituary summarized his life work.

As I sat and listened to the loud roar of the train, I couldn't help but feel there was something amiss, something most foul about this case. Could Holmes have been successful in his translation, and the full story too horrible for Monroe to comprehend? And what of Holmes? Could a similar fate befallen my comrade?

When the train arrived at the Baker Street Station, I forced my way through the throngs of people and moved with a mercurial speed to 221b.

I burst into our sitting room and found Holmes standing before the hearth. He turned to me at my loud entrance and I saw on his face not an expression of concern nor fear, but one of anger and frustration.

I noted balled pieces of paper in the fireplace burning away.

"Holmes, are you alright?"

"Of course I'm, alright, Watson. Just . . . perturbed . . . at wasting my time over the last few days."

"Wasting?" I asked. "Holmes, do you mean you did not decipher *In the Realm of the Wretched King?*"

Holmes's upper lip moved into a sneer, and he grumbled, "No, I was successful. You can see the fruits of my labor crackling in the fireplace."

"You . . . you burned it?" I stammered. "But why, Holmes? The future – "

"Is not contained in a trite penny dreadful unworthy of publication. I burned the manuscript, my dear Watson, because that is what one does with rubbish."

I was baffled and said as much to Holmes. There had to be something to the story, something to the cause of my nefarious dreams.

"My dear Watson, you know of my opinion on the matter of the supernatural. Keep that which belongs in Heaven and Hell *in* Heaven and Hell. There is plenty of mystery on this Earthly realm."

"But the story?" I began.

"Was just that, Watson, a story, a poorly written story that Adam Smith conceived but never drafted."

"Never drafted? But Holmes, this does not add together. What exactly have you been deciphering then?"

"Nothing, Watson. I have been deciphering nothing," Holmes said firmly, his cheeks reddening again. He motioned for us both to sit. After making ourselves comfortable and listening to Holmes mumble complaints to himself, he explained all.

"Adam Smith never wrote *In the Realm of the Wretched King.* Don't say a word, Watson. Let me speak, for I believe all of your questions shall be answered. Adam Smith was a folklorist who explained many unexplained phenomena and also exposed a number of charlatans. He also had a jolly sense of humor.

"When Monroe brought the case to me, I noted in his retelling of Smith's life story that the tale of the Wretched King was hidden within the confines of the latest edition of his complete work, not just his complete work. That indicated Smith had no intention of dying, that this edition was not to be his last. After analyzing the manuscript and the text of the story, I began to suspect that there was nothing there, and that the tale of Smith's hidden romance was nothing more than a myth created by the author himself. This conclusion was proven when we met with Mr. Walker yesterday."

"But Walker had deciphered additional pages?" I interrupted.

"Watson, please," Holmes glared at me, and I could see I had raised his ire. I silenced myself and allowed him to finish his explanation. "When I began my games with Walker, I saw he had created an elaborate pattern, with each move indicating the placement of a word or even groups of letters from the complete work of Adam Smith. As I removed the words, I could see the story emerging, but the story came not from the mind of Smith but from the mind of Walker.

"What I mean, Watson, is that Walker had been privy to a copy of Smith's original pages of *In the Realm of the Wretched King*, pages that were never hidden within the words of his actual text. In his madness at not finding the remainder of the story, Walker created his own demented pattern to write his own narrative by yanking random words and even letters out of Smith's complete work.

"The smouldering pages you see were the gibberish of a crazed mind." Holmes paused shook his head sorrowfully then continued.

"I was going to explain all to Mr. Monroe this morning, but sadly the man passed before I had a chance. Without a signed contract, I'm afraid that not only was my time wasted, but my promised exorbitant fee was cancelled."

"But . . . ." I started quietly, not wanting to upset Holmes. He seemed fine with me asking questions now that he had finished the majority of his tale. "Why did Smith send the beginning of his manuscript to his publisher and claim it was contained within his complete work?"

"To prove a point, Watson. Smith wanted to show how easy it can be to con the public. Over the last few nights, I have spent time conducting research at private libraries which never close their doors. I have learned much about Smith. He hated charlatans, hated those who tried to muddy the truth with the supposed unexplained. So, Smith created his own mythology surrounding his work. He created the myth of the spirit visiting him at the Indian burial ground and that of the Wretched King. I believe he planned on allowing the story to spread and waited to see different deciphered versions of his text before announcing that the entire claim was a sham. He could then use the self-debunking as a lesson in trusting to scientific research and not to those who practice séances and Theosophy."

My mind was reeling at this information, and I confess that I felt deflated, for I believed through the story we could see that which

322

would come. Then I dared pose one more question to Holmes. "But – my dreams Holmes?"

"What do you mean, Watson?"

I explained my continued night terrors to Holmes and he looked almost disgusted with me.

"Really, Watson, you, yourself, are a medical man. Can you not see the obvious before you?"

"I confess to being blind on the matter."

"Very well," Holmes spat through gritted teeth. "This case has caused you to have memories of your time in the war. The mentioning of the horrible prophecies, coupled with the current news of the war between America and Spain, has caused brutal visions to occur within your sleeping mind. I believe, now that a rational explanation for the Wretched King has been presented and when the current war draws to its conclusion, your dreams will return to more pleasant subject matters."

And that should have been the conclusion of Holmes's seemingly non-adventure. However, there were two exceptions. First, Holmes was only correct in part about my dreams. Though they did lessen over time, the ovens and oily smoke continued to haunt my sleep.

The second occurred when I saw Lefty at the Cambridge Medical Conference that summer. I asked my chum about Walker, and he looked horrified at my mentioning of the name.

"You mean you didn't hear?" Lefty asked. "I thought since Holmes was a friend of the family, you would have heard about it. Dreadful business. Nearly exposed our facility."

"Lefty, what are you on about?" I inquired.

"Johnny, it was terrible, old boy. A few days after you left, Walker went mad. He claimed someone had stolen his ugly china doll. He attacked one of the guards, and nearly ripped the man's face off. There was a tussle with the other security men, and in the melee, Walker took a hit to the back of his head. The blow proved to be lethal."

"That's terrible!" I said, horrified. Then I asked. "And the doll, what of it?"

"Funny you should ask. We never did find Caliban."

When I returned home from the conference, I brought this information to Holmes and asked what he thought on the matter. "I have no opinion, Watson. The man was a lunatic. For all we know, he could have destroyed the doll himself. Then, when it was gone, he could have believed someone else to have committed the crime. I don't know and quite frankly, finding out does not interest me. That case was one of my most disappointing. Now, tell me about the sessions you attended . . . ."

That was the last time Holmes and I spoke on the matter of the Wretched King. That should have concluded the matter, and yet, for me, it did not, for I have found my mind drawing a very different conclusion from that of Holmes. Perhaps the tale of the Wretched King truly was buried within the work of Adam Smith. Perhaps Holmes deciphered the work, and perhaps he did not work alone. I keep thinking back to the other corpulent Holmes who visited Walker that morning, of how Walker did not tell Holmes "*Shall we begin?*", but rather "*Shall we continue?*" his games.

Could the Holmes brothers have worked together to decipher the document? It is possible. Perhaps they were being directed by one of Mycroft's superiors. Perhaps the knowledge they discovered was deemed too horrifying to be released to anyone in the general public. Perhaps that is why Holmes burned the manuscript of *The Wretched King*. Perhaps Mycroft's superior arranged for Monroe's weak heart to stop beating. Perhaps he arranged for the Caliban doll to disappear. Perhaps this superior even arranged for Lady Espinoza to become ill and to call me away from Walker's chamber. The thought is horrifying, I know, yet I can't help but wonder. There is much that is done to keep our Empire safe, and the deaths of a madman and an aged munitions manufacturer is a small price to pay to keep our kingdom afloat.

Over the years, I have thought to this theory. I have chuckled and dismissed it as the foolish thoughts of an old man. I have thought of how rational the explanation presented by Holmes and yet, I can't help but wonder. I have even attempted to get my own copy of *The Complete Work of Adam Smith*, but I've never been able to obtain one. When a bookstore or antiquarian claims to have a copy for sale, it always seems to go missing or I am outbid. Could the British government be snatching up all copies? Could they fear the public discovering what lies ahead in our world's future?

I hope my fears are unfounded. I pray we don't face the ovens or the gases on the battlefield, and I pray the most for my nightmares to finally come to a close.

The Case of the
Little Washerwoman
by William Meikle

It was a cold night in September, one of those early chills that preludes the winter to come and far too cold to be standing on the doorstep of 221b Baker Street. But that is exactly where I found a rather well-to-do gentleman when I arrived to take supper with Holmes after my rounds. The man appeared to be in quite a state, but had obviously stopped short of going so far as to knock on the door. He was not the first gentleman to be in two minds over consulting my friend Sherlock Holmes, and there is no doubt he will not be the last.

He almost took a blue funk and fled at my approach, but my hand on his arm and a smile from me did much to allow the man he obviously was to come to the fore.

"I would ask you to unhand me, sir," he said, in a slightly accented voice that was used to being obeyed. Fortunately I had more than enough army experience to know how to counter such utterances.

"Mr. Holmes is not accustomed to leaving his clients standing on the doorstep," I replied. "Please, come inside, and allow me to make your introductions for you."

And so it was I enticed him in off the street, and was able to introduce Holmes to Lord MacAlpin of MacAlpin, a Scottish Lord, and by far the most frightened man I have met outside of the field of war.

Once I got him upstairs and seated, Lord MacAlpin perched at the front of the fireside armchair, as if afraid that it might devour him should he sit back, and would not look either Holmes or myself in the eye. He took to Holmes's brandy readily enough though, and what with that and a smoke, his tongue finally loosened and his story came all at once across the fireplace.

"It's the curse from the auld country," he began, as if that was meant to make any kind of sense to us. "It has followed the family these three-hundred years or more since we came over from Ireland. It spares some, skips a generation, maybe even two, but we all know it is never really gone, and the best we can hope for is that it passes us by as it works through the lineage. But I have not dodged this bullet – it has come for me – *she* has come for me – and if I have to hear that dashed screaming one more night, I might well throw myself off the roof and spare her the trouble of killing me."

It had all come out of him in a rush, and letting go of it raised his spirits somewhat. He allowed himself a thin smile, although not much of it reached his eyes.

"You must think me a terrible mouse, Mr. Holmes, but this thing has me in a funk. And it is not just me – it is the staff here in town too. They have all left me, apart from old John, and he only stays because he has got nowhere else to go. I am at my wit's end over the whole bally affair. Please say you will help me?"

Holmes rested his elbows on the arms of his chair, steepled his long fingers at pursed lips, and studied the man across the fireplace. Some clients take this extended stare as a sign of insolence in my friend, but I knew it for what is was: It was the method at work.

Whatever Holmes managed to glean in those ten seconds of scrutiny, it made up his mind to work with his Lordship on the matter, for otherwise he would normally have dismissed an outlandish story such as MacAlpin had given out of hand. His voice was low, calm, and measured when he spoke, without a hint of sarcasm.

"Am I to take it, sir, that you believe you are under the curse of a Banshee?"

He spoke so low that I almost did not catch it, and he had to repeat it for his Lordship, who didn't appear to have heard him at all the first time. Holmes spoke the same words, louder this time, and MacAlpin chewed on his cigarette as if his life depended on it before answering.

"It is more than a belief, Mr. Holmes, it is a blasted fact. The terrible shrieking has come these last five nights. If the legend speaks true, I only have two left to me before the end."

"And this has all occurred here in London, at your townhouse in Belgravia?"

His Lordship nodded.

"Every bally night, at five minutes to midnight by the big clock in the hall."

"Are there any manifestations? Any visible phantoms, spooks, or specters? Ghostly ladies at the window, perhaps?"

His Lordship looked directly at Holmes, thinking he was being mocked, but there was no amusement in Holmes's stare, nor was there any sign of malice of intent.

326

"There is only the shrieking, Mr. Holmes, but that is enough, for it is a most terrible thing all on its own. I pray you never have to hear it."

Holmes nodded, as if the reply had confirmed some aspect of his deduction, then suddenly clapped his hands together, the slap as loud as a gunshot in the room.

"Then it is settled. Tonight we shall break the pattern. You will be our guest here for the duration, and Watson and I shall stand guard to ensure you are not unduly disturbed. With such a course of action, I am confident I can get to the bottom of your problem in short order. Are we agreed?"

MacAlpin seemed very relieved to have unburdened himself, and agreed readily enough to Holmes's plan, so I headed off to make arrangements with Mrs. Hudson for the wellbeing of our new houseguest.

We had the history of the MacAlpin family curse over our late supper.

"The story stems from the first of our name, Callain Alpin, 1st Earl of the line in Ireland, some time back even before the Normans," MacAlpin told us over a glass of ale and a mutton pie. "He was a great hell raiser in his day, sowing wild oats all across the country. Until, one day in late autumn, he met a girl washing the family clothes at a ford. He asked her for a kiss and when she dismissed him, he took her anyway, defiling her such that no man would want her again.

"Three days later, the girl died in agony . . . and the singing began. On the seventh day after her death, it reached its height. Callain spent his last night on this earth in abject terror. It is a terror the male members of the family have been subjected to ever since, down these long years. It happens right when we reach Callain's age at the time of his death, which was several months before his fiftieth birthday . . . and exactly the age I have reached this year."

He told the story flatly, without emotion, as if it was something that had been dwelling on his mind so long that it had lost its power.

"And your father? Holmes asked. "He also suffered this affliction in his fiftieth year?"

MacAlpin smiled thinly.

"Unfortunately not. The old man was spared it, although if anyone deserved it, it was certainly him, for he inherited our Irish ancestor's lusts, as could be attested by many a Scottish servant girl who had to be sent away to the London house for a few months. No, the last of the line to suffer from the fate was my great-grandfather, Andrew. We all thought, wrongly as it turned out, that the curse had been lifted. But here the damnable thing is again, right on schedule."

"We?" Holmes asked. "You have spoken to someone else about this legend?"

MacAlpin laughed again, although there was little of any humor in it.

"It was all anyone ever talked about in the auld house on the shore in Ayrshire when I was a lad," he said. "Family, servants, even the townsfolk – everybody knew the tale."

"And by family, you mean your father?"

"Yes, and my brother, George."

"And George? Where is he now?"

"If you are wondering about a plot to take my title with my life, you can have no worries on that score. We lost poor George at Isandlwana to a Zulu *assegai*. I am the last of my line. The title dies with me . . . maybe that is for the best."

Ever since Mrs. Hudson started to serve supper, our guest had been snatching occasional – and now not-so-occasional – glances at the tall clock in the corner. And now that it was approaching midnight, MacAlpin grew increasingly anxious, and took to the drink rather alarmingly, first the ale, then more of Holmes's best brandy, not savoring it, but drinking in great gulps, a drowning man desperate for air. By the time the minute hand reached five minutes to the hour, he was well on his way to being deep in his cups.

But it did not save him from what awaited for us.

Holmes was first to spot it.

"Do you hear that, Watson?"

At first all I heard was the clatter and clink of glass on glass as MacAlpin, with an unsteady hand, partook of more of the brandy. Then it came to me. It was just a distant high whine at first, like a far off wind, but getting louder quickly, more strident until it seemed to ring and echo inside my head, driving out all other noise, all other thought. I saw that poor MacAlpin was in some agony, his mouth wide open and obviously screaming, but all I could hear was that high insistent whine. The volume went up a notch, then became louder still. It screamed, filling my skull with its rage, sending sympathetic vibrations through my jaw, my chest, and my gut until I thought my flesh and bones might be shaken to pieces.

Holmes got out of his seat unsteadily and lurched, almost staggered, toward the front window. Just as he reached it and pulled back the curtain to look over the street, a crack ran all the way up the largest pane. Dust shook down from the ceiling and the floor thrummed underfoot, even while cutlery, plates, and glasses jiggled and marched across the tabletop.

And still the noise roared with a wail like a wild beast in pain. Then, just as I thought I might not be able to take any more, the sound cut off, like a wax cylinder suddenly disengaged from the mechanism, and the room fell silent, save for the piteous sound of MacAlpin's sobbing.

Holmes left the room at a run and I heard his footsteps clatter away down the stairs and the front door slam as he left.

As for myself, I felt quite wrung out, sweating as if having undertaken strenuous exercise, yet at the same time chilled to the very bone. Every muscle felt heavy and tired, and my ears rang with the fading echo of that terrible scream. It took me several deep breaths to quite recover my dignity and a minute after that to ensure that his Lordship was of stout heart and not about to expire at the table. I was administering him some medicinal brandy when Holmes returned, his face like thunder.

"Missed them, by Jove, but not by much. They had a carriage in the street."

"They?"

"The perpetrators of this deed, of course," he replied. "Banshees are not in the habit of waking half of London, breaking windows and rousing babes from slumber, as far as I know. No, the threat here is quite physical, as I have suspected ever since our Lord here came in the door."

"How do you come to that conclusion, Holmes?"

Holmes pointed toward where Lord MacAlpin was slumped in his chair.

"It is obvious, is it not? He has a slight waver in his step, and a tendency to favor his left ear. I suspect he sleeps with that against the pillow. Did you not notice how he did not even flinch at my sudden loud handclap earlier? He is most certainly more than a tad deaf, and I believe it is mostly the right ear, and that it has been damaged by the assault of the sound these past five nights."

"And you are convinced the sound came from out on the street?"

"Most definitely," Holmes replied, turning to address the man at the table, "although I do not yet understand the mechanics of the matter. Trust me, your Lordship, there is indeed malevolence at work against you, but it is of an all-too-human nature. I think we can all agree that banshees do not need to use London carriages to make their escape into the night."

I took Holmes aside as his Lordship made further inroads into the brandy.

"I am not sure it matters whether the banshee is real or not, Holmes. The poor man's nerves are shot to pieces, and another shock like that might well kill him."

"I agree with your prognosis, Watson," Holmes replied. "Time is against us. We must find the perpetrator of this campaign of terror and put a halt to it before its cruel objective is achieved. I managed a good look at the carriage as it sped off. Shall we see if we can track it down?"

I knew Holmes's working habits of old, of course. Now that he had the bit between his teeth there would be little time for sleep, and even food would be more of a necessity for fuel than a pleasure, at least until the job was done. I helped myself to some cold meat pie from the table to sustain myself through what was to come, then went to fetch my service pistol. By the time I returned from my room, Mrs. Hudson was shepherding a rather unsteady Lord MacAlpin to his bed in the guestroom.

"He'll sleep," Holmes told our landlady, "but maybe not too well. Keep an eye on him for us, Mrs. Hudson. We will be back before we are needed again, one way or the other."

And at that, I followed my friend downstairs and out into the chilly London night air.

Our first port of call was to the carriage rank that served both Paddington Railway Station and the Great Western Hotel. Holmes frequently uses the drivers there as a source of information, for they travel far and wide in this great city, and see much that eludes the eye of less frequent travelers. I heard Holmes's bag of florins rattle as we approached the rank, and knew it would be rather lighter by the time we left.

Holmes approached the lead cab, and addressed the driver directly by name, a trick of his I have never quite been able to master, not having his ability to match faces with people and remember it forever afterward.

"Mr. Jones," he said, "I wonder if you could help me? I am looking for the whereabouts of a tall carriage that I saw in Baker Street but twenty minutes ago. It had a large, somewhat heavy, load up top, and a squeaky wheel at the back left."

Jones, a lean, mousy looking chap with a wispy beard and a coat that had seen its best days years before, sucked hard at his teeth.

"That ain't much to go on, Mr. Holmes, and you know me, I would tell you if I had seen it. I will pass the word among the lads in town that you're after it though."

Holmes thanked the man, passed him a florin, and moved down the line to the next carriage. He handed out four florins before his patience was rewarded.

"I seen it," the driver, one John Appleton said. "No more than ten minutes ago near Euston Station. It was stopped up around the near side of The Nag's Head. Didn't recognize who were driving it though. It were a small chap in a big coat and hat, ain't nobody I seen afore. He went into the pub. As far as I know, he's still there."

Holmes repaid the chap with two florins and the added bonus of employing his services in taking the carriage over to the aforementioned bar. We checked the alley on the eastern side of the bar before entering, but there was no sign of Holmes's squeaky-wheeled carriage.

The Nag's Head bar, situated across from the main façade of Euston Station, is a huge barn of a place full of mirrors, mahogany, and chandeliers, with a gaudily painted ceiling and a riot of color in murals and frescos on every wall. I have rarely seen a more opulent establishment, even in the palaces of the Raj. It was also, despite the hour, full of people seeming intent on getting inebriated as fast as they were able. The air hung heady with smoke and liquor and the hum of conversation was loud, almost too much so given the recent battering taken by my poor eardrums.

Holmes showed no sign of noticing the noise, and proceeded to work his way through the crowd, with a question here, a nod of greeting there, ghosting among the throng, at once part, and yet always apart, from the common people gathered in the bar. I knew of old that this too was part of the method, a part that might take some time. I headed for the bar, bought a flagon of ale, and lit up a smoke, all the while keeping an eye open for anything out of the ordinary.

I was halfway down my ale when I spotted a shadowy figure in a doorway behind the bar itself, looking in my direction. He was slight, and his features were hidden below a wide brimmed hat, such that all I could see was a clean shaven chin, his body obscured by a heavy dark overcoat, but he certainly fit the carriage driver's description of our quarry. I turned to look for Holmes, only to spot that he too had taken note of the man and was already pushing his way through the crowd in that direction.

I saw that I had no time to follow, not through the crowded bar, so leapt over the top of the counter, much to the amazement of the poor barman that I had to push aside to try to keep pace with Holmes. I made it to the door, and was right behind Holmes when I heard it again, the same soft whine I'd noted in Baker Street.

Holmes had also taken note of it, and clamped his hands over his ears. I followed suit. The dampening effect helped a tad, but the noise, when it came, thundered through the bar like a shot from a cannon. The roar, like that of an enraged elephant, sent the chandelier's swaying, tumbling bottles falling from the gantry, and the gathered crowd screaming in agony, their wails lost in the cacophony of sound that felt almost solid all around us.

Holmes, his hands still pressed firmly to his ears, pressed forward, hunched as if straining to walk into a gale. I followed as best I could, but it was like walking through ever thickening molasses, and the noise gripped my head so tight that I feared my skull would split open under the pressure.

Finally, after what seemed like an age, the noise abated, not cutting off sharply this time, but fading away into the far distance, receding away from us at some speed.

When Holmes and I emerged from the bar into the back passage behind the building, we were just in time to see an overburdened carriage turn a corner fifty yards away. It almost toppled over as the extra weight on top of it threatened to send it off balance, but it made the corner, and swung away out of sight.

Even then Holmes was intent on making a pursuit, but neither of us were in any fit state for exertion. Our legs felt weak beneath us, and we had to cling to each other for balance. We made for what we hoped would be the safety of the bar, only to find the place in chaos.

The simple act of covering our ears had obviously protected us from the brunt of the attack, but the patrons of the bar had not been so fortunate. Many were bleeding from nose and ear, and some were unconscious, draped across chairs and tables. The large mirror behind the bar was cracked in a spider-web pattern across its whole surface, and the floor was awash with broken glass and spilled liquor and ale.

My medical training took over and, for the next half-an-hour, I was busy tending to the afflicted as best I could. I took little note of Holmes, although I saw that he spent some time in conversation with the same barman I had so roughly shoved aside immediately before the attack.

The next time I looked up, it was not the barman who had

Holmes's attention, but an old ally and sometime friend, Inspector Lestrade of Scotland Yard.

More medical help turned up soon afterward, and I was finally able to leave the task in the hands of others and join Holmes and Lestrade at the bar in a most welcome smoke. Listening to their conversation, I realized that Holmes had told the inspector the tale of our pursuit so far.

"His Lordship is safe?" Lestrade asked.

"For the time being," Holmes replied. "Our quarry is following the pattern of the family legend. The final attack will most likely come at five minutes to midnight tonight."

Lestrade motioned around the bar.

"And these poor blighters? What do they have to do with it?"

"They had the misfortune to be in the way when I caught up with our quarry," Holmes replied. "I did not anticipate the strength of his resolve."

"And you have no idea who the blaggard might be?"

Holmes looked pensive.

"Not the exact person, although I may have some idea as to why he is doing it. To prove it, I need access to Somerset House to search the records. That is why I have been frank and open with you on this case, Lestrade. I need you to get the Records Office opened up for us, and I need it before morning."

I will not bore you with the details of our night's endeavor in the depths of the Records Office. Suffice to say that even with the help of three of Lestrade's constables, it was a dashed boring task, enlivened only by copious cups of sweet tea and stolen smoke breaks. Holmes had us looking for needles in haystacks. Children born in the MacAlpin house in London from the middle of the century onward, to unwed mothers from Scotland with no father's named on record. Such a search involved much crossing to-and-fro between many subsets of the filing system, but at least Holmes had let us in on his thinking. He did indeed have a suspect in mind, but as he'd said to Lestrade, the exact person yet eluded him.

By morning we had four names to go on, three boys and a girl. Holmes took the two oldest boys, Lestrade the other of the three. I was left to chase up the current whereabouts of one Elizabeth Wiggins, the presumed bastard daughter of our client's father. All I knew was that she had been born in London in 1874 to the big house's laundry servant Margaret Wiggins. There was no other pertinent fact to go on but that.

But it was a start.

I spent much of the day traversing various government departments and utilizing the facilities that Lestrade had at his command. My paths crossed several times with either Holmes or Lestrade, but none of us had much to report and time was passing quickly. I was only too aware that his Lordship would be facing another night of terror all too soon if we did not succeed.

Finally, in late afternoon, I found my girl, via a circuitous route of a dead mother, the workhouse, and on to taking domestic service in a country house in Northumberland more than a decade ago. There the trail went cold. I could do no more than telegram the house asking after her current whereabouts, before hurrying back to join Holmes in Baker Street, it being late afternoon, and time to agree a plan of action for the coming night.

Holmes, Lestrade, and I discussed our options over a light supper. Neither of them had uncovered anything pertinent in their investigations, and we were at rather a loss as to how to proceed. His Lordship did not join in the conversation. He sat, staring morosely into the fire smoking a succession of cigarettes and not speaking, as if he was already resigned to his fate.

Our talk led nowhere and, as darkness fell, we knew we had to move fast. In the end, Holmes suggested the simplest of subterfuges. His Lordship and I were of similar builds, and it was an easy matter for us to switch clothing. Several minutes after that was achieved, Holmes and MacAlpin, wearing the largest overcoat and hat we could find for him of mine, left, very visibly and very slowly by the front door of Baker Street. Holmes made quite a scene of calling a carriage at the side of the road to ensure their departure would be noted by anyone watching the door.

Lestrade and I gave them ten minutes start, then made a similar scene of our own, although I kept my head down and let his Lordship's hat hide my features. I walked unsteadily and, as Holmes had suggested, favored my left ear, as if I was hard of hearing on the right. I will admit to being rather proud of my performance as we stepped up into the carriage and headed off for Belgravia, while Holmes was headed in the other direction, after promising to see his Lordship safely domiciled, and also promising to meet us later.

Upon arrival in Belgravia, we again took our time, disembarking and loitering on the street for several minutes, with me keeping my head down while Lestrade spoke to a solitary constable.

The plan was to make it appear that Lestrade was concerned enough to put one man on guard, but not enough to do much more than that. Once I was inside the house, Lestrade left again, and the somewhat bored looking constable took up a watching brief on the doorstep.

Then all there was to do was wait.

His Lordship's man, Old John, ensured that my stay in the house was a comfortable one. I was plied with a tray of cold meats and cheeses, fresh bread, and a pot of fine ale from MacAlpin's cellars, so I wanted for nothing. I was, however amused to see that the old gentleman had what appeared to be wads of cotton stuffed in his ears, such that I had to shout to make my wishes, and thanks, heard. It was only after I was left alone in the parlor with my smokes that I began to consider the wisdom of it, and I took time to tear up one of my best handkerchiefs to roll into balls that fit comfortably in my own ears. It provided a certain distance and dissociation from the world outside my head, and I knew I would have to keep my wits about me for what was to come, but I felt all the better for the protection.

The wait dragged on. I found it hard to settle, and spent quite some time at the window, although I was circumspect enough to stay in shadow lest I be recognized by anyone lurking outside. There wasn't much to see. The policeman shuffled from right foot to left foot, obviously in an attempt to keep warm, and then was relived just after ten by another officer who appeared much more still and alert. We had arranged earlier that Lestrade would have more men around the property at strategic points, but try as I might, I could not see hide nor hair of them.

I found that I could not keep my gaze from my pocket-watch as the minute hand crept, ever so slowly, round to five to midnight.

It was almost time.

Finally, the allotted hour came round. I was looking at my watch, counting down the time. Either my timepiece was late, or the attack was early, for it came at six minutes to the hour, catching me ever so slightly off guard.

The handkerchief plugs performed most admirably at first, with the initial whine sounding like no more than an annoying buzzing insect. But in a matter of seconds, the whine rose to a wail, and then a full-blooded roar that threatened to drive all rational thought from my head.

I was, however, doing better than some others nearby. I leaned on the window, feeling the glass thrum and warp under my fingers, and looked out to see two men, obviously from the Yard, stagger out of the shrubbery, already bleeding at nose and ears and fit to collapse at any second.

Much to my amazement, the constable on guard at the door did not seem to be the slightest bit affected, and turned his head from side to side, attempting to pinpoint the source of the sound. It was only when he turned to his left and I caught a glimpse of his profile that I saw that it was Holmes himself. Even as I recognized him, he walked away from the doorstep, heading off to his left at some speed.

Despite the raging howl of the noise all around me, I was able to move, far better than I had managed the night before in the Euston Bar, and quickly made my way downstairs to try to follow him.

I was almost too late.

As I stepped down off the doorstep, a carriage came barreling round the corner from my left, heading straight for me, attempting to trample me underfoot and have the wheels finish the job. I just had time to see the white face of the driver, lips turned back in a snarl, as the roaring bellow of sound rose to a crescendo. The carriage leapt forward to bring doom down on me, rolling violently from side to side, threatening to topple at any moment.

Holmes appeared at a run and leapt up to take hold of the nearest passenger door. His added weight provided just the impetus required. The carriage took a sudden lurch to one side, almost righted itself, then finally toppled. Holmes rolled away just in time to avoid being crushed beneath it and the whole shebang crashed over to the cobbles mere yards from where I stood. The poor horses, suddenly free from their tethers, clattered away into the silent night.

I walked over, slowly so as to calm my frayed nerves, and joined Holmes in standing over the body of the driver that had been thrown off to one side. It was a young woman, her neck broken, her pale face staring, lifeless, at the stars.

Holmes turned and spoke to me, and I remembered the earplugs. As I removed mine, he removed a pair from his own ears. Where mine were cotton, his were thick wax. When he spoke again, his voice echoed and rang in my head, but I heard him clear enough.

"Well met, Watson. And I presume this is must be our Miss Wiggins?"

The tumbled carriage had spilled its load as it fell, and after

336

ensuring the woman was indeed past any of my help, Holmes and I went to inspect the heavy item that caused the instability. It proved to be a disc around four feet in diameter, sitting atop a cube some three feet on a side, and it had been strapped to the top of a carriage with thick strips of leather that now lay, torn asunder, on the street.

The large disk was made of some material I did not recognize, like thin cotton but with a slightly metallic sheen to it. The box below was mahogany with brass fittings, a cranking handle on the right, and an aperture on the left from which a long tubular hose extended.

I walked around the box, examining it from all angles, but no matter how much I looked at it, I still had no idea of its function. Holmes, as usual, seemed to grasp it almost intuitively. He bent and turned the crank handle, two then three turns.

"As I understand it, this cranking serves to compress a column of air inside the contraption which, when released, vibrates against the material of the disc. You release the latch, and speak in here," he bent and lifted the hose, putting the far end at his mouth, "and it comes out, amplified, here. "

He waved a hand at the metallic looking material at the top of the disc and whistled one sharp note into the hose.

The noise echoed through the whole of Belgravia.

It was not until the morning when Holmes hosted a breakfast for his Lordship that we were able to put all the pieces of this particular puzzle together.

I had a telegram from Northumberland that, among other things, told me that Miss Wiggins was on the run from her employer, one Samuel Parsons, an inventor of some distinction involved in the science of acoustics.

The other, and final, piece was provided by Lestrade who, having a nose for such things, arrived in time for breakfast and brought with him a note found in the dead woman's pocket. Holmes read it first, then passed it to me without comment.

> *Either he is done, or I am done, it matters not which. All that matters is that he has had a taste of what my mother had to suffer at the hands of his father. While I am right sorry to Mr. Parsons for stealing his machine, I knew as soon as I heard it that it was just what I needed to pursue my revenge.*

337

The last thing Mother ever spoke of was her hope that the Banshee would speak for her in the hereafter. I have ensured her final wish has come to pass, and if I have done ill to his Lordship in the process, I am glad of it.

It was signed in a clear hand: *Elizabeth MacAlpin*

The Catacomb Saint Affair

by Marcia Wilson

Autumn in 1898 had been so mild that second crops entered London and lawns were fresh and thriving until long after November's Ides. Oaks sat proudly green and the gardens were, in the vernacular of the press, "gay with flowers". Alas for scientific progress; there were noisome voices which took fault in this windfall, and ripe strawberries and blooming snowdrops were their listed proofs of future cataclysms. A rare aurora upon the 9th of September was added to this list, and hail in the north a few days after. Lastly, there was the Hallowe'en funeral of Sir Reginald Errol, a man of such fame that it would be redundant of me to recite his accomplishments here.

His sudden illness and subsequent passing had been a surprise, but he had prepared for his final journey with much pomp and show and the funeral would march through the heart of Central London. Unhindered with free weather and perfect skies, the streets were congested. Holmes and I observed the procession from our sitting-room window, and cheered the street Arabs that ran for the tossed confections.

"I daresay a few will proclaim this funeral proof of misfortune, Holmes."

"You are not normally of such a frivolous mind, Watson."

"I shall claim the season." For effect I stabbed at *A Study in Scarlet*. "I have re-organised your cases, and Constable Rance created the thought in my mind."

"His belief in the supernatural, no doubt." Holmes yawned. "For it is the Hallowe'en Season and one may expect a ghoulish turn of thought, just as we may expect to feel camaraderie at Christmas, or defiant optimism at Easter."

I lowered my voice in a poor attempt to imitate Rance's naturally rich consonants: "*I ain't afeared of anything on this side o'the grave; but I thought that maybe it was him that died o' the typhoid inspecting the drains what killed him. The thought gave me a kind o'turn.*"

Holmes scoffed. "Policemen laugh at the public's fears and cozen, but they are as vulnerable to nonsense as everyone else.

339

Besides, a mark of superstition is its relationship with fear. A proper mind in possession of reason should be absent of both."

"And yet we approach a holiday known for its willful suspension of rationality."

"One could say that about most holidays, Watson."

Through this turbulence came our client: A messenger from Inspector Lestrade.

"Lestrade is begging for your presence at the Church of the *Virgo Fortis* – to help him out of a fog." I read aloud the note.

Holmes pointed to a dozen pricks sunk deep through the paper. "He has used his leg as a writing-desk again. See the little stab wounds as he hammers it with his pencil, wondering how much he should say! His fastidious self is overwhelmed with his urgency. And at *Frère* Jerome's little house of worship! It should be diverting, if nothing else. We still owe them a few candles and pocket-lamps since that trouble with the falconers. Do you have time to come along?"

We soon found ourselves in the mews adjacent to London's only church wholly dedicated to the bearded saint. Normally swarming with life, the dead man in its gutters had cleared the narrow street, leaving only the Chapel's row of chicken-coops and two stable-hands. The adjacent pig-sty was curiously empty, for we had not yet had that first hard frost that marked the backyard butcher's trade. From the shadows gleamed the shaved heads of *Frère* Jerome's pupils. There were always at least ten hovering about, and as Holmes chatted with Lestrade, I saw them step out of the shadows with brooms, their dark, suspicious eyes upon the three Constables guarding the perimeters.

"Here, now!" Lestrade yelled. "I've told you no work until we've cleared this place! No cleaning!" To us he explained: "They've got a horror of getting sacked, and they can't wait to finish sweeping it all clean! As if Jerome would dismiss a child!" He snorted and shook his head. "Mind you, don't drop anything on your person without diving for it, gentlemen. They'll have sold it to the dustman or bone-grubber before you have the time to miss it."

"You are having a stimulating morning, friend Lestrade," Holmes sympathised.

"I've never seen anything like this, and honestly, I had hoped to stop saying that years ago. This time, I've gotten you away from your fire and a hot breakfast."

It was plain the little detective had been working long hours with little sleep, but he stood straight as ever, and the cluster of uniformed policemen were canny to watch his every move.

"Tut-tut, Lestrade. I am always here for a pretty problem. It was smart of you to call me before you carted him off."

Lestrade looked at us dumbfounded, for our friend has many good points, but imagination is not one of them.

"We aren't being 'smart', Mr. Holmes. The cart broke down on its way over here and has to wait for the Duke's funeral to clear the roads."

"Ah, my apologies. And he has not been moved?"

"No, and Barkley can swear to it. He's who found him." Lestrade nodded to a gangly young patrolman, who picked his way over amidst the ground-up mud and straw.

"I smelled the gin before I even got there," the young man reported bashfully. "There he was, all flopped over, head in the gutter and his arms wrapped around his bottle like a baby. I seed a lot of the dead folk in the gutters, sir, but not never one like this."

"He has an interesting coat." Holmes had bent to lift the tail up, and beneath the shabby wool rested many small pockets.

Lestrade groaned. "Artful Dodger come back from Australia. He's got more pockets than my tailor's shop!"

"Well then! I suppose I should add my learned opinion." Holmes handed me his gloves before kneeling. "Watson, what do you make of this?"

I knelt and pulled back the filthy rag of the dead man's shirt. The angry brown mottling underneath was a shocking contrast to the grimy white skin, and in some places the man had tried and failed to scratch himself with his ragged fingernails. My startled cry made Lestrade jump like a natterjack.

"Warn a fellow next time, Doctor!" The policemen looked ready to bolt and run.

"My apologies, Lestrade. Very curious. I have seen something almost identical to this rash before, in America."

"Do you say? Could this be the same thing?"

"I do not know how. The 'Woodsman's Rash' is an allergic reaction from the large conifers of the great forests. We have nothing like that here." Lestrade's face fell and I continued my examination. "The man must have been miserable! Drinking against his discomfort, no doubt. His bottle of gin took hold and he fell. There was no sense of urgency thanks to the warmth of the drink, and he tried to cool himself on the cold cobblestones. He only curled his body inward to protect his bottle from any prying eyes, for I daresay a chapel will not look kindly upon those who drink in its shadows." I pointed to the gutter the dead man had been using as a pillow.

"So we can say drink and the chill of the stones was the cause of death?"

"Without further tests, this is how the dead man appears to have died. The underlying cause – "

"Right!" Lestrade barked. "You heard the man, gents! Get the canvas back over him! The cart should be here any minute! Turnbull, you're in charge until I get back!"

To our astonishment, Lestrade grabbed Holmes up under the arm and half-pushed him across the mews and into the back door of the Chapel, where the police had set up a makeshift office.

"Now's not the time," Lestrade hissed under his breath at our protests. "I'll tell you everything as soon as I get away. Meet me upstairs at the *Frère's* office." To the Desk Sergeant piling papers upon an old kitchen-table: "Hart! As soon as that cart gets here, get the papers signed for the Morgue. The Coroner's waiting." And with that, he clapped his hat upon his head and hared back into the rising mist.

"A disgrace," the sergeant said mournfully. "Puir Mr. Lestrade. Hallowee'n's a fearful enough season without a dead man in it, but now we have a curse to worry about too."

"You say a curse?" I asked in astonishment.

"Don't know what else it might be," was the solemn answer. "Johnny Sheetpaper's a seasoned old man of the streets. It would take more to kill him than a bottle of gin. I'd seen him drink twice that and nebber sway and nebber with those marks."

"One cannot stay immune to drink, and tainted alcohol can cause strange marks."

"True, sir, true. But it wasn't like him to be in a gutter, neither. Johnny wouldn't rest where he could be found and made to leave." The sergeant stroked his tobacco-yellow mustaches sadly. "We're always moobing his lot, for we can't hab 'em sleeping on the streets. Against the law! He was divr'ent. If he sat it was to tie his shoe. Or look-over the next building to rob."

"A man of many talents, eh?" Holmes murmured

"One ob our best informants when he wasn't stealing, and too slippery to get caught for either. Best mouth we had! I'd hab trusted him to turn in his own mother."

"A rare endorsement," Holmes agreed wryly. "Did he steal from the Chapel of the *Virgo Fortis*?"

"If anyone dared! The common folk hab no fear of the Devil. Either way, it's caught up with him and the rest."

I was as puzzled as Holmes at this garbled intelligence.

"The rest, my good man?"

"The rest of them dead, of course," the Sergeant exclaimed. "Haben't you heard the news?"

"I fear we must have missed the papers."

"Not that news! The real news, Mr. Holmes – not that stuff in ink! Don't you listen to what's said on the streets?"

"Alas, we rarely have the time to be as well-informed as yourself, Sergeant. I apologise for my ignorance. If you would enlighten us?"

"Well. First Brother Jerome gets a crate in the mail. He opens it up, and there's a murdered woman inside it, all decked out in gold and jewels! He asks Mr. Lestrade to find who sent the thing to him, and the inspector tracks it to anobber dead man, and so is ebberyone else who touched those puir lady's bones. And Johnny's not the only thing dead here. The hogs hab died; the rats and mice, too, but the cats are walking live and free! All signs point to a curse."

I believe I was the only one to hear Holmes mutter, "And Hallowe'en." It was easy to forgive him this cynicism, for though he was unfailingly patient with those in need, his loathing of the supernatural admixed into a synergetic concoction every year when Hallowe'en approached.

"Do you believe in this curse, sir?" I asked.

"I don't think it matters what I believe. I'm no man of God, so I'm not qualified to say. But if it is, it's out of my hands, isn't it? Still, I'm hoping for a scientific reason."

"That is most gratifying, Sergeant," Holmes cheered.

"Just bein' practical, sir. Got no protocols in the books for arresting dead people, or how you could stick a curse in a file cabinet?"

"Well done!" Holmes clapped. "Sergeant, your practicality will take you far! Watson, I think we owe it to our kind host to learn what we can at the Chapel!"

"Mind you the draughts coming in from the stair-well," Hart cautioned. "There's bubbles in me tea."

Holmes released his pent-up mirth once we were alone.

"Mischief Night is early, Watson! A dead man in the middle of a lowly church mews, and the police both eager for and afraid of my verdict. Did you see how Lestrade barely noticed my rifling through the dead man's pockets?"

"I thought that, though he summoned you, he was more interested in my verdict."

"Agreed. Lestrade does not believe our man died of drink, but he wanted his men to believe it in order to stifle some threat of hysterics. And now a deskbound savant foretells the precipitation in his cup, and we are on our way to pull up another three yards of scarlet thread. I hope that is not the last of our homespun wisdom today. It remains to be seen what Brother Jerome will offer us."

"I am troubled at that rash. I know that just because a rash appears to be identical, it does not guarantee. And besides, the Woodsman's Rash was not fatal. I fear the police have seen two separate cases – a rash and death – and drawn a fanciful conclusion in involving curses."

"All data has the potential to be useful, Watson. We have not yet collected enough to know. Nor, I should add, have you or Lestrade evaluated your own worth in this investigation. I shall take a moment and look around the Chapel . . . . Give the *Frère* my regards. I shall be no more than a few minutes, I think."

I made my way through the long corridors to the stairs, my mind muddled at the confusion Holmes's words had inspired. The Chapel was old and very fond of strange carvings, half-barbaric in nature, and there were images of the *Virgo Fortis'* attendant, a small, almost dwarflike fiddler merrily grinning up into my face. On a normal day the fiddlers inspired me to smile, but today I felt glum and impatient. Despite my excellent memory, I could think of nothing that I or Lestrade had said that would show we did not understand our worth.

When Holmes chooses to keep something from someone, he merely says nothing. Despite his love of staging situations, he does not spin lies and scenarios. However, he had often lamented that so many people failed to trust in the evidence of their senses to solve a problem. He had just set a clue down for me to solve, but as hard as I was trying, I could not grasp a single crumb of enlightenment.

In a brown study, I nodded at the children I passed, busy cleaning or repairing. Jerome had been a policeman before inheriting a considerable sum of money and going on a world tour. He returned with a new purpose in life, aimed to the spiritual and care for the poor. Police and poor alike respected him, and much of his money had restored the chapel into a solid shelter that welcomed all.

Hart's forecast arrived by a light rain as I cleared the flight of steps to the friar's office. I paused for a moment to ease my old wounds, and looked out the dripping windows to the streets below. From window-ledges across the street lurked faces cut of old turnips, mangels, and beets. Once night fell, they would be lit and gibbering with flickering light behind their uneven teeth. Men and women pushed carts back and forth, selling hot drinks and bags of nuts. In the Irish and Scotch quarters, fires could be found within the rubble of tumbled-down buildings in their ancient Celtic belief that fire drove away evil – or perhaps preparing for Bonfire Night. The smoke of nut-hulls was thick. It was easy to see where lived the more old-fashioned citizens, who called this Nutcracker Night.

The *Frère* was sweeping the hall as one of the Chapel's orphans collected dust into a basket. When he saw me he waved happily, and when Lestrade's uneven stamp shook the stairs, he waved with both hands. Holmes appeared as mysteriously as he had left, and as usual with no more explanation as ever, but I saw from the peculiar flush upon his thin, white face that something had pleased him.

Before long, the four of us were ensconced in a tiny library and drinking smoky black tea. When I exclaimed on the flavor, he beamed bashfully and admitted his family was fond of giving him largess, which he could never enjoy it unless he was with friends.

"Thank you for finding them, Geoffrey. And, Sirs . . . ." He blinked his watery blue eyes and clasped large, brawny hands to the rope belting the waist of his humble robe. "I am a terrible story-teller, but I will try to tell you what has been happening. I hope we may see a quick end to this tragedy."

"If time is of the utmost importance, you may tell us your side of the story, and Lestrade can fill in the gaps," Holmes assured him. "Are we drinking in honour of The Saltwater Duke, or is it because he gave you this excellent Russian Caravan?"

Brother Jerome laughed. "How did you know?"

"The poorest of parlour-tricks: A nose for gossip. The newspapers reported his ship from the Black Sea last month, and tea was one of his primaries. Russian Caravan tea is not well-known outside of the London Embassies. 'Largess' is a word frequently attached to your cousin, but I shall be bold and presume tea was not his only business south-and-east of our shores."

"You are correct." Jerome praised. "Geoffrey suggested I appeal to you for aid, as he has been overwhelmed with the speculations in the church and Yard. Superstition is an embarrassing fault, and he said I could trust you. I already know to trust him."

"It isn't dead people that make me nervous. Glowing demon dogs are different." And Lestrade scowled at Holmes, which was his response whenever anything of a supernatural nature rose in our conversation.

"On last Monday," said Brother Jerome, "my cousin sent an unmarked crate to this Chapel. It may be unseemly, but I have learnt suspicion for boxes. Unpleasant things have been found in them, and for years we had cause to fear dynamiters.

"You cannot imagine my shock to find a Catacomb Saint inside!" Still shuddering at the memory, Jerome held his tea close to his trimmed grey beard. "I saw them in the wilds of Old Romish Europe, but they belong there, mouldering peacefully away in their quiet little hamlets! Their sad days are numbered. Rulers and churchmen are embarrassed at the reminder they pose for the older, more credulous days of worship, not to mention the fortune the Vatican once spent in creating these saints."

"I have never seen one for myself, but I recall skeletons from unearthed crypts that were exhumed and sent to convents to be clad in fine linens and jewels, given names for saints, and purchased by towns in need of their own spiritual patron," Holmes mused. From his faraway grey gaze, I could tell his thoughts were headed to a place that we could not follow. "Once dressed and given a fictitious history, the 'Saint' was venerated by the villages who chose to purchase them – to the extent that one could reliably guess the name of said saint by noting the most common baptismal name among the village."

"Saint Isabella Afra is a bit more than that, Mr. Holmes. The villagers swear she was martyred on their soil. They say she was a black slave caught by her Roman master in war. When her grave was discovered, she was sent away to be 'clad like the others' during the Reformation."

"He called me." Lestrade picked up the story. "Of course, he was concerned on the legality of the box, and the letter that followed was more a hasty note. By then, Sir Reginald was too ill to have visitors, so it took me some time to prove it was an authentic Catacomb Saint, collected as a work of art!"

Jerome smiled on the little detective. "I shall not waste time sermonizing. The waters have been stirred, and we must find the bottom of this well. Geoffrey did prove that saint came from the village of Ascher, just outside Ilanz in the Grey League. They speak Romansh over there, so he had an interesting time with the wires. Mr. Holmes, deaths have been attributed to these remains, and there are rumours that the bones themselves are protected by a curse from the angry saint."

"I've never seen so many people eager to run or witness in my entire career!" Lestrade added. "It was underhanded of me to treat you as I did earlier, but as soon as you made it look like Johnny died of drink, I got him off the streets. Those men are too eager to talk!"

"I take it you believe the man died of natural causes? No angry ghosts? No curses?"

Lestrade groaned. "Whenever you're involved in a case, no matter how spooky it looks, or how much it seems like something past the Veil . . . you can always find a scientific, educated reasoning for it. I may feel there is nothing ghostly about a death, but it is on me to prove it to the Crown and to my own men. And for that I need you, because if a ghost ever materilised in front of you, I am sure that it vanished just as quickly out of sheer disgust at your refusal to accommodate it."

"Why, thank you." Holmes was surprised and touched.

"Don't thank me just yet," Lestrade grumbled. "We're working against time. After the bones arrived, the pigs were found dead without a mark on their bodies – and the rats too! But the cats and hens are untouched. It looks strange and unsettling, and though the Chapel is a safe place for the poor at night, they won't come in until it's sorted. This soft weather won't last forever, and people have been skittish for omens since September's aurora and that hailstorm up north."

"And if you aren't wrapped up on a case, your in-laws will press you into lating the witch tonight," Jerome retorted with a large grin. "Forgive the informality; I've known this man forever. His mentor was one of my old mates on the Force."

"And I've been regretting it ever sense," Lestrade mock-complained, but he was pleased and opened a leather folio fat with neatly layered papers. "Mr. Holmes, the records are the best we could gather with what we had. I am aware there are many missing pieces in it. Those I had hoped to question were either unwilling to talk, or dead." In a fettle, the little detective saucered his tea. "But mostly, dead. Johnny's the latest. He was hired to watch over the box while Jerome signed for the papers."

"You needn't glare at me so, Geoffrey. I knew it was a risk to ask him, but he was already here looking for work when the cart pulled up, and I'd rather risk the temptations of a grown man than a child any day."

"Jerome . . . ." Lestrade wearily rubbed at his forehead. "Jerome, you don't see what's plain on your face at times. Those children aren't going to rob you. They're too terrified that you'll toss them back out on the street! They're so terrified, they've stayed here when everyone else has fled this Chapel! Think, man! Anyone with working eyes could see this!"

"A moment, Lestrade," I protested. "I would like to know more about these dead animals."

"We keep two pigs in a coyte behind the garden, Doctor," Jerome answered. "Three days after the Saint's arrival, the children who feed them came to find them dead without a mark on their skins. The cats who do their part in killing the vermin are walking about untouched. You must admit it is a queer coincidence."

"A coincidence lacks personality," Holmes answered thoughtfully. "Lestrade, may I examine your folio?"

"Certainly. I have no idea what you will see as useful, so I put everything I could glean here in chronological order." The little detective handed over the leather journal.

"Who precisely is this Saint Isabella?" I wondered. "What is her story?"

"An African slave woman caught in war and brought to the Roman villa where the village sits now," Jerome said. "As was common among early Christians, she refused to touch the pigs in his keeping or take out the poisoned vermin, and in a fury he killed her with a blow of one of her people's two-headed axes. The stroke split open her breast but the weapon rebounded and crushed his skull. He was cremated as a Roman and she was tossed on a midden, to be buried in secret until the era of the Catacomb Saints emerged centuries later."

"One moment." Holmes held up one of Lestrade's papers. "The Duke's purchase of the Saint is established, gentlemen, but not how he became interested."

"I apologise. He went through Hans Gmelin, an art dealer. Gmelin 'discovered' this saint lying in her mouldering chapel in the middle of Aschergot, and offered to take this embarrassing relic of illiterate Catholicism off their hands. The Mayor Richter had outsider blood and was quick enough to give permission. Money greased palms, and the Mayor and Art Dealer were happy to move that poor woman's skeleton out of its bier and into a box as the Duke held the lantern." Lestrade's sallow face was twisted in distaste. "The citizens were not violent about it, but they followed the cart and

348

then the train as long as they could, weeping and begging for the return of the bones."

"An art dealer in collaboration with their own mayor over the removal of their saint?" Holmes repeated. "Indeed, the peasants would be upset."

"It wasn't a week after, the mayor was found dead in his bed."

"Coincidence." Holmes yawned. "If the Saint had anything to protest, it would have been during the transaction, do you not think?"

"The Mayor had also been overseeing the repairs of the Chapel where the Saint rested."

"Obviously a black-hearted knave."

"Mr. Holmes, I am merely trying to show there is a connexion, however small, between the contact with the Saint and mysterious deaths. Perhaps it is only co-incidence, but they add up."

"You present ephemeral data regarding the mayor and the Saint, but Herr Gmelin was unaffected, and he had far more guilt to his purchased grave-robbing than Mayor Richter."

"But Herr Gmelin *did* die. He died a few days after he sent the crate to England, and while I have no proof, I was assured that he died in bed with a peculiar rash about his flesh."

"Well! That adds an unexpected piece to your puzzle. What did the Duke think of his new acquisition's unpleasant history?"

"I cannot say. Before he died, he had the crate sent to this little chapel, where it remains well out of sight of the public."

Holmes looked upon Brother Jerome. "Have you any threads to offer this tangle?"

"Reggie kept to his profession and I to mine."

"His profession?"

"Money. My cousin purchased the Saint for his own reasons. Perhaps I should show Mr. Holmes the letter? Or memo, really. Too short to be a real letter. It was sent out the same day as the bones, but two days late in the arrival. Poor Geoffrey lost a lot of time in his hunting before it came." He bent into his desk and after a great deal of rummaging, pulled out a wrinkled envelope, clumsily split by a dull letter-opener.

It was indeed more of a memo, with miniscule writing covering barely half the paper. Holmes put it in his lap so we could both read:

Dearest Cousin,

We have had our differences. You have scolded me for being floral and now I must be blunt. I am dying, old

349

friend, and I want you ready when my solicitor comes knocking.

You know my weakness for collecting period jewelry. I purchased this crate from an art dealer who was also the assistant to the mayor of the village of Ascher, outside of Ilanz in the Grey League. Mr. Hans Gmelin is his name and will help you with any information you may need. We met because he wished to know if I, an Englishman unaffected by the Roman tastes that survive in these isolated mountains, would care to purchase a unique work of art with "all its remarkable pieces complete".

I accepted his offer, for he had sold me interesting examples in the past (you recall the Weathering Exhibit I donated to the Museum for an entire season) and could be trusted to show me something new.

What he showed me was the contents of this box. Isabella Afra, the Saint of this small village, patroness of the victims of injustice. The shrine was about to be destroyed and I was convinced it would be kinder to purchase the Saint, which would preserve her from ruin. There were some trifles to endure, but it was all legally purchased.

I am weak now, Cousin, and I shall stop. I have wrapped her back in her wooden house despite the effort. Welcome this Saint into your Chapel, and see to her remains in ways which please you. My superstitious servants whisper, convinced that I am bearing the consequence of dabbling in forbidden matters. I insist that my motives were pure, for this is a unique relic of our past. Isabella Afra was no ordinary Catacomb Saint, for the village insists she has always been one of them, and only removed once in order to clad her in the robes of her martyrdom. I fear that upon my death they will destroy it, and that I shall not tolerate.

"It looks as though he wished to say more," added Holmes, "but decided not to or was too weak. The hesitation in his crossed t's and the over-emphasis of underlined words is telling." He frowned and returned the papers. "I should like to look at these later, but for now if I may, a viewing of your guest."

Despite my self-appointed title as a gentleman experienced in art, as well as the ways of worldly affairs, I have never been so amazed as by the sight in the chapel's private viewing-room.

The skeleton was astonishingly well-kept. The bones were given another skin by cobweb-fine shrouds, with each limb and join carefully wrapped as if to give the Saint, if she should suddenly desire to prove another miracle, the freedom to move.

Her movements would be ungainly nonetheless. Her heavy robes were that ancient shade of red known as the purple of the classics. Jewels had been sewn across every available inch of that red cloth.

Much of the larger pieces were glass, wondrously clear and sparkling. I saw the rare Chartres Blue, that perfect shade of the rosemary blossom with its alchemy now lost to time. Gold thread gleamed in waves about the Saint's hems and cuffs, with corals and pearls of every hue. There were beads of precious metals, wonderfully small. The long finger bones were so laden with rings it was a wonder the weight had not disarticulated the joints.

In all of this fulsome barbarity there was no mistake of murder. The breast of the Saint's robe was cut away and basted with gold thread, exposing the blow of martyrdom and a glowing spring green undercloth padded inside her ribs as if to replace the natural organs, long dissolved to dust. The exposed bones had not escaped the ministrations of the convent: They were varnished with some sort of white paint and wrapped with stripes of red and green poppyseed beads, and bore up the weight of a golden chain ending at the Saint's throat. The skull itself was left clean, and only the fine shrouding and a hood matching the robes touched its face.

"And this is the alleged killer?" Holmes murmured. "My good man, I am not attempting to be sacrilegious, but I must point out that so far I see proof of *a* murder, but no evidence that these mortal remains are responsible for another death."

We were interrupted by a hasty knock and the arrival of a young constable, his face cherry red from running. He gasped as he gave a tiny box to Lestrade, and quickly stepped away with a pointed lack of interest in the bones within the casket.

"One moment, gentlemen," Lestrade said in a tired voice. He opened the box and pulled out a small piece of paper to read while we waited. "Well," he said at last, "That is one question answered.

They found positive proof Mr. Sheetpaper did more than watch over these bones." And he tipped the box forward to show a fine freshwater pearl that should have been pale and pure, but it was instead a remarkable shade of spring green, and, when we looked closely, there was a corresponding absence of a pearl within the rib cavity's gems.

"All of the pearls are green," Holmes commented. "And there is a little of the staining within the corals – they are porous, moreso than the painted bones."

"That green stain could only come from this." *Frère* Jerome pointed to the brilliant mossy cloth within the rib cage of the saint. "Oh, and look how crumbly. And the rats have found their way in here! This has not borne up the test of time." He looked at all of us with a mournful face. "The wage of sin is death, but I had hoped Johnny would have more time to listen . . . ."

"*Frère* . . . ." Lestrade rested his hand on his old friend. "Be patient just a little longer. All Souls will be here before you know it." He turned to my friend. "Mr. Holmes, if you could offer a scientific explanation for this before then?"

"I can give you my explanation now. First, I must beg all of you to step away from these venerable bones." Holmes drew me by the arm to the far side where the chapel windows had cracked open to allow a little fresh air, and the others followed.

"Lestrade, *Frère*, I have made organic chemistry one of my life's pursuits, and you know of my expertise. Did any of your men touch the Saint's clothing?"

"Certainly not, sir!"

"Be at peace, old friend. I was thinking of their own safety. As soon as I saw the cavity of the bones I knew I had part of my answer. The cloth is a unique shade of green, for its main source is a lichen within the conifers of the Saint's land. *Letharia vulpine*, commonly called *Fox* or *Wolf Lichen*, mixed with meat to poison the beasts that threaten man's property. One meal is all it takes. The wolf is dead. In the old days, ground glass was mixed with the poison, but it has no need of any help, so virulent is this death. Now, Lestrade, why did you suspect Mr. Sheetpaper swallowed any ill-gained loot?"

"What!" Lestrade stared. "I never said such a thing!"

"No, but you were eager to have the body taken to the morgue with your hand-picked constables without the *Frère*'s knowledge."

"You are right. Johnny was known for that trick. I didn't want Jerome to know if . . . if I didn't have to tell him."

The Friar only sighed.

352

"How did you know?"

"Because Wolf Lichen can cause a rash." Holmes wagged a finger under my nose. "Watson, Watson! You had the answer, but you decided it was impossible. The logger's rash exists because the Pacific Forests of North America are one of the other rare parts of the world that has Wolf Lichen."

"You mean that the men who have died in relation to Isabella Afra had swallowed her jewellry? This is obscene!"

"No. The cloth is rotting and dry. Inhaling the dust from the air when the bones were transported was enough reason. The letter is clear that the peasants were no help and the thieving was done by the purchasers. The Duke was the last to die, because it was his task to hold the lantern for the other grave-robbers, and so he received the least amount of dust in his lungs, but he put himself at fresh risk by lodging the bones in his collection. The poison manifests as a rash only on the outside of the body – if it shows at all. With proper treatment, it will never cause any adverse reaction. But a guaranteed fatality is in inhalation or ingestion into the lungs or stomach. And this is how our friends met their ends."

"That doesn't explain the death of the pigs." Lestrade protested. "Mr. Holmes, this is a wonderful explanation and I want to believe it – but there will be rumours of why only the desecrators and the animals the Saint called unclean were the only ones to die. The pigs were nowhere near her."

"Ah, and I believe I can satisfy you curiosity to that fairly quickly. *Frère*, can you show us a room where we can look out and see your little stables?"

Frowning in confusion, the little friar took us to a small room close to the top floor.

"Excellent." Holmes nodded and reached into his pocket. To our united shock, he produced a dead rat from his pocket.

"Constable," Holmes said to the baffled young PC, "If you step within the foyer, there is a small church-urchin with a broom. Would you tell him that Mr. Holmes is finished with his things and to please ask him to come here?"

In less than a minute, the child came, holding a single bony hand out expectantly.

"Thank you, Ricker." Holmes set the rat, handkerchief at all, into the grimy palm. "No, no. You can keep the handkerchief. I have plenty."

Like a bolt, the boy took off and Holmes turned to the window. "Watch, gentlemen."

As we watched, the tiny child entered the mews and went straight to the wall of chicken-cages against the stable walls. Poor *Frère* Jerome clapped a hand over his mouth to see the rat fed to his precious hens.

"A curious thing about that poison," Holmes commented. "It only affects carnivorous mammals if it is in the lungs or stomach. The rats paid for their interest in the soft, crumbling cloth, but your hens are safe, Brother."

"But how could the cats be unharmed?" Jerome protested.

"Ah, you may owe that to your generosity, *Frère*. Cats and rats are the most vicious of enemies, it is true, but while a rat will eat a cat, only a starving cat will eat a rat. They will kill them with great eagerness, but they will not eat them if there is a choice."

"God pardon the dead." Lestrade shook his head. "Jerome, I can see to it the lady is returned to her village. Can you assure your people it will be safe to return?"

"I can try, but they shan't feel safe until the Saint has left."

Jerome went to find his staff, so it was left to Holmes and me to sit with Lestrade and decide the details of shipping Isabella Afra back to her village. The little detective was restless as always, and as we talked he wandered aimlessly back and forth among the gazes of the *Virgo Fortis* smiling down upon us and the little fiddler at her feet, appearing to smile up.

"A penny for your thoughts, Lestrade." I said at last.

"I'm not sure they're worth that much." Lestrade tried to smile. "Jerome told me something after I learnt of Saint Isabella's origins, and my mind keeps going to it." He finally sat in one of the ancient pews and toyed restlessly with his watch. "He thought it right and natural that a girl murdered for standing up to a cruel master would find sanctuary here, in all the places of London."

As we watched, his eyes went up to the carving of the crucified woman above us.

"The Strong Virgin is a rare saint." Holmes reminded us. "I can think of only one other fitting address on the Isle, and that is Westminster Abbey." He leaned back, tapping his ink-pen like a cigar. "This one is far more approachable, if less opulent. The two often pair.

"Do you know the legend of the *Virgo Fortis*? It comes from Portugal. When her father demanded she marry against her will, she prayed to be repulsive. Overnight her face bearded. Her father crucified her in rage, but she died triumphant, and an unmarried

354

virgin. Women and girls from all over the world plea for her support when they feel the encumbrance of men."

"And I've buried too many of them," Lestrade answered with a sharpness not directed to us. "I've tried to forget the number of times where I've stood in court and spoke under oath, and my words will or will not grant justice to a woman or woman-child. I've seen things where I could only believe it was as bad as life could get . . . but I never dreamed I would see the bones of a woman kidnapped into slavery, only to be murdered and then lawfully stolen from the only home she'd known for hundreds of years, and shipped to another foreign land! Jerome said 'like calls to like', like the right singer can make a water-glass sing. I don't know if that's true, but I chill to think what would have happened if she'd been sent to any other chapel but this one. Jerome will pay to return her to her people, for though she was not born in that village, they have welcomed her for their own."

"Ah, but perhaps you give the story too much credit." Holmes offered. "It is more than likely her name is derived from the isabelline colour of her shrouds, and the 'Afra' is someone's concocted appellation to note her exotic and unlikely origins in Africa. The odds for an African slave to survive, even within the folds of folk-tales, is astronomically high."

"Perhaps, Holmes." I answered. "But as a physician, I can assure you that the skeleton is that of a woman. And an African at that."

And, as Hallowe'en night slipped into the Chapel, we found ourselves with nothing else to say.

The Affair, as we think of it, ended as quietly and peacefully as its origins had been furtive and murky. Brother Jerome used his unexpected windfall of his cousin's fortune to bring over the priest devoted to Isabella Afra's chapel. Before one could pass a simple *Fa plaschair*, the priests were fast friends, and together they escorted the bones of the lost Saint back to Ascher. The Saltwater Duke's benefice extended enough that her Chapel was discreetly restored, and Jerome returned to do the same for the eternal needs of his own house of worship. Even now, the two chapels are firm allies, or "sisters", as the holy brothers and sisters of their care proclaim.

Lestrade was deeply relieved at the bloodless conclusion, but admitted there were some final surprises at the end of this case. The first was the passage of a law amongst the authorities of the Grey League that strengthened the protection of "Swiss residents both living and dead". The second was that a small carving of a fiddler now rested at the feet of Isabella Afra, a farewell gift from her sister in hospitality, the *Virgo Fortis*. Thirdly, a new necklace rested upon the worn wooden carving of the *Virgo Fortis*, but the delicate shade of its green pearls was a surprise to very few.

The Curious Case of
Charlotte Musgrave
by Roger Riccard

Chapter 1

I must confess, the case which I am about to record here is somewhat controversial. That is, it is a bone of contention between myself and my celebrated friend, the consulting detective, Mr. Sherlock Holmes.

While he sees it as a fairly straightforward matter of deduction and conclusion, there were aspects which he dismissed, but which I, with a different viewpoint and perspective, was not entirely comfortable ignoring, fantastic as they might have been.

It was some years after Holmes's return to London, following his three-year absence, subsequent to the Reichenbach adventure, and I was again living with him in our old rooms at 221b Baker Street. I arose late one morning to find Holmes clad in his mouse-colored dressing gown and smoking an early pipe as he sat by the fire, going through the first post of the day, a cup of coffee at his side.

"Ah, there you are, Watson," he greeted. "Do be good enough to ring for Mrs. Hudson. I believe a hearty breakfast is in order."

"A hearty breakfast is *always* in order, Holmes," I replied as I pulled the bell rope which would alert our dear landlady to our needs. "What makes it worthy of your interest on this particular day?"

"I foresee we have a day of travel ahead, if you would be good enough to join me, Doctor."

He handed me a letter and envelope, which I took over to the window to read by what daylight penetrated the poisonous yellow fog of this dreary London morning.

Imitating his methods, I studied the envelope first, noting that it was addressed in a strong feminine hand, fanciful, yet with determined purpose in its broad strokes. I was a bit taken aback when I saw the return address.

"Hurlstone Manor, Sussex?" I queried.

"Indeed, old friend. I thought that might pique your interest. Read on," commanded Holmes.

I unfolded the letter within and found a different hand had written out this supplication. It was in a neat masculine fashion, yet the writing varied at points, switching from block letters to cursive and back again.

I read through the document, which enquired as follows:

My dear Holmes,

I take up my pen at the urging of my wife to request your presence at Hurlstone to use those unique powers of yours to investigate a strange incident in which we believe the police have not been as thorough as they might have. You may recall that two years after your visit, in which you solved the mystery of my family ritual and the incident of butler, Brunton, I married Miss Elizabeth Ryan. I understood your absence from my wedding, due to your involvement in a case on the Continent at the time. But in the intervening years we have had a daughter, Charlotte, who is now sixteen years of age. She is a gregarious child. However, she has a unique condition which would be easier explained in person than in writing.

Upon her sixteenth birthday, I hired a footman specifically to see to her needs and protection as a lady to the manor born. This gentleman, however, had not been on the job a month before he was found dead in the stables on Sunday last.

The police have ruled it death by misadventure, in that they are convinced he was killed by a kick from a horse. My protests, in spite of my rank as MP for the district, have been brushed aside, even though there are obvious clues which remain unexplained.

My wife is well aware of our school ties and your part in recovering the crown of Charles I, which now adorns our family heirloom collection. Of course, Dr. Watson's writings have made your powers known far and wide, and we have agreed that you are the only man qualified to investigate this mystery.

Since the police have closed the case, I would understand if your own business priorities make it inconvenient for you. However, if at all possible, we would be ever so grateful if you and Dr. Watson could come down, for we believe his medical opinion would be invaluable as well.

Please advise if you consent and I will have your train met.

Respectfully yours,

Sir Reginald Musgrave, MP

"I take it you wish to go down to Hurlstone," I stated, rather than asked.

"Only if you would be good enough to accompany me, dear fellow. I have no pressing cases requiring my attention for the next few days. However, this familial situation could well be trying to my patience. You will note the variety of handwriting by my old schoolmate. This indicates several intruding thoughts of hesitation on his part. The fact that his wife has addressed the envelope suggests a strong urging on her part, and it would not surprise me, given Musgrave's personality and character, if his wife were not the true ruler of the household."

I snickered at Holmes's intimation, "The world is changing, old chap. Women are gaining more recognition for their abilities, and this Lady Elizabeth Musgrave may be an ideal complement to her husband. She could easily be an Irene Adler, rather than the hen-pecker you suspect."

The mention of the one woman who had ever bested Holmes brought him up short for a brief moment. Then he replied, "A woman of that stripe would not be attracted to a fellow like Musgrave. He is a decent chap and serves his district well in Parliament, but his shortcomings would be intolerable to someone of Miss Adler's intellect."

"Well, whatever the case," I said as I ruefully looked out at the dreary city atmosphere. "I shall be glad to accompany you to the countryside of Sussex whenever you wish to leave. Anything to get out of this noxious climate."

At that moment, Mrs. Hudson arrived with breakfast. As I sat down to eat, Holmes checked his Bradshaw for train departures and wrote out a telegram for Mrs. Hudson to give our pageboy to take to the telegrapher's office.

Holmes joined me at the table, scooped up eggs, bacon, and bread onto his plate. This act alone convinced me that he was indifferent about the situation. Normally, he would forgo such a meal at the beginning of a case, not wishing to waste energy on digestion when it could be used for deductive reasoning.

"There is a train from Victoria leaving at one o'clock for Horsham," he informed me. "I have advised friend Musgrave that we shall be on it." He leaned conspiratorially toward me and said, "If we have time, the fishing at Hurlstone is quite excellent, for they have their own lake. However, Watson, given that a murder is suspected, I suggest you bring your revolver, in case hunting becomes the sport of our trip."

Chapter 2

The trains were running well that day and we stepped off our carriage before two-thirty at the venerable Horsham Station. The half-century old brick building with its arched windows stood well back from the tracks.

As we disembarked, we found ourselves in a picturesque setting of blue skies, evergreen trees mixed with deciduous ones (which had lost most of their brightly colored leaves) and a sleepy hamlet with quiet country lanes. Walking out of the station, we were approached by a groom who doffed his cap and enquired, "Would you be Mr. Holmes and Dr. Watson, gentlemen?"

"I am Sherlock Holmes," said my friend. "And this is my colleague, Dr. Watson. You are from Hurlstone Manor, I perceive."

"Indeed, sir," said the elderly man. He was a thin fellow, bundled up against the cool day with an ulster and a brightly colored scarf about his neck. He put his top hat back upon his head, covering the thinning brown hair tinged with grey. "I'm Sutton, Sir Reginald's driver. Have you luggage, gentlemen?"

As Sutton went to retrieve our bags, even I could note the Musgrave crest upon the door of the carriage parked in front of the station. I turned to my friend.

"Did the family crest always look like that, Holmes? The inclusion of the crown should have given them a clue long ago to the mystery of the ritual."

Holmes shook his head, "No, Watson. The rest of the crest has not changed, except for the icons appearing smaller to make room for this new addition. Apparently, Musgrave has chosen to advertise his family's allegiance and the part they played in supporting Charles II."

Sutton appeared with our bags and we boarded the enclosed carriage for the drive to Hurlstone Manor. The inside of the conveyance was quite opulent, with thick upholstery and finely embroidered curtains. Even the window shades were decorated with representations of fine art from the Renaissance period.

"It appears your friend is quite the wealthy gentleman, old chap, and not afraid to display it," I remarked, gazing about the fine interior.

"Humpf!" declared Holmes, "This is not Musgrave's doing. He can be a bit foppish with his apparel and he certainly kept up the appearance of that section of the manor used for social gatherings. But he was a maintainer of tradition and the status quo, Doctor. He felt the old place was quite well-suited to his needs with what was passed down by his ancestors. Gas lighting and indoor plumbing were quite enough of an improvement for him. This," he said, waving his hand about the carriage, "this speaks of a lady's touch, and I've no doubt the fair Lady Elizabeth is the author of this manuscript to affluence."

Holmes raised the window shade to take in the view and we noted little traffic about on this cold, yet sunny, day. The clear skies belied the fact that there was still snow on the ground in many places and the bright sun held little warmth. The feeling of coldness was not alleviated by our coming into view of Hurlstone Manor. It was an L-shaped structure, the short arm representing the ancient keep with its grey stone walls and mullioned windows. This section is that which is first espied from the road, and its ancient lichen-covered walls seemed to emanate a cold and dreary mien.

Rounding about its southern end, however, the long arm of the manor came into view. The modern wing, with its Georgian architecture of red brick, white framed windows, and tall white columns and railings presented a welcoming site. Further on to the west, we could see the vast parkland with its ancient oaks and elms surrounding pleasant pastures. Through the trees, I thought I even caught the glimmer of sunshine reflecting off the lake.

Sutton stopped under the portico and unloaded our bags as we stepped down to the pavement. An eager young man, not yet twenty by the look of him, stepped quickly from the front door and took up our luggage to carry inside. He was about my height, that is, a couple inches short of six feet, with brown eyes and wavy brown hair. His frame was thick and muscular, even though he had not likely reached his full grown stature. I supposed that young girls would call him a handsome fellow, and he certainly exuded confidence. He hefted our bags like feathers and led the way inside.

As we entered the foyer, we were greeted by a gentleman who could only be Reginald Musgrave. I'd only had Holmes's description of him, dictated when he had apprised me of "The Adventure of the Musgrave Ritual". The figure before us looked very much like Sydney Paget's illustration of him when *The Strand* had published my story in 1893. Only this version was grey around the temples and a bit stooped in the back. He also wore gold wire-rimmed glasses. He thrust his hand forward at the sight of his old school mate.

"My dear Holmes, how decent of you to come at such short notice," he declared as he pumped the detective's hand vigorously.

"Nonsense, Musgrave. We are delighted to come to the aid of old friends. London is quiet at the moment, from the criminologist's point of view anyway, so this little sojourn is a breath of fresh air. This is my esteemed colleague and friend, Dr. John Watson."

Holmes's tone had told me that he had chosen to play this hand as the affable old friend rather than his usual persona as the taciturn detective. I likewise chose to follow suit.

The Parliamentarian turned to me and grasped my hand in both of his. "An absolute pleasure, Dr. Watson. Your recording of Holmes's adventures has been a source of delight to me and my family."

"Sharing Holmes's cases has been a pleasure, I assure you," I replied in my most amiable fashion. "I only hope what assistance I can offer will be helpful in your case as well."

"I'm sure your medical expertise will be of tremendous help in this instance, Doctor. But come, come. Let us go to my study where there is a warm fire, excellent brandy, and fine cigars to enjoy as I lay out our case before you."

Holmes held up his hand, "If you please, I think we should waste no time in examining the scene of the crime, especially if there are outdoor elements to consider. Any sign of an intruder could already be lost to the elements, and are certainly in danger, if they still exist, to the whims of Mother Nature."

Musgrave's face fell momentarily. Apparently he was not used to having his well-laid plans changed so abruptly. He rallied quickly, however.

"Of course, I should have realized that would be your priority. And it is well you mention it, for I have preserved what I thought relevant, in spite of the police's dismissal of any possibility of murder. Peter," he said, turning to the boy who carried our bags, "take the gentlemen's luggage up to their rooms and meet us out in the stables."

The young man nodded his assent and took up our bags. Musgrave went to a closet, retrieved an overcoat, scarf, and slouch hat, then led us out to the stables.

Upon entering the barn, he explained the scene of the crime. "The body of my footman, William Hancock, was found in a stall back there, with my daughter's horse presiding over it. Damage to his skull and other broken bones seemed to indicate that he had somehow frightened the horse, which kicked and trampled him to death."

"Yet you, yourself, do not believe this to be the case," Holmes stated without question.

"No, my friend, I do not. First of all, there was no reason for Hancock to be out here at that hour, for it was well after dinner and near bedtime for most of the staff. Ah, Peter, just in time. Give me a hand here."

The boy had caught up to us and was standing by to do his master's bidding. Musgrave took us off to one side, where a large canvas tarpaulin was laid upon the ground. The first action he had to take was to shoo off a large black cat which lay upon it. "Move off there, Othello. Go on, scoot!"

The cat looked up in disgust at having his nap interrupted. It stretched slowly, yawned and sauntered off with a flick of his tail.

The nobleman then had the young man assist him in raising the canvas carefully, so as not to disturb the ground beneath.

"Second of all," he paused dramatically as the tarpaulin was laid aside, "there was this."

His declaration hung in the air as Holmes and I looked at the newly revealed ground. As for myself, I saw nothing remarkable. Holmes knelt into a crouching position and said nothing as he examined the area. His silence spoke volumes to Musgrave, who sputtered.

"What! This . . . this is impossible! There was a small pool of blood here, Holmes! I'll swear to it, as well as drag marks that indicated a body was moved.

"Peter," cried Musgrave, "do you know who moved this tarpaulin?"

The boy seemed taken aback. "Why, no sir. It's laid in that spot since you set it down the day of the accident. No one's touched it as far as I know. You gave us strict orders not to."

"Very well, you may go," ordered our flustered host with a dismissive wave.

After his departure, Musgrave informed us, "Peter is the son of the butler and housekeeper I hired to replace Brunton and Rachel [1]. He is a bit proud above his station, but I doubt that he would lie to me. In fact, he is a conscientious worker and has the makings of a skilled craftsman."

Holmes hummed in distraction and continued his examination of the ground as he asked, "Did anyone know why you covered this area?"

Musgrave shook his head. "I did it myself and merely told the groom to leave the tarp laid out here until I directed him to move it. No one was aware of my suspicions, except for the police and my wife."

Holmes examined the ground, but it was rock hard from centuries of use as the Musgrave stables. "Where exactly did you see these signs?"

Holmes's old schoolmate pointed out the spot where he said there had been blood – at least a couple of spoonful's by his reckoning. Then he indicated the area where he was sure there had been two drag marks scraping the surface, as from the heels of boots.

"How long were these marks and how far apart?" enquired the detective.

Musgrave closed his eyes as if picturing the scene in his mind. "They were about a foot apart and perhaps two or two-and-one-half feet in length."

I spoke up at that, "They did not lead all the way to the horse's stall?"

"No, which is why the police disregarded their significance."

Holmes was down on his knees at this point, examining the ground with his lens. He occasionally blew off some little dust to take a closer look, but said nothing. Suddenly he stood and asked, "Where was the body found?"

364

Musgrave led us back to a stall where a beautiful white mare was lazily munching hay from its manger. We stood outside the gate, looking over the railing, as the horse gave us the merest glance, then went back to its food.

"How exactly was Hancock's body positioned?" asked my friend.

"He was here," indicated Musgrave, pointing to just inside the gate. "Lying on his stomach with his feet almost touching the gate."

"And his wounds?" requested Holmes

"There was a major gash to his forehead, which probably killed him outright. The back of his coat was torn from the effects of the horseshoes where he had apparently been trampled upon. The coroner has verified several broken ribs in his back."

"And the horse has never shown any sign of violence prior to this?"

"None, Holmes. I would not let my daughter anywhere near an animal that I thought dangerous. She has always been the most gentle of creatures. See here."

He gave a short whistle and the animal ceased its meal and came right over.

"Hello, Guinevere. How are you today, girl?" He spoke soothingly, patting the snow white neck as the horse stood contentedly still.

I reached out slowly and stroked the mare's muzzle. I had a great deal of experience among horses while serving in the army in Afghanistan and this was one of the most gentle creatures I had ever encountered.

"She is certainly not fearful of strangers," I remarked.

Holmes joined me in patting the animal and, convinced it was not dangerous at the moment, opened the stall gate and proceeded to examine the floor and the gate itself. The horse stood by as I continued to stroke its neck. It nodded its head sharply at Holmes's trespass, but settled quickly when the detective did not approach it.

"Was there any blood found in here?" he asked Musgrave, as he used his lens to get a close look at the boards of the gate.

"Only some few smears on pieces of straw where the head lay."

Holmes nodded in understanding, then straightened up and rejoined us outside the stall. "Does anyone care for the horse other than Sutton and your daughter?"

Musgrave thought a moment, then replied, "Well, Hancock of course, and occasionally Peter would saddle her when Charlotte wanted to go riding. I also took her out occasionally when we first got her, to ensure she was gentle enough for my little girl."

"I presume this incident has not produced any fear in your daughter," I asked.

"Oh no, Dr. Watson. Quite the opposite. She is adamant that the animal is innocent."

"Indeed," enquired Holmes, "what has inspired her trust in face of the damning evidence?"

The nobleman's shoulders fell in resignation. He put his hand upon a stall rail and gazed intently at the beautiful white mare within. At last he spoke. "You must understand, gentlemen, that my daughter is quite normal in all respects save one. She is attractive. She does well at her studies. She plays the violin beautifully. And she is an accomplished horsewoman. She won the blue ribbon at her riding academy this year.

"But there is one characteristic in her personality which manifests itself often and causes all manner of awkwardness for her in social settings. It is why I requested your presence as well as Holmes, Dr. Watson."

"Pray, what is the issue?" I asked, hoping to be helpful.

"She firmly believes she has a *pooka*."

Chapter 3

"A *pooka*?" I repeated, to ensure I had heard him correctly.

He looked at me in all earnestness and replied, "Yes, Doctor. One of those mythical creatures who can portend either good or evil, but is mischievous in any case."

"Come, Musgrave," responded Holmes, his grey eyes skeptical under questioning eyebrows. "Surely you do not believe in such a thing? Spirits who manifest themselves as goats or rabbits – or horses – and go about helping or hindering mankind as they see fit."

"Of course not, Holmes," said the embarrassed father. "But the point is, she believes it, and I'm afraid she has used it as an excuse for actions that she herself has taken from time to time."

I spoke up, "Surely you do not suspect your daughter of having a part in Hancock's death?"

"Oh, no," answered the man. "But she is insistent that it was her *pooka* that has confided in her the truth of the man's death, and that it was not her horse who brought it about."

Holmes held his reactions in check and asked the obvious question. "And what, pray tell, does she have to say?"

Musgrave lowered his grave face until his chin sunk deeply into his scarf as he rubbed his thumb and fingers on his forehead. "She will not tell us, Holmes. I know that this terrible secret is gnawing at her, for she has been morose and withdrawn. I was hoping that perhaps, together, you and Dr. Watson could draw it out of her."

Seeing his old friend in such a state, Holmes softened momentarily and put a hand upon his shoulder.

"I am sorry for your predicament," he sympathized. "I shall do what I can, but by definition I am not equipped, nor desirous, of dealing with the supernatural. I shall observe, examine, investigate, experiment, and deduce through logical and scientific means. The realm of *pookas* is not within my purview. Watson here, with his imaginative, literary bend of mind, is far better qualified to do so. What say you, Doctor?" Holmes asked, turning to me. "Shall we pool our resources and give friend Musgrave the best of both worlds?"

I answered without hesitation, "I shall be most happy to assist, Sir Reginald. Indeed, I find myself anxious to speak with your daughter to learn more of her . . . ." I searched for the right word and finally finished with, "condition."

"Excellent!" cried the great detective, obviously happy to not have to deal with hysterical or superstitious young ladies.

"One more thing, Musgrave," he continued. "Is the body of this unfortunate footman still available for us to examine? I should like to satisfy myself on one or two points."

"Yes, Holmes. I've had it kept at the coroner's office in Horsham, rather than any funeral parlor. Hancock's people won't be down until next Sunday to retrieve it and take him home for burial in the family plot."

"Where are his people from?" asked the detective.

"Up Preston way, north of Liverpool. He had thoughts of going to sea, but the waters of the Channel are less forgiving than those of the Irish Sea. He left his ship in Brighton and was making his way overland to London when he came upon our path. Elizabeth suggested the idea of hiring him on as footman for Charlotte. She subscribes to the notion that large footmen are a status symbol, and the lad was six feet and five inches in height."

"Indeed?" queried Holmes. "Not an easy man overpower, then?"

"He was no musclebound giant. More of a beanpole, but with a sinewy strength that served him well, and he was quite agile."

"Ah," pondered my friend. "That is helpful."

367

Taking one more look about the stables, the famous detective clapped his hands together and declared, "I believe I have gathered what I can from here for now. I should like to continue collecting all the empirical evidence before tainting my thoughts with testimony of witnesses who did not actually witness the event. Would it be convenient for you to return to Horsham with us and introduce us to the coroner, so that we may examine the remains of this unfortunate fellow?"

Musgrave, obviously a man who lays out his plans and does not deal well with them when they go astray, was hesitant with his reply. However, after checking his watch, a fine silver Hunter, engraved with the family crest and on a thick chain, he acquiesced and sought out Sutton to drive us back into town.

As we passed the front of the manor, an attractive woman of about forty years stepped out onto pavement beneath the portico and flagged us down. She was about five feet and four inches in height with a trim figure, clad in a simple mauve-colored gown. Her heart shaped face was surrounded by lustrous locks of red hair, and her green eyes queried our departure.

"You're not leaving so soon, Mr. Holmes?" she asked. Her tone was almost on the verge of a command, but also held a trace of fear that she could not stop us.

Musgrave made the formal introductions of myself and my friend to Lady Elizabeth.

Holmes quickly allayed her fears. "On the contrary, madam, I've only begun my investigation. However, it is imperative that Dr. Watson and I examine the corpse before any further deterioration affects the evidence. We shall return in time for tea, I assure you."

A graceful hand with long slim fingers rose toward her throat and rested upon her breastbone. "Thank goodness," she replied. "Charlotte would be so disappointed to not meet you and explain all that she knows. She believes only you can absolve Guinevere from this unfortunate accident."

I spoke up at that, hoping to stem off any unfortunate remark which Holmes might make.

"I am looking forward to meeting Charlotte, Lady Elizabeth. I assume that is she, in the window?"

The mother looked around and confirmed, "Yes, that is our daughter."

The curtains were pulled wide apart from one of the front windows. The young lady of the house was at one side of the opening, holding the curtain in her right hand. The other side must have been tied off. Seeing us looking at her, she put her left hand to her mouth and leaned to that side, as if speaking to someone out of our sight.

"I had better go and assure her that you will be back," declared Mrs. Musgrave. "I will have tea prepared when you return."

Lady Elizabeth's departure encouraged Sutton to whip up the horses once again, and we made a quick pace to the coroner's office in a very short time.

The coroner was a wizened old gentleman of about fifty. Stocky of build with short white hair, he greeted us amicably. Musgrave introduced him as Dr. Samuel Hazlett.

Upon hearing Holmes's name, he became animated. "I've read several of your monographs, sir. Most impressive. I particularly enjoyed the piece on *Poisons of the Southern Hemisphere.* Very enlightening, indeed."

Holmes nodded his appreciation. "Thank you, Doctor. I presume you've ruled out such poisons in this case of young Hancock. Do you have an official cause of death?"

"Oh, indeed, gentlemen. Come with me."

He led us to a back room where the temperature was precipitously lower, nearly as cold as outside. There were two examination tables containing *corpora delecti*, both covered in white sheets. Hazlett proceeded to one and removed the muslin.

On the slab, laying face up, was the long, sinewy figure of William Hancock. Proceeding to the head, Hazlett pointed with the little finger of his right hand to a severe indentation of the forehead.

"There is your fatal blow. A severe cranial fracture caused by forceful contact with a horseshoe or similar curved metal object. You'll note the lack of bruising on the body, despite the fractures of several ribs. Those injuries were post-mortem. Death had occurred immediately upon this impact and blood had ceased to flow."

He stepped back and gestured for me to have a look. I peered closely at the head wound and then gently felt around the skull and the back of the neck.

Wiping my hands on a nearby towel, I voiced my observations.

"I am surprised that the force of the blow from such a large animal did not break this fellow's neck. The damage to the brain was certainly immediate and devastating."

Hazlett replied, "I wondered about that as well. But it is really a matter of angle as well as force."

Holmes stepped forward and drew out his lens for a closer look at the traumatic injury. He then asked if we could turn the fellow over. Hazlett and I helped him to do so, at which point Musgrave left the room looking somewhat green.

My friend examined the back of the head and upper back, paying particular attention to the shoulder blades. When he finished, he threw the cloth back over the man.

"May I see his clothes and boots?" he asked.

"Certainly," replied the old doctor. "I have them in the other room."

Returning to the office area, we found Musgrave seated by a wood-burning stove, his colour much improved. Hazlett unlocked a cabinet and handed over the belongings of the former footman.

Holmes gave a cursory glance to the few items found amongst the deceased's pockets, which included only some keys, a multiplex knife, an inexpensive watch with no chain nor fob, and some few coins. He spent considerably more time examining the young man's clothing, particularly his boots and the back of his jacket, where there were several abrasions, apparently from the horse's hooves. He examined the rear of the trousers and the back of the man's shirt as well. He even pulled some tracing paper from his inner coat pocket and sketched the shape and pattern of the boot print, and used his pocket tape to ensure correct measurements.

He appeared finished when a new thought seemed to strike him. "Dr. Hazlett, if Sir Reginald can identify these keys as belonging to various locks upon his estate, may he sign for their custody and take them back with us?"

"Why, certainly, Mr. Holmes," answered the aging physician. "The case is closed as far as the police are concerned. Any items belonging to Sir Reginald are his for the taking."

"Excellent!" cried Holmes. "Musgrave, if you would be so kind as to retrieve the keys, I believe we have gleaned all that we can from here.

"Dr. Hazlett, you have been most thorough and helpful," continued my friend. "I would only call your attention to one other significant detail."

"What's that, Mr. Holmes?"

"The most unusual curvature of the blow to the forehead."

"It appeared to be normal for a horseshoe."

"Normal in size and shape, perhaps, replied the detective. "But I suggest you consider it from another direction."

Without another word, he led us back out to our waiting carriage.

370

Chapter 4

True to her word, Lady Elizabeth Musgrave had hot tea and biscuits awaiting us in the parlour, where a substantial fire alleviated us of the chill of our journey from town. Once we had settled into our seats, she asked the question that was on all our minds.

"How is your investigation progressing, Mr. Holmes? Is there reason to suspect foul play after all?" She glanced anxiously at her husband and put her hand upon his forearm.

Holmes sipped his tea deliberately before answering. At last, he set down his cup and turned toward our hostess and Sir Reginald, who were occupying a settee opposite to our wing-backed chairs.

"It is a capital mistake to draw conclusions before one possesses all the facts," he said – a comment I have heard him make often, usually to a policeman. "However, I can tell you at this stage that there are certain inconsistencies which need further investigation."

"But if the horse is innocent, then a murderer may be living amongst us," observed Musgrave. "The very possibility I feared, which made me call upon you."

"Of course Guinevere is innocent!"

This loud declaration came from the doorway where their daughter, Charlotte, appeared. She was a pretty young woman, with the same auburn hair as her mother, but the broader face of her father. This last was made more emphatic by the last vestiges of baby fat which still lent her a child-like appearance, despite her sixteen years.

"Charlotte," scolded her father gently. "It is not polite to interrupt."

"We're talking about *my* horse," she stated, emphatically. "I know she did not kill poor Willy, as sure as I am standing here. Isn't that right?"

She turned her head at this last remark, as if making it to someone standing next to her.

"Charlotte," said her mother gently. "You should introduce your friend to our guests."

"Oh, of course. How rude of me. I am sorry. Dr. Watson, Mr. Holmes, this is my very good friend, Stewart. Stewart, these are father's friends from London."

She walked toward us and I naturally, as good manners demand, stood upon the presence of a woman entering the room. She held out her left hand to me and I bowed over it with courtly propriety. She then took her right hand as if she were guiding someone else's and brought it toward mine.

"Shake hands with Dr. Watson, Stewart. He's going to help prove Guinevere innocent."

With both her hands wrapped around mine, it would have been difficult to gauge the presence of a third person's in that tangle of palms and fingers. I could only make a mental note that her hands seemed abnormally strong for their size.

"And this is the famous detective, Sherlock Holmes," she continued, turning toward my companion.

Holmes had stood and bowed to the young woman, but did not extend his hand. "I am afraid my hands are still a bit contaminated from handling . . . things at the coroner's office. Forgive me, Miss Charlotte."

"Oh, we quite understand, Mr. Holmes. I would insist that you handle anything you need to prove the innocence of my poor Guinevere."

"And to find the true killer of Willy Hancock?" he responded.

A dark shadow passed across her face, but was gone instantly as she rejoindered, "Of course, Mr. Holmes. Justice must be done, after all."

"I am pleased to hear you say so," replied the detective. "I cannot guarantee to exonerate your horse. However, to do so will likely point to the actions of a human being. I only hope that the exposure of such an individual will not be too painful for you."

Musgrave spoke up at that, with some agitation "What are you implying, Holmes?"

"I wish to imply nothing, my friend. There are too many unanswered questions to make implications at this time. I should like to observe the stable and the grounds once more before we lose the daylight. Perhaps you and I should do so together. Watson," he said, turning to me. "I am well aware that your old wound is troubling you in this cold weather. You can best help me if you stay here, off your feet, and speak with the ladies about the staff and habits of the house."

Though my wound was acting up a bit, it would not have precluded me from accompanying Holmes and his old schoolmate. But I understood that he was giving me the excuse to question the girl for more detail and I played along with his request.

After Musgrave and Holmes left us, I continued to enjoy my tea and biscuits with the women. Lady Elizabeth kept the conversation going.

"I've read many of your accounts of the adventures you have shared with Mr. Holmes, Doctor. But I've never been sure, where exactly were you wounded? If you don't mind my asking."

"Not at all," I answered, setting down my cup. "I was wounded in Afghanistan."

My attempt at levity was met with a smile by her Ladyship. "If it's too embarrassing, Doctor, I understand." She smiled, giving me back a little bit of my own.

Clearing my throat I replied in earnest, "I actually suffered two wounds, Madam, during the Battle of Maiwand and its aftermath. I was first hit in the shoulder and Murray, my orderly, was able to heft me up astride a horse, which he led along the line of retreat under enemy fire. During that perilous escape, a second bullet struck my leg near the knee. It is that wound which gives me trouble to this day, especially when it's cold.

"But old war wounds are not the topics to discuss with young ladies." I smiled charmingly and looked at Charlotte. "Tell me, my dear, how did you and Stewart meet?"

The teen aged girl was all smiles as I engaged the topic of her friend. I could only imagine how often the presence of this *pooka* was met with derision or pity towards her.

"He is actually a friend of mother's," she answered. "He'd been gone for some time since she grew up, but now he's come back to be *my* friend and guardian."

I looked quizzically at Lady Elizabeth, who cast her eyes downward momentarily. Drawing upon some inner resolve, she turned to me and responded.

"Yes, Dr. Watson, it's true. Growing up in Ireland, Stewart came to me as a young girl and was a spiritual force in my life from the age of thirteen until my twentieth year. He was not so bold then, and demanded I keep his existence a secret. But he was an advisor and protected me on occasion from physical harm. He left me when he felt I no longer had need of him. But now that I've my own daughter, he has returned to continue his role for her sake."

I must admit that this confession took me completely off guard. I'd heard of cases of mental instabilities affecting girls as they entered puberty. But this was the most bizarre and outlandish tale I'd come across. I wondered if the mother were merely placating the child, but her manner seemed so sincere it was hard to fathom that it might be an act.

Recognizing that I must be careful of upsetting the delusion, I chose my words carefully.

"I see. I was not aware that *pookas* attached themselves to families for generations. Stewart," I said, looking to Charlotte's left, pretending in all earnestness that I was speaking to a living entity, "I've never studied *pookas* in depth, but my understanding is that they take on many forms. I'm not quite sure I recognize this manner in which you present yourself."

Charlotte burst out laughing, "Why, Dr. Watson, Stewart only allows himself to be seen by others on rare occasions. Any impression you are having must be based upon the evidence of his size and indications he leaves in his wake. As long as I've known him, he has taken on this form, which is erroneously referred to as a centaur in mythology."

She stopped and leaned to one side, then continued her conversation with me.

"Stewart says he must go now and see what your friend is up to. He knows Guinevere is innocent and wants to ensure that the guilty party is dealt with."

"Has he told you who it was that killed Mr. Hancock?" I asked.

Suddenly the door to the parlour, which had been ajar, closed solidly. I jerked my head in that direction but, of course, saw nothing. Almost immediately however, the butler, Madison entered and I assumed it was he who had accidently closed the door while reaching for it and then re-opened it. He enquired as to our desire for further refreshment and we all declined.

The three of us alone again, Miss Charlotte picked up the conversation.

"He refuses to tell me, Doctor. He says it would be better if I did not know, but that he will ensure that I'm not in danger and that my horse shall not be harmed."

I nodded. "Well, for what it's worth, Holmes appears to have reason to believe your horse is not guilty. If anyone can find the truth, it is he."

Lady Elizabeth spoke again, "Thank you, Doctor. That is quite reassuring. Charlotte, dear," she said, turning to her daughter. "You've had a very long day. I think it would be best for you to go and lie down for awhile. I'll have Mrs. Madison wake you in plenty of time for dinner."

"Very well, mother," answered the young woman. She stood and curtsied to me. "Thank you, Dr. Watson. You have given me great hope."

Alone now with Lady Elizabeth, I felt I could at least ascertain her role in her daughter's delusion.

"Your daughter's condition is one of the most unusual I've come across, Lady Elizabeth. Have you consulted any doctor on her behalf?"

She looked at me with a most perplexed expression.

"There is no 'cure', Dr. Watson," she stated, matter-of-factly. "Stewart will leave her when he feels she has reached adulthood safely. Just as he did with me."

I had my answer. What good it would do Holmes, I had no idea.

Chapter 5

I went out to the foyer to see about grabbing my coat and hat to join Holmes and Musgrave outside, but just as I was about to do so they returned. Our host invited us to join him for cigars in his study to discuss the day's events.

Once settled into comfortable arm chairs before a substantial fireplace, we were offered some fine Cuban cigars, and soon a blue haze had pervaded the room.

"Well, old friend," enquired Musgrave, "can you offer any enlightenment into this tragedy? Was I correct in surmising a criminal act rather than a 'misadventure'?"

Holmes exhaled a long stream of smoke as a preamble to his voicing his thoughts. At last he spoke.

"All the physical evidence, in addition to your observations and the fact that they were eliminated, point to a human culprit, Musgrave. Watson, you may wish to make note of these facts, for we will surely wish to lay them before the police."

I took my ever-present notepad and pencil from my inner breast pocket and assumed a writing position on the end table by my chair.

"The evidence you attempted to preserve," continued Holmes, "the blood and drag marks, indicate that that spot is where the murder actually occurred. Hancock was struck in the forehead by an object resembling a horseshoe. He fell to his back, his head rolling to one side. Bleeding profusely as head wounds are wont to do, the pool of blood which you observed spilt out. The murderer then grabbed the victim under the arms and dragged him up into a position where he could get a shoulder under him to carry him back to the horse's stall. The short drag marks of the boots on the ground, and the scraping of the backs of his boot heels which I observed, confirm this. Also, there was dirt upon the rear of the trousers and the back of his shirt, where his jacket had ridden up when he was dragged into position. This does not match up with his being struck from the front by a horse's hoof and falling onto his chest."

Holmes took another puff of his cigar as he contemplated his next words.

"Our killer must be someone of considerable strength. Although Hancock was a lean young man, his weight still measured at least one-hundred-and-seventy-five pounds. Not a small feat to lift upon one's shoulders and carry for some thirty feet to the stall. He is also quite methodical to have constructed a weapon which resembled a horse's shoe and somehow lure the footman out into the stables at that time of night. It was a well thought-out scheme and likely would have succeeded, as the police have fallen into his plan with their erroneous conclusion.

"They, however, failed to note that such a blow as Hancock was purported to have received would have thrown him back against the wooden stall gate with tremendous force and, as the Good Doctor here has observed, would likely have broken his neck. The gate shows no signs of receiving such a forceful impact, and the man's neck was intact."

Musgrave interjected, "But what of the broken ribs and the damage to the back of his jacket?"

"Our culprit likely used the same instrument of death to pound Hancock's back, in order to simulate the trampling by the horse."

I spoke up at that remark, "What would the mare be doing all this time, Holmes? Would she not have reacted to this violence in her presence?"

"As you must have noted, Watson, the stall is fairly large, some twenty-feet square. It is my belief she was lured into a corner with some enticement, extra hay or lumps of sugar perhaps, and ignored what was happening several feet away. The victim was already dead, so there were no cries for help nor howls of pain. Nothing really to upset the horse until the smell of death began to permeate the area, by which time the killer was long gone."

Holmes's friend shook his head and mumbled, "I knew it! There's a devil afoot here, Holmes! How do we catch him?"

"For that I shall require more data," answered Holmes. "I would like to question the staff, determine their whereabouts, see if anyone noted any strangers to the area."

"Ascertain a motive, I presume?" I offered.

"Indeed, Watson. That will be our primary object." He looked at me questioningly and asked, "What did you learn from Miss Charlotte?"

I glanced at our host, who nodded, knowing what was likely to come forth from my answer.

"I should like to learn more of the history and mythology of *pookas*," I answered. "Both Lady Elizabeth and her daughter appear to be convinced of their guardianship by this 'Stewart' creature. Charlotte insists that he knows the truth behind this murder but says he will not tell her anything, other than to assure her that the mare is innocent."

"I can help you with that, Dr. Watson," Musgrave offered. He stood and walked over to a bookshelf where he retrieved a well-worn volume. He handed it to me as it automatically opened to a much-read page. I glanced at its significance and then read aloud:

> *The* pooka *or* puca *is long entrenched in mythology throughout Europe and Scandinavia. There are English, Welsh, Scot, and Irish versions of this creature, who has been described as both evil and benevolent; a demon and a fairy.*
>
> *Their origins can be traced back to the satyrs and centaurs of Greek mythology. The character of Puck in Shakespeare's* A Midsummer Night's Dream *is derived from the legend of the pooka.*
>
> *The pooka is a shapeshifter who can take on many forms. As an animal it is commonly black, though not always, and manifests itself as a cat, dog, goat, rabbit, horse, or other domesticated creature. In other cases, it takes on the form of hobgoblin, leprechaun, or fairy. Throughout the ages, many have reported seeing it as half beast and half man. The human portion is usually a male, sometimes bare-chested from the waist up, other times dressed in the fashion of the day.*
>
> *It is known to lead travelers astray, sometimes to their doom. In other instances it will perform work in return for reward. It is believed to be benevolent to farmers and will sometimes take up guardianship of certain individuals whom it deems worthy and needful of advice or protection . . . .*

"It goes on, Holmes," I said, "but these are the essential facts as they pertain to this case. Lady Elizabeth claims this Stewart creature came to her upon reaching puberty and acted as her protector until the age of twenty."

Musgrave spoke up, "Puberty is when Charlotte first spoke of his existence. Some three years ago now."

It was Holmes turn to question, "What form does your daughter claim this creature to have taken?"

Musgrave spread his hands and replied, "Her description is that of a centaur, half-horse, half-man. Although she claims that moniker is erroneous, according to Stewart."

"Most interesting," mumbled Holmes around his cigar, which had burnt down significantly. "Musgrave," he suddenly declared, throwing his cigar butt into the fire, "I should like to examine Hancock's quarters immediately, if you please."

"Certainly, Holmes," our host replied. "I'll take you there now."

The footman's room was in the servant quarters in the old wing of the manor. No longer occupied, it was quite chilly. Musgrave lit the lamp on the table, as the setting sun cast little light through the small window.

Holmes went through the closet, checking the pockets of Hancock's modest collection of garments. They yielded nothing. Nor did his old sailor's trunk, for which Musgrave had the key amongst those retrieved at the coroner's office, which held some books, extra shoes, small tools, and personal mementos. There was a small writing desk opposite the bed and, when Holmes opened the drawer, it appeared that he had found a significant clue at last. He rapidly skimmed the latter pages of what appeared to be a personal journal or diary.

Turning to our host he queried, "This could be key evidence. The police did not search this room?"

"Only a very cursory examination," answered our host. "I saw the chief constable with that very book in his hand, but he set it back in the drawer, attaching no significance to it."

"How foolish of him," declared the detective. "I should like to borrow it for the evening to examine it more closely. I shall return it tomorrow so that it can be packed up with his other things for his people to retrieve."

"By all means, Holmes, if you think it will help."

Holmes held the book up, like a college professor to a roomful of students. "I believe this contains the trigger to the motive for Hancock's death."

Without explaining that remark, he led us from the room, stating that there was no more to learn there. By now it was approaching time to dress for dinner and the three of us went our separate ways, Musgrave promising that the servants would be made available for Holmes to interview after the evening meal.

Chapter 6

The repast which was laid before us at dinner was overseen by Lady Elizabeth's exacting standards. Yet it was clear that the servants performed out of loyalty and good will toward their mistress, rather than fear of retribution for any mistakes. It spoke well of the household that the camaraderie among the staff was so pleasant. To my way of thinking, this bode well for Holmes's upcoming interviews.

At the beginning of our meal, I chose to make some small talk with Miss Charlotte, who was sitting between her mother and me.

"Does Stewart ever join the family for meals?" I asked, as conversationally as I could.

As if it were a natural question, she answered me directly.

"No, I'm afraid not, Dr. Watson. He is very particular about his eating habits and chooses to dine in private. He also likes a good ale now and then and sometime imbibes too much for company's sake, so he prefers his privacy."

Surprisingly to me, Holmes spoke up at that.

"It's not a good idea for anyone to drink alone, Miss Charlotte. It is far too easy to indulge to excess, and alcohol can have the most devastating effects upon a person's, or even a *pooka's*, behavior. Sometimes to the point where they do not remember their actions the next day."

The young lady frowned at that remark and the conversation turned to other things. When the meal was done, Musgrave arranged to have each staff member in turn meet with my friend in the study.

I sat by, taking notes as servant after servant came under Holmes's scrutiny. When we were finished at last, Musgrave himself came in to ascertain what we had learned.

"As I feared," stated the detective, "no one really saw or heard anything on the night in question. Young Peter cast some aspersions about the way Hancock looked at his charge on occasion, but no one else noticed anything untoward in his behavior."

379

Musgrave pursed his lips, "Peter has been Charlotte's playmate for years now, but they are growing into adulthood and I'm afraid he has taken too keen an interest in my daughter."

"And you do not trust him," stated Holmes, matter-of-factly.

"I suppose, like most fathers, I am wary of any young man where my daughter is concerned. But he's never truly given me reason not to trust him. In fact, I believe he is so smitten with her that he would do anything to protect her."

"Including murder?" I asked.

The Member of Parliament looked aghast, "Oh no, Doctor. I did not mean to imply that at all."

Holmes sat silent for several seconds as he lit his pipe. He then turned toward Musgrave, who sat between us and the door to the hallway, and declared forcefully, "In the absence of an obvious motive, I suggest the next step is to search for the murder weapon. First thing tomorrow morning, Musgrave, I believe we should start with the servants' quarters, then proceed to the stables themselves."

"But, what are you looking for, Holmes?" the parliamentarian asked. "What could mimic a horse's kick?"

"Why, a horseshoe, old man, naturally."

It was approaching ten o'clock and we agreed to take our leave of each other then reconvene at seven in the morning. As we departed the study and turned the corner, we noted the butler Madison near the front door, speaking with Sutton. They glanced our way and then Sutton left, while Madison turned off in the direction of the kitchen.

As Holmes and I ascended to the second floor rooms we had been provided, he called me to join him in his room, I presumed for a nightcap, as each of our rooms had a small liquor cabinet.

Instead, he bade me sit in the chair by the dressing table.

"We've a long night's work ahead, Watson," he said in hushed tones. "Our culprit is indeed a member of the household, and I hope to catch him red-handed with the murder weapon tonight."

"Who is it, Holmes?" I asked, "Why not merely confront him now and force his confession?"

"I've narrowed his identity, Doctor, but there are still three possibilities. Someone was listening outside the study when I loudly announced my intention to search the quarters. Unfortunately, the floor in the hall was wood and gave up no shoeprints. But by stating our plan, I believe it will force the culprit to move the weapon tonight, and we shall be there to catch him."

"But, Holmes," I asked. "Wouldn't he have rid himself of it after using it? Its existence would surely be a danger to him."

"I believe his only safety was in a clever hiding place until he could dismantle it," replied the great detective. "He could not risk it being found and destroying the theory of the horse as the culprit. But now we have forced his hand. All that remains is to apprehend him."

He went on to lay out his plan. He would take up a position out front, where he could see the main entrance to the house and servants' quarters and both ends of the stable. I would be in his line of sight, but off toward the rear of the house where I could see the exits from the kitchen, the rear of the servants' quarters, and the French doors from the parlour. If either of us saw our prey, he would light a candle out of sight behind a tree, and the other would make their way across to assist in capturing the murderer.

We bundled up against the cold of the early winter's evening. Fortunately, no storm threatened and it was a clear cold night with a three-quarter moon to light the grounds.

The time ticked by slowly. Fortunately, we had brought our heavy winter coats, gloves, and mufflers. I managed to bundle up with my ears and lower half of my face well covered by the woolen scarf, which had been a gift from my wife years before. Still, sitting in complete quietude wore on my constitution, and along about one o'clock my eyelids were weighing heavily. I had just made up my mind to stand and stretch, remaining out of sight behind a large oak, when windows in the house began to shimmer with light. First the ground floor and then a first floor bedroom came to life with gas lamps. Suddenly a woman's muffled scream pierced those old brick walls. I looked toward Holmes, not sure if he would treat this as a diversion to keep us from our quarry, or a significant event requiring our presence.

He waved me toward the kitchen entrance while he ran deliberately toward the front door, both of which he had taken the precaution to unlock when we took up our posts. A second woman's cries were heard as I entered the kitchen. The cold night, having a deleterious effect on my leg, had caused me to arrive several seconds behind Holmes. When I entered the foyer, I found him kneeling over the body of young Peter Madison at the bottom of the staircase. His mother was crying into her husband's shoulder as he tried to comfort her, though visibly shaken himself at the sight of his son's still body, lying awkwardly and unmoving. Lady Elizabeth had her hand upon the woman's back, attempting to offer comfort.

Holmes motioned me to join him, but it was clear from the look on his face that the boy was gone. A diagnosis I confirmed when I felt his neck, clearly broken from an apparent fall down the stairs.

When I looked toward Holmes to verify the obvious, I found him gazing up the staircase to see Musgrave holding his sobbing daughter in his arms. He climbed the stairs and spoke briefly back and forth with our host. Then Musgrave and Charlotte descended and Holmes quickly examined the landing.

Since I had often assisted police investigations in the past, it was felt we could legally move the body and send for the official coroner in the morning.

With the boy safely wrapped away in the cool of the basement, the entire household was gathered into the dining room. The housemaids were all crying as they were allowed to sit at the long table. Madison and his wife were at the far end while Musgrave, Lady Elizabeth, and Miss Charlotte occupied the head of the table. I kneeled near the hearth, stoking a fresh fire to warm the room. Holmes, hands thrust deep into his pockets, still wore his overcoat and hat. He had removed his gloves when checking the boy's pulse. He briefly paced the room while the rest of them settled into their seats, then proceeded with his questions.

Addressing the master of the house first, he enquired for all to witness, "Pray, Sir Reginald, tell us what you know."

"I was sleeping rather fitfully," he responded. "Not wishing to wake my wife, I decided to go down to my study, read for a bit, and have some wine to calm my nerves. This whole business of Hancock's death has affected me more than I realized.

"Just as I opened my bedroom door and stepped out into the hallway, I heard a gasp and then a cry, followed by the sound of what must have been Peter, tumbling down the stairs. I rushed to the staircase and almost immediately Charlotte came out of her bedroom and raced to my side. Seeing her friend at the bottom of the staircase, she screamed, which woke the household. When Mrs. Madison and her husband came in from the servant's wing and saw their son, Mrs. Madison screamed as well. Madison knelt by the boy, checked for signs of life and looked up at me, shook his head, then went to hold his wife. Charlotte was shaking and I held her while Elizabeth came out, saw the situation, and went to Mrs. Madison's aid. The other servants soon arrived, then you and Dr. Watson. What I don't understand is, where was he going? He had no business upstairs."

Mrs. Madison spoke up at that. "Peter was concerned for Miss Charlotte, Sir Reginald. He told me he used to stand guard near her door because he didn't trust that Hancock fellow."

"But Hancock is dead," I said. "Why would he stand guard now?"

Mrs. Madison, through her tears, said, "He heard Mr. Holmes and the master speak about Hancock being murdered. If there was a stranger about, killing people, he was determined that Miss Charlotte be safe."

Holmes spoke up at last. "It appears that your son slipped on a loosened rug at the top of the stairs. The stair runner has pulled loose from a carpet tack. He may have reacted in fear and caught his foot as he turned when Sir Reginald opened his bedroom door unexpectedly, or he may have merely tripped while trying to keep quiet by walking on tiptoe."

This idea became generally accepted and soon everyone went their separate ways. Holmes again called me to join him in his room. When we entered, I noted a canvas duffel bag upon his bed.

"What is this, Holmes?" I asked. "It wasn't here when we left to take up our posts outside."

"This, dear fellow, contains the answer to our mystery. But I have asked Musgrave to join us once he puts his daughter back to bed. Then I will explain all."

We sat and smoked for several minutes until our host could rejoin us. He quietly closed the door behind him and explained that he'd had a difficult time settling Charlotte down.

"She told me some additional facts that may be pertinent to the case, Holmes," he stated. "It seems that after the death of Hancock, Peter took it upon himself to tell her that he loved her and wanted to court her. As you can imagine, with all this *pooka* business, my daughter is still child-like in many ways. She is not yet inclined toward romance and told Peter she only wanted their friendship to remain as it was. Apparently he was bitterly disappointed, and they have not spoken these last few days."

I was concerned at this news and spoke up, "Then why would he be going to her room in the middle of the night? Surely he did not think he could harm her without discovery?"

Holmes stood and walked over to the bed. Lifting the duffel bag he dumped its contents onto the mattress. "This is why, Doctor. You could not see it from the bottom of the staircase, but it was off to the side on the landing near where the carpet had torn loose. I retrieved it while you all were taking the body to the basement and brought it here."

Musgrave and I joined Holmes at the bedside and observed the strange items that lay there.

"You said the boy had the makings of a craftsman, Musgrave," said my companion. "I presume that craft was leatherworking."

Our host nodded and he and I each picked up a strange looking boot which had been constructed in an unusual shape and size and used horseshoes for the bottom of the heels.

"This is the most telling item, gentlemen. He used those boots to hide his presence and create the impression of the trampling, but this is the actual murder weapon."

He held out a stout club with a D-shaped handle like a shovel and about as long as a walking stick. On the bottom it, too, was fastened to a leather boot-like object which also had a horseshoe as its foundation. Holmes grabbed the club in two hands and thrust it upward in demonstration.

"Hancock had several inches reach over Peter. But this apparatus, especially if delivered unexpectedly, could negate that advantage quickly.

"I also found this note crumpled in the bag. I believe it explains much."

Musgrave took the note and read it aloud, "'*Meet me in the stables at ten o'clock. – Charlotte.*' This was a common occurrence, Holmes. Charlotte would often have Peter saddle Guinevere for her, so she could take a morning ride before lunch."

"Let me explain my hypothesis based upon the facts we now have," said the detective. "Somehow Peter got this note, innocently received from Miss Charlotte at an earlier date, to Hancock on the afternoon of the murder. Hancock's journal reveals that he was indeed smitten with the girl. Finding this note, he was likely pleased to participate in what he thought would be a rendezvous. Instead, arriving at the stable after all have gone to bed, he is confronted by Peter. There may or may not have been accusations thrown back and forth, but before rising voices could alarm anyone, Peter smashed this club into Hancock's face. Even he may have been surprised by its instantaneous killing of his rival, but the deed was done. I have noted Peter's strength in his muscle tone and the way he handled our luggage. He dragged Hancock into a position where he could lift him over his shoulder and carried him to Guinevere's stall. There he distracted the horse and went about stomping the lifeless body with

384

these boots. To all the world it would appear to have been an accident."

"But," I interjected, "what was he doing bringing these items upstairs tonight?

"Ah, there we enter into the subject of conjecture. He may have believed if he hid them up here we would not find them, not suspecting the family members. Or," his face darkened, "he may have thought to implicate the girl who spurned him by planting the evidence in her room."

We discussed the various options into the wee hours and, by the time we sent for the local police in the morning, had settled upon a scenario that would absolve the horse and spare the Madisons' feelings regarding their son.

Holmes deciphered the evidence in such a way that it appeared Hancock had surprised someone who was trying to steal Charlotte's mare. This unknown assailant struck the footman with a horseshoe taken off a bench in the stable during their altercation, then placed the body in with the mare and got away before anyone could come investigate the noise of their struggle, which he thought would arouse the house.

He convinced the constable by one salient fact.

"As I told Dr. Hazlett, one must consider the horseshoe print on Hancock's face from another direction. The fact that it was curved upward, like a smile, indicated it was done artificially. A horse would face a threat head on and strike with its fore hoof. Thus, the shoeprint would curve downward, like a frown."

The police, reluctantly, agreed to a widespread search of the area, looking for any strangers – though with several days gone by, there was little hope of apprehending the culprit. With that settled, Peter Madison's death was ruled an accident due to the faulty carpet tack and subsequent fall.

We spent the rest of that day catching up on sleep and prepared to depart Hurlstone Manor the next morning to return to London.

Epilogue

We took our leave of Lord and Lady Musgrave after breakfast the next day. It was unseasonably warm, thus we had the carriage windows wide open as Sutton drove us at a leisurely pace to the train station. Before we had actually left the grounds of the ancient manor, I noted a rider in a meadow adjacent to the old section of the house. My observation revealed that it was young Charlotte, for there was no mistaking that auburn hair flowing behind her as she cantered along, moving away from the road we took.

Suddenly, she stopped. Turning to look back over her shoulder, she gazed at me in deep concentration. The effect was almost hypnotic. Then a most extraordinary thing happened. From in front of her, a young man suddenly appeared, peering around her shoulder and following her gaze to stare intently at me. He was fair with blond curly hair and clean shaven. It appeared at first, that they were riding double. As more of his torso was revealed however, I realized that he wore no shirt and I could see no horse's head beyond him.

"Sutton, stop!" I cried, looking up toward our driver. Grabbing my companion's sleeve I exclaimed, "Holmes, look there!"

Unfortunately, in taking these actions, I had looked away from the unbelievable sight. Turning back, with Holmes questioning, "What is it, Doctor?" in my ear, I found the scene to be completely normal. Miss Charlotte had turned her horse, which now had all the appearance of Guinevere, and was riding toward us, completely alone in the saddle.

She slowed her mare to a walk as she approached, then she stopped and spoke.

"Gentleman, we do so want to thank you again for proving Guinevere innocent," she said, patting her horse's neck.

"Why, Dr. Watson, are you all right?" she asked in all innocence as she noted the look on my face, but I could see the smile behind those whimsical green eyes.

I stammered, "I . . . I thought I saw . . . ." My voice trailed off, not knowing what to say.

"Oh, you had the mushroom omelet for breakfast, didn't you? They seem to have an odd effect on people's vision." she offered. "We've had that problem before with some of our guests. I've warned poor Mrs. Madison about where to pick her mushrooms."

Guinevere shook her head and pawed at the ground. "If you'll excuse us gentlemen, we need our exercise. Have a wonderful trip back to London!"

"What was that all about, Watson?" asked Holmes. "What did you think you saw? Surely not Stewart?"

I wiped my forehead with a handkerchief and bid Sutton to drive on.

"As you said at the beginning of this case, Holmes, you handle the logical and leave the imaginative to me. Let's just leave it at that for now."

NOTE

1 – Rachel Howells was the maid who was spurned by Brunton and disappeared the night of his death in "The Musgrave Ritual" by Sir Arthur Conan Doyle (acting as Watson's agent, of course!)

The Adventure of the
Awakened Spirit
by Craig Janacek

It was a dark and stormy afternoon in early November when an uncommon client called upon my friend, Mr. Sherlock Holmes, asking for help of a most peculiar nature. The new century was almost a year old, though upon the day in question both Holmes and I were feeling like relics of a more ancient era. Holmes was listlessly drawing a bow across the strings of his violin, while I was rather drowsy and dreamy, an old tale by Mr. Irving resting upon my breast. Our repose was shattered when the bell announced a visitor.

I glanced over at Holmes. "Undoubtedly a new client," I opined.

His heavy dark brows rose, and a glimmer of interest appeared in his suddenly sharp, piercing grey eyes. "How can you tell, Watson?"

"Because Mrs. Hudson shut the door quickly. When it is a tradesman, she typically natters with them for a while."

"It might have been an express district messenger," said Holmes. "They rarely have time for small talk. Nothing less than attempted murder will keep the London message-boy from speeding upon his way."

I shook my head. "I heard someone enter. A messenger would not have done so."

"It might be a friend of mine?"

"Except that you have none. In the almost twenty years of our partnership, I can count upon one hand how many social visitors you have received."

He snorted in wry amusement. "You may have missed a few during those times when you deserted our little suite at Baker Street. But, very well . . . it might be one of Mrs. Hudson's cronies?"

"That is highly improbable, Holmes."

I had the rare opportunity to witness a look of confusion upon Holmes's face. "Why ever not?"

"Because I had a conversation with her at tea, and she specifically noted that she was planning upon a quiet evening with her knitting. She would not have made such a claim if she was expecting the visit of an acquaintance."

Holmes threw back his head and laughed. "Well, even if the case turns out to be a dull one, I have our visitor to thank for your rousing display of my methods at work."

"So you agree?"

"I do, Watson. However, your reasoning remains faulty."

"How so?"

"Pray tell, how do you know that it is not Lestrade or Gregson or some other perplexed member of the Yard?"

I considered this for a moment. "I suppose it could be."

He shook his head. "It is not."

"And how can you tell with such certainty?" I asked, puzzled.

"Because at this very moment I hear our visitor's tread upon our seventeen steps, and it is both distinct and unfamiliar. I would know the presence of Lestrade or Gregson long before they ever opened our door. The man who is about to enter shall be rather unusual. I would wager that he is tall, thin, and endowed with rather large feet."

As Holmes concluded, a knock upon the door was followed by the entrance of a man who uncannily matched his prediction. He was tall and exceedingly thin, with narrow shoulders, long arms and legs, and hands that appeared to dangle out of his sleeves, despite the fine cut to his suit and vest. Black leather shoes could not hide enormous flattened sole, and his whole frame seemed to loosely hang together. Contrastingly, his head was small and rather flat, with large ears, bulging brown eyes, and a long point of a nose.

Holmes welcomed the visitor inside and bade him take a seat in the basket chair. "I am Sherlock Holmes, and this is my friend and confidant, Dr. John Watson. What can I do for you, sir?"

Once the man was settled, his face quivered with something which resembled fear. He had taken off his bowler hat and was nervously spinning it around by its brim. "My name is Peter Cannon. I come on behalf of my father-in-law, Sir Randolph Russell. Do you know him?"

Holmes shrugged, as if the name meant nothing to him.

"The celebrated jurist?" I interjected.

"The same," answered Cannon.

"Ah, yes," said Holmes. "I remember now. He heard the case of Patrick Cairns, did he not? I recall that the papers reported that he had been unusually lenient in the sentencing."

"Indeed," replied Mr. Cannon. "Sir Randolph rarely allows for a quality of mercy. His judgements on the High Court, while never unfair, are seen by some as harsh. Nevertheless, he is expected to soon rise to become Lord Chief Justice of the Queen's Bench."

"Indeed. I hope to never have to stand in his dock!" laughed Holmes. "And what problem of the Honorable Sir Randolph requires my humble services?" asked Holmes.

"The matter concerns Sir Randolph's home."

"Has it been burgled?" I asked, for I had seen nothing to that effect in the morning edition of *The Times*.

Cannon shook his head. "No. I wish it was as straightforward as that, Doctor. A theft we could simply bring before Scotland Yard. I am afraid that the problem is rather more complex and peculiar than a mere burglary."

Holmes leaned forward, his interest piqued. "Pray tell, Mr. Cannon. I recommend you start at the beginning."

"Very well. Sir Randolph resides at No. 100, Barclay Square in Mayfair." [1]

"And you are staying with him temporarily upon your holiday from Cambridge?"

The man started in surprise. "How could you know that, Mr. Holmes?"

Holmes pointed to the man's hat. "Your bowler hat has a tag inside which plainly reads '*Ryder & Amies, Cambridge*'. It would be a rare London gentleman who would travel to Cambridge simply for a hat which one could easily purchase at any haberdashery on Savile Row. Therefore, I presume that you live and work in Cambridge."

"I see. Very clever," said Cannon, nodding appreciatively. "You are correct, Mr. Holmes. I am a Professor of Philosophy. I was formerly at UCL, but received a Jacksonian Chair at King's eight years ago. However, Penelope and I pay a visit to Sir Randolph every year at this time in order to mark her birthday."

"And where is your wife now?" I asked.

The man appeared stricken and did not answer.

"Watson, it is plain that Mr. Cannon is a widower," interjected Holmes. "And from the location of that golden strand of hair upon your vest, I would estimate that his daughter is no more than ten years of age."

Our visitor composed his face and continued. "That is correct, Mr. Holmes. Penelope was born just over ten years ago. Tragically, my sainted wife Dorothy died shortly thereafter from puerperal fever."

"And the reason for your visit to us, Mr. Cannon? The house?" urged Holmes.

"Ah, yes. Well, the house came into Sir Randolph's possession some twenty years ago."

"Who owned it before that?" I asked.

Cannon shook his head. "It has changed hands several times, Dr. Watson. I believe it was originally built by a former Premier, and after he died, it was occupied by an aged spinster. I am told that Sir Randolph bought it from an eccentric gentleman by the name of Thomas. The son of an MP, Mr. Thomas was something of a recluse. He was rarely seen in the neighborhood, and typically opened the door of his room solely in order to receive food from his servant. At the end, Mr. Thomas was said to be fully mad, rambling about the house making strange sounds."

"I see," said Holmes, dryly. "And the current problem?"

"As you must know, two days ago was All Soul's Day. [2] We therefore visited Nunhead Cemetery. We decorated my wife's grave and lit candles. We brought some soul-cakes and had a bell rung in her memory. However, when that bell rung, I think something happened," he finished, an ominous tone in his voice.

"What?" I exclaimed.

"I believe, Doctor, that we set up a spiritual resonance. On that day – when the boundary between this world and the otherworld thinned – a gateway was opened."

"And what came through?" I asked, with morbid curiosity.

"The spirit of my deceased wife. It followed us home that afternoon."

Holmes sniffed dismissively. "Are you claiming that Sir Randolph's house is haunted?"

"That is correct," said Cannon, nodding eagerly. "However, I assure you, Mr. Holmes, that I am not the only one who believes this to be true. The house has long been considered to be a magnet for spirits."

"According to whom?" I asked.

"Well, Doctor, when you talk to the neighbors, you find that the stories go back to the first days of the house. It is is known for eerie noises, which primarily emanate from the attic room. I understand that many years ago, a young woman killed herself there. She flung herself from the window after being abused by a cruel step-father."

"Threw herself, or was thrown?" asked Holmes, with a grimace. "I am aware of similar tragedies."

Cannon shrugged. "I know nothing more of the matter, Mr. Holmes. Simply what the servants tell me. The young woman's spirit typically takes the form of a brown mist, though upon occasion it can materialize as a white figure."

"Fairy tales," said Holmes, waiving his hand dismissively.

"That is not what my father-in-law's friend, Lord Spencer, said after seeing the apparition himself."

"What happened?" I asked, eagerly.

"This was before I met Dorothy, of course. However, from what I hear, Lord Spencer was intrigued by the house's stories, so he asked permission of Sir Randolph to spend the night locked in the attic. He brought his fowling piece, and during the night, the other occupants of the house heard the gun fire once. In the morning, Lord Spencer appeared to be paralyzed with fear. Although he couldn't speak for days afterwards, there was no sign of anything else in the attic . . . save only the spent cartridge. Two years later, his health ruined, Lord Spencer hurled himself down the stairs of his London home and broke his neck."

Holmes raised his eyebrows speculatively. "It sounds like the man had a melancholy disposition."

Cannon shook his head again. "That is what Sir Randolph said. He hated the ghostly rumors, and wished to dispel them once and for all. Shortly before Dorothy and I became affianced, Sir Randolph convinced a friend in the Admiralty to loan him a contingent of sailors from the *HMS Bellerophon*. Twelve brave lads went into that attic, and by morning, one was dead. The poor boy had thrown open the door, and in a state of abject fear, tripped upon the stairs. His head was bashed in by the fall. The survivors noted that they had been aggressively approached in the night by the spirit of the madman, Mr. Thomas. They unanimously refused to ever set foot in the attic again, not for all the gold in Threadneedle Street."

"These are old stories, Mr. Cannon," said Holmes. "However, you speak as if something has transpired recently?"

Our visitor nodded fretfully. "You are correct, Mr. Holmes. After the tragic incident of the sailor, it seemed that the ghosts' lust for blood had been sated. They passed on to the great Beyond. Nothing more was heard from the attic room for many years, save only the standard creaks and groans of an old house. And yet, two nights ago something changed. A ghost returned to the house."

"And you believe this to be the ghost of your deceased wife?"

"I do."

"Have you seen it yourself?"

"I have not, heavens be praised. I could not bear to look upon Dorothy's face again."

Holmes frowned. "Then how do you know that there is a ghost?"

"We began to hear noises. Sounds that could not be produced simply by an aging house."

"Such as?"

"Knocking upon the walls. Furniture moving. Chains rattling."

Holmes shrugged. "All easy to imitate."

"Perhaps," said Cannon, nodding in an unconvinced fashion. "But not the voices."

"Voices?" I asked, my interest aroused.

"Voices unlike anything you have ever heard before, Doctor. Deep and sonorous. Sometimes I think it's almost a song . . . but no earthly song. Only something that has passed to the Beyond could make such a noise."

Holmes sniffed. "And what, pray tell, is your exact question for me? Do you wish for me to perform an exorcism of some sort? I am a detective, not a priest."

Cannon shook his head. "No, Mr. Holmes. I simply wish for you to determine whether you are in fact able to prove a supernatural explanation, or whether this is some cruel fraud. If the former, I need to do whatever I can in order to allow Dorothy to pass to her place of eternal rest. If the latter, I would know who is tormenting us so."

"And what does your father-in-law have to say about the matter?"

"Sir Randolph is most displeased. However, he is inclined to ignore the noises. It was with some reluctance that he first permitted me to hire Henry Worth to investigate the case."

Holmes frowned. "I believe that I am acquainted with all of my supposed rivals – both within London and without. However, the name Henry Worth is unfamiliar to me."

Cannon laughed nervously. "Oh, no, he is not a detective, Mr. Holmes. No, indeed. He is the Secretary of the Ghost Club."

"The what?" I exclaimed.

Holmes eyebrows rose with apparent interest. "I have heard of them, but to date have paid little heed to their activities, as they do not typically overlap with our purview." He turned to me. "Watson, if you could reach the *G*, we might see what they are all about."

Acceding to his request, I took down the index volume in question and handed it to Holmes. He placed a side pillow upon the table, and used this as an impromptu stand to facilitate his rapid scan through the wide and varied cases of his career.

"*Genius loci*," he read. "Gerard, the Gascony lieutenant. What a vain fool, that one! The German Master's murder. I have a memory that you wrote the case up, Watson, though the product was overly-romantic, as per your typical wont. Geyser of Craig. Terrible death, that! The Ghazi's *shamshir*. The Ghibelline code. [3] Here we are! Good old index. It will be many moons before someone invents a superior system. Listen up, Watson. '*Ghost Club. Founded 1855, Trinity College, Cambridge, in order to undertake practical investigations of spiritualist phenomena. Counted Charles Dickens as an early member, dissolved upon his death*' – though it seems that his spirit most unkindly refrained from coming back and assisting in their research, eh, Watson!" He chuckled at his little humor. "'*Re-launched 1882 by A.A. Watts and the Reverend Stainton Moses, in parallel with the Society for Psychical Research. The membership roster is a secret. However, the current iteration appears to operate from the* Established Hypothesis'."

"What do you mean by that, Holmes?"

"The empiricist, Watson, operates from the 'Null Hypothesis.' That something is not true, unless so proven. On the other hand, the Ghosties – as we shall call them – are already convinced that ghosts are a verified fact. This is a scientifically unsound method. They merely seek to try to convince others, and thus are no different than any other cult or religion."

"So, will you take the case, Mr. Holmes?" asked Cannon, pitifully.

Holmes smiled broadly. "You may be certain of it, sir. Please return to your father-in-law's house and tell him to expect us at eight o'clock tonight."

"You won't come straightaway?"

"No, Mr. Cannon, there is one stop to make first," said Holmes, shaking his head. "However, we shall see you soon, do not fear."

Holmes showed his new client to the door and then turned to me with a shrewd smile. "I presume you intend to accompany me, Watson?"

"I wouldn't miss it for the world! However, it sounds as if this ghost might prove to be dangerous, Holmes. You may need a weapon. There's something of the kind in the drawer at your right, if I recall correctly."

Holmes shook his head. "If Lord Spencer's fowling-piece was of little use, then my Webley revolver won't be either. No, I think my hunting-crop will prove to be sufficient for the matter at hand."

"Where are we headed, Holmes?" I asked, as we strolled along Baker Street in the direction of Marylebone Road. I was concerned that Holmes intended a long jaunt despite the dismal weather.

"There are times, Watson, when the great plethora of clubs in London astonishes me. There are political clubs, military clubs, clerical clubs, artist clubs, merchant clubs, adventurer clubs, clubs for the learned and the literary, and clubs for the dissolute. Even clubs for the unclubbable, such as my brother. And now, we shall visit one of the most peculiar of them all . . . a club for the imaginary! According to the Index, we shall find it at No. 49 Marloes Road, Kensington."

"So you do not believe that there is any chance we will prove Sir Randolph's spirit to be real?"

"Do not be absurd, Watson. There's as much truth in ghosts as there is water in the Sahara. There will be a man behind all of this, mark my words."

He turned at the corner and led us into the Metropolitan Railway Underground entrance. Any further conversation was limited by the noise in the carriages. When we reached the High Street Kensington stop, Holmes motioned for us to disembark. From there, it was a brief walk to our destination, which I found to be an unremarkable, white-painted, terraced house. There was no sign or other marking to inform the average passerby that it was the gathering place for individuals of a decidedly-spiritualist bent.

Holmes knocked upon the door, which was promptly opened by a footman. Holmes explained that he wished to speak to Mr. Worth, and we were promptly shown into the library.

The man in question was studying a book when we entered. Worth proved to be an elderly man, only a few years shy of seventy, unless I missed my guess. His hair was already receding away from a brow which appeared heavily furrowed. His large flat nose and long arms gave him the appearance of a loose-limbed simian, though his dark brown eyes shone with intelligence. His vested suit was rather rumpled, but a golden watch chain bespoke of no want of funds.

"Welcome to the Ghost Club, Mr. Holmes!" Worth exclaimed, animatedly. "I never thought to see you grace our presence. I was under the impression that you were rather skeptical of ghosts?"

"Your impression is correct," said Holmes, tersely.

"And yet, the overwhelming evidence suggests the contrary."

"Is that so?" Holmes asked, mildly. "Perhaps I have yet to examine all of the available evidence?"

"You are welcome to peruse the volumes in our library any time you wish. I will ensure that you are given unlimited access by the warden. Not as a member, of course. Not unless you become convinced and wish to join officially? No? It will be, shall we say, a sort of 'by courtesy' appointment. Herein you may read, for example, the *Diary* of Samuel Pepys. This is someone we universally consider to be an accurate and honest eyewitness to the events of his age . . . the Restoration and Second Dutch War, the Great Plague, the Great Fire, etcetera. And in those pages you will find his thoughts on the Drummer of Tedworth, a '*strange story of spirits and worth reading indeed*'. Do you know it, Mr. Holmes?"

"I do not."

"In 1661, John Mompesson, a landowner in Tedworth, began to be plagued by nocturnal drumming noises after he won a lawsuit against a vagrant gypsy drummer named William Drury. But Mompesson was hardly the only one to hear the noises. It was heard by his children and servants, as well as the philosopher Joseph Glanvill. How do you explain that, Mr. Holmes?"

"Perhaps a *folie à deux*?"

Worth shook his head sadly. "A shared delusion? Come now, Mr. Holmes. Soon you will have Dr. Watson regaling me with tales of exotic powders which stimulate the brain centers in order to create visions."

Holmes smiled wanly. "Nevertheless, I think Sir Randolph would be well served to have a second investigator glance over the scene of the haunting."

"And what do you think that you will find that I missed?" asked Worth, a hint of irritation entering his voice.

"I suspect that we will encounter a fraud. Something akin to the Cock Lane Ghost."

"Scratching Fanny?" said Worth, smiling thinly.

"Indeed." Holmes turned to me. "Are you familiar with the case, Watson?"

I considered this for a moment. "Not that I can recall. Should I be?"

"As a man of letters, Watson, you might have caught mention of it in some of Dickens' work, as he was quite taken with the tale. [4] It is a long and sordid account, regarding how one Fanny Lynes supposedly returned from the dead. in order to accuse her lover William Kent of poisoning her with arsenic. It drew great crowds to Cock Lane, but was eventually proven – by a committee composed of Dr. Samuel Johnson and others – to be a trick played in revenge by the daughter of Kent's landlord." Holmes turned back to Worth. "Or do you doubt the conclusion to that case, Mr. Worth?"

"It may surprise you to learn, Mr. Holmes, that we in the Ghost Club are not credulous fools. We know that there are more Fox

396

Sisters out there. [5] We take our work earnestly, and are fully cognizant of the fact that false sightings do terrible damage to our cause. They tend to induce people to empty the baby out with the bath, metaphorically-speaking. In fact, one of my first assignments with the Club was to help debunk the spirit cabinet of the Davenport Brothers. However, I also investigated the Brown Lady of Raynham Hall, and I could find nothing that would contradict the notion that the spirit of Lady Dorothy Walpole still walks those halls." [6]

"And the residence of Sir Randolph?" asked Holmes. "What have you concluded from your investigation within?"

A grave look appeared upon Worth's face. "It is a most serious matter, Mr. Holmes. I went round to Barclay Square first thing this morning and inspected the attic chamber. I also questioned all of the residents, as well as the servants. I assure you that the reports were unanimous regarding the sounds of unholy revelry that were heard to issue from the attic last night. This is the genuine article."

"Revelry? I thought Mr. Cannon was under the impression that it was his wife who has crossed the pale, and come back to haunt her father's home? She seems an unlikely sort to be engaged in a loud festivity, does she not? I would think moans, and perhaps chains to rattle, would be more along her line."

Worth's eyes narrowed. "Perchance you would be of another mind if you learned that Mrs. Cannon died shortly after a soiree thrown in celebration of her daughter's birth?"

Holmes shrugged. "No, I assure you that such a snippet of information does not alter my opinion of the case one iota."

"And yet, I find it rather compelling, Mr. Holmes. Mrs. Cannon has returned from the Beyond for some reason. It is our job to determine the nature of her message."

"Why can she not simply tell it to us? Why make us guess?"

Worth shook his head. "I cannot pretend to understand the laws that govern how the universe functions, Mr. Holmes. I only know that – in every case I have investigated – the ghost in question is barred from direct communication."

Holmes snorted derisively. "That seems to be rather opportune for the medium. If I was inventing such a thing, I too would place strict rules upon who is allowed to converse with the dead."

"So you believe it to all be faked, do you, Mr. Holmes? You do not admit to even the slightest possibility of real ghosts?" asked Worth, reasonably. "I find that most of mankind may disagree with you. It seems to me that there are two sorts of men. There are those who at least admit the chance of the existence of ghosts, and who would make some effort to witness one. And then there are those who profess to not believe, but whom are in secret mortally afraid of them."

Holmes chuckled at this modest insult. "Perhaps I am a third sort? I find that there are inherent contradictions which make their existence exceptionally implausible."

"Such as?" asked Worth, frowning.

"For example," said Holmes, "I put to you the question: Are ghosts insubstantial?"

The ghost hunter nodded. "All ghost-hunters agree that is the case. There are many reports of them being able to pass through solid objects, even people."

"And yet they can also slam doors shut and throw objects across rooms? To be able to do so would suggest that they are, in fact, material. Unfortunately, the law of physics is such that it must be one or the other. Nothing can exist in both states."

"I appreciate your attempt to explain the essence of ghosts in scientific terms, Mr. Holmes, I really do. You are a one of those folks who only believes in what you can touch – *quod tango credo*. Someone who walks in the narrow path of certain fact, and this is quite reasonable given your profession, I suppose. However, that does not rule out the possibility of the unseen and the supernatural. Things beyond the currently understood laws of nature."

"Then what *are* your ghosts composed of, Mr. Worth?"

"The common supposition is that they are spirits of the dead who have gotten lost on their way to the Afterlife. All of the great religions of the world tell us that when a man dies, he casts off all the cares and troubles of the world and becomes a pure and ethereal spirit. But it is not possible that a man – or woman, mind you – could be harried from this world with his soul steeped with some single all-absorbing passion, such that it clings to him even after he has passed the portals of the grave?"

"Human souls, then?" asked Holmes.

"If you will."

"And yet they wear clothes? And carry canes? And what of the supposed ghost-animals or ghost-carriages? Does a train have a soul, Mr. Worth?"

"Now you mock me, sir," said Worth, heatedly.

"Not at all. You share your beliefs with many illustrious sorts. Even the Bard himself made much use of ghosts. The murdered victims of Richard III returned to torment him on the eve of his death. Macbeth was haunted by the ghost of murdered Banquo. And without the prompting of his father's ghost, Hamlet would never have been set upon the path to his destruction."

"Those tales all ended poorly, Mr. Holmes. Do you fear something untoward happening to Sir Randolph?"

Holmes shrugged. "That is precisely what I intend to discover. A good day to you, Mr. Worth."

Upon our exit from the house, I deduced that Holmes had seen enough of the Underground on this gloomy day, for he promptly engaged a black hansom cab to take us from Kensington to Mayfair.

"You are rather quiet, Watson," noted Holmes as we rode. "Upon what are you reflecting?"

I shook my head. "I am concerned, Holmes, that you are proceeding counter to your typical methods."

"What do you mean?" asked he, sharply.

"Rather than waiting for fuller knowledge of the facts of the matter and avoiding the formation of a provisional theory, in this instance, you do not appear to give any credence to the possibility of a genuine haunting."

"Surely, Watson, you do not think there is anything to the ideas of Mr. Worth?"

"I will admit, Holmes, that I find his theories intriguing. Certainly, I was taken by the idea of a ghost emerging when a person perishes while still possessed by a deep passion. This need not solely be dark feelings of hatred or revenge, but also love, or patriotism, or some other pure and elevating passion. I could imagine such things – even after death – obstructing the poor soul, so that it cannot pass onto the other side. This would account for the many unexplainable things which have happened even in our own time, and for the deeply rooted belief in ghosts which has existed in every age. Odysseus consulted the ghost of Achilles. Pliny the Younger tells of a villa in Athens haunted until the bones of an old man bound with chains were found buried in the courtyard and properly interred. As far back as tales go, the idea has persisted. Can so many be wrong?"

"You will again accuse me of a monstrous egotism, Watson, when I say – with confidence – that yes, so many can indeed be wrong. There is a madness in crowds. Take the South Sea Bubble, for example. The Railway Mania, the various 'witch' trials, even the poor souls wanting to join the Red-Headed League." [7]

"'*I can calculate the movement of the stars, but not the madness of men.*'"

Holmes smiled. "Precisely, Watson. Newton is always pithy."

"I still think it possible that a psychic residue could remain after a particularly tragic death."

He shook his head. "I, for one, refuse to subscribe to the dogma of purgatory – souls forced to wander the earth for eternity. There is no sound rationalistic principle to support such a fantasy."

"Then what happens to us after we perish, Holmes?" I asked. "Are we simply dust and shadow? Is there nothing eternal?"

He was silent for a moment. "No one knows the answer to that, Watson. Anyone who says otherwise is a liar or a fool. We all have to wait until we cross over to that Undiscovered Country."

"But surely you must believe in something?"

He shrugged. "I find the standard version, derived as it is from the Greek Hades and Elysian Fields, unsatisfying. If pressed, I suppose I would say that my time with the Great Lama has made it such that I consider the Buddhist concept of eternal re-birth to be the most convincing explanation. Though, secretly, I hope that Poetic Edda is correct. I think that some humble corner of Valhalla sounds like a pleasant place in which to pass eternity."

My eyes narrowed. "Are you mocking me, Holmes?"

"Certainly not, Watson!" said he, his eyebrows rising in surprise. "I would assume that you will join me there! You, too, have fought your fair share of battles."

I shook my head in dismay at Holmes's flippant tone and, instead of conversation, settled for staring grimly out of the window into the darkening evening.

The driver deposited us next to a lamplighter, who was just extracting his pole from the street light situated immediately in front of our destination. Like many such residences in the area, No. 100 Barclay Square was set off from the pavement by a small wrought-iron fence. I had half-expected some tumbledown old pile, with a garden choked up by rank weeds and girt round by pools of stagnant water. Instead, it proved to be a tidy, four-story, flat-roofed Mayfair townhouse, constructed of white-grey Portland stone. A series of small flues poked out above, suggesting multiple fireplaces within. The ground floor had a solid black door flanked by two windows, while a small balcony ran along the length of the first floor. However, it was the highest windows which attracted my attention.

"Holmes!" I exclaimed. "The attic windows are bricked up!"

"Indeed, Watson," he replied, studying the front of the house carefully. "That is certainly suggestive."

"Of what?"

"That the legend of the haunted attic is – as Mr. Cannon noted – not a new one. The tales of the house's ghost must be deeply ingrained in all who reside or work here."

"Surely you don't suspect one of the servants of faking the ghost?"

"Why ever not, Watson? It is a perfectly valid explanation for what Mr. Cannon described."

"Why would a servant want to do such a thing?"

He shook his head. "Now you are asking me to theorize in advance of the facts, Watson. Let us first examine the members of the household."

As we climbed the steps, the front door was opened by Mr. Cannon himself. He expressed his gratitude for our visit, and said that he would take us up to see Sir Randolph immediately. He showed us into a great, gray-curtained study. There the eminent jurist awaited us, as aloof, self-contained, and remote as a ruin in a desert. Cannon excused himself so that we could consider Sir Randolph's independent opinion of the matter at hand.

Sir Randolph glared at Holmes. "I have heard good things about you, Mr. Holmes, from Lord Holdhurst. I am surprised to find you wasting your time with such nonsense."

Holmes raised his dark eyebrows with interest. "So, you do not accept a supernatural explanation for the events transpiring in your residence?"

"Balderdash!" the judge exclaimed. "Of course, that was the conclusion of the charlatan we had by earlier."

"Do you refer to Mr. Worth?"

"A credulous fool. Let me tell you something, Mr. Holmes. I have heard a great many terrible things in my forty years upon the bench, and I have sent many a worthy cad to face Jack Ketch. If ghosts were real, it would be one of them haunting my every step. Not my poor Dorothy! She was the treasure of my life."

"But you did hear something the last two nights?"

"Of course!" he cried. "A deaf man could have heard them!"

"And what do you propose it was?"

"It was my mother!" a voice suddenly exclaimed.

Holmes and I turned and found that a young girl had entered the room. She was a striking lass, pale-faced and dark-haired, with piercing, ice-blue eyes. This could only be Mr. Cannon's daughter, Penelope. Her cheeks were red with embarrassment.

"Little girls are meant to be seen and not heard!" Sir Randolph thundered.

Penelope's eyes widened in alarm, and she turned and fled.

"I apologize for my grand-daughter, gentlemen. Cannon is not a bad chap, but he is hardly a replacement for Dorothy. The girl has grown up without a mother, surrounded by moldy books and impractical professors. Hence, she has little sense of proper decorum."

"Hmm, yes, I can see that," murmured Holmes.

"In any case," Sir Randolph continued, "there can be no truth to these ghostly rumors. It is a hoax of some sort, I tell you."

"I share your opinion of the matter, and intend to prove it. With your permission, I would like to have a word with your housekeeper."

"Mrs. Bosworth? Why ever do you need to speak to her?"

"I assure you, Sir Randolph, that I intend to investigate this case with the same thoroughness that I do any other. I would be a poor detective if I failed to interview all the potential witnesses."

"Very well," the judge agreed.

"And afterwards, I take it I have your permission to examine the attic room? If so, I will ask Mrs. Bosworth to show it to us. No, no need to get up. I am sure we can find her without difficulty."

Taking our leave from Sir Randolph, we made our way back into the hall. I assumed that Holmes would head for the lower levels in order to locate Mrs. Bosworth, but to my surprise he stopped in his tracks.

He stood there quietly for a minute and then smiled. "You may come out now, Penelope," he called.

Moments later, the little girl that we had briefly seen in the study appeared from behind one of the pillars. "Yes, sir?" said she, shyly.

"You are a clever girl, Penelope. Most people would never have sensed you hiding behind that pillar."

Her eyebrows rose with interest. "How did you do it then?"

"I am not most people." He pointed at a gas jet upon the wall. "That light casts a shadow, and the edge of the pillar was not as straight as it should have been. In fact, it was decidedly curved, much like a human form."

She shrugged. "It might have been a servant."

"Are your grandfather's servants in the habit of hiding behind pillars?"

She considered this for a moment. "No, I suppose not. Mrs. Bosworth wouldn't fit behind a pillar. And Wooten would never think of such a thing."

"Who is Mr. Wooten?"

"My grandfather's butler. He's almost a hundred years old, and has no sense of humor whatsoever."

"And the other servants?" Holmes asked.

She shrugged. "There is a charwoman who comes in early in the morning to light fires, clean boots, and scrub the front steps."

Holmes's eyebrows rose in surprise. "No valet?"

She shook her head. "My grandfather prefers to do those tasks himself."

"Surely a secretary?"

"There is Simon, who comes round from Westminster on days when grandfather doesn't go in, but he doesn't live here."

"So there you go, Penelope," said Holmes, spreading out his hands. "With so few others in the house, who else could it have been?"

"It might have been the ghost!"

"Do ghosts cast shadows?" asked Holmes.

She frowned as she thought about this question. "I don't know. The stories never mention it one way or the other."

"What stories, my dear?"

"Well, there is Mr. Dickens' signal-man. [8] That's a mighty fine tale. Or the ones my daddy's friend from Cambridge likes to tell. Whenever he comes over for supper, afterwards Mr. James tells me all about ghosts and goblins, as well as haunted fields, brooks, bridges, and houses. He knows about direful omens and portentous sights and sounds in the air, and frightens me so with speculations upon comets and shooting stars." [9]

Holmes smiled. "I see. Very good, Penelope. You have been most helpful. I hope to talk with you more later."

"Goodbye, sir," said she with a curtsy, before departing.

Holmes watched her go for a moment and then turned to me. "Most instructive, wouldn't you say, Watson?"

"I suppose so, Holmes. It is odd that Sir Randolph has such a limited staff."

"Hmm, indeed. Well, let us go find Mrs. Bosworth and see what she has to say about the matter."

We found her in the look-out cellar kitchen. As Penelope had suggested, the comfortable-looking Mrs. Bosworth would not have fit behind one of the pillars in the upper hall. After Holmes had introduced himself and explained his purpose in the house, the housekeeper consented to an interview.

"Now, then, Mrs. Bosworth, you have been with Sir Randolph for how long?" asked Holmes.

"Eighteen years."

"And has your employment been a satisfactory one?"

She pursed her lips as she considered this question. "I would reckon so. Sir Randolph is a stern man, but very fair. If you do your job well, he notices and appreciates it."

"And if you do not do your job well?"

"Then your term in this house is limited," said she, with grim finality.

"It must be a lonely house, with just Sir Randolph and the butler?"

"We used to have more, but with just Sir Randolph residing here now, the needs are less. Wooten is a fine cribbage player, and Sir Randolph generously permits me two evenings out with my friends every week. That is sufficient for me."

"Surely it was once more gay, back when Sir Randolph's daughter was alive?"

Mrs. Bosworth's face fell and a glisten appeared in her eyes. "You are correct, sir. Miss Dorothy was the apple of Sir Randolph's eye. And after she died, not two months later, Lady Russell was carried off by a apoplexy." She shook her head sadly. "I always thought that Lady Russell died from sadness."

"Ah, so the appearance of Penelope was the herald of two other deaths?"

"You can't blame the poor lass, Mr. Holmes! She was just a little baby! She is a good girl, mayhaps a touch different. But who can fault her, raised as she has been by her father and a bunch of eccentric old professors?"

"And what is your opinion of the attic ghost?"

She peered at Holmes. "Call me a fool, if you will, but I have heard it with my own ears."

"Since when?"

"Since the day I came to work for Sir Randolph."

Holmes's eyebrows rose with surprise. "Truly?"

"Everyone knows that this house attracts spirits. For a while it bothered me. One of the neighbors told me that a maid had slept in the attic room and was found mad the following morning. An old waiting-maid of Lady Russell's told me that a young man had once been locked in that room, fed only through a hole in the door, until he went mad and died." She shook her head. "After some time, I realized that neither I – nor anyone I knew – was being bothered by

404

the ghosts, and I suppose I simply got used to the noises. Like the passing of the hansom cabs in the street outside."

Holmes smiled and nodded. "You have been most helpful, Mrs. Bosworth. I would very much like to inspect the attic room before it draws much later. I suppose it is locked?"

"Of course. I possess the only key. Sir Randolph is most adamant that no one is to ever enter, though he earlier gave permission to that Worth fellow, so I suppose you two can also take a look. Make sure you bring the key right back, mind you. And you best take a torch, or you won't see much."

Acquiring the suggested item from a storage closet, Holmes and I found our way up the staircase which led to the attic. As we walked, I asked Holmes why we had not questioned the butler Wooten.

He shook his head. "That would be a waste of time, Watson. You heard Penelope's characterization of the man. Even if – with the carelessness of youth – she exaggerated his age, Penelope noted that he was completely devoid of humor. The young can be surprisingly perceptive, Watson. I doubt such a man would be capable of manipulating such a hoax."

"So you still think it is all a fraud?"

"Let us say that my views upon the matter have begun to shift. I think an inspection of the troubled garret will prove to be informative."

The entrance to that room was located at the right hand landing of the lofty staircase's top floor. The massive oaken door was secured by a padlock. A gas jet was set in the wall next to the door, and its flame shone a fair amount of light into the otherwise dark corner.

As Holmes bent to insert the key, he nodded in the direction of the door. "Observe, Watson, the lack of a hole through which Mrs. Bosworth's mythical young man was fed."

"The door might have been replaced."

Holmes finished removing the padlock, and knocked upon the stout wood. "These houses around Barclay Square were built about a hundred years ago. I suspect this door is no younger."

He pushed open the door and we caught our first glimpse of the terrible place beyond. The room was bare and unfurnished, save only a dilapidated wicker chair. It was a place of undisturbed solitude and darkness. As I had noted upon our arrival, the room was entirely cut off from the light of the outer world by the bricking up of its solitary window. I was about to set foot inside, when Holmes barred the way with his hand.

"Hold a minute, Watson. Although I would recognize your footprint anywhere, it will be easier to observe the dust upon the floor if only one of us enters."

He trotted carefully into the room and – much like the night of our very first adventure together in the Lauriston Gardens – he proceeded to examine the room with the utmost of care. Once his inspection of the floor and chair was complete, he used his tape to measure the walls, and then tapped upon each one with his loaded hunting-crop. Finally, he replaced his glass and tape in his pocket and turned back to me.

"Did you fancy sleeping in your own bed tonight, Watson?" he asked with a smile.

I frowned in confusion. "I was unaware that there is somewhere else I need to be?"

"Yes, your assistance will be invaluable. For we are going to pass the night in this haunted house. And by morning, we shall either have solved the mystery of its spirits, or we shall ourselves – perhaps – be mad."

After he replaced the door's padlock, I followed Holmes back down to the study, where he explained his plan to Sir Randolph and Mr. Cannon.

"This is most irregular, sir," the jurist protested.

"I assure you, Sir Randolph, that this is the only way to get to the bottom of the matter. Either your house is truly haunted, or someone is playing a cruel trick upon you. Send Mrs. Bosworth and Mr. Wooten to a local hotel for the night. That will remove them from the equation. I will then personally go around and ensure that there are no secret modes of ingress by which an external party might enter the house undetected. Once we are alone in the house, I shall bunk in with you, while Dr. Watson will reside with Mr. Cannon. It is hardly the first time that he and I have held a long sleepless vigil through the night."

Cannon shook his head. "What of Penelope?"

"We shall make certain that she has everything she requires and then – for her own safety – we shall lock her within her room."

Cannon looked troubled at this plan, but Sir Randolph appeared to have been won over. "It is a sound strategy, Mr. Holmes, for proving that this is all claptrap. But when there are no noises tonight, how will we determine the identity of this hoax's perpetrator?"

406

Holmes smiled. "I assure you, sir, that I too have considered that very question. I will explain further in the morning if the expected course comes to pass."

Sir Randolph rang for his butler and housekeeper, while Mr. Cannon went to inform Penelope of the situation for the evening. Meanwhile, I drew Holmes aside.

"I thought you had excluded the butler, Holmes. So you must suspect that Mrs. Bosworth is involved? But what could be her motive?"

"Ah!" exclaimed Holmes. "That is exactly the question that I asked myself some time ago, Watson. It is the question that shines light where everything else is dark." He nodded. "You will see soon enough, if I am not mistaken. But keep an eye on Mr. Cannon, too, Watson. I have not yet determined whether he is involved in this matter. Oh, and keep that torch. We shall need it later."

He left me to inspect the house, while I pondered his words. I knew Holmes suspected a human agency rather than some force from outside our narrow understanding of the world. However, I could not be so certain. Mrs. Bosworth seemed an unlikely perpetrator, and in any case, she had been banished from the house along with the butler. I was certain that Peter Cannon firmly believed the spirit of his wife had returned from beyond the grave, and it was inconceivable that Sir Randolph himself was involved. Holmes was not infallible. He had been beaten at least four times by men – as well as a woman. Surely his prejudices against the spiritual world could be blinding him to the possibility that the long-standing tales of this house were actually based in fact?

And thus it was with a dreadful foreboding that I settled into my night watch. Mr. Cannon attempted to read, but I saw him nodding off several times. I, for one, was able to wait silently without signs of flagging. Hours by Holmes's side had trained me well. I had pulled out my pocket watch and noted that midnight had just passed when I heard the noise. It was very clearly the sound of a chair being moved, followed by the rattling of chains. Even if I had suspected the unlikely involvement of Holmes or Sir Randolph, I knew these sounds were not coming from the neighboring bedroom. They were coming from the floor above, where no being resided!

And then came a sound which chilled me to my bones. It was the sound of a human voice, but one distorted beyond one's ken. I could almost make out the words, though the deep roar made it impossible to be certain. The only thing I knew was that it was it was not the voice of a living human being. This horrible sound cut off as quickly as it began, only to be replaced by the chair moving again.

Cannon had startled awake and looked at me with wide eyes. "Now do you believe, Dr. Watson?" he gasped. "My Dorothy has returned."

I sprang to my feet and raced for the door. Throwing it open, I stumbled into the hallway at the same time as Holmes.

He looked at me with a deep exhilaration in his eyes. "Watson!" he yelled. "To the attic!"

Sir Randolph and Mr. Cannon had followed us into the hall, and Mr. Cannon moved towards Penelope's door. But Holmes forestalled him. "No, Mr. Cannon, hold a minute. If she had been awakened by the sounds, she would have cried out in terror. We heard nothing, so she is safe. Follow me, if you please."

Holmes led the way up the stairs back to the padlocked door. He rapidly opened the lock with the key which he had retained from earlier, and then he threw open the door. I shone my torch inside, but there was no one to be seen, nor any chains to make that ratting noise. The only thing of note was that the chair had plainly moved from its last location, and was now closer to the far wall. I knew that Holmes had not moved the chair in this locked room, so who had? A shiver passed down my spine.

After Sir Randolph and Mr. Cannon had silently inspected the room from the doorway, Holmes indicated that we should repair back down to the study. However, on the way, he stopped in front of Penelope's door. "I think we should have your daughter join us, Mr. Cannon. Would you unlock the door, please?"

Cannon nodded and did as Holmes instructed. Cannon went inside to rouse Penelope from her bed while Holmes followed him, presumably to ensure her safety. When the two of them returned with the little girl, Holmes wore a satisfied smile upon his face.

The five of us had settled into the study. Sir Randolph took his accustomed arm-chair, I sat in the chair across from him, and Cannon and his daughter took the sofa. Holmes refused a seat and began to pace up and down the Persian rug.

"Your situation is, to my knowledge, unique amongst all others which have come before me," said Holmes. "I have investigated countless cases and never seen its like."

"So you admit the possibility of a ghost?" exclaimed Mr. Cannon.

"I thought you did not believe in the possibility of the supernatural, Holmes," said I.

He turned his piercing gaze upon me. "That was true, Watson. However, this case has forced me to question those assumptions. First, when we inspected the attic room, both this evening and just now, I noted the complete absence of footprints in the dust. Therefore, we must ask ourselves how the chair was moved. Furthermore, the sound of chains was very clear, and yet I can say with confidence that there are no chains in that room."

Sir Randolph appeared much upset. "I cannot believe it, Mr. Holmes! Do you mean that the ghost is real?"

Holmes pursed his lips. "I can wholeheartedly assure you, Sir Randolph, that there was no man behind the noises emanating from the attic. In fact, I sense that the spirit behind these apparitions is with us still. It will not rest until it has achieved its goal."

"I shall leave the house at once!"

Holmes shook his head. "I assure you, sir, that this spirit is not confined to the house. It will follow you wherever you go."

"Then what should I do?" said he, his voice trembling with dismay.

"I would ask yourself . . . *what does the spirit want?*" said Holmes, severely. "What mistake could you have made in order to have awoken this spirit? Only then will you find peace."

"I do not know!" the jurist wailed.

"Mr. Cannon and your granddaughter believe this to be the returned spirit of Dorothy. If this is indeed the ghost of your daughter, would she be happy to see you shun your own blood?"

Sir Randolph's face quivered and his eyes moistened. He sat there for a moment in silence and then turned to Penelope, his hands outstretched. The little girl shyly moved over to him, and he wrapped her in his arms. Knowing that the great judge would not wish for strangers such as Holmes and I to witness this private reconciliation, it was clear that it was time for us to depart. I sincerely hoped that this small action would sanction a final rest for Dorothy's ghost.

As we sat in the hansom back to Baker Street, I shook my head in wonderment. "Holmes, I am thoroughly amazed. I never thought to see you admit to the presence of a ghost."

He looked at me sharply. "Who said anything about a ghost, Watson?"

I frowned in confusion. "Well, you did."

Holmes shook his head. "In point of fact, Watson, I did not. I told Sir Randolph that a spirit that was behind the sounds, and in so doing I spoke the literal truth. However, I never claimed that said spirit had ventured from another plane of existence. Do not you and I have a spirit that distinguishes us from the animals?"

"But you and I watched Sir Randolph and Mr. Cannon the entire time!" I protested. "There was no one else in the house!"

"Watson, you have made the same mistake as Sir Randolph. You have overlooked the most obvious spirit of them all. The spirit of a little girl who has never received an ounce of love from her grandfather because she – through no fault of her own – was the instrument of her mother and grandmother's demise." He reached over and deposited a long strand of dark silk into my hands.

"Penelope!"

"Indeed."

"I don't understand," I exclaimed.

"It is simple, Watson. Like all investigations, this case boiled down to means and motive. The means was relatively easy to determine. First, that room was locked with a single key, which never left the possession of Mrs. Bosworth. And yet, someone was making noises within. Therefore, there must have been a second entrance. When we stood outside the house, you pointed out the bricked-up window. However, I was estimating the width of the building. Once I measured the attic room, I knew that there must be a secret door, a fact I confirmed with my series of knockings upon the wall. I did not bother to trace the passage behind, but I deduced that it led down to Penelope's room. I can only assume it was built upon the orders of one of the first owners – perhaps as a method to facilitate assignations with one of the maids – and the curious Penelope accidentally discovered the other side of the passage."

"I am amazed, Holmes. What else made you suspect a human agency?"

"Second, for a room that was never visited, it was shockingly free of any dust upon the floor. Penelope must have swept it regularly in order to mask any signs of her visits."

"But the chains?"

"Hidden behind the secret door, and rattled after she tugged upon that monofilament string, the other end of which was tied to the chair. As I little desired to disrupt her show, I cannot say with certainly. However, I suspect that she tied the chair with a highwayman's hitch or thief's knot, in order to facilitate the rapid untying of the string, should someone investigate either the attic room or her own whereabouts. I found that silken strand in her room and removed it as a souvenir, especially since she will not be needing it any longer."

"So her 'haunting' career is over?"

"Of course, Watson. Penelope has achieved what she desired. Her grandfather has stopped unreasonably blaming her for causing the death of her mother and grandmother. I told you that the motive was the key. Once I knew what the perpetrator wanted, her identity was plain."

I considered this for a moment and then realized the error in his conclusions. "But the horrible voice! Surely, Holmes, little Penelope did not make that noise!"

He smiled wanly. "I confess that I didn't expect that. Even though Mr. Cannon had warned us, I didn't believe it until I heard it with my own ears and – for a moment – I was frozen in my seat. Fortunately, my time in Lhassa gave me the answer."

"What? How can your travels in Tibet have anything to do with it?"

"The monks there have fostered a rather unique form of chanting – though I have determined that it can also be found amongst the Tuvan people of Siberia – in which the singers develop the ability to create sounds from their vestibular folds."

"The false vocal cords!" I exclaimed.

"Indeed. I must admit, Watson, that earlier today, I was starting to think that I had seen it all. Fortunately, Penelope made me realize that there are still surprises in the world."

I shook my head. "But you said that today forced you to question the possibility of the supernatural!" I protested.

"And so it did. For a brief moment, I questioned it. And then I realized that there was a far more human reason for those sounds. We spoke before of Shakespeare, did we not, Watson? Many years ago, before I settled into my chosen profession, I performed the Danish play in Chicago and in New York. I recall how the stage manager had borrowed Henry Irving's idea of burning limelight in order to magnify the ghost's otherworldliness. And even then I was struck by the ghost's power. If the deceased king had not incited Hamlet to move against his uncle, the entire tragic chain of events might have unfolded far differently. Did Shakespeare believe in actual ghosts, or was he merely using it as a symbol of Hamlet's secret regrets? If I may be excused for once more paraphrasing the Bard, men often make their own ghosts from the wicked deeds or intents within their hearts. [10] Surely such was the case of Sir Randolph, don't you think, Watson? Thankfully – due to the actions of a clever little girl – it can certainly be hoped that Sir Randolph will henceforth conduct his life filled with a more charitable spirit."

NOTES

1 – There is no "Barclay Square" in London, though Admiral Sinclair is also said to have a home at that locale. ("The Adventure of the Bruce-Partington Plans").

2 – All Soul's Day is celebrated on 2 November.

3 – Unfortunately, Watson neglected to write up any cases which included a Gascon lieutenant, someone dying at the Great Geysir of Iceland (upon land owned by Lord Craigavon), a Ghazi's scimitar-like weapon, or a cipher belonging to one of the rival factions in the politics of medieval Italy.

4 – The Cock Lane Ghost was mentioned in both *Nicholas Nickleby* (1839) and *A Tale of Two Cities* (1859).

5 – The Fox Sisters were American girls who began to report ghostly rappings in 1848, when they were twelve and fifteen years of age. They eventually became spiritualist mediums, eventually confessing to faking everything in 1888.

6 – The Davenport Brothers were American magicians who claimed to possess a cabinet filled with musical instruments which were played by spirits of the dead. They were debunked in the 1870's while touring in England. The ghost of Lady Dorothy Walpole (1686-1726) has been reported by many individuals to wander the halls of Raynham Hall since as early 1835.

7 – The South Sea Bubble (1720) was one of the earliest stock market crashes, and the Railway Mania (1846) was another collapse which occurred closer to the Victoria era. Various witch trials, such as the one in Salem (1692) resulted in the deaths of some forty-thousand women over a period of three centuries. The last "witch" in Scotland was executed in 1727.

8 – Clearly a reference to his 1866 short story, "The Signal-Man", about a railway monitor who is haunted by a phantom warning him of impending disasters.

9 – Montague Rhodes James (1862-1936) was an English author, most famous for his ghost stories. The first collection, *Ghost Stories of an Antiquary*, was published in 1904. He lived for many years, as an undergraduate, don, and provost, at King's College, Cambridge.

10 – "Angels, and ministers of grace, defend us! / Be thou a spirit of health, or goblin damn'd. / Bring with thee airs from heaven, or blasts from hell. /

Be thy intents wicked or charitable. / Thou com'st in such a questionable shape, / That I will speak to thee." (*Hamlet*, 1.4).

The Adventure of the Theatre Ghost
by Jeremy Branton Holstein

I

If there is one truth that I have discovered throughout my years of accompanying Sherlock Holmes on his many adventures, it is that he is a gentleman of many contradictions. While capable of differentiating between over two-hundred different types of tobacco ash, he is ignorant of the fact that the Earth moves around the Sun, as he deems the knowledge superfluous to his chosen career. He is the wisest man I have ever known, yet has foolishly made himself slave to cocaine's needle. It is these same contradictions, maddening though they are to his chronicler, that make Holmes the most brilliant detective of his age, able to find light amidst the densest darkness, to find the truth lost in the most tangled forest of deceptions.

I can recall no more vivid demonstration of these contradictions than the affair of the Charing Cross theatre ghost, an adventure which exposed me to a period of my good friend's history that had previously been unknown to me.

It was the autumn of 1901, and I was still living in my old rooms at Baker Street. Holmes's fame as a consulting detective was at its peak, and he was able to choose which cases he would accept, as his attentions were always in great demand from both the highest and lowest in the land. His name was even now being immortalized on the stage, as the American actor William Gillette had opened an adaptation of some of Holmes's earliest adventures at the Lyceum Theatre to some critical acclaim. I was sitting in my armchair, studying an advertisement for the production in *The Strand* magazine, when Holmes's voice broke into my thoughts.

"The answer is no, Watson," said Holmes.

"But why not?" I said. "Surely it would be an honor to see yourself – " I stopped in mid-sentence. "Now, really, Holmes. How did you know what I was thinking?"

"We have known each other for over twenty years, Watson. Surely you are familiar with my methods by now. As for the theatrical production, I simply see no point in subjecting myself to

414

seeing my methods of scientific deduction transformed on the stage into the very lowest form of melodrama."

"The play is quite popular," I said. "I'm surprised the theatre has not issued you an invitation."

"They did," said Holmes. "I refused it."

"But why?" I asked.

"Because," said Holmes, "unlike yourself, Doctor, I neither seek nor desire accolades for my profession. The work itself is my own reward."

Before I could argue this point, the door to our study opened and Mrs. Hudson entered.

"A foreign gentleman to see you, Mr. Holmes," she said, holding a small piece of cardboard at arm's length. "His card."

Holmes took up the card from Mrs. Hudson, glanced at it, and handed it over to me. "We seem to be practically swimming in Americans today," he said.

I looked at the card. There was only a single name printed upon its surface, in large bold letters, no address or title. "'*William Hodge*'," I read aloud, and frowned. "The industrialist? I did not know he was in London."

"Nor did I, which is both unusual and curious," said Holmes. "Show the gentleman in, Mrs. Hudson."

"Yes, Mr. Holmes," said Mrs. Hudson, and departed. A moment later she ushered Mr. Hodge into our sitting room.

William Hodge was a small, yet extremely sturdy man whose slicked back hair and thin mustache belied his reputation for ruthlessness. Dressed in the sombre formal-wear adopted by so many of our American cousins, he eyed the room and its clutter with obvious distaste.

"Which of you is Holmes?" he asked.

"My name, sir," said Holmes.

Hodge ran his eyes appraisingly up and down my friend before turning his burning gaze to me. "Which would make you Doctor Watson," he said. "I've read your stories in *Harper's*, Doctor, but I must say, neither of you looks anything like the illustrations."

Holmes laughed. "I cannot control my portrayal by the American illustrators," he said, "nor the way that the doctor romanticizes my investigations. I fancy I might try recording a case myself one day, if only to finally see an accurate portrayal of my methods. Now, what brings you to Baker Street, Mr. Hodge?"

"Aren't you going to do it?" asked Hodge.

"Do what, pray tell?" asked Holmes.

"That trick of yours," said Hodge. "That one where you look me up and down and tell me everything about my history."

"Hardly necessary," said Holmes. "Your family history has been covered at length in the press. I know that you are roughly thirty-two years old, born in London but shipped by your father to an American boarding school at a young age. That exile to America has apparently served you well, as you have thrived into a successful businessman whose reputation for ruthlessness is somewhat offset by your occasional bursts of charity. I did not know that you were here in England, an oversight in my intelligence gathering that I shall have to correct, although I can deduce that you arrived here yesterday on the steamer *Essex*, checked into the Hotel Metropole, and have since visited the site of a fire. It is logical to assume that this fire was the reason for your abrupt voyage across the Atlantic, so, given the timeframe, I must assume that the site you visited was the Icarus Theatre, which suffered a catastrophic fire only two weeks ago."

Hodge burst out with a cry that soon changed to laughter. "Very good," he said. "No doubt there are traces of ash on my boot, and I must not have pushed the receipt for the Metropole deep enough into my pocket. My history is, as you say, a matter of public record. But how in thunder did you know about the *Essex*? Unless, of course, you've memorized the comings and goings of international ships."

Holmes smiled. "Well, Doctor," he said. "It would seem that your stories have not been entirely in vain. You are quite correct, Mr. Hodge. I must compliment you on your deductions."

"One does not get to where I am in business without a decent head on your shoulders," said Hodge. "And you, Mr. Holmes, seem to have quite a decent head as well. You'll do."

I became angry at Hodge's presumptuous manner, but Holmes, knowing my tempers when I thought him mistreated, warned me off with a glance. "Gratified that I am to hear your approval of my methods," said Holmes, "I cannot help but wonder what it is that's brought you across the Atlantic and, finally, to our door in Baker Street."

"It's very simple, Mr. Holmes," said Hodge. "I want you to get rid of my father."

II

"Surely you misspoke," I said, in disbelief.

"Not at all, Doctor," said Hodge. "My father continues to be a thorn in my side, even after that damnable fire."

"Your father is dead then?" said Holmes.

"Oh, very," said Hodge.

"Then I'm afraid you have come to the wrong address, Mr. Hodge," said Holmes. "Watson and I do not trade in the disposal of the dead. Perhaps that Carnacki fellow – "

"I don't want Carnacki!" said Hodge, his voice rising to the steel tones that had assured him success in his chosen field. "I do not want some so-called ghost finder predisposed to the supernatural. I need a man of rational thought, one who will seek a scientific explanation. Do not suppose, sir, that I came here by accident. I chose you, Mr. Holmes, very deliberately."

"Perhaps," I offered, "you might sit down and explain yourself."

William Hodge did as I bade, taking Holmes's own armchair by the fire, and began to speak.

"You are both familiar with the tragedy at the Icarus Theatre?" he said.

"Only what I have read in the papers," said Holmes. "An accidental fire in one of the dressing rooms. There were fatalities."

"Indeed, Mr. Holmes," said Hodge. "But it was not fatalities, only a single death. My father."

"You have my condolences," I offered.

Hodge did not even glance in my direction. "Your summary of my history was quite correct," he said. "I have never truly known my father. My earliest memory is of the man putting me on that damned boat that would take me to America. In that moment, he abdicated both his parental responsibilities and my affection. Yet, despite my misgivings, I cannot deny that my life has been the better for my father's actions. The New World has proved a wealth of opportunity for me, and I have become very rich. Indeed, it has been so good to me that this is my first trip back across the Atlantic since that fateful day."

"You mean to say that you have not seen your father in almost thirty years?" I asked, astonished.

"There seemed no need," said Hodge. "My father had made it quite clear on that day that he wanted nothing to do with me, so I have merely returned the compliment. His letters in the post were enough contact for my taste. Through his missives I have been able to track my father's progress, or, rather, lack thereof."

"We know full well what happened to you after your departure to America," said Holmes. "What became of your father?"

417

Hodge snorted in derision. "My father," he said, "freed of the whelp he had brought into this world, dedicated his remaining life to the arts, specifically the theatre. Together with a troupe of actors, he founded a theatre near Charing Cross, funded by no less esteemed a person than W.S. Gilbert, who, I am told, was my father's childhood friend. It is my understanding that they experienced some modest success before the tragedy."

"Watson," said Holmes, "would you kindly consult my index for any articles on the Icarus?"

Holmes kept an ongoing system of documents for tracking items of interest throughout London and beyond. Despite my complaints that I little understood his filing methods, he continued to ask that I locate and present him information from within. Quite frankly, I think my difficulty in understanding his system amused him, though he would never admit it. After some difficulty I located the article between a rather unique draft of *Hamlet* and a monograph upon a Professor who claimed to have discovered living dinosaurs.

"'*Icarus Theatre*'," I read aloud. "'*Located in Charing Cross between the Lord's Bank and the Snyder Gallery. Built in 1889 through financing from the distinguished lyricist W.S. Gilbert, it has run with some success for more than a decade before a recent fire ravaged the dressing rooms, resulting in the death of its founder, Francis Hodge*'."

"I've come back to England," said Hodge, "to put my father's affairs in order, and to pay my last respects. As my father's only son, it has fallen to me to dispose of his remaining possessions and properties. One of these is the Icarus Theatre itself."

"Admirable," said Holmes, "but not why you are here."

"No," said Hodge. "I am here because of what occurred to me last night when I visited the Icarus."

"Pray," said Holmes, "describe your visit to the theatre. Be precise as to the details."

"It was just as you said, Mr. Holmes," said Hodge. "I arrived only yesterday morning by the steamship *Essex*. I promptly checked into the Hotel Metropole, which, I have been assured, is among the finest in London."

"So they say," said Holmes. "I have, in my career, seen both its glamor and its underside."

"Oh, you've investigated cases at the Metropole?" asked Hodge.

"Nine," said Holmes. "But only two were murder."

"I only have five in my notes," I said.

"Another time, Watson," said Holmes. "Continue, Mr. Hodge."

418

"Very well," said Hodge. "You have already deduced that the Icarus was the second place I visited upon my arrival in London, as my father has long since been buried. I told myself it was to evaluate the property, but I think part of me wanted to see the place where my father met his untimely end. Once I had stowed my luggage at the hotel, I hailed a cab and made my way over to the Icarus to begin my arduous task.

"Arriving in Charing Cross, I was met at the door of the Icarus by its acting manager, one Mr. James Walsh, a most distasteful man. I took an instant dislike of the fellow, as he kept pushing to give me a full tour of the premises. I declined, wanting only to see my father's rooms, but he was most insistent. I could sense his agenda – that if he were able to impress upon me how grandiose an establishment my father had built, he might persuade me to continue the theatre's funding. I knew from my father's recent letters that the Icarus was in difficult financial shape, a situation I had steadfastly chosen to ignore. But now, in the wake of my father's death, I found myself less decisive, less sure how I should proceed. For the sake of my father's memory, I agreed to Mr. Walsh's tour.

"Despite Mr. Walsh's intention to impress, his tour provoked in me the exact opposite reaction. No amount of window dressing or hyperbole could hide the truth: The theatre was dilapidated, in desperate need of repair. Yet none of this seemed to bother Mr. Walsh, whose eyes seemed blinded by love for his art. 'It's a grand building, Mr. Hodge,' he kept saying, over and over as he guided me through the halls. 'We have all put our hearts and souls into this humble stage.'"

"One moment," said Holmes. "Who is the 'all' that Mr. Walsh referred to?"

"My father maintained a troupe of actors under the exclusive employ of the Icarus, a company that would stage various productions under his direction. He mentioned them frequently in his letters. Some of them have worked for the theatre for nigh on a decade."

"Did you meet any of these actors during your tour?"

"I'm afraid not. In the wake of the fire, and the Icarus's uncertain future, many of the actors have departed for other venues, but there are some who remain loyal to my father's memory. Mr. Walsh assured me that we would meet two of that loyal company when we return to tour the Icarus together this afternoon."

"I fear you may be getting ahead of yourself," said Holmes. "I have not yet accepted your case."

"But you will, Mr. Holmes, for I have now reached the most mysterious, the most extraordinary part of my tale."

"Leave the hyperbole to the doctor, Mr. Hodge," said Holmes. "I require only the facts."

"Very well," said Hodge. "I quickly tired of Mr. Walsh's attempts at aggrandizement, and asked for him to show me the dressing room where my father had died. Mr. Walsh could not hide his obvious disappointment in my disinterest, but acceded to my request. He guided me down to the theatre's basement, and into the rear dressing room which still bore my father's name upon the door. Extracting a large keyring, he opened the door beyond.

"The room was charred by fire, but still structurally sound. Singed debris, papers, and clothing were scattered everywhere, with only my father's dressing table, wardrobe, and standing mirror still remaining untouched against the blackened wall.

"'It's just as it was the day Francis died,' said Walsh. 'I hadn't the heart to clean it out just yet. Your father was very dear to me.'

"I asked Mr. Walsh for a moment alone, a request which he granted, assuring me that he would be nearby. I began going through the remains of my father's dressing table, sorting some of his possessions, some clothing, some scraps of paper, when, despite myself I felt a wave of emotion. I fell to the floor, and, for the first time in many years, I cried."

"Perfectly understandable," I said.

"Watson," said Holmes, warning me from further outbursts.

Hodge had seemingly not even noticed my words, so lost was he in his memory. "It was then," he said, "that I heard a voice, a strange, ethereal voice, calling my name. When I opened my eyes again, my father was standing there, not ten feet from me in the corner of the dressing room. But this was not my father as I remembered. This was an apparition, a ghostly image of a man, reaching his thin hand out for me. I shrank back in disbelief. It had been years since I had seen him, and he had grown so very old.

"Good Lord," I said, unable to help myself.

"You may think me mad, Doctor, but I swear every word I tell you is God's honest truth. The apparition who approached me looked more spirit than flesh, yet I'd swear upon my hard won fortune that it had my father's own voice."

"You had not heard your father's voice since childhood," said Holmes. "How can you be sure it was he who spoke?"

"One does not forget the voice of one's father," said Hodge. "I will always remember him ordering me, commanding me, that I was to leave my life in England and be shipped off to America. Those words and the voice which spoke them are forever etched in my memory. It was my father's voice, I'd swear to it."

"It is true, Holmes, that trauma can cement certain sounds or smells within the memory," I offered.

"Very well," said Holmes. "Pray continue."

"'William,' it said. 'William, if you ever bore me love as your father, listen to me. You must not sell this theatre. Men will come to you, will offer you riches, but you must resist. Honor my memory. Honor my request. Know that everything I did was because I loved you.'

"And then, even as I watched, he dimmed into the shadows, as if he were nothing more than a dying candle flame, and disappeared entirely. I ran to where my father had been only moments ago, but the space was now empty, with no sign that my father had ever been standing there. I called out for Mr. Walsh, who soon appeared. Together we searched both the dressing room and the theatre beyond for any sign of the apparition, but, alas, we found nothing."

"Think hard, Mr. Hodge," said Holmes. "You are certain there was nothing? No smells? No sounds? No subtle marks upon the floor?"

"Mr. Holmes, I'm ashamed to say that I felt so overwhelmed by the experience I cannot rightly say."

"Try," said Holmes. "Any details you can provide might prove to have the greatest importance."

Hodge closed his eyes, thinking back. "The room smelled of cinders. The ash crackled under my feet as I walked. There was a faint sound, like the faintest of winds, but I was crying so hard I thought I must have imagined it." Hodge opened his eyes again, and fixed my friend with a gaze of such intensity and need that I felt relieved I was not its focus. "Sir," said Hodge. "I have always prided myself on being level headed, capable of noticing the faintest details. Yet at that moment, my senses and wits deserted me. I felt as lost as I had that day nearly thirty years ago when I boarded the steamship. I have never believed in ghosts, yet I saw my father with my own eyes, heard his voice with my ears. I do not know what to believe anymore, and so I turn to you. Can you help me?"

Holmes sat silently in his chair, his fingers tented before his face in deep thought. It was this lack of response from Holmes that drove many of his visitors mad with impatience, yet I knew from experience it meant he was pondering the merits of his potential client's case.

"How quickly did Mr. Walsh respond to your cries for help?" asked Holmes at last.

"Within a minute," said Hodge. "He must have been quite close."

"And what are your intentions toward the Icarus Theatre, Mr. Hodge?" said Holmes.

"I have not as yet decided," said Hodge. "It is true the sale of the building was my original intention when I arrived in London, but my father's words have left me unsure."

"Then let us reassure you," said Holmes. "It do find it an intriguing little problem. I will accept your case."

"Thank you," said Hodge. "I am most grateful for your assistance."

"Now," said Holmes. "It is just past eleven, and I have some pressing matters to attend to, but if you would be so good as to meet both Watson and myself at the Icarus Theatre just past four this afternoon, we will see if we cannot dispel your ghost."

III

The weather had not yet turned cold, so Holmes and I decided to forgo a cab and instead enjoy a constitutional from Baker Street to Charing Cross. As we strolled, we discussed the case.

"What do you make of it all, Watson?" asked Holmes.

"I think Mr. Hodge experienced a delusion," I said. "It is not unusual for a man under emotional duress to suffer hallucinations, especially when sleep deprived from such an arduous voyage."

"What you say might be true," said Holmes, "but I cannot help but feel there is something more to his tale. Does the circumstance not strike you? A father's ghost come to haunt his son?"

"It reminds me of Shakespeare," I said. "The Danish Prince."

"Yes, and I cannot help but think that it is intentional," said Holmes. "There is a theatricality to this case, if nothing else."

We walked on in silence for a time.

"Have I ever told you of my days in the theatre, Watson?" said Holmes.

"No, I cannot say that you have," I answered. "Certainly nothing in detail."

"I do not generally speak of my life prior to Baker Street," said Holmes. "It rarely serves a point."

"That is an understatement," I said. "We had lived together for some time before you deigned to mention that you had a brother."

422

Holmes smiled. "Yes, Mycroft. Someday I may tell you of our childhood together, should circumstances warrant."

"Tell me of your days on the stage," I said. "I never knew you to take more than a passing interest in such matters."

"Oh, I take interest in whatever knowledge suits my vocation," said Holmes. "My career in the theatrical arts began just after Cambridge when I was casting about for a direction in life. You might even be familiar with the gentleman who recruited me to the stage, a Cambridge man I knew then as Lord Peter, but whom you now might know better as Langdale Pike."

"The scandal monger?" I cried.

"I'm sure he would prefer instead to be called a societal columnist," said Holmes. "I toured with Langdale for less than a year, in both London and America, but during that time we studied all aspects of the theatrical arts voraciously. The skills I developed on the stage have served me well in my career as a consulting detective. Makeup and disguise are essential arts to both the actor and the sleuth, along with the ability to both stage a scene and recognize when one has been staged. This in particular has been quite useful."

"But why did you leave the stage?"

"Theatre is a cruel mistress, Watson. One lives and dies by the reviews of the public. And, quite frankly, it was not my calling. I walked away from the stage to create the profession of private, consulting detective. I believe that choice was the right one, and I do not regret that decision."

"And Langdale Pike?"

Holmes smiled. "You will have to ask him that question yourself, Watson. I'm sure our paths will cross again one day. Ah, here we are. Wait for me, won't you?"

Holmes walked into the Office of Records, and returned ten minutes later with a rolled up document under his arm.

"I have everything we need to proceed in the case," he said. "Let us now make our way to the Icarus."

IV

The Icarus Theatre was small by the standard of the grand music halls to which I had become accustomed as Holmes's companion. A solid granite wall with ionic columns lined the front, with a small double door leading to the lobby beyond. William Hodge was waiting for us on the front step, accompanied by a second man who I took to be James Walsh. The contrast between the two could not have been starker. While Hodge was short, stocky, and well attired, Walsh was tall, lanky, and dressed in the mismatched and eclectic garb that seemed to be the hallmark of his chosen profession.

"Well met, Mr. Holmes," said Hodge upon spotting our approach. "Gentlemen, this is James Walsh, the current manager of the Icarus Theatre."

"I've heard of you, of course, Mr. Holmes," said Walsh. "And dare I hope that your companion is the famous Doctor Watson?"

"I am," I said.

"I must say, this is a great honor," said Walsh. "I have read all of your stories, Doctor. Indeed, I feel as if I know both of you personally."

"I would not believe everything you read in the Good Doctor's writings, Mr. Walsh," said Holmes.

"So you have said," said Hodge. "Now, gentlemen. Daylight is wasting. If you would please show Mr. Holmes and Doctor Watson the theatre?"

"Of course," said Walsh. "This way." Mr. Walsh led us through the entrance and into the theatre beyond. Hodge followed just behind.

We emerged into a cramped lobby, its walls decorated with artifacts of the Icarus's past triumphs. Aging posters, programs, and even costumes were pinned everywhere creating, to my eye, a cluttered rather than romantic look.

"As you can see, gentlemen," said Walsh with an unmistakable air of pride, "the Icarus has a rich and vibrant history. We have performed for both royalty and commoners, everything from comedy to grand opera. Once we have affected repairs to our dressing rooms, our forthcoming season promises to be our greatest to date." While this seemed to be directed to all of us, I could tell that the real focus of his words was William Hodge, the man whose temperament would soon decide the theatre's future. Hodge, for his part, kept his opinions behind a stoic facade, and said nothing.

Holmes pointed to a framed portrait of two smiling, well-fashioned gentlemen which had been hung next to the Box Office. "Is this man your father, Mr. Hodge?"

"Yes, that's the scoundrel," said Hodge. "The tall man standing to the right of Mr. Gilbert."

"That photograph was taken the day the Icarus first opened its doors," said Walsh. "A marvelous day! Simply marvelous! A triumph for both your father and, if I do say so, Sir William as well.

Have you ever met him? He is a most talented lyricist, and very generous besides."

"I have not had the pleasure," I said. "Have you, Holmes?"

It was at this moment that I realized Holmes was no longer at my side. Looking about I spotted him in the corner of the lobby, studying an old, ornate but faded concert poster still mounted on the wall. "Holmes?" I said.

"A moment, Watson," he said. He reached out, and ran his hand over the faded image of an American contralto. I recognized her at once.

"I had not realized she sang here," I said.

"Oh, yes," said Walsh. "Miss Adler enjoyed a lengthy engagement here at the Icarus shortly after it first opened. I personally attended every performance. She was magnificent."

"Magnificent," echoed Holmes, an odd expression of emotion on his face that I have rarely seen in all our years of association. A moment later it was gone, replaced by the familiar visage of the great detective. "Thank you, Mr. Walsh. Now, if you would, pray, proceed with your tour."

"Very well," said Walsh. "This way to the main stage, gentlemen."

We followed Mr. Walsh through the stage doors, and down a dimly lit corridor, emerging into the theatre itself. The performance space was an enormous room dominated by a proscenium stage and a dilapidated set of seats in the pit below. Even I, with my limited knowledge of the theatrical arts, could see that this had once been a grand theatre, but evidence of neglect was everywhere, from grime in the shadowed corners to small tears in the stage curtain which had been clumsily mended by a haphazard hand.

On the stage two performers, both as grimy with dirt as the theatre that surrounded them, were busy rehearsing a dramatic fight amidst a haphazard set made from piles of metallic debris. Seeing that they now had an audience, they dropped their metallic implements and approached us.

"I say, Walsh!" said the taller of the two actors. "You had promised us privacy."

"We cannot be ready to dazzle our audience unless we can focus on our craft," said the shorter, and stouter. "And, frankly, we look a mess. We are not ready to face our adoring public."

"My apologies, but it cannot be helped," said Walsh. "Gentlemen, these are two stars of the Icarus stage, Mr. Bradly Night and Mr. Norman Wilde."

425

Both men bowed low. "At your service, sir," said the taller one, whom I took to be Bradley Night. "And just whom do we have the honor to be addressing?"

"This is Sherlock Holmes."

Both men started in recognition, a response to which I had grown accustomed over the years. Holmes's fame rarely failed to provoke a response, something I knew he found to be a double-edged sword in his profession. "Ah! Yes, of course," said the stouter actor. "The famous detective. I've read of your many adventures in *The Strand*. Really, sir. You should hire yourself a better biographer. Some of that prose he uses is positively lower-class drivel."

Walsh cleared his throat.

"What?" answered back Wilde.

"This second gentleman," said Walsh, "is Doctor Watson."

I took some mild pleasure in watching the color flush from Wilde's face, as he struggled to find words. Night laughed, greatly amused by his companion's plight.

"Hah! It's always been your trouble, Norman," he said. "You always did rush to say your lines. A thousand apologies, Good Doctor, for my ill-read companion. I happen to enjoy your efforts. Have you ever considered writing for the stage?"

"It had honestly never occurred to me," I answered.

"Well, it should. That play about your companion there is positively bringing down the house over at the Lyceum. I'm sure you could easily write circles around that American."

"You're too kind," I said.

"I'm dreadfully sorry," Wilde mumbled, recovering his voice at last. "If only I had known – "

"But you didn't, Norman," said Night, "and now you've landed yourself in the butter again. But, wait! There are three of you with Walsh! Sherlock Holmes and Doctor Watson – The third wouldn't be Inspector Lestrade, by any chance? Pray tell, who is the third gentleman accompanying you this afternoon?"

"This," said Walsh, "is William Hodge."

Both actor's faces fell in an instant from bemusement into sorrow. "My most sincere apologies and condolences, Mr. Hodge," said Wilde. "I knew your father well. Indeed, I owe him my career. He helped me recover from a difficult period in my life."

"My admiration for your father knows no bounds," said Night. "He gave everything to this theatre, and, thus, also to me."

"Thank you, both" said Hodge, clearly wanting to move this encounter along.

"But what brings the celebrated Sherlock Holmes to our humble theatre?" said Night. "Surely there can be no question of the circumstances behind Francis' demise? It was a fire, plain and simple."

"He is not so much concerned with what happened that dreadful night," said Walsh, "as he is with what happened after."

"You pique my interest, Walsh!" said Wilde, recovering his bluster at last. "Tell us all!"

"There's not much to tell," said Walsh. "Young William here visited the theatre only last night, to see the room where his father died, and he thought he saw . . . ." Walsh trailed off, unsure he should finish the thought. Holmes watched this exchange with great interest.

"My father," said Hodge. "I thought I saw my father's spirit. In the very room he died."

"Did you now?" said Night. "Why, that's positively Shakespearian!"

"But you were mistaken," said Wilde. "Surely you were mistaken."

"Afraid of a ghost, Wilde?" needled Night.

"I assure you both, I saw him as clearly as I see you now," said Hodge. "The experience was a vivid one, but I am seeking a rational rather than a spiritual explanation. This is why I have brought Mr. Holmes here."

"I see," said Night. "And have you any theories to explain young Hodge's vision, Mr. Holmes?"

"Before I arrived here, I saw four possible explanations," said Holmes. "Now there are five. Gentlemen, it has been a distinct pleasure, but I am anxious to continue my investigation. Mr. Walsh, if you would take us to Francis Hodge's dressing room, I would be most obliged."

"Of course," said Walsh. "This way."

Walsh guided us away from the actors and down a set of steps which led below the stage. As we walked along a lengthy corridor, I sidled up beside Holmes

"Tell me, Watson," asked Holmes, his voice low. "What did you observe about Mr. Night?"

"He seemed far more gracious than his companion," I said. "Lower class drivel, indeed."

"Social graces aside, did you notice anything about his height? His build?"

I considered. "He seemed remarkably thin," I said. "But they do say that a man does not join the stage if he enjoys eating well."

"I would estimate him to be roughly just over six feet tall," said Holmes. "The same height as Francis Hodge, if the photograph in the lobby is any indication."

"Holmes, you're not suggesting – " I began.

"I suggest nothing, Watson," interrupted Holmes. "It is merely an observation. I would point out that Mr. Walsh shares the same height and build as well. A most remarkable coincidence, would you not agree?"

Before I could answer, Walsh stopped before a fire-damaged door. Its woodwork was blackened and singed, yet we could still read the name of "Hodge" imprinted high on a gleaming metal plate.

"Here we are, gentlemen," said Walsh. He stepped forward, extracted his key ring, and opened the door for us.

The room beyond showed every evidence of being the site of tragedy. Like the surface of the door outside, everything within was covered by a layer of ash, with several items showing clear evidence of being damaged by fire. A broken chair sat before a singed dressing table, and a rack of clothes had entirely collapsed, many of its garments now either blackened or destroyed. A large wardrobe had been pushed against the wall, its doors hanging by the loosest of hinges. The only item which still gleamed within was a full length standing mirror, which, based upon its appearance, had somehow been spared the ravages of fire.

Holmes took one of his exhaustive, all-encompassing glances about the chamber. "The room is just as you saw it yesterday? Nothing has been moved or disturbed?"

"Nothing," said Walsh.

"Don't be daft," said Hodge. "Of course things have been disturbed. We both moved some of the debris and furniture about in our search for my father's spirit."

"That is most unfortunate," said Holmes. "Although – " From his pocket he produced a glass, and dropped to his knees, examining the traces of ash which covered the floor. He then stood, and pushed the dressing table toward the wall, adjusted the standing mirror, and pushed the wardrobe to the left. "There," he said. "Is this how you found the room last night, gentlemen?"

"I think that it was," said Walsh, uncertain.

"Yes," said Hodge. "That's it, exactly. Mr. Holmes, I believe you have seen something in this room that we do not."

428

"No," said Holmes. "I believe we have all seen the same room. Now a moment, gentlemen. There is work to be done."

Holmes again dropped to his knees, and began to crawl slowly around the periphery of the walls, examining with his glass traces in the dirt and ash that only he could see. For ten minutes we watched in silence as Holmes diligently surveyed every detail until, at last, he stood again in satisfaction.

"I believe I have seen everything I need to see here," he said. "Mr. Walsh, if you could now show us the rest of the theatre?"

Walsh subsequently led us through the rest of the building, including the other dressing rooms, the rear entrance, the balconies and offices. However, despite his request, Holmes displayed only a cursory interest. At length we concluded our visit, bade Walsh goodbye, and made our way back to Charing Cross.

"Well, Mr. Holmes?" said Hodge.

"A pretty little problem, Mr. Hodge," said Holmes. "Thank you for bringing it to me."

"You've solved it, then?"

"I believe that I have."

"Then, for pity's sake, tell me! Just what was it that I saw last night?"

"Patience, Mr. Hodge. All shall soon be revealed. Now, are you game for a bit of theatre of our own? You must follow my instructions to the letter and without question."

"If it will bring this matter to a close, then certainly."

"Good man. What I am to suggest might sound unorthodox, but I do believe that it will bring our drama to a close. Tonight, just before nine, you must summon Walsh, Night, and Wilde to the Icarus theatre. Give them no explanation as to why. Escort them to the interior of your father's dressing room, and then inform them that you have decided to sell the theatre. They will of course attempt to persuade you otherwise, but remain steadfast in your determination. Then dismiss the lot of them, telling them that you wish to be alone with your father's memory. Be sure to lock the door after they depart, and remain within until first light. Do you understand?"

"Perfectly," said Hodge. "But what do you hope to accomplish with this ruse?"

Holmes smiled. "I would think that was perfectly obvious. Good night, Mr. Hodge. We shall expect you back at Baker Street by first light."

Then, to both my own and Hodge's astonishment, Sherlock Holmes walked away before his client could offer another word.

"I've fired people for less incivility," said Hodge.

"Trust Holmes, Mr. Hodge," I said. "His methods may seem strange, but he generally brings his cases to successful conclusions."

"Generally?" said Hodge. "I've never read of a failure in one of your stories, Doctor."

"The public does not like to read the failures," I said, and then ran after Holmes, leaving our client standing alone before the Icarus Theatre.

V

I quickly caught up with Holmes. "Holmes, you were damnably – " I began.

"Damnably rude?" interrupted Holmes. "Then I shall offer my apologies once this affair has been concluded. I assure you, my dear fellow, that my behavior tonight has been calculated to provoke a response in the cast of this drama. We are, after all, playing a game for long odds. Now, Watson. We have a long evening ahead of us. I think there is just enough time for a quick dinner at Longberry's before our excursion. What do you say?"

We dined as the sun set over London, and soon returned to Baker Street. Holmes dispatched two telegrams, and asked that I collect my service revolver for the night ahead. I did so without question, and when I saw Holmes pack up his burglary kit, I knew that we would be spending an evening operating outside of the Queen's Law.

This time we took a cab to the Icarus, letting ourselves out two streets away, lest we be seen. Stealthily we made our way through the back streets and to the alley behind the theatre, whereupon Holmes withdrew his lock-pick from his black bag and set to work on the rear entrance door.

"It is important that no one knows we are here tonight, Watson," said Holmes. "We must be careful to remain unobserved."

"But you did not ask Hodge to summon Walsh and the others until nine," I pointed out. "The theatre is empty."

"So it may seem," said Holmes. "but theatres are never without their ghosts. Ah, but hello! This is very strange."

"What is it?" I asked.

"This lock is no lock at all. It is merely a prop, intended to create the appearance that the rear door of the theatre is barred. Look here. I merely depress this nodule, and – there." I heard a click, and the lock securing the door released.

"Illusion after illusion," I asked. "But what does it all mean?"

"We shall soon find out," said Holmes. "Come, Watson. Silently, now. Make not a sound."

We walked as quietly as we could down the silent corridors. I followed Holmes, knowing, though it remained unsaid between us, what our destination would be. Soon we stood again before the dressing room of Francis Hodge. This door was locked, but it was no match for Holmes's skill with the lock pick, and we quietly entered, silent as the very ghost we hunted.

"The wardrobe, Watson," said Holmes. "I believe it is large enough to conceal the both of us."

We climbed within, and swung the door closed behind. The wardrobe was cramped, but still allowed both of us to stand, with some minor discomfort. We settled in for our vigil, peering through the cracks in the double doors into the murky room beyond.

Time passed slowly. I carried with me no watch, lest the sound alert others to our presence, but far off I could hear the chimes of a clock, and knew that the hour had just struck nine. Soon the dressing room door opened again and Walsh, Night, and Wilde were escorted within by our client. All seemed agitated.

"Really, Hodge, I don't understand why this couldn't have waited until the morning," said Walsh.

"I quite agree," said Wilde. "Why, if it were not for my respect for your father's memory – "

"I am not a man who is fond of waiting," interrupted Hodge. "When I have made a decision, I act upon it. And that, gentlemen, is why I have summoned you all here. I have made up my mind. I have decided to shutter the Icarus Theatre, and put it up for sale, immediately."

There was stunned silence in the room.

"You can't!" said Night at last. "You simply can't!"

"Your father would not have approved," said Wilde.

"More than that," said Walsh. "This is contrary to his dying wish!"

"I've made my decision," said Hodge. "You will, of course, be compensated, but my decision is final."

"But the ghost!" said Night. "What about the ghost?"

"I've given the ghost all the consideration it deserves," said Hodge. "Indeed, this seems the best way to put my father's memory, at last, to rest."

The assembled argued fervently, but Hodge was as steely as his reputation belied and would not budge from his decision. The tension

431

in the room turned hostile. Wilde curse Hodge, and Night even took a swing at our client before being restrained by Walsh.

"You'll regret this," said Night, as Wilde and Walsh pushed him from the room.

"I think not," said Hodge. "If anything, your behavior has reinforced my decision."

"You're upset," said Walsh. "Tired from your long journey. Why don't you sleep on it, and we will discuss the matter further in the morning."

"I've said all I care to say," said Hodge. "Now leave me. I want a last moment alone with my father's memory."

Walsh grimaced in frustration, but did as he was bade, closing the dressing room behind him.

Finally alone, Hodge sat upon a stool before the dressing table. With shaking hands he picked up a damaged photograph of his father from the table's surface. Then, even as Holmes and I watched, the steel of the man broke, and he let loose with sobs of grief. I made to exit the wardrobe, to comfort our client in his moment of need, but I felt Holmes's hand upon my shoulder.

"Steady on, Watson," whispered Holmes. "The drama is not yet concluded."

Indeed, even as Holmes spoke, a small sound reached my ear; a soft, grinding noise, like something being dragged along a stone. It was followed by some most unsettling words.

"William," said an unearthly voice, its tones tinged with a rasp of the grave. Despite myself I shrank back into the wardrobe, and steeled my grip on the hilt of my revolver.

William Hodge started from his grief and sprang from his stool, gasping in disbelief. Even as we watched, the light in the corner of the room where the mirror stood seemed to dim, and then, to my astonishment, drew together into a tall, shadowed figure.

"Father," whispered Hodge.

"My son," said the spirit, advancing slowly, his arm outstretched, his bony finger pointing in accusation. "You have disrespected my final wishes. I begged you to spare the theatre, but you would not listen."

"I listened to you, father," said Hodge.

"Silence!" cried the spirit. "Do not speak foul lies to me. I heard every word you spoke within this room. I know you are intending to sell the theatre."

"You are dead," said Hodge. "This building is now mine to do with as I wish."

"So it is," said the spirit. "A situation I shall have to correct."

The figure leaped at his son, but my eyes had difficulty in following what was occurring. Even as the spirit advanced, his ghostly figure seemed to lose substance, becoming nothing more than a wisp of darkened light in the foul dressing room air, but this did not stop his son from crying out as very real hands clutched their fingers around his throat – not from the spirit who advanced before him, but coming from behind where he was defenseless.

"Now, Watson!" cried Holmes, springing forward.

We burst from the wardrobe together, only to be confronted by one of the strangest sights I ever saw in my long career of adventures with Sherlock Holmes.

A tall figure had seized our client from behind, his fingers clasped tightly around Hodge's windpipe. Clad entirely in black robes, his face caked with black tar, Hodge's assailant seemed a figure straight out of a child's darkest nightmares. Surprised by the suddenness of our entrance, the ghost dropped Hodge to the ground, even as Holmes tackled him headlong. The two wiry men began to tussle, Holmes's skill in baritsu seemingly matched by the desperation of the ghost. I leveled my pistol, but dared not shoot, lest the bullet strike my friend.

Suddenly the door of the dressing room burst open, and a most unexpected figure entered, leading two police constables behind him.

"No one move!" cried Inspector Lestrade, leveling his own weapon at the head of the specter. Presented with such overwhelming odds, the black cloaked individual fell back and threw up his hands in surrender. He was promptly hauled to his feet by the waiting constables.

"Well met, Lestrade," said Holmes.

"Happy to lend a hand," said Lestrade. "Got your message, and came straight down to the Icarus. I must say, this is one of the strangest collars I've ever had. Not many police inspectors can say they'd caught a ghost."

"Your timing, as ever, is impeccable, Lestrade," said Holmes. "Were you successful?"

"Of course," said Lestrade. "They were just where you said they'd be, and we snapped up the lot of them. Walsh, Wilde, and Night are all in custody."

"But, Holmes!" I said. "If none of the theatre staff was portraying the ghost, then just who have we caught here?"

"He is exactly who he purports to be, Watson," said Holmes. "Gentlemen, I would like you all to meet the late Francis Hodge – formerly deceased, now very much alive."

VI

Francis Hodge refused to utter a word, not to Holmes, Lestrade, or his astounded son, so he was taken away without protest to Scotland Yard. Holmes requested that Inspector Lestrade and William Hodge visit Baker Street in the morning, where he promised to discuss the details of the case.

The next day, both Lestrade and Hodge arrived promptly at nine, the pair of them anxious for answers, but Holmes insisted that we all first partake of one of Mrs. Hudson's excellent breakfasts. This clearly irritated both gentlemen, but they ate their kippers with stoic patience. At last, after Holmes had finished his second cup of coffee, there was a knock on the door.

"A telegram for you, Mr. Holmes," said Mrs. Hudson.

Holmes accepted it, and cried aloud in excitement. "My case is complete!" he said.

"That's all well and good, but could you please explain everything that's been going on?" said Lestrade.

"Of course, Lestrade," said Holmes. "I was only awaiting the telegram which tied up the last thread of this tangled skein. I can now explain in full."

"Then, please," said Hodge. "Do so."

"There really was no great mystery in this case," said Holmes. "Indeed, the ghost himself was kind enough to confess his motivation, which simplified things enormously. He wanted to save the Icarus Theatre. It was thus merely a matter of matching the motive to the perpetrator. That it might have been your father, Mr. Hodge, occurred to me immediately."

"But, Holmes, everyone believed Francis Hodge to be dead," I said. "How in heaven did you know he was alive?"

"Oh, come now, Watson," said Holmes. "This is hardly our first case where those believed deceased prove later to be still in the land of the living. Besides, I did not know for certain. It could just as easily have been the theatre manager, Walsh, or the remaining actors employed, Night or Wilde. It was important to suss out the guilty party, and to that end I contrived a little drama of my own."

"Putting your client in mortal danger," pointed out Lestrade.

"The danger was minimal," said Holmes. "Both Watson and I were observing the scene from within the wardrobe, and you yourself, Inspector, were only moments away."

"But why didn't you tell me?" said Hodge. "The experience was unsettling to say the least. I might have felt safer if I'd only known you were there."

"Because, Mr. Hodge," said Holmes, "despite your reputation as a ruthless business man, I did not know your abilities as an actor. You were, after all, dealing with at least three individuals skilled in the craft, and they might sense your deception. This was, after all, a case of deceptions. The faked fire within the dressing room, for example."

"Faked fire?" I said. "What on earth are you talking about?"

"Oh, come now, Watson. The fact that Francis Hodge is still alive should be enough for you to conclude the tragedy was faked. Combine that fact with a door singed by flame, yet still featuring a gleaming brass nameplate, along with a room we are meant to believe suffered a fire so intense that it killed its inhabitant, yet somehow spared the dressing table, wardrobe, and mirror. The conclusion is obvious. The scene was staged by Walsh and the elder Hodge for the benefit of the wealthy son. They knew that he would never agree to fund the failing theatre while his father lived because of the years of animosity between them, but hoped that his son might agree to do so in honor of his dead father's memory. To this end, they dressed the room, first to stage Francis Hodge's death, and subsequently a spectral reunion between father and son."

"But the ghost, Mr. Holmes!" said Hodge. "How did they achieve the ghost?"

Holmes lit his pipe, and began to puff smoke rings into the air. "Have you ever, by any chance, heard of the Lord Peter illusion?"

Hodge shook his head. "I cannot say that I have."

"It was a theatrical effect created for a production of *Hamlet* by a member of my own former troupe, a man then going by the name of Lord Peter, but now doing business under the moniker of Langdale Pike. It was based upon the famous Pepper's Ghost illusion, but far more practical to stage, as it only utilizes a standing mirror and a rear projected light. The backing to the mirror is removed, a light is shone through the glass, and, provided the angle of the glass is correct, a ghostly figure appears. You saw him standing in front of you, Mr. Hodge, but he was, in fact, standing behind."

"Impossible," said Hodge. "There was no one else in the room. I would swear to it."

"Not at first," said Holmes, "but then through cleverly concealed sliding panels, two participants entered the room. The first was your father, who opened a panel obscured by the mirror. This was the sound you heard, Mr. Hodge, that you described as wind, or that you, Watson, later described to me as something being dragged against stone. Thus positioned, he began to speak. Then, when your attention was drawn to the far wall by your father's voice, a hidden panel was opened behind you, allowing Walsh, now dressed in the ghostly guise of your father, to enter the room and position himself so as to be seen in the mirror. The stage thus set, your father lit his lamp, which shone light through the mirror's glass, allowing the image of a ghost to appear before you. It is a very simple, yet effective, illusion. Light the rear lamp, the ghost appears. Dim the lamp, and the ghost will appear to fade away. By the time you turned around, both Walsh and your father had retreated behind their respective sliding panels, and you were, again, alone."

"I searched that room extensively," said Hodge. "I saw no sliding panel."

"You did not know how to look," said Holmes. "It is ironic that the very ash your father and Walsh scattered about the dressing room to simulate fire also created the trail which showed me precisely where the two hidden doors were located. Your subsequent search of the room had destroyed much of the evidence, but enough remained. Besides, I had stopped off at the records office earlier in the day, and obtained this."

Holmes produced the rolled up sheet of paper from the day before, which he spread out over the table.

"These are the architectural drawings for the Icarus Theatre. The architect made sure to include hidden panels and passageways throughout the building, including the sliding panels to access the dressing room. Note, gentlemen, the name of the architect."

We all stared. "Francis Hodge!" said Lestrade.

"Precisely," said Holmes. "The elder Hodge and Walsh chose the dressing room because they knew of the hidden panels. Indeed, Francis Hodge had even placed them there himself over a decade before."

"You've managed it very neatly, Mr. Holmes," said Lestrade. "I'll draw up charges for both conspirators, Hodge and Walsh, and arrange for the release of the actors, Wilde and Night."

436

"I would not be so quick as to let that pair loose, Lestrade," said Holmes.

"And why not?" said Lestrade. "It would seem they are innocent in the attempt to defraud and murder Mr. Hodge here."

"And so they are," said Holmes, "But they are, none the less, guilty of attempted robbery. I recognized the pair of them instantly. Frankly, Lestrade, I'm surprised you did not spot them as well."

"Oh?" said Lestrade. "And why's that?"

"They may now be trading under the names Night and Wilde," said Holmes, "but you may know them better as Fonzetti and Lorenzo."

"The art thieves?" said Lestrade, astonished. "I put them away myself back in '91."

"With some assistance from Sherlock Holmes," I pointed out.

"Yes, yes," said Lestrade. "I admit that Mr. Holmes's advice was of some minor help in the case, but I personally made the collar. Are you sure it's them? I didn't recognize either man, and last I heard they were in Blackgate."

"Both men have undergone a transformation since last you saw them," said Holmes. "Fonzetti has put on considerable weight, and Lorenzo has lost both his hair and his beard, but it is them, I assure you. One can change many things about one's appearance, but your height and your ears remain unmistakable. It is Fonzetti and Lorenzo, practicing the art of thievery once more. As for Blackgate, here is the response to the telegram I sent out only last night. The warden of Blackgate informs me that the pair was released some three years ago for good behavior."

"Even supposing it really is Fonzetti and Lorenzo," said Lestrade, "I cannot arrest them unless there is evidence of attempted theft, and, as you yourself pointed out, Mr. Holmes, the Icarus Theatre has very little worth stealing."

"True enough, Lestrade," said Holmes, "but the Icarus is not their intended target."

I realized something in that moment, a memory that fell into place within my mind. "The dirt," I said.

"What was that?" said Lestrade.

Holmes smiled. "Very good, Watson," said Holmes. "I will let you explain to the inspector."

"I thought this was just part of the theatrical scene they were practicing, but when I first saw the pair both men were covered in dirt. It seemed in line with the general conditions of the Icarus, but, on reflection, I realize now that the dirt was mainly on their hands and knees."

"Precisely," said Holmes. "And what else?"

"The debris," I said. "I assumed at the time that it was merely scenery, but now that I think back – "

"Yes?" said Holmes.

"It was tunneling equipment," I said. "Shovels, spades, and buckets."

Holmes smiled. "You progress, Watson. You really do. Yes, Fonzetti and Lorenzo claimed to be rehearsing a theatrical scene, but they were, in reality, using their requested privacy to tunnel their way from the Icarus to the museum next door. If you revisit the Icarus, Lestrade, and examine the stage, I believe you will discover a tunnel, hidden somewhere behind a curtain or theatrical flat. That should be more than enough evidence to put the pair of them away again, at least for a little while."

Lestrade seemed quite chuffed at the prospect of having arrested a con man, an attempted murderer, and two thieves all in the same haul. He thanked Holmes and left, leaving us alone with Mr. Hodge.

"Well, Mr. Hodge," said Holmes. "I'm sorry the case turned out as it did."

"As am I," said Hodge. "I've gone from mourning my father to the realization that the same man attempted to both defraud and kill me. But I do thank you, Mr. Holmes. You have brought the affair to a successful conclusion, even if it is a personally difficult one."

"What will you do now?" I asked.

"I've no wish to ever see my father or his theatre again," said Hodge. "I will return to America. Once returned, I will have my accountant send you a bank cheque for your services. Oh, and should the Good Doctor ever decide to immortalize this as one of your adventures, I will, of course, expect a small commission."

"That is most acceptable," said Holmes.

"I quite agree," I added.

Hodge rose from his chair, shook both our hands in his typical, aggressive manner, and departed. I watched him go from the window of Baker Street. He seemed smaller, somehow, as if the experience had diminished him.

"One point that confuses me, Holmes," I said.

"Yes, Watson?"

"The lock," I said. "Why did the Icarus have a fake lock on the rear door?"

438

"I cannot say for certain, Watson," said Holmes, "but I do have a suspicion. Remember that Francis Hodge had to pretend to be dead for almost two weeks' time, a long time for anyone to be willingly confined indoors. I believe that, as most men of London would, he wished for the outside air. It would not fit with their deception if the late Francis Hodge were seen exiting his own theatre by the front door, especially not on the off-chance that he might run headlong into his son, newly arrived from America, so he confined his visits outside to the alleyway behind. The fake lock would allow him to come and go as he pleased. Surely you observed the myriad of cigarette ash scattered about on the ground outside?"

"I confess that I did not," I said.

"But, alas, this is all speculation," said Holmes. "Should Francis Hodge ever decide to confess his sins, we may clarify that point. Until then, we can only wonder."

We sat by the fire for some time in silence, Holmes smoking his pipe while I recorded my notes upon the case.

"Are you free this afternoon, Watson?" asked Holmes, suddenly.

"I just have these notes to complete," I said, "but, otherwise – "

"I have reconsidered," said Holmes. "I do not often indulge in nostalgia, but I confess that this case has reignited my interest in the theatrical arts. I believe I will take Mr. Gillette and his company up on their offer to see his new production."

"Really!" I said. "Holmes, you surprise me."

"I am glad I can still do so after so many years," said Holmes. "Would you care to accompany me?"

"I'd like nothing more in the world," I said.

"Good fellow," said Holmes. "I think we might even swing by his St. James Street club to pay a visit to Lord Peter. I'm sure Langdale Pike would also enjoy both a seat at the most popular show in London, as well as a chance to converse together about old times."

The Adventure of the
Glassy Ghost
by Will Murray

I have rarely been reluctant to join my esteemed friend Sherlock Holmes in one of his fascinating investigations, but the law of averages, not to mention the inexorable wheel of fate, both conspired in an attempt to block me from participating in the tantalizing mystery which I will now I relate.

Let me be clear that it was not an absence of curiosity, but rather a surfeit of energy that caused me to all but miss out on one of my dear friend's most baffling intrigues.

I had been away in the country for a week, visiting distant relatives. What had promised in the beginning to be a relaxing period of welcome respite from city life ultimately devolved into a dismal and unnaturally depressive and forced captivity.

The rain had commenced at mid-week. In spite of periodic respites, the elements had whipped themselves into an electrical froth, culminating in the night of 12 October, 1901. A thunderstorm of such ferocity that the house periodically shook is if the earth were being made to convulse by burrowing creatures raged half the day and well into the night. Slumber was impossible. The house lights, which were illuminated by electricity, failed miserably and had not returned. When morning came, it was time for me to take the train back to London.

Fortunately, by that hour the beastly rain had abated. The air smelled clean, as well it should have, having been relentlessly washed by successive downpours. Despite that, hailing a cab at Victoria Station proved to be an ordeal. The skies were still an ugly slate hue, and the fear of fresh downpours motivated even the most hearty hikers to avail themselves of any cab that rolled up to the station entrance.

Impatience was getting the better of me when finally my turn arrived. The coachman dutifully accepted and stowed my luggage, and I climbed aboard a feeling that the clap of the coach door closing upon me was one of the most welcome sounds ever to impinge upon my hearing. For the homey sound signified that quite soon I would be safely ensconced in my own domicile, perfectly dry, and prepared to catch up on my sleep, which I fully expected to restore frazzled nerve strings.

The short ride through London's muddy streets showed that the familiar metropolis had not escaped the fury of the overnight elements. The overcast sky hung low and oppressive, promising more dreary misery.

As the cab pulled up before 221b Baker Street, I alighted. I happened to glance up at the windows overlooking the thoroughfare from the first floor apartment we shared, Mr. Sherlock Holmes and I.

I recognized Holmes, almost cadaverous in his vertical gauntness, looking down upon the muddy prospect, his hawk-like features wearing a predatory if slightly worried cast.

His sharp eyes glanced my way and he threw off his singular immobility. Swiftly, he disappeared from view. In my overwhelming fatigue, I took no special import from his sudden vanishment. Nor did I then imagine that Holmes had been standing sentry, awaiting my return. That I was expected upon this day did not rise to the level of my conscious thinking, for I desired but one thing. That was bed rest. And I was determined to have it as quickly as I could shrug off my garments and fling myself upon by familiar mattress.

As the coachman was unloading my luggage, the door abruptly flew open and Holmes stalked out, displaying the weird nervous energy the characterized him, even when he was in repose.

"Your timing is hardly perfect, Watson," he snapped out, "but it will have to do."

"I beg your pardon, Holmes?" I sputtered.

"No time for idle chat," snapped Holmes. "Have the coachman place your belongings inside. He will convey us to our destination."

I confess that my nerves have been abraded to a rawness that caused me to snap back impatiently, "The only thing I seek at the moment is my bed!"

Holmes appeared momentarily taken aback. "Have you not just returned from a restful week in the country?"

"I have returned from the country, yes," I shot back. "But restful it was not!"

Holmes stepped back, and his keen eyes raked me up and down. Owing to long association with his canny ways, I was not surprised by his next statement.

"No sleep, I take it," he enjoined.

"Not so whatsoever in two nights. Although last night was the worst."

"The thunderstorm, no doubt."

"The very same," I allowed. "Now if you'll excuse me, Holmes, as much as I would normally be pleased to accompany you to your destination, you will have to make your own arrangements with the coachman. I am really exhausted and without interest in anything other than temporary oblivion."

Holmes's expression was fixed and firm. A sparkle was in his eyes, very deeply held.

"This is regrettable, for I have waited nearly an hour for your expected return. And now you fail me."

"I am doing nothing of the kind. I will be happy to join you after a suitable interval of rest, provided my presence is required. But I trust you can carry on without my limited insight in the interim."

"I see that I shall have to," murmured Holmes slowly. "But it is a pity. This promises to be one of the most intriguing mysteries to come my way in months."

I nodded. Curiosity did not awaken in me one iota. Instead, I waited for Holmes to carry on, and avail himself of the convenient carriage.

But he did not. Instead, he remarked, "You are familiar with the solicitor, Morland?"

"Yes, yes. Of course I know the name."

"It appears that the poor fellow perished last night at the height of the thunderstorm."

"Murder?" I returned dully.

"I have formed no firm convictions on Morland's demise, one way or another. The manner of his death may or may not be explicable. But it is what happened to him after his death that intrigues me."

Now Holmes had me. "Did you say *after*?"

"I did, Watson. For after the man expired, it appears that the window glass of his office on Oxford Street captured his departing soul, and it is now displaying it there for all to see."

"Extraordinary, if true," I burst out in spite of myself.

"Extraordinary if *not* true," countered Holmes, "for several persons claim to have seen the dead man's spirit after it had been captured by the window pane."

At these words, my tongue became still. I momentarily lost the power of speech. I stood rooted.

Sherlock Holmes eyed me with his appraising gaze. No doubt he was searching my face to discern if I wavered in my resolve for slumber.

I inquired, "This took place on Oxford Street?"

442

"It did. Not five minutes away by cab. Surely, you could accompany me that far. I promise to hold the driver, who will take you back if you are not up to a complete investigation."

Fatigue will do many things to a man's brain. It will dull it, stupefy it, and work other mischief upon its pliable grey matter. In this particular instance, I fear it robbed me of my resolve, if not my better judgment.

"I can spare fifteen minutes, Holmes. Perhaps twenty. But that is my limit." I spoke these words firmly, but I might as well been a man who was sodden with drink. I had no will of my own before the master of psychology who was Sherlock Holmes.

Before I could change my mind, Holmes urged me back into the cab and the doors were shut, the driver having deposited my luggage in the entryway and closed the outer door firmly.

And so we were off on what promised to be in a truly baffling mystery. And so it proved to be. I only wish that I had the clarity of thought necessary to fully participate in its unfolding.

During the brief journey, Holmes recounted what was known of the matter to date.

"Morland happened to be working late last night, and failed to return home at a reasonable hour. It was initially believed that the downpour had stranded him in his office, but when midnight came and went, his wife braved the elements and entered the place. It was dark and the lights were inoperative. Fumbling about the office, she all but tripped over the cold corpse of her late husband. The police were immediately summoned, and under the light of the electric torches, they pronounced the unfortunate solicitor deceased."

I nodded, too fagged to comment.

Holmes resumed his account. "It was in the torchlight that the apparition in the window pane came to light. It was a head, not much more than a silhouette. The wife was still present when torch illumination brought it to light. At the site of the stark image, she let out a hysterical scream and fainted. Upon being revived, she swore that the silhouette was that of her late husband. She particularly remarked that the unruly hair could belong to none other than Sylvester Morland, Esquire. The shape of the head also convinced her, for Morland's skull was very broad at the crown and tapered to a rather narrow pointed chin. Only one ear could be discerned by its shape. This, too, Mrs. Morland pronounced to be evidential."

This choice of words roused me. "Evidential! Is that not the word spiritists employ to complement a so-called medium that they consider genuine?"

Holmes nodded. "I believe you are correct, Watson. You are not so sleepy headed as you imagine yourself to be. My use of the term was inadvertent. But it augers for intriguing times ahead, does it not?"

"I should hope so, Holmes," I said, rather dispiritedly, for my thoughts kept careening back to my comfortable pillow, upon which I dearly wished to lay my tired head.

Within minutes, we were dropped off before the Oxford Street offices of the late attorney. They were those of a man of middling achievement, as the shabby-genteel appointments suggested once we entered.

Inspector Lestrade was there to greet us. Our initial conversation was perfunctory and to the point. The body of late Morland had been born off to the morgue and little remained of the death scene, other than the empty office.

Pleasantries abandoned, Holmes snapped, "Show me the window in question, Lestrade. I am keen to examine it."

"Would that I could, Mr. Holmes," said the police official. "But I fear it has been removed to Scotland Yard for minute examination. A glazier has already set the replacement glass in its place, the apparition understandably attracting a noisy crowd."

"Then my own examination must await official permission. Now then, I understand from the morning newspaper that Mr. Morland was discovered lying upon the floor." Holmes cast his penetrating gaze about the office. He pointed to an inner wall, remarking, "I would say that the corpse was found upon that spot."

"Why, exactly upon that spot," returned Lestrade. "However did you puzzle that out, Holmes?"

"There was no doubt considerable scuffling following the discovery of the deceased, and scuff marks, many of them moist from the recent rain, display that trampling to even the casual eye. One spot, however, appears relatively untrammeled." Holmes strode over to the spot and began surveying the immediate surroundings.

There was nothing of interest there, but his attention became fixed on the electrical switch controlling the ceiling light. This consisted of a black knurled knob. Reaching out, he gave it a turn, producing a click, but no illumination from the light fixture overhead.

"It appears to be due to defective wiring," Holmes pronounced.

"That may be so," said Lestrade. "Perhaps the evening thunderstorm had something to do with it. As you doubtless noticed, lightning lashed the heavens continually for several hours."

"It was quite a performance," agreed Holmes. "One could readily imagine why less sophisticated men in olden times came to believe in thunder gods of various sorts. Tell me, Lestrade, were there any unusual marks upon the body?"

"A bruise on the left temple. That was all."

"I see. No doubt it was occasioned by the dead man's fall."

"There is no reason to suspect the man was dead before he fell," countered Lestrade.

"On the contrary," returned Holmes. "There is no doubt upon the matter."

The inspector's eyes became unnaturally narrow.

Cord wiring ran from the electrical switch to the ceiling fixture, held in space by hasps and staples set into the plaster wall and baseboard. Holmes was examining this closely.

"When will the autopsy be performed?" he asked suddenly.

"There will be no delay. It may have already commenced."

I confess that I heard the proceedings as if through a curtain that smothered my senses. The lively exchange was not without interest, but was insufficient to rouse me from my low state.

Abruptly, my overwhelming sleepiness was shattered – along with the sharp sound of breaking glass.

The spartan desk was suddenly littered with shards of glass, and the cobblestone rebounded off its polished surface, banged off a wall, and came to rest under the desk.

"Hullo?" Holmes expounded. "What have we here?"

A constable has been posted on guard outside, but he had wandered up to the corner. Now he came hurrying back.

Holmes dashed out into the street and it was he who spied the street urchin ducking around a corner. He gave chase, the constable and Lestrade hot behind him.

I was content to step out onto the pavement and await developments. My energy was not up to hot pursuit.

Not long after, Holmes returned, the urchin in tow. The latter was squalling in the most unbelievable manner and his words were hardly articulate.

Marching the boy up to Inspector Lestrade and the constable, Holmes instructed him firmly, "Repeat now what you have just told me."

"I fear to do so, sirs," sobbed the boy.

Holmes gave him a rough shake. That was all that was needed.

"A fellow I never saw before gave me a gold crown and asked me to do the deed."

"To break a window pane?" demanded Lestrade.

"No, sir, to break a particular window pane. The man was very particular about the exact one. He wanted nothing broken but that particular pane."

"Did the fellow say why he wanted this done?" demanded Holmes.

"He did, sir. But I fear to relate it to you."

Holmes directed, "Fear not. Simply speak the plain truth."

"This fellow Bob said that a man's spirit has been captured by the window glass and needed to be liberated to complete his journey heavenward. He was so sincere in his words, that I took them to heart. He told me that if I did this, I would be doing the poor unfortunate fellow who have died a great service."

"My word!" I exclaimed.

"Describe the fellow," encouraged Holmes. "It will go better on you if you do a good job."

The distraught lad did the best he could, but his powers of speech were insufficient to the task.

"The man was neither very tall, nor was he short. He did not dress in a gentlemanly fashion, but rather rough, sirs. I did not like his eyes, but it was his hair that was most arresting thing about him. It was wild and unruly."

"What color, boy?" demanded Lestrade.

"The hair or his eyes, sir?"

"Both, if you would."

"The eyes I should say were a rather sad blue color, verging upon grey. His hair reminded me of a chestnut mare, one that had not been groomed in a fortnight."

Holmes interjected, "I take it he did not introduce himself formally."

"He said his name was Bob. Just plain Bob. I've never seen him before in my life. But the gold crown swept my senses away. After he flashed it, I was his to command."

Lestrade said tightly, "Now you are the law's to command. Constable, take this young scalawag away. The charge will be disorderly conduct and wanton destruction of property."

The officer dragged off the sobbing, unresisting boy. We repaired to the late solicitor's office to consider matters.

Holmes said, "It need not be overemphasized that the boy was importuned to shatter the window upon which the apparition had been inscribed."

446

Again the choice of words caught my attention. Lestrade also noted this, for he remarked, "Inscribed, did you say? Whatever do you mean, Mr. Holmes?"

"I merely using a convenient word, for I have no inkling as yet as to the truth of the matter. Once I see the window pane, I may have a theory to offer. But first I would like to examine the body while it is still fresh and reasonably intact."

The growler was still standing by the curb, and we three availed ourselves of it after shutting up Mr. Morland's dingy office.

By this time, my interest in the matter was overcome by fatigue and I went along without resistance. Although I must add without great relish, either. It was not that I was determined to see it through, but rather that I lacked the force of will to remove myself from the rush of events.

We soon found ourselves in the morgue. The body was rolled out of its metal drawer, still clothed. Holmes gave the man's corpse careful scrutiny, then he lifted the hands by their wrists, one at a time, examining the fingernails, the palms, the tips of the fingers, and apparently nothing else.

I noted that the man's features seemed stark and vexed, as if a great fright had been experienced prior to the moment of death. His head of hair was rather full, but very carefully arranged. Death had not greatly disordered it. The smell of pomade, although faint, lingered about him. This made me think that he was more fastidious about his hair than his attire, for the latter was a trifle worn here and there, especially at the cuffs and elbows.

One ear protruded, the left. It did not match its opposite appendage. To my physician's practiced eye, I took this to be a malformation present at birth, and not the result of disfigurement.

"I have seen what I expected to see," announced Holmes, after opening one eyelid to ascertain the color of the hidden orb. "Let us examine the window pane next."

This caused Lestrade's jaw to sag slowly. He regained control of it sufficiently to blurt out, "What did you see that I failed to discern?"

"Time enough for that later. The window glass, if you please."

The specimen had been carefully placed in a wooden box large enough to encase it, and this was brought out and placed upon a work table. The lid was lifted and Holmes reached in and raised it to a vertical position. He rested the lower edge upon the work table and moved the glass back and forth, peering into it with the steady intensity of a soothsayer staring into a crystal ball.

I joined him in this endeavor.

"I fail to perceive any image, ghostly or otherwise," I admitted frankly.

Inspector Lestrade was gaping openly at the smooth surface. It appeared to be unblemished.

"I examined this window pane while it was still in its casement," he said tightly. "The silhouette was as plain as day. Now I do not see it."

Then Holmes made a remark that utterly baffled me. "That does not mean that it is not there."

Lestrade turned to him. "Whatever do you mean by that, Holmes? It is either there, or it is not there. My eyes inform me it is no longer there."

"My eyes communicate the same information. Perhaps it will return. Perhaps not."

Without another comment, Holmes laid the glass carefully in its wooden receptacle and said, "I should like to examine this more closely."

"If you think it will do any good," allowed the inspector. "But if I had not seen the window glass with my own eyes earlier this morning, I would doubt the testimony of all witnesses, including my own constables."

When the box was carefully sealed, Holmes said, "I wish to speak with the widow next."

En route to the Morland domicile, Inspector Lestrade ruminated, "Whatever could have been the motive for hiring the wayward boy to shatter the replacement window pane?"

I ventured, "Is there someone who cared very much for the late Mr. Morland, and the repose of his spirit? Or, conversely, someone who hated him thoroughly?"

Holmes astonished me with his next remark. "Neither motivation is exclusive of the other."

As the growler rumbled along, Lestrade and I stared at Holmes with undisguised astonishment. But Holmes kept his own counsel. His eyes were exceedingly thoughtful.

Understandably enough, Mrs. Morland had taken to her bed. As the maid showed us in, and I beheld the widow resting comfortably in her soft bed, I felt pangs of envy, but suppressed them.

Inspector Lestrade introduced us. "This is the renowned Mr. Sherlock Holmes, and his friend, Dr. Watson. They would like a word with you if you would, Mrs. Morland."

"I regret that I cannot properly greet you gentlemen, but I am sure you understand my situation."

"It is a grievous one," allowed Holmes. "I have a very few questions. I beg you to pay attention to them closely."

"Proceed, Mr. Holmes," invited the bereaved woman.

"Had Mr. Morland lost any significant cases in recent weeks?"

"Two."

"Did either of his clients quarrel with him, or deny him his fee?"

"There was trouble with both gentlemen. But I do not know the particulars."

The inspector interjected, "No doubt the details can be gleaned from court records."

"No doubt," agreed Holmes. "Mrs. Morland, tell us why you believed the apparition shown in the window pane was that of the late Mr. Morland."

"It was the shape of the head. Sylvester's skull was rather distinct. Broad at the top, it tapered down, rather like a turnip. But it was the hair. The way it stuck out, the wildness of it. That was my husband's hair most mornings upon awakening. You see, he tossed turned in his sleep. As a result, his hair became as disordered as a rag mop."

"I beg your indulgence for the following indelicacy, Mrs. Morland," said Holmes carefully. "I have just examined Mr. Morland's remains. And his hair was rather well cared for."

"Yes, no doubt it was. Sylvester took great pains to keep it under control. The wildness was something he only tamed through careful grooming and the liberal application of pomade."

"I take it that his hair was in place when you found him?" pressed Holmes.

"It was, sir."

"Then why is it, Mrs. Morland, I beg you to say, do you believe that that was his spirit was captured upon the window pane?"

"For they identical reason I told you. That was Sylvester's hair apparent in the glass. Also one ear had stuck out, and was the proper shape. The shape of the head, combined with the formation of the ear, surrounded by the crown of unruly locks, could only be my late husband. Please accept my word upon that."

"I do. Yet I find myself dissatisfied."

"In what way, Mister Holmes?"

"Why would the soul of a man display the wildness of hair when his body lay on the floor correctly coiffed?"

"I do not know. But something in the aspect of the silhouette upon the window suggested sudden fright. Perhaps his spirit was taken aback by his sudden and unfortunate passing and expressed itself by reverting to his natural appearance."

At this point I was forced to interject, "That is an extraordinary statement, Mrs. Morland, if I do say so."

"This is an extraordinary eventuality, Dr. Watson," returned the woman gravely.

"Had Mr. Morland any relatives?"

"A brother. They were estranged. We had not heard from him in years. He lives in Harwich."

"His profession?"

"I believe he is, or was, a chemist. I do not know any other particulars. As I said, they were estranged, a condition that was mature when I first married Sylvester nearly eleven years ago."

"I see," said Holmes. "I am sorry for your misfortune, Mrs. Morland, and I want to assure you that I will do everything in my power to bring the murderer of your husband to justice."

The statement was delivered with such calmness that it nearly escaped my notice. But I beg to remind the reader that I was extremely fatigued. Inspector Lestrade, however, was not. His rejoinder was sudden and sharp.

"Murderer, you say!" he exclaimed. "What brings you to that conclusion, Holmes?"

"The evidence of my senses, Inspector. Nothing more and nothing less. Now we must take a leave of you, Mrs. Morland. My condolences to you. You will be hearing from Scotland Yard in due course."

Mrs. Morland said nothing. She had clapped her hands to her face as if her grief had suddenly become overwhelming, and she was no longer able to control herself.

I felt pass over me a great wave of sympathy for the unfortunate woman, and we quitted the room as quietly as practical.

Standing by the waiting cab, Holmes addressed the inspector.

"Watson and I must take leave of you, Lestrade. I imagine you are going to look into court records."

Lestrade nodded vigorously. "No doubt they will prove illuminating."

"No doubt. And I would be eager to hear of your discoveries when you have made them."

"Good day to you, Mr. Holmes," said Lestrade, turning on his heel and departing.

450

As we piled into the faithful cab, Holmes remarked, "That will keep Lestrade occupied while we pursue more fruitful lines of inquiry."

"Such as?"

"Such as may be found in my private library. And if not there, in my chemical laboratory."

I imagine that I looked a trifle blank, or perhaps it was sheepish. But I was grateful when we returned to 221b Baker Street and Holmes released me to my bed chamber and an unbroken a sleep that lasted nearly twelve blissful hours.

I saw little of Sherlock Holmes the remainder of the day and that evening. He was shut up in the sitting room, and I could hear the occasional clinking of glass, as if he were mixing chemicals. To what end, I could not imagine.

Most alarming to me were the flashes of light visible round the edges of the closed door and through the keyhole. It was as if the fellow were brewing a tempest in the chamber.

I knocked once to inquire if he needed anything.

His retort was abrupt. "I require solitude, Watson. Nothing more, nothing less. Thank you."

So I left him to his alchemy, and dined alone.

Inasmuch as I had slept late, I took an evening stroll rather than retire at my usual hour. When I returned from my walk along the Strand, I chanced to look up to see the intermittent flashes so much like indoor lightning coming from the sitting room windows that I could not imagine if he were emulating the Norse thunder god, Thor, or experimenting with electrical apparatus.

I considered the irony that Sylvester Morland had died at the height of a thunderstorm in a chamber whose electricity had been extinguished. These two thoughts I attempted to combine, braiding and unbraiding possibilities, but accomplished nothing for all that mental exertion.

I can only wonder as to my dear friend's line of experimentation, for it was baffling.

Inevitably, the hour came when I needed to retire, and while sleep did not come swiftly, it did finally arrive. It was interrupted once by a low grumble of thunder, and I imagined that Sherlock Holmes, not the elements, was the responsible party.

Fortunately, the noise was not repeated and my slumber resumed, this time without any unwelcome breaks.

Morning found Holmes bustling about the apartment, looking for all the world like a fox hound unable to catch a proper scent.

"Difficulties, Holmes?" I inquired.

"Complications, Watson," Holmes responded shortly. "I have reconstructed pieces of the puzzle, but I do not know yet if they constitute a whole, or merely an unmeasured portion of the entire skein."

The ringing of the doorbell stopped Holmes in his tracks.

"Ah," he announced. "That would be Inspector Lestrade, possibly bearing other parts."

I imagine my expression communicated my surprise. For, noticing it, Holmes remarked, "The inspector employs his thumb to ring the doorbell. He lets it rest there far too long. His calling is as distinctive as a fingerprint. Let us not keep him waiting, Watson. Show him in."

Moments later, I brought Lestrade up to the sitting room and we all settled into comfortable chairs.

"Once again," the inspector began, "I must complement you, Mr. Holmes. You correctly deduced murder where mere misadventure was what met the casual eye."

Holmes waved the compliment away impatiently. "Please get on with your report, Inspector."

Unruffled, Lestrade produced a small square notebook and began reading from it.

"The bruise to the left temple was determined to precede the fall, and was not caused by it."

Holmes interrupted shortly, "That was obvious. The man fell on the opposite side, according to the crushed state of his hair. What produced the disabling blow? A hammer?"

"That is the likeliest implement," rejoined Lestrade with no trace of injured pride. "Someone struck Morland, knocking him down, if not out. Whether conscious or not, the man would certainly have been dazed by the blow."

"Rendered helpless, in any event," I remarked.

"What was the pernicious substance injected into his veins?" demanded Holmes.

Astonishment made Lestrade's eyebrows shoot upward. I have no doubt that my own greying brows matched their acrobatics.

Rather impatiently I thought, Holmes related, "I detected the needle puncture mark visible in the cloth of Morland's coat, but was undecided on the point of the lethal brew injected."

"The autopsy suggests that it was a solution of arsenic."

Holmes frowned. "Too common a substance to point the finger of guilt towards a definite party." His expression darkened. Faint shadows of unreadable thoughts paraded across his sharp features, making his eyes cloudy. At length, he lifted his head and asked, "Have you any suspects among aggrieved clients?"

"Two. Both were recently represented by Morland, who failed to win their cases."

"Their names?"

Lestrade said, "A Mr. Robert Daisley and a Mr. Donald Thorson."

Holmes caused the inspector's eyebrows to perform miracles with his next question.

"Which of the two gentlemen was by profession an electrician?"

Lestrade sat momentarily speechless. Finally he said, "The latter gentleman."

"Then that is the man we must interview," cried Holmes, rising to his feet.

Mr. Donald Thorson lived in a respectable house in the suburb of Earls Court.

En route to the residence, the lowering skies commenced to grumble and I cast a worried glance upward.

"Rain in the offing," I muttered.

"A downpour for a certainty," answered Holmes flatly.

I shivered inwardly. I had had enough of rain in recent days.

Inspector Lestrade accompanied us, of course. It was he who knocked upon the door of the modest dwelling.

Donald Thorson answered the door himself, and seemed startled by the trio of strangers confronting him. He was a bluff fellow, as wide of face as a bear, with hair and eyes grey as the storm clouds marching over our heads.

"Mr. Donald Thorson?" demanded Lestrade.

"The same," replied the man. "Who is it calling upon me?"

Lestrade identified himself and presented Sherlock Holmes and myself.

"The celebrated sleuthhound himself!" Thorson marveled. "To what do I own the rare and unexpected pleasure?"

He seemed truly impressed, and not at all concerned by our unannounced arrival on his doorstep.

Lestrade answered officially. "We are investigating the death of Sylvester Morland, with whom you are professionally acquainted. We would like a word with you."

Thorson hesitated only momentarily, and then threw the door wide while stepping back to permit our entry. "Enter at once."

We were seated in his little parlor a moment later.

Holmes regarded the man with his canny grey eyes and remained silent while Lestrade opened the proceedings.

"Well, no doubt you have read of Mr. Morland's untimely passing in the newspapers," the inspector began.

Thorson laughed raggedly, "Strike me, I have. And quite a shock it was, too. I had seen him on the night in question."

Lestrade blinked rapidly, rather like a animal who sights unexpected prey.

"Do you mean upon the night he perished?"

"I do, Inspector. Mr. Morland rang me up, requesting my immediate services. After a bit of haggling, I agreed to come out and restore his electrical service. The blasted storm had knocked it out."

"It is our understanding," said Lestrade, "that you and Mr. Morland had had a falling out over services rendered in a recent legal matter."

"I do not deny it. On the contrary. I had been dawdling on the matter of settling the bill, for I felt that Morland had let me down in his representation of my case. It was a simple matter, and I should have prevailed in court. But I did not. It cost me dearly. The details are neither here nor there."

"So how was this settled between you?" pressed Lestrade.

"Well, as I have said," continued Thorson pleasantly enough, "Morland rang me up and suggested a settlement. Namely, that I restore his electrical service in lieu of paying the outstanding bill. I was hesitant, for I was still nursing a bit of a grudge. But upon reflection, Morland convinced me that this was a reasonable resolution for our impasse. He had previously hinted that he might sue me for the balance due, which was his perfect right, of course. But I did not hold that against him. I hurried out into the storm, found him holding forth in his office – in the dark as it were – and resolved the matter, at the same time concluding our business amicably. That is all there is to it. And that is the last time I beheld poor Morland alive."

During this interview, the intermittent grumble of distance thunder grew into a clamor of increasing detonations. Rain began cascading down, all but drowning out the man's words, which were couched in a forthright but low tone, as befits discussing the recently deceased.

454

All the while, Holmes simply regarded the man without comment. It was uncharacteristic of him not to probe with questions of his own, and I took this to mean that my friend accepted the electrician's account without qualm.

I was soon to be disabused of this assumption. I should not have been greatly surprised. But I confess that I was.

A streak of lightning slashed the heavens framed in the window behind Thorson's head. He jumped up. His head turned about, and he stared out the window at the jagged electrical bolt. It was like a luminous artery fading from sight.

"My word!" he exclaimed. "From the sound of it, we are in for another beastly round of weather."

Lestrade said, "Pray resume your seat, Mr. Thorson. To return to the matter at hand, have you nothing else to offer?"

Donald Thorson gave the question no great consideration. He answered readily. "Once I had completed my work, I left Mr. Morland to his own toil. I daresay we were both well satisfied with the resolution to our disagreement, but of course I should only speak for myself."

Another bolt hurtled earthward and the entire room lit up with a blue-white discharge that made us all resemble startled ghosts. I know that I felt that way, and Thorson's stark aspect in the searing electrical light gave me that impression.

Again the electrician jumped out of his chair and looked about rather nervously.

Holmes spoke for the first time. "For a man who works with electricity, you appear to be apprehensive when it manifests in its natural state."

Slowly, carefully, Thorson sat down again, but this time his fingers clutched the arms of the overstuffed chair and he looked as if he were prepared to propel himself to his feet at the slightest excuse. Had it not been for the resounding storm, I would have judged him guilty of something.

"Mr. Holmes," he said carefully, "I work with the Jovian stuff. Who would know better than I of its potentials for destruction?"

"Elegantly stated," agreed Holmes. "Now I have a question or two, if you do not mind." This was pitched to both Lestrade and Mr. Thorson, both of whom nodded wordlessly.

"When Morland was found deceased upon the floor of his office," said Holmes carefully, "the electrical lights were not functioning. How do you explain that fact if you restored service?"

"You don't say! Let me see, I left around nine-twenty that evening. The storm raged more than half the night. It is possible, in fact it is quite likely, that an errant thunderbolt undid all of my hard work."

"Yes," agreed Holmes. "Both possible and plausible. Let me ask this: Did Mr. Morland give you a receipt for the work done?"

"No, he did not."

Thunder grew louder in the background.

"Did Morland provide documentation that the debt between you were settled?"

"He did not, Mr. Holmes. As professional gentlemen, we simply shook hands on the matter. That sealed it forever."

"At least, it was sealed forever," mused Holmes thoughtfully. "But by death rather than by any human agency."

Thorson batted his eyes several times nervously. From his expression, it was clear that he did not know what to make of that laconic comment. Nor did Sherlock Holmes enlighten him.

An interval of silence came and went. I noted that Thorson's fingers on the arms of his comfortable chair became tenser, as if in expectation of something unpleasant.

Holmes supplied that ingredient with his next words. "You might be wondering why we are so interested in the death of Sylvester Morland."

"It had crossed my mind, yes."

Holmes's next words shocked me. "We are considering the theory, still unproven, that Morland was electrocuted by the very wiring you claim to have restored."

A wild little laugh shook itself out of the electrician's mouth. His eyes lit up strangely. "What are you gentlemen suggesting – that Morland was done away with deliberately?"

"If you take that implication from my words, you were taking them too far," said Holmes flatly. "My suggestion was merely that Sylvester Morland might have met his fate through faulty electrical work."

Thorson became slightly indignant. "My work is considered to be of impeccable quality. And your accusation a canard. If the electricity went out after I had departed Morland's office, it was through no fault of mine. You might as will blame almighty Zeus as me."

Sherlock Holmes appeared to be leading up to something, but that same deity invoked by Morland seemed to intervene.

Another bright thunderbolt manifested, followed by booming thunder. The house shook noticeably.

This time, Morland sprang from his chair with the feral look of a tiger. He turned this way and that, then his eyes fixed upon the window pane to his right. They widened, and out of his mouth came a strange scream, trailing off into a wail.

"Look! Look it's the accusing devil himself!"

At those words, we were all up on our feet, staring in the direction the quaking man had indicated.

I confess in retrospect to experiencing a shock unlike anything I have ever before felt. I am not a believer in the supernatural, but for a moment, my scientific convictions were shaken to the core.

For the lower pane of glass framed a face, a countenance I had beheld once before. But not in life – in death!

In the semidarkness, it appeared to be the face of the late Sylvester Morland!

With a fearfully shrill outcry, Donald Thorson bolted in the direction of the kitchen. Holmes, followed by the Lestrade and myself, rushed in the opposite direction.

We went out the front door, and pounded towards the parlor window on its opposite side.

There was no one lurking there. The pane was perfectly transparent, unblemished by anything other than dripping raindrops.

"Quickly!" yelled Holmes. "Search in all directions. The ghost is abroad."

We three dispersed, inspected bushes, peered around corners, and rushed about in the rain, all the while fearful of another punishing thunderbolt.

Holmes vanished to the rear of the house, after first examining the muddy ground which had accumulated so much rain water that tracks were not easily discerned.

When finally we were forced to conclude that our quarry had either successfully fled, or was not in any way, shape, or form physical, we returned to the welcome shelter of the parlor.

Donald Morland could not be found. He had fled out the back way, apparently in utter terror.

When his absence was firmly established by search, Lestrade turned to Holmes and demanded, "What do you make of it, Mr. Holmes?"

"I make of it murder."

"That fact has already been established – by you."

Holmes waved the statement aside. "I'm not referring to the late Mr. Morland. But to another party."

"Thorson?"

"Perhaps. Perhaps not."

Holmes strode up to the very parlor window through which the apparition had appeared. He gazed into the glass a long time, as if expecting to discern something there. Finally, he turned to address us.

"I found this in the mud," said Holmes. "Dropped, no doubt, by one of the parties who fled."

Out of a pocket he produced a long white envelope, very wet and soiled. It was addressed to Donald Thorson. There was no stamp or postmark upon the envelope, nor any return address. It was sealed. Holmes took the liberty of opening it.

From within, he took and unfolded a sheet of plain stationary. It bore no salutation or signature. Instead, there was a blob of India ink, in which three smeared words were visible.

I read the running letters aloud: "*Pay your debt!*"

"What does that mean?" demanded Lestrade.

"On the surface, it would suggest that the ghost of Sylvester Morland is continuing to dun Mr. Thorson for an unpaid debt incurred in life," intoned Holmes.

The seriousness of his utterance took me aback. This infuriated Inspector Lestrade, who burst out, "You cannot be serious, Holmes!"

"There is one fact which I consider to be both unassailable and unimpeachable. And that is this: Mr. Morland is demanding that Mr. Thorson pay him."

Neither Inspector Lestrade nor I knew what to say to that.

Without another word, Holmes stalked out into the elements and we were forced to follow.

Huddled in the rain, Sherlock Holmes turned to Lestrade. "Inspector, let me suggest that you muster a number of your constables and search for Donald Thorson. If your men prove swift, they may be able to forestall another murder."

"I will do as you say, Holmes," returned Lestrade, "but I would expect an explanation first."

"There is no time for explanations," snapped Holmes. "If your men can lay hands upon Thorson, you may lawfully arrest him on the charge of murdering Sylvester Morland."

"Really, Holmes!" I interjected. "Thorson seemed perfectly innocent during the course of our conversation, and only became nervous at the approaching thunderstorm. How can you so casually deem him a murderer?"

Holmes did not answer directly, but instead took us around to the back of the house where he had previously sought the missing electrician.

In the rear glowed a small single-pane window. The window was sheltered by overgrown bushes, which Holmes thrust aside.

In the light from the street lamps, we could see the glass. Distinct as if edged etched there was fixed a frozen face. Its features were shadowy and not discernible, but the unkempt halo of hair and protruding right ear were outlined perfectly. But to my eye it was all but identical to the fearsome silhouette that we had been told was somehow impressed into the glass of Sylvester Morland's office window pane.

Lestrade pushed forward, placed one hand upon the glass, and rubbed it vigorously. The image did not fade or disappear.

"I confess I do not know what to make of this," he said, withdrawing in frustration.

Holmes stated, "Consider that Mr. Thorson is being haunted by his misdeeds, Lestrade. If you will be good enough to mobilize the local constabulary, you may have your man before midnight."

Looking rather bleak, the inspector rushed off to do exactly that.

Holmes turned to me. "Quickly, Watson. We must catch the next train to Harwich."

"Harwich? Whatever for?"

"Because I have no doubt that Donald Thorson has in mind to take that very train."

We found an unoccupied cab, availed ourselves of it, and were rushed to the train station. But, alas we were too late. The train to Harwich had departed only ten minutes before.

A hasty consultation with the ticket agent brought forth the fact that a rain-soaked individual had boarded the late train to Harwich. "He was a wild-haired sort," the agent averred. "I did not see his face very clearly. But in a rush, he was."

Holmes next described Donald Thorson.

"That fellow also purchased a ticket," the agent offered.

"Thank you," said Holmes.

Taking me aside, he said, "Thorson trailed the revenant and they are on the same train. No doubt the quarry is unaware of his pursuer."

"Do you expect violence to be done?"

"Not upon a moving passenger train, no."

Holmes possessed a remarkable memory. One might call it phenomenal in its retentive powers. Without consulting a timetable, he announced, "The train to Yarmouth will be along in twenty minutes. It stops at Ipswich. We will get off there, and hire a cab to take us to Harwich."

I objected slightly. "Do you not think that Lestrade will be put out once he discovers that you have sent him off on a wild goose chase?"

Holmes frowned. "I rather doubt that Lestrade ever arrives at that particular suspicion. Inasmuch as I could not be certain of Thorson's ability to make the Harwich train, it was a reasonable suggestion, circumstances being what they are."

In due course, the train pulled in and we boarded.

As it rattled through the intervening towns, Sherlock Holmes unburdened himself of certain facts.

"Thorson was clever enough," said Holmes. "But he made a number of slips, one of which was to volunteer that he had been with Morland on the night in question. Most of what he related was substantially true, save for certain particulars. I descried no sign of electrical wiring repair in the Morland office, and the lights had not been restored, the electrician's representations notwithstanding. No doubt the solicitor summoned him for the very reasons stated, but Donald Thorson was playing a deeper game. Namely, to revenge himself.

"As proof of his fabrications, we have Thorson's failure to produce written proof of the resolved debt. Watson, have you ever heard of a man of the law failing to draw up a memorandum attesting to the receipt of funds or services rendered?"

"Never!"

"I rest my case," said Holmes. "Furthermore, did you mark the man's swift assumption of a murder accusation when I implied nothing of the sort?"

"I did, but not immediately."

Holmes nodded. "Thorson's failure to bring up the subject of the apparition in Sylvester Morland's office window is also suggestive of guilt."

"How so?"

"Why would he avoid what the newspapers have made a sensation?" asked Holmes.

"Perhaps he puts no stock in ghosts," I ventured.

"Yet he fled in terror from what appeared to be a visitation from the revenant."

"So he did. Puzzling."

"Not puzzling when you comprehend all the skeins in this particular web."

"Holmes, why did you suggest that Morland was murdered by electricity?"

"Why, to make it appear that I was not on the correct track. Thorson was doing a credible job of appearing to be an innocent person. I was encouraging him in the belief of his successful imposture, the better to trap him, you see. Unfortunately, the thunderstorm disrupted the placid snare of my interrogation."

After a pause, Holmes scrutinized me silently for some moments, then inquired, "Why have you not leapt upon the most basic question of all, Watson?"

I managed a blank frown, I suppose.

Holmes smiled thinly. "You failed to ask how I knew that among Morland's dissatisfied clients, one must be an electrician?"

I smiled. "That was elementary, my dear Holmes. Who else would be present at such a late hour under the circumstances?"

Holmes suppressed a dry chuckle. "I accuse you of reasoning backwards from subsequent facts, but no matter. That was my thinking."

The train soon arrived and I found myself sitting beside Holmes in a rain-slickened hansom cab, rushing to an address he told the driver. The address meant nothing to me, but it was within sight of the Harwich High Lighthouse.

As we raced along, Holmes broke his silence. "I trust you have your revolver, Watson?"

"I have it."

"Would you lend it to me? That's a good fellow."

Holmes carefully checked the weapon, saw that it was loaded, but that the chamber under the hammer was empty. This was a common precaution against accidental discharge. Only when he was certain that the weapon was safe to pocket, did he conceal it on his person.

As we approached our destination, Holmes asked that we be let off two streets short of the stipulated address.

We walked the remainder of the distance in the rain, which was steady but not extreme. Fortunately, there was no electrical activity present in the clouds massing above our heads.

The home to which Holmes led me be proved to be dilapidated and in the state of disrepair, but not distressingly so. It was an

461

ancient cottage and the years had not been kind to it. Evidently, the occupant had given it a little attention in recent years.

Holmes approached cautiously, one hand stuffed in the pocket of his coat where the revolver rested.

He stalked up the front walk, whose flagstones were cracked and loose. Holmes appeared to be determined and not at all inhibited in his bold stride.

"I pray that we are in time," he said to me, "but I fear that the interval between trains will prove decisive."

A muffled report coming from the confines of the house stamped a grisly period at the end of Holmes's sentence.

Rushing forward, he assaulted the door. It proved to be unlocked. Holmes thrust himself inside, the revolver in hand.

A strange voice cried out, "Murder! Murder!"

The familiar voice of Donald Thorson screamed in rage, "Not murder, you low blackmailer! Doom! Righteous doom!"

Another shot rang out. It came from the far room.

Heedless of the danger to himself, Sherlock Holmes barged into the room in question, I myself not far behind him.

Sharp shots were traded! One gouged a door frame perilously close to my head. I heard the ugly sound of a body falling to the floor, followed by another.

When I entered the room, I was greeted by the spectacle of Sherlock Holmes standing over the bodies of two men. One I recognized instantly. It was Donald Thorson. A smoking pistol was clutched in one hand, but the fingers would never again move of their own accord. The fellow was dead.

Kneeling, Holmes removed the pistol and then turned his attention to the other corpse.

The body in question was jittering in its death throes, and soon completed them. The nervous tension in the muscles relaxed, and it was as if the newly dead man was gaining in stature even though he was stretched out upon the floor. A modest lake of blood seeped out from beneath him. The powder marks of two point-blank gunshots showed blackly on the man's shirt front. But my attention did not linger there – they went to the fellow's face.

I knew it. Or thought that I did. For I had seen the identical cadaver stretched out before me in the London morgue. It appeared to be the face of Sylvester Morland!

"There is your ghost, Watson," pronounced Holmes solemnly.

All but tongue-tied, I blurted, "How can a newly-dead man produce a ghost three days in the past?"

462

"Of course, he cannot," Holmes returned sharply. "Any more than the spirit of a dead man could become trapped in glass. For all is not what it seems to be, despite the seemingly inconvertible certainty of otherwise unfathomable evidence."

I offered nothing, for I had nothing to say. I was utterly baffled. Staggered would not be too strong a word.

"Kindly explain yourself, my dear fellow," I entreated Holmes.

"Do you recall mention that Sylvester Morland had a brother? One who lived in Harwich."

"Well, now that you remind me, I do. Is this his twin then?"

"Not a fraternal twin, no," said Holmes. "My research revealed, they were but a year apart in age, as you might surmise from this man's general appearance. You will note the wild hair not tamed by pomade, as well as the protruding right ear, which is not precisely the same configuration as the one that I noted in the morgue. That was one of my first clues that the image in the solicitor's window was not that of the dead man himself. The differences were subtle, true, but also undeniable."

"How, then, did the image come to be embedded in the window?" I wondered.

"Come, come, Watson. Surely, now that the supernatural explanation has been discarded, it should not be hard to deduce the obvious."

"Obvious to you, I have no doubt, but I confess that I remain flummoxed."

"You cannot be ignorant of the fact that glass negative plates remain the most common means of capturing images for photographic reproduction."

"Well, yes. Of course I am familiar with glass negatives. Who is not?"

"From the sensation caused by the original glassy image, one might conclude that few were," said Holmes dryly. "The late Mr. Artemis Morland here is – or was – a chemist. And if we investigate his basement, I am sure we will find the inevitable photographer's darkroom, as well as all that is necessary ingredients to coat ordinary window glass with the proper emulsion that will make it sensitive to retaining photographic impressions when subjected to bright light."

"By what means were these images imprinted?"

"During the time that you were taking your extended sleep of recovery," said Holmes, "I was exceedingly busy. I had already formed a possibility in my mind, which I verified by consulting a local photographer, as well as going to the Royal Observatory where,

463

as I am sure you will recall, photographs of the stars are captured on glass plates. In our sitting room, I studied the original window pane closely and attempted to duplicate the process by means of flash powder. I would have preferred a lightning bolt, but the elements were uncooperative."

Holmes continued, "All whom I consulted agreed that it was possible for images to be imprinted upon glass by lightning flashes. This has occurred in the past, but it is a rare phenomenon. I might note that similar occurrences have given rise to credible reports of haunted houses. This is what happened on the night Morland was murdered."

I was now even more baffled than before, for Sherlock Holmes appeared to be suggesting a different murderer than the one named previously.

"My thoughts are tangled, Holmes. Your assistance in straightening them out would be greatly appreciated."

"Mr. Artemis Morland was the estranged brother of Sylvester Morland, the solicitor," Holmes related. "The reasons are somewhat obscure, but discreet inquiries revealed that Artemis Morland greatly lamented being excluded from his brother's life. He dearly yearned to alter that circumstance, but the stubborn solicitor rebuffed all fraternal overtures. The younger brother, Artemis, a chemist of modest repute, hit upon a scheme that was as fantastic as it was unlikely to move his obdurate older brother. He had developed an ingenious colloid emulsion that could be applied to the surface of a window in such a way that when illuminated by flash powder, the image of anyone staring in or out of the pane would be imprinted upon it, albeit without impressive clarity or fidelity. It had the regrettable limitation of fading within days, making it commercially of doubtful value.

"It was the younger brother's thinking that by surreptitiously coating his brother's window by night, during a thunderstorm, an interesting effect would be produced. This is surmise, Watson, but I give it great weight. Artemis appears to have hoped that by marking his distinctive countenance upon the window as a perplexing reminder of the unresolved issues existing between them, his brother would weaken and relent in time."

I was moved to say, "That sounds preposterous, to put it mildly."

"Absurd might be equally descriptive, I will grant you," said Holmes. "But this was the scheme, and during the recent stormy night Artemis Morland set out to implement it. As it happened, he arrived at his brother's office at an inopportune moment, and witnessed the cold-blooded murder of his own brother. During that interval, a lightning bolt streaked through the sky in such near proximity that the abrupt flare imprinted a perfect outline of his own head upon the glass. This later was incorrectly assumed to be the image of the dead man, when it was not."

"I see. Obviously, after this Morland fled the scene."

"Obviously," returned Holmes. "What he witnessed was shocking in the extreme, and there was nothing he could do about it. Sensational newspaper accounts published the next morning apprised Artemis of the silhouette created on the window, for the murder prevented him from igniting flash powder in his possession. No doubt he feared being accused as an accessory to the crime – hence the appearance the next day of 'Bob', who inveigled the poor street urchin into hurling a cobblestone at the incriminating window pane."

"May we assume that Bob was acting upon the orders of Artemis Morland?"

"We assume nothing of the sort," shot back Holmes. "Call to mind the boy's description – unruly hair and blue eyes. Attributes of the dead solicitor, as well as his younger sibling."

"Ah! I see now. Bob was Morland the younger."

"In any event," continued Holmes. "Sylvester Morland's brother hit upon a fresh game. Blackmail. In some way, he discovered the identity of the murderer, I suspect by following him to Earls Court, and set about to apply his foiled plan to this new endeavor. First, he painted the emulsion to one of Thorson's windows, imprinting his own face upon it by igniting flash powder when the man was not home. No doubt he was inspired by the newspaper reports of the original haunted window pane. I also do not doubt that at least one letter or note of demand was sent to Thorson – the one I discovered that was dropped before being slipped into the electrician's mailbox. As you will recall, it exhorted, '*Pay your debt.*' Here, then, was a demand for blackmail, not an unpaid bill."

"Remarkable," I said.

"If you're referring to my deductions, Watson, I must deflect a great deal of your praise, intended or otherwise. But if you are referring to the schemes of Artemis Morland, I will agree that they are remarkable, although also pathetic and tragic at the same time. All he wished was to reconcile with his brother, and now they are both deceased. This is a tragedy, Watson. And a testament to the folly of bruised feelings and unbending egos."

"You hint that you know more about the estrangement than you let on," I suggested.

"I would let the details be buried with both men. They are no longer important. Now, we must inform Inspector Lestrade of the unfortunate outcome of these proceedings."

As Holmes turned to seek a telephone, I remarked, "There was never a ghost then, Holmes?"

"Or to put it another way," replied my friend, "now there are three."

The Affair of the Grange Haunting
by David Ruffle

The fire in our sitting-room supplied a pleasing warmth that was altogether absent in the outside world. Although spring had very definitely arrived, winter was not giving way without a fight. I had buttoned up my overcoat, had wrapped my warmest scarf around my neck, and done battle with the elements in order to collect the morning newspapers, which unaccountably had not been delivered. Holmes was leafing through his correspondence and sifting the various missives into two unequal piles. By far the smaller of these two piles contained only those letters whose contents had piqued his interest. I stretched out my feet towards the flames and devoured a piece in *The Times* which seemed an unduly pessimistic view of the chances of Middlesex landing the County Championship in the coming cricket season. I glanced at the two piles of correspondence.

"It looks like a barren day for you, Holmes."

"In an unceasing run of barren days," he replied, shaking his head ruefully.

"Something will turn up, you mark my words."

"Ah, Watson, the eternal optimist. Your well of boundless enthusiasm is fathoms deep, I only wish I shared it. My correspondents are certainly a cross-section of society from the highest in the land to the humblest, the wisest to those who could best be described as potential inmates of Colney Hatch asylum. Ah, I believe this illustrates my theory perfectly," he added, holding a sheet of paper above his head, brandishing it like a weapon. "Listen to the opening lines, Watson. *"Mr. Holmes, I am at my wit's end. My only hope is you, or failing that . . . a priest!"*

"If he requires some form of moral guidance, I would recommend a priest, Holmes."

"Thank you. I knew I could rely on you for a response along those lines."

"I presume this correspondent of yours goes on to outline his problem?"

Holmes put up a hand to stay me as he scanned the rest of the text. A few grunts and sighs later he declared himself finished.

"Well?" I asked.

"Mr. Caleb Charles of Middleton Cheney appears to have moved into a haunted house. In his letter, he details the manner of this haunting in admirable detail, a trait much to be admired."

"Admirable indeed, I'm sure, but why on earth would he write to you about the matter?"

"Perhaps your chronicling of my adventures, as you term them, leads people to believe I am a universal panacea for anything and everything. He does, however, mention a mutual acquaintance, Thomas Cromwell."

"I had not realised you went back so far," I laughed.

"Other than the fact of his being also a son of a blacksmith, my Thomas Cromwell has little in common with his more illustrious namesake, and certainly seems duty bound on keeping his head intact on his shoulders. He was, for he is retired now, an inspector with the Northamptonshire Constabulary. We met several years ago when we were both retained to look into the action of the counterfeiters who went by the charming name of The Press Gang. Most of them were rounded up and deposited in several of Her Majesty's prisons."

"Notwithstanding that connection, do you intend to answer Mr. Charles with your regrets that you will not be able to look into his problem?"

"You race ahead too quickly, Watson, unlike the horses upon which you place your money. We are due, are we not, at the Oxford Assizes to present evidence in the Bennett case? It is but a short train ride to Banbury, and from there no distance at all to Middleton Cheney, where we can see first-hand the problems that burden Mr. Caleb Charles. Namely these *knockings, unearthly wails, and other unexplained phenomena* as he puts it in his rather lively letter."

"Surely, you do not put any credence in this tale, you of all people!"

"You are correct. I do not think for a moment Mr. Charles is plagued by spirits. Yet he may well be plagued by something else."

"I dare say it is his own fevered imagination."

"I am surprised to hear you say it, for surely you have a far more open mind than I do, for what may be termed by some, supernatural events."

"Once, maybe. The older I get, the less inclined I am to believe."

"I certainly cannot chide you for that. In essence, you are a man of science, as am I, and while there may be things that we cannot explain at the moment, I am confident that science will shine a light into those areas of darkness. As for our man in Middleton Cheney I will wire Thomas Cromwell and ask him for his recollections of Caleb Charles, and then plan accordingly."

Our trip to Oxford was not due to take place for two weeks, and during that time Holmes received the information he required from Thomas Cromwell regarding that gentleman's connection with Caleb Charles. The connection, as it turned out, was quite superficial. In fact, Cromwell had difficulty in even placing the man. This paucity of information, however, did nothing to dampen Holmes's enthusiasm for visiting Middleton Cheney. As for me, I was not enthusiastic in the slightest, but I reckoned I would once more be falling into step with Holmes's plans as so often before.

In the days leading up to our departure for Oxford, I had seen very little of Holmes – not that there was anything unusual in that. He came and went in a variety of disguises from an Anglican clergyman to a jobbing builder. The stage lost a fine actor when Holmes decided to turn to sleuthing for a living. I was no less busy myself, for I had taken on a few of Anstruther's patients, as he had taken the decision to lessen his workload in preparation for his retirement. All these new patients seemed to be in the thralls of hypochondria, and my own workload increased dramatically and quite unnecessarily. The result was to ponder my own retirement, something I had given much thought to of late. My life was very full indeed, what with assisting Holmes in whatever cases he may have on hand, not to mention writing up the notes of those cases in readiness for publication. I had heard Holmes mention retirement himself, although it was not something I could readily imagine.

The proceedings at the Oxford Assizes turned out to be laboriously slow. Holmes, although an expert in the application of law, found such trials very tiresome, and was vociferous in declaring his displeasure to all and sundry. Holmes's evidence in this particular case was crucial to the prosecution, and he manfully endured a torrid cross-examination by the defence barristers. Despite a few muttered oaths under his breath, he came through with flying colours. After two days spent in the courtroom, Holmes was heartily glad that he was released from his duties.

The following morning, we left the Randolph Hotel and made our way to Oxford Station, where we caught the ten o'clock service to Banbury. The train pulled into the Merton Street Station, which was alongside the cattle market. We could see young boys, for the most part looking thoroughly miserable, guarding the gates to prevent any escapees. A fellow traveller explained that the boys would stand there the best part of the day while their fathers conducted their business. The proximity of the market was reinforced when we alighted, for the air was thick with the cries of drovers, the bellowing of cattle, the bleating of sheep, and the squealing of pigs. Coupled with the stench, it was a veritable assault on the senses.

We had arranged to see Caleb Charles in the early part of the afternoon, which gave us a little time to explore this market town. I particularly wanted to see Banbury Cross, famed as it was in the nursery rhyme, *Ride a Cock Horse to Banbury Cross*, a ditty that was one of the very first things I had learned to recite as a child. I was disappointed to find the cross was a modern structure on the site of the original, which had long since been torn down. However, I did get my first taste of Banbury Cake, a confection filled with currants, other fruits, and spices. It more than made up for the disappointment occasioned by being unable to see the fabled cross.

Our attempts to obtain transport to the village of Middleton Cheney were fraught with difficulty. The first cabbie we saw declared, "Sorry, sirs, but I don't go abroad."

"Abroad? We only ask you to take us to Middleton Cheney, and we will pay handsomely."

He leaned into us as though he was going to divulge a state secret. "But that's over the border, my duck. It's in Northamptonshire."

"Could you recommend anyone?" I asked.

"There's always your legs," he said, drily.

In the end, after other fruitless enquiries, we indeed found ourselves walking to the village. I reckoned the distance to be just under three miles, but as the greater part of it was uphill, it made little difference to my mood which was expressly one of disillusionment and disappointment.

We came to The Grange, Caleb Charles's house, after a solid forty-five minute walk. It had the appearance of a farmhouse, perhaps of the 17th century, constructed out of locally quarried stone (as I learned later), which gave it rich, honeyed look, both warm and inviting. To the side of the building were various outhouses which seemed to have been given over completely to the storage of bicycles and carts of all shapes and sizes.

Mr. Charles, an elderly yet sprightly gentleman, greeted us warmly and bade us enter. He guided us into a large and sparsely furnished sitting-room where a large fire blazed in the inglenook. Truth be told, although the weather was mild, the house, even with a fire lit, did feel a little cold.

470

"Would you care for tea, gentlemen? It will only take me a few minutes to prepare."

"You have no housekeeper or other servant, Mr. Charles?" Holmes asked.

"No," he answered, chuckling wheezily. "The house has a certain reputation, which has the effect of scaring off the ladies of the village from any gainful employment here."

"Is the reputation one that has been gained recently?"

"No, Mr. Holmes, it has acquired this notoriety over many, many years. Let me gather our tea together. Then we can discuss the house at our leisure."

I warmed my hands by the fire, feeling the need to rid myself of this unaccountable cold. "Do you feel a chill, Holmes?"

"I am perfectly warm, thank you. Perhaps your older bones account for the fact you are feeling it."

"Speaking as a medical man . . . ."

Holmes cut me off before I could finish my sentence by raising his hand in my direction. He was staring intently at what appeared to be a family portrait captured in a photograph. He produced his magnifying lens and studied one of the faces.

"No doubt, Watson. You have heard me say that I never forget a face."

"I do not believe I have ever heard you say that, Holmes."

"Well, it is of no matter."

Mr. Charles appeared in the doorway and attempted to steer a lop-sided trolley laden with teapot, cup, and saucers through the gap. I sprang to his assistance, and after safe negotiation to the heart of the sitting-room, I poured our tea, and we awaited Caleb Charles's account of this so-called haunting.

"First of all, you must know," he started, "that I had never even heard of The Grange until a few weeks ago, nor indeed Middleton Cheney. I had for myself a small dwelling in Tring, where I worked as a clerk for the Hertfordshire Council. The position was quite humble, but adequate for my needs and wants. I have never put any great store in ambition, and was content just to knock along as I was."

"A few weeks ago, I was contacted by a solicitor who practiced in Brackley, who informed me that a cousin of mine, who I assure you I would not know from Adam, had left a property and a small sum of money to me."

"The cousin's name?" interjected Holmes.

"Samuel Waters. I gave notice at the council, put my affairs in order, and uprooted myself. Would that I had not!"

"The family portrait on the wall there. Is that the Waters family?"

"The housekeeper who was here when I arrived to take up residence told me it was. The gentleman on the left is Samuel, the woman on his right was his late wife, Lavinia. The young man is Samuel's son, James, and the burly man is Clive Merry, who is James's cousin. Mrs. Mold mentioned some trouble connected with Merry, but did not burden me with any details, nor did I want any."

"Is James still living?" I asked. "I only ask because, if he was, he would surely inherit."

"As far as the Waters's family solicitor is aware, it is more than possible that James is alive, but no one, it seems, has seen sight or sound of him for some years."

"Now, as to your recent troubles?" nudged Holmes.

"All was quiet for a week then I began to hear whispered voices, and footsteps overhead on the deserted upper floor. I heard bangs and curious tappings and scratching noises at all hours of the day and night. Often, I awoke to see the grey shape of a man at the foot of my bed."

"Can you be sure it was the figure of man?" asked Holmes.

"I am absolutely sure."

"The housekeeper you mentioned – was she a witness to these events?"

"No, Mister Holmes, I had to let her go immediately. The small sum of money I inherited if I invest it wisely will cover my living costs, but will not stretch to the payment of wages."

"Did you consult her regarding your experiences?"

"Yes. I visited her and asked her if she had experienced anything of a similar nature. She professed she had not, but there had been talk in the village for many years of odd occurrences here."

"Did your housekeeper live in before your arrival?" I asked.

"Yes, Mrs. Mold had been in residence for many years. I felt very guilty about letting her go."

"I am sure you were," said Holmes in an impatient manner. "So the house, as far as you are aware, has never lain empty in recent years?"

"I think it is fair to assume that, yes. Is it important?"

"It's entirely possible it could have some bearing on the matter, but I fear I get ahead of myself."

472

I was puzzled as to what the fact of the house being empty or not could have to do with it and, although I was still of the opinion that our visit here was a waste of our precious time, I posed a question of my own.

"Did the tales Mrs. Mold told you differ essentially from your own experiences here?"

"They covered the whole gamut of the recognised signs of a haunting. The only difference to what I have seen or heard myself is the stories that tell of a young girl who haunts the house, going from room to room bouncing a ball, imploring all those who see her if they will play with her. A legend, no doubt, but an entertaining one all the same."

"You are not a believer in the supernatural then, Mr. Charles?" I asked.

"Oh, I try to keep an open mind, but I have seen or heard nothing to convince me that such things happen – until now of course."

"And yet you come to me, a detective, rather than a priest, for instance."

"I do not want to believe there is a anything other-worldly going on, and as I have followed your exploits closely, I felt sure you would be the man to reveal the truth of what is happening in this house."

Almost on cue, there came a tremendous bang from somewhere above us, like a heavy piece of furniture had fallen or been thrown to the floor.

"Quick, Watson, the stairs!" shouted Holmes, without asking for any form of assent from Mr. Charles.

I heard, or seemed to hear, footsteps as we ascended the stairs, followed by three large thuds that reverberated throughout the building. Upstairs, we could find nothing during a cursory search that appeared out of place in the sparsely furnished rooms, and nothing that would account for the noises we heard. Holmes then commenced a rather more thorough search, laying himself down across the floorboards in each room, running his fingers along the edges of each plank. Walls were examined in much the same manner, with what furniture there was being pulled away from the walls. Holmes rapped hard on the wood panelling and plasterwork, but we heard nothing suggestive of the hollow cavities or tunnels that I assumed rightly, as it turned out, that he was looking for.

There were two doors on the upper floor that were locked, and after finding the keys in a kitchen drawer, we returned upstairs to

473

resume our search. Behind the first door we tried was a large cupboard with shelves filled with long-forgotten bedding, rotting and discoloured.

After unlocking the other door, we found some dilapidated wooden steps which took us up to a large attic. It appeared to run the whole length of the house, and contained a jumble of detritus of families past: Retired household appliances jostled for space with clothes, furniture, children's toys, and even garden implements and, oddly enough, several bird cages.

"What do you think caused the noises we heard, Holmes?

"If one lives in a big old house, you have to accept that occasionally things go bump, creak, tap, crash, and groan in the night. In our family home, I remember seeing effects caused by changes in humidity that would have been instantly ascribed to spirits had they occurred here. Wood increases its width as humidity rises. Rapid changes in humidity can have spectacular effects. If one walks down a stair so that the boards jam, they will release later with a sound like a footstep.

"If a layer of dryer air rises, the footsteps go up the stair as the wood shrinks and springs back into shape. If boards have been too tightly laid, the skirting boards can creak as if someone is creeping around the edge of the room. Taps on a door, or in a piece of furniture, can happen as the panels move against the frames. A change of air moving along a lengthy corridor, as when someone leaves an outside door open, can cause a shift in the woodwork that sounds for all the world like someone in slippers moving along. Perhaps these are the ghosts of the Grange, Watson. But possibly there is more at work here than meets the eye."

"There is a human element to this, you think?"

"The family portrait, coupled with the existence of the bird cages, renders it very probable indeed."

"I don't quite follow you."

"Forgive me, Watson. I sometimes forget you do not share my knowledge of sensational crimes."

"Something of which I am heartily glad, I can tell you! What is our next step, should there be one?"

"A wire to Thomas Cromwell should be enough, if I am on the right track."

Caleb Charles informed Holmes there was a post office in Queen Street, and he promptly left the house to send his wire. He was back a few minutes later, telling us that a boy would be dispatched to the Grange as soon as a reply was received.

474

Once more, we made ourselves comfortable in the sitting-room with a freshly brewed pot of tea. Holmes leaned back in his chair, his fingers steepled together, eyes shining.

"Now, gentlemen," he announced. "A few years ago, there were several bank robberies the length and breadth of Northamptonshire, with occasional forays into Oxfordshire. The gang were a nasty bunch, with much violence meted out to bank clerks and managers who had the temerity to resist. Eventually, acting on a tip-off, the gang were apprehended at their hideaway in the village of Turweston. All but the nastiest of them were captured then and there. He went on the run, but was picked up in the village of Thenford."

"Where is that?" I asked.

In reply, Holmes pointed out of the window. "That road opposite goes to Thenford."

"Was the stolen money recovered?"

"Some, but by no means all. The gang numbered five and all were sentenced to lengthy prison terms, the longest being reserved for the leader and most violent, one Clive Merry."

"James Waters's cousin!" I exclaimed.

"Indeed, Watson. One member of the gang received a lesser sentence for, from all the witness accounts, he had not once joined in the violence and was described even by fellow gang members as being gentle. It was said he formerly trained canaries. Anyway, Jim Wilson, known as *Wilson the Canary Trainer*, received a sentence of twelve years only."

"J.W. . . . bird cages," I spluttered. "Jim Wilson was *James Waters*?"

"That is my belief, Watson."

"When did these events occur, Mister Holmes?"

"Ten years ago."

Just then there was a knock at the door. Holmes leapt up and disappeared into the hallway to answer it. He came back into the room brandishing Cromwell's reply.

"Ah, it seems the man known to the law courts as 'Jim Wilson' was released early from his gaol term, owing to his excessively good behaviour."

"When?" I asked.

"Just a few weeks ago."

"Then you are saying in effect that James Waters is responsible for the events here? But how? Or indeed, why?"

"The obvious conclusion is that he believes that Merry, during his flight, hid what was left of their loot in this house, and it is his intention to recover it."

"I am at a loss to see how Merry could have made his way in here and found a hiding place. Surely, Waters's family would have been in residence."

"We can confirm or deny that by asking Mrs. Mold what she can remember of that time. Do you know her address, Mr. Charles?"

"Yes, Mr. Holmes. It's Archery Road, No. 13. But from what little she has told me of the family history, I believe it was around ten years ago that Samuel Waters took his wife on an extended visit to Switzerland, hoping such a holiday would benefit her failing health. Sadly, it did not work, and Lavinia died shortly after their return."

"Do you think Waters has hidden himself in the house, Holmes? And why the noises of a haunting?"

"As we have learned, he is not a man of violence, so his probable intention is to scare his kinsman away, and as that appears not to be working as yet, he no doubt performs a limited search while Mr. Charles is soundly asleep."

"We must institute an immediate search," I said decisively.

"Ah, Watson, always the man of action. I believe we can save ourselves the labour and allow Waters to reveal himself."

"How can we do that?"

"With a little subterfuge and a little oil," he replied enigmatically.

From the sparse pickings in the kitchen, we managed to construct ourselves a meal, Holmes revealing unexpected culinary skills. It was decided that we would stay the night, and Holmes would reveal his plan to us in the morning. The bedrooms were as sparsely populated as the kitchen, and the best we could do was to attempt to sleep using our overcoats as blankets for warmth. I was not optimistic of obtaining a good night's sleep, and so it proved.

After what seemed like no more than a few minutes fitful sleep, I was awakened by a noise I could not readily identify. The moon was shining reasonably bright, and as my eyes adjusted, I could make out a shape by the door. Thinking immediately of James Waters, I leapt out of bed ready for a confrontation. On doing so, I very suddenly came to the realisation that this could not be he, for the shape was more childlike. This mystifying shape became more defined and even before I was aware of seeing it, I could plainly hear the sound of a ball being bounced onto the floor. The thuds and the recognition of what it meant paralysed me. I opened my mouth to

476

speak and no words would form. Fully fledged in front of me was a young girl of perhaps six or seven years old, her eyes fixed on me as she bounced that infernal ball. She opened her mouth and I clasped my hands to my ears, having no wish to hear the words I knew she would utter. I was transfixed with terror and chilled to the bone. I knew no more until I awoke with the early morning sun streaming through the window.

Still feeling chilled, I slipped on my overcoat and descended the stairs. Holmes and Charles were in the kitchen with a freshly brewed coffee apiece.

"Ah, Watson, we had almost given up on you," Holmes quipped. "Do I detect a disturbed night?"

I had already resolved to keep my experience to myself for fear of ridicule more than anything else. My reply was consequently vague.

"A little, maybe. Have you resolved a plan of action?"

"Indeed I have, my dear fellow. I have located some oil," he replied, tapping a can which was sitting on the table, "and we are about to go an excursion."

"Could I have breakfast first, at least?"

"I am very much afraid that our meal of yesterday evening over-stretched the Grange kitchen's resources somewhat. Take a sip of coffee and follow me into the hall."

I gulped down as much as I could manage in my disordered state and joined Holmes and Charles at the bottom of the stairs.

"Now, I have a squeaking hinge to see to," Holmes said.

Holmes crossed the hall to the door, opened it, and proceeded to oil the hinges before putting the lock to the latch position. After positioning himself once more at the foot of the stairs, he announced in a stentorious manner: "Well, gentlemen, if you are ready, we will go. Firstly to Archery Road, and then I fancy a trip to Banbury is in order to get some supplies in for dinner tonight."

We followed Holmes out of the door, whereupon we turned to our left and walked around a bend, where Holmes promptly sat himself on a bench, pulled out his pocket-watch, and lit a pipe.

"Come and join me, gentlemen. We need not be here long, I assure you."

We spent thirty minutes or so sitting there. Holmes was content to smoke his pipe and discourse on English stately homes and the deplorable rise in the price of tobacco. He suddenly got to his feet.

"I think that should suffice. I would be grateful if you both observe silence for the next few minutes."

477

We eased ourselves through a now silent door. Holmes halted and stood stock still for a few moments before setting off in the direction of the kitchen.

Standing outside the door, we could plainly hear a tapping noise, a creaking of wood, and also a sharp intake of breath.

Holmes crashed through the door and there, prostrate on the floor grappling with a floorboard, was the recognisable figure of James Waters. He sprang to his feet and made a dash for the back door, a look of alarm on his face.

"Please, Mr. Waters, there is no need of flight. We mean you no harm," stated Holmes.

Waters paused in his flight, looked at us intently, and in that moment decided we could be trusted.

"It was a nice trick you played there, and I fell for it completely."

"You have been playing tricks yourself!" protested Caleb Charles.

"Yes, I have. I saw as it the only way to give myself the time I needed for a thorough search of the house. If I frightened you unduly, I apologise. Who are you two other gentlemen?"

"My name is Sherlock Holmes, and this is my colleague Dr Watson. You may have heard of me and any small reputation I possess. You are obviously of the belief that your cousin Clive Merry hid a sum of money here, your ill-gotten gains from your bank robberies."

"I am convinced of it. Oh well, it will be for someone else to discover now. If you wish to send for a constable, I will come quietly."

"I have no intention of so doing. I am not aware that you have committed a crime, other than those you have already paid the penalty for. By rights, this is your house, and as I see it, you are entitled to do as you wish in it, including searching for the proceeds of your crimes."

"But, Holmes," I protested. "The money is the property of the various banks it came from. It is not for you to decide what happens to it."

"It may be that I am compounding a felony, but the banks will have been compensated by their respective insurance companies. It may be that they have had to pay a few extra pennies on their premiums – nothing they cannot afford, and as I just stated, Waters has paid his debt to society."

He turned to Waters: "If Mr. Charles is agreeable to you staying here whilst you continue to search, then that is my recommended course of action. Of course, when and if you find the cash, you may wish to offer some of your bounty to Mr. Charles. Tell me, where did you secrete yourself?"

"There is a further room in the attic space. I have been camping out there with my meagre supplies. I could certainly do with a square meal, I can tell you."

Holmes threw his head back and laughed. "You are not the only one, I assure you. One more question, if I may: The tip-off the police received. Did that come from you?"

"Yes. I was sickened by the violence I saw. I wanted it all to end."

"My advice is simple. Take the money and make a fresh start far away from here."

"Thank you, Mr. Holmes. That is exactly what I intend to do."

We heard later from Caleb Charles that the loot had been discovered and James Waters had sailed to Australia to begin his new life. He added as an afterthought that all notions of the house being haunted had of course now dissipated.

As to my own experience, I tell myself often that it was a waking dream and my imagination supplied the images and sounds. But, all the same . . . I know what I saw.

I think of it still.

The Adventure of the Pallid Mask
by Daniel McGachey

<u>THE CAST</u>

SHERLOCK HOLMES – *The famous consulting detective*

DR. JOHN H. WATSON – *His associate, chronicler, and friend*

INSPECTOR LESTRADE – *One of the best of the Scotland Yarders*

ACTRESS – *A member of a theatre troupe, playing "Cordelia" and "Cassilda"*

HUBERT WARBURTON-BRANCHE – *A flamboyant Victorian actor/manager*

MONSEIUR HAWKSPUR – *A mysterious translator of uncanny works*

MRS. LONGBRACE – *A shabby London landlady*

MR. MYCROFT HOLMES – *The enigmatic older brother of Sherlock*

Narration by Watson, Branche, and Holmes is presented in italics

<u>MUSIC: OPENING MUSIC UP AND UNDER</u>

WATSON: *Of the many Scotland Yard officials who trod the well-worn stairs to our sitting room, none was a more frequent, nor more welcome, visitor than the one who called upon us on a torrential autumn morning in the latter days of Sherlock Holmes's tenure in Baker Street.*

SOUND EFFECT: THE SITTING ROOM OF 221b: THE CLOCK TICKING, THE FIRE CRACKLING, AND RAIN OUTSIDE HEARD THROUGHOUT. A KNOCK, THEN THE SITTING ROOM DOOR OPENS

LESTRADE: Good morning, Dr. Watson. Mrs. Hudson said for me to just come up.

WATSON: Quite right, too. No need to stand on ceremony with you, old chap. Take a seat by the fire. (CALLING OFF) Holmes! Inspector Lestrade is here! (TO LESTRADE) It's still raining, then?

LESTRADE: Great Heavens, you've been learning tricks from Mr. Holmes, I'd swear!

WATSON: Not at all, your hat and coat are . . . . (THEN, WITH A CHUCKLE) Ah, very droll. You have a case for Holmes? Something bizarre or out of the ordinary, perhaps?

LESTRADE: Well, I think what I have promises those baffling features paramount in gaining Mr. Holmes's attention.

SOUND EFFECT: HOLMES'S BEDROOM DOOR CLOSING SOFTLY AS HE ENTERS

HOLMES: I'll be the judge of that, Lestrade. And you, Watson, can stop looking so eager, too.

MUSIC: LOW AND MOURNFUL UNDER NARRATION

WATSON: *But I was eager to hear what Lestrade had to say. With little of late to tax Holmes's ferocious intellect, he had lapsed into a dejection which had worsened with each new day, until finally he had abandoned his sullen meditations, only to stalk off into the night.*

SOUND EFFECT: THE DOOR SLAMS. CLOCK TICKS THE PASSAGE OF TIME. THEN, UNDER THE FOLLOWING, THE DOOR OPENS, FOOTSTEPS ENTER, AND BOTTLES AND RETORTS CLINK AND RATTLE

WATSON: *It was only after several days' absence that he had returned, unshaven, and laden down with bottles containing soil, clay, and gravel, which he pored over as if examining the facets of a great diamond. It was then that I was suddenly required in my professional capacity, rather than as a friend. For, following his intense study of these relics of his expedition, he had thrown up his hands with a cry of disgust and crashed headlong into a fevered swoon.*

HOLMES: (A CRY) Trickery! This cannot be! All lost!

SOUND EFFECT: A CRASH OF FURNITURE AND GLASS

WATSON: Holmes? What on earth . . . ?

HOLMES: (PUZZLED, DELIRIOUS) Watson? It is you . . . I . . . I thought you were . . . lost . . . .

WATSON: Then I'm sure if anyone would have the ability to find me, it would be you. Now, let's get you to your room . . . .

SOUND EFFECT: RAIN, GROWING IN INTENSITY, AS THE WIND HOWLS

WATSON: *Now on this chill day, with the skies unleashing a deluge upon the city, it was surely the fever in whose grip he had spent the previous days that caused his apathy as Lestrade described his latest problem.*

SOUND EFFECT: RESUME CLOCK, FIRE, AND DISTANT RAIN

LESTRADE: . . . and, being blunt, Mr. Holmes, I'm not one for reading, beyond the *Illustrated Police Gazette* and Dr. Watson's rather . . . fanciful retellings of your escapades, so I didn't instantly grasp what was odd about this play when Mr. Warburton-Branche told me of its loss.

WATSON: Hubert Warburton-Branche? Who you say introduced himself as the actor-manager of the Lyric Theatre in the West End?

LESTRADE: Announced himself! I don't know who pointed him in my direction, but I knew he was a theatrical from the instant he burst into my office yesterday morning. Overwrought doesn't even begin to describe it.

HOLMES: Then I wish you would confine yourself to terms which *do* describe it. Otherwise this discourse will prove entirely unenlightening, and therefore pointless.

LESTRADE: Look, I've got my hands full, what with vandalism in Burke Court and some nasty business with a dead body down by the river. But I reckoned there was something odd that might appeal to your interests for someone to risk stealing a thing they can neither spend nor sell. Then there's the play itself. I can't do justice to the wild things Mr. Warburton-Branche told me about it, so it would save us all some time and trouble if you would come and meet the gentleman in person.

HOLMES: And it would save me even more of both if I declined to do any such thing, and occupied myself in more pressing pursuits than chasing up your cast-offs.

SOUND EFFECT: HOLMES'S FOOTSTEPS GOING SWIFTLY OFF. HIS ROOM DOOR OPENS THEN SLAMS

WATSON: My dear Lestrade, I can only apologise for Holmes's behaviour. He has been rather out of sorts of late . . . .

LESTRADE: "Of late"? If that's the cause of his blasted rudeness, he's been out of sorts all the years I've known him!

WATSON: We know where to find you, Inspector. The Lyric Theatre. I'll have a quiet word with Holmes . . . when he wakens, hopefully in a better frame of mind . . . .

483

LESTRADE: Thank you, but I wouldn't bank on it, Watson. If there's a right side of bed to get out of, that's the one thing he hasn't detected yet. Good day to you.

WATSON: (LOUD ENOUGH TO BE HEARD THROUGH A CLOSED DOOR) Holmes! I know you're not sleeping, so I know you can hear me. Good Lord, man! The dearth of stimulating problems is such a frequently heard litany within these walls that I considered having Mrs. Hudson embroider it to hang above the mantel. So I cannot help but marvel at your perverse refusal to find a shred of interest in the loss of the single copy known to exist within these Isles of a play as controversial and mysterious as the one that has been stolen!

SOUND EFFECT: HOLMES'S ROOM DOOR OPENS

HOLMES: And if I were to find this lost manuscript, what next? Recovering mislaid newspapers? Or possibly I could expand beyond mere paper products to the thrill of finding lost bicycles and locating wandering spouses?

WATSON: This is no ordinary manuscript, though, Holmes. This is notorious! Blasphemous, even! Some say utterly nightmarish! Holmes, this is *The King in Yellow*!

MUSIC: EERIE AND FORBIDDING UNDER THE FOLLOWING

HOLMES: You speak as if I should immediately know the title.

WATSON: A scandalous and deplorable work, if you were to heed the references in those Continental newspapers that you use to adorn our dining table and carpets . . . .

HOLMES: To which I subscribe in order to keep abreast of criminal affairs from beyond our shores, not for the theatrical notices.

WATSON: I know very well your indifference to drama and poetry. Even so, this play's origins are steeped in intrigue, its author is

484

unknown or untraceable, and it is said to have so startling an effect on those who see it performed that it might be thought possessed of some power that is . . . unnatural . . . Certainly unhealthy!

HOLMES: Then might it not be better if it remained unaccounted for, if it has these extraordinary consequences?

WATSON: Extravagant claims to incite public curiosity. You can't tell me that this isn't *recherché* enough to incite your own? Besides, you've said yourself often enough that you can never resist a touch of the dramatic.

HOLMES: (A LAUGH) Well put, Watson. And as it would be churlish to resist your earnest entreaties, we shall meet this theatrical entrepreneur who has the recklessness to attempt mounting so notorious a production, then.

WATSON: Finally! (STEPPING AWAY) I'll fetch our overcoats, if we're to brave . . . .

HOLMES: Tomorrow. You can send word to friend Lestrade to preserve the scene until then. I haven't the energy for overwrought impresarios today. Besides, it was no lie when I said I have pressing matters to attend to – namely sleep. Kindly remove that look of reproach, Watson. It has never suited you. And you are forever telling me that I must not misuse myself so freely.

SOUND EFFECT: HOLMES'S ROOM DOOR FIRMLY CLOSING AS HE EXITS

WATSON: Yes, but I had no idea you ever listened.

MUSIC: SOFT, MELANCHOLY UNDER NARRATION

WATSON: *A telegram was sent, though given his treatment, I was unsure how gratefully Lestrade would receive it. In truth, it was I who was grateful to the inspector. Though it had been many years since Holmes had sought chemical stimulus as a release from boredom between cases, I was all too aware that the temptation may simply have been lying dormant within him.*

485

HOLMES: (UNDER NARRATION. FEVERED, DELIRIOUS, AND LARGELY UNINTELLIGIBLE) Strange is the night . . . black stars . . . strange moons . . . laid aside disguise . . . no mask . . . I wear . . . I have seen the yellow . . . mask?

WATSON: *Having administered to him as he'd weaned himself from that wretched habit, his nightmarish delusions as he sweated through his recent fever brought memories of those alarming weeks vividly to mind. Once more I found myself sternly lecturing against that destructive drug, reminding him of his many astonishing achievements, which would have been impossible had he continued to allow his vice to hold him in its thrall.*

WATSON: . . . and with a mind addled with poison, would you have unmasked the real evil behind the curse that roamed the great Grimpen Mire?

HOLMES: (FEVERED) Mask? No, no mask! It was the hound in human form, the curse stalking on two legs instead of four . . . .

WATSON: *In those long gone days, distraction from the commonplace had been the only answer, so I was relieved that Lestrade had delivered just such a distraction to ensure those days remained long gone.*

SOUND EFFECT: FADE THROUGH TO INSIDE A COACH, HOOVES AND WHEELS SPLASHING THROUGH PUDDLES, AND THE RAIN STILL POURING OUTSIDE

WATSON: You seem more refreshed and buoyant today, Holmes.

HOLMES: Buoyancy would be a fine attribute on such a day, old boy. The city's streets are more like canals. And those unlucky enough to roam them have taken on the look of denizens of some long-drowned city.

WATSON: Well, I think I recognise that example of the walking drowned approaching us now.

SOUND EFFECT: THE RAIN INTENSIFIES AS THEY LEAVE THE COACH, FOOTSTEPS SPLASHING

486

HOLMES: Whatever your Mr. Warburton-Branche may claim, his theatre lies in rather too easterly a direction to be truly in the West End, Lestrade.

LESTRADE: And a good morning to you, too, Mr. Holmes.

WATSON: Still, it's grand in its own faded way. New paint on the boards, fresh varnish on the doors, and the brass handles and parquet floor polished to gleaming.

SOUND EFFECT: AUDITORIUM DOORS CREAK OPEN AND SHUT, CUTTING OFF THE RAIN

(Below the next piece of narration, echoey sounds of a rehearsal may be heard . . . .)

ACTRESS/CORDELIA: "How does my royal lord? How fares your majesty?"

BRANCHE/LEAR: "You do me wrong to take me out o' the grave: Thou art a soul in bliss; but I am bound, Upon a wheel of fire, that mine own tears, Do scald like moulten lead."

ACTRESS/CORDELIA: "Sir, do you know me?"

BRANCHE/LEAR: "You are a spirit, I know. When did you die?"

WATSON: *The masks of tragedy and comedy leered down upon pale, shrouded forms as lengths of canvas protected the seating, while pails and mops awaited an attack on the years of dust and nicotine staining the woodwork. And facing onto this was a stage, upon which a troupe, struggling to give life to the tragedy of* King Lear, *became aware of their unexpected audience . . . .*

BRANCHE: (DROPPING CHARACTER) What is this intrusion? Is it he? Has he returned?

WATSON: You weren't exaggerating his tendency for melodrama, Lestrade. He's stepping down from the stage like Zeus descending from Olympus.

487

HOLMES: The scarlet robe doesn't lessen the similarity. However, I doubt Zeus wore such an obvious toupee.

BRANCHE: (APPROACHING, LOUDLY) Ah, Lestrade. This is all too much! Two disappearances in so many days, and I really cannot say what is to be made of it, I honestly cannot . . . .

HOLMES: Sir, your tones are doubtless modulated to reach the further away seats in the auditorium, but you are no longer on the stage, and we can hear you quite clearly.

BRANCHE: (A FURY) What do you mean by . . . ? (MELLOWING) Why, is it not Mr. Sherlock Holmes and, yes, of course, Dr. Watson? It really is too much, gentlemen. I am a man driven to his limits. Please, one moment . . . .

WATSON: *With that, he shooed the assembled players away, the troupe dispersing with more enthusiasm than they had shown in their rehearsal.*

SOUND EFFECT: TRUDGING FOOTSTEPS AND MUTTERING GOING OFF

BRANCHE: This grievous crime has rendered us despondent, and I thought it better to dismiss them. They are such sensitive souls and . . . Well, your pardon, Inspector, but there's nothing less aesthetic than a Scotland Yard official going about his trade. (CHEERING CONSIDERABLY) Now here, gentlemen, we have something quite otherwise.

HOLMES: The effusiveness of your handshake belies your self-proclaimed despondency.

BRANCHE: I have long desired to meet you both. Doctor, your narratives of Mr. Holmes's exploits positively teem with dramatic possibilities. Have you ever considered an adaptation of your more thrilling tales for the stage?

WATSON: Well, there was this American fellow once, who . . . .

488

HOLMES: (INTERRUPTING BRISKLY) Mr. Warburton-Branche, you speak of two disappearances. The first, clearly, is this notorious manuscript. And the second?

BRANCHE: Why, Nightingale! Frederick Nightingale, a most promising member of the company. He failed to materialise for yesterday's rehearsal – not that we can proceed with the rehearsal I had foreseen, following the vile intrusion of Tuesday night – nor has he emerged today, and no reply to the messages I've sent to his lodgings.

HOLMES: With nothing to rehearse, his presence would seem redundant.

LESTRADE: I insisted on his being here, Holmes. Same with all of the company, in the event one of them should be connected to the theft.

BRANCHE: And as I told you, Inspector, I can imagine no-one less likely to have committed this barbaric act than Frederick Nightingale. He would have neither the strength nor the constitution. He's so delightfully pale and aesthetic. Just the perfect aura for tragedy. And such a powerful tragedy would have been played out upon our stage, if fact had not overtaken fiction within these very walls! Such a debut it would have been . . . .

WATSON: His debut? Then he's not been with your troupe long?

BRANCHE: Mere weeks, yet he has made himself invaluable in so many ways.

HOLMES: And how long have you pursued a desire to stage *The King in Yellow*?

BRANCHE: Mr. Holmes, just to set eyes upon a copy of the text has been a tangle of lengthy searches, lost trails, and dead ends. Until that prize package was delivered on Tuesday afternoon, all I had were tantalising hints, garbled accounts – surely exaggerated, and full of flights of fantasy! Even so, when I first glimpsed a pale, bearded figure outside my theatre declaiming the sonnets for passing pennies, it was clear that I had found the very incarnation of "the Stranger" whose arrival signifies the doom of the lost kingdom of Carcosa. Perhaps even the tattered King himself in his pallid mask!

WATSON: *For reasons that I could not yet fathom, these brief mentions of alien names and places chilled me. There was something familiar, yet just out of my grasp . . . .*

HOLMES: What a stroke of good fortune for you to find him, then, on your very doorstep, just as you had secured the text holding a role seemingly made to measure for him. And a great misfortune for you to lose him again.

WATSON: And just as the play too has gone. The arrival of this fellow and his departure seem peculiarly well-timed. The one might be a coincidence, but both together strike as rather suspicious.

LESTRADE: But hardly conclusive. Doctor, I've had dealings with so-called actors in the past. Little more than gypsies, most of them, moving on from place to place. Mostly they leave only bad memories, broken promises, and broken hearts behind them. (REMEMBERING WHO HE'S WITH) No offence meant, Mr. Warburton-Branche.

HOLMES: From your tone, Lestrade, I take it you wish me to continue to view the case as one of missing property, and not missing persons?

LESTRADE: Quite so, Mr. Holmes. Unless, of course, our elusive Mr. Nightingale proves to be involved in the break-in.

BRANCHE: Entirely out of the question, Inspector. The man is an artiste, not a common cultural vandal.

LESTRADE: Cultural vandals aren't as common as all that.

HOLMES: Mr. Warburton-Branche, I think it would be best if you were to tell me the facts from the beginning.

MUSIC: SOFT UNDER THE FOLLOWING

490

BRANCHE: If I may just set the scene for you, then, Mr. Holmes. Our little company is relatively young, and while my own name has a certain cachet, it cannot yet match that of the great Irving. Such are the slings and arrows faced by the artiste, and when the Warburton-Branche Dramatic Company took up residency here, the once flourishing Lyric had descended to little more than a music hall, shunned by those who crave artistry.

WATSON: Yet you're clearly making great strides in restoring it.

BRANCHE: I was on the verge of letting the tumblers and chorus girls back on the bill when whispers reached me of the extraordinary *coup de theatre* creating such ripples on the Continent. A play whose grip on its audience was so strong that some became inextricably caught up in the fantasies it wove. It had become the scandal of the season, with talk of it being banned outright by the authorities of more than one nation. I can readily believe it truly is a work that obsesses the minds of all who have witnessed it, as I was most assuredly obsessed with it, sight unseen. If I secured exclusive rights to mount the London premier of the piece, would that not be the audacious move that would draw the crowds away from Irving and his ilk?

HOLMES: Audacious is as good a word as any.

MUSIC: GROWING EERIE AND DISCORDANT

BRANCHE: Throughout my enquiries, I heard either that the author had taken his own life as penance for summoning such a work into being, that he had been murdered – or given up as an offering – by those who saw his work as a true and faithful history relayed by unearthly means and merely transcribed by him. Yet others swore that he still lives and strives in increasing despair in his futile attempt to match the perfect note of art that he has achieved in his fledgling offering. How terrifyingly maddening his efforts must be! And how much more terrifying for us all should he succeed!

WATSON: (SOFTLY) Holmes, he's speaking like a fanatic . . . .

HOLMES: (SOFTLY) Even so, let us hear his account and judge if his fanaticism is misplaced.

BRANCHE: I thought to have located an agent representing the author in Paris, but the man proved to be a delusional liar. The news later reached me that he took his own life, as well as those of several innocents whom he had grown convinced were revolutionaries plotting against him in his entirely hallucinatory position as ambassador of some undefined kingdom.

WATSON: Dear Lord! Some grotesque monomania . . . .

BRANCHE: Such are the dangerous individuals one encounters when dealing with the chronicles of the King! Others were opportunists, frauds, and confidence tricksters who attempted to claim exorbitant finder's fees. I was taken in more than once, shame on me. Then, I found Monsieur Hawkspur, the translator! Rather, I should say, Monsieur Hawkspur found me . . . .

MUSIC: EERIE CHORDS RISE IN PITCH, THEN OUT

SOUND EFFECT: BRANCHE'S OFFICE. A SHEET OF PAPER UNFOLDING

BRANCHE: *Upon yet another frustrated returned from Paris, I received a note, the hand somewhat curious, but the English impeccable . . . .*

HAWKSPUR: (DISTANT) "Monsieur Warburton-Branche, your quest has become known to me, so I write to propose that I deliver into your hands not simply the play as I have obtained it, in my native tongue, but the entire work in translation."

BRANCHE: *He asked none of the ridiculous sums I had grown to expect – merely his regular fee for translating the text.*

HAWKSPUR: (DISTANT) "You may also find enclosed references to my previous experience in preserving in translation the essence of the author's intent in numerous other dramatic works across several nations."

BRANCHE: *Having been so foolhardy in my spending, I checked these references and found them genuine. And as I awaited the completion of Monsieur Hawkspur's task, my company continued in our routine of rehearsals by day and our best efforts presented by night. Until, to my joy, I received the telegram announcing that he would soon be on our shores with the finished work! In a state of nervous expectation, I dismissed the company early, rather than face them should I be left waiting in vain, and sat alone in my office, growing evermore convinced that I was awaiting a phantom.*

SOUND EFFECT: FIRM KNOCK AT THE OFFICE DOOR. BRANCHE'S EAGER FOOTSTEPS, THEN THE DOOR OPENS

BRANCHE: Monsieur . . . . (STARTLED) Monsieur Hawkspur?

HAWKSPUR: Naturally, sir. This is the appointed hour, is it not?

BRANCHE: *Monsieur Hawkspur was . . . rather unusual. Like many of his countrymen, he possessed a certain elegance of dress and of speech. But the most striking thing about him was that he was entirely blind, his eyes concealed behind dark-tinted spectacles.*

SOUND EFFECT: HAWKSPUR'S STEADY FOOTSTEPS, BEFORE HE TAKES HIS SEAT

BRANCHE: *He made no mention of his affliction, and found his way easily through the unfamiliar surroundings of my office to lay the precious manuscript on my desk. My own eyes kept flicking between the neat, handwritten pages before me and those black lenses which threw the distorted image of my startled features back at me. I was grateful that he was unable to see the confusion I saw reflected in my expression. So, I suppose it must have been something in my voice that betrayed me.*

HAWKSPUR: Naturally you cannot conceive how a man deprived of his sight can take a composition in one language and reproduce it in another. Here is no great mystery. I was not always this way, and I learned as we all do how to put ink to paper. It always pleased me, the ability to transmit thoughts and ideas from the internal recesses of the brain through such simple means. And after my loss, I strove to retain that ability through practice and exercise. My own thoughts, alas, are of interest to no-one. I am but a medium through which the ideas and fantasies of others may

493

be spread. I may no longer have the means to see those written thoughts, but it is an inconvenience simply overcome. I employ someone to read to me. What my ear hears, my mind visualises, still as words which appear upon a white page. The movement of the hand is quite mechanical.

SOUND EFFECT: A SHARP DRUMMING OF FINGERS

BRANCHE: *His fingers drummed upon the desk as if operating a typewriter. Gloved though he was, I could hear the clatter of nails that I took to be unnaturally long.*

HAWKSPUR: The mind is where the true work is done. I am assured that the results are quite presentable.

BRANCHE: *I could only add to that assurance. The pages before me were as legible as any type-sheet.*

HAWKSPUR: It relieves me to have completed your commission. I finished it with little time to spare, as the secretarial agency on which I have so long relied now refuses to send anyone to read for me. Toward the end there were too many who became . . . erratic in their actions.

SOUND EFFECT: HAWKSPUR'S FOOTSTEPS FADE INTO DISTANCE, AS WE FADE UP AUDITORIUM

BRANCHE: The last sight I had of him was as he moved, with little effort and considerable grace, through the crowds on the street. And I was relieved to have him gone. In part, because I wished to be left with my long-sought prize. But mainly as his presence had unsettled me.

WATSON: A blind man sounds harmless enough.

BRANCHE: He had claimed to have been blind since childhood, yet behind those dark lenses I could see fresh scars amongst those turned white with age. My peculiar fancy was that mere blindness wasn't enough. That he still tore at those sightless eyes with long, yellowing nails, in an effort to remove the images that existed only in his own internal darkness.

494

HOLMES: That is indeed a peculiar fancy. And then, left alone, you finally read the play?

BRANCHE: No, Mr. Holmes. I did not.

WATSON: After seeking it so long? Why-ever not?

BRANCHE: I tell myself it was caution, in case the pages proved some elaborate forgery, yet I could see no gain in playing such a trick for so paltry a sum. Did I fear it would fall short of those delirious expectations I'd harboured? A few stolen glances told me that there was beauty there. And horror too! I wanted nothing more than to lock my door and let my eyes devour those words, such was their hold on me. And it was this hold – this compulsion – that frightened me. So I sat gazing at it without ever touching it, until the clock chimed six and I had my excuse to go.

WATSON: Why? What is it that occurs at six o'clock?

BRANCHE: That, sir, is when I partake of my ritual. It must be observed, and I . . . but, look at me! Still robed and crowned for Lear . . . If you will kindly excuse me . . . .

SOUND EFFECT: BRANCHE'S FOOTSTEPS CROSSING THE STAGE

HOLMES: (CALLING) This "ritual" you speak of . . . ?

BRANCHE: (OFF) We actors are a notoriously superstitious lot. If a rehearsal goes well, I remain behind to raise a toast to the Gods of Tragedy and Comedy whose masks gaze down on all poor players.

WATSON: And if it goes badly?

BRANCHE: (OFF) I raise several toasts elsewhere, well beyond the reach of their baleful eyes, and beseech Bacchus to put it from my mind for a few hours.

HOLMES: And the rehearsal had gone badly?

SOUND EFFECT: BRANCHE'S FOOTSTEPS AS HE RETURNS

495

BRANCHE: (COMING BACK) Props misplaced. Costumes in disarray. I held myself responsible. My eagerness for the afternoon's appointment had made me careless.

WATSON: *The figure who strode back out across the stage wore a velvet coat I suspected was cut from the same roll as King Lear's gown, and a waistcoat across whose folds a thick watch-chain gleamed. Even out of costume, the actor looked like he might still be playing a role.*

BRANCHE: What did the rehearsals matter? Oh fickle, faithless artist! I would exchange Lear for another, tattered yet altogether more formidable eminence. My dread would have flown by the morn, and the ritual would at least ease me into sleep. *"To sleep, perchance to . . . ."* (TROUBLED) No, perhaps not that . . . .

HOLMES: And what of the manuscript while you indulged?

BRANCHE: I have a strongbox in my desk. It normally holds the evening's takings, but there are none at the moment. Our planned season of classical Greek drama was cancelled, to no great outcry, and I chose to devote my energies to the material needs of the building itself. We have pigeons in the roof and the moth is rampant in the costume store. But what you see is a theatre in the process of being born afresh!

HOLMES: What would be more instructive for us to see would be your office and this strongbox.

SOUND EFFECT: AUDITORIUM DOORS OPENING, THEN A MURMURING HUBBUB AS THE ACTORS RETURN. THE DOORS SWING CLOSED ON THEM AS FOUR SETS OF FOOTSTEPS ECHO ALONG A CORRIDOR

WATSON: *We left the auditorium as the actors returned, their tunics and robes replaced with rolled sleeves and smocks, to take up pails and brushes. I've heard the term for an actor not performing is "resting", but as I glimpsed a flushed Cordelia take a scrubbing brush to a stained cherub, the term seemed entirely unsuited.*

BRANCHE: Please, come in. This is my throne room, from where I command my kingdom. Or it will be again, once I'm allowed to do more than stand and admire the view.

WATSON: *The office walls were adorned with framed playbills, on which the name Warburton-Branche was prominently emblazoned, while a desk and bureau were cordoned behind rope barriers.*

SOUND EFFECT: HOLMES'S FOOTSTEPS CROSS THE ROOM

HOLMES: The entry was made by the removal or breaking of a pane in the window, allowing the intruder to reach inside and unfasten the lock.

BRANCHE: Aha! The detective in dramatic reconstruction of the crime. If I may take on the part of the dumbfounded client . . . This is extraordinary, Mr. Holmes! I never said that the window had been the means of ingress!

LESTRADE: Ho! Just like in one of your stories, Doctor.

HOLMES: (POINTEDLY) Quite, Watson! But, it is perfectly simple. There is a single pane of glass noticeably cleaner than those that surround it, which, on closer inspection, shows fresh putty in its frame.

LESTRADE: I ordered the repair, rather than leave an unsecured window to put temptation in the way of any passing rogue.

HOLMES: Really, Lestrade, how much data will you rob me of? Did you have the furniture rearranged and the room redecorated while you were at it?

LESTRADE: No, but I did take pains, if you'll forgive the pun, of having the pane of glass preserved in this cloth for your inevitable inspection.

497

HOLMES: My apologies, Inspector. I see you've taken at least a moment's notice of my methods over the years. Well, now. A perfectly circular hole.

WATSON: This suggests to me a diamond-tipped glass cutter. An invaluable part of the housebreaker's box of tricks, but something unlikely to be in the possession of any spur-of-the moment opportunist.

HOLMES: An opportunist would have done considerably more ransacking upon the discovery of a strongbox devoid of takings. It would be unlikely that he would settle for some reading matter in its stead. Where did you find the extracted glass, Lestrade?

LESTRADE: In the alley, surprisingly unbroken considering the traffic that passes through there at all hours. The alley serves the back entrances of several public houses and a restaurant, so there are deliveries in the early hours. If there was anything else to be found out there, it was trodden underfoot before we were called in.

HOLMES: Evidently another part of our intruder's box of tricks is a pair of gloves, as he's left no trace of himself on the glass. And the drawer (CROUCHING) hasn't been forced. Nor, I see has the strongbox.

SOUND EFFECT: SHARP RAP OF KNUCKLES ON METAL, AND A DULL ECHO FROM WITHIN

HOLMES: Sturdy enough, and entirely undamaged. (STANDS) You, of course, have the key, Mr. Warburton-Branche. Has any other?

SOUND EFFECT: A JINGLE OF KEYS ON A CHAIN

BRANCHE: No-one, Mr. Holmes. And that's the mystifying thing. I have the keys to the desk and strongbox here upon my watch chain, you see. The chain, and the keys, never leave my waistcoat.

HOLMES: You have been rehearsing the role of King Lear. And does the King wear a waistcoat?

BRANCHE: Why, naturally, not. Preposterous! I change, with the help of a dresser, who takes charge of my day to day clothes while I am onstage, and . . . Oh . . . Oh, no?

HOLMES: Might this dresser have been Mr. Nightingale, who "has proved so useful while awaiting his debut"?

BRANCHE: But he is an actor amongst fellow actors! Oh, now, is that it? Hubert Warburton-Branche, how can you have been so monstrously dull-witted? A talent like that going undiscovered? Impossible! He had been discovered, oh, yes, but by a rival! By an enemy! Yes, he is an actor indeed, and he played his role to the hilt!

WATSON: It was known, then, amongst the acting fraternity, of your intention to produce *The King in Yellow*?

BRANCHE: Naturally, Dr. Watson. One cannot present a theatrical coup when no-one knows about it. Word of mouth plays a vital part. But there's no way of knowing whose ear that word will reach. There are jealous foes all around that would prevent my triumph.

LESTRADE: A rival company attempting sabotage is a plausible explanation. But I'm not going to march up to Sir Henry Irving and ask him if he's taken up burglary.

BRANCHE: (RISING IN PITCH) But can't you see what they would deny me? When this theatre has achieved its renaissance, it will be the magnet toward which all minds possessed of a love of art will be drawn. There will be royalty in attendance, of that I can assure you. What has happened here is treason! You must make your enquiries!

HOLMES: We are endeavouring to do so. Now, the alley, as Lestrade informs us, is a veritable procession of drays and delivery boys, and even had anything instructive survived such an onslaught, it would still have been carried away by the rains.

Therefore, we must confine our search to our immediate surroundings.

BRANCHE: (MOOD SHIFTING TO EXCITEMENT) Ah, the famous magnifying lens! I had hoped to see the renowned hawk-like gaze brought into play!

HOLMES: (IMPATIENTLY) You will observe here, and here, tread marks with a distinct bluish grey hue. I can think of a dozen locations where such a clay is to be found, but only two in which street-works, which would be likely to unearth it in any great quantity, are being carried out.

SOUND EFFECT: A SHEET OF PAPER UNFOLDING

LESTRADE: I have been thinking on similar lines, Mr. Holmes. I have a list of public works, and I sent men out to take samples from each. I'd narrowed it down to Norwood Avenue and . . . let me see now . . . Hardwicke Lane.

HOLMES: You match my nominees precisely. Do you regularly stroll through a park, Mr. Warburton-Branche?

BRANCHE: I've scarcely the time, with so many preparations . . . .

HOLMES: Capital. Of the two locations specified, only Hardwicke Lane lies in a direction that would necessitate traversing any of the city's great parks, these being the very places in which one is liable to gather leaf mould such as that caught up in the clay.

SOUND EFFECT: SCRAPING OF PAPER ON A FLOOR

WATSON: *Holmes scraped a smear of the substance into an envelope, before producing a second envelope and dropping once more to brush the open edge of the envelope across the floor, then rising to show us the glimmering contents.*

LESTRADE: I don't know how I could have missed those.

WATSON: They look to me like brass shavings.

HOLMES: Precisely. Now when I say that not only are there new sewer pipes being laid in Hardwicke Lane, and not merely that this thoroughfare lie beyond a large park, but also that there is a watch-repairer and key-cutter's shop which offers rooms for rent, what does that suggest?

LESTRADE: It suggests we should be at Hardwicke Lane now!

SOUND EFFECT: A HORSE AND CAB HURRYING THROUGH THE RAIN, FADING THROUGH TO INSIDE THE CAB

WATSON: I'm not sure I should have left Warburton-Branche in his agitated state without a draught to calm him. He does have an unhealthy fixation on this play.

LESTRADE: It's my opinion that all actors are in some way crazy. (SMILINGLY) You know, it often surprised me you didn't take up the profession, Mr. Holmes.

WATSON: You did admit that his theory about a rival actor might have possibilities.

LESTRADE: Even the mad can be right about some things.

HOLMES: There is another possibility. From all we know of the play's history, it has inspired fanaticism, both for and against it. Might not someone driven by an opposition to its very being and a conviction that there is danger in its pages feel compelled to act in order to prevent it from being seen?

LESTRADE: It certainly provokes fanatics. And we've just met one. Does he really think that royalty is going to trade a night in the Palace for a dollied-up music hall?

HOLMES: I rather fear our actor friend expects – to use his own words – "a more tattered yet formidable eminence".

MUSIC: EERIE AND UNEARTHLY

SOUND EFFECT: CAB WHEELS AND HOOVES COME TO A HALT. FOOTSTEPS OF HOLMES, WATSON, AND LESTRADE IN THE RAIN

501

LESTRADE: Here we are . . . and there are the workmen's ditches and mounds of blue clay, just as we both anticipated.

SOUND EFFECT: SHOP BELL RINGS AS DOOR OPENS AND CLOSES. MANY CLOCKS AND WATCHES TICK AND ECHO IN THE TINY INTERIOR

WATSON: *Longbrace's Emporium was a cramped shop with a couple of floors perched above. Mr. Longbrace himself seemed to have adapted to the limited confines, so that we were greeted by a shrivelled pate perching atop a hunched, gnomish frame as he laboured on the intricate workings of a timepiece.*

HOLMES: We've come about your rooms for let.

SOUND EFFECT: A HEAVY TREAD AND A CURTAIN RUSTLES

LONGBRACE: No use asking him, love. He has eyes for nothing bigger than a dial or cog, and he hears nothing if it doesn't tick or chime.

WATSON: *The woman who emerged from behind a shabby scrap of curtain to the rear of the shop was as large and smooth as the man was small and wrinkled.*

LESTRADE: We didn't see you there, Mrs . . . ?

LONGBRACE: Mrs. Longbrace. If it's rooms you're after, you talk to me, though I fancy you gentlemen'll seek something a bit more up-market than what we can offer.

HOLMES: (CHEERILY) Ah, more's the pity. We sought a billet for our associate here, who frequently finds his duties leave him late in the city and unable to make the journey home. I'm sorry to have troubled you. Come, Mr. Watson, I'm sure there are other landlords who are more in need of a guinea a week.

LONGBRACE: But, then, who am I to dictate the tastes of others? I'm sure I'm not one to pry into the doings of others. The stairs are at the back. You'll have to go one at a time.

502

HOLMES: (SOFTLY) As ever, the promise of money opens doors quicker than any threat of the courts could. And if you'd direct your gaze to the workshop floor . . . .

LESTRADE: (SOFTLY) Strewn all about with twists and strands of brass. Just like the floor of the theatre office.

SOUND EFFECT: FOUR SETS OF FOOTSTEPS ON CREAKING STAIRS. A DOOR OPENS

WATSON: (QUIETLY) What a dismal, dingy place.

HOLMES: This won't do, Mrs. Longbrace. It overlooks a tannery. The fumes would make our friend quite bilious. Surely you have something more salubrious? We are prepared to stretch to double your usual rent.

LONGBRACE: There's only mine and Longbrace's rooms on the floor above, and this one next door is taken . . . though I might ask Mr. Starling if he'd consider switching.

LESTRADE: (SHARPLY) "Starling"? Just like . . . .

HOLMES: (INTERRUPTING) Yes, you're right, we do know a fellow by that name, don't we?

LESTRADE: Why, yes! I wonder if he could be the same man? Would you describe your Mr. Starling as . . . ah . . . "wonderfully pale and aesthetic"?

LONGBRACE: I might. If I knew what it meant. Pale? I'd say he was. Like a ghost. And not just to look at. Quiet as one, too. *Most* nights. You're not prone to sleepwalking, Mr. Watson, or nightmares? Don't cry out in your sleep, do you? I couldn't be doing with another like that.

WATSON: I assure you, dear lady, I am not given to any of these habits.

503

LONGBRACE: Only he wasn't like that to start with. Here a week and not a complaint, except when he'd come looming out of the dark on the stairs and frighten me half to death, that great white face of his floating there. Still, no-one can help the face they're given, can they? And he paid prompt, so I thought there was no harm in it. More fool me for a kindly thought! Then, being wakened in the night with his pacing and ranting and muttering.

WATSON: Ranting? Did you catch what he said?

LONGBRACE: Odd, foreign words that I didn't much like the sound of. I gave the floor a proper hammering and told him to pack it in, but the damage was done. The disturbed nights I've had since. (A SHUDDER) The dreams . . . .

SOUND EFFECT: A SHRILL OF WIND, THE FLAPPING OF TATTERED CLOTH

WATSON: *She turned suddenly, as if startled, though the only movements to be seen were the fluttering edges of ragged curtains caught in the pale yellow tint of a sun that struggled valiantly to break through the clouds.*

LONGBRACE: (RECOVERING HERSELF) Now don't you worry yourself that he'll be disturbing you, Mr. Watson. I'll have words for him about that and put him out. If he even comes back.

HOLMES: Not here then? And when did you last see him?

LONGBRACE: Not so much "see", but I'm sure I heard him creep back this morning, then out again to wherever he disappears to for days on end. I'll show you the room. You'll see it's more to your tastes.

SOUND EFFECT: FOOTSTEPS ON THE LANDING AND A DOOR OPENING

WATSON: *The room was identical to its twin. Just a table, a lone chair, a sink in one corner, and a low cot in the other. But I forgot the drab surroundings as my eye fell upon the burnt down remains of a candle next to a sheaf of papers on the table. None of*

504

us made a move toward it until Holmes had placed a shining coin into a waiting hand and Mrs. Longbrace made her exit.

LONGBRACE: So nice to have real gentlemen about the place.

<u>SOUND EFFECT: THE DOOR CLOSES, HER FOOTSTEPS RECEDE. THEN THREE SETS OF FOOTSTEPS RACE TO THE TABLE, AND PAGES RAPIDLY TURN</u>

HOLMES: Dr. Watson . . . Inspector Lestrade . . . Permit me to present *The King in Yellow.*

WATSON: It's so neat. Precise. Yet written by a blind man's hand?

HOLMES: You've heard me detail how handwriting can give the key to the author's character more precisely than any biography, Watson. Pride can be found in capitals and doubt in curtailed strokes. It is rather chilling to look on handwriting that gives nothing of its owner away.

WATSON: What was it the strange Frenchman told Warburton-Branche . . . ? That he had nothing of himself to share . . . .

HAWKSPUR: (A GHOSTLY ECHO) . . . I am but a medium through which the ideas and fantasies of others may be spread —

<u>SOUND EFFECT: PAGES BEING TURNED</u>

HOLMES: Then we may find something of the original author. You see? The first act is devoid of any characteristic, which in itself may be taken as a characteristic. Look now at the final pages of Act Two. Can this really be the same hand? There is importance here and massive self-regard. Yet it vies with a sense of impotent rage, as if the desire to exert its power is thwarted. What a proper analysis would reveal of the hand behind this! But that is not our business here today. That was to recover these papers, and this we have done.

LESTRADE: But where is this man, Nightingale? And if he wanted to ruin Warburton-Branche's plans, or was one of your fanatics, why didn't he just destroy the thing?

HOLMES: Perhaps once it was in his possession, he found he could not. As to his whereabouts, I think our Mr. Nightingale . . . or Mrs. Longbrace's "Starling" . . . has flown, and I don't imagine either will be heard of again. However, we may find some trace of his true identity, eh, Lestrade?

LESTRADE: More mud and leaves? Or, with a Starling and a Nightingale, should we be looking for feathers?

MUSIC: EERIE AND UNEARTHLY UNDER THE FOLLOWING

WATSON: *I left them to peer and prod as, giving in to morbid curiosity, I leafed through the script. The imagery of the alien realm of Carcosa, the shores of Hali, the Phantom of Truth, Cassilda and her mournful song, the Stranger, and the fate who awaited all who saw the dreadful Yellow Sign . . . these all brought back an uneasiness I had first felt when Warburton-Branche had spoken of these fictions. But the chill dissipated when a hand relieved me of the pages.*

SOUND EFFECT: PAGES RUSTLE LIGHTLY

HOLMES: I'd advise against delving too closely there. Whatever reputation this piece has may be well earned.

WATSON: And Nightingale?

LESTRADE: Gone, and nary a trace of him to be found.

WATSON: A pity he didn't take the text with him, then! Must we return it? I speak mainly for the sake of Warburton-Branche's mental well-being. And for his audience.

HOLMES: When I shake a hand where the nails are chewed to the quick, I know I am greeting a highly-strung individual. Our friend will regain his composure once his property is returned. He may continue to suspect some plot, but the feeling of persecution will pass. Indeed, if he has any genuine feel for theatrics, he will use this little adventure to add publicity for his production. As for the audience, as any child will tell you, "Sticks and stones may break my bones . . . ."

WATSON: "But words can never hurt me." Let us then hope we can rely on the wisdom of children.

HOLMES: Now, Lestrade, you may restore Mr. Hubert Warburton-Branche's property to him, and then get back to your vandals and your riverside corpses.

LESTRADE: Oh, we've moved on from that. A bucket of carbolic for one and a line struck through the name of a regular villain for the other. But there'll be plenty of reports waiting for me at the Yard. Despite your complaints to the contrary, crime never stops. They might not be peculiar enough to engage your interest, Mr. Holmes, but someone has to work them through nonetheless.

SOUND EFFECT: A HORSE AND CARRIAGE RECEDE, FADING THROUGH TO TICKING CLOCK AND FIRE OF 221b

WATSON: *We went our separate ways, the inspector to Scotland Yard, and Holmes and I to Baker Street. Yet, the events of the day still did not quite sit easy with me.*

WATSON: (A HEAVY SIGH)

HOLMES: Your mind is wandering, Watson?

WATSON: Indeed. It has so far wandered to Carcosa, and Hali . . . and beyond. These are names that I've heard before. And recently too.

HOLMES: (LANGUIDLY) Really? Where?

WATSON: In these very rooms. And from your lips, Holmes.

MUSIC: A TENSE UNDERTONE

HOLMES: (A FLASHBACK. AS EARLIER, DELIRIOUS AND GARBLED) Strange is the night where black stars rise . . . And strange moons circle through the skies . . . But stranger still is Lost Carcosa . . . Have you seen the yellow sign?

507

WATSON: In your fever you spoke of these impossible things. They made little sense at the time, but now the sense is chillingly clear. And I see that your burglar kit has been removed from the shelf. You think I'd forgotten how you used just such a glass cutter to enter the home of that vile blackmailer, Milverton? I recognised the tool instantly, but I now perceive the hand that applied it. Who else but the precisely minded Sherlock Holmes would have cut such a perfect circle?

MUSIC: A DRAMATIC STING

SOUND EFFECT: A MUFFLED CLATTER OF METAL AND GLASS OBJECTS IN A CANVAS BAG LANDING ON THE TABLE

HOLMES: You'll find the burglary kit here, Doctor. To save you the trouble of checking, within you'll also find jars of pale make up, a set of whiskers, and a hairpiece. You see, Frederick Nightingale has not flown far, though Lestrade will never find him. I disposed of the counterfeited keys, but retained a sample of the shavings from their manufacture to allow my sleight of hand today. It's rather a cheat on the inspector, I admit, considering he'd done so well up until then.

WATSON: That business with envelopes? There never were any brass shavings on the floor. Until you put them there!

HOLMES: The placing of clues may be an even more painstaking business than the detection of them. Lestrade has invariably picked up some of my methods, even if only through osmosis. I might risk his spotting one or two of the clues I had carefully left in my wake, but not all three. I could easily have used my adaptable picks to open the desk and that ludicrously ineffective strongbox, but the manufacture of fake keys not only strengthened the case against poor Nightingale, but also gave us a location in which to locate his lair. The clay and the leaf mould provided a suggestion. The particles of brass turned suggestion into insistence.

WATSON: You were the actor and the thief!

HOLMES: One and the same, yes.

WATSON: You've frequently mused on what you might achieve if you were to turn your attention to the creation rather than the deduction of crime. Yet I fail to see what you've gained by this charade. It strikes me as nothing more than some grotesque joke upon an already anxious man, upon Lestrade, and upon myself, for your own amusement.

HOLMES: I certainly would never play such a joke on you, my good Watson. Would you view it as a joke if this damaging play was allowed to work its course? And would it be an amusement to watch as the madhouses fill around you?

WATSON: Then all those days and nights when you wandered off, you were on a case? You let me think you were dangerously bored. You let me believe you were ill!

HOLMES: I was ill, I assure you. It can be a considerable strain living behind a mask for any prolonged period.

WATSON: You might at least have told me what you were about!

HOLMES: You're too good a friend. If I had explained the dangers involved, you would have endeavoured to stop me. Watson, I apologise unreservedly for any deception on my part. You deserve better. And you also deserve the full account. But I'm not the man to give it to you.

WATSON: Then who?

HOLMES: Be so good as to order a cab to Pall Mall, and you will have the truth of it.

SOUND EFFECT: A HORSE AND CAB UNDER NARRATION

WATSON: *I had no need to ask who we were to meet, as Pall Mall could only mean the Diogenes Club. And a visit to that singular institution meant an audience with a man I had already learned was even more remarkable than Sherlock Holmes – his brother, Mycroft.*

SOUND EFFECT: MIGHTY DOORS OPEN

HOLMES: (WHISPERED) Not a word now, Watson, but I'd urge you to glance – surreptitiously, yet with an eye for detail – at the members as we proceed through the club.

SOUND EFFECT: A LIGHT "SHUSH" OF FOOTSTEPS ALONG A CORRIDOR

WATSON: *I was unsure what I was looking for, but until we had reached the Stranger's Room I could only do as I was bid without question.*

SOUND EFFECT: THE STRANGER'S ROOM DOOR QUIETLY CLOSING

HOLMES: You are aware, Watson, that outside of this room silence is the strict maxim within these precincts. And yet, without a single word being spoken aloud, the air is positively alive and crackling with communication.

WATSON: All I saw was a collection of antisocial men who favour their books or newspapers over the company of their fellows.

HOLMES: Which is precisely what you are expected, indeed desired, to see. However, when I observe a fellow in these environs immersed in a copy of *The Times* from the day before, it raises questions.

WATSON: I did note a chap reading *The Times*. But how do you know that it was yesterday's edition?

HOLMES: The headline on the page so prominently displayed to the man seated opposite refers to the recent anarchist troubles that have plagued the Bohemian government. There is no mention of Bohemia or its problems in any of today's editions. When I also note that by the elbow of this same avid devourer of old news is a volume of nautical adventures, its spine also directed outwards, and that he is beating out a soft yet steady five note tattoo with his fingers on the arm of his chair . . . .

SOUND EFFECT: FINGERS LIGHTLY DRUMMING ON TABLE

510

HOLMES: . . . . I cannot help but surmise that the man seated in the corresponding chair will shortly be leading a party of five on a sea voyage to Bohemia, in order that certain unofficial enquiries may be made into the situation.

WATSON: Perhaps he had merely recalled an article which caught his interest but which he hadn't time to read yesterday?

HOLMES: I hardly think a man in Viscount Alderton's position within government circles would have need of a day-old situations vacant column, old boy, for that is what you'll find on the corresponding page.

WATSON: Well, no. I imagine not. I know, of course, that your brother holds sway in certain . . . secret areas of officialdom. Even so, can you really suggest that this Club, which seems nothing more than a resting place for taciturn officials, is a centre for disseminating confidential information and assigning missions into the perilous waters of international espionage?

HOLMES: I simply offer the suggestion.

WATSON: Then what is suggested by the large bearded fellow who was avidly scrutinising the menu while constantly checking his watch?

SOUND EFFECT: A DOOR SOFTLY CLOSING

MYCROFT: It suggests that he is trying to decide between the oysters and the veal. He will choose the veal. It is always the veal with Colonel Stockwill, so I cannot fathom why he chooses to torment himself with thoughts of delights he will never savour.

HOLMES: Mycroft, your footstep is as light as you are not.

SOUND EFFECT: A CREAK OF LEATHER AS MYCROFT SQUEEZES HIS FRAME INTO A CHAIR

MYCROFT: (SIGHING) I do wish you would call at more civilised times, Sherlock. Supper is almost upon us. And Doctor, I believe your turn for the lurid has begun to rub off on my brother. His conjectures may amuse, but it would be less amusing if we had to confiscate any journal that might publish such claims.

HOLMES: I have decided to take Watson into my confidence over the Yellow King Stratagem. You can be assured that nothing of this matter will see publication within our lifetimes.

MYCROFT: Very well. I can trust your judgement, even if I cannot always officially applaud your methods. Dr. Watson, my brother has been acting upon my instructions, and on a higher authority than I can mention.

WATSON: But to what purpose? Why would you sanction what amounts to little more than a case of petty theft?

MYCROFT: Would you describe preserving the British way of life and preventing war between the nations as petty?

WATSON: Well . . . no . . . No, of course not!

MYCROFT: No. But our very reliable analysis suggests that if this subversive literature is not checked, then war is a very likely outcome in the not too distant future. Now, I'm given to understand brandy to be effective against shock, Doctor. Would you pour some, Sherlock?

SOUND EFFECT: DECANTER CLINKS AS BRANDY IS POURED

MYCROFT: In those nations where this play has seized the public imagination, unrest has grown at an alarming rate. Paranoia and agitation run rife. The balance of power is a fragile thing, and it is constantly shifting.

HOLMES: In such an unsteady arena, where tiny but ambitious princedoms jostle for recognition amongst tired and bloated empires, there is no room for the arrival of anarchists and assassins of a kingdom with no corporeal existence in our world.

MYCROFT: But such troublesome individuals have begun to emerge at a rate that is unacceptable. Men and women who

512

abandon all laws to pledge their loyalty to this supposed King in Yellow and his realm.

WATSON: It sounds like sheer madness.

MYCROFT: Mad they may be, and their actions fuelled by mere fantasy. But these actions still pose a threat to the smooth handling of the ebbs and flows of command. War will come, of course. It's inevitable wherever there is humanity. But it will not be predicated on the desires of invisible governments! How can one predict the influence of a realm whose agents can be found anywhere and everywhere, yet with no embassies with which to bargain or borders to blockade? We cannot make treaties with shadows, nor can we wage war on phantoms! Yet this is the dilemma we face, and the root of the problem lies with this play.

WATSON: If this is so, why didn't you just seize the manuscript before that deluded soul could attempt to present it?

HOLMES: Prohibition would only excite further curiosity and bring an influx of printed editions from unscrupulous publishers. The spread would increase a hundredfold.

MYCROFT: A thousandfold! Sherlock is correct; we have no wish to suppress the work. Hubert Warburton-Branche must be allowed to perform it. Though when he does it will be in a subtly altered form.

HOLMES: The play which has been delivered back to him is not the one he lost, though in facsimile it is impossible to distinguish from the original. But it has been changed.

WATSON: But what good will this do?

MYCROFT: As a literary fellow, Doctor, you will grasp how the alteration of a single word may profoundly change the sense of a phrase, the modification of a phrase can radically alter the effect of a paragraph, and a changed paragraph may shift the emphasis of an entire chapter. We calculate that by making many such miniscule alterations, we can neutralise the effects this play possesses. The changes are minor – a substitution of "forgotten" for "lost", of "rags" for "tatters", "robes" for "vestments", and so

513

on – yet the effect is cumulative. The play will attract the public, but leave no actual damage. Warburton-Branche will not lose on his investment, however. Many will still clamour to see this curiosity before interest wanes. He will be feted for his daring, which is, after all, his genuine desire.

WATSON: But to achieve this in so short a time? It's incredible!

HOLMES: It's entirely credible when you realise the assets to hand, Watson. There are laboratories and libraries and arsenals the length and breadth of this country where the work of the Diogenes Club proceeds apace. Yet those who toil there are not always aware in whose service they labour. Nor are they always drawn from honest and respectable backgrounds.

MYCROFT: What a waste a blade would be if it could not be turned to save a life as well as to take one.

HOLMES: I'd imagine the division of work was split between graphologists, linguistic experts, and calligraphists on the one hand, and cunningly skilled forgers on the other, both to speed the work along and to prevent any of the effects their efforts are designed to counteract.

MYCROFT: Our intelligence tells us the First Act is innocuous enough, the easier to lull the unsuspecting into the horrors that await as Act Two unfolds. Those working on the earlier pages were allowed a scene each in its entirety. No single operative was to view a complete scene of the fatal Second Act.

HOLMES: And yet . . . ?

MYCROFT: Yet somehow pages became transposed in transit, and one unfortunate – a man named Henry Lynch – received the wrong set.

HOLMES: Henry Lynch? Son of Victor. You recall, Watson?

WATSON: Victor Lynch, the forger . . . He devised compromising letters so convincing that even their alleged writers momentarily believed them genuine. Your substitution will surely go unobserved if the son has inherited his father's eye for detail.

514

MYCROFT: The inheritance was strong.

HOLMES: "Was", Mycroft?

MYCROFT: A terrible mistake. But one which apparently cost him his reason. His final act, before throwing himself from the roof of a shipping warehouse, was to daub some peculiar sigil in yellow paint upon the doors of a hotel called "The Crown and Gown".

HOLMES: That's in Burke Court. Here we have Lestrade's vandal and his nasty little riverside business in one.

WATSON: (DISTANT, RECALLING) "He had seen the Yellow Sign . . . ."

HOLMES: (SHARPLY) What was that, Watson?

WATSON: Ah . . . just . . . musing on the coincidence of three of the inspector's cases being linked in such a twisted manner since chance drew him into this business.

MYCROFT: "Chance", Dr. Watson? There was no chance to it that Lestrade was given the case. The combination of the Good Inspector and a peculiar crime guarantees a visit to Baker Street will follow. Did you know that Colonel Stockwill – he with the taste for veal – is intimately involved in the running of the Metropolitan Police Force? It *is* rather a coincidence that Lestrade would be attached to the Lynch business, though.

WATSON: *Privately I considered that coincidence had no play in the matter. Lestrade had become embroiled in the affairs of the Yellow King, and the touch of that dread monarch was not easy to leave behind.*

HOLMES: The Diogenes Club doesn't make mistakes, and their actions invariably function on several levels at once. While they may have spared an unsuspecting nation from a corrupting force, I am in no doubt that, even now, attempts are being made to unlock the secret of the potency in the confiscated text. And to emulate it.

WATSON: (APPALLED) But to what possible end?

515

HOLMES: Brother Mycroft speaks to us of phantom kingdoms and of invisible governments, even as we stand in the very heart of just such a one. And even phantom kingdoms need their weaponry.

MYCROFT: Let us suppose what you suggest has some basis in reality, Sherlock. Consider the defensive possibilities. Encrypted into decoy messages and ciphers, it could eliminate entire networks of foreign agents operating within our boundaries.

HOLMES: But if we consider the matter of defence, we must also look at the issue of offence. As an act of aggression, let us say with "infected" notices placed in newspapers of any nation we choose, the result could be swift and merciless in its totality.

WATSON: That is utterly monstrous! It's obscene!

HOLMES: If such a use has crossed my mind, Mycroft, you cannot deny that it has already been factored into the calculations of the Diogenes Club. Think of the original text – the one delivered to Henry Lynch, whose background among the criminal class will see less surprise elicited at his untimely fate than if he had been some privileged professor – as a prototype, to be refined and enhanced. And prototypes need testing.

SOUND EFFECT: FADE UP STREET NOISE UNDER THE FOLLOWING

WATSON: *The coolness with which Mycroft Holmes listened to his brother's accusations left me eager to leave the confines of that club, whose silent operation now gave off the reek of stealth and sinister secrecy. And so we strode off in the direction of home under skies which darkened once more, as if to match my frame of mind.*

WATSON: I can hardly believe that you would have had a hand in allowing such a vile weapon to be brought into being.

HOLMES: Had I destroyed the manuscript, they would simply have their agents locate a copy that could be translated to suit their purposes. And it suited *my* purpose to be the one who delivered it into their hands. I suppose you consider my study of the characteristics of hand-writing as purely theoretical? It has its practical applications also, and the late Henry Lynch wasn't the only one capable of producing a convincing forgery.

WATSON: Then they don't have the wretched play?

HOLMES: Oh, they do. Rather, they have roughly 90 percent of it in its original form. I hadn't time to alter more than a few random pages. Not enough to prevent poor Lynch's fate, alas. But I'm confident that I introduced sufficient corrupting anomalies to wholly compromise the Diogenes Club's every experiment. And the pages I extracted had their own use, as they were the basis for that most warming fire we enjoyed yesterday.

MUSIC: LOW UNDER FOLLOWING

WATSON: *War did eventually come, and of that I need hardly add to what is widely known and written and remembered. Mycroft's other predictions, regarding Warburton-Branche's presentation of* The King in Yellow, *were also proved accurate.*

SOUND EFFECT: FADE THROUGH TO AUDITORIUM, THE ALTERED PLAY IN PROGRESS

ACTRESS/CASSILDA: "You, sire, should remove your mask. Truly, it's time. All have laid aside costume but you."

BRANCHE/THE KING: "But no mask do I wear."

ACTRESS/CASSILDA: (IN UTTER HORROR) "No mask? No mask!"

SOUND EFFECT: GASPS FROM A CROWD, DISTANT AUDIENCE APPLAUSE, THEN FADE

WATSON: *The show was a minor hit for a single season. The reviews were unanimous that the play both moved and appalled, yet there was none of the overwhelming terror or delight the work's reputation had promised. No doubt the script had lost something in translation.*

WATSON: *The last we heard from the actor was when he sent us tickets to the opening performance of* The King in Yellow. *Neither Holmes nor I attended. But I pasted them, alongside other souvenirs of our adventures, in one of several large scrapbooks following my fellow lodger's departure. And it was to these scrapbooks that Holmes looked on one of his rare returns to London following his – not entirely complete – retirement.*

SOUND EFFECT: PAGES TURNING, THEN PAUSING

HOLMES: Such a nest of lies, fictions, and concealed purposes. You never did get the entire truth of the matter, and you were always too diplomatic to ask.

WATSON: I knew better than to try.

HOLMES: You recall, of course, the Cornish horror. I believe you chronicled that deadly business some years ago.

WATSON: At your suggestion, yes.

MUSIC: AN EERIE AMBIENCE RISING UNDER THE FOLLOWING

HOLMES: Indeed. I had been ruminating on Warburton-Branche's misadventure, and this brought to mind a particular detail of our ordeal in Cornwall. As we were recovering from the fumes of the so-called Devil's Foot root, you told me of the visions that had afflicted you as the drug did its damnable work. I may often accuse you of being overly dramatic, but your words frequently register. You spoke of a sense of creeping menace, of the approach of something monstrous . . .

WATSON: ". . . *the advent of some unspeakable dweller upon the threshold, whose very shadow would blast my soul.*"

HOLMES: Those words might well have been capturing my own tortured thoughts as *The King in Yellow* entered my life. In my delirium, I caught glimpses, nothing more, and of that I am

518

thankful. What I thought to have seen was something that lurks and waits with unbearable patience . . . and the only movement it ever displays is the endless stirring of the tatters of its robe.

WATSON: You read it! You read the play!

HOLMES: I cannot proceed without data. In creating Nightingale, I had to adopt the characteristics Warburton-Branche sought in order to insinuate myself into his company. How else could I observe his habits at close enough quarters to learn that a carefully sabotaged rehearsal would set him off on a ritualised drowning of sorrows, leaving the play unguarded? Even as I first donned my guise, I was immersed in the fragments of information that had fed his own obsession. Can you condemn my curiosity when the play itself came into my grasp?

WATSON: I can scarcely believe Mycroft would have exposed his own brother to such danger!

HOLMES: You have noted that I am unmoved by literature and poetry, and no-one knows me more fully than do you. Mycroft knew it also – I suspect because your writings told him so – and by his reasoning, no-one could be more immune to the effects of some phantasmagorical romance than I. A calculating machine cannot be thrown out of gear by mere emotions. But no-one can long withstand a close association with one whose very feeling soul is as open and on display as is yours without feeling some effect. The machine has become a man, thanks to your humanizing influence, Watson.

WATSON: (MOVED, BUT STOICALLY HIDING THE FACT) Holmes, I . . . Well, might Mycroft not have factored in your own subterfuge? Perhaps that was his actual reason for choosing you for this mission?

HOLMES: There. Your charity reinforces my picture of you. My brother never had such a friend, thus his calculations could never have predicted such a factor. The pieces of the great chessboard lying perpetually before him could neither weep when they were taken nor rejoice when they advanced. They served but one function.

WATSON: To take the King.

HOLMES: Indeed. The prize was mine and I succumbed to the lure of its riches. Mesmerists use certain rhythms and the repetition of key words and phrasing to achieve their effect. Logically I know this to have been the case here. But logic had temporarily fled. Nightingale was a fiction, designed to exist but briefly and then be discarded. Yet in those days, I grew to question which life was the true fiction. Was I a detective wearing the mask of an actor, or was the detective the mask and the actor the reality? Was there not, perhaps, some world running parallel to ours upon which a genuine actor named Nightingale performed for his King, and had some substitution somehow taken place?

SOUND EFFECT: 221b FADES, TO BE REPLACED BY CITY STREET SOUNDS, DISTANT AND DISTORTED

HOLMES: After I laid down the pages, I stepped outside to regain myself. Here I saw the city I know so well transformed. Between the cracks in the brick facades I perceived the shimmering walls of a long buried city breaking through. I . . . I became lost, Watson!

WATSON: Lost? You've mapped London's every twist and turn!

HOLMES: I thought to follow the stars, but when I turned to the heavens, I gazed into an altogether different sky. So I wandered aimlessly in no longer familiar avenues . . . .

SOUND EFFECT: DISTANT CHEERING, DISTORTED AND HARSH

HOLMES: *There was a procession in the streets. In the parks and cemeteries, the troops of a returning army buried their dead. Or perhaps they were not laying them to rest but raising them up to press them into further service against an enemy of whom I could scarcely conceive.*

HAWKSPUR: (DISTORTED) Onwards! Carcosa must not be lost!

HOLMES: *A phalanx of soldiers charged past in response to the rallying cry of a scarred officer who lead them blindly while*

520

issuing instructions in a voice that was not his own. There amongst them was my friend, the former army medic, in full dress uniform, looking as he must once have done under the burning Afghan sun.

WATSON: (HARSH, DISTORTED) For Carcosa and the King!

HOLMES: *But his skin was pale and had a yellow tinge to it, as though the sun he fought under carried little warmth. I tried to call to him, but on opening my mouth, I found I could no longer remember his name. Then he was gone, no recognition in his eyes as he charged past.*

SOUND EFFECT: HORSES CHARGE AND FADE. WATER LAPS, A GREAT RIVER FILLED WITH HEAVING FORMS

HOLMES: *I found myself on the brink of a lake in whose depths cyclopean beasts coiled and swam, and whose shores lay awash with lustrous gems. Was this my reward from my ragged sovereign for providing him with such vivid entertainment? I was so entranced by these trinkets that my wanderings somehow took me back through the maze of columns and spires to Baker Street.*

SOUND EFFECT: (EXACTLY AS WE HEARD IN THE OPENING MOMENTS) THE DOOR SLAMS. CLOCK TICKS THE PASSAGE OF TIME. THEN, UNDER THE FOLLOWING, THE DOOR OPENS, FOOTSTEPS ENTER, AND BOTTLES AND RETORTS CLINK AND RATTLE

HOLMES: *Here, the familiarity of our rooms let me see these treasures for the pebbles they were, and I felt myself lurch between worlds. On the one hand, a great kingdom of majesty and jewels, on the other the prosaic, grey London that I had so long loved and wished to return to. Nightingale and Starling fought well, but as soon as I focused on that clammy grey rock in my grip their hours were numbered.*

HOLMES: (EXACTLY AS EARLIER – A CRY) Trickery! This cannot be! All lost!

SOUND EFFECT: (AS EARLIER) A CRASH OF FURNITURE AND GLASS

521

WATSON: (AS EARLIER) Holmes? What on earth . . . ?

HOLMES: (AS EARLIER) (PUZZLED, DELIRIOUS) Watson? It is you . . . I . . . I thought you were . . . lost . . .

<u>SOUND EFFECT: FADE UP THE COMFORTING SOUNDS OF THE CLOCK AND THE FIRE</u>

HOLMES: I was quite recovered by the time Lestrade came knocking, though I had to extend my period of convalescence by an extra day to allow the counterfeit manuscript to be prepared. But I was fully myself – quite literally – thanks to your diligent ministrations and your insistence that I rise above myself.

WATSON: I'd thought . . . .

WATSON: (AN ECHO OF EARLIER, DISTANT) . . . a mind addled with poison . . . .

WATSON: It was an unworthy thought, Holmes.

HOLMES: Yet well meant. It takes a true friend to acknowledge faults in another and to list them to his face, and there was never a truer friend than you, dear Watson. And without you repeating my own words and deeds back to me, I might never have regained myself and thrown off the mask I had donned. Even yet, in the theatre of my own imagination, I might still have remained convinced that I was nothing more than a player in the court of the King.

<u>SOUND EFFECT: AN EERIE, UNEARTHLY WIND AND THE RUSTLING OF TATTERED GARMENTS SOUNDING LIKE THE DISTANT ECHO OF COLD, MALICIOUS LAUGHTER DRIFTS IN THEN DWINDLES INTO THE FAR DISTANCE</u>

<u>MUSIC: FADE IN</u>

The Two Different Women
by David Marcum

As his gaze shifted to something beyond me, I saw my friend's eyes narrow with the slightest indication of irritation. Having known Mr. Sherlock Holmes at that time for nearly a quarter-century, I had long ago learned not to twist like a new constable and attempt to see what had provoked that most subtle of reactions.

Holmes, being who he was, had of course noticed that *I* had noticed his glance, and he didn't need to evince his uncanny skills, sometimes mistaken for mind-reading, to understand my unspoken question.

"A pesterment, Watson," explained. "Nothing more." Then, as almost an afterthought, he added, "Give me your opinion."

Free now to pivot in my seat, I laid down my fork and turned slightly, looking across the common room at the man and woman seating themselves at a nearby table. The woman was concentrating on getting situated in her chair, and I realized that she was, in fact, well into her second term. The man paused beside his own chair, caught in the act of looking rather despairingly in our direction. Turning my attention his way caused his focus to shift slightly from my friend to me, and our gazes met. Then his eyes dropped, rather nervously I thought, and he settled into his own seat beside his companion.

I took another moment to frankly study him while he gestured, almost angrily, toward the bar. I noticed that he had a head that was much too large for his narrow shoulders, before realizing that it was actually normal, and that it was his body that was smallish. His lower lip, underneath a Bismarck moustache waxed at the tips, rested above an average chin and was pursed with a natural petulance. This didn't not improve when a large whisky was set before him. Although he appeared to be in his mid-thirties, his high forehead was quite lined and topped by thin brownish hair, parted on his left and already going gray at the temples. Those same eyes which had looked my way were underscored with dark circles, along with an underlying shiftiness that would certainly have been there before whatever was worrying him now had begun, and would still be there in future days as well.

"His wife?" I asked rather foolishly, turning back to my own dinner, a magnificent piece of roasted pork with a thin layer of flavorful fat forming an outer layer, crisped and awaiting my further attentions. I suspected that, as the friend of Sherlock Holmes, I was being rewarded. Holmes, with a similar slab upon his plate, seemed indifferent.

"Obviously. But what else did you see?"

I shifted my eyes, gazing into the distance and concentrating a moment before replying. "Moderately wealthy," I began, recalling the excellent quality of the couples' clothing – at least what I could see across the dim dining room.

"The clothing," agreed Holmes, nodding and following my thinking, still serving as something of a teacher after all these years. "And?"

"American," I added as I envisioned the peculiar cut of the garments that suggested ostentatiousness without a corresponding level of class. Holmes began to pounce, but I held up a hand. "Wait. The clothing was *purchased* in America, I should say. It has something of the western styles that I saw in San Francisco years ago. But it wasn't obtained recently, as it seems rather worn. Based on that fact, along with the man's moustaches and gestures, and a few other random indications from his lady, I should say that they are actually of German descent, having moved to America at some time in the past, where they had enough money to the purchase moderately expensive clothing. But for some reason they haven't purchased new clothing since traveling here."

Holmes dropped his napkin and clapped with a smile and a rather loud, "Ha!" which caused an elderly man at the adjacent table to start and drop his spoon with a clatter. Holmes ignored the resulting scowl and replied, "Really, Watson, that was excellent. If I wasn't already retired and rusticating here in my self-imposed apiaristic seclusion, I would have to consider leaving things in your capable hands!"

I snorted, replying, "We both know that your 'retirement' has ended up being almost a hobby, as you still become involved in nearly as many cases now as when you lived in London. You have your brother to thank for that, if not your own curiosity. Else, why would I be down here?"

We both knew the answer to that, as I had arrived only that afternoon from the capital on the Eastbourne train, carrying with me the final evidence that would prove the guilt of Vincent Berne, the False Parson of East Dean. It was a tragic tale, spiraling out from one

524

of Holmes's long-past cases, and set into motion by the untimely death of Berne's own son who, upon learning what his father had done to his mother, had tragically jumped over the high cliff of Beachy Head, directly across from Holmes's own retirement villa.

"I should point out," continued Holmes, "that the gentleman and his wife, both of whom are actually both from the Kingdom of Bavaria, did live in the western United States for several years before returning to the German Empire late last year, apparently choosing to retain their American clothing throughout the trip rather than purchase something new in their native land.. They have one daughter, less than a year old, currently upstairs in the care of a nurse. They are now returning to the United States, but have inexplicably stopped in this little inn in this out-of-the-way village, where they seem determined to stay for an indefinite period of time."

I was beginning to feel that usual amazement when Holmes meticulously revealed all the hidden layers of anyone that fell under his scrutiny. And then I remembered his short statement referring to the man as a *pesterment*. "You've met him before," I said.

"Indeed. Three days ago. He introduced himself and attempted to solicit my services. As he had been here for nearly two weeks at that point, and as my reasons for 'retirement' include being aware of all things German, I had already become curious about – and wary of – him. I naturally wonder about any Germans who stay around here for too long, and for no apparent reasons. Therefore, I instigated some inquiries through my brother, and also with friends across both the eastern and western seas. In short, this is not a man with whom I wish to associate."

Having known Holmes for so long, I realized that he would reveal nothing more. However, circumstances were such that I was soon to be introduced to the traveler and his wife, although by an unexpected source.

For at that moment, our table was approached by Tom Keller, the proprietor of the Tiger Inn where we supped. At the time of this narrative, mid-June 1905, I had known Keller for a little under two years. Not long after Holmes announced his retirement from active London practice in October 1903, with the intention to settle east of Birling Gap (which I have referred to in some of my notes as "Fulworth" – something of an inside joke), I had travelled down to visit. During the course of that first stay, Holmes and I had naturally walked the mile or so from his "villa" (as he liked to call it), across the fields to the Tiger Inn on the East Dean common. It was an old smuggler's inn, like so many others dotting the landscape of these seacoast hamlets, dating back half-a-thousand years or more – although that was still young compared to some of the nearby churches, now approaching their first millennial birthdays.

Holmes, as a nearby resident, made the trip from his Sussex home to the common regularly, as he had an arrangement with the village estate office to serve as a mailing address. It was at that same building, west across the green and visible through the window where we now sat, that we had confronted Vincent Berne only a few hours earlier. After that unpleasant encounter, it had been only natural to repair to the inn. Stepping through the low door, clearly built for men of another age, we had been greeted by the owner and shown to a fine table near the window. The late afternoon sun had long since disappeared, leaving only massing clouds behind the brick buildings lined across the far side of the green.

Keller had recommended the pork, and had also brought us ale. "On the house," he added, in a tone that brooked no argument. As he walked away, I raised my eyebrows.

"A benefit related to little service that I performed for him several weeks ago. A trifle."

Realizing that this was another of Holmes's investigations that I would likely never add to my notes, I instead questioned him about some more details from the Berne affair, which I hope to publish in due course, as my restriction against placing narratives of Holmes's adventures in *The Strand* was lifted upon his retirement. The food arrived, excellent as expected, and we proceeded through the meal to the point where we had observed our fellow diners, the Bavarians, and so on to Keller's arrival at our table, asking, "Is it all right, then?"

"Excellent!" I beamed.

Keller nodded and turned his head towards Holmes, who added with a more leveled enthusiasm, "Indeed."

The proprietor nodded, as if he expected no other response, but his eyes didn't seem as if he were truly listening. He appeared distracted, and he said in a lowered voice. "A word please, Mr. Holmes? When you and the Doctor are finished?"

Holmes, long accustomed to surreptitious conversations, simply nodded. "I'll be in my office," Keller added, turning away and gesturing toward his daughter Katy. She went into motion, resulting in her smiling appearance beside us a moment later with two fresh ales standing beside our plates.

At that point, Holmes began to finish his meal, but in a steady workmanlike way, rather than savoring the brilliance of the preparation. I turned toward the window, observing with some uneasiness the piling clouds in the west. There was a storm coming.

Within moments, Holmes had finished and, seeing that I had also concluded my portion, he arose and walked towards the foreign man and his wife without casting either of them a glance, whereas both of them were clearly watching us. I tried not to look at them either, but instead followed Holmes around the end of the bar, and so into Keller's small office behind it.

"What can we do for you, Mr. Keller?" asked Holmes as we found our seats. The big man didn't answer for a moment, and then he ran his hands over his face in a curious washing motion before releasing a sigh.

"I hate to ask it, Mr. Holmes, especially so soon after what you did to help Katy." Holmes waved a hand in dismissal, but Keller continued. "No, it's true. I'll always be in your debt, and have no right to be bothering you again, and especially so soon. And during your dinner, no less. But he's been pestering me about it for a couple of days, and I told him no, but then you and the Doctor walked in, and . . . and I decided to go ahead and ask anyway."

"The *he* that's been pestering you," said Holmes, "is surely *Herr* Siegen, now in the dining room with his wife."

"It is. He told me how he spoke to you the other day, and that you turned him down. Rightly so, I might add. If doesn't like it, he can go somewhere else. I don't know why he stays, to be honest, if he's that unhappy."

"I asked him the same question," said my friend. "He had no good answer. That, and what I already knew about him, led me to turn down his initial request."

"Excuse me," I said, interrupting as I had a thousand times before in an attempt to find the trail. "What would Mr. Siegen's problem be, exactly?"

Holmes's lips tightened. "He feels that he is being persecuted by a ghost."

By now, nothing surprised me, and knowing Holmes, I understood why he had declined the case. Keller interjected, "The White Lady wouldn't persecute anyone. She was a healer in life."

"The White Lady?" I asked, as the door opened, allowing Katy Keller to slip inside.

"That's what we call her," answered Keller, glancing toward his daughter. "We don't know what her real name was."

"She's been here for several hundred years, at least, or longer," added Katy, taking a seat beside her father. "All the stories agree that

527

she was a nurse, or at least someone who cared for the ill and wounded. There are stories that she first worked for the Estate as a servant, but that she also tended to the injured who were placed in the houses just next door during the wars with Napoleon. Others think that she has been here much longer than that – since The Plague in the 1600's."

"And like all of these spirits," added Holmes, with a touch of sarcasm, "she would rather stay here than move on."

"She *can't* move on, you see," said Keller. "Whatever she saw in life – the suffering, the pain – affected her in some way, and now she stays." He looked from one to the other of us as if that explained it. "We've all seen her, you know. At different times. In the hallways or on the stairs. In the kitchen, or in the bar when it's late and closed and when there's no bright light to obscure her."

A sudden burst of wind outside rattled the window, causing me to start involuntarily. Keller and his daughter also looked unnerved, and Holmes smiled slightly to himself.

"Sometimes I wake up, and she's standing by my bed," said the young lady softly. Keller nodded, as if this didn't surprise him.

"I've seen her since I was a little girl," continued Katy. "I . . . I used to think it was my mum." She glanced at her father, whose eyes dropped, and then continued. "But now I know better. Mum . . . Mum has let me know in other ways that she's watching over us. The White Lady is someone else. She watches too, but in a different way. She's good – I can feel it. She never does anything hurtful. Sometimes she just moves things, or shuts doors or windows."

"The usual ghostly forms of amusement," added Holmes, with just the hint of sarcasm. I knew that he could say more. Often in days past, he and I, along with our friend the spiritual investigator Alton Peake, would sit in Baker Street, sharing a glass and telling tales. It was always one of Holmes's sticking points that a spirit, free from the body and physical obligations and limitations, and with a world – nay *a universe* – to explore, should instead choose to remain in one location and drop books and slam doors to get attention. Peake would shake his head with a tolerant smile and give us yet another example of why such a behavior, in his experience, was caused by a torment that the poor spirit could not overcome. Peake had debunked many a false claim, but he also insisted that he had seen the real thing, and he told us that in many cases he had exorcised these souls, allowing them to finally achieve peace. Holmes was a skeptic, but he also respected Peake, and therefore he – usually – held his tongue.

528

Now, he was clearly doing the same in Keller's office. "This is what Siegen asked you about?" I said to Holmes. "To protect him from the Tiger Inn's ghost?" He nodded, and I added, "I understand why you declined, but why did you not refer him to Peake in London?"

"Because I didn't want our friend to have to deal with this man any more than I wanted to." Holmes shifted his gaze to Keller. "You know something of my background," he said. "I am a cautious man, and part of that is to be aware of my surroundings, and those who populate them. Word reached me through the usual local gossip – your cook by way of Mrs. Hudson – that this man Siegen was staying here for quite a long time and for no apparent reason, and that he seemed to be unhappy while doing so. It wasn't sinister *per se*, but it was a bit unusual. I sent a few messages here and there to learn more about him. He is . . . unsavory.

"His name, loosely translated, means *triumph*, but I find his history anything but. He is originally from Kallstadt, in Bavaria, near Mannheim. When he was in his teens, he moved to the United States, where he lived with relatives for a number of years in the East. At some point, apparently related to the gold discoveries in the West, he traveled, and when settled he began to scramble, revealing his true character. He was able to worm into a series of questionable shipping investments and land deals, and he began to build a modest fortune. However . . . ." At this point, Holmes paused for just a moment, glancing at Katy before continuing, ". . . However, his greatest source income came from establishing a sizeable bordello along the routes to the gold fields. Upon this shaky ground, his wealth multiplied exponentially.

"At some point, he became a citizen of the United States. Returning to Bavaria for a visit a few years ago, he ended up marrying a woman who is a number of years younger than he. Then they returned to America, where they have lived until last year, before returning to Kallstadt for a visit. After only being back there for only a short while, there was some sort of scandal, and Siegen was ordered to leave. Rather than returning directly to their home, they traveled, first to France, and then on to London, before eventually washing up here – to your consternation, Mr. Keller."

Keller ran a hand over his whiskers and nodded. "Consternation is right, Mr. Holmes. I had no idea about his past until now, but I've never liked him much anyway."

"Then why let him stay?" I asked. "Surely you can find a way to turn him out."

529

Keller dropped his eyes, and then glanced at his daughter, who smiled. "It's the money, you see," she said. "He's rented all of the upstairs rooms – the whole floor – and is paying twice the normal rate to keep them."

The innkeeper glanced back up. "We've made some improvements in the last year or so. You can't see them, as they relate to the piping and the drains and so forth. But there was some expense involved, major expense, and I'm still paying for it. The extra money . . . well, I can't lie and say that it doesn't help."

"*Twice?*" said Holmes, fixating on Keller's earlier statement. "He is paying twice your rate?"

"He is. He made the offer when he first arrived, without prompting. And as Katy said, that's for all of the upstairs rooms."

"His own, one for the nurse and the baby . . . ."

"And one for his wife too. They are not lodging together. The rest stand empty"

"Twice the rate," muttered Holmes to himself. "That is significant in and of itself." Looking back at Keller, he asked, "Why would he do that – why would he wish to stay here, especially as he seems to be suffering under the illusion that this White Lady is tormenting him?"

"I cannot tell you," said Keller, even as his daughter spoke at the same time: "I can't believe that she would do that!"

"The Lady has always been gentle," added her father. "Although I will say that since Siegen has been here, she's been acting up quite a bit. She's agitated. And more of her mischief has occurred than usual. Katy and I have seen her often of late." The girl nodded in agreement.

Holmes shook his head, as if annoyed by a gnat. "And what do you want me to do for Herr. Siegen?"

"Well, it's this way," said Keller. "He has asked me . . . he . . . asked me to ask *you* to speak to him once more. To have mercy and see if you can't give him some assistance."

"Battling the supernatural does not fall within my purview," said my friend shortly.

"I understand. I appreciate that. But as a favor to me – to us – " I could see that the man hated being put in this position, but he also would do what was needed to keep the added funds flowing toward relieving his debt.

Holmes scratched his forehead and then cupped his chin in thought. Then, tapping his forefinger, he seemed to reach a decision. "May we use your office to speak with him?"

Keller seemed relieved, standing abruptly. "Of course. We'll go and get him. And . . . and thank you, Mr. Holmes."

As they left us, I glanced at my friend. "What changed your mind?"

"The Kellers, of course. They wouldn't have asked if it were not important to them. Otherwise, I have no interest in proving or disproving the existence of a White Lady, and certainly not in helping *Herr* Siegen."

He had made no effort to lower his voice, and he concluded this sentence even as the man in question was being shown into the office. He must have been waiting, poised on the edge of his seat to see if he would be summoned. As he walked in, the little man clearly heard Holmes's declaration, and his eyes narrowed. Siegen's wife, who had accompanied him, quite frankly looked rather angrier than her husband at this sleight.

Keller introduced me, and Katy slipped past him, setting down a tray with a full bottle of brandy and glasses. Then they both nodded and backed out, closing the door behind them.

Holmes and I had stood in deference to Mrs. Siegen. "My wife, Berta," said our prospective client, providing us with the lady's heretofore unspoken first name and clearly trying to be as charming as he knew how. He still had something of an accent, which his recent sojourn in Germany had likely sharpened.

Up close, I could see that Mrs. Siegen was quite a bit younger than her husband, as reported. She had classic Bavarian features, but they were marred by a cold and calculating expression that would only harden as she aged.

We found our seats, and Siegen reached for the brandy. He was already exhibiting the early signs of inebriation, which was no surprise, as he presented unmistakable indications of alcoholic tendencies, which were quite obvious up close. After pouring himself a tall measure, he remembered his manners and looked at Holmes and me, gesturing toward the other glasses. We declined. He made no such offer toward his wife – rightly so, I thought, for a woman in her condition, although I douted if that was his reasoning.

Holmes began in a curt tone. "Mr. Siegen, I only agreed to speak with you again at the request of my friends, the Kellers. As I explained to you the other day, I do not waste my time on pointless investigations of the supernatural."

Siegen started to speak, but he was interrupted by his wife, allowing him to take a deep swallow of the brandy. *"Gott in Himmel, Friedrich!"* she hissed. *"Du machst dich selbst zum narren!"*

531

Holmes's German was excellent, and mine passable. Her criticism of him, telling him that he was making a fool of himself, caused his eyes to narrow, and he slammed the empty brandy glass onto the table.

"I am an American, now," he said in English, "and my name is *Fred*, not *Friedrich.*" And then he filled the glass, raised it to his lips, emptied it, and proceeded to fill it again.

His wife turned to us. "I have tried to tell him! He is only imagining this White Woman that torments him so. He stays in his room all day, brooding and only coming out for meals. He drinks too much – " and she glared at him, where his own actions seemed to be proving her point " – and he is having problems sleeping. He has heard these innkeeper stories about a ghostly woman walking the hallways and causing mischief, and he has started to imagine that he's seeing her."

"I *have* seen her," muttered Siegen in a surly tone.

"After what happened in Kallstadt," continued his wife, "it's no wonder that he's upset. When we return home to New York, all will be well."

"And what happened there, in Kallstadt?" asked Holmes, having noticed, as did I, that Siegen winced when his hometown was mentioned.

The downtrodden little man cleared his throat. "It . . . well, you see, my brother died while we were there." Another swallow. Then, before the glass was emptied this time, he topped it off again.

"Really," said Holmes blandly. "Was he murdered?"

Siegen's eyes widened. "What? No! Don't be absurd. He had a bad heart, and it finally caught up with him."

"And that is why you are upset?"

"Of course."

"Ah. I had heard differently, you see. My information was that there was some scandal there, necessitating your hasty departure. Perhaps, as I need to have an understanding of *all* of the relevant facts to determine why this spirit is harassing you, you will share that story as well."

Siegen scowled and looked at his wife, who returned the expression. Then, with a nod, she released him to speak.

"It was determined – falsely, I would add – that when I first moved to the United States, it was to avoid service in the military of the German Empire. Nothing could be further from the truth. Upon my return last year, this was . . . discussed with me by the authorities, and based upon that, I was told to leave the country."

Holmes nodded. "And then, instead of returning to America, you have buried yourself here in this English village, specifically within this establishment, where I'm told you have reserved the whole upstairs floor and pay above the going rate, in spite of clearly being unhappy and feeling as if you are being victimized by a dead woman." His skepticism was palpable. "Why would you do that, Mr. Siegen?"

Holmes's tone had sharpened as if he were a prosecutor interrogating a lying witness. Siegen looked again to his wife, but she seemed to have no advice or direction for him this time. He swallowed and said, "When I first departed for America, twenty years ago, my brother – the one who has just died – went with me. We had plans to make our fortunes. He was a carpenter, and I, while having no special skills, was willing to work hard. We left home and began to make our way in a leisurely fashion, eventually reaching England. With no plan in mind, we explored a bit, and almost by accident we ended up in this village, staying in this very inn. We had a bit of money at the time, a gift from our grandmother for the journey, and those were happy days – at least at first. But my brother quickly became homesick, and we fought while we were here. Finally, he decided to return home and we parted – he to go back to Kallstadt, while I journeyed onward.

"Last year, my wife and I were both missing our old home after all those years away, and I especially wanted to visit and spend time with my brother, whom we had learned was ill. I tried to regain the closeness that we'd had when we were young, but it seemed as if we couldn't rebuild the bond from twenty years ago. There were too many different experiences between us since then. He had grown to regret his decision to return home, and hearing about my adventures in the west had only fed his resentment. He was very ill during our entire visit, often unconscious, and when he died, there was no understanding between us. Then, soon after, we were asked to leave Germany, and we wandered a bit before I had the idea that if I stayed here, in the very inn where he and I had parted, I might obtain some sort of comfort."

"Instead," said Holmes, "you find yourself, not making peace with the shade of your brother as you'd hoped, but rather being visited by a stranger, an English woman dead for hundreds of years."

"It is not just me," said Siegen, with something of a whine creeping into his voice. "Gerda has seen her too."

"Gerda?"

"The nurse," snapped Mrs. Siegen. "She has mentioned something of the sort. But she is a simple-minded girl, and cannot be trusted."

"Nevertheless," said Holmes, "I shall want to speak to her. Is she available?"

"She is not," said the wife firmly. "She is with the baby."

"Ah. Perhaps tomorrow, then." He turned back toward Siegen, who was pouring yet more brandy into his glass. "Does the nurse's account agree with your own experience?"

Siegen nodded and took a drink, and his wife snapped, "It is foolish. I have seen nothing of this *geist*. Friedrich is hoping for a message from his brother, and instead his imagination creates some woman moving about his room."

"Is that what she does?" I asked. "Appear in your room and move around?"

"She does," answered the man. "Each night, my sleep is troubled. I fall asleep without incident, even when I try to stay awake, but I always become aware that she is there. I don't know the exact time that she appears or leaves. It is as if I am paralyzed, but I can see her, glowing, as she moves from here to there about the room, intent on something, but often pausing to turn her gaze toward me, frowning in disapproval. Eventually, I fall back to sleep, awakening in the morning exhausted, as if I've had no true rest."

"Then again I ask you: Why stay?" asked Holmes. "You've been here for several weeks now. You have been ignored by your brother's spirit the entire time, and yet you continue to place yourself in a situation that only disturbs you."

Siegen nodded. "You are right. I can only say that I feel that my business here is not yet finished, and if I must face this White Woman to do so, then so be it. But I would feel better if you could advise me, Mr. Holmes, and perhaps find a way to make her leave me alone so that I may rest."

Holmes shook his head, and I thought that he was going to refuse, but he said, "I'm not clear on what exactly that I can do, as I know nothing about exorcising spirits, but I will make some sort of effort, if only because my friends the Kellers have requested it. However, I will need to do a bit of research, and the hour is late. May I call on you again in the morning?"

Siegen seemed to have a moment of emotion, possibly as he considered that night was approaching, and that he was facing another encounter with the inn's resident phantom. But he nodded, rising and lurching slightly from the quantities of alcohol that he had just consumed in such a short time. "Thank you, Mr. Holmes. Doctor. I believe that my stay here will conclude successfully soon, but in the meantime, I will hope that your intervention can make the remaining days more tolerable."

He turned to his wife. "It is as I've told you, Berta. Mr. Holmes can see things that others cannot. If anyone can get to the bottom of this, it is he."

Mrs. Siegen simply frowned and nodded at our wishes for a good night. We let them proceed us out of the office, and I was amused to notice Siegen reach out for his wife's hand. With a flick of her wrist, she swatted his fingers away before they could touch her, leaving him slumping as he shambled forward, attempting to retain his drunken balance. In a low voice, she began to berate him with a nearly continuous string of guttural billingsgate as they moved away from us.

We exited into the common room, now considerably emptier than it had been a half-hour earlier. In fact, Tom Keller was in the act of sending one last patron out the door and into the windy darkness. The Siegens also made their way to the front door, which opened onto a small vestibule. There, as was curiously the way in the construction of these old buildings, a separate doorway opened to the stairs leading up to the upper floor, wherein their rooms were located. We watched them open that door and begin to climb, the woman's complaints never ceasing. As the door to the common room shut, we turned to Keller, who was now standing behind the bar.

"Can you help them?" he asked.

"Possibly. I told them that we'd be back tomorrow morning."

At that moment, the wind rose afresh, throwing small pebbles against the front window. "Well, then," said Keller. "I won't hold you up. It promises to be a right night of it, or so the old fellows at the bar were saying before they scooted off home."

I nodded in his direction and moved toward the entryway, taking my coat from the hook as I did so. Pulling the door open, I looked back to see that Holmes had moved in the opposite direction, leaning toward Keller and saying something quick and quiet and short. With a puzzled look on his face that quickly turned canny, Keller nodded. Then Holmes joined me, grabbing his own coat and hat as we ducked our heads, stepping into the vestibule. The area was shallow, just a few square feet across, with the doors to both the common room and the upstairs pressed close beside us. I started ask a question, but Holmes, in the act of adjusting his fore-and-aft cap, put a cautionary finger to his lips. Then he led me out onto the village green.

As we had perceived from inside, the wind had steadily risen, and dark clouds were moving with great speed across the sky toward us. In the distance I could see lightning. There was no thunder yet, as so far this was only some electrical disturbance in the high atmosphere. But I knew that it would arrive soon, along with the rains that undoubtedly follow.

"We should hurry," I said, "or we're going to be drenched."

"No need," said Holmes. "We want to stay here and see what happens."

I understood. "So you told Keller – "

" – to join us in five minutes."

"And your promise to return in the morning . . . ?"

"As you will have realized, old friend, that was simply a way to make sure that whatever has been happening on previous nights will also happen on this one. As soon as it is perceived that we will be taking a more focused interest in the matter, ostensibly in the morning, the conditions will change. I want to give the impression that there will be one more night wherein things can proceed as they have been doing before our further involvement skews the matter into a different direction.

"In science," he continued, leading me across the green toward the estate office, "sometimes the simple act of *observing* a reaction is enough to *affect* the reaction. For instance, measuring an electrical current with a voltage meter necessarily diverts some quantity of that current, no matter how minute, to power the measuring device, causing a slightly false reading of the true current. A thermometer must use some energy, thermal converted to kinetic, in order to move the mercury, again taking energy away from the thing being measured. Even checking the pressure in an automobile tire causes some air to be inadvertently released, resulting in a slightly inaccurate reading. Thus, the introduction of the two of us as variables into this situation will change the conditions of the experiment, and before that is expected to happen on the morrow, we need to allow it to play out tonight, as it has every night."

I was about to make a contrary and less-scientific statement about "*A watched pot never boils*" when the door to the inn opened, and Keller slipped out. He looked around, spotted us in the dim light, and walked across to where we stood in the shadows of the estate office. "It's going to be a raw night for sure," he said, handing each of us Mackintoshes that he had thoughtfully gathered. Although both

Holmes and I were wearing overcoats, for the day had been cool, we gratefully put on the waterproof coverings.

"I think that I understand the upstairs layout," said Holmes, gesturing back the hundred or so feet toward the inn. "There is, unfortunately, nowhere to hide within the hallway itself, or I would have suggested it. The steps leading up from the entryway there in the vestibule open at the top into the hallway, which then leads along the front of the building where behind those windows there. The rooms in question are each situated along the backside of the building. Do they also have windows?"

"Of course. They look down on the courtyard."

"Excellent. Then I'm afraid there is nothing to do but wait. I have a key to the estate office, and if the rains begin we'll certainly step inside, but for now we'll be able to see much better from out here. It shouldn't take long. Mr. Siegen is already quite inebriated, and will no doubt be asleep very soon."

"What do you expect to see?" asked Keller, glancing back and forth from the inn to Holmes.

"Why, your White Lady, of course. With the knowledge that our investigation begins in earnest tomorrow, things will have to intensify tonight. No doubt she will appear. Eyes sharp, now."

And in truth, it did not take very long at all before we saw signs of something in the hallway windows. On the left a light suddenly glowed, near where the stairs down to the outside door were located. "Ah," said Holmes. "She is confident enough that there is no need to put out her own bedroom light when she opens her door."

"Who?" asked Keller. "Mrs. Siegen?"

"Indeed. Watch."

It was hard to see, but there was some movement across the windows as the woman moved down the hallway from our left to right. "Mr. Siegen is in the last room?" asked Holmes.

"He is. Their rooms are separated by that of the nurse."

The light vanished to the right, apparently as the woman entered Siegen's room. After several moments where nothing happened, I was moved to ask, "What do we expect to see?"

"That, for whatever reason, Mr. Siegen's specter is really his wife, as just indicated by her visit to his room."

"Surely," I countered, "it isn't completely unusual for a wife to visit her husband's room – even such an unpleasant couple as the Siegens. Perhaps he is ill, and she is checking on him."

"I suppose so," replied Holmes, "But we must be certain. Keller, is there a ladder near the back courtyard, long enough to reach the first floor windows?"

"Mr. Holmes, I – " He swallowed whatever objection was about to be voiced and said, "Yes. In the open shed."

"Excellent. I shall return momentarily." And with that, he vanished into the ever-growing darkness, leaving Keller and me looking at one another with puzzled and somewhat uncomfortable expressions. It didn't surprise me that Holmes would leave no stone unturned, no fact unverified. In the meantime, I was aware that the wind was increasing, and the first hints of rain – those fine, almost non-existent drops that brush one's face or the back of one's hand and might only be imagined – seemed to be increasing.

We had stood there in silence for nearly five minutes, and I was considering leading us to a more sheltered location, when Holmes reappeared, a smile barely visible upon his face. "As I expected. Siegen is lying on the bed, still fully clothed, flat on his back and apparently passed out – no doubt helped down that path by whatever was slipped to him by his wife. You didn't see it? Well, you were facing the wrong direction. While he was turned to request yet another whisky at dinner, she passed a hand over his glass. I could just see something drop from it. At the time, it was none of my business. But now? It becomes amazingly relevant. As of just a few minutes ago, she is frantically searching his room. She must be looking at night for whatever it is that he has been seeking unsuccessfully during the day. What a pair! The promise of our involvement and interest has motivated her to try even harder than before."

"Wait," said Keller. "You're saying that she's been drugging him, and then going into his room at night to look for something hidden there?"

"Undoubtedly. Siegen probably learned of whatever it is that they seek from his dying brother, who must have hidden it there in that room twenty years ago when they first stayed at this inn. That's why he came back here now, and why he rented out the whole upstairs, and why he's been spending his days in his room. He's searching for something – and his wife also wants to find it – apparently without his knowledge. But time is slipping away from him – from both of them. And no doubt Mrs. Siegen has been drugging him with something of an evening to render him unconscious – thought not enough so that he is completely unaware of when she is moving about the room. His fogged mind has

538

convinced him that what he sees, combined with the induced paralysis, is the result of the ghost that he has heard inhabits the place."

While Keller and I considered Holmes's conclusions, the storm began to arrive in its entirety. The lightning, so silent and distant earlier, was now nearly on top of us, along with the related thunder. The light raindrops had begun to solidify into larger pellets. Holmes glanced up and said, "We've let this go on long enough. I shall gather Mrs. Siegen, and we'll discuss the matter in the common room." And once again, as he had just a few minutes earlier, he vanished into the darkness.

At that moment, the storm broke in full force, and a flash of lightning revealed that Holmes had already covered the thirty yards or so to the inn door and was stepping into the vestibule, pulling open the door of the stairs leading to the upstairs rooms. Keller and I stayed put for a moment, reluctant to venture out of the protection of the estate office and into the now-driving rain. We saw the dark shadow of Holmes pass in front of the first floor hall windows, left to right, and then after a moment or so, return more slowly along the same path, now lit by Mrs. Siegen's lantern as he moved with a light-shaded bulk that could only be the lady in question. Seconds later, the hallway returned to darkness and the door at the bottom of the steps opened, revealing the two of them in the vestibule, pulling open the second door to the common room.

Realizing that it was time to join Holmes, I took a deep breath and prepared to spring through the rain, only to be stopped by Keller's oddly quiet voice. "There she is," he whispered flatly, pulling at my arm and pointing toward the inn.

I followed his gaze and saw her, standing in the window to far right, the side located near Siegen's room. She was tall and thin, nearly reaching the top of the window, and nothing like the dumpy silhouette of the woman who had just passed that way. There is no other way to describe it – she was illuminated somehow from within, not throwing any light of her own, but possessing light nonetheless. It was a cool glow, slightly greenish in cast but not unpleasant, and it seemed to pulsate with faint regularity, although that may have only been from the beating of my own heart, as my pulse was suddenly throbbing anxiously.

"The nurse," I whispered, my voice raspy. "It must be the nurse."

"No, it can't be," said Keller, an edge to his tone. "She's a tiny girl, no bigger than Katy. See how tall this woman is?" His grip tightened on my arm, and I realized that I hadn't noticed that he'd never let go from before. "She's there. It's her. *It's the Lady*. But I've never seen her so clear before."

And clear she was. Although a hundred feet separated us from that window and where we stood, I felt as if I could see the very expression upon her face. It was one of great beauty, and infinite sadness. The features were visible in that greenish glow, although they shouldn't have been at that distance. Her eyes were each a black abyss, framed in pain and wisdom, yet mysterious nonetheless. Even as I watched, she gestured, indicating in some way that gave me an instinctive understanding that I was needed. Yet, I was paralyzed, continuing to watch her while my feet remained locked to that patch of ground by the estate house doorway. Only when she gestured again, this time sharper and with what almost looked like urgency and impatience, did I gain the impetus to break free and move.

"Come on!" I called to Keller, and set off running.

There was a blinding crack of lightning, and that, along with the sudden shock of the freezing rain instantly soaking through my clothing, left me gasping. I ran blindly, and as my vision cleared, I realized that I was already about half the distance to the inn. Looking up at the window, I saw that she was gone. That window was now as dark as the others along the same hallway, as if it had always been so.

Reaching the alcove, I wrenched open the door to the common room, seeing Holmes and Mrs. Siegen standing there facing one another, both with attitudes of tension. They turned their heads in my direction, and I summoned my breath to cry, "Holmes! Upstairs!" And then, letting that door swing shut, I opened the adjacent one and pounded up the steps, aware that Keller was right behind me.

Swinging around at the top, I ran along the hallway, sparing a glance as I passed the window where I had observed the woman, yet realizing without pause that there would now be nothing there to indicate her presence. I turned to the nearby door and was immediately joined by Keller. Thinking we would need a key, I reached for the knob, only to find it unlocked. I pushed open the door and entered.

The now nearly continuous lightning illuminated the room to reveal a low ceiling, crossed by ancient wooden beams, their bare unfinished appearance in contrast to the shadowed plaster bracketing them. Stepping closer to the bed in the center of the room, I perceived a foul smell hovering nearby, indicating that someone had been ill. And as there was only one person in the room, there was no question as to whom.

"Light a lantern," I snapped to Keller, moving toward the bed, where Siegen was lying on his back, as Holmes had described. I reached and turned his head toward the window, revealing the *vomitus* running alongside his mouth, down one cheek to puddle on the bed covering. Was it possible that he had aspirated it, too drunk or drugged to do otherwise? I was feeling his clammy forehead when simultaneously Keller lit the lamp and Holmes arrived.

"Mrs. Siegen?" I asked.

"She isn't going anywhere."

I could see that Siegen was in a bad way. His breath was quite shallow, and his eyes rolled up into his head. There was a distinct brandy-like odor wafting from his lips, along with a sour smell that could be anything from simple illness-related matter to poison.

"Keller," I snapped. "Black coffee. Not too hot – we have to get it into him as fast as possible. And find someone with an automobile."

"I have the remains of today's last pot beside the stove," said the innkeeper, moving toward the door. "And I'll wake up Clayton at the tobacconists across the way. He has a car."

"Have him go to Holmes's cottage. Bring my bag."

"Right."

"And send up Katy."

"I'll wake her."

After he left, Holmes helped me turn Siegen onto his side, instinctively understanding that the man was suffering from some likely combination of a narcotic and alcohol. "I don't believe that she intentionally poisoned him," I muttered as we effected respiration techniques. "This was likely an accident, spooked into using too much of what she's been giving him, combined with the increasingly large amounts of brandy and whisky that he consumed tonight. His respiration is dangerously suppressed."

"Agreed," said my friend. And then, "How did you know? To check him?"

I continued my efforts in silence for a moment before glancing up. "You won't believe me when I tell you."

In just a moment, Katy looked in, alerted by her father as he departed to seek an automobile. When she asked if there was anything that she could do, I sent her next door to check on the nurse, Gerda. Soon she reported that the girl was sleeping heavily and could not be awakened – "I pinched her!" – no doubt drugged, as had been Siegen, but she appeared to be in no danger.

Nearly half-an-hour was to pass before Keller finally returned, carrying my bag. I fished around for a stimulant, and used my stethoscope to verify what I'd already tried to hear without it – namely, whether the man's lungs were filled with any fluids from when he was ill while unconscious and on his back. They appeared to be clear, but I knew that he wasn't out of the woods yet.

It was touch-and-go for a while, but eventually he began to rally, and the stimulants brought him further around so that he could sit up and drink the cold coffee. Soon we had him up and walking, although he was not yet coherent at all.

When Siegen was somewhat better, I went next door and checked on the nurse, finding that the tiny figure was as Katy had indicated. Gerda might feel terrible in the morning, but for now she was in no danger.

I returned to Siegen's room to find that, in my absence, Anderson of the Sussex Constabulary had arrived, and that Holmes was apparently examining one of the low beams crisscrossing the ceiling with great satisfaction.

Even as I entered, he slipped something into his pocket, unseen by Anderson and Keller, who were both looking at Siegen, now slumped and groaning on the side of his bed, his hands on his head.

"Watson, you might give a short sketch of tonight's events to Anderson. In the meantime, I must tie up a few loose ends. I'll return with a full explanation shortly."

And with that, he slipped past us and out the door, leaving Anderson looking my way expectantly.

I pulled out my watch to discover that it was already approaching five in the morning. Where had that time gone? Glancing at Siegen, and not wanting to reveal too much in his presence, I nodded toward the hallway. Anderson joined me and, after pulling the door shut, I gave him a short *précis* of the night's happenings, from the time we were asked to meet with Siegen and his wife, to the observation of Berta Siegen going to her husband's room and Holmes's subsequent revelation of her nightly searches, followed by the discovery of Siegen's condition. Thankfully, Anderson didn't ask how I knew to check on the man, and I didn't volunteer it. "What are they looking for?" was his only question, and I had no answer for him.

We checked on Siegen one more time. He was still very sleepy, but as his condition had improved, letting him go back to bed now and sleep normally would only help his recovery, as he was out of danger. Downstairs, Keller and Katy had prepared coffee and an early breakfast, and we ate at one side of the common room, while Mrs. Siegen sat alone at the other. No one attempted to question her, or otherwise engage her in the least. At one point, she stood, indicating that she wished to check on her baby, but Katy quickly said that she would, and Mrs. Siegen could see that Anderson would accept no arguments otherwise.

It was nearly eight before Holmes returned. He bounded in, looking fresh and energetic as he crossed the room to the cold leftovers and made up a plate. Eating it quickly while standing, he watched us all with amusement, occasionally turning his gaze toward the glowering woman sitting by herself.

"Mr. Keller," he said, "would you and your daughter summon Mr. Siegen and the nurse? Thank you."

There was no conversation in the twenty minutes or so that we waited while the drugged individuals readied themselves. Eventually they entered, each looking befuddled and confused. They were led to seats near Mrs. Siegen, where they watched with puzzlement. Katy cuddled the baby, still sleeping, to her shoulder.

Turning to Mrs. Siegen, Holmes said, "Did you also drug the child?"

The woman looked startled. "No!" she said. "*Mein Gott*, no! She's always been a good baby, sleeping through the night."

"For your sake, I hope that's the truth." Then, "Mr. Siegen!"

His sharp tone focused the little man's attention. With a cough, he said, "Yes?"

"I want you to know that prevarication is useless. I have found the jewel. So far I believe you to be innocent. Now all I need from you is the truth."

"The . . . the jewel? What do you mean? I cannot think . . . ."

"The jewel that was stolen from Countess Brazelton in Bad Dürkheim in 1885. Your brother was a suspect, but there were others, so he was never seriously investigated. When you and he left the country at approximately the same time, it was considered suspicious, but when he returned alone a few months later, with no signs of increased wealth, it was finally decided that he was innocent, and the search focused elsewhere. The jewel has never been found."

At that point, he placed a thumb and forefinger in his waistcoat pocket, pulling out a sizeable emerald that winked in the morning light as he turned it this way and that. "Until now."

"The . . . the jewel," said Siegen, now more alert. "But . . . how did . . . how did you . . . ?"

"Yes, how?" snapped his wife, her harsh tone shocking us."

"It was inserted into one of the beams crossing the ceiling over the bed. Considering that your brother had been a carpenter, I assumed that whatever you were searching for would be cleverly concealed in some wooden object, but apparently that fact never crossed your minds. Or it did, but your imaginations were limited to articles of furniture, and you were unable to see the tell-tale marks that gave away the previous work when your brother opened a cavity in the beam.

"As for my deciding an object was concealed in the room in the first place? Last night, I considered why you were spending so much time in that room, in a place that you hadn't visited in twenty years. Your story of attempting to achieve a closeness with your deceased brother was, frankly, poppycock. I considered seven separate possibilities, but the most likely was that something was hidden there. But not by you, or you could have retrieved it on the first night. No, you didn't know where it was – thus, your continued stay, and willingness to reserve the rooms at double the rate to ensure that you would not be turned out. Clearly whatever you sought was worth more than whatever you were paying to keep the upstairs rooms free.

"You gave me the rest of the explanation when you explained that your brother, who had been here with you, had recently died. What else could it be, but that *he* was the one who had hidden the item here on his earlier visit, failing to return over those long years, and had at the last told you where it was – but not *precisely* where."

Siegen nodded sadly. "When we left Kallstadt as boys, I didn't know that he had taken it. He had been in Bad Dürkheim, making a repair at the spa, and discovered that the jewel was left unsecured. He walked out with it, and though he realized that no one suspected him, he decided that it would be a good time to go to America, something that we had long discussed. Our grandmother gave us some money, and we decided to see the world along the way. Arriving in England, we traveled along the southern coast, intending to work our way to Bristol.

"But here in the inn, a random stop on our way to see some of the nearby white cliffs, Otto revealed the jewel to me, and how he had obtained it. I was appalled, and certain that we would be arrested immediately. By then, he also regretted taking it, but he was afraid to return it, and unwilling to completely abandon it. Unknown to me then, he hid it somewhere in our room, where he could sever his

544

association with it, but find it again in years to come if he changed his mind. We continued to argue, and finally agreed to part ways.

"I proceeded to America, and gave only passing thoughts to the emerald over the next twenty years. Even when I visited Kallstadt a few years ago, and married Berta, Otto and I didn't discuss it – unwilling, I suppose, to open old wounds. But then I heard that he was sick, and Berta was missing the old country, so we went back again. This time, Otto wanted to tell me what had happened to the jewel, but the cancer had almost overwhelmed him at that point. He was only conscious long enough to relate that he'd hidden it in the old room upstairs, but was unable to share any other information.

"I should have let it go. But . . . but since selling out my business interests in the west and moving to New York, my finances have been . . . precarious. The possibility of getting the jewel became tempting. And . . . and I had told the story to Berta, and she was most anxious that we should find it."

His wife glowered by said nothing. However, Holmes addressed her.

"Mrs. Siegen. You gave the impression during our conversation last night that you were ready to leave for New York as soon as your husband could be convinced. And yet, you were actually as anxious as he to retrieve the jewel. Why argue to leave when you also wanted to stay?"

"Because," she snapped, "I knew that he would stay regardless of what I said. And I didn't want it to seem as if I was too interested in finding it."

"Because he might get suspicious at your interest, of course, if it was actually greater than his." She didn't answer, and he continued. "What were your plans if you found it?"

"Why, to sell it, of course. We can always use the money."

"Ah, but if it was to be used for the both of you, the 'we' to which you refer, then why did you feel the need to search in secret? Why not help your husband during his daytime searches? Why drug him at night, so that you could search on your own, if not to find it on your own, keeping the knowledge to yourself."

Siegen looked at his wife, shocked understanding crossing his features. "Berta?" he said, his voice small. "You . . . you drugged me?"

She stood up abruptly, her voice cutting like a whip. "Of course I drugged you, *dummkopf*! You, who were too stupid to take the jewel when you had the chance! You, who would have gone back home without trying to find it!"

545

"But . . . but I was trying to find it for us. Why would you try to keep it for yourself?"

"Why not? What have you ever done for me?"

"The house? The business? They were always for you."

"You spineless *kretin*! What kind of business do you have now? You had the chance to be a rich man and threw it away!"

"But I sold the . . . the club out west because I didn't want you to be embarrassed."

"You fool! That business would have made us rich! And now you won't even consider starting something similar in New York." She stood and rested her hands on her mid-section, where Siegen's unborn child rested. "This one, and Etta upstairs, are all that I need. If I could have found the jewel, I would have been able to leave you and find a real man!"

Siegen unexpectedly sobbed and lowered his head into his hands, while the rest of us looked on in mortified silence. He muttered something about the raging woman being "his life", to which she said, "Do you think that I don't know about the others? *Heuchler!* The lawyer's wife? Mrs. Allyn next door? *This one!*" And she flung out a hand toward Gerda, the nurse, who turned bright red before standing and fleeing from the room. Siegen made no reply.

"Mr. Siegen," said Holmes, his quiet voice cutting through the tension. "Your wife has been drugging you to search your room each night. Doubtless is it some opiate that didn't quite put you to sleep, but caused you to hallucinate that it was a ghost moving about your room, when in reality you were seeing her search. Last night, a combination of several things nearly resulted in your death: Your greater-than-normal drinking and her decision to use a higher dosage level, as her search had become more urgent, knowing that Dr. Watson and I would be investigating today, possibly finding some indication of her involvement, or even the jewel itself.

"I do not believe that she intended you any true harm . . . *this time*. But I must warn you – *this is a dangerous woman*. Should it suit her, and if she believes that she can accomplish it without consequences, *she will kill you*. Possibly not this year, or even this decade, but should the need arise, you will die, and likely in a way that seems natural and above suspicion."

He turned to the woman, who had sat back down and was hunched like a cornered beast. "After I had some idea of what had happened, I sent telegrams early this morning to Kallstadt. The wires sizzled between Germany and Eastbourne. Sorting through their records, they provided information that allowed me to narrow down

546

what had likely happened twenty years ago, giving me a direction to search. But along the way, a great deal of information, madam, was sent this way about you too. It is their contention that you, as they say in America, are *a piece of work.*

"I will have my eye on you," he added. "And, as much as I dislike Mr. Siegen, he is now under my protection. Should something happen to him, I will know the reason why. Do you understand me?"

Of course, she made no acknowledgement. But I could see in her eyes, now stripped of all pretense, the dangerous animal lurking underneath, like some venomous lizard moving in and out of the light. So could Siegen, who was looking at her with raw fear.

"I can't tell you what to do, Mr. Siegen," concluded Holmes, "and I suspect that you'll return to New York with this woman. You are a weak man. But have a care, sir. Have a care!"

Of course, as the world now knows, Siegen did indeed come to a bad and unexpected end, and Holmes kept his promise, although things did not end quite as either of us expected.

I never saw the White Lady again – at least, not until last week, when I received an urgent message requesting my presence from Katy Hollander *née* Keller, still at the Tiger Inn, and fast approaching the date of her confinement. I was honored that she would contact me, in London, before even reaching out to Holmes. I rushed down to her aid . . . but that is another story.

Later in the afternoon following the recovery of the jewel, after the Siegens had been left in one another's custody and Holmes and I had returned to his villa, we found ourselves sitting in his study, discussing the recent events. My own questions had all been answered, and I sensed that we were circling closer to that matter which still puzzled him and of which I had yet to speak. Without making him ask, I explained.

"It was the White Lady," I sighed. "At least I suppose that it was. If I can make myself believe in such a thing." I went on to relate, as best I could, how she had become visible to both Keller and me from our vantage in the storm.

As expected, Holmes scoffed. "Nonsense," he said, lighting his pipe. "You somehow connected all of the alcohol that the man had been drinking with my report that his wife had drugged him, and you feared the results."

I shook my head. "It was Keller who drew my attention to her."

"Then it was the nurse," he said confidently.

"Not possible," I said. "She was also drugged."

"Perhaps she drugged herself after signaling to you from the window."

"Now why would she do that? And in any case, Mrs. Siegen has confirmed that she gave the opioid to the girl an hour or so earlier. There is no way that, at that dose, that she could have been up and walking by the window, let alone signaling for help. And soon after we found Siegen, Katy confirmed that the nurse was asleep."

"Katy, then," said Holmes, clutching at straws. "She was the one at the window."

"She said she wasn't, and you and I both know she wouldn't lie. The woman that Keller and I saw was too tall for Katy – and also for the nurse. And in any case, what business would Katy have had up there, in a hallway where you and Mrs. Siegen had just passed by seconds before?"

"Then it was a flash of lightning – your eyes were affected by the glare. Or a reflection on the wavy window glass."

This time I didn't answer at all, and Holmes fell silent. We both sipped our whisky. Then, to my great surprise, Holmes murmured, "When you have eliminated the impossible . . . ."

I lowered my glass. "Holmes! That is the last response that I would have expected from you."

"Good to know that I can still surprise you after all these years," he smiled. Then his smile failed. "How sad," he said.

"What?"

"If one admits the existence of a ghost – and do not mistake this conversation for such an admission on my part! – then why doesn't this nameless woman who spent her life serving others – a nurse or something like that, we're told – merit some sort of special dispensation for her soul, rather than being compelled to exist, year after year, century after century, in that place in-between, by whatever means that we do not understand – a phantom, prevented from going to her deserved rest? Is she somehow punished for having such a good and generous heart that she must remain to provide further help when needed, even across the generations?

"And yet, a creature such as Mrs. Siegen will barrel onward through her own misbegotten life, shedding misery around her in every direction, and no doubt poisoning the lives of her children and her children's children. Who can tell how far her evil influence will spread, and how much pain and suffering it will cause?

"Two women," he finished after a moment. "So different, and both with such very different fates."

I tried to think of some response. I knew that Holmes could occasionally find his way down these existential rabbit holes, and I was determined to prevent it. I took a deep breath, not knowing what to say, but trusting that I would think of something. But before I could begin, I heard the sound of a motorcar arriving. I raised my eyebrows.

"Just in time," said Holmes with a smile. "When I divined what might have happened to direct your attention to Siegen's bedroom – what you *think* might have happened – I took the liberty of inviting Peake down, in order for him to hear your story. He might have some valuable insight."

Soon our old friend had joined us, and it turned out that he did.

NOTE

It is claimed that The Tiger Inn in East Dean has been haunted by a figure known as *The White Lady* for several hundred years. Accounts vary as to her identity, with one possibility being that she was someone who was once employed by the family that owned both the village of East Dean and the surrounding estate. Another is that she was a nurse in a nearby hospital that was set up in the three buildings located immediately adjacent to the inn. At some point in the past, either during the Plague Years or the later Napoleonic Wars – accounts vary – her experiences were such that she has been unable to find any peace, even to the present time. The staff at The Tiger Inn reports slamming doors, falling pictures, and occasional appearances by the Lady.

In September 2013, I was able to make my first (of three so far) Holmes Pilgrimages, with a stop in East Dean to see the country around Holmes's retirement villa, nearby Hodcombe Farm. I stayed overnight in The Tiger Inn, having no idea at that time about the inn's connection with The White Lady. Coincidentally, I stayed in the same room that, from its description in this narrative, was used by Friedrich Siegen in 1905. During the night, I had one of the three (so far) supernatural occurrences that have happened to me in my life. I awakened from my sleep to find the room extremely cold, objects knocked to the floor, and flickering lights. I saw no shapes and heard no noises, but I felt that I wasn't alone. I wasn't scared, and after a few minutes, the incident ended, although I still felt as if I were being watched. Still, I eventually drifted back to sleep.

Sadly, I was too exhausted from my rambles over the Downs the day before to wake up further and investigate when the incident occurred. I did, however, mention the affair to the inn's owner and staff downstairs at the bar the next morning, asking them innocently if they had a ghost. They were strangely reticent, which puzzled me, as I would think they would be proud of their ghost. It was only later, after coming into possession of this

Watsonian manuscript that it occurred to me to verify through further research whether The Tiger Inn is known to be haunted. Unsurprisingly, I learned that The White Lady has been a long-time resident of the inn.

I only wish I had known that before I stayed there. I might have been better prepared to pay more attention when she was carrying out her shenanigans . . . .

D.M.

About the Contributors

The following contributors appear in this volume
The MX Book of New Sherlock Holmes Stories
Part VIII – Eliminate the Impossible: 1892-1905

Deanna Baran lives in a remote part of Texas where cowboys may still be seen in their natural habitat. A librarian and former museum curator, she writes in between cups of tea, playing *Go*, and trading postcards with people around the world. This is her latest venture into the foggy streets of gaslit London.

Brian Belanger is a publisher and editor, but is best known for his freelance illustration and cover design work. His distinctive style can be seen on several MX Publishing covers, including *Silent Meridian* by Elizabeth Crowen, *Sherlock Holmes and the Menacing Melbournian* by Allan Mitchell, *Sherlock Holmes and A Quantity of Debt* by David Marcum, *Welcome to Undershaw* by Luke Benjamen Kuhns, and many more. Brian is the co-founder of Belanger Books LLC, where he illustrates the popular *MacDougall Twins with Sherlock Holmes* young reader series (#1 bestsellers on Amazon.com UK). A prolific creator, he also designs t-shirts, mugs, stickers, and other merchandise on his personal art site: *www.redbubble.com/people/zhahadun*.

Derrick Belanger is and educator and also the author of the #1 bestselling book in its category, *Sherlock Holmes: The Adventure of the Peculiar Provenance*, which was in the top 200 bestselling books on Amazon. He also is the author of *The MacDougall Twins with Sherlock Holmes* books, and he edited the Sir Arthur Conan Doyle horror anthology *A Study in Terror: Sir Arthur Conan Doyle's Revolutionary Stories of Fear and the Supernatural*. Mr. Belanger co-owns the publishing company Belanger Books, which released the Sherlock Holmes anthologies *Beyond Watson*, *Holmes Away From Home: Adventures from the Great Hiatus* Volumes 1 and 2, and *Sherlock Holmes: Before Baker Street*. Derrick resides in Colorado and continues compiling unpublished works by Dr. John H. Watson. For this story, the following students completed research as part of their 7th grade IB project at Century Middle School in Thornton, CO: Dante Avilez-Cruz, Isaiah Buckner, Larissa Garcia, Doramay Jones, Cooper Kehmeier, Brooklyn Ossowski, Conner Phillips, Zoey Pilcher, LaShawn Prince, and Dylan Wright. Without their contribution, this story could not have been written.

Ben Cardall is *The Deductionist*, a man who has spent the better part of his life in pursuit of the skills of Sherlock Holmes and how much of a reality they are. He spends his days working as a Mentalist and has made it his business to know what others don't or simply cannot, essentially splitting his time between writing, researching, and testing/performing these feats that were only previously thought to be works of fiction and legend. Contained within is the very first pastiche he has ever written, carefully guided under the expert tutelage of David Marcum.

Nick Cardillo has loved Sherlock Holmes ever since he was first introduced to the detective in *The Great Illustrated Classics* edition of *The Adventures of Sherlock Holmes* at the age of six. His devotion to the Baker Street detective duo has only increased over the years, and Nick is thrilled to be taking his first, proper steps into the Sherlock Holmes Community. His first published story, "The Adventure of the Travling Corpse", appeared in *The MX Book of New Sherlock Holmes Stories – Part VI: 2017 Annual.* A devout fan of The Golden Age of Detective Fiction, Hammer Horror, and *Doctor Who*, Nick co-writes the Sherlockian blog, *Back on Baker Street*, which analyses over seventy years of Sherlock Holmes film and culture. He is a student at Susquehanna University.

Lee Child was fired and on the dole when he hatched a harebrained scheme to write a bestselling novel, thus saving his family from ruin. *Killing Floor* was an immediate success and launched the series which has grown in sales and impact with every new installment. *Forbes* calls it "The Strongest Brand in Publishing". His series hero, Jack Reacher, besides being fictional, is a kind-hearted soul who allows Lee lots of spare time for reading, listening to music, the Yankees, and Aston Villa. Visit *LeeChild.com* for more info, or find Lee on *Facebook: LeeChildOfficial*, *Twitter: LeeChildReacher*, and *YouTube: leechildjackreacher*.

Michael Cox started his working life as an actor in the theatre, but the habit of eating regularly drove him into advertising. From there he was grateful to join Granada TV as a floor manager in 1961, and to train as a programme director in 1963. His credits as a director or producer include: *Coronation Street*, *Mr Rose*, *Murder*, *A Family at War*, *Holly*, *Victorian Scandals,* and *Sam*. He was appointed Head of Drama Series in 1980, and was the original producer of the *Sherlock Holmes* series with Jeremy Brett. He published a book about the series, *A Study in Celluloid* in 1999. He is now retired and lives in Cheshire with his wife Sandra and their small dog.

Sir Arthur Conan Doyle (1859-1930) *Holmes Chronicler Emeritus.* If not for him, this anthology would not exist. Author, physician, patriot, sportsman, spiritualist, husband and father, and advocate for the oppressed. He is remembered and honored for the purposes of this collection by being the man who introduced Sherlock Holmes to the world. Through fifty-six Holmes short stories, four novels, and additional Apocryphal entries, Doyle revolutionized mystery stories and also greatly influenced and improved police forensic methods and techniques for the betterment of all. *Steel True Blade Straight.*

Cindy Dye first discovered Sherlock Holmes when she was eleven, in a collection that ended at the Reichenbach Falls. It was another six months before she discovered *The Hound of the Baskervilles*, and two weeks after that before a librarian handed her *The Return*. She has loved the stories ever since. She has written fan-fiction, and her first published pastiche, "The Tale of the Forty Thieves", was included in *The MX Book of New Sherlock Holmes Stories – Part I: 1881-1889.* Her story "A Christmas Goose" was in *The MX Book of New Sherlock Holmes Stories – Part V: Christmas Adventures.*

Steve Emecz's main field is technology, in which he has been working for about twenty years. Following multiple senior roles at Xerox, where he grew their European eCommerce from $6m to $200m, Steve joined platform provider Venda, and moved across to Powa in 2010. Today, Steve is CCO at collectAI in Hamburg, a German fintech company using Artificial Intelligence to help companies with their debt collection. Steve is a regular trade show speaker on the subject of eCommerce, and his tech career has taken him to more than fifty countries – so he's no stranger to planes and airports. He wrote two novels (one a bestseller) in the 1990's, and a screenplay in 2001. Shortly after, he set up MX Publishing, specialising in NLP books. In 2008, MX published its first Sherlock Holmes book, and MX has gone on to become the largest specialist Holmes publisher in the world, with over one hundred authors and over two hundred books. MX is a social enterprise and supports two main causes. The first is Happy Life, a children's rescue project in Nairobi, Kenya, where he and his wife, Sharon, spend every Christmas at the rescue centre in Kasarani. In 2014, they wrote a short book about the project, *The Happy Life Story*. The second is the Stepping Stones School, of which Steve is a patron. Stepping Stones is located at Undershaw, Sir Arthur Conan Doyle's former home.

Melissa Farnham, Head Teacher of Stepping Stones School, is driven by a passion to open the doors to learners with complex and layered special needs that just make society feel two steps too far away. Based on the Surrey/Hampshire border in England, her time is spent between a great school at the prestigious home of Conan Doyle, and her two children, dogs, and horses, so there never a dull moment.

David Friend lives in Wales, UK, where he divides his time between watching old detective films and thinking about old detective films. He's been scribbling out stories for twenty years and hopes, some day, to write something half-decent. Most of what he pens is set in a 1930's world of non-stop adventure with debonair sleuths, kick-ass damsels, criminal masterminds, and narrow escapes, and he wishes he could live there. He's currently working on a collection of Sherlock Holmes stories and a series based around *The Strange Investigators*, an eccentric team of private detectives out to solve the most peculiar and perplexing mysteries around. He thinks of it as P.G. Wodehouse crossed with Edgar Allen Poe, only not as good.

Wendy C. Fries is the author of *Sherlock Holmes and John Watson: The Day They Met* and also writes under the name Atlin Merrick. Wendy is fascinated with London theatre, scriptwriting, and lattes. Her website is *wendycfries.com*.

Mark A. Gagen BSI is co-founder of Wessex Press, sponsor of the popular *From Gillette to Brett* conferences, and publisher of *The Sherlock Holmes Reference Library* and many other fine Sherlockian titles. A life-long Holmes enthusiast, he is a member of *The Baker Street Irregulars* and *The Illustrious Clients of Indianapolis*. A graphic artist by profession, his work is often seen on the covers of *The Baker Street Journal* and various BSI books.

Paul D. Gilbert was born in 1954 and has lived in and around Lindon all of his life. He has been married to Jackie for thirty-nine years, and she is a Holmes expert who keeps him on the straight and narrow! He has two sons, one of whom now lives in Spain. His interests include literature, ancient history, all religions, most sports, and movies. He is currently employed full-time as a funeral director. His books so far include *The Lost Files of Sherlock Holmes* (2007), *The Chronicles of Sherlock Holmes* (2008), *Sherlock Holmes and the Giant Rat of Sumatra* (2010), *The Annals of Sherlock Holmes* (2012), and *Sherlock Holmes and the Unholy Trinity* (2015). He has finished *Sherlock Holmes: The Four Handed Game*, to be published 2017, and is now working on his next novel.

John Atkinson Grimshaw (1836-1893) was born in Leeds, England. His amazing paintings, usually featuring twilight or night scenes illuminated by gas-lamps or moonlight, are easily recognizable, and are often used on the covers of books about The Great Detective to set the mood, as shadowy figures move in the distance through misty mysterious settings and over rain-slicked streets.

Arthur Hall was born in Aston, Birmingham, UK, in 1944. He discovered his interest in writing during his schooldays, along with a love of fictional adventure and suspense. His first novel, *Sole Contact,* was an espionage story about an ultra-secret government department known as "Sector Three", and was followed, to date, by three sequels. Other works include three Sherlock Holmes novels, *The Demon of the Dusk, The One Hundred Percent Society,* and *The Secret Assassin,* as well as a collection of short stories, and a modern detective novel. He lives in the West Midlands, United Kingdom.

Jeremy Holstein first discovered Sherlock Holmes at age five when he became convinced that the Hound of the Baskervilles lived in his bedroom closet. A life long enthusiast of radio dramas, Jeremy is currently the lead dramatist and director for the Post Meridian Radio Players adaptations of Sherlock Holmes, where he has adapted *The Hound of the Baskervilles, The Sign of Four,* and "Jack the Harlot Killer" (retitled "The Whitechapel Murders") from William S. Baring-Gould's *Sherlock Holmes of Baker Street* for the company. Jeremy has also written Sherlock Holmes scripts for Jim French's *Imagination Theatre.* He lives with his wife and daughter in the Boston, MA area.

In the year 1998 **Craig Janacek** took his degree of Doctor of Medicine at Vanderbilt University, and proceeded to Stanford to go through the training prescribed for pediatricians in practice. Having completed his studies there, he was duly attached to the University of California, San Francisco as Associate Professor. The author of over seventy medical monographs upon a variety of obscure lesions, his travel-worn and battered tin dispatch-box is crammed with papers, nearly all of which are records of his fictional works. To date, most have been published solely in electronic format, including two non-Holmes novels (*The Oxford Deception* and *The Anger of Achilles Peterson*). He recently released paperback editions of many of his Sherlock Holmes works, previously only available in electronic versions, including: the short trilogy *The Assassination of Sherlock Holmes*; *Light In the Darkness,* containing the four adventures previously collected as *The Midwinter Mysteries of Sherlock Holmes* and the four stories from *The First of Criminals*; and a Watsonian novel entitled *The Isle of Devils.* Craig Janacek is a *nom de plume.*

Christopher James was born in 1975 in Paisley, Scotland. Educated at Newcastle and UEA, he was a winner of the UK's National Poetry Competition in 2008. He has written two full length Sherlock Holmes novels, *The Adventure of the Ruby Elephant* and *The Jeweller of Florence,* both published by MX, and is working on a third.

Roger Johnson BSI, ASH is a retired librarian, now working as a volunteer assistant at the Essex Police Museum. In his spare time, he is commissioning editor of *The Sherlock Holmes Journal,* an occasional lecturer, and a frequent contributor to The Writings About the Writings. His sole work of Holmesian pastiche was published in 1997 in Mike Ashley's anthology *The Mammoth Book of New Sherlock*

Holmes Adventures, and he has the greatest respect for the many authors who have contributed new tales to the present mighty trilogy. Like his wife, Jean Upton, he is a member of both *The Baker Street Irregulars* and *The Adventuresses of Sherlock Holmes.*

Andrew Lane is a British writer with thirty-odd books to his credit, a mixture of fiction and non-fiction, adult and young adult, and books under his own name and ghost-written works. Most recently he has written eight books in a series (sold in translation to more than twenty countries at the last count) imagining what Sherlock Holmes would have been like when he was fourteen years old. *A Study in Scarlet* was the first book that Andrew Lane bought with his own pocket money. He was nine years old at the time, and the purchase warped his life from that moment on.

Rand B. Lee is a freelance writer whose fiction has appeared in *Asimov's* and *The Magazine of Fantasy & Science Fiction.* He is the youngest surviving child of Manfred B. Lee, co-author with Frederic Dannay of the *Ellery Queen* detective stories. Rand lives in Santa Fe, New Mexico.

Michael Mallory is the Derringer-winning author of the "Amelia Watson" (The Second Mrs. Watson) series and "Dave Beauchamp" mystery series, and more than one-hundred-twenty-five short stories. An entertainment journalist by day, he has written eight nonfiction books on pop culture and more than six-hundred newspaper and magazine articles. Based in Los Angeles, Mike is also an occasional actor on television.

David Marcum plays The Game with deadly seriousness. He first discovered Sherlock Holmes in 1975, at the age of ten, when he received an abridged version of *The Adventures* during a trade. Since that time, David has collected literally thousands of traditional Holmes pastiches in the form of novels, short stories, radio and television episodes, movies and scripts, comics, fan-fiction, and unpublished manuscripts. He is the author of *The Papers of Sherlock Holmes Vol.'s I* and *II* (2011, 2013), *Sherlock Holmes and A Quantity of Debt* (2013, 2016) and *Sherlock Holmes – Tangled Skeins* (2015, 2017), and the forthcoming *The Papers of Solar Pons* (2017). Additionally, he is the editor of the three-volume set *Sherlock Holmes in Montague Street* (2014, recasting Arthur Morrison's Martin Hewitt stories as early Holmes adventures,), the two-volume collection of Great Hiatus stories, *Holmes Away From Home* (2016), *Sherlock Holmes: Before Baker Street* (2017), *Imagination Theatre's Sherlock Holmes* (2017 – Forthcoming), and most recently the ongoing collection, *The MX Book of New Sherlock Holmes Stories* (2015-   ), now at eight volumes, with two more in preparation as of this writing. He has contributed stories, essays, and scripts to *The Baker Street Journal, The Watsonian, Beyond Watson, Sherlock Holmes Mystery Magazine, About Sixty, About Being a Sherlockian* (Forthcoming), *The Solar Pons Gazette,* Imagination Theater, *The Proceedings of the Pondicherry Lodge,* and *The Gazette,* the journal of the Nero Wolfe *Wolfe Pack.* He began his adult work life as a Federal Investigator for an obscure U.S. Government agency, before the organization was eliminated. He returned to school for a second degree, and is now a licensed Civil Engineer, living in Tennessee with his wife and son. He is a member of *The Sherlock Holmes Society of London, The Occupants of the Full House* and *The Diogenes Club of Washington, D.C.* (both Scions of *The Baker Street Irregulars*), *The John H. Watson Society* ("Marker"), *The Praed Street Irregulars* ("The Obrisset Snuff Box"), *The Solar*

Pons Society of London, and *The Diogenes Club West (East Tennessee Annex)*, a curious and unofficial Scion of one. Since the age of nineteen, he has worn a deerstalker as his regular-and-only hat from autumn to spring. In 2013, he and his deerstalker were finally able make his first trip-of-a-lifetime Holmes Pilgrimage to England, with return pilgrimages in 2015 and 2016, where you may have spotted him. If you ever run into him and his deerstalker out and about, feel free to say hello!

Daniel McGachey Outside of his day job – which, over the past quarter century has seen him write extensively for comics, newspapers, magazines, digital media, and animation – Scottish writer Daniel McGachey's stories first appeared in several volumes of *The BHF Book of Horror Stories* and *Black Book of Horror* anthology series, and *Filthy Creations* magazine. In 2009, Dark Regions Press published his first ghost story collection, *They That Dwell in Dark Places*, dedicated in part to M.R. James, whose works inspired the creation of the collected stories. Since 2005, he has reviewed television and radio adaptations of James's stories for *The Ghosts and Scholars M.R. James Newsletter*, while his sequels to several of James's original tales appeared as the Haunted Library publication *Ex Libris: Lufford* in 2012. Moving from M.R. James to his other lifelong literary hero, his 2010 Dark Regions Press collection pitted Sir Arthur Conan Doyle's rational detective against the irrational forces of the supernatural in *Sherlock Holmes: The Impossible Cases*. His radio plays have been broadcast since 2005 as part of the mystery and suspense series *Imagination Theater*, including entries in its long-running strand of new Holmesian mysteries, *The Further Adventures of Sherlock Holmes*. He recently completed a new "impossible case" for Sherlock Holmes and Dr. Watson in the novel, *The Curse of the Devil's Crown* for Dark Renaissance Press.

William Meikle is a Scottish writer, now living in Canada, with over twenty novels published in the genre press and more than three-hundred short story credits in thirteen countries. He has several Sherlock Holmes books available from Dark Regions Press and Gryphonwood Press, and his Holmes pastiches have appeared in a number of professional anthologies and magazines. He lives in Newfoundland with whales, bald eagles, and icebergs for company. When he's not writing, he drinks beer, plays guitar, and dreams of fortune and glory.

Will Murray is the author of over seventy novels, including forty *Destroyer* novels and seven posthumous *Doc Savage* collaborations with Lester Dent, under the name Kenneth Robeson, for Bantam Books in the 1990's. Since 2011, he has written fourteen additional Doc Savage adventures for Altus Press, two of which co-starred The Shadow, as well as a solo Pat Savage novel. His 2015 Tarzan novel, *Return to Pal-Ul-Don*, was followed by *King Kong vs. Tarzan* in 2016. Murray has written short stories featuring such classic characters as Batman, Superman, Wonder Woman, Spider-Man, Ant-Man, the Hulk, Honey West, the Spider, the Avenger, the Green Hornet, the Phantom, and Cthulhu. A previous Murray Sherlock Holmes story appeared in Moonstone's *Sherlock Holmes: The Crossovers Casebook*, and another is forthcoming in *Sherlock Holmes and Doctor Was Not*, involving H. P. Lovecraft's Dr. Herbert West.

Sidney Paget (1860-1908), a few of whose illustrations are used within this anthology, was born in London, and like his two older brothers, became a famed illustrator and painter. He completed over three-hundred-and-fifty drawings for the

Sherlock Holmes stories that were first published in *The Strand* magazine, defining Holmes's image forever after in the public mind.

Robert Perret is a writer, librarian, and devout Sherlockian living on the Palouse. His Sherlockian publications include "The Canaries of Clee Hills Mine" in *An Improbable Truth: The Paranormal Adventures of Sherlock Holmes*, "For King and Country" in *The Science of Deduction*, and "How Hope Learned the Trick" in *NonBinary Review*. He considers himself to be a pan-Sherlockian and a one-man Scion out on the lonely moors of Idaho. Robert has recently authored a yet-unpublished scholarly article tentatively entitled "A Study in Scholarship: The Case of the *Baker Street Journal*'. More information is available at *www.robertperret.com*

Tracy J. Revels, a Sherlockian from the age of eleven, is a professor of history at Wofford College in Spartanburg, South Carolina. She is a member of *The Survivors of the Gloria Scott* and *The Studious Scarlets Society*, and is a past recipient of the Beacon Society Award. Almost every semester, she teaches a class that covers The Canon, either to college students or to senior citizens. She is also the author of three supernatural Sherlockian pastiches with MX (*Shadowfall*, *Shadowblood*, and *Shadowwraith*), and a regular contributor to her scion's newsletter. She also has some notoriety as an author of very silly skits: For proof, see "The Adventure of the Adversarial Adventuress" and "Occupy Baker Street" on YouTube. When not studying Sherlock Holmes, she can be found researching the history of her native state, and has written books on Florida in the Civil War and on the development of Florida's tourism industry.

Roger Riccard of Los Angeles, California, U.S.A., is a descendant of the Roses of Kilravock in Highland Scotland. He is the author of two previous Sherlock Holmes novels, *The Case of the Poisoned Lilly* and *The Case of the Twain Papers*, as well as a series of short stories in two volumes, *Sherlock Holmes: Adventures for the Twelve Days of Christmas* and *Further Adventures for the Twelve Days of Christmas*, all of which are published by Baker Street Studios. He has another novel, a new series of short stories, and a non-fiction Holmes reference work in various stages of completion. He became a Sherlock Holmes enthusiast as a teenager (many, many years ago,) and, like all fans of The Great Detective, yearned for more stories after reading The Canon over and over. It was the Granada Television performances of Jeremy Brett and Edward Hardwicke, and the encouragement of his wife, Rosilyn, that at last inspired him to write his own Holmes adventures, using the Granada actor portrayals as his guide. He has been called "The best pastiche writer since Val Andrews" by the *Sherlockian E-Times*.

David Ruffle was born in Northamptonshire in England a long, long time ago. He has lived in the beautiful town of Lyme Regis on the Dorset coast for the last twelve years. His first foray into writing was the 2009 self-published, *Sherlock Holmes and the Lyme Regis Horror*. This was swiftly followed by two more Holmes novellas set in Lyme, and a Holmes children's book, *Sherlock Holmes and the Missing Snowman*. Since then, there has been four further Holmes novellas, including the critically acclaimed *End Peace*, three contemporary comedies, and a slim volume detailing the life of Jack the Ripper. When not writing, he can be found working in a local shop, "acting" in local productions, and occasionally performing poetry locally. To come next year is *Sherlock Holmes and the Scarborough Affair*, a collaboration with Gill Stammers, in which David is very much the junior partner.

At the age of ten, **Aaron Smith** walked in on his father watching an episode of the Jeremy Brett series of Sherlock Holmes dramatizations. He was fascinated by the intensity of the character on screen and the mystery that had to be solved. Two decades later, Smith was thrilled to have, as his very first published work, "The Massachusetts Affair," in Airship 27 Productions' *Sherlock Holmes: Consulting Detective Volume 1*. Since then, Smith has contributed eight Holmes mysteries to that anthology series, seven of which were collected into a Kindle edition in 2016. His other Holmes-related work includes the Doctor Watson novel *Season of Madness* and a Holmes/Van Helsing crossover. "The Cocoon of His Dreams," as part of 18th Wall Productions' *The Science of Deduction* series. He can be followed on Twitter as *@AaronSmith377*

Sandor Jay Sonnen is a crime writer who taught government and history for twenty-five years in Los Angeles. After retiring, he found the time to begin writing mysteries and hasn't stopped. He has written a novel featuring a detective thrown into having to solve a murder, aided by his sort of competent attorney. *Who Can Impress The Forest* introduces Anhur Lennox, forced to prove his innocence, concerned in the death of his wife, by finding the real killer, while his lawyer works to help him by drinking vodka, smoking cigars, and avoiding the wrath of his wife, secretary, and the F.B.I. He has also written three short stories featuring two graduate students who run around southern California solving puzzles and finding treasure while surrounded by the crazy people who are their friends. This series, *There Was A Star Danced*, introduces Ridge Wesley and Jennifer Gayle, who aren't certain why they are placed in the circumstances in which they find themselves. Yet they uncover clues and figure out where things are and manage to stay half-a-step ahead of the authorities. For now, Sandor especially enjoys writing Sherlock Holmes stories, those that are alluded to by Dr. John Watson in the Doyle stories, but ones Watson never got around to writing and publishing. He lives and works in Palos Verdes, California. His e-mail address is *sandorjaysonnen@yahoo.com*.

Tim Symonds was born in London. He grew up in Somerset, Dorset, and Guernsey. After several years in East and Central Africa, he settled in California and graduated Phi Beta Kappa in Political Science from UCLA. He is a Fellow of the *Royal Geographical Society*. He writes his novels in the woods and hidden valleys surrounding his home in the High Weald of East Sussex. Dr. Watson knew the untamed region well. In "The Adventure of Black Peter", Watson wrote, *"the Weald was once part of that great forest which for so long held the Saxon invaders at bay."* Tim's novels are published by MX Publishing. His latest is titled *Sherlock Holmes and The Nine Dragon Sigil*. Previous novels include *Sherlock Holmes and The Sword Of Osman*, *Sherlock Holmes and The Mystery of Einstein's Daughter*, *Sherlock Holmes and The Dead Boer At Scotney Castle*, and *Sherlock Holmes and The Case of The Bulgarian Codex*.

Marcia Wilson is a freelance researcher and illustrator who likes to work in a style compatible for the color blind and visually impaired. She is Canon-centric, and her first MX offering, *You Buy Bones*, uses the point-of-view of Scotland Yard to show the unique talents of Dr. Watson. This continued with the publication of *Test of the Professionals: The Adventure of the Flying Blue Pidgeon*. She can be contacted at: *gravelgirty.deviantart.com*

*The following contributors appear
in the companion volume*
**The MX Book of New Sherlock Holmes Stories
Part VII – Eliminate the Impossible: 1880-1891**

Hugh Ashton was born in the U.K., and moved to Japan in 1988, where he remained until 2016, living with his wife Yoshiko in the historic city of Kamakura, a little to the south of Yokohama. He and Yoshiko have now moved to Lichfield, a small cathedral city in the Midlands of the U.K., the birthplace of Samuel Johnson, and one-time home of Erasmus Darwin. In the past, he has worked in the technology and financial services industries, which have provided him with material for some of his books set in the 21st century. He currently works as a writer: Novelist, freelance editor and copywriter, (his work for large Japanese corporations has appeared in international business journals), and journalist, as well as producing industry reports on various aspects of the financial services industry. Recently, however, his lifelong interest in Sherlock Holmes has developed into an acclaimed series of adventures featuring the world's most famous detective, written in the style of the originals, and published by Inknbeans Press. In addition to these, he has also published historical and alternate historical novels, short stories, and thrillers. Together with artist Andy Boerger, he has produced the *Sherlock Ferret* series of stories for children, featuring the world's cutest detective.

S.F. Bennett was born and raised in London, studying History at Queen Mary and Westfield College, and Journalism at City University at the Postgraduate level, before moving to Devon in 2013. The author lectures on Conan Doyle, Sherlock Holmes, and 19th century detective fiction, and has had articles on various aspects from The Canon published in *The Journal of the Sherlock Holmes Society of London* and *The Torr*, the journal of *The Poor Folk Upon The Moors*, the Sherlock Holmes Society of the South West of England.

Mike Chinn has published almost sixty short stories, from westerns to Lovecraftian fiction, with all shades of fantasy, horror, science fiction, and pulp adventure in between, along with a tale of the good Professor in *The Mammoth Book Of The Adventures Of Moriarty* (2015, Robinson). The Alchemy Press published a collection of his Damian Paladin fiction in 1998, whilst he has edited *Swords Against The Millennium* (2000) and *The Alchemy Press Book Of Pulp Heroes* Volumes 1, 2, and 3 (2012, 2013 and 2014 respectively) for the same imprint. 2015 saw the publication of his short story collection *Give Me These Moments Back* (The Alchemy Press), and a Steampunk Sherlock Holmes mash-up, *Vallis Timoris* (Fringeworks). A new Damian Paladin collection, *Walkers in Shadow*, and a Western, *Revenge Is A Cold Pistol*, are to be published by Pro Se Productions.

Jan Edwards is a British author. She was born near Horsham, Sussex, UK, but now lives in Staffordshire Moorlands with her husband, Peter Coleborn, and the obligatory three cats. She has a life-long passion for folklore and the supernatural, and draws on this for her fiction. To date, forty-plus of her short stories have seen publication in magazines and anthologies, including *The Mammoth Book of Dracula, The Mammoth Book of the Adventures of Moriarty*, and *Terror Tales of the Ocean*. Much of her published short fiction is reprinted in the collections *Leinster Gardens and Other Subtleties* and *Fables and Fabrications*. Jan won a Winchester

561

Slim Volume Prize for her rural novel *Sussex Tales*, was short-listed for a BFS Award for Best Short Story as an author, and short listed three times as editor of anthologies. She edits anthologies for the award winning Alchemy Press and also for Fox Spirit Books. In a previous existence she has been Chairperson for both the *British Fantasy Society* and *Fantasycon*. Other works by Jan Edwards include *Leinster Gardens and Other Subtleties*, *Sussex Tales*, and *Fables and Fabrications*. Anthologies edited by Jan and Jenny Barber include *The Alchemy Book of Ancient Wonders*, *The Alchemy Press Book of Urban Mythic*, *The Alchemy Press Book of Urban Mythic:2*, and *Wicked Women*. Jan's World War II crime novel *Winter Downs* is due for publication in 2017. For more details on Jan and her fiction visit *http://janedwardsblog.wordpress.com/*

Anna Elliott is an author of historical fiction and fantasy. Her first series, *The Twilight of Avalon* trilogy, is a retelling of the Trystan and Isolde legend. She wrote her second series, *The Pride and Prejudice Chronicles*, chiefly to satisfy her own curiosity about what might have happened to Elizabeth Bennet, Mr. Darcy, and all the other wonderful cast of characters after the official end of Jane Austen's classic work. She enjoys stories about strong women, and loves exploring the multitude of ways women can find their unique strengths. She was delighted to lend a hand with the "Sherlock and Lucy" series, and this story, firstly because she loves Sherlock Holmes as much as her father, co-author Charles Veley, does, and second because it almost never happens that someone with a dilemma shouts, "Quick, we need an author of historical fiction!" Anna lives in the Washington, D.C .area with her husband and three children.

Thomas Fortenberry is an American author, editor, and reviewer. Founder of Mind Fire Press and a Pushcart Prize-nominated writer, he has also judged many literary contests, including the Georgia Author of the Year Awards and the Robert Penn Warren Prize for Fiction. Another Sherlock Holmes story appeared in the anthology *An Improbable Truth*.

James R. "Jim" French became a morning Disc Jockey on KIRO (AM) in Seattle in 1959. He later founded *Imagination Theatre*, a syndicated program that broadcast to over one-hundred-and-twenty stations in the U.S. and Canada, and also on the XM Satellite Radio system all over North America. Actors in French's dramas have included John Patrick Lowrie, Larry Albert, Patty Duke, Russell Johnson, Tom Smothers, Keenan Wynn, Roddy MacDowall, Ruta Lee, John Astin, Cynthia Lauren Tewes, and Richard Sanders. Mr. French states, "To me, the characters of Sherlock Holmes and Doctor Watson always seemed to be figures Doyle created as a challenge to lesser writers. He gave us two interesting characters – different from each other in their histories, talents, and experience, but complimentary as a team – who have been applied to a variety of situations and plots far beyond the times and places in The Canon. In the hands of different writers, Holmes and Watson have lent their identities to different times, ages, and even genders. But I wanted to break no new ground. I feel Sir Arthur provided us with enough references to locations, landmarks, and the social conditions of his time, to give a pretty large canvas on which to paint our own images and actions to animate Holmes and Watson."

Jayantika Ganguly BSI is the General Secretary and Editor of the *Sherlock Holmes Society of India*, a member of the *Sherlock Holmes Society of London*, and the *Czech*

Sherlock Holmes Society. She is the author of *The Holmes Sutra* (MX 2014). She is a corporate lawyer working with one of the Big Six law firms.

John Linwood Grant is a writer and editor who lives in Yorkshire with a pack of lurchers and a beard. He may also have a family. He focuses particularly on dark Victorian and Edwardian fiction, such as his recent novella *A Study in Grey*, which also features Holmes. Current projects include his *Tales of the Last Edwardian* series, about psychic and psychiatric mysteries, and curating a collection of new stories based on the darker side of the British Empire. He has been published in a number of anthologies and magazines, with stories range from madness in early Virginia to questions about the monsters we ourselves might be. He is also co-editor of *Occult Detective Quarterly*. His website *greydogtales.com* explores weird fiction, especially period ones, weird art, and even weirder lurchers.

Dr. John Hall has written widely on Holmes. His books includes *Sidelights on Holmes*, a commentary on The Canon, *The Abominable Wife* on the unrecorded cases, *Unexplored Possibilities*, a study of Dr. John H. Watson, and a monograph on Professor Moriarty, "The Dynamics of a Falling Star". (Most of these are now out of print.) His novels include *Sherlock Holmes and the Adler Papers*, *The Travels of Sherlock Holmes*, *Sherlock Holmes and the Boulevard Assassin*, *Sherlock Holmes and the Disgraced Inspector*, *Sherlock Holmes and the Telephone Mystery*, *Sherlock Holmes and the Hammerford Will*, *Sherlock Holmes and the Abbey School Mystery*, and *Sherlock Holmes at the Raffles Hotel*. John is a member of the *International Pipe-smoker's Hall of Fame*, and lives in Yorkshire, England.

Mike Hogan writes mostly historical novels and short stories, many set in Victorian London and featuring Sherlock Holmes and Doctor Watson. He read the Conan Doyle stories at school with great enjoyment, but hadn't thought much about Sherlock Holmes until, having missed the Granada/Jeremy Brett TV series when it was originally shown in the eighties, he came across a box set of videos in a street market and was hooked on Holmes again. He started writing Sherlock Holmes pastiches about four years ago, having great fun re-imagining situations for the Conan Doyle characters to act in. The relationship between Holmes and Watson fascinates him as one of the great literary friendships. (He's also a huge admirer of Patrick O'Brian's Aubrey-Maturin novels). Like Captain Aubrey and Doctor Maturin, Holmes and Watson are an odd couple, differing in almost every facet of their characters, but sharing a common sense of decency and a common humanity. Living with Sherlock Holmes can't have been easy, and Mike enjoys adding a stronger vein of "pawky humour" into the Conan Doyle mix, even letting Watson have the second-to-last word on occasions. His books include *Sherlock Holmes and the Scottish Question*; *The Gory Season – Sherlock Holmes, Jack the Ripper and the Thames Torso Murders* and the Sherlock Holmes & Young Winston 1887 Trilogy (*The Deadwood Stage*; *The Jubilee Plot*; and *The Giant Moles*), He has also written the following short story collections: *Sherlock Holmes: Murder at the Savoy and Other Stories*, *Sherlock Holmes: The Skull of Kohada Koheiji and Other Stories*, and *Sherlock Holmes: Murder on the Brighton Line and Other Stories*. *www.mikehoganbooks.com*

Steven Philip Jones has written over sixty graphic novels and comic books incl-uding *Curious Cases of Sherlock Holmes*, the original series *Nightlinger*, *Street Heroes 2005*, adaptations of *Dracula*, several H. P. Lovecraft stories, and the

1985 film *Re-animator*. Steven is also the author of several novels and nonfiction books including *The Clive Cussler Adventures: A Critical Review, Comics Writing: Communicating With Comic Book , King of Harlem, Bushwackers, The House With the Witch's Hat, Talisman: The Knightmare Knife,* and *Henrietta Hex: Shadows From the Past.* Steven's other writing credits include a number of scripts for radio dramas that have been broadcast internationally. A graduate of the University of I-owa, Steven has a Bachelor of Arts in Journalism and Religion, and was accepted - into Iowa's Writer's Workshop M.F.A. program.

James Lovegrove is the author of more than fifty books, including *The Hope, Days, Untied Kingdom, Provender Gleed,* the *New York Times* bestselling *Pantheon* series, the *Redlaw* novels, and the *Dev Harmer Missions.* He has produced three Sherlock Holmes novels, with a Holmes/Cthulhu mashup trilogy in the works, the first being *Sherlock Holmes and the Shadwell Shadows.* He has also sold well over forty short stories and published two collections, *Imagined Slights* and *Diversifications.* He has produced a dozen short books for readers with reading difficulties, and a four-volume fantasy saga for teenagers, *The Clouded World,* under the pseudonym Jay Amory. James has been shortlisted for numerous awards, including the Arthur C. Clarke Award, the John W. Campbell Memorial Award, the Bram Stoker Award, the British Fantasy Society Award, and the Manchester Book Award. His short story "Carry The Moon In My Pocket" won the 2011 Seiun Award in Japan for Best Translated Short Story. His work has been translated into over a dozen languages, and his journalism has appeared in periodicals as diverse as *Literary Review, Interzone,* and *BBC MindGames.* He reviews fiction regularly for the *Financial Times.* He lives with his wife, two sons, cat, and tiny dog in Eastbourne, not far from the site of the "small farm upon the South Downs" to which Sherlock Holmes retired.

Adrian Middleton is a Staffordshire-born independent publisher. The son of a real-world detective, he is a former civil servant and policy adviser who now writes and edits science fiction, fantasy, and a popular series of steampunked Sherlock Holmes stories.

James Moffett is a Masters graduate in Professional Writing, with a specialisation in novel and non-fiction writing. He also has an extensive background in media studies. James began developing a passion for writing when contributing to his University's student magazine. His interest in the literary character of Sherlock Holmes was deep-rooted in his youth. He has also released his first publication of eight interconnected short stories titled *The Trials of Sherlock Holmes* earlier this year.

Jacquelynn Morris, ASH, BSI, JHWS, is a member of several Sherlock Holmes societies in the Mid-Atlantic area of the U.S.A., but her home group is Watson's Tin Box in Maryland. She is the founder of *A Scintillation of Scions*, an annual Sherlock Holmes symposium that is in its eleventh year. She has been published in the BSI Manuscript Series, *The Wrong Passage*, as well as in *About Sixty* and the upcoming *About Being a Sherlockian* (Wildside Press). Jacquelynn was the U.S. liaison for the Undershaw Preservation Trust for several years, until Undershaw was purchased to become part of Stepping Stones School. This is her first opportunity to have the honor of working with David Marcum and MX Publishing

Mark Mower is a crime writer and historian whose passion for tales about Sherlock Holmes and Dr. Watson began at the age of twelve, when he watched an early black-and-white film featuring the unrivalled screen pairing of Basil Rathbone and Nigel Bruce. Hastily seeking out the original stories of Sir Arthur Conan Doyle and continually searching for further film and television adaptations, his has been a lifelong obsession. Now a member of the *Crime Writers' Association* and the *Sherlock Holmes Society of London*, Mark has written numerous books about true crime stories and fictional murder mysteries. His first Holmes and Watson tale, "The Strange Missive of Germaine Wilkes" appeared as a chapter in Volume I of *The MX Book of New Sherlock Holmes Stories* (MX Publishing, 2015). His own collection of pastiches, *A Farewell to Baker Street* (MX Publishing, 2015) appeared shortly afterwards. A forthcoming collection, *Sherlock Holmes: The Baker Street Case Files* will be released in late 2017. His non-fiction works have included *Bloody British History: Norwich* (The History Press, 2014) and *Suffolk Murders* (The History Press, 2011). Alongside his writing, Mark lectures on crime history and runs a murder mystery business. He lives close to Beccles, in the English county of Suffolk.

Gayle Lange Puhl has been a Sherlockian since Christmas of 1965. She has had articles published in *The Devon County Chronicle*, *The Baker Street Journal*, and *The Serpentine Muse*, plus her local newspaper. She has created Sherlockian jewelry, a 2006 calendar entitled "If Watson Wrote For TV", and has painted a limited series of Holmes-related nesting dolls. She co-founded the scion *Friends of the Great Grimpen Mire* and the Janesville, Wisconsin-based *The Original Tree Worshipers*. In January 2016, she was awarded the "Outstanding Creative Writer" award by the Janesville Art Alliance for her first book *Sherlock Holmes and the Folk Tale Mysteries*. She is semi-retired and lives in Evansville, Wisconsin. Ms. Puhl has one daughter, Gayla, and four grandchildren.

Geri Schear is a novelist and short story writer. Her work has been published in literary journals in the U.S. and Ireland. Her first novel, *A Biased Judgement: The Diaries of Sherlock Holmes 1897* was released to critical acclaim in 2014. The sequel, *Sherlock Holmes and the Other Woman* was published in 2015, and *Return to Reichenbach* in 2016. She lives in Kells, Ireland.

Shane Simmons is a multi-award-winning screenwriter and graphic novelist whose work has appeared in international film festivals, museums, and lectures about design and structure. His best-known piece of fiction, *The Long and Unlearned Life of Roland Gethers*, has been discussed in multiple books and academic journals about sequential art, and his short stories have been printed in critically praised anthologies of history, crime, and horror. He lives in Montreal with his wife and too many cats. Follow him at *eyestrainproductions.com* and *@Shane_Eyestrain*

Robert V. Stapleton was born and brought up in Leeds, Yorkshire, England, and studied at Durham University. After working in various parts of the country as an Anglican parish priest, he is now retired and lives with his wife in North Yorkshire. As a member of his local writing group, he now has time to develop his other life as a writer of adventure stories. He has recently had a number of short stories published, and he is hoping to have a couple of completed novels published at some time in the future.

S. Subramanian is a retired professor of Economics from Chennai, India. Apart from a small book titled *Economic Offences: A Compendium of Crimes in Prose and Verse* (Oxford University Press Delhi, 2012), his Holmes pastiches are the only serious things he has written. His other work runs largely to whimsical stuff on fuzzy logic and social measurement, on which he writes with much precision and little understanding, being an economist. He is otherwise mainly harmless, as his wife and daughter might concede with a little persuasion.

Thomas A. Turley has been "hooked on Holmes" since finishing *The Hound of the Baskervilles* at about the age of twelve. However, his interest in Sherlockian pastiches didn't really take off until he wrote one. "Sherlock Holmes and the Adventure of the Tainted Canister" (2014) is available as an e-book and audio book from MX Publishing. Another (non-Holmes) story, "The Devil's Claw", appeared in *The Book of Villains* (2011), a Main Street Rag anthology. Currently, Tom is hard at work on *Sherlock Holmes and the Crowned Heads of Europe*, a new collection of historically-based cases that will include the one found in this volume. Although Tom has a Ph.D. in British history, he spent most of his career as an archivist with the State of Alabama. He and his wife, Paula, (an aspiring science fiction novelist,) live in Montgomery, Alabama. They are the proud parents of two grown children and one bossy little yellow dog.

Charles Veley has loved Sherlock Holmes since boyhood. As a father, he read the entire Canon to his then-ten-year-old daughter at evening story time. Now, this very same daughter, grown up to become acclaimed historical novelist Anna Elliott, has worked with him to develop new adventures in the *Sherlock Holmes and Lucy James Mystery Series*. Charles is also a fan of Gilbert & Sullivan, and wrote *The Pirates of Finance*, a new musical in the G&S tradition that won an award at the New York Musical Theatre Festival in 2013. Other than the Sherlock and Lucy series, all of the books on his Amazon Author Page were written when he was a full-time author during the late Seventies and early Eighties. He currently works for United Technologies Corporation, where his main focus is on creating sustainability and value for the company's large real estate development projects.

Daniel D. Victor, a Ph.D. in American literature, is a retired high school English teacher who taught in the Los Angeles Unified School District for forty-six years. His doctoral dissertation on little-known American author, David Graham Phillips, led to the creation of Victor's first Sherlock Holmes pastiche, *The Seventh Bullet*, in which Holmes investigates Phillips' actual murder. Victor's second novel, *A Study in Synchronicity,* is a two-stranded murder mystery, which features a Sherlock Holmes-like private eye. He currently writes the ongoing series *Sherlock Holmes and the American Literati*. Each novel introduces Holmes to a different American author who actually passed through London at the turn of the century. In *The Final Page of Baker Street*, Holmes meets Raymond Chandler; in *The Baron of Brede Place*, Stephen Crane; in *Seventeen Minutes to Baker Street*, Mark Twain; and *The Outrage at the Diogenes Club*, Jack London. Victor, who is also writing a novel about his early years as a teacher, lives with his wife in Los Angeles, California. They have two adult sons.

The MX Book of New Sherlock Holmes Stories
Edited by David Marcum
(MX Publishing, 2015-   )

"This is the finest volume of Sherlockian fiction I have
ever read, and I have read, literally, thousands."
– Philip K. Jones

"Beyond Impressive . . . This is a
splendid venture for a great cause!
– Roger Johnson, Editor, *The Sherlock Holmes Journal,*
The Sherlock Holmes Society of London

The MX Book of New Sherlock Holmes Stories
Edited by David Marcum
(MX Publishing, 2015-   )

Part I: 1881-1889
Part II: 1890-1895
Part III: 1896-1929
Part IV: 2016 Annual
Part V: Christmas Adventures
Part VI: 2017 Annual
Part VII: Eliminate the Impossible – 1880-1891
Part VIII: Eliminate the Impossible – 1892-1905

In Preparation
Part IX – 2018 Annual
Part X – Some Untold Cases

. . . and more to come!

569

MX Publishing

MX Publishing is the world's largest specialist Sherlock Holmes publisher, with several hundred titles and authors creating the latest in Sherlock Holmes fiction and non-fiction.

From traditional short stories and novels to travel guides and quiz books, MX Publishing caters to all Holmes fans.

The collection includes leading titles such as *Benedict Cumberbatch In Transition* and *The Norwood Author*, which won the 2011 *Tony Howlett Award* (Sherlock Holmes Book of the Year).

MX Publishing also has one of the largest communities of Holmes fans on *Facebook*, with regular contributions from dozens of authors.

www.mxpublishing.co.uk (UK)
and
www.mxpublishing.com (USA)